V. V.'s Eyes

IS THIS MISS HETH? (p. 44)

V. V.'s Eyes

BY

HENRY SYDNOR HARRISON

AUTHOR OF "QUEED"

WITH ILLUSTRATIONS

BOSTON AND NEW YORK

HOUGHTON MIFFLIN COMPANY

The Riverside Press Cambridge

1913

To my first, second, and third reader

NORVELL

Who raises books by hand

CONTENTS

I

Contents

VIII

IX

X

XI

XII

XIII

XIV

XV

XVI

Contents

XVII

Contents

Contents

XXXIII

XXXIV

ILLUSTRATIONS

From drawings by Raymond M. Crosby

V. V.'s Eyes

I

*Two Houses, with a great Gulf between; of V. Vivian, M.D., and
what he thought of John the Baptist.*

V. VIVIAN, M.D. by the paint upon his window, dwelt in
the Dabney House; Mr. Heth — pronounced *Heath* if
you value his wife's good opinion — dwelt in the House
of his cognomen. Between the two lay a scant mile of city streets.
But then this happened to be the particular mile which traversed, while of course it could not span, the Great Gulf fixed.

In one sense (though the wrong one) the Dabney House was the
more impressive of the pair of domiciles: for it was seven stories
tall and had two hundred rooms; while the House of Heth was
only four stories and basement, and had but fourteen rooms,
counting in the trunk-room. But physical size is size only:
whereby hang few tales. Over and in the Heth House there prevailed the most charming air of ease with dignity, of taste plus
means, that you could well imagine: while the circumambient
atmosphere of the Dabney House, not to put too fine a point on
it, was the abomination of desolation, or that abomination's
little brother. Before the one stretched a brilliant street where
imposing residences crowded each other just as close as they
could crowd, and still be imposing, and residences. Behind the
other stretched the likeliest the city could show in the way of
slums, and, farther back, just over the brow of the sinister Hill,
something less cheering than honest slums. One glittered upon
the future; the other decayed into the past. And it would cost
you — to clinch the comparison with the true and only — two
thousand dollars a year, say, to secure Mr. Heth's house, nego-

I

tiating with his executor at that; while in the great pile of the eponymous Dabney, you could have all of three rooms and (portable) bath for twelve dollars a month, though strictly cash in advance. . . .

Cartographers, with their miserable mathematics, called this a statute mile, which, as we say, a brisk man can walk in the smoking of a cigarette. But the authors of the Blue Book, grave fellows who have better struck the scales from their eyes, would have computed you this distance at N, which is infinity: and so closed up the book. For what bridge shall cross the uncrossable, what ferryman ply for silver pounds on the Great Gulf? An image-breaking age; no doubt; but there are limits, in decency. No thread of destiny or clue of circumstance shall connect two Houses set upon the poles of the world. . . .

So spoke the Blue Book: judging somewhat by the look of it, after all, pronouncing not without a touch of the weary wisdom which comes of knowing too much. But is it not written how the hussy Appearance wears a painted face, justly open to interrogation? — how there stands a summit from which a man shall see yet more sharply than his most admired authors, above referred to? Hence, look down. And behold, against the sunny day two clues now visible upon the bosom of the Gulf, to wit: the dark-eyed lad so oddly taking hired-carriage exercise up and down Washington Street, between eight-thirty and ten-thirty A.M.; and yon half-column of winged words in "The People's Forum" column of this morning's "Post," under the caption (supplied by the editor): "Severe Arraignment of Local Factory Conditions."

The Dabney House felt the pluckings first. They were Nobodies there; and by that token they were early risers.

She was fluttered to-day, was Mrs. Garland, by the nocturnal reappearance of her errant husband, Mister, as simply called: but she did not forget the iron rule. The "Post" was under the door by seven o'clock. Dr. Vivian perused by seven-fifteen. He perused with a peculiar and paternal gusto: for doctoring was not his meat and drink, and he had written these winged words himself. But of the vehicular lad he heard nothing till some hours later, when Labor Commissioner O'Neill, skirting the old park from Centre Street, where he had been for cigars, dropped in on the way back to his office.

Even here, the words came first. O'Neill had a "Post" in his hand.

It was then nearing eleven o'clock. The doctor sat at a tall old "secretary" between his windows, swinging round with expectancy as his friend entered. There were still people of a sort, human beings in a manner of speaking, in the waiting-room; but he let them wait now, that being what the room was for.

"Well? . . . How 'd it strike you?"

The Labor Commissioner mopped his brow with a snowy handkerchief, which released into the office the scent of cologne. He was a stoutish man, and the morning, for autumn, was astonishingly warm.

"Well, it's ill-timed, V. V.," said he, without ill-humor. "And — kind of extreme. I told you the other day how I felt about it."

The face of the medico fell.

"I thought you said you approved of a good, pertinent letter, to show that the laity were backing you up!"

"I said a mild, easy-tempered letter might be all right. But —"

"Why, Sam, don't you think that's an awfully mild letter? You ought to see what I edited out of it."

"Well, you left in enough to let the 'Post' in for a damage suit, all right. You, too. . . . Only you won't have much to lodge a judgment against, long's you have n't got a billhead printed and charge regular fees like I told you."

"I'm perfectly responsible — far as that goes. Don't you worry."

The doctor's look showed that he considered O'Neill's pleasantry in bad taste, to say the least of it. He had told Sam often enough, one would think, that he meant before long to put in a good businesslike system of fees, small fees . . .

The Commissioner was continuing: "Point is, V. V., there's nothing gained getting these people's backs way up. They're sore now. A little tact, a little bit of —"

"Tact!"

3

"Sure thing. Look here, old boy, remember it's only a week since my report was in the papers, practically blacklisting those four plants, and I've already called personally on every one of 'em, putting it right up to 'em. You heard me at Heth's and the Pickle people's, yourself. I guess I put it up about as strong as could be done, hey? And that's all can be done till I get me some more law. Put it right square . . ."

But V. Vivian, gazing steadily over the chair-back, had obviously been stoking his inner fuel.

"Ah! Rousing public opinion's no use at all? . . . Why, don't you *know* that public opinion is the grandfather of your little statute-book laws? Don't you —"

"Yair. Know. See you say that in your letter."

"Well, it's a *great truth!* . . . How tactful will you feel some day, when one of those floors at the Heth Works collapses and kills a hundred people?"

Labor Commissioner O'Neill seemed unterrified by the grisly picture. He was strolling about the very large, bare, and strange-looking medical office, flicking cigar-ash where he would: a good-natured-looking Commissioner of thirty, wearing a glossy brown suit and strong yellow gloves. And his present pacific air was undoubtedly to his credit; certainly he had been annoyed when his eye first fell on the "Severe Arraignment," over his morning rasher. . . .

"And that isn't the worst of it," shot the doctor again, flinging out an arm. "It's only a detail, I say, this factory end of it; only a symptom, don't you see? What we're dealing with is the most dangerous element in the life of this city! Tact! . . . When fire couldn't sweep through that new house of yours faster than the corrupting ideals of these people'll lick through this community!"

"Whe-ew!" said Sam O'Neill, this ground being not unfamiliar. . . . "Got to take 'em along slowly, Doctor, all the same. Rome wasn't built in a day."

"But mark my words, the vandals kicked it down in about fifteen minutes."

O'Neill felt vaguely worsted by this riposte. He was the older

4

man, the practical man, with a proven ability to make money out of real estate; but old V. V., though talking like an anarchist of late, was admitted to have a verbal dexterity at debate. Argument was forced upon Sam, as it were. He demanded authority for calling these people corrupting; desired to know if V. V. knew any of 'em personally. And presently he was reading aloud from the letter in the "Post," reading retributively; one swingeing phrase after another.

"And here — here! Listen to this, will you? — 'Why should we stand by and permit these shameless egoists of industry to bleed the strength from the community's sinew and grow rich by homicide at the cost of the race?' . . ."

Severe, indeed, the Arraignment seemed when read aloud to you in that tone. Gusto ebbed a little, mayhap. But it was clear that the medical author did not propose to retract; quite the contrary, in short.

"Permit! Ought to have asked why we applaud them, court them, *envy* them —"

"'Shameless homicides'! — and he calls it mild! Now, here, honor bright —"

"It's what they are — and more! You ask me if I know these people personally? I reply that in the truest sense I do know 'em, very well, for I've made a study of the type, d' you see? . . ."

Then the office door from the hall opened about a foot, a fat head in a gaunt bonnet protruded through the crevice, having rather a decapitated look, and a deep inflectionless voice said:

"Excuse me introodin', Doctor, I'm sure, but your sick here raskin' me kin they see you soon."

"In five minutes precisely . . ."

Morning sunshine streamed through the unwashen windows. V. Vivian had risen in the ardor of his argument. Quite a different-looking man from the Commissioner he was observed to be, tall where the Commissioner was thick, eager where the Commissioner was easy-going. Rather a long face he had, sensitive about the mouth, lucid about the gaze, and hair of a tan shade which waved a little, no matter how crisply cut. The faded gray suit he wore contrasted unfavorably with his friend's new brown;

on the other hand, his movements were not devoid of a certain lank grace such as the gods have denied to rotundity.

Yet when he stepped out from his quaint desk, it was suddenly to be seen that the young man limped, on his left foot: that this limp was not accidental or temporary. . . . A lame doctor: so it was with him. And yet the fire with which he spoke was surely not born of the pharmacopœia. . . .

"Take it in the large — that's all I ask! Look at your job from a social standpoint. I tell you, it's just these Huns, these yellow-rich Heths and Magees and Old Dominion Pickle people who're rotting the heart out of this fine old town. And the root of the whole trouble's in their debased personal ideals, don't you see? 'Get on' at all costs, that's the motto: slapping their money in their neighbors' faces and shouting, 'Here's what counts!' — spreading their degraded standards by example through the community — yellow materialism gone mad. . . . Oh, I know! — I know it is n't your slave-driving captains only. It's mainly the women pushing from behind — fat horse-leeches' daughters always screaming 'more, more' — when there's —"

"Leeches! Peaches, you mean! You ought to see —"

"When there's no way to get any more but to bleed it out of — Corinne Garland here! — which is duly done. Brutal egoism, that's the philosophy —"

"Police!" cried O'Neill, puffing good-humoredly. "Why, V. V.! — They're personally some of the best people in town! If you knew 'em you'd be the first to say so. Take the Heths now, just to show you —"

"Huns all! I do know them, I say, through to their little pre-hensile souls! You don't seem to get me. . . . Why, I feel *sorry* for them, Sam! I would n't mind much what they did if they were only *happy with it!* But, good heavens! . . . D' you know what this age needs, my boy? *A voice crying in the wilderness. . .*"

"H'm! Don't know about that. You'll find, where it's a matter touching their pockets, people don't listen to voices much, either in —"

"They listened to John the Baptist!"

6

"What?" said Sam, rather disliking these constant references to the ancient days.

"I say they listened to John the Baptist!" cried tall Dr. Vivian, slapping one impetuous hand into the other. "Yes, and came running and sweating to the desert, just to get a tongue-lashing from him — the very same old scribes and Pharisees that drive motor-cars down Washington Street to-day! And they'd run to him to-day, never fear! I tell you, there's a voice the heart is never deaf to! And that's what this age needs, Sam, — since you ask *me*, — a big, fierce prophet on the outskirts of the city; a great, grim, uncompromising *hater*, with a tongue that bites like a blacksnake whip. By George, they'd listen to him! He couldn't hide where your yellow Huns wouldn't come to him on their knees!"

"Let him do it, then, — go's far as he likes. Only don't ask *me* . . ."

O'Neill had not failed to perceive how the talk wandered from the Labor Commission. Now, drawing on his gloves, he was struck by a humorous thought.

"You're looking for work, for trouble, you say. Why don't you sign on this John the Baptist job yourself?"

Oddly, the small gibe seemed to disconcert the orator. His cheek acquired a pinkness; unexpectedly, too, he seemed to lose the thread of his headlong thesis. However, he brandished his arms, gazing hard.

"That's as it may be! As it may be, my dear fellow! All I . . . Ah," he said hurriedly, turning. "One minute . . . There's some one knocking . . ."

And he went striding off with his unequal step toward his visitors' door — not his sick's — though it did seem that "Come in" would really have answered just as well as usual . . .

The stoutish Commissioner glanced after him, dimly surprised.

Boyhood friends these two, their ways had long parted while the younger followed away the descending fortunes of his father, the inventor of a double-turbine which would never quite work. Their reëstablished intimacy now was of the thorough-going sort:

7

witness Sam's letting him trot along on factory inspection the other day, something he'd have done for no other amateur, not on your life. Yet old V. V. was kind of puzzling at times, as now; wild-talking, then kind of reserved all of a sudden, like pulling down a shade on you. Talked different at different times. . . .

Business awaited the Commissioner at his office in the Capitol, as he now recalled. However, V. V. was opening his dingy old door.

Without, in the corridor, there was seen standing a scraggly-bearded individual in a ragged shirt, which offered glimpses of a hairy chest in need of soap. A stranger this chanced to be, but the genus was by no means unfamiliar in the environs of the Dabney House. The young doctor's speaking countenance, confronting him, appeared to fall a little. Doubtless he had learned by now the usual business of such as these.

"Good morning," he said, in rather a firm way. "What can I do for you?"

The caller, having turned a china-blue gaze upon his host, wore a confused air. He spoke in a furry, plaintive voice, professional in its way.

"Jes lookin' fer the Doc a minute, sir, that's all. You ain't him, are yer?"

"Why not? . . ."

And then it came over Vivian who this man must be: surely no other than the Dabney House prodigal, spouse of his own fellow-lodger, landlady, and *blanchisseuse*. Upon that thought he stepped out into the hall, closing the office door behind him upon Sam O'Neill.

"Yes, I'm the doctor — and you're Mr. Garland, are n't you? Your wife and daughter are friends of mine . . ."

Mr. Garland accepted the introduction with signs of abashment, but stated his business simply.

"Doc, could you he'p me out with a coat like?"

"Oh. . . . A coat, you say?"

"Rags to my skin, sir. I 'clare you can see my meat . . ."

The bearded one inspected himself downward with feeble cackles, hollow parodies of gay derision. And he added, with the

8

same mock dash, that he did n't mind his situation for himself, being used to taking them as they come; 't was his missus seemed sort of shamed *fer* him . . .

The pleasant-faced young man stood stroking his chin.

"Yes — yes — I can fit you out, I dare say," said he. "I — ah — have a coat in here that I think 'll do you. Very nicely. . . . S'pose you wait here a moment, and we 'll see — what we shall see . . ."

He disappeared through a door down the hall, and returned presently, carrying a black coat of the sort commonly known as a cutaway.

"There 's the vest that goes with it, too," said he. "You might as well have that — though of course Mrs. Garland may have to let it out a little . . ."

The man received the gifts in a somewhat awkward silence. Having eyed the proffered coat, — which in this dim light appeared to be quite a good one, newer-looking, indeed, than the one worn at present by the doctor, — his gaze wandered up and then stealthily away. His air of hesitancy was a little surprising.

"In the seams, you know," said V. V. "Make it bigger. She 'll understand . . ."

Then thanks came from the furry voice, effusive yet somehow rather sheepish: perhaps the man was n't as experienced at this sort of thing as he looked. However, he shambled away with speed, appearing at least to know that when you had got what you wanted, that, and no other, was the moment to go.

Far down the corridor of the old hotel, he turned once, looking back furtively over his shoulder. . . .

Vivian reappeared in his office, to be greeted with a grin by Sam O'Neill, who, having just thrown his cigar-end into the ruined fireplace, was ready to go.

"'Nother beggar, hey?"

"No — no . . . Oh, no!" said the doctor, hastily. "Just a — ah — sort of a fellow wanted to see me . . ."

He halted in the middle of the room; stood absently pushing back his hair; and his gaze, turned toward the window, became introspective, a little dreamy. . . .

"What we were speaking of, Sam . . . Just to show you I'm not so opinionated — so eccentric — as you seem to think. I read a great little thing the other day . . . In a magazine article, it was, describing one of those so-called public balls — in Chicago, this one was. You know the sort of thing — an orgy: rounders and roués, young cheap sports, old rakes, all the demi-monde, rivers of alcohol . . . Drunken women kicking men's hats off and lying where they fell . . . Regular bacchanalia. Well, about one o'clock two men in evening clothes came into the gallery and stood looking down into that — maelstrom of infamous faces. . . . Then one of them said: '*John the Baptist would have 'em all grovelling in three minutes*' . . ."

He had told his story with a certain youthful expectancy, the air of one who confides, counting upon a delicate understanding. But Sam O'Neill, though perfectly willing to be delicate, could only say, after an anti-climacteric pause: "Is that right? Well, that bunch needed to grovel all right" — which was a little vague, say what you would of it, chilling somewhat. . . .

"Well, what's your coryphées' ball but life?" muttered Vivian, knocking the ashes from the dead pipe he had been holding. . . .

And then, turning away with the fire gone out of him, he added:

"All I say about these people is they'd be so much happier with their shells hammered off. What's getting rich but building a wall between yourself and the great common? . . . Seems to me God meant us all to be citizens of the world . . ."

"That's right," said Sam, reassuringly. And then, as the two men walked toward the door: "Oh, I don't say that letter there'll do any *harm*, V. V. Maybe a little stirring 'em up's just as well . . ."

At the door, O'Neill recollected, and spoke again: "Oh, say, V. V.! Saw your gay young friend Dalhousie just now. Had a pretty nice little load of bananas too . . ."

V. V. halted dead, his look changing abruptly. Trouble gathered on his brow.

"Where?"

"Driving down Centre Street in a hack, looking sober as a judge, but —"

"What sort of hack?" demanded Vivian, as if a good deal might depend on that.

"Reg'lar sea-going," answered the Commissioner, confirming the worst. "Kind with the fold-back top, like you see principally at nigger funerals and aldermen's parades . . ."

But it was evidently no merry matter to V. V.

"Then he's off," said he, slowly, and glanced at his watch. . . . "He seemed all right when I saw him last night. Only you never can tell, with him. . . . I wonder if I could catch him . . ."

The Commissioner thought not. "He was headed straight for Centre Street Station, and that was a half-hour ago. Had a bag out front in the sea-going, too. Oh, thunder, he's all right. Little trip'll do him good . . ."

Left alone in his office, V. Vivian stood still, staring intently into space.

New-returned to his old home town, this young man was deep in love with twenty gallant schemes, from the general reform of the world, by his own system, to the repairment of the stomachic equipment of Tubby Miggs, aged six. But O'Neill's tidings of the vehicular lad knocked them all from his mind. He forgot the Huns; forgot John the Baptist; forgot even his sick, till one of the weller of them (as we may assume) knocked memorially upon his door. . . .

What trouble was brewing for his frail friend Dal?

Upon this matter, now and henceforward, the other House was to have information first. Dusk of that day had fallen before the word came to the deserted hotel. But when it did come, the lame doctor broke his evening office-hour without notice, and caught a train by thirty seconds.

II

Two Persons of More Importance, and why they went to the Beach in October; Miss Carlisle Heth, and how she met an unwelcome swain at Sea; how this Swain could swim enough for one.

MR. HETH perused the Severe Arraignment of himself about nine o'clock, over his second cup of coffee. He perused with indignation; but, being long since trained to keep a neat partition between downtown and uptown, he did not divulge his sentiments to the breakfast-table, and even carried the paper off with him to the office. By such demeanor, he abdicates our present notice. Mrs. Heth, hours later, bought a copy of the "Post" from a uniformed newsboy, to see what they had to say of the Associated Charities meeting on the evening preceding, and of her remarks in accepting the office of First Vice-President. Absorbed by this particular piece-in-the-paper, — for so the good lady named all journalistic efforts, from dry-goods advertisements to leading editorials on Trouble in the Balkans, — it was past three-thirty o'clock, post-meridian, or well after luncheon, before her eye chanced to alight on the Dabney House's winged words.

At this hour the ladies sat at ease in their private sitting-room on the seventh floor of the great handsome caravansary by the sea. For to-day, as it falls out, the House of Heth, just as we have it so firmly fixed on Washington Street, had split and transplanted itself; all that mattered of it, the soul and genius of the House, having flitted off seventy miles to the Beach for an over-Sunday rest.

It was the 29th of October, which should have meant grate-fires. On the contrary, two windows in the rented sitting-room were open, and Miss Carlisle Heth, laying down "Pickwick

Papers," by Dickens, the well-known writer, now rose and flung wide the third.

"Whew!" said she, just as an ordinary person might have done. "It's stifling!"

Her mother, a lifelong conservative, presently replied:

"It isn't the heat, it's the humidity."

Carlisle looked out over the sunny sea, and wondered if her mother were never going to take her nap. She was twenty-three years old, and, Hun or no Hun, was certainly not displeasing to the fleshly eye. Also, she much desired to pass the time with a little sail, having already privately engaged a catboat for that express purpose. There was no reason whatever why she shouldn't have the sail, except that her mother was opposed on principle to anything that looked the least bit adventurous.

"There are cinders on me yet, in spite of my bath," added Mrs. Heth, whisking through the less interesting pieces in the "Post." . . . "Willie's train arrives at four-thirty, I believe?"

Miss Heth confirmed the belief.

"I wonder, really," mused the dowager, not for the first time, "what attraction the place can offer Mr. Canning. Men are strange in their choice of amusement, to say the least."

"He's tired of the hermit life, and wants to let down his bars and have a little fun."

"He could have all the fun he wants in town, Cally. He has only to make a sign —"

"Of course! — and be snowed under with invitations which would be odious to him, and probably roped in for something by Helen and Sue Louise Cheriton, say. He can have fun here, without its leading to anything."

She added, with perverse merriment: "At least he thinks he can, not knowing that two enterprising strangers are camping right across his little trail."

Mrs. Heth frowned slightly. She was a slim, rather small lady, and her fair face, at first sight, suggested an agreeable delicacy. To herself she acknowledged with pleasure that she was "spirituelle." To the observer, after a glance at her attractive upper face, the thick jaw and neck came as a surprise: so did the hands and feet. The feet, seen casually in a company, were apt to be taken for the belongings of some far stouter woman, sitting near. They were Mrs. Heth's, however; and she had also a small round birthmark on her left temple, which a deft arrangement of the hair almost concealed, and a small dark mustache, which was not so fortunately placed. She was sane and sound as to judgment, and her will had raised the House of Heth as by a steam derrick.

Miss Heth, gazing down at three or four hardy bathers, who splashed and shouted at the hotel float, said, laughing:

"Truly, mamma, what do you suppose the Cheritons would have given Willie for the splendid tip?"

Mrs. Heth's frown at her newspaper deepened; otherwise she made no response. She learned with difficulty, like a Bourbon; but many years' experience had at last convinced her that her daughter's occasional mocking mannerism had to be put up with. Conceivably there were people in the world who might have liked this mild cynical way of Carlisle's, seeing in it, not indeed a good quality, but, so to say, the seamy side of a good quality; the lingering outpost of a good quality that had been routed; at least the headstone over the grave of a good quality that maybe was only buried alive. But of these people, if such there were, Mrs. Heth was positively not one. . . .

And Carlisle's next remark was: "What would you wear to-night, for the occasion? . . . Oh, there's a big motor-boat going by like the wind."

For though she might sometimes jeer aloud over processes, the daughter was known to be quite as serious at heart as her mother, over the great matters of life. Otherwise, look you, she might not have been at the Beach at all to-day. The fact was that she and mamma had not *positively* decided on this recuperative excursion (though they had *practically* decided) until after the arrival of Cousin Willie Kerr's notelet at breakfast: in which notelet Willie mentioned laconically that he and Mr. Canning were themselves going Beachward by the three o'clock train, and concluded his few lines with *verbum sap*, which is a Latin quotation.

Standing idly at the window, the girl had indeed been thinking of Mr. Canning before her mother spoke; and thinking with most pleasurable speculations. Truly he was worth a thought, was Mr. Canning, proud stranger within the gates — "house-guest," as the society column prefers it — for whom, if reports were true, many ladies fair had sighed, sickened, and died. And she, alone in her maidenly coterie, had already met the too exclusive metropolitan — four days ago, by the lucky fluke of turning in at the Country Club at an out-of-the-way morning moment, when she might have motored straight on home, and had been within an ace of doing so. An omen, was n't it? Five minutes she and Mr. Canning had talked, over so-called horses' necks provided by his sedate host, and before the end of that time she had perceived an interest dawning in the young man's somewhat ironic eyes. With the usual of his sex one could have counted pretty definitely on the thing's being followed up. However, Mr. Canning, the difficult, had merely saluted her fascinatingly, and retired to re-maroon himself in the rural villa of his kinsmen, the Allison Paynes, where he halted for a week or two on his health-seeking progress southward.

It looked like a parting forever, but was n't, owing to that help which comes ever to those who help themselves. . . .

To the sensible query, Mrs. Heth, lightening, replied: "Of course, the gray crêpe-de-chine."

"I think so, too. Only there's a rip at the bottom. I'm sure Flora has n't touched it since Mr. Avery put his large foot straight through it."

Having turned from the window, Carlisle yawned and glanced at the clock. The two ladies conversed desultorily of draped effects, charmeuse, and why Mattie Allen imagined that she could wear pink. Mrs. Heth ran on through the "Post." Carlisle put up "Pickwick," by Dickens, sticking in a box of safety matches to keep the place. Then she examined herself in the mirror over the mantel, and became intensely interested in a tiny redness over her left eyebrow. She thought that rubbing in a little powder, and then rubbing it right off, would help the redness, and it did.

"I asked Mattie why she said such long prayers in the mornings. That was what made me late for breakfast. Her feelings were quite hurt. Is n't her devoutness quaint, though?"

"She uses my house," murmured Mrs. Heth, "like a hotel. One would think it might occur to her that if she *must* mummer like a deacon she ought to get up —"

She broke off, her wandering eye having just then fallen upon the Arraignment.

"She didn't like our packing her off right after breakfast a bit either. . . . I'm devoted to her," said Carlisle, gently rubbing off the powder, "but there's no denying there's a great deal of the cat in Mats."

"Hmph! . . . Why, this is outrageous! I never read such a thing!"

"What is it?" said the daughter, not turning, clearly not interested.

"Here's a man saying he visited the Works with the Labor Commissioner, and that conditions there are *homicidal!* I never! Mmm-m-m. Here! 'I speak particularly of the Heth Cheroot Works, but all four stand almost equally as burning blots upon the conscience of this community' —"

Carlisle's attention was not diverted from her eyebrow. "The Works! He's crazy. . . . Who is the man?"

"A piece in the paper here — let me see. Yes, here's his name. Vivian. *V. Vivian!* There's no such man! . . ."

"Oh," said the girl, absently, "it's only some notoriety-seeking nobody. . . . Like the man who threw the brick at papa that election night."

"But nobodies haven't any right to publish such untruths!" said Mrs. Heth, more grammatical than she sounded. "They ought to be punished, imprisoned for it. 'Public opinion is the grandfather of statute-book law.' Where's the sense in that? . . ."

"It's probably one of those Socialistic things . . . They said the man who threw the brick at papa was a Socialist."

"'Shameless egoists of industry — grow rich by homicide!' I'm greatly surprised at Mr. West for printing such fanatical stuff. I trust your father did not see this. He gave forty dollars to the tuberculosis fund, and this is his reward."

She fumed and interjected awhile further, but her daughter's thought had dreamed far away. From her childhood days she had carried a mind's-eye picture of the dominant fourth member of the family, the great Works, lord and giver of her higher life, which completely refuted these occasional assaults from socialists and failures. Their malicious bricks flew high over her girlish head. Presently Mrs. Heth rose, looking about for her novel, which was a glittering new one, frankly for entertainment only, and not half-cultural like "Pickwick." The two ladies moved together for the bedrooms.

"You had better get a little nap, too," said Mrs. Heth, "to be fresh for the evening."

"It's so early now. Perhaps I may stroll down for a few minutes first."

"Well — it's so quiet I feel as if we had the place to ourselves. But come up in plenty of time for a nap before dinner. .... You're here to get two days of good rest."

"I'll shut the door between," said Carlisle.

Before long, from the mother's side of the door so shut, certain sounds arose indicating that after the morning's fitful fever she slept well. Carlisle, on her own side, quickly donned a white boating-dress, a blue fillet for her hair, and white doeskin shoes with rubber soles. That done, she went out through the sitting-room, shot down in the lift, traversed the forsaken lobby, and emerged upon the long empty boating pavilion which ran from the hotel's side-entrance well out over the water.

"The bell-boy gave you my message, Mr. Wedge?" said she, to the weather-tanned renter of boats. "How do you do? I'm late. How's the little Lady Jane?"

"How you, Miss Heth? Glad to see you back again, Miss. Lady Jane's trim as ever. Yes'm. And there's a little sou' breeze coming up — puffy, but just suit her."

"Bring her up a little more."

"Yes'm — there now! Feels most like summer, don't it?"

"But it does n't *look* like it!" smiled Miss Heth, and glanced about at the emptiness of things.

"You'd ought to of seen her afore the hot spell," replied Mr. Wedge, with artificial hilarity. . . .

Then the light air took the little sail and Carlisle slid away with the sunshine on her hair.

For half a week the breath of summer had confounded October, mid-autumn plucking a leaf from July's best book. Now, with the half-holiday at hand and a Sabbath to follow, a few others beside the Heths and the Willie Kerr select party had deemed it worth while to go down to the sea where the breezes blow. Only a few, though: the desolate quiet of a summer place out of season yet clung and hung over all. In a solitary corner of the vast piazza four coatless men sat idly drinking the rickeys of summer. These, indeed, watched the embarkation of the girl with interest, and when she stood a moment to get a knot out of the sheet, revealing the figure of the Huntswoman (though she was by no means one of your great Amazons), one of them might have been heard to say:

"Well, she can have *me* any time. . . . And, by crackey, she can *sail!*"

The remark betrayed the hypnotic influence: for she really could not sail very well. No athlete this lady; she had even let her saddle-horse go after the purchase of the second car; the sail now stood as her sole sporting activity, and that but lately taken up. However, she handled her bark with a tolerable efficiency. Keeping prudently inshore, yet feeling delightfully venturesome, she skimmed along by the row of shut-up cottages, and was soon lost to the stare of the rickey-drinkers, of whose interest she had been quite unaware, or, let us say, practically unaware. . . .

Not for the eyes of anonymous transients or liberal-minded drummers had Carlisle Heth donned this charming boat-dress and put out upon the bounding blue. Not just to break the tedium of the afternoon, either; not even exclusively for the vast exhilaration of sailing, though undoubtedly she thrilled to that. But the interesting coincidence, giving a peculiar point to it all, was that the three o'clock train from town was due within the half-hour, and her present course lay dead across the line of the street from the station.

Travel-worn young men; desolate Beach; chagrin at coming;

and then, presto, upon the jaded vision:—blue, sunny water, white-sailed boat, beautiful nymph. Great heavens, what a tableau! . . .

We well know how resistlessly the male of humankind is drawn to the female, at the mere glimpse of her flinging aside the tools of his trade, whatever it may be, and furiously pursuing to the ends of the earth. And we know, too (for the true poets of all ages have told us), how the female of our species goes her inno-cent ways full of artless fancies and sweet girlish imaginings, all unaware that an opposite and uproarious sex is in headlong pur-suit. And how she springs up startled from her otherworldly dreams, to hear the thundering feet behind . . .

Yet we do know also of cases everywhere which make familiar principles not merely out of place, but fairly grotesque. You are hardly to conceive Miss Heth's pretty tableau as staged for, her prospecting journey to the Beach as concerned with, some or-dinary male, of whom one could expect that he would pursue even extraordinary maids in an ordinary way . . .

The nymph sailed gayly, stimulated by agreeable anticipa-tions. The minutes danced by with the skipping waves. A gust of wind slapped the solitary little canvas, and Carlisle's small but not incapable hand tightened upon the sheet. Her eye went dreamily over water and strand. Far down the shore, boys were swimming with faint yells, but the hotel bathers had tired and gone in. She seemed to have the great Atlantic to herself, and the fact seemed nice to her, and refined. . . .

The years had passed since Carlisle Heth had formulated the careering importance, even the nobility, of marrying high above her. Aspiration, not your ditchwater cynicism, was the main-spring of her real being, as her mother well knew; and this su-preme fulfilment had long glittered ahead as the ultimate crown, not of triumph only, but of happiness consummate. A little too long, perhaps: waiting princesses grow discontented. Vague dis-satisfactions possessed the girl at times, for all her large blessings; mild symptoms stewed and simmered from her which surprised her in reflective moments, and her mother at all moments. These things, she knew well, came all from a single want. Her reach far exceeded her grasp. Her sighs were Alexander's.

Now, in the smiling and anticipatory afternoon, a limpid brook of girlish imaginings beguiled her with enchanting music, while realer water lapped her shallop, and the substantial breeze whipped her glorious hair about her yet more glorious face. This face, it is time to say plainly, attracted more than rickey-drinkers. Good men might here read their dearest dreams come true; had so read them. The fact deserves capitals, being enormously important. With one half the world only, as all know, is character destiny: the rest is bent and twisted, glorified or smashed, by Physiognomy, the great potter.

And this girl's destiny was obviously magnificent. Experience had long since convinced her, personally, of that. Hoarse testimonials from the pursuing sex she had had in superabundance from her fifteenth year. Yet, while these were duly valued as indicating the strong demand, she had waited, stanch to her destiny. Were not Alexandrine sighs her right? One so endowed could hardly be asked to rest content with the youth of the vicinage. . . .

The cottage row was now well astern; the long string of empty bathhouses slid by; water foamed under the swelling sail. Gliding with the bark, dreamy retrospect met and joined hands with solider prospect. Carlisle threw round a measuring eye, and perceived that she had covered more distance than she had thought; had passed the limits of the board-walk and the beach, which was quite far enough, considering. She luffed cleverly, having a splendid blowy time of it, and put about. This done, she permitted herself to glance for the second time over the purview.

No cloud of smoke stood upon the horizon stationward, no human being appeared within such view of the strand as the cottages and bath-houses left to her. The train, evidently, was late. Well, as far as that went, there was no special hurry about getting back to the hotel. Mamma could only scold a little, as usual.

Carlisle smiled to herself, rather tickled by the thought of the brilliant march she and mamma had stolen upon the world. In five minutes, under stiff Mr. Payne's eye at that, she had indubitably interested Mr. Canning. And now, thanks chiefly to Willie Kerr's loyal enterprise, . . .

Her returning eye fell upon a bobbing object in the water, very near her, and her heart missed a beat. Her lips moved soundlessly. *Jack Dalhousie!* . . .

The bobbing object, in fact, was the head of a man of the sea; a youthful swimmer who had come up on her unseen — behind her till she had put about. The lad was swimming rapidly, though with a curious waste of motive power, and was so close that Miss Heth seemed to herself to be staring full into his face. His course was laid dead across her bows; for other reasons, too, his piratical intentions were instantly obvious to the girl in the boat.

How did he dare! — after all these months . . .

For an exciting second she plotted escape by flight, but the impulse was all but still-born. He would be on her before she could put about. The girl sat entirely still, regarding the swimmer in a kind of fascinated silence. The irony of fate, indeed, that, at a moment when her whole mind and heart were toward the rose-pink future, this scapegrace ghost from her only "past" should have risen out of the sea upon her. To dream of a Canning, and be entrapped by a Dalhousie! . . .

The youth sloshed alongside, laid hold of the boat's nose, and methodically and with some difficulty pulled himself in. The weight of his ingress tipped the gunwale to the water's edge, but Carlisle made no outcry. She was clear of head; and the heart of her desire was to be free of this misadventure without attracting attention from the shore.

She said in a sharp, clear voice: "Mr. Dalhousie, are you perfectly crazy?"

Dalhousie, in his swimmer's suit, sat stiffly forward, sluicing water into the bottom. He was a big and well-built boy, with a face that had no viciousness; but his dark eyes, with their heavy silken lashes, were hardly meant for a man. Neither was his mouth, for all that he sought to set it so firmly now.

"Mr. Dalhousie," he repeated with elaborate distinctness. "When d' I — draw that — title?"

The girl sat eyeing him with frosty calm: a look which covered rage within, not unmingled with perturbation. . . .

He was a neighbor of hers, this audacious youth, though not of Washington Street; impecunious, and hence negligible; moreover somewhat notorious of late for a too vivid behavior: the distant bowing acquaintance of many years. This till the moment of indiscretion last May; when, encountering his dashing attractions in the boredom of a dull resort, far from her mother's restrictive eye, she had for an idle fortnight allowed the relation between them to become undeniably changed. Foolish indeed; but really she had thought — or now really thought she had thought — that the impossible youth took it all no more seriously than she. Not till her return home last month had he revealed his complete untrustworthiness: presuming, as she termed it, making claims and advances, putting her to trouble to keep her vernal unwisdom from her mother. Still, she *had* thought she had disposed of him at last. . . .

Now there sat the unwelcome swain, her boarder, so close that she could have touched him. And her gaze upon him was like arctic snowblink: an odd look in pretty young eyes.

"You've no right to force yourself upon me in this way," said she. "You must get out of my boat at once."

"Oh, no, I must n't, Carlisle. That's where you make — mistake. You've put me off — too often. Now — the time's come."

"You must be out of your senses. This is outrageous. I insist —I demand that you get out of my boat *immediately*."

"When d' ju — listen when I — demanded?"

His heavy resoluteness reduced her suddenly to the weakness of saying: "A gentleman would n't do such a thing. . . .You will regret this."

"Man," said Dalhousie, with the same labored slowness, "comes before gen'leman. An' the regrets — will be yours. I've come — to have a talk."

In the momentary silence, the drip, drip from his bathing-suit became very audible. The lad leaked like a sieve, all over her boat. Miss Heth glanced swiftly and vexedly from him, over the unchanged panorama. Empty water lapping empty beach; no one watching. Only now, in the sky over the station, there hung a haze of train-smoke. . . .

Her eyes came back: and now she observed with some girlish anxiety the young man's unwonted solemnity, the strange brilliance of his eyes. A certain nervousness began to show through her cold calm: her unconscious hand wound the taut sheet round and round the tiller, an injudicious business in view of the gusty breeze. How to be rid most quickly of the interloper? . . . She might, of course, put ashore with him: but she particularly did not care to do that, and have all the piazza loungers and gossips see her in his somewhat too gay company. Most particularly she did not care to have her mother glance out of her upstairs window and be stunned by the same sight, with apoplectic cross-examination to follow . . .

"Jack," said Carlisle Heth, hurriedly, in rather a coaxing sort of voice, "if you will leave me now, I will — I promise to see you in town next week."

A flicker touched Dalhousie's eyelid; but he said huskily, after a pause: "Promise? What's your promise worth? You've promised me before. You said — you loved —"

"I can't talk now. But on Monday afternoon — in the park — or at my house — whichever you prefer . . . I — I'll explain. I give you my word of honor —"

"No! You've done that before — too. Explain! Howc'n you explain? Go on. Try now. Why've you — refused to see me? Why —"

Red stained the girl's cheeks.

"Then you'll force me to put in immediately," she said, with an angry reversal of tactics, — "and subject me to the humiliation of being seen with you. What a coward!"

"Humiliation!" Dalhousie repeated, flushing vividly. "You say that?"

"Can't you understand that it would be? Are you really so stupid? Haven't you learned yet that I don't ever want anything more to do with you? . . ."

Such remarks brought action and reaction. The lad's look must have warned Miss Heth that all this went rather far. In fact, she began a sort of retraction, a hurried little soothing away of her impolitic and fairly conclusive remarks. But Dalhousie interrupted her, rising unsteadily in the boat, his young face quite strange and wild.

Who would scrutinize the dying flickers of last summer's flirtation? All that mattered was only too well seen from the shore.

It was the smallest of the rickey-drinkers who bruited the mishap abroad, his eye having happened to stray through a slit between a cottage-side and a boat-house. At this time, with the approach of evening coolness, the hotel piazza was filling up a little; and at the man's word, the place was instantly in a turmoil.

There started, in fact, all the horrid rigors of amateur rescue work: of which the least said the soonest mended. It was presently noted by some coolhead that the renter of boats, having seen the disaster first, had already put out for the scene of trouble, rowing lustily. Nobody could beat him to his garlands now; that was clear; clear, too, that there really wasn't much peril, after all. So the motley gathering of idlers became content to stand upon the edge of the boat pavilion, gazing most eagerly, gossiping not a little. . . .

The bystander, like the Athenian, ever desires to see or to hear some new thing. And really this spectacle was new enough to satisfy the most exacting.

Perhaps a mile over the water, a hundred yards or so from shore, the little boat Lady Jane lay side up on the sea. To it clung a young girl, well above water; near her appeared the head of a young man, a swimmer. So far, so good. But there was something wrong about this swimmer, something grossly discordant in his position in the picture. It developed upon close examination that the interval between him and the overturned boat was not decreasing. It was widening indeed; widening quite steadily. . . . Yes, there it was; unfortunately no longer open to doubt. The man was pulling for the shore and safety, leaving the girl to sink or swim as she preferred.

The sight was a strange one, resembling a defiance of established law. It staggered the eye, like the sight of water running uphill. People had seen the Hanging Gardens of Babylon and kissed the Pope's toe; but they had never seen anything like this.

A nasal, hawk-nosed individual in eye-glasses voiced the sentiments of all: "If that's your Southern chivalry, Warlow, the less I see of it the better."

Another spoke more sympathetically, yet with unchanged point: "Poor Dalhousie — born to trouble! Rye whiskey an' marryin' cousins — that's what's killed him."

A third, an elderly woman, with a rich voice, said: "I wonder what there was between those two. . . ."

The actual rescue proved a tame affair. Suddenly attention was diverted from it by the cry of a certain winsome young thing, who, when the alarm was raised, had been among the first to scream.

"Oh, *look* at that little man. He *hit* him!"

"Where? — Who? — Oh!"

"Serves him ri — Ah-h!"

It proved as the screamer said. The smallest rickey-drinker, not content with sounding the alarm, had gone brilliantly bolting down the beach. Taking his stand there at a given point, he had flung himself upon the youth who had so ably saved his own skin, as the latter waded ashore, and struck him savagely in the face. It was observed that the man from the sea seemed surprised by this attack. He stared at his small assailant in a confused sort of way; and then with passionate swiftness plucked hold of him by two favorite points of vantage, and threw him bodily into the water. This movement, as it chanced, turned his gaze seaward. The youth was seen to stand an instant, rigid as a bather in marble, staring out over the water he had traversed . . .

Then he turned, heedless of the brandishings of the little man behind him, and went away toward his bath-house in the manner that is best described as a slink.

III

MISS CARLISLE HETH sat cold and proud in the approaching lifeboat, picking at her sopping skirts. She ignored, hardly hearing, the conversation of her rescuer, hinting broadly that she should reveal these mysteries to him. Revelation, as she understood herself, was the contrary of her desire. The occurrences of the last quarter of an hour had actually dazed her; but the net result of them was sufficiently manifest. Her purpose had been to detach herself unnoticed from Dalhousie's gay fame. And now: — *Look at the boat pavilion . . .*

It was the bitterest moment of Miss Heth's well-sheltered young life. Of notoriety, of a vulgar sensation such as this, of malicious gossip, of all that was cheap and familiarizing, she had a deep-seated horror. Of the moment of reckoning with her mother, whose objections to noisy rumor rather surpassed her own, she felt a wholesome dread. There was also the matter of her personal appearance, which she conceived to be repulsive: she was confident that she looked a hideosity and a sight. Her eyes fastened from afar upon the staring faces on the pavilion. She saw hungry curiosity stalking there, naked and unashamed, and the sight sickened her.

For these faces, as individual faces, she felt indifference and contempt. But in the mass they seemed to assume the enormous importance of good or ill repute. What these people were saying of her and Dalhousie to-day, the world would say to-morrow.

To know what this was, she would have given on the spot all the money she possessed (eight thousand dollars, birthday and Christmas presents, in United States bonds). But to run the gauntlet of those questioning faces was just a little more than she could endure. She was quick in action. She said:

"Land me here, Mr. Wedge. And you must walk with me to the hotel."

As she directed, so it was done. They landed there, and Carlisle and Mr. Wedge struck out hurriedly up the strand for the main entrance of the hostelry. When the cunning ruse became plain to the staring gallery, it was practically too late to do anything about it. You could not have caught the escaping pair without a sprint. However, each man promised himself to be the first to interview the boatman . . .

After the humiliating cut-and-run, which stretched out interminably, Carlisle found herself, at length, in the haven of the brilliantly lighted elevator. Water dribbled from her skirt's edge; she was aware of the elevator boy's African side-glances. If she had been a different sort of girl, she could no longer have refrained from bursting into tears. Fine ending to her rosy journey this! — a sensational "scene" played out before a house of loafers, and now the babel of thousand-tongued gossip, linking her name amorously (so she suspected) with the red-painted ne'er-do-well. Charming background, indeed, for a remeeting with the heir of the Cannings.

Her plight was crushing to the distracted girl; but her anger, the wild resentment of a high spirit feeling itself abominably mistreated, made it impossible for her to be crushed. She would not lie down tamely and be trampled upon by malicious mischance. She would *not* . . .

Mrs. Heth, just risen from her refreshing nap, heard the sounds of arrival in the adjoining room and opened the door between. Then she leaned back against the door-frame, her ladylike eyes starting from her head.

"*Carlisle!* . . . Oh, merciful heavens! What? — *What on earth's happened?*"

Miss Heth, already beginning to free herself of her soaking clothes, braced for the explanatory ordeal. Having no plan of procedure except to put herself in as praiseworthy a light as possible (thus avoiding a useless scene), she began in a hard, dry voice:

"I went out for a little sail. I thought it would be a nice thing to do, the sea was so smooth and calm. A — a man was out swimming near me, and he climbed into my boat. I ordered him out, and — and he jumped out, and — I upset. He swam off — leaving me in the water — and the boatman had to come out and bring me in. Oh, mamma! — *I'm the talk of the place!*"

Mrs. Heth took two swift strides into the room. She came like a cat, claws out, ready to pounce. Her splendid hair hung loose about her head, revealing the birthmark upon the temple, a round spot the size of a silver half-dollar. Ordinarily dull pink, this spot was slowly mottling in blues and purples: though evidently not with reference to the perils of the deep, so narrowly escaped by her only child.

"The talk of the place! — what do you mean?" she asked in a voice that sounded dangerous. "A man! — what man? Speak? What right did he have to get into your boat?"

"Of course he had *no* right to get into my boat, mamma," said Carlisle, dribbling water. "None whatever. That is what I told him, from the beginning. His name is Dalhousie. I — that part makes no dif —"

"Dalhousie! Colonel Dalhousie's son! — that young sot! Why, you don't know him, do you? — you never met him in your life —"

"Please don't storm and rant, mamma. It only makes things worse. As I was saying, when you interrupted, I — I met this man once — a long time ago. Some one introduced him, I suppose. That must have been it. I — I've never seen him from that time. He had n't the faintest right to get into my boat — not the faintest. He —"

"But what did he do it *for?* What did he want? What was his purpose, I say?"

Carlisle turned away with a wet skirt to hang. It was certainly very difficult to explain things to mamma.

"Oh, mamma! — How can I tell you why he wanted to get into my boat? All this just wastes time. Perhaps he thought he would have a little flirtation. Perhaps he wanted to rest from his —"

"What did he *say* when he got in? He did n't just step on like you were a street car, did he? Speak up! What ex —"

"That's just it! That's just what he did. He climbed in, and did n't say a word. I at once told him to get out. That is what we talked about *entirely*. Then at last he got out, in — in an angry way — shaking the boat, and then I — I went over —"

"It passes belief! The young ruffian, after upsetting you, simply deserted — Were you in the water long? Are you cold? Do you feel like you were going to have chills?"

"No — I feel well enough, physically. . . . But — mamma — "

"You're going to have chills — that's it. No wonder! Wait! I never in my life! . . ."

She whisked into her bedroom, and, returning with the travelling-bag, produced a bijou flask with a silver top that turned into a little drinking-cup. Into the top she swiftly poured a thimbleful of excellent French brandy.

"Drink this. It will keep them off." And she added: "It passes belief. . . ."

And then she walked the floor, her unexpected hands, so oddly stubbed and thick, clasped before her.

"You called out to him, of course? You screamed for his assistance?"

Carlisle, choking over the inflammatory draught, set the silver top down on the bureau. There was a gratifying absence of cynicism in her manner. She was always, as her mother knew, a serious girl at heart. She had to drink nearly half a glass of water before she could dislodge all the brandy from her larynx.

"Oh, mamma — how can I remember just exactly what I did? Please be reasonable. I was too excited and frightened, suddenly plunged into the water, to think what I was doing. The point —"

"You must have cried out. Of course you screamed for his assistance. And the young blaggard . . . What time is it? Five o'clock? Then Willie's train is already in . . ."

The spoken thought brought a full stop to the good lady's ejaculations, shot her mind in dead silence round a corner. She stopped walking, stood intently still. After all, what so serious had happened? Her daughter was, indeed, the talk of the place, which was an exceedingly undesirable thing; especially since an "exclusive" girl's name is so tender a bloom, and Mr. Canning was very probably downstairs listening to it now — the talk, that is. But, after all, young Dalhousie's dissolute misbehaviors were so well known, nobody could possibly . . .

"They can hardly say anything to reflect upon *you*," the mother summed up aloud, frowning intently. "You have been foolish, most indiscreet. How you ever permitted anybody to introduce such a character to you passes my understanding. However — any attractive girl is likely to draw the attacks of ruffianly men. His conduct surpass —"

"Yes — but do you think everybody 'll understand that?" said Carlisle, hurriedly, and rather felt that the worst was over. "That's just it, mamma, — don't you see? How do we know what sort of gossip is being bandied about downstairs now? You know people *always* put the worst possible construction they can on a — an episode like this! . . ."

Her mother wheeled on her, struck afresh in her dearest possession, namely: her pride in the prestige of the name of Heth in an envious and backbiting world.

"How do you mean, construction? What construction could they possibly —"

"Why, anything, mamma! — anything their horrid minds can think of. That I'm a great friend of this charming man's, for instance, — engaged to him, perhaps! That this exhibition in the boat was only a refined little lovers' quarrel —"

"How under heaven could any fool say —"

"Well, you *know* they'll wonder why he got into the boat in the first place, and say the hatefullest thing they can think of . . . There are plenty of people who would like to see us h-humiliated."

Mrs. Heth, staring at her with an intake of the breath, then said slowly: "*Ah—h!*" And she took in a whole range of new possibilities with one leap of her immensely constructive mind.

"It is n't fair," said Carlisle, nervously, slipping into a pretty pink negligee. "And you know how a gossipy story flies, growing all the time —"

"I know," murmured her mother, intensely, as one who has suffered much from just that demeanor of stories. . . .

The falling sun shot a ray into the white-and-cherry bedroom;

peeped at the lovely girl sitting stiffly on the bed's edge, turned thick mote-beams upon the lady of deceptive delicacy who stood, with flowing brown hair and still more flowing robe de chambre, silent upon her peak in Darien. The leather-shod clocklet, which always accompanied these two upon their travels could now be heard ticking. Carlisle looked at her mother, and there were both apprehensiveness and dependence in her look. She herself was the cleverer of the two women, but very comforting it was to her to feel this rock-like support behind her now.

Into Mrs. Heth's gray eyes had sprung a kind of glitter, the look of a commanding general about to make an exterminative rush upon the enemy. Hugo Canning to be maliciously informed that *her* daughter was, had been, or ever should be engaged to Jack Dalhousie! Not while she retained her love of justice, and the power of locomotion in her limbs.

"Oho!" said she. "Well, I'll fix *that* . . . I'll stamp upon their miserable lies . . ."

The room telephone rang loudly, hastening decisions. Carlisle winced visibly. In her mood of acute sensitiveness, she was for not answering at all. But Mrs. Heth, the fighting man now in full possession of her, tossed off the receiver with a brigadier air.

"Well?" demanded she sharply; and then, continuing: "Yes. Oh, yes! Howdedo, Willie . . . You've arrived, have you? (It's Willie Kerr, Cally.) What? Oh, yes. She's quite well, though naturally somewhat upset by the shock. It is a most unpleasant occurrence, and I feel deeply for the young man's father, and his friends if he has any. Certainly, Willie. We want the whole affair perfectly understood. Our position demands it. Yes. I want to talk with you about it, at once. Will you meet me in the Blue Parlor in ten minutes? Very well. Mr. Canning came with you, I suppose? . . . Ah, yes . . . What? *No*, Willie! Not a *line!* You must put your foot down on that! This is entirely a personal matter and I will not allow a piece in the paper about it. I won't have it. . . . Ah. All right, then. I'll trust that to you. In ten minutes, Willie. . . ."

The capable little general turned from the telephone to find the eyes of the lieutenant or private fixed fearfully upon her.

"Willie," she explained, hurriedly, "says there's a newspaper reporter hanging about — think of it! — trying to pick up something scandalous for his wretched sheet. Willie has promised to attend to *him*. He says he knows the editor or correspondent or whoever it is, and there won't be the slightest trouble in shutting him up. There shan't be either. Now to business."

At her best in action, mamma glided through the door into her own room, slipping off her robe as she glided. In an amazingly short time she was back again, breathing hard, and dressed for no-quarter affray.

"You did n't talk downstairs, Cally? No one pumped you as to what had happened?"

"No, I spoke to no one."

Mrs. Heth wielded hatpins before the mirror, the glitter surviving in her eyes.

"I am putting on a hat," she threw out, "to give matters a casual air. A public hotel's a hotbed of gossip. Everything depends on the story's being started right — on just the right note. . . . Thank God, I'm here!"

"Lie down," added Mrs. Heth, and Carlisle lay down.

The most exhaustive details of the affair had not, perhaps, been laboriously collected as yet, but luckily Mrs. Heth was not the sort that requires a mass of verbose testimony and dull statistics. The right note awaited her touch six floors below, and time was pressing. Already her mind had flown well ahead, perceived with precision just what was required. Willie must be seen, and at least two ladies, of different sets, great gossips, for preference; and to these she would confide, with some little just indignation but without excitement, the astounding truth about the young blackleg who, having boarded and upset her daughter's boat, turned coward and scuttled off, ignoring her frightened cries. Nor would she fail to express her sincere sympathy for Colonel Dalhousie, whose heart (she understood) the behavior of his degenerate son had broken before now. . . .

"Do you want Flora with you?"

"No — I 'd rather be alone."

"Remain quietly here till I return."

Briefly framed in the doorway, Mrs. Heth added: "You must get some sleep to be fresh for the evening . . . *I'll* nail their slanderous falsehoods."

Her daughter's glance upon her was touched with a flash of admiration, the more striking in that she herself was quite unconscious of it.

Exact definition of desire and a simple strength of purpose from which all aims of others bound back stone-dead: what brilliance of genius or quintessence of mother-wit can hope to outdo this immortal combination?

Echo, solitary, answers . . .

Mrs. Heth's return to the upper regions, an hour later, trumpeted complete victory. The right note was struck; all was settled. Carlisle, it appeared, had trusted insufficiently to the virtue of the Heth name. Of horrid gossip there had been, at the worst, no more than a bare hint or two, an attenuated suggestion. Malicious as the world was, few, indeed, had dreamed any justification of Dalhousie's blackguardism. Already, it appeared, the hotel rang with objurgations of it, and him. Still, Mrs. Heth had struck the note, and struck hard.

Carlisle was bidden to sleep, after her trying experiences, to regain her poise and color for the evening. . . .

Alone again in the twilight bedroom, the girl snuggled beneath a pretty pale-blue quilt, and absently scrutinized her pink and very shiny little finger nails. After the excitement and strain of the last hour and a half, she felt that she was now at peace. Nothing at all was going to happen. Nobody could say anything the least bit horrid about her, the least bit injurious to her position. She stood exactly where she had stood when she went out for the sail. She was not even going to have chills . . .

She decided to dismiss it all from her mind and go to sleep, but her mind for a time refused to come into this agreement. Though that was exactly what she had meant not to do, the girl presently found herself thinking back over the whole occurrence, from the moment when she first saw Dalhousie in the water. In time vague doubts gathered and clouded her perfect brow. She became a little oppressed by the recollection of certain variations between what she had said and really intended to say to her mother upstairs, and what her mother appeared to have said to Rumor downstairs. For instance, she had never said that Dalhousie *literally* upset her boat, or even that he was exactly *in* the boat when it upset; and *never* said that she had screamed again and again for his help when she found herself in the water. No, she had particularly avoided saying those things, for justly angry and excited though she was, she had n't considered it right to say anything that was n't strictly true. Mamma just jumped right on ahead, though, paying no attention to what you said.

The whole thing had happened very unfortunately, she saw that clearly now. Of course, she could n't tell mamma that she and Jack Dalhousie had quarrelled terribly in the boat and he had looked as if he meant to strike her, for then mamma would have asked, How could you have had such a terrible quarrel with a man that somebody barely introduced to you once, a long time ago? And if she had said pointblank, No, I don't think I screamed, mamma would have asked, Why under heaven did n't you scream? — and all this would have meant stopping for a long explanation right there, just when there was so much else to think about, and mamma almost bursting a blood-vessel as it was.

Still, she wished now that it had all been started differently. In the excitement, of course, she had not had time to think out every single thing carefully and definitely. It occurred to her now, after some meditation, that she might simply have said to mamma: "He had frightened me so by getting into my boat, that when I upset and I knew I was n't going to drown, I did n't want to call him back " . . .

Darkness crept into the white-and-cherry bedroom. Till now, what with nearly drowning and mamma and everything, she had really thought very little about it from Dalhousie's point of view. Now it came over her, rather dubiously, that what everybody seemed to be saying of him downstairs did put him in quite a disagreeable position. But then, of course, everybody was a little worked up and excited just now. In a day or two they would forget about it, and the whole thing would blow over. Besides, he deserved the severest punishment for the way he had treated her; and as for anything he might say now (though as a gentleman he would hardly say anything and try to blacken a lady's character), of course nobody would listen to him for a minute.

And as far as that went, nobody would listen to her either. People never did. She regretted the whole occurrence as much as any one, but you could *never* correct flying gossip; everybody knows that. People always arrange the little details as they want them arranged, according to what makes the most exciting story, and they never pay the smallest attention when you come in with a just, mathematical face and say: "You haven't got it quite right *there*. There's a little mistake *here*. . . ."

Worry, clearly, was out of place. It never does any good, as all philosophers agree; and besides, it brings wrinkles in or near the forehead. Carlisle turned on her other side and snuggled with more relaxation beneath the pale-blue quilt. Drowsiness stole over her, seducing thought. Presently she slept, and dreamed of Mr. Canning.

IV

*Mr. Hugo Canning, of the well-known Pursuing-Sex; how the
Great Young Man pursued Miss Heth to a Summer-house, and
what stopped his Thundering Feet.*

NOR were the figments of sweet sleep too fanciful or far-
flown. About eight-thirty o'clock, when Mrs. and Miss
Heth stepped from a descending lift into the glaring publicity of the main floor, the first object that their eyes fell upon
was Mr. Hugo Canning in the flesh. The second was Cousin
Willie Kerr, even more in the flesh, trotting loyally at his side.
At this precise instant, in short, the celebrated transient quitted
the dining-room for the relaxations of his evening.

The coincidence of the moment was pure: one hundred per
cent, as they say commercially. One takes it to mean that
Destiny, having handled a favorite child somewhat roughly for
a time, now turned back its smiling mother-face. The ladies
Heth, having dined refinedly in their sitting-room, descended in
search of cooling breezes, or for any other reason why. Over the
spaces of the great court, half lobby, half parlor, Miss Heth had
seen the masculine apparitions an instant before they saw her:
or just in time, that is to say, to be showing them now her flawless profile. . . .

It is easily surmised that Miss Heth's manner in action was
contained, her habit the very reverse of forward. One seeing her
now would be cheaply cynical, indeed, to say or dream that, with
reference to some such conjuncture as the present, this girl had
left a happy home many hours before. Her presence shamed
every unworthy surmise. With a lovely unconsciousness she
was spied walking her innocent ways toward the piazza with
mamma, even now girlishly unaware that an opposite and uproarious sex was in headlong pursuit . . .

If this pursuit — to be doggedly literal — appeared to lag for a moment, if it did not seem to start with that instant *élan* which one had a right to expect, be sure that there was a complication of sound reasons for that. Kerr, in the circumstances, was the appointed leader of the chase; and Kerr hesitated. Canning's desire to avoid the local society and be left free to outdoor exercise and sleep was, in truth, only too well known to him. And to-night, worse luck, the distinguished visitor appeared even less socially inclined than usual: annoyed when the select little party he had expected from northerly haunts had been found represented at the Beach by a telegram instead; increasingly bored by the desolate air of the all but empty hostelry. "When's the next train out of this hell-hole?" — such was Mr. Canning's last recorded remark up to this not uninteresting moment.

Kerr, when he saw Mrs. and Miss Heth over the distance, merely made a genial exclamation, and then gazed. He was nearing forty, was Willie, short and slightly bald, with an increasing appreciation of the world's good things and as much good nature as his round figure called for. Canning's acquaintance he had by the chance of a lifelong friendship with Mrs. Allison Payne. By reason of a native clannishness and certain small obligations of a more material nature, he was more than ready to share his privileges with his brilliant cousins. But . . .

"So that's the drowned lady," said Canning's voice, rather moodily, at his elbow. . . . . "Well, then, I know her."

"Dandy girl, Carlisle," exclaimed Willie, instantly. "Great little piece of work . . ."

One hundred feet away, opportunity unconsciously receded toward the piazza. Willie, having hesitated through no unfaithfulness, plunged with no want of tact.

"Got to speak to 'em a minute — make inquiries — cousins, y' know. D' ye mind?"

"My dear chap, why should I?"

"Awright — just stop and say howdedo," said the plump diplomatist. "Won't take a minute . . ."

And Canning, perceiving then that Kerr expected to make this stop in his company, said with an assurance not unbecoming to his lordly bearing: "If you please. And don't start anything, for pity's sake. I'm for bed in fifteen minutes."

So it all fell out, according to the book. So it was that the pursuing feet were free to thunder. So Mrs. Heth heard the voice of the leal one, subdued from a distance: "*Howdedo, Cousin Isabel! How're you an' Carlisle this evening? . . .*"

And so the maid turned, startled from her other-worldly dreams . . .

He was the greatest parti that had ever crossed her path, that was ever likely to cross her path. But Miss Heth faced him with no want of confidence; received his greeting with a charming bright negligence. One saw readily that such a matter as "making an impression" was far indeed from this maid's mind. If doubts, a vague uneasiness relative to the afternoon, still fretted the hinterlands of her mind (and they did), she was much too well trained, too resolute withal, to let them appear troublously upon the surface. Moreover, the nap of forty minutes, not winks, had been like the turning of a new leaf; and she was fortified, woman-wise, with the knowledge that she looked her best. Over her shoulders there clung a shimmering scarf, a pretty trifle all made of the scales of a silver mermaid. It was observed, however, that the gray crêpe-de-chine quite justified its choice. . . .

The meeting of four had been effected in one end of the wide garish space: among the loungers of the lobby, all eyes were turned in that direction. There were salutations; the introduction of Mr. Canning to Mrs. Heth; inquiries after Miss Heth's health. Quite easily the square party resolved itself into two conversational halves. Mrs. Heth, it was clear from the outset, preferred Willie Kerr's talk above any other obtainable at that time and place. She was, and remained, absolutely fascinated by it . . .

"It seems quite unnecessary," Mr. Canning was saying — but he pronounced it "unne's'ry" — "to ask if you are any the worse for the ducking . . ."

"Oh, no — I'm quite well, thank you. We've suffered nothing worse than the spoiling of all our plans in coming here!"

The man's look politely interrogated her. "Oh, really? I'm sorry."

"We came, you see, to be very quiet. And we were never so frightfully noisy in our lives."

He smiled; made his small distinguished bow.

"You've reason to feel annoyed on all scores then. At any rate, it's charming to find you as our fellow guest."

And his eyes flitted from her toward Kerr, and then turned briefly upon mamma, and her strange little downy mustache.

Carlisle now perceived the disinterestedness, if not the faint weariness, in Mr. Canning's manner; she saw that he had forgotten the five minutes at the Country Club. The strong probability was, moreover, that he thought the worse of her for allowing herself to be nearly drowned in so vulgarly public a way. However, she was untroubled; she thought him, for her part, adorable to look at and of a splendid manner and conceit; and aloud she inquired, with her air of shining indifference, if Mr. Canning was not delighted with the Beach in October.

"Well, you know, I think I've been here before" — he said *bean*, most deliciously — "only I can't be quite sure. It seems to me a most agreeable place. Only, if it isn't indiscreet to inquire, what does one do in the evening?"

"Usually, I believe, one goes to bed directly after dinner. If one does this, and dines extremely late, the evening slips by quite nicely, we find."

"But the afternoons? Wouldn't they perhaps loom a thought long at times, waiting on for dinner?"

"There's napping provided for the afternoon, you see. And many other diversions, such as reading, walking, and thinking."

"Perhaps one should arrange to spend only afternoons at the Beach. You make them sound simply uproarious."

"We're a simple people here, Mr. Canning, with simple joys and sorrows, easily amused."

Mr. Canning looked down at her. However, Carlisle did not meet his gaze. Having already, in a quiet way, given him two looks where they would do the most good, she was now glancing maidenly at mamma, who conversed vice-presidentially of her Associated Charities policies.

"They must be brought to help themselves!" Mrs. Heth was saying. "Wholesale, thoughtless generosity is demoralizing to poverty. It is sheer ruination to their moral fibre."

"Promiscuous charity! — ruination! Just what I always say," chirped Willie. "Look at ancient Rome, ma'am. Began giving away corn to the poor, and, by gad! — she fell!" . . .

"Delightful ! I see I shall like it here," Mr. Canning was observing — and was there perceptible the slightest thawing in his somewhat formidable manner? . . . "I too," said he, "have dwelt in Arcady."

The girl looked over the spaces, a little smile in her eyes.

"Ah, then you did n't need to be told that the sandman comes early there."

"But not, I think, when the moon shines bright — and the simple amusements you speak of seem to be waiting? Surely games in the evening are not altogether forbidden, or does my memory of the place deceive me?"

"You seem to remember it perfectly. But I thought your complaint was that there was nothing at all amusing to do in Arcady."

"Ah," said Mr. Canning, "but I'm having my second thoughts now."

She had given him a third, uptilting look with her speech; and now it was as if the great eligible had seen her for the first time. If the gaze of his handsome eyes became somewhat frank, this girl had been fashioned to stand all scrutiny victoriously. A mode which defined the figure with some truthfulness held no terrors for her; rather the contrary. Her skin was fine and fair as a lily, with an undertone of warmth, dawn pink on the cheek; the whiteness of her neck showed an engaging tracery of blue. Her mass of hair, of an ashy dull gold, would have been too showy above a plain face; but the case was otherwise with her. Her mouth, which was not quite flawless but something better, in especial allured the gaze; so did her eyes, of a dusky blue, oddly shaped, and fringed with the gayest lashes . . .

"Besides," added the man, looking down at her with a certain lightening in his gaze, "as I remember, I did not say that there was nothing amusing to do. I merely, as a stranger, came to you begging some guidance on the point."

"I see. But I very much doubt my ability to guide you in that way, Mr. Canning —"

"I can only observe that you've thrown out a number of perfectly ripping suggestions already — walking on the piazza, for example. Might n't we steal that diversion from afternoon temporarily, don't you think? Perhaps Mrs. Heth would agree to pursue the missing breeze so far?"

"That would be nice," said Carlisle.

You could distinctly hear his thundering feet now . . .

Strolling for four was agreed upon, and that simple afternoon amusement started. But, arriving at the piazza, the dowager discovered that, after all, the night air was just a little cool for her, and turned back, not without some beaming. She mentioned the Blue Parlor as her port of call, where smoking was forbidden. Willie, doing his duty as he saw it, dropped his cigar into a brass repository. He had faults like the rest of us, had Willie, but his deathless loyalty deserved a monument in a park.

Carlisle and Mr. Canning strolled on alone. She walked outwardly serene as the high-riding moon, but inwardly with a quickening sense of triumph, hardly clouded at all now. As she and mamma had planned it, so it had fallen out. . . .

Many eyes had followed this shining pair as they quitted the common gathering-place. She, as we have seen, was inviting as a spectacle. He, to the nobodies, was simply one of the sights of the place, like the Fort. And his distinguished House was still a small one, at that, not yet arrived where another generation would unfailingly put it. If the grandfather of Hugo Canning had founded the family, financially speaking, it was his renowned father who had raised it so fast and far, doubling and redoubling the Canning fortune with a velocity by no means unprecedented in the eighties and nineties. To-day there were not many names better known in the world of affairs, in the rarer social altitudes, even in the shore-hotels of the provinces. . . .

And the son and heir of the name and fortune, who now trod
the Beach piazza with Miss Carlisle Heth, was obviously more
than many sons of wealth, much more than a mere trousered
incident to millions. This one saw in the first glance at his
Olympian bearing; but Carlisle Heth knew more than that.
Upon this young man the enterprising vehicles of modern history had, long since, conferred an individual celebrity. Often had
the Sunday editors told their "public" of his exploits in the
sporting and social realms, as they called them; not rarely had
journals of a more gossipy character paragraphed him smartly,
using their asterisks to remove all doubt as to who was meant.
Before such an evening as this had ever crossed her maiden's
dreams, Carlisle Heth had read of Hugo Canning. . . .

It was a bad throat, a God-given touch of bronchitis or what-
not, that had sent the great young man south. This was known
through Willie Kerr, and other private sources. Also, that he
would remain with his Payne cousins through the following week;
and in December might possibly return from the Carolinas or
Florida for a few days' riding with the Hunt Club. Meantime
he was here: and it was but Saturday, mid-evening, and a whole
beautiful Sunday lay ahead. . . .

From the piazza, after a turn or two, Miss Heth and Mr.
Canning sauntered on to a little summer-house, which stood on
the hotel front-lawn, not far from the piazza end. She had
hesitated when he commended the pretty bower; but it was
really the discreetest spot imaginable, under the public eye in all
directions, and undoubtedly commanding a perfect view of the
moonlight on the water, precisely as he pointed out.

In this retreat, "What a heavenly night!" exclaimed Miss Heth.

Canning, still standing, looked abroad upon a scene of dim
beauty, gentle airs, and faint bright light. "Now that you say
it," he replied, "it is. But depend on it, I should never have
admitted it quarter of an hour ago."

"Oh! But isn't it rather tedious to deny what's so beautifully
plain?"

"Should you say that tedious is the word? A better man than
I denied his Lord."

"Yes," said Carlisle, not absolutely dead-sure of the allusion, "but he was frightened, wasn't he, or something?"

"And I was lonely. Loneliness beats fear hollow for making the world look out of whack."

"Doesn't it? And is there a lonesomer place on the globe than a summer resort out of season?"

"But we were speaking of fifteen minutes ago, were we not?" said Canning, and sat down beside her on the rustic bench.

The walls of this little summer-house were largely myth, and lattice for the rest. Through the interstices the dim brightness of the moon misted in, and the multitudinous rays from the hotel. There reached them the murmur of voices, the languorous lap of water. A serene and reassuring scene it surely was; there was no menace in the night's silvern calmness, no shadow of stalking trouble. . . .

Carlisle imagined Mr. Canning to be capable of a rapid advance at his desire, and was opposed on principle to such a course of events. Still, she was saying, a moment or two later:

"And in the Payne fort on the Three Winds Road — I suppose you never feel lonely there?"

"Why fort, if one might know?"

"I've been told that you were awfully well barricaded there, prepared to stand any sort of siege."

Canning seemed quite amused. He declared, on the contrary, that neglect and unpopularity were his portion in a strange land.

"I'm an invalid on sick-leave," said he, "and my orders are to go to bed. Please don't smile, for it's all quite true . . ."

He appeared to develop a certain interest in the moonlit talk. He proceeded in a voice and manner no longer purely civil:

"And, to bare my soul to you, I'm no fonder of being lonely than another man. . . . Do you know that, but for Kerr, you're my one acquaintance in all this part of the world? What shall we say of that? I sit at dinner, consumed by blue devils. I emerge, and behold, you walk across the lobby. Haven't I some right to feel that the gods are with me even at the Beach?"

Perchance she might have given him some information there, but instead she laughed musically.

"The god of the pretty speeches, at any rate! Must I tell you that you did n't look quite overjoyed when dear Willie came dragging you up?"

"I've no doubt I looked all sorts of ways, for I'd never felt more unfit for any society, including my own. The more is my debt to you for chasing my devils away. . . . But perhaps I owe you no thanks after all, as one guesses that you do these little services for others without any particular effort."

Carlisle glanced at him, smiling a little from her dusky eyes.

"Your experience is that most people find it a great effort to speak pleasantly to you, I suppose?"

"Again I point out to you that our talk is not of most people, but of you."

"Oh! And is there something particularly original about me? This grows exciting."

"I, for one, think that beauty is always original," said Canning, with sufficient impersonality, but no more. . . . "Still, we know, of course, that unaided it cannot drive the blues of others very far."

"After the sugar-coating comes the pill. Tell me in what way I have been deficient."

"Ah, that's yet to learn. To be charming by habit is an agreeable thing; but you have n't convinced me yet, you know, that you know how to be kind."

Her lashes fell before his masculine gaze; she did not answer. About them was the sweet hush of the night. She was aware that he had moved nearer upon their bench; aware, too, of a faster beating of her heart. And then, quite suddenly, a new voice spoke, so close that both started sharply; a rather shy voice, yet one possessed of a certain vivid quality of life.

"I beg your pardon — but *is* this Miss Heth?"

They turned as upon one string. At the door of the summer-house stood the blurred figure of a man, bareheaded and tall. The light being chiefly behind him, he showed only in thin silhouette, undistinguishable as to age, character, and personal pulchritude. Stares passed between the dim trio.

44

"I am Miss Heth."

"Could you possibly let me speak to you — for a moment, Miss Heth? I realize, of course, that it's a great intrusion but —"

Canning started up, annoyed. Carlisle, without knowing why, was instantly conscious of a subtle sinking of the heart: some deep instinct rang a warning in the recesses of her being, as if crying out: "This man means trouble." She glanced at Mr. Canning with a kind of little shrug, suggesting doubt, and some helplessness; and he, taking this for sufficient authority, assumed forthwith the male's protectorship.

"Yes? What is it that you wish?"

The tall stranger was observed to bow slightly.

"As I say, I beg the favor of speaking to Miss Heth a few moments — privately. Of course I should n't venture to trespass so, if the matter were n't vitally important —"

"Who are you?" demanded the great young man with rather more impatience than seemed necessary. "And what do you wish to speak to her about? Speak plainly, I beg, and be brief!"

The two men stood facing each other in the faint light. Ten feet of summer-house floor was between them, yet something in their position was indefinably suggestive of a conflict.

"I should explain," said the intruder, dim in the doorway, "that I come as a friend of poor Dalhousie — the boy who got into all the trouble . . . Ah . . . "

The involuntary ejaculation, briefly arresting his speech, was his perfect tribute to the girl's beauty now suddenly revealed to him. For Carlisle had unconsciously leaned forward out of the shadows of the bench just then, a cold hand laid along her heart.

"This afternoon," the man recovered, with a somewhat embarrassed rush. "I — I appreciate, I need n't say, that it seems a great liberty, to —"

"Liberty is scarcely the word," said Hugo Canning, fighting the lady's battle with lordly assurance. "Miss Heth declines to hear . . ."

But the stranger's vivid voice bore him down: *"Do you, Miss Heth?* . . . The situation is terribly serious, you see. I don't want to alarm you unnecessarily, but — I — I'm afraid he may take matters into his own hands —"

Canning took an impatient step forward.

"Nevertheless, it's pure impudence for him to send to this lady, sneaking for favors now. Let's —"

"Mr. Canning, I — I'm afraid I *ought* to speak to him!"

"What?" said Mr. Canning, wheeling at the voice, as if stung. *"Oh! . . . That's kind of you!"*

Carlisle felt, under Mr. Canning's incredulous gaze, that this sudden upwhirl of misfortune was the further refinement of cruelty. She hardly knew what to do. Scarcely thinkable as it was to dismiss Hugo Canning from her presence, it seemed even more impossible to pack off this nameless intruder. Inconceivable malignity of chance, indeed! Only one doubt of its all being settled and blown over had lingered on to trouble her; and now without warning this doubt rose and rushed upon her in the person of the sudden stranger — and before Mr. Canning, too. It occurred to her, with ominous sinkings of the heart, that she had relied mistakenly upon Dalhousie's gentlemanliness. What horrid intention was concealed behind these strange words about his taking matters into his own hands? And suppose she refused to see the emissary alone, and he then said: "Well, then, I'll just have to speak before your friend." . . . What would Mr. Canning think of her then? What was he going to think of her anyway?

Carlisle, having risen, answered her protector's gaze with a look of appealing sweetness, and said in a low, perturbed voice:

"I'm so dreadfully sorry. But I don't quite see how I could refuse just to — to hear what he has to say. Under the circumstances, would it — would n't it be simply unkind?"

Canning said, with small lightening of his restrained displeasure: "Ah! I'm to understand, then, that you wish to give this — gentleman an audience alone?"

It was, of course, the last thing on earth she desired, but God clearly was out of his heaven to-day, and Mr. Canning would like her better in the long run if he stepped aside for a space now. She said, with a restraint which did her credit:

"*Could* you forgive me — for five minutes? You must know how I — dislike this. But *ought n't* I —"

The great parti gave an ironic little laugh.

"As you please, of course. I shall await your pleasure on the piazza."

And he stamped out and away into the moonlight, passing the silent intruder with a look which said loudly that he would have kicked him if it had promised to be worth the trouble.

The silver cord was loosed. The village-clock, quarter of a mile away, struck nine, and all's well. Hugo Canning's stately back receded. Coincidently the shabby-looking stranger who had displaced him stepped forward into the summer-house. The first thing Carlisle noticed about him was that he was lame.

V

Dialogue between V. Vivian, of the Slums, and Mr. Heth's Daughter (or his Niece); what the lovely Hun saw in the Mr. Vivian's eyes, just before he asked God to pity her.

DALHOUSIE'S tall friend advanced with a limp, in silence. He halted at a courteous distance; it was seen that one hand held a soft hat, crushed against his side. A faint wave of the ethereal light immersed the man now, and Carlisle dimly descried his face. She observed at once that it did not seem to be a menacing face at all; no, rather was it kindly disposed and even somewhat trustful in its look. It was the second thing that she noticed about him.

Perhaps no girl in the world was less like the popular portrait of a fat horse-leech's daughter than this girl, Carlisle Heth. Surely no advance ever less resembled the charge of a hating prophet upon a Hun than this man's advance. Carlisle, to be sure, was never one to think in historical or Biblical terminology. But she did note the man's manner of approach upon her, and his general appearance, with an instant lifting of the heart. The whole matter seemed desperately serious to her, full of alarming possibilities, a matter for a determined fight. And she felt more confidence at once, the moment she had seen how the emissary looked, how he looked at her.

Chiefly for strategic reasons, she had sat down on the bench again, well back in the shadows. She did not speak; had no intention of speaking till speech might gain something. And the stranger, silent also, wore an air of hesitancy or confusion which was puzzling to her and yet quite reassuring, too. If he had come to say that Dalhousie would talk unless she did, would he be this sort of looking person at all? . . .

The man began abruptly; clearly nothing plotted out in advance.

"He's quite crushed. . . . I — I've just come from him . . ."
And then, hurriedly running his fingers through his hair, he
retraced his steps for a better start.

"I should first say how kind it is of you to receive a — a
stranger, in this way. I need hardly say that I appreciate it,
greatly. . . . And I bring his hope that you can be merciful, and
forgive him for what he did. He is badly broken, that I promise
you. . . . It's all so curiously confused. But it does n't seem that
he can be quite so bad as they're saying here to-night . . ."

The stranger hesitated; he was gazing down with grave intentness.

"Miss Heth, Dal swears he can't remember the boat's upsetting at all."

His tone expressed, oddly, not so much a contradiction of anybody as a somewhat ingenuous hope for corroboration: Carlisle's
ear caught that note at once. She was observing Jack Dalhousie's
shabby friend as a determined adversary observes. He had
moved a little nearer, or else the pale light better accustomed
itself to him. And she saw that his face, though manifestly
young, had an old-fashioned sort of look which seemed to go
with his worn clothes; a quaint face, as she regarded it, odd-
looking in some elusive way about the eyes, but, she felt surer
and surer, not dangerous at all.

Now her gaze, shifting, had fastened upon his tie, which was
undeniably quaint; a very large four-in-hand showing pictori-
ally, as it seemed, a black sea holding for life a school of fat white
fish. And then there came a lovely voice from the shadows —
lovely, but did it sound just a little hard? . . .

"Perhaps you had better begin at the beginning, and tell me
who you are, and what it is you want."

"Yes, yes! Quite so!" agreed the author of the Severe Arraignment, rather hastily. . . .

A little easier said than done, no doubt. Yet it may be that
one of the young man's inner selves still hovered over the belief
that this girl must be Mr. Heth's (of the Works) niece, or haply a
yet more distant relative. . . .

"I mentioned that," said he, "because it was naturally uppermost in my mind. I — ah ... But to begin at the beginning, as you say ... I got a telegram in town, telling me that Jack Dalhousie was in serious trouble. It was from Hofheim, a fellow, a sort of druggist, who happened to know that I was one of his best friends. So I caught the six-ten train and Hofheim met me at the station. *My* name's Vivian ... "

He stopped short, with an odd air of not having intended to stop at this point at all. So bystanders have watched the learning bicycle rider, irresistibly drawn to his doom against the only fixed object in miles. However, no association of ideas woke in the mind of the silent girl upon the bench. Not easily at any time did brick-throwing Socialists gain foothold there; and this day had been a disruptive one for her, beyond any in her experience.

"The name," hastily continued the young man, with an intake of breath, "probably conveys nothing to you. I — I merely mention it. . . . Well, Hofheim, this sort of — fellow, was n't in the hotel when the — the occurrence took place, but he told me what everybody was saying, as we came up in the 'bus together. I feel very sure you can have no idea. . . . Shall I repeat his story? I don't, of course, want to trouble you needlessly."

"Do."

So bidden, he swiftly epitomized the narrative told him by the fellow Hofheim, who had got it at fifth or sixth hand after Mrs. Heth's striking of the right note. The Hofheim rendering seemed to include such details as that Dalhousie (being an entire stranger to Miss Heth) had overthrown her boat with homicidal hands, and that, as he swam away, he had laughed repeatedly and maniacally over his shoulder at the girl's agonized screams.

"They don't say that he struck you — with an oar," the man concluded, sad and satirical. "I believe that's the only detail of the sort they omit. . . . As a matter of fact, Miss Heth, Dal says he never heard you scream at all."

Then he clearly paused for a reply, perhaps a reassuring burst; but there was only silence. The harried girl on the bench was thinking, intently but with some bewilderment. Somewhat aghast as she was (truth to tell) at the way in which the minor variations had been maliciously distorted, her attention had been closely engaged by the curious way in which Mr. Dalhousie's friend was going at things. Why did he sound less like a challenge and a threat than like somebody whistling hopefully to keep up his courage?

The question irresistibly emerged. Carlisle's slim fingers furled and unfurled the end of her mermaiden's scarf, and she looked up at the tall stranger in the dusk and sweetly spoke for the third time.

"But I don't understand. If he has told you all about it, I — I don't see why you have come to me at all."

Then the man appeared to recollect that he had omitted the most important part of his narrative — of course she did n't understand, no wonder! — and spoke with some eagerness.

"I should have explained that in the beginning! — only of course I don't like to trespass too far on your time. . . . You see — unfortunately — Dal's hardly in position to speak about the matter at all. I —"

He paused, as if seeking how to put it, and then spoke these doubt-destroying words:

"It is very perplexing, but the truth is — he says so himself — he does n't know at all what took place."

"Oh! . . . *He does n't know!*"

"I don't wonder you're astonished at his saying so," said the young man, in quite a gentle way. "And yet I do believe him absolutely . . ."

He now explained, in well-selected phrases, that Jack Dalhousie had been very drunk when he boarded the boat, having taken a running start on the evening preceding. Though he might have seemed normal enough, through long experience in control, he was actually quite irresponsible; and drink had played strange tricks with his mind before now. The boy could remember getting into the boat, it seemed; remember that — ah — that she had objected (very properly) to his presence; remember standing up in the boat, very angry, and the wind blowing in his face. The next thing he remembered was being in the water, swimming away. And then, when he landed, a man standing there on shore

cursed him and struck him in the face . . . Then he had looked
out over the water; he saw the upset sailboat and the boatman
rowing out, and the people, and it rushed over him what he must
have done. Till then, he said, he had never dreamed that anything had happened. He could hardly believe it, even with the
evidence of his own eyes. Then later Hofheim, the sort of fellow,
had gone up to see him, and told him what people were saying,
which so much more than confirmed his worst suspicions. Hofheim was a stranger, but he meant well. . . .

Dalhousie, in short, was in the singular position of having to
implore others to assure him that he had n't done all these terrible things. And it appeared that Miss Carlisle Heth was the one
person in the world who could possibly give him that assurance.

So spoke the stranger. That he had scattered lifelines, that all
his oratory had come agrapple with nature's first law, evidently
did not cross his mind. He gazed down at the girl's dimly limned
face, and his gaze seemed full of an unconquerable hopefulness.

"The boy's behavior has been inexcusable in any case," he
said. "And be sure he's been punished, and will be punished
severely. But . . . it must be that either the — the trouble
did n't happen at all as this story says it did, or if — at the worst
— it did happen that way, Dalhousie was simply out of his
mind, quite insane, and did n't know what he was doing. He
is n't, of course, a ruffian or a coward. Won't you help to make
them understand that?"

The girl raised her eyes, which in the twilight were darker
than the 'depth of water stilled at even.'

"I don't see the necessity for that," she said, in a firm voice.
" I— I'm afraid I can't consent to be involved in it any further."

Over the little summer-house hung the sweet beauties of the
serene night. About it stretched the calm lawn in chequers of
large faint brightness and gigantic shadows. Within it stood the
tall stranger, rooted in his tracks. Then it seemed to occur to
him that there was some misunderstanding; that at least, in his
anxiety about his friend, he had n't allowed sufficiently for the
properly outraged feelings of the lady — this so unreasonable-
looking daughter of Mr. Heth of the Works, or his niece . . .

"It's all tremendously trying for you, I know," he said, with the same sort of gentleness. "I assure you the situation has distressed me greatly — from every aspect. And I think it's most kind and — and generous of you to let me speak with you when you must feel that you've been so badly treated. . . . But you see — as it stands, you are involved in it, really, more than any one else. I'm sorry, but in fact the whole issue is in your hands."

"I can't see that. He has given you his — his version of what took place. No one will prevent him from saying the same thing to whomever he wishes."

"But who will believe him?"

Carlisle perceived a rhetorical question, though she did n't know it under that name; she made no reply. She would really have preferred no more questions of any sort — what was the use of them? In her, as in all the Maker's creatures, the instinct for self-preservation was planted to work resistlessly. Small wonder, indeed, if, in the unexpected discovery that dependence on Dalhousie's dubious gentlemanliness was unnecessary, the uprush of relief should have swept away all lesser considerations, flooded down all doubts. All was settled again in a trice, as by a miracle: the miraculous agent here being, not the Deity (as she vaguely suspected), but only the Demon Rum, he who had taught the frail lad Dalhousie to be so mistrustful of himself . . .

She had had a harassing day, including three momentous *tête-à-têtes* with three different and widely variegated men, mostly comparative strangers: Jack Dalhousie, Mr. Canning, and now this Mr. Vivian. She was very tired of being dogged and nagged at and interfered with, and she wanted very much to terminate this interview, which she saw now had been extorted from her by a pretty sharp piece of deception. And through her mind there skipped a beckoning thought of Mr. Canning, conceived as feverishly pacing the piazza . . .

"You see, his defence," Mr. Vivian was saying, with some signs of nervousness, "is merely his own word that he had no idea you were upset. I believe him absolutely, because I know he would n't lie, and he admits, to his own disadvantage, that his

memory is n't at all clear. But — it 's all so muddled and confused somehow — I 'm afraid everybody else will think that a
rather silly fabrication, invented by a desperate man to put
himself in the best light possible. That is — unless his word is
corroborated."

His inflection invited remarks, nay, urged them, but there was
only silence.

And then within V. Vivian, M.D., there woke a cold doubt,
and gnawed him.

"Miss Heth — I must ask — for the whole moral question
hangs on this . . . *Did he know that you were upset?*"

Miss Heth cleared her throat, preparatory to rising. She saw
now that she ought never to have consented to talk with this
strange man at all. Mamma would have known that in advance.

"It is — rather absurd — for me to be asked to decide what
he knew. He has assured you that —"

"But — I don't make myself clear, I see — the fact is that
yours is the only assurance that will carry the smallest weight on
that point. . . . He was n't — may I ask? — actually *in* the boat
when it went over, was he?"

"N-no. As to that — I believe he had just got out, but —"

"Did you think at the time that he knew you were upset?"

"Unfortunately, I am not a mind reader," she began with dignity, objecting seriously to these obstacles in the way of ending
the interview. "Thrown without warning into the water, I could
not look into his thoughts and see —"

"Quite so. But did he show in any way that he knew you were
upset?"

A kind of chill had crept into the stranger's voice. The two
young people gazed at each other. The man had strange eyes
(they were the third thing she had noticed about him), gray, she
thought, and gifted with an odd sort of translucence, singular
and speaking.

"Let me see. No, he did not. That is what I said at the time
— that he did n't take the slightest notice of me —"

"He swears he never dreamed anything was wrong till he
landed. Don't you feel that that 's quite possible, at least? Or . . .

did you scream out for his help, so loudly that he *must* have heard you, if he 'd been himself?"

"The — the first few minutes in the water were very confusing. I can't pretend to say exactly what I did or did n't do. I had to think about saving my life —"

"Of course. But if you'd screamed a number of times in saving your life, you would be likely to remember it, would n't you?"

"Really I can't acknowledge your right to —"

"Miss Heth — *why did n't you scream ?*"

His swift cross-examination touched the quick of her spirit; and she came to her feet, trembling a little, and feeling rather white.

"I will not allow you to catechise me in this way. I will not . . ."

Dr. Vivian, from the Dabney House, over the Gulf, stood still, quite silenced. . . .

The thought had struck V. Vivian, and shot him down, that this girl was lying, deliberately suppressing the truth that meant more than life to Dal. She had n't screamed. Dal had n't known she was upset. . . . Yet was it thinkable? In the fiercest denouncing of the yellowest Huns, who had ever dreamed anything so base of them as this? *Lying ?* With that face like all the angels, that voice like a heavenly choir? . . .

The tall doctor saw that his suspicion was unworthy and absurd. His was no simple choice between his friend's shameful cowardice, and this girl's criminal falsehood. No, Dal was crazy-drunk at the time, and himself cried out in his misery that the worst that they said of him was probably true. And even supposing that this girl was no more than a fiend in seraphic shape, what conceivable reason could she have for such infamous suppression? Motive was unimaginable. . . . No, the fault must be his own. He had pressed too hard, pried too tactlessly and inquisitively, not made her understand sufficiently the dire swiftness of the poor boy's need . . .

These two stood face to face. Carlisle saw that Jack Dalhousie's friend was becoming excited; but then, so was she. The man spoke first, in a low, hurried voice:

"I don't mean to catechise — indeed, I don't. You must try to forgive me for the liberties I seem to be taking. . . . The thing's so serious, so pitiful. This story already flying around back in town — making him a base coward — he'll never live it down. And it's to-night or never, a — a misstatement travels so fast and far, and has so long a life —"

"You should have reminded him of all this," said Carlisle, her rounded breast rising and falling, "before he got into my boat."

"Oh, you have a right to say that! He's been wrong, insanely wrong! But does he deserve disgrace — ostracism — ruin? You alone stand between him and —"

"I don't feel that it — it's right for me to be brought into it further. I've explained that. And I must ask —"

"But you *are* in it already, you see. Whatever anybody does or leaves undone, now and for the future — *you are in it . . .*"

The enemy paused, gazing at her; and then suddenly, before she could make just the right opening to go past him, he abandoned restraint, and flung himself upon entreaties.

"Could n't you make a statement — just a little statement — saying that you feel certain he did n't know the boat was upset? that perhaps in the excitement you forgot to scream? — that you know he would n't have left you if he'd understood you were in trouble? Could n't you at least give him the benefit of the doubt? — say or do something to show you've no bitter feeling toward him? —"

"Did he show any regard for my feelings? I must ins —"

"All the finer is your opportunity — *don't you see?* . . . Even strain the truth a little for him, if that's necessary. God," said the shabby young man, quite passionately, "would count it a virtue, I know, for it's now or never to save a man. . . . Could n't you do that? I promise you you won't be bothered any more about it. I know how awfully hard it's all been for you. Could n't you say *something* to help him a little?"

Miss Heth, facing him, imperceptibly hesitated.

For a second, offended though she was by his religious reference (she never heard the name of God mentioned in polite society), this quaint begging Mr. Vivian had her upon the balance. Her flying thoughts swept down the parting of the ways. But they flew swiftly back, stabbing all hesitancies. . . .

She wished as much as any one that it had all been started differently, as it might have been had she been perfectly certain in advance that no one would dare say anything the least bit horrid about her. It was not her fault that gossip was so notoriously unreliable. And now it was simply impossible to rake up the whole subject again, just when it was all settled, and go through another long explanation with mamma. Of course she didn't believe all this about Dalhousie's being ruined and disgraced forever: that was just the man's way of working on her feelings and trying to frighten her. She knew very well that the whole thing would blow over in a few days, if just quietly left to itself.

And what use, whispered the returning thoughts, would the unknown make of the "little statement" he begged so for? What would mamma say, for instance, to a black-typed piece-in-the-paper in the "Post" to-morrow? And what of Mr. Canning —nudged the wise thoughts — the happiness symbol on the piazza, whose princely feet were so plainly twitching to thunder behind? . . .

No; clearly the only sensible thing to do was to end all the talk and quibbling at once, definitely. Carlisle took a step forward over the dim chequered floor, resolute as her mother.

"I can't add anything to what I've already said. I cannot let you detain me any longer."

Her advance had brought her fully into what light there was, falling mistily through lattice and door. And at the look in her eyes, young Dr. Vivian's hands fell dead without a struggle at his sides. His tall figure seemed mysteriously to shrink and collapse inside his clothes. He said, oddly, nothing whatever. Yet an hour's oration could not have conveyed more convincingly his sense of irreparable disaster.

The instantaneous cessation of his verbal flow curiously piqued the girl's attention. Face to face as they stood, she was struck quite sharply with an elusive something that seemed to cling to this man's look, a subtle enveloping wistfulness which she had vaguely noticed about him before, which somehow seemed, indeed, only the sum of all that she had noticed about him before. It may have been this look that briefly checked her withdrawal. An odd desire to justify herself somewhat more clearly fluttered and stirred within her. Or — who can say? — perhaps this was no more than the beautiful woman's undying desire to appear at advantage before every man, however far beneath her.

"You — you must not think me unfeeling," she said in a sweet hurried voice. "I want to be as considerate as possible. I am terribly sorry for him — terribly — and you must tell him so, from me. But I — I am in a peculiar position. I am not free to —"

"I see. I understand now."

His strange tone fell upon her ears as a challenge, quiet though it was; and it was a challenge which Carlisle, though instantly regretting her generosity (when she might just have walked away), saw no entirely dignified way of avoiding.

"You see what?" she said, faltering a little. "I don't know what you mean."

The man replied slowly, almost as if he were thinking of something else, and the thought rather hurt him:

"I see your only thought is to gain some point for yourself — you alone know what — no matter what pain your silence may give to others . . . Ah, that's sad . . ."

Angry and a little frightened, too, Carlisle Heth drew her gossamer shawl more closely about her shoulders, with a movement that also wore the air of plucking together her somewhat wavering hauteur.

"You are at liberty to think and say what you please," she said, distantly; and with a slight inclination of her head started past him.

But he did not seem to hear the dismissal order; stood unmoving, blocking her progress; and looking up with now tremulous indignation, Carlisle ran once more full on the battery of his speaking eyes. . . .

Perhaps it was not difficult to guess what John the Baptist

would have said, in such a case as this: but then the young man
V. V. was not thinking of John the Baptist now. He was not
feeling grim at all at this moment; not fierce at all. So in his look
there was to be seen nothing of the whiplash, not one thing reminiscent of the abhorring fanatic on the outskirts of the city. His
eyes were filled, indeed, with a sudden compassion; a compassion
overflowing, unmistakable, and poignant. And from that look
the richly dressed girl with the seraph's face instantly averted
her gaze.

She heard a voice: the lame stranger speaking as if to himself.

"All that beauty without, and nothing at all within. . . . So
lovely to the eye, and empty where the heart should be. . . .
God pity you, poor little thing . . ."

And then Carlisle passed him quickly and went out of the summer-house upon the lawn. The escape, this time, presented no
difficulties. For the last syllable had hardly died on the young
man's lip before self-consciousness appeared to return upon him,
staggering him, it may be, at the words of his mouth. He
turned, abruptly, and fled in the other direction.

So the audience in the moonlit summer-house concluded
precipitately, with the simultaneous departure of both parties
from opposite exits. Carlisle Heth went hurrying across the lawn.
Within her, there was a tumult; but her will was not feeble,
and her sense of decorum and the eternally fitting hardly less
tenacious. Strongly she ruled her spirit for the revivifying remeeting that awaited her just ahead . . .

But it was not Mr. Canning's voice which greeted her as she
stepped up on the hotel piazza. It was the low, angry challenge
of her soldier-mother, nipped in the act of charging upon the
summer-house.

"*Carlisle!* . . . In heaven's name, what have you been doing?"

Facing mamma on the deserted piazza-end, Carlisle explained
in a hurried sentence that Mr. Dalhousie had sent a pleading
friend to her, whom she had felt obliged to see. . . .

"Are you *mad* to say such a thing? Was it for wild antics of
this sort that I threw everything to the winds to bring you down
here?"

59

"Oh, mamma — please!" said Carlisle, her breath coming fast. "I've had about enough. . . . I — I could n't run the risk of his starting heaven knows what scandalous story. Where is Mr. Canning?"

Mamma looked as if she wanted to shake her.

"You may well ask," she said, savagely, and turned away.

"I do ask," said Carlisle, with returning spirit. "Where is he?"

Mrs. Heth wheeled on her.

"Did you suppose he would hang about kicking his heels for hours while you hobnobbed with low men in dark summer-houses? He just excused himself on the ground of a cold caught on the piazza, and has retired for the night. You shall do the same. Come with me."

Carlisle went with her.

And next morning, Sunday, the very first news that greeted the two ladies, upon their appearance for a late breakfast, was that Mr. Canning and Mr. Kerr had left the Beach for town by the nine-twenty-two train.

VI

Of Carlisle's Bewilderment over all the Horrid Talk; of how it was n't her fault that Gossip was so Unreliable; of the Greatest Game in the World; also, of Mr. Heth, who did n't look like a Shameless Homicide.

THE explosion that followed the boat occurrence at the Beach came as a complete surprise to the heroine of the small affair. When she had terminated the interview in the summer-house, she understood that she was giving the signal for talk to cease and all trouble to proceed to blow over. The want of coöperation on the part of talk and trouble was gross, to say the least of it. The tide of excited questions and comment that poured in on and around Carlisle, upon her return to town on Monday, resembled the breaking of floodgates. Her small and entirely private misadventure had become her world's sensation. And within a day there came a climax which secretly astonished and frightened her not a little. The primal blood-tie itself was severed for offended righteousness' sake. The proud old widower, Colonel Dalhousie, already sorely tried by his son's wildnesses, could not stomach his flagrant cowardice. It was shouted about the town that he had cut Jack off with a curse, and turned him finally out of his house.

Unplagued by the curses of imagination, Carlisle had, indeed, anticipated nothing in the least like this. She was dazed by the undreamed hubbub. For the first few days after her homecoming, she remained very closely in the house, to avoid all the worrying and horrid talk; and one day, the day Mattie Allen ran in with popping eyes to tell her about Jack Dalhousie, she pretended to be sick and stayed in bed, and really did feel extremely badly.

In these days of uneasiness, Carlisle wished far more than

ever that the whole thing had been started differently; and she wondered often, and somewhat fearfully, if Dalhousie's friend, Mr. Vivian, would try to force himself on her again. That did not happen; nothing happened; and the more and more calmly she came to think about it all, the more clearly the girl saw that she personally was not to blame for the misunderstanding. It was plainly seen as one of those unfortunate occurrences which, while regretted by all, herself as much as anybody, you simply could not do a single thing about. And if it had seemed impossible to rake it all up again even that night, how much more unrakable was it now, when days had passed, and everybody had accepted everything, for better or worse, as it was? Fate and gossip had proved too strong. Deplorable, indeed; but it was to be, that was all.

It was very plain, of course, that all the initial excitement and pother could not possibly last. Withhold food from gossip, and it starves and dies. Carlisle simply stayed quiet and held her tongue; and as the days passed without more developments of any sort, she found her philosophical attitude thoroughly justified by events. Town-talk, that bugbear of the delicate-minded, shot off first to the Hoover divorce, and then to the somewhat public disagreement between the Governor of the State and Congressman Hardwicke, at the Chamber of Commerce luncheon for the visiting President; finally to a number of things. By the time six weeks had passed, the Beach had dropped completely from the minds of a fickle public. Dalhousie, it seemed, had considerately vanished. Talk ceased. The boat trouble blew over, much as the boat had done. . . .

About this time, namely, about the middle of the seventh week, one of Willie Kerr's cryptic messages lay beside Mrs. Heth's breakfast plate on a morning. It ran:

> I think he will come at 5.30 o'clock
> Wednesday. Better arrive first?
>
> W. K.

Willie's cipher (he liked to write as if he lived in Russia, with the postal spies after him like hawks) was no mystery to Mrs.

Heth, she being, in a certain measure, its inventor. Having taken the telegraphic brevity upstairs to show to Carlisle, she disappeared into the telephone booth, to rearrange her afternoon. If all subscribers to the telephonic system were as tireless users as she, probably fewer people would have made large fortunes by the timely purchase of forty dollars worth of stock.

This was a Wednesday morning in mid-December. Carlisle, recuperating from a gay débutante rout on the evening preceding, remained in bed. By this time the "season" was well under way: all signs promised an exceptionally gay winter, and Carlisle was, as ever, in constant demand. She had meant to spend the morning in bed anyway, and then besides her mother had pointed out the necessity of being fresh for the afternoon. . . .

From the moment of their abrupt parting at the Beach, Carlisle had not set eyes upon Mr. Canning, though he was known to have lingered as a house-guest all through the following week. The circumstance had surprised her considerably at the time, until she had thought out some satisfactory explanations for it. To-day her maidenly thoughts assumed a wholly prospective character, very agreeable and cheery. Mr. Canning, having arrived yesterday from some southerly resort of his choice, was again staying at the Payne fort on the Three Winds Road, his reported design being to ride a few times with the Cold Run hounds, otherwise barricading himself as unsocially as before. Still, he expected to remain for a week at least, which was very nice; and under these circumstances it was as natural as possible that his connoisseurship should be asked to pass judgment on the new little bachelor apartment in Bellingham Court, where his friend Kerr was just comfortably installed. . . . Where, also, no impossible stranger could intrude himself upon the company of his betters, with revivalist vocabulary and killjoy face.

The clock stood at eleven. The drawn shades imparted a restful dimness to the bedroom, but the reliable maid Flora had been in to shut the windows and start a merry fire in the grate. This room had been done over last year in gray and old rose, with the "suit" in Circassian walnut, and wainscoted walls which harmonized admirably. It was a charming cloister, all most captivating to the eye, with the possible exception of the dressing-table, which rather bristled with implements and looked just a thought too businesslike.

Carlisle loafed and invited her soul. Her glorious ash-gold hair, whose habit of crinkling from the roots was so exasperating to contemporaries of her own sex, swept loose over the pillows, charmingly framing her face. . . .

While the Beach episode itself was now long since closed and done with, it was not unnatural that the memory of Dalhousie's friend, the Mr. Vivian, should have remained in Carlisle's mind, for Mr. Vivian had addressed such words to her as had never before sounded upon her ears. These words had clung by their sheer astounding novelty. To have God petitioned to pity you by a shabby nobody in a pictorial tie: here was an experience that invited some elucidation. For a time the girl's thoughts had attacked the nobody's sincerity: he was merely failure pretending to despise success. But, not ungifted at self-suasion though she was, she had not seemed to find solid footing here; and she had early been driven irresistibly to quite a different conclusion. Evidently this man Mr. Vivian was a queer kind of street-preacher type, victim of a pious mania which rendered him dangerously unsound in the head. This, obviously, was the truth of the matter. On no other theory could his pitying her be satisfactorily explained.

It was true that, with the dying down of her own sense of vague ambient perils, she herself had come once more to feel dreadfully sorry for Jack Dalhousie, and even to admit in her meditations that she could have afforded to be more magnanimous in defending him from gossip. But then that did not at all change the fact that Dalhousie deserved the severest punishment for all the trouble and worry he had brought her. It clearly was not right, was not moral, to make things too easy for wrongdoers. She had gradually come to see herself as a custodian of the moral law in this quarter, a tribunal of justice which, while upholding the salubriousness of punition, yet strives to keep as large and generous as it can.

Therefore it followed as the night the day that Mr. Vivian,

who could work himself up to the condition of feeling sorry for
her as she discharged her painful duties (while admiring her loveliness), was a sort of camp-meeting madman. He was an advanced kind of religious fanatic, nearly in the foaming stages,
something like a whirling dervish. His emotional gibberings
were beneath the notice of sane, wholesome people.

Still, in lengthening retrospect, Carlisle had become quite
dissatisfied with the manner in which she had permitted the
summer-house interview to terminate. It was somewhat galling
to recall the tameness with which she had allowed a Shouting
Methodist such a last word as that, entirely unreproved. Because unreproved, the staggering word had stuck fast; in spite of
all efforts, it remained as a considerable irritation in the background of her mind. Many times she had resolved that, if she
ever saw the man again (which seemed unlikely, as nobody appeared ever to have heard of him), she would make a point of
saying something pretty sharp and definite to him, showing
him how little she cared for the opinions of such as he. And
then, at other times, she decided that it might be best simply
to ignore the man altogether, turning her back with dignity, after
perhaps one look such as would completely show him up. Let
sleeping dogs lie, as they say. . . .

She rose, in excellent spirits, shortly after noon, and began an
unhurried toilet. The toilet was so unhurried, indeed, that
she had hardly finished and descended to the family sitting-
room on the second floor when her father's latch-key was heard
clicking in the front door. This sound was the unofficial lunch-
eon-gong. The House of Heth proceeded to the dining-room,
where Mr. Heth kissed his daughter's cheek in jocund greeting.

"Good-*afternoon*, Cally! And you just up — well, well!
Times have changed —

> ' Early to bed, early to rise —
> That makes us all healthy,
> Wise and wealthy —'

That was my father's rule, and Lord, he kept us to it. . . ."
Mrs. Heth, already seated, bit her lip slightly, which seemed

to confer prominence upon her little mustache. Her consort's habit of quoting, and especially of misquoting, was trying to her, but she now knew it to be incurable, like her daughter's occasional mannerism. She sat as usual rather silent, plotting out the next few hours of her busy time, her remarks being chiefly of a super-fluous managerial nature to that thoroughly competent African, Moses Bruce.

Carlisle, having so lately risen, ate but a *déjeuner*. Mr. Heth, on the contrary, attacked the viands with relish, restoring waste tissues from two directors' meetings, a meeting of the Conven-tion Committee of the Chamber of Commerce, and an hour in his office at the bank. He was a full-bodied, good-looking, amiable-mannered man, of sound stock and excellent digestion, and wore white waistcoats the year round, and fine blond mustaches, also the year round. He certainly did not look to the casual eye like a shameless homicide, but rather like an English country gen-tleman given to dogs. He was fifty-four years old, a hard worker for all his indolent eye, and his favorite diversion was about twelve holes of golf on Sunday morning, and his next favorite one table of bridge by night in the library across the hall.

Greetings over, Mr. Heth said "Catch!" to his wife and daughter, referring to the ten-dollar goldpieces from the direc-tors, and remarked that he had n't been near the Works for two mornings, and that money made the mare go. A sober look touched his fresh-colored face as he voiced these observa-tions, but then he was tired and hungry, and nobody noticed the look anyway. This fashion of the 1.30 luncheon had been one of the earliest of their Yankee innovations which had caused the rising Heths to be viewed with alleged alarm by ante-bellum critics, dear old poorhouse Tories who pretended that they wanted only to live as their grandsires had lived. The Heths, unterrified, and secure from the afternoon torpor inflicted on up-to-date in'ards by slave-time régime, dispatched the exotic meal with the cheerfulness of Property.

"Effete, Cally, — that's what this age is," said Mr. Heth, pushing back his chair, and producing his gold toothpick. "Everybody looking for somebody else's neck to hang on to.

And makin' a lot of grafters out of our poor class. Look at this Labor Commissioner and his new-fangled nonsense. Nagging me to spend Lord knows how many thousands, making the plant pretty and attractive for the hands. Voted for the fellow, too."

"I never heard of such a thing. What sort of things does he want you to do, papa?"

"Turkish baths and manicures and chicken sandwiches, I guess. I don't listen to his rot. Law 's good enough for me. Point I make is that 's the spirit of the poor nowadays. I pay 'em wages that would have been thought enormous a hundred years ago, but are they satisfied? Not on your life! . . ."

Winter sunshine, filtering in through cream-colored curtains, touched upon those refinements with which the prosperous civilize and decorate the brutal need : upon silver, growing flowers, glittering glass, agreeable open spaces, and fine old mahogany. It was an exceptionally pleasant room. The Heths might be "improbable people," as Mrs. Berkeley Page was known to have said on a certain occasion and gone unrebuked, but their material taste was clearly above reproach. And all this was to their credit, proving efficiency in the supreme art, that of living. For the Heths, of course, were not rich at all as the word means nowadays: they were far indeed from being the richest people in that town. Their merit it was that they spent all they had, and sometimes a little more; and few persons lived who could surpass Mrs. Heth in getting a dollar's worth of results for each dollar expended. . . .

Carlisle and her father chatted pleasantly about the remarkable spirit of the poor, and the world's maudlin sentiment towards it and them. The lovely maid professed herself completely puzzled by these problems.

"We're always giving them money," she pointed out, spooning a light dessert in a tall glass, "or getting up bazaars for them, or sending them clothes that have lots more wear in them. And what do they do in return, besides grumble and riot and strike and always ask for more? And they stay poor just the same. What is going to happen, papa?"

Mr. Heth lit a cigar — not one of the famous Heth Plantation Cheroots. He requested Cally not to ask *him*.

"Never be satisfied," said he, "till they strip us of everything we've worked our lives away earning. They'll ride in our motorcars and we'll sit in their workhouse. That'll be nice, won't it? How'll plain little girls like that, eh?"

She was the apple of papa's eye; and she rather enjoyed hearing him talk of his manifold business activities, which was a thing he was not too often encouraged to do. To-day the master of the Works was annoyed into speech by recent nagging : not merely from the Commissioner of Labor, but from the Building Inspector, who had informally stopped him on the street that morning. . . .

"Don't you think, papa," Carlisle said sweetly, "that it will all end in something like the French Revolution?"

Mr. Heth thought it extremely likely.

"Well," said he, "I shan't be bothered by their college folderol. O'Neill's easy enough managed. All I need to do is invite him and Missus O. to dinner."

"Who's O'Neill?" demanded Mrs. Heth, gliding in.

For the second time during the meal, she had been absent from the table, on a telephone call. She always answered these summonses personally, regardless of when they came, appearing to fear that otherwise she might miss something.

"And who," she added, "is going to invite him to dinner?"

Mr. Heth explained, and said that nobody was. He'd only mentioned the possibility if the fellow ever got troublesome, which was most unlikely. His wife was a climber — social bug, you know. "Pays to know your man, eh, Cally? . . ."

"I should say! And O'Neill's wife manages him?"

"Don't they always?" said he, pinching her little pink ear. And thereupon he bethought himself of a thoroughly characteristic quotation, which he rendered right jovially:

"'Pins and needles, pins and needles,
When a man marries, his trouble begins,'

"As the fellow says," concluded Mr. Heth; and so departed

for The Fourth National Bank. Mrs. Heth, reminding her daughter about being fresh for the afternoon, glided to her writing-desk in the library. Carlisle confronted three hours of leisure before the prospective Great Remeeting. She went to the telephone, and called up her second-best girl-friend, Evelyn McVey. It developed that she had nothing special to say to Evey, or Evey to her. However, they talked vivaciously for twenty minutes, while operators reported both lines "busy" and distant people were annoyed and skeptical.

That done, Carlisle went to the upstairs sitting-room, and sat by the fire reading a Christmas magazine, which had come out on Guy Fawkes day, the 5th of November. Presently she slipped off her pumps the better to enjoy the heat: and assuredly there is nothing surprising in that. It is moral certainty that Queens and Empresses (if we knew all) dearly love to sit in their stocking-feet at times, and frequently do so when certain that the princesses-in-waiting and lady companions of the bath are not looking. The telephone interrupted Carlisle twice, but she toasted her arched and silken little insteps well, read three stories, and thought that one of them was quite sweet. Where she got her hands and feet she often wondered. They were so clearly neither Heth nor Thompson. By this time her unwearied mother had gone out to "get in" three or four calls; also an important Charities engagement at Mrs. Byrd's, where Carlisle was to call for her in the car at five o'clock *sharp*, for their visit to the Bellingham. Carlisle now became conscious of a void, and ate five chocolates from a large adjacent box of them, the gift of J. Forsythe Avery. Then she yawned delicately, and picked up "Sonnets from the Portuguese" (by Mrs. Browning); for she, it must be remembered, had a well-rounded ideal, and believed that it was your duty to cultivate your mind. Life is n't all parties and beaux, as she sometimes remarked to Mattie Allen. . . .

There came a knock upon the door, breaking the thread of culture. The seneschal Moses entered, announcing callers, ladies, in the drawing-room. Carlisle sighed; recalled herself to actuality. After glancing at the cards, she conceded the injudiciousness of saying that she was out, and told Moses to announce

that she would be down in a moment. She kept the callers waiting twenty moments, however, while, in her own room, she
made ready for the street. She was donning a hat which in shape
and size was not unlike a man's derby; it was of black velvet,
lined under the brim with old-blue, and edged with a piping of
dark-brown fur. At a certain point in or on it, there stuck up two
stiff straight blue plumes. The hat was simply absurd, wildly
laughable and ridiculous, up to the moment when she got it on;
then it was seen that it had a certain merit after all. It was a
calling-costume (as one believes) that Carlisle assumed for the
Bellingham; a blue costume, of a soft material which had been
invented only about a month before, and which was silk or satin,
according as you looked at it, but certainly did not shine much.
The coat, or jacket or wrap, which completed the suit was arresting in design, to say no more of it. Less original were the
muff and stole of darkest sable; but they were beautiful.

Carlisle, it need hardly be said, went downstairs in her hat.
"Oh," the visiting ladies would say, "but you are going out."
"Oh, not for half an hour yet," she would protest. "I'm *so* glad
you came."

About 4.30, J. Forsythe Avery, who had no office hours, was
ushered into the stately Heth drawing-room. The lady callers
withdrew promptly, but not so promptly as to make it too
pointed. It was generally believed at this time that Miss Heth
"had an understanding" with Mr. Avery, though it was quite
well known that she, personally, much preferred young Robert
Tellford. The figure, however, at which a famous life insurance
company commanded Robert's undivided services made him a
purely academic interest. With J. Forsythe the case was totally
different: from the environs of his native Mauch Chunk the
Avery forbears had dug principal and interest in enormous quantities.

J. Forsythe remained for twenty minutes, the period named
when he had telephoned. Having failed to secure any extension
of time, he went away, and Carlisle skipped upstairs to look in
the mirror, and put on the concluding touches indicated above.
Descending and emerging into the winter sunset, she sent the

waiting car on ahead to the Byrds', and set out to do the five blocks afoot. Exercise makes pink cheeks.

It was a splendid afternoon, sharp and clear as a silver bell. Carlisle walked well, especially when one considers the sort of shoes she wore: she had the good free stride of one who walks for the joy of it and not because that is the only conceivable way to get somewhere. Nevertheless, just as she reached the Byrd door-step, she was overhauled by the Cooneys, her poor but long-step-ping relatives. There were only two of them this time, Henri-etta and Charles, better known, from one end of the town to the other, as Hen and Chas.

The Cooneys, who were young people of about her own age, greeted Carlisle with their customary simple gaiety. Both exclaimed over her striking attire, Charles adding to his sister:

"Let Uncle Dudley stand next to Cally there, Hen — I'm better-looking than you, anyway."

"I'd like to see a vote on that first. Recognize *mine*, Cally?" cried Hen — "the brown you gave me last fall? First appearance since I steamed and turned it. It'll stand a dye next year, too. But we have n't seen you for a long time, my dear. Did you know Aunt Rose Hopwood's staying with us now?"

"Oh, is she? I had n't heard, Hen. How is she?"

"She's bad off," said Chas, cheerfully. "Deaf, lame, and cruel poverty's hit her right at her old home address. I guess she'll come live with us later on. Come walk out to King's Bridge for an appetite."

Carlisle, with an impatient foot on the Byrds' bottom step, glanced from Chas to Hen, smiling a little. Her cousins were well-meaning young people, and she liked them in a way, but she often found their breezy assurance somewhat amusing.

"Thank you, Chas," said she, "but I've an engagement with mamma. I'm to pick her up here now. I hope Aunt Molly's well?"

"Fine," said Hen. "Come and see us, Cally. Why don't you come to supper to-morrow night?"

The lovely cousin obviously hesitated.

"Aw, Cally does n't want to come yell in Aunt Rose Hop-wood's trumpet, Hen —"

"Aunt Rose Hopwood's going home to-morrow."

"First I've heard of it. Frankly I doubt your word."

For that Hen idly smote Chas's shins with her silver-handled umbrella (Carlisle's gift three Christmases before), at which Chas cried *ouch* in such a manner as to attract the attention of bystanders. Henrietta liked this umbrella very much and commonly carried it, like a cane, through all droughts.

"But," said she, reconsidering, "I think Hortense 'll be off to-morrow, that's so. Well, come the first soon night you feel like it —"

Carlisle had been doing some considering also, her conscience pricking her on account of the cousinly duty, long overdue.

"I've an engagement to-morrow — so sorry," she said, rather hastily. "But how about one night early next week, say — Thursday, if that would suit — ?"

Chas and Hen agreed that it would do perfectly. Pot-luck at seven. Sorry she would n't walk on with them. Bully day for Shanks's mares. And so forth. . . .

Carlisle, an eye-catching figure in her calling costume (assuming that this is what it was) glanced after her poor relations from the Byrds' vestibule, and was amused by her thought. How exactly like the Cooneys' lively cheek (and nobody else's) to propose a country walk with them as a perfectly satisfactory substitute for an hour's *tête-à-tête* with Hugo Canning!

VII

How the Great Parti, pursued or pursuing to Cousin Willie Kerr's apartment, begins thundering again.

BELLINGHAM COURT was the very newest of those metropolitan-looking apartment hotels which the rapid growth and complicating "standards" of the city was then calling into being. It was on the most fashionable street, Washington, in one of the most fashionable parts of it. And it had bell-boys, onyxine vestibules, and hot and cold water in nearly every room.

It also had a fat black hall-porter in a conductor's uniform, and this functionary informed Mrs. Heth that Mr. Kerr was momentarily detained at the bank, but had telephoned orders that any callers he might have were to be shown right up. The Heth ladies were shown right up.

Willie's new apartment consisted of a sitting-room, a fair-sized bedroom, and a very small bath. About the sitting-room the ladies wandered, glancing disinterestedly at the Kerr Penates. Presently Mrs. Heth opened doors and peeped into what lay beyond.

"It's a good thing he's small," said she. "H'm, that thing looks like a foot-tub."

Carlisle, looking over her mother's shoulder, laughed. "You could n't splash about much. . . . You shave at that, I suppose."

"I don't. One shaves. There's a better apartment he could have got for the same price, but manlike he did n't find it out till too late. What's this — bedroom? . . . Yes, there's the bed."

They stepped back into the sitting-room, and Carlisle, strolling aimlessly about, became a little silent and distrait.

It is possibly true, as crusty single-men affirm, that a certain solacing faculty inheres in beautiful ladies: the faculty, namely, of explaining all apparently unwelcome situations upon theories quite flattering to themselves. But Carlisle surely needed no such make-believe in this moment of rather excited expectancy.

Of course she knew well enough what inferences Evey and Mattie, for instance (in both of whom there was a certain amount of the cat), would have drawn from the fact that Mr. Canning, last month, had not seemed to follow up in any way their very interesting meeting at the Beach. She alone knew the real circumstances, however, and it had become quite clear to her that Mr. Canning's demeanor was only what was to be expected. He was the proudest of men, and (that awful night at the Beach) she had expelled him from her presence like a schoolboy. Naturally he had been annoyed and offended — stung even into the rudeness of abandoning her in a summer-house to an entire stranger. How could you possibly wonder (unless feline) that he, great unsocial at best, had thereafter remained silent inside his fort? . . .

"How like a man," breathed Mrs. Heth, glancing at her watch, "to pick out this day of all others to be detained at a bank."

She had sat down in one of the bachelor chairs, to take her weight from her feet, which hurt her by reason of new shoes half a size too small. The sitting-room was pleasant enough in a strictly orthodox fashion, and was illuminated by an electric-lamp on the black centre-table. Mrs. Heth, who had helped Willie with his furnishings, had considered it the prettiest electrolier that fourteen dollars would buy in the town during the week before last. Carlisle had come to a halt before the bookcase. It was a mission-oak case, with leaded glass doors. For the moment it might be said to represent rather the aspirations of a bibliophile than their fulfilment, since it contained but seven books, huddled together on the next-to-the-top shelf. Carlisle swung open the door, and examined the Kerr library title by title: "Ben Hur," "The Little Minister," "Law's Serious Call to a Devout and Holy Life" (from his loving Grandma — Xmas 1904), "Droll Tales," "Religio Medici" (Grandma again — Xmas 1907)," "The Cynic's Book of Girls" —

Carlisle laughed merrily. "Willie has two copies of 'The Cynic's Book of Girls.' . . . I'd never thought of him as a divil with the women somehow."

"He could never get Helen Tellford to *look* at him."

"'Religio Medici.' Is it religious or medical? It might be either, by my Latin."

"One of those faith-healing things, I suppose. Emmanuel Movement. I'd sit down if I were you. . . . Ah! There's Willie at last. Mind, Carlisle, — don't you hear the steps?"

"Well, we're invited to look at his things — aren't —"

Her careless voice died, as both together became aware that these could not possibly be the steps of a proprietor. The approaching feet halted decorously without, and instead of the door's bursting open there came only a manly knock upon it. Carlisle looked at her mother, and found that her mother was looking at her with quite a tense expression. This certainly was not the way they had wanted things to happen. . . .

"Possibly it's only a tradesman," murmured Mrs. Heth, with hope; and she added in a commanding voice: "Come in."

The door opened, with a certain stately dubiousness. Full on the threshold stood Mr. Hugo Canning, no less: an impressive presence in loose motor-coat of black fur. Mr. Canning stood agaze; it was to be seen that he was taken considerably by surprise.

For the smallest known fraction of a second, the tableau held. Then action began, dashingly.

"Why, Mr. Canning!" cried Mrs. Heth, heartily, rising. "What a very pleasant surprise! So you're back with us again? Delightful!"

Mr. Canning came forward; he bowed with fine civility over the proffered hand, voicing great pleasure in this remeeting. And then his eye went flitting, with a certain interrogativeness, from mother to daughter.

"Such an agreeable coincidence," beamed the good little lady. "Or perhaps this is not your first visit here, like ours? When did you return? Carlisle . . ."

Carlisle, having forgotten more about the Great Game than

75

her mother would ever know, was far from effusive. Advancing half a step from the bookcase, and offering the tips of white-gloved fingers, she said, smiling perfunctorily:

"How nice to see you. And Willie Kerr, our very delinquent host, — do you bring us news of him?"

"I'm told that he's unluckily detained downtown. But, indeed, it's charming to find you awaiting him too, Miss Heth."

Mrs. Heth sparkled, and declaimed of Willie's remissness. Canning stood in the middle of the floor, hat and stick under his arm, looking without pretences at Carlisle. Under the agreeable indifference of his seemingly amused eye, she felt her color mounting, which only brightened her loveliness. Perhaps it was not quite so easy to maintain the reasoning of beautiful ladies here on the firing-line, as in the maidenly cloister at home.

"Why are men the unreliable sex, Mr. Canning?" said she, laughing. "Here Willie begs us for days to visit him at his rooms — I believe he thinks there's something rather gay and wicked about it, you know, though mamma picked them out for him! — and assures us on his honor as a banker that he is in every afternoon by five at the very latest. So we inconvenience ourselves and come. And now — look!"

"At what, Miss Heth? I trust nothing serious has happened?"

"Ah, but our time is so valuable, you see. We must leave without even saying how-do-you-do. Don't you think so, mamma?"

"So it seems," said Mrs. Heth, and sank into a chair.

Canning smiled.

"Very pleasant little diggings he has here," he observed casually — "my first glimpse of them. I happened to be coming in town on business, and Kerr invited me particularly to drop in to see them, at half after five sharp."

"Really! How *very* fortunate we are! But, oh, why didn't you come a little earlier and charitably help us through the wait? We've had nothing on earth to do but read and reread 'The Cynic's Book of Girls.'"

"Had I ventured to hope that you were to be here," said he, with a little bow — and was there the slightest, most daring stress upon the pronouns? — "you may be sure I should have arrived long ago."

Carlisle, dauntless, looked full at him and laughed audaciously.

"I recall you now as a maker of the very prettiest speeches. And the worst of it is — I like them! . . . Mamma," she added, with fine, gay courage, "it is sad to go just as the guests arrive. Yet don't you think, really —"

"I'm afraid we must, my dear. Willie's evidently —"

But the need for tactics was fortunately at an end. If Carlisle had drawn it rather fine, it was yet not too fine. The door flew open, and in bounded Willie. Destiny climbed to the wheel once more.

Willie, though heated with hurry and worry, handled the situation loyally and well, expressing just the right amount of surprise at the coincidental assemblage, in just the right places. Of his detention at the bank (where, as we may infer from his long incumbency, he discharged a tellership to the complete satisfaction of the depositing public), he spoke in bitter detail.

"If you'll excuse the French, ma'am," he summed up, "a man might's well be in hell as ten cents out."

"Why, I do think, Willie," said Mrs. Heth, "that rather than take all that trouble, I should simply have paid the ten cents from my own pocket and said no more about it."

But even Willie, perfect host though he was, did not see his way clear at the moment to explaining the banking system to a lady.

"You might call it sporting pride, ma'am," he said, patiently, and proposed a little tour of the rooms.

The tour, in the nature of the case, was a little one, almost a fireside tour, and soon over. Willie simply did not have the material to spin it out indefinitely. Then refreshments were hospitably insisted on: tea — muffins — something of that sort, you know — and Willie cried down his order through the telephone, which had already been duly admired — one in every room, etc. Next from a hidden cubby he produced siphon-water, glasses, and a black bottle of Scotch. Needed it, said he — digging two hours for ten cents out.

"Like the quarters, hey, Canning? Gad, may move again. Man across the hall — bigger rooms — wants to sublet. Like you to look at 'em sometime, Cousin Isabel. Say, Cousin Isabel, by the bye," he added, expertly putting ice into three glasses, "ran down that chap V. Vivian for you, just now. Fact. Old Sleuth Kerr — catches 'em alive. He's Armistead Beirne's nephew — just turned up here — what d' you think of that?"

"Mr. Beirne's *nephew!*" echoed Carlisle Heth, without the slightest strategy.

"Vivian? Who on *earth*, Willie?" demanded Mrs. Heth, puzzled; and looked, not at Willie, but at Carlisle.

"Don't you remember? — chap that wrote that fierce slush attackin' the Works, month or so ago? That's the bird. — Got rye right here, if you prefer it, Canning. — Walked a block with him and old Beirne just now. Remember Amy Beirne — eloped with some inventor fellow — what's his name — oh, sure, Vivian, haha! Lived in Alabama. Here's regards."

Mrs. Heth now recalled the name, and also having asked Willie, long since, to identify it. However, she thought the topic just a little inopportune at the moment.

"Ah, yes. Mr. Beirne's nephew — well! I hope you made this *very* mild, indeed, Willie? You know I rarely consent to . . . He might be better employed, one would think, than vilifying the Works, but there's no accounting for tastes, as I always say."

"Just water with a dash, ma'am. Oh, he's one of these slumming chaps, seems — kind of a Socialist, y' know —"

"The Works?" queried Mr. Canning. "Ah, yes! Mr. Heth's — of course! Is a cigarette permitted? . . ."

Carlisle, who had been gazing into the fire and acquiring information, roused. "Oh, here's your tea, Willie!" said she. "How very good it looks!"

Unlike mamma, she did not in the least mind Mr. Canning's hearing mention of the Works, even under attack. Shame at trade was not in her: she was confidently proud of the great mute author of her brilliant being. And it was by this pride, dating back many years and untouched by any late personal impression, that no "attack" could gain standing in her mind.

At seven, she had one day asked her father, "Papa, what *are* the Works?" — and papa had smiled and answered, "It's the place where all our money comes from." To this day, her mind's eye called up a great white marble palace, something like the New York Public Library, only bigger, from the front of which, through an enormous cornucopia, poured a ceaseless flood of golden dollars. . . .

"I've no patience with Socialism," said Mrs. Heth, rising. "Where do you want your things put, Willie? Divide all our property up equally with the lazy and drunken classes, to-day, and by to-morrow the hard-working, well-to-do people would have won every bit of it back again. I'm surprised everybody can't see that, aren't you, Mr. Canning?"

"I'm astonished at their blindness," said Canning, gazing at the floor. "Vivian is clearly off his chump at all points."

"That's right — screw loose," said Willie, genially. "Set 'em here, boy. From the feller's literary style, I'd expected a regular riproarin' fire-eater. Gad, no! Face like a child's, kinder cute-lookin'! Fact. Polite as peaches. You pour, Carlisle, will you?"

The folding-table was set. The tea-things were tenderly arranged upon it by the dusky waiter. The little company moved and shifted. Host Kerr surveyed the pleasant scene with no little secret pride of proprietorship. His room — his tea the ripping-looking girl was serving on his patent table — his hireling just backing out of the door . . . However, his also was the manifest duty in the premises; and, bestirring himself, he fetched tea and cakes for Mrs. Heth and invited her to sit with him beside the mission-oak bookcase.

Canning had dropped into a chair near the fireplace, one yard from the tea-table. He wore without concealment the air of waiting to be entertained. Carlisle poured, and thought that in ten minutes, or at most fifteen, this would be all over: if the present *tête-à-tête* was to lead to another, and so on through a gorgeous climacteric sequence, it was now, or it was never. Here was an exciting thought, with stage-fright possibilities to some; but Carlisle, confident through her many testimonials, merely smiled prettily and asked Mr. Canning if he would not take one or more of the cunning little pink cakes. It appeared that Mr. Canning would; pink, he said, was his color.

"I believe we parted rather suddenly," said Carlisle, continuing to smile a little to herself, "the last time I had this pleasure. Do you remember?"

He desired to know if she could possibly conceive his memory to be so short.

"I was immensely mortified," said she, "to learn that I had given you a cold — it was a cold, was n't it? — or whooping-cough? — by keeping you so long in the night air that evening. I 've worried so about it all these weeks. *Am* I too late to inquire?"

"I kick myself to have gone away leaving you anxious," said Canning, with entire gravity. "The attack, as it chanced, was transitory. There was no coughing — whooping or otherwise. The trouble was purely localized, in the head, and —"

"In the imagination, might one almost say?"

"In the head. You must have heard somewhere of cold in the head? A well-known though unfashionable complaint, throughout the north. I, on the other hand, was much troubled about you, whom I was compelled, by your command, to leave to the mercies of the nocturnal caller. However, Kerr assured me, before I was obliged to go away, that you had come through alive and uninjured."

"Ah, but did I?". . . She added, after a brief pause: "Should you call a biting lecture on one's shortcomings from a strange man no injury?"

"But surely, speaking to that topic alone, my supplanter could not have spun it out for two hours, while I, luckless one, tramped alone on the piazza."

"Two hours? . . . As I say," Carlisle laughed at him, nibbling a little pink cake, "I like your pretty speeches."

The fire crackled merrily. The masculine paraphernalia stood convenient. Canning stretched out an indolent but man's sized hand and refilled his glass. From across the room Kerr's voice sounded, conveying enthusiasm founded on the solid rock of patience:

"And this little poem about roses and how cold your nose is —
I must really show you that, ma'am. Spicy, you know! And the
witty picture!"

"I'll compromise on an hour," said Canning. "And what hideous foibles did the visitor charge you with to banish me that
long?"

"With being quite heartless."

"Oh."

"With having nothing inside to be kind with. For these reasons he felt quite sorry for me."

"Ah! Is it possible that you could remember *my* suggesting,
just a thought before him —"

"I do remember. But, you see, this man is quite crazy. I suspected it then, but I know it now, for you said so not five minutes ago."

Canning looked at her.

"Your words," said Carlisle, "were that he was off his chump
at all points. I hope mamma is n't listening, for she does n't like
me to use slang, and will not believe me when I say the men teach
it to me."

"Oh! . . . Was *that* Vivian!"

Carlisle nodded. "It makes it all quite interesting, does n't it?
To be felt sorry for by a man who writes really wicked attacks on
one's father's perfectly lovely business. Only I knew all along he
was n't really quite right. . . . I hope you 've had a very happy
trip?"

"Thank you. I don't believe I have, particularly."

"Oh, I'm sorry! . . . Have you suffered at all from the blues,
since you got well of the cold and escaped at midnight from
your little fort?"

Canning continued to look at her.

"I 've felt lonely," said he, "when the moon shines bright."

"You?"

A knock fell upon the door, making all look up; and Kerr
bustling forward, first opened the door, and then stepped out
into the hall. He returned in a moment, his round face puckered
dubiously.

"It's Johnson," he explained — "chap across the hall, with the better apartment. Wanted to show it to me now. He's living down the river, and's going off in half an hour. H'm. Well, guess I better let it go till the next time he's in."

"Don't mind us, old chap," said Canning, without hesitation.

"If you wanted mamma to look at it with you, Willie? Perhaps —"

Mrs. Heth was already on her feet.

"Nonsense, Willie! Of course get the man while he's here — and *I'm* here too! Across the hall? — it won't take us five minutes —"

"All right 'm — thank you," agreed Willie, with evident pleasure. He added, smiling roguishly: "You two be trusted five minutes without a chaperon?"

Carlisle laughed dazzlingly.

"Five years, Willie. Mr. Canning is absolutely safe."

Mrs. Heth, saying archly that they would not absent themselves quite so long as that, glided out. Willie followed, engrossed in Johnson. The door was left half open. Johnson was presented. Their voices died away across and down the hall. . . .

A momentary silence fell upon Mr. Canning and Carlisle, thus deserted in the Kerr sitting-room. It appeared to embarrass neither. Having risen, Canning stood at the mantel, sipping his Scotch and looking down at her. Carlisle went on cutting bread and butter, or something of that sort. She felt agreeably excited. In the manner of the shining passer-by she had observed just that progressiveness noted on the occasion of their two other meetings: faintly ironic boredom yielding slowly to passive interest, passive interest warming steadily. . . .

She had taken off her coat, at Kerr's solicitation; she sat with lowered lashes, the glow of the fire upon her cheek. To what measure she engaged and intrigued the eye, Mr. Canning had had seven weeks to forget. No dull wit, we may suppose, in appreciation of feminine masterpieces, he seemed to see it suddenly with some force now, standing and sipping the pleasurable Scotch. And he began to speak in a voice not previously heard in Kerr's apartment.

"Lonely, Miss Heth, when the moon shines bright — blue, too, now that I think of it. — You are good enough to ask if I've had a happy trip. Happy! . . . Weeks of moping from dull place to duller, months ditto staring one in the face, and for this present — the rural villa of one's estimable cousins, with the sun and the stars for company. Really does it seem such a trifle to you to be plucked up by the ears from one's environment, transplanted bodily league on league, and set down on an empty road four miles from nowhere?"

"Nowhere? You are cruel, Mr. Canning. Four miles travelled in the right direction might bring you to a good deal. Only mountains never really come to Mahomets, not in life."

"Ah, but I'm no Mahomet in these months, alas! to scale mountains or not as the whim strikes me. If I were! . . . But no, no! — my sentence, you see, is expressly to avoid all mountain-climbing with whatever else is pleasant — to play the invalid, to rest, breathe deep, sleep and coddle. And for excitement — it is my revered mother's own suggestion — why, write a book if I like — my impressions of the New South, or any other reason why! Write a book! What have I to do with writing, think I, of a long morning or a longer night! I'm no scrivening professor, but blood and flesh. . . . You couldn't imagine the number of times I've been tempted to chuck all the mild climate tomfoolery, and cut away for lights and home!"

Carlisle gazed up at him, her chin upon her ungloved hand. Was there pose in these depictions of Mr. Hugo Canning as a morose recluse? She thought not: his light bitterness rang true enough, the note of a man really half-desperate with ennui. And she read his remarks as a subtle sign of his confidence, an acknowledgment of acquaintance between them, a bond. . . .

"But you can't do it, I suppose? — if your health demands that you put up with us a little while longer?"

"I seem rude? — of course. But my meaning is quite the contrary. . . . May you, Miss Heth, never know the sorrows of the transplanted and the idle —"

He broke off, staring with apparent absentness.

Much interested, Carlisle said, toying with her teaspoon:

"I did n't think you rude at all. It seems to me perfectly natural that you should be both bored and blue — especially if you don't feel quite well. . . . But surely a little mild pleasuring during rest hours is n't forbidden as injurious to throats?"

"A little?"

"Of course you think we have n't much to offer, but really there is *some* amusement to be had here. Really! Perhaps a little gambolling now and then —"

"My curse," said Canning, turning his dark eyes down upon her, "is that I can't learn when to stop. Once I begin, I am never satisfied till I 've gambolled all over the place."

Carlisle's eyes fell before his gaze. "This," said she, drawing on a glove, "is a small place."

"You appear to invite me to gambol?"

"I? Oh, no! These are matters that men decide for themselves."

"Possibly the fact is that you invite without desiring to do so."

"Then what," said she, suddenly laughing up at him, "should I have to think of your rudeness in declining my invitation all these days?"

She rose on that, looking about for coat and furs.

"But you must not think of going," said Canning, instantly.

The thundering of his feet grew very audible now.

"The instant mamma comes back. She is staying a long time, is n't she? Do you realize that we 've been here hours and hours, and that it looks like midnight outdoors?"

"Still, it would be a satisfaction to finish one conversation with you. We seem to remain all beginnings."

"What end is there to such conversations as this, Mr. Canning?"

"Conversations end in many ways, Miss Heth. I have known them to end like journeys."

The man left the fire, advanced to her side, took the modish wrap from her hands. But he did not at once offer to hold it for her. He stood two feet away from her, and a gleam came into his eyes, faint and a little cold.

"But I wonder," said he, musingly, "if what two men told you in a summer-house one night is n't quite true, after all."

"That I have no heart, you mean?"

"And don't know the meaning of being kind. Easter lilies are pretty on a tomb, but they were never my favorite flowers."

"No," she said, "it is not true. My heart is here" — she touched the place — "it is large — and I am, oh, very, very kind."

"You are rather adorable, you know," said his abrupt voice. "Here is your coat."

She was warm to the eye, animating, of an exquisite figure. Her nearness released a faint fragrance. She slipped her left arm into the sleeve he offered, and looking up at him, half over her shoulder, said with a mocking little laugh:

"And *you* know that kind-hearted girls are always awfully credulous . . . I sweep you off your feet. My eyes *intoxicate* you, drive you *mad!* Go on. I've told you that I like your pretty speeches."

"I do not always stop with speeches — you wild, sweet thing . . ."

So Mr. Canning; and with that speech he did in fact stop most abruptly, and at once turned a step away. In the sharp brief silence, Carlisle put on her other sleeve for herself.

From the hall, almost at the door, it seemed, had sounded the brisk approaching voices of Mrs. Heth and Kerr; presumably also of Johnson. Destiny, having had its way with their absence, was returning them upon the dot. In the sitting-room, talk of such matters as Miss Heth's wild sweetness necessarily came to a sudden conclusion.

The big man lounged with folded arms. His look was slightly annoyed.

"One more beginning, and you have your way again, after all! This becomes a habit," said he, with his faint ironic note. "Miss Heth, I am as you say quite dull and safe: the dullest of all creatures, a play valetudinarian, bored to ill-manners at times, as you have observed, by large overdoses of my own society. Could you take pity on me? Could you and Mrs. Heth give me the pleasure of dining with me, and Kerr, at the Arlington, perhaps, — or wherever else you may prefer, — on the first evening you can spare for deeds of mercy?"

Carlisle looked at him, buttoning her glove. Her lips smiled; but in truth she was a little unsteadied by the exciting moment just passed through, by the buoyant sense of triumph welling up within her. Were not all men, however exalted or difficult, alike her playthings at her pleasure?

"Of course I shall first beg," added Mr. Canning, "to be permitted to pay my respects to you and Mrs. Heth — might I say to-morrow afternoon at five?"

"We shall be so glad to see you, if you care to come," said Carlisle, looking away from him. "As to dining, that would be very nice, of course, — but are you sure your health would —"

"Oh, confound my health!" cried the great hermit. "Promise me now that you will never speak the word in my presence again."

"I promise . . . Only really — if my invitation to gambol should lead you to —"

"You are as God made you, Miss Heth. It's not your fault that you invite."

He gave her a look, and, turning, swung wide the door for the chaperon.

VIII

Supper with the Cooneys: Poor Relations, but you must be Nice to them; of Hen Cooney's friend V. V., as she irritatingly calls him; also relating how Cally is asked for her Forgiveness, and can't seem to think what to say.

THE Heths' poor relations, the Cooneys, lived in a two-story frame house on Centre Street, four doors from a basement dry-cleaning establishment, and staring full upon the show-window of an artificial-limb manufactory, lately opened for the grisly trade.

The interval between the families of Heth and Cooney was as these facts indicate. If Thornton Heth had married an ambitious woman, and he had, his sister Molly had displayed less acumen. The Cooney stock, unlike the Thompson as it was, deplorably resembled a thousand other stocks then reproducing its kind in this particular city. The War had flattened it out, cut it half through at the roots, and it had never recovered, as economists count recovery, and would n't, for a generation or two at the least. Accursed contentment flowed in the young Cooneys' blood. They had abilities enough, but the sane acquisitive gift was not in them. They were poor, but unashamed. They were breezy, keen, adventurous, without fatigue. They claimed the gasoline-cleaning establishment as their private garage, challenging any car under six thousand dollars to beat the expensive smell. A large and very popular group of family jokes centred about the plant of the legman.

Carlisle Heth "came to supper" with the Cooneys, as agreed, on the Thursday following the magic afternoon at Willie's apartment. The week intervening had been, as it chanced, one of the most interesting and titillating periods of her life; by the same token, never had family duty seemed more drearily superfluous. However, this periodic, say quarterly, mark of kinsman's comity was required of her by her father, a clannish man by inheritance, and one who, feeling unable to "do" anything especial for his sister's children, yet shrank from the knocking suspicion of snobbery. In the matter of intermealing, reciprocity was formally observed between the two families. Four times per annum the Cooneys were invited in a body to dine at the House of Heth, Mrs. Heth on these occasions speaking caustically of her consort's relatives, and on Christmas sending gifts of an almost offensively utilitarian nature.

The noisy cousins filled the dingy little parlor to overflowing; this, though Mrs. Cooney and Hen, having rushed out for the welcome, had at once rushed back to the preparations for supper. For it appeared that Hortense was absent once again, having asked to "git to git" a night off, to see her step-daughter allianced to a substitute Pullman porter. The two ladies, however, were only gone before, not lost, and through the portières joined freely in the conversation, which rattled on incessantly in the Cooney style.

Carlisle sat on the rusty sofa, listening absently to the chatter. Her unaspiring uncle-in-law, the Major, who was vaguely understood to be "in insurance" at present, parted his long coat-tails before the Baltimore heater, and drifted readily to reminiscence. Louise and Theodore (as the family Bible too stiffly knew Looloo and Tee Wee) sat together on a divan, indulging in banter, with some giggling from Looloo — none from grave Theodore. Chas informally skimmed an evening paper in a corner, with comments: though the truth was that precious little ever appeared in any newspaper which was news to the keen young Cooneys. . . .

"And I said to Hen," observed Major Cooney to his fashionable niece, having now got his short history of the world down as far as the '80s — "now stop your whining around me, Miss. If you've got to whine, go down to the cellar and stand in the corner. Well —"

"Why could she whine in the cellar, father? That point is n't clear, sir," said Tee Wee's deep voice.

"Because it was a whine-cellar!" cried Hen, through the portières.

There was mild laughter at this, rather derisive on the part of all but the Major; but when Chas, glancing up from his paper, remarked crisply: "Aw, Miss Mamie! Like to speak to you a minute, please!" — the merriment seemed mysteriously to acquire a more genuine ring. Carlisle politely inquired who Miss Mamie was.

Looloo, who alone seemed the least bit awed by the presence of her dazzling cousin, undertook to explain.

"She's Mamie Willis, Cally, — I don't believe you know her. Well, you see she's always making the most atrocious puns, and is very proud of them—thinks she's quite a wit. So, you see, when anybody makes an awfully bad pun, like Hen's —"

"Brightest thing I've heard to-night," screamed Hen, defiantly, through the curtains.

"Aw, Loo!" came her mother's soft voice from the unseen. "Run upstairs and get half a dozen napkins, my child. The wash is in the basket on my bed."

"We always pretend like we're repeating it to Miss Mamie, just for fun," concluded Looloo. "Yes 'm, mother!"

"Oh! I see," said Carlisle.

She had donned for the coming to supper a plain house-dress of soft dark-green silk, two summers old and practically discarded. ("This old thing, my dear! Why, it positively belongs in the *ragbag!*") She never dressed much for the Cooneys. Also, by wholly mechanical processes of adjustment to environment, her manner and air became simpler, somewhat unkeyed: she unconsciously folded away her more shining wings. Nevertheless, there was about her to-night a fleeting kind of radiance which had caught the notice of more than one of her cavalier cousins, notably of pretty little Looloo, who had kissed the visitor shyly (for a Cooney) at greeting, and said, "Oh, Cally! You do look *so* lovely!" Cally herself was aware of an inner buoyance oddly at variance with the drab Cooney *milieu*. Recent progress in the great game had more than blotted out all memory of little mishaps at the Beach . . .

Starting aloft for the napkins, Looloo was adroitly tripped by Tee Wee, and fell back upon him with a little shriek. Instead

of checking the tumult that followed, Major Cooney, including
Carlisle in the proceedings with a mischievous wink, called
out: "Give it to him, Loo! Give it to him!" Loo, having got her
small hand in his hair, gave it to him, good-fashion. Tee Wee
moaned, and Chas made a fairly successful effort to gag him
with the newspaper. In the midst of the uproar, Mrs. Cooney's
gentle voice could be heard calling, "Supper, supper," and Hen,
entering with a large dinner-bell, conceived the whimsey of ringing it loudly in everybody's ear.

Presently, after much noise and confusion, they were seated at
the antique mahogany, with the dent near one edge where a
Yankee cavalryman had rested his spurred foot too carelessly
once upon a time. It was then observed that Hen, having silenced
her great clapper, was unobtrusively gone from the midst. The
circumstance proved of interest to the younger Cooneys.

"She's nursing a little bunch of violets she got three days ago,"
Tee Wee explained to Carlisle. "Says she's going to wear 'em
to the Masons' to-morrow, though anybody can see they can't
possibly live through the night."

"I thought I saw a purple box in the front window as I drove
up," said Carlisle. "Is it a secret who sent them?"

"'Bout forty," said Chas, making a fine one-hand catch of a
napkin. "You'd hardly call 'em a bunch, Tee Wee — more like
a nosegay."

"Pass this coffee to Cally, son."

"Bob Dunn sent 'em, Cally, down at the bookstore," said
Looloo, sweetly. "And he wrote Hen a love-letter Thanksgiving
beginning, 'Darling Miss Cooney.'"

"That so?" said Tee Wee, who was just home from the University for Christmas and not up on all the news yet. "How'd
he sign it — 'Your loving Mr. Dunn'?"

"'Ave some werry nice 'am, Cally?"

"Yes — thank you. But do go on and tell me about Mr.
Dunn. Does Hen like him?"

"No, but she loves violets," said Tee Wee. "Made me sit up
half of last night, fanning 'em for her."

"Loo, pass Charles's plate, daughter."

Carlisle surveyed the noisy table as from some lofty peak. She knew that the Cooney habit of monopolizing all conversation, and dashing straight through every topic, was only their poor-but-proud way of showing off: sometimes it was a little irritating, but to-night only rather fatiguing to the ear-drums. The children came two years apart, as regular as some kind of bi-annual publication; Looloo, seventeen, being the youngest, and also the best-looking and the most popular in the family. But then all the Cooneys were good-looking, including the Major, and all were popular in the family. In fact, they were more like a house-party than a family at all: and in some ways they rather resembled a queer little secret fraternity, enjoying strange delights and responding with shrieks to unintelligible catchwords.

To-night the talk was more than usually disjointed, owing to the regrettable absence of Hortense. There was constant jumping up, infinite "passing." Mr. Tee Wee, manipulating the water-pitcher from the side-table, complained aside to his mother at the universal thirst. Chas, it seemed, had charge of the heating-up of the later crops of biscuits: he kept springing off to the kitchen, now and then returning with a heaping platter of what he called his little brown beauties.

In the midst of the confusion, Hen strode in, looking somewhat defiant, and instantly drew the fires of all.

"How 're the little patients, Hen? Number 9 looked pretty sick to me this —"

"Best thing I know is running 'em up and down the hall, and then brisk massage —"

"Gargled 'em yet, Hen?"

Hen, laughing wildly, stood her ground.

"That's all right!" she retorted to the last sally, which happened to be Chas's. "There are swains in this town who might boost their standing a little if only *they'd* patronize the florist once in a while!"

This drew loud approbation, and Chas (who was understood to be very attentive to a Miss Leither — *Leither!* — of the Woman's Exchange), laughing with the majority, threw up his hands, saying, "Hellup! Hellup!"

He fled to the kitchen to look after his little brown beauties. The noisy supper proceeded. Presently Major Cooney, the easy-going and reminiscent, gave the conversation a new tack.

"And where are your violets, Cally, my dear?" he asked, directing one of his mischievous winks at Looloo. "You must have a flower-shop full at home, if what we hear is true."

Carlisle, on the point of saying something slightly caustic about Chas as a swain, found the tables abruptly turned. All the Cooneys were looking at her. She said with equanimity that, on the contrary, she got so few flowers that when she did have any, she sat up at night with them just like Hen.

"And I'll wear 'em to the Masons' to-morrow night, too!" said Hen, throwing round a look which challenged contradiction.

"Now, cousin, what's the use?" said Chas, reëntering with his platter. "The Visitor is giving you the rush of your young life, and we're all on. Take a handful of my beauties."

"You mean Mr. Canning? My dear Chas, if he only were!"

There was no rebuffing the Cooneys. They began their little third-degree system.

"He called on you last Thursday afternoon, did n't he, Cally?" said Looloo, laughing, with a little face for her daring.

"One call, my dear child!"

"You went motoring with him on Friday," said Theodore, gravely, "and stopped for tea at the Country Club at 6.20, you taking chocolate —"

"One motor-ride!"

"You dined with him at the Arlington on Monday night, table decorations being small diamond necklaces —"

"Good heavens!" laughed Carlisle, coloring a little. "All this is terribly circumstantial! I had no idea my movements were —"

"Movement is useless — don't move, lady! We have you covered —"

"There, there, children! — stop showing your jealousy," laughed Mrs. Cooney; and her eyes rested with a brief wistfulness on the shining niece who plumed eagle's feathers for flights where her daughters would never follow. "You'd all give your eye-teeth to be half as pretty and attractive as Cally . . ."

"Yes'm," said Chas. "Well, then, Cally, have one more sardine, *please*. Nothing on earth for the complexion like these fat saline fellows that mother catches fresh every morning with her little hook and line. — Mind, *Loo!* You're joggling The Bowl."

Carlisle was hardly to be overwhelmed by the Cooneys' teasing, nor perhaps was she seriously displeased by it. Even less did the detail of her eccentric cousins' knowledge surprise her. If there was a fight or a fire, a *bon mot* launched or a heart broken, money made or a death died, it invariably happened that one of the Cooneys was "just passing." . . .

In the middle of the table stood an object of shiny green crockery, which seemed to be a cross between a fruit-dish and a vase. Most of the table service was quite familiar to Carlisle, not a little of it having started life as Christmas presents from the Heths. But this crockery piece was new, and, upon Chas's admonition, its shiny hideousness caught and riveted her attention.

"Aunt Rose Hopwood's parting gift," said Tee Wee, softly, following her fascinated gaze. "Oh, Cally, ain't it boo'ful!"

"Theodore," said his mother, quite sharply, "I don't think your stay at the University has improved your manners."

Theodore colored abruptly and deeply. "Why, I — I was only funning, mother."

"I think that's a very poor sort of funning. And this applies to you, too, Charles."

"Yes'm," said Charles, starting.

The eldest-born made no other reply to his mother, nor did Theodore: meekness under parental reproof being another of the odd Cooney characteristics. Conversation seemed about to languish; but Mrs. Cooney, as if to show that the episode was closed, said equably:

"By the way, Cally, Cousin Martha Heth is coming next week to make us quite a visit. If you are not too busy, do try to come in some time, and cheer her up. She is going to take treatment for her nose and also for flatfoot, and I fear is very miserable."

After supper Carlisle sat on the sofa, feeling rather sardiney, and had an irritating talk with Aunt Molly, the subject being Chas's affair with his Leither, for the furtherance of which he was reported to be even now arraying himself upstairs. The complacence with which Aunt Molly regarded the threatened alliance — all possible objections being answered in her mind by a helpless, "If she is the girl he loves?" — was most provokingly characteristic of the Cooneys' fatal shiftlessness. And they were popular, too, in their way, and Chas might easily have married some socially prominent girl with money, instead of bringing a nameless saleslady into the family. It was impossible for Carlisle not to contrast her aunt's flabby sentimentalism with her own and her mother's sane, brilliant ambitiousness. If nothing succeeds like success, how doubly true it was that nothing fails like failure.

Carlisle had reached a point where she longed to shake her aunt, when Hen, who had been "scrapping up" with Looloo, came in, putting an end to the futile talk.

To her mother's demand if they had stayed to wash the dishes, Hen replied that they thought they might just as well: there were n't many, and the water was nice and hot. And Chas, hearing the clatter from aloft, had slipped down the backstairs in his suspenders, and lent a hand with the wiping. Mrs. Cooney chided, saying the dishes should have been left for Hortense, to-morrow morning before breakfast. She asked Hen whether Chas knew that his white vest had come in with the wash, and though Hen was pretty sure he did, Aunt Molly presently made an excuse and slipped away upstairs. She was a great hand for being by when the children were dressing to go out, and no one in the family, not even Chas, could tie a white lawn bow half so well as mother. . . .

Looloo lingered in the dining-room, the family sitting-room of evenings, where Theodore had engaged his father at checkers. Hen, dropping into a chair by the sofa as if she were rather tired, asked Cally for gossip of the gay world, but Cally answered briefly out of regard for the chasm between: how contract the name and fame of Mr. Canning to fit this shabby little "parlor"?

Hen was thin, colorless, and sweet-faced, and was known in the family (for the Cooneys, strange to say, knew of enormous individual differences among themselves) as the most thoughtful and considerate of the children, and as alone possessing the real Ambler nose. She rather suggested some slender pale flower, made to look at its slenderest and palest beside her cousin's rich blossom. Still, Hen was accounted a fine stenographer: they paid her sixty dollars a month at the bookstore, where she earned double at least.

For five minutes the talk between these two girls, of about the same age and blood but, it seemed, almost without a point of contact, was considerably perfunctory. Then, by an odd chance and in the wink of an eye, it took on a very distinct interest. Carlisle inquired if Hen had ever heard of a man named V. Vivian, said to be a nephew of Mr. Beirne; and Hen, with a little exclamation, and a certain quickening of countenance, replied that she had been raised with him. Moreover, she referred to him as V. V. . . .

Though the Cooneys knew everybody, as well as everything, and though Carlisle had thought before now of putting an inquiry to Hen or Chas in this particular direction, the manner of her cousin's reply was a decided surprise to her, and somehow a disagreeable surprise.

"Oh! Really?" said she, rather coldly. "I understood — some one told me — that the man had just come here to live."

"He's just come *back*," explained Hen, with interest. "Why, he was born here, Cally, three doors from where we used to live down on Third Street — remember? Well, Dr. Vivian lived right there till he was sixteen or seventeen —"

"Why do you call him Dr. Vivian?"

"Well, that's what he is, you see. He's a doctor — medical man."

"He does n't look in the least like a medical man to me," said Carlisle, as if that ought to settle something.

"Oh! You know him, then?"

"I have spoken to him," replied Carlisle, her gaze full on Hen's face. "You see a great deal of him, I suppose?"

"No, we don't," said Hen, with an odd air, suggestive of regret. "He keeps so terribly busy. Besides being sort of a missionary doctor, he's always working on dozens of grand schemes of one sort or another. His latest is to raise about a million dollars and buy the Dabney House for a Settlement! How's that for a tall one? He just mentioned it to me this morning, *en passant*, and says I must help him raise the million —"

"I suppose you did n't know that one of his grand schemes was to write a terrible article in the paper attacking papa and the Works?"

"Oh!" said Hen, plucking a thread from her old black skirt. "Oh, that letter in the 'Post,' long ago, you mean? Yes, I — knew about that; I wanted to speak to you about it at the time. Did you read it, Cally?"

"I glanced at it," said Cally, shortly.

Full of the interest of thundering feet as the week had been since Willie and mamma had given her the connecting link, Carlisle had in fact made a point of getting hold of a copy of the old paper containing that particular piece. Not being at all familiar with Works and newspapers, she had found the process involved with considerable perplexity and trouble, but she had felt amply rewarded in the end. The piece came to her hand like a weapon, against any possible remeeting with its remembered author.

Now she regarded Hen with steadily rising annoyance.

"What was your friend's idea in writing such outrageous stuff, do you know? Is he really crazy, as they say, or is he just an ordinary notoriety seeker?"

Colorless Hen looked rather hard at her pretty cousin. She allowed a perceptible pause to fall before she said:

"I thought you said you knew him."

"No; I said that I barely spoke to him once."

"If you only said good-morning to him — if you only *looked* at him once, on the street — I don't see how you could possibly imagine . . . Why, Cally, he's about the least self-seeking human being that ever lived. He's so absolutely un-self-seeking that he gives away every single thing he's got, to anybody that comes along and wants it. In the first place, he's giving away

his life . . . Some of his ideas may be visionary or mistaken,
but —"

"I should think so, after glancing at his article. What *was* his
object, then, my dear?"

"Well, that's simple, I should think. He went to the Works,
and thought that conditions there were bad, and being what
would be called the reformer type, I suppose he thought it his
duty to tell people so, so that the conditions would be cor-
rected —"

"Well, really, Hen! Don't you know, if conditions *were* bad
at the Works, — whatever that may mean, and I for one have
never felt that working-girls were entitled to Turkish baths and
manicures, — don't you *know* papa would correct what was wrong
without being called a homicide by — by eccentric medical
men?"

Hen hesitated, and then began: "Well, business is hard, Cally,
and men in business —"

"Why does n't your friend try attending to his own, then, the
medical business, instead of interfering all the time with other
people's?"

The Cooney answered quite easily: "You see, he 'd say this *was*
his business." Then she smiled a little, thoughtfully, and said:
"He'd say, Cally, that the world's all one family, and everybody's responsible for everybody else. The cute part about it
is that he absolutely believes it. . . . And it worries him that
people are n't as happy as they ought to be, the poor because
they have n't anything to be happy with, the rich because they
have too much. He and Mr. Beirne argue about that for hours.
He's absolutely the only person I ever saw who really does n't
care for —"

"Why, my *dear!*" interrupted Carlisle, smiling rather dangerously. "You'll make me believe that you *admire* the man
immensely."

Hen laughed, and replied enigmatically: "Well, it's nice to feel
free to admire what 's admirable, don't you think so?"

"You do admire him very much?"

"I think he's perfectly precious," said Henrietta Cooney.

A peal of triumph from the rear room indicated that Major
Cooney had reached the king-row in the teeth of bitter opposition.
The peal came from Looloo, who should have been reading "Le
Bourgeois Gentilhomme" with a big dictionary instead of hang-
ing over her father's shoulder. Footsteps above suggested that
Chas and Aunt Molly were making a careful toilet indeed for
his call upon the obscure inamorata.

In the Cooney parlor, the two girls looked at each other. Carlisle tried hard to stare Hen down, and failed. In this moment
she felt that she positively disliked her commonly negligible
cousin. She had proved and re-proved to her own almost complete satisfaction that the man who had spoken the affronting
words to her in the summer-house was a virulent religious fanatic,
or (since she had read the piece) a crazy Socialist, like the man
who had thrown the brick at papa, or both; almost certainly both.
She was, it might be said, deeply and irrevocably committed to
these beliefs: they settled and explained everything, and no
more need to think or worry. It was simply not to be endured
that Henrietta Cooney should cheekily sit there and try to unsettle everything, pretending. . . .

"But understand me, Cally," Henrietta was saying, with provoking calm. "Of course I did n't like that letter a bit. You
see — Heth was n't any more than a name to V. V., a sort of
symbol, when he wrote it. But I think it was a mistake all
through, and I scolded him well at the time —"

"Oh, did you?" said Cally, her cheeks very pink. "I imagined you thought it perfectly precious of him to call papa a
shameless homicide."

"Why, you know I never thought anything of the sort, Cally
dear," answered Hen. . . .

She seemed surprised by the signs of her cousin's displeasure
(which really did seem excessive for a business controversy
nearly two months old) and went on in what was evidently intended to be quite a soothing manner:

"You know, men are always hammering each other over things
like this — it 's really not nearly so awful as it sounds! . . . And
honestly, Cally, that letter was n't at all representative of V. V. —

even though he probably thought it was! I mean . . . he may
talk in that fierce way about whole classes, but when it comes
down to people — individuals — he's about the kindest person.
What he really thinks is — well, that *everybody's good.* . . .
Here's what I mean, Cally," said Hen, laughing a little, but with
a certain eagerness too, as if it were of some importance for Cally
to see what she meant. . . . "You know him, you say — slightly,
of course. Well, instead of writing any more letters about the
Works, do you know what it would be exactly like him to do
now?"

"Throw a bomb in at papa's office-window?"

"No, speak to *you* about it!" laughed Henrietta, unabashed —
"some time when he sees you at Mr. Beirne's or somewhere —
ask you in the nicest, most natural way to ask Uncle Thornton
if he won't build a new Works! And you'd see from the way he
looked at you that he was perfectly *sure* you were going to do it,
too!"

Cally gazed at Hen silently for at least ten seconds.

"I'd enjoy immensely having him try it," said she slowly.
"*Immensely!* I — I've wanted for some time to say a few words
to him. . . ."

At that moment the broken Cooney doorbell rang feebly,
and within one minute V. Vivian came walking into the little
parlor.

Supping at the Cooneys was not usually so interesting as this.
When the bell rang, Looloo, springing up from the Major's
side in the dining-room, hurriedly pulled shut the folding-doors
between. She apologized to her cousin through the diminish-
ing crack, saying that it was probably awful Bob Dunn, and
Cally could come hide in there with them if she'd rather. But
Cally said briefly that she was not afraid, and had to go home in
a little while anyway.

In the same moment Carlisle heard the voice of the caller in
the hall, for whom Hen had just opened the door. She recognized
this voice at the first word. And she involuntarily rose in the
Cooney parlor, feeling the oddest, suddenest, most unreasoning

impulse to go at once into the dining-room, after all, and be with Looloo, and watch them play checkers for a little while. . . .

It was the surprise of it; nothing more. And Carlisle overcame that impulse. She remained standing motionless, reconsidering as by lightning flashes the quite complicated point of etiquette that so suddenly confronted her. What was a lady's proper attitude toward a nobody who has called her father a shameless homicide and herself a God-pitiful poor little thing? There was no experience to guide here. But clearer and clearer it seemed to become to Cally that to hold any converse with such an one could only be, after all, essentially debasing. Icy indifference was the stingingest rebuke. . . .

Henrietta came through the door, with the lame medical man behind her. Without looking at him, Cally gathered that the man found the sight of her properly disquieting.

"You know my cousin, Miss Heth, I believe — *Doctor* Vivian, Cally."

"Oh! . . . How do you do!" said the doctor.

Carlisle, not advancing from the sofa-side, said:

"I remember Dr. Vivian."

"Well, sit down, both of you," said Hen.

And then Henrietta, with that audacious forwardness which the Cooneys mistook for humor, smiled treacherously at her cousin over the caller's shoulder, and said:

"And entertain each other a moment, won't you? I have *got* to speak to mother. . . ."

On that Hen left them. Through some bias in its ancient hinges, the parlor door swung to behind her. It shut with a loud click. From behind the other closed doors, the merry voices of the checker-players and rooter grew very audible.

Despite the hostess's cordial injunction, the two young people in the shut Cooney parlor did not immediately sit down and begin to entertain each other. Both remained standing exactly where Hen had left them, and there ensued a hiatus of entertainment just long enough to be quite distinctly appreciable.

Then the absurdity of her — Miss Heth's — feeling constraint before this Mr. — no, Dr. — Vivian, this friend of the Cooneys and malicious attacker of the Cooneys' relatives' characters, rushed over the girl inspiritingly. Then it occurred to her simply to incline her head coldly, and leave the man without a word: dignified that, yet possibly open to misconstruction. So, taking one graceful step toward the door, Carlisle said, with a sufficiency of distant hauteur:

"You can entertain yourself, I hope? I am going."

The tall young man removed his gaze from the blank space left by Hen's exit, with a kind of start, and said hurriedly:

"I hope you are n't letting *me* drive you away? I — I merely stopped a moment in passing, on a — a professional matter. . . ."

"Why should you imagine that I am anxious to avoid you?"

He said, with gratifying embarrassment: "I naturally could n't hope that — you would wish to see me —"

And then suddenly all her just and fortifying resentment seemed to return to her, and she said with frosty calm:

"Yes, I 've rather wanted to see you again. I did n't quite place you when — I had this opportunity before . . ."

The man regarded the floor. He looked as if he knew what was coming.

"I 've recently read your letter in the 'Post' about my father. Tell me, what pleasure do you find in writing such wicked untruths about people who 've never harmed you?"

In her mind it had seemed exactly the thing to say, the rebuke which would put him finally in his place on all scores, show him up completely to himself. But the moment it was out, it acquired somehow the wrong sound, jangling and a little shrewish and somewhat common, and she rather wished she had n't said it. She had never seen anybody turn pale so suddenly. . . .

The man wore the same clothes he had worn in the summerhouse, she thought; indubitably the same large four-in-hand, floating the fat white painted shad, or perch. He was rather better-looking in the face than she had supposed; and in this light she observed more clearly the rather odd expression he wore about the eyes, a quality of youthful hopefulness, a sort of confidingness: not the look of a brick-thrower, unless you happened to know the facts in the case. All this, of course, was his own lookout. If he wanted to say and do outrageous things, he had no right to appear so pained when he got his merited punishment. He had no right to put on that appealing look. He had no right to be lame . . .

"It is perfectly natural for you to say and think that," he was saying with an odd air of introspection, quite as if he were reassuring somebody inside of him. "I don't think there was anything untrue in that letter, but — no doubt it must have seemed so. And of course . . . I *don't* suppose you can go to the Heth Works much, or be very familiar —"

"It isn't necessary for me to go to the Works to learn that my father is not a homicide."

Her voice had lost something of its first ringing assurance. It seemed to shake a little, like an indignant child's.

The young man said hurriedly:

"No, no! Of course not! I — indeed, I think you misunderstood what I meant to say in — in that letter. I must have expressed myself badly. I did not intend so much a — a criticism of individuals, as of society, for —"

"Oh, please don't apologize. That's always rather silly, I think. I like to see people with the courage of their convictions, no matter how wrong they are. Good-evening."

"Don't go," said the slum physician, instantly, much as Mr. Canning had said at a similar yet totally different moment — "that is — *must* you — go at once? I — there is something I've wanted very much to tell you."

She stopped still; stood in silence gazing at Dalhousie's friend, the shabby author of the two Severe Arraignments. Undoubtedly there was a sinking feeling within her, unsteadying in its way. But she was spirited, and into her eyes had come a hostile challenge. Passionately she dared this man to ask God to pity her again. . . .

Her eyes were oval and lifted the least bit at the outer corners. The bow of her upper lip drew up a little most engagingly at the middle (like Teresa Durbeyfield's), an irregularity more endearing to the eye than any flawlessness. There was the possibility of tenderness in this mouth; more than the promise of strength in the finely cut chin. Her thick lashes began pure gold, but changed their minds abruptly in the middle, and finished jet black....

She was the loveliest thing this man's eyes had ever rested upon. And as at the Beach, he seemed to begin with a plunge:

"Jack Dalhousie's gone away, Miss Heth — gone to Weymouth, Texas, to live. I had a letter from him, day before yesterday. He's got work there, on a stock-farm — among strangers. He has n't taken a drink since — October. He's making a new start, with nothing to remind him of what's past. I . . . hope he will be happy yet."

Carlisle's breast rose and fell. "Why do you tell this to me?"

"Because," said Vivian, "I've felt I — did you such a wrong — that night . . . "

Under the flickering Cooney gas, the two stood staring at each other. The young man hurried on:

"I've had it on my mind ever since, and have wanted very much to tell you. . . . I've felt that — what I — I said to you was all wrong — most unjust. . . . "

He hesitated; and the gold-and-black lashes, so piquant and gay, fell. "Take your jump! Take your jump!" called Major Cooney in the dining-room. You could hear him plainly, straight through the folding doors. And young V. Vivian, who was merciless as a social philosopher but somewhat trusting as a man, took his jump with a will.

"I was much upset about it that night — and excited, I suppose. I can't account for — for what I said in any other way. I've hoped for the opportunity to tell you . . . Why, of course I don't believe that at all. . . . It was all so confused and mixed up; that was the trouble. But of course I know that you — that you would n't have said anything that — that was n't entirely consistent with the facts. . . ."

He paused, expectantly it seemed; but there came no reply.

Cally Heth, indeed, stood in a dumbness which she seemed powerless to break. Well she knew what sort of reply she ought to make to these remarks: what was the man saying but what she had already said a hundred times to herself? He was simply making tardy admission that her position had been exactly right all along; that was all. Yet somehow the sane knowledge did not seem to help much against this sequence of unique sensations she was at present experiencing, — odd, tumultuous, falling sensations, as of bottoms dropped out. . . .

"I suppose," said the man's faraway voice, sounding a sudden loss of confidence, "it's rather too much to hope that — that you can forget . . ."

Again his words dropped into the brief, expectant silence. . . . It seemed that he had happened to say the one thing to which no reply was possible. And somehow the effect of it was worse, even, than the never-forgotten moment in the summer-house.

"And forgive," finished the voice. . . . "I've felt — "

And then, in good season, there sounded welcome footsteps, Hen's, in the hall. They broke at a stroke the strange petrifying numbness which Carlisle had felt mysteriously closing over her. She murmured the name of Henrietta, and turned away. And her voice was the voice of Lucknow, as the friendly columns poured in. . . .

Hen came walking in, saying something lively and Cooney-esque, and glancing with an air of interested expectancy from her friend V. V. to her cousin Cally. But Cally only said once more that she must be going, and asked where Aunt Molly was. She then let fall the word good-night for Hen's caller, while looking at a point some ninety degrees removed from his whereabouts: by which the caller understood that his forgiveness was problematical, to say the least of it.

IX

Concerning an Abandoned Hotel, and who lived there; also of an Abandoned Youth, who lived somewhere else, Far Away; how a Slum Doctor dressed for a Function, such as involved Studs; and how Kern Garland wishted she was a Lady.

MRS. GARLAND, catching sight of Doctor as he came up the decayed grand-stairway, cried out, well, she never, just in the nig of time! Why, the words was no more 'n out of her mouth that the stoo was just done to a hair, she did declare, and Kern she said, quick as anything, what, a hair in the stoo, now, mommer, that 'd never do. . . .

The clocks of the city had just struck six for the last time that year. Dr. Vivian, having placed his suitcase and overcoat on the second-hand operating-table in the office, washed face and hands, brushed his coat-collar with a whisk whose ranks had been heavily thinned in wars with dust and lint, and, repairing in sound spirits to the Garland combination dining- and living-room, with the kitchen in the corner, made his interesting confidence relative to the suitcase. He made it in mouth-filling phrases, with many teasing generalizations about the ways of the world and the evils of modern society, which was only his gempman's way when playful. But by close application his auditors soon got at the heart of his meaning, to wit: Doctor actually was going uptown to his swell Uncle Beirne's swell Noo Year's reception to-night in Mr. O'Neill's fulldressuit.

Naturally the Garlands were much interested and excited by the tidings, which brought them so close to great events that, practically speaking, they themselves became members of the fash'nable set: and Mrs. Garland publicly thanked God that she was not as other women were, lazying and keeping back their gentlemen's shirts till Saturday night, or worse. Laid away tidy in the second bureau drawer, her shirts were. The doctor himself seemed not a little enlivened by the evening's prospect. It is imaginable that the Dabney House grew a little lonely at times. . . .

"And to think your swell uncle wants you so special, sir!" said Mrs. Garland, in her harsh, inflectionless voice. "A compliment, I 'm sure. And his party all a fizzle unless you come, and his gai'ty a mockery! Well!"

Such indeed was the way in which Vivian had been pleased to depict his fashionable uncle's attitude. He smiled slightly, sipped his feeble coffee and said:

"Bear in mind that he 's a bad, bad (though personally not displeasing) old man, ridden by ruinous ideas about the almightiness of the dollar, or lucre as we term it. . . . I have observed for some time that he desires to corrupt me with his Persian luxuries."

"Persian! Well, I never!"

Mrs. G., a stout woman and a dress-reformer by the look of her, got hot corn muffins from the kitchenette in the corner, and added:

"Them rugs is beautiful."

"He said lux'ries, mommer, like lowneg dresses, and tchampagne, and ice-cream all like animals," said Kern.

"I do declare! Well, they do say the mawls of some of them swells is something nawful. Not alloodin' to your uncle now, well, of course, sir."

"I know a girl named Sadie Whirtle," continued Kern, "and there was a man named Toatwood made a lot of money, corn-tracting, and his wife she took some of the money and went to Europe in a steamer and stayed more 'n two months buying clo'es. And one day Sadie Whirtle goes up to him and says, 'Mist' Toatwood, hear your wife 's come home with some fine Parisian clo'es.' And Mist' Toatwood says, 'Shucks ' — on'y he says somep'n worse 'n shucks — 'Shucks,' says he, 'why, my wife never been to Persia in her life.'"

Kern was eighteen, with six years of bread-winning behind her, but she told her story exactly in the manner of a child of eight. That is to say, she told it in a monotone without evincing, and clearly without feeling, the slightest amusement in it, and at the end, continuing quite grave, watched for its effect on others with a curious, staring interest. Her immobile, investigatory expression made the doctor laugh, which seemed, of late, to be the object in life of all Kern's anecdotes.

"Where'd you get that story, Corinne?"

His odd habit of so calling her had often been privately discussed between Kern and her mother, who had so long ago shortened their own original Kurrin that even that had passed from memory. They had concluded that this was only one of his jokey gempman's ways.

"Off Sadie Whirtle," said Kern, rocking backward and forward in her chair. "On'y I don't see anything comical in it."

And then she giggled for some time.

The talk and stoo went forward cheerfully. Beside the Goldnagels, on the ground floor, these two women were the doctor's only fellow lodgers, for Mister Garland, of the wanderlust, had not visited his family since the day in October, and so hardly counted. In the early weeks of the doctor's tenancy, which began only last September, he had walked three times a day to the Always Open Lunch Room, known among the baser sort as the Suicide Club, and had then become possibly the most discriminating judge of egg-sandwiches in all the city. Later, having made the better acquaintance of the Garlands, he had rightly surmised that the earnings derivable from a medical boarder might not be unacceptable in that quarter. The present modus vivendi, then worked out, had proved most satisfactory to all, from both the financial and the social viewpoints.

"I wisht I had a red satin dress, and a necklace all pearls, and was going to the party, too, and had a dark sad-faced man with a mustache and a neye-glass engaged to me, like a count. I wisht I was a Lady," said Kern.

"You don't need a red satin dress to be a lady."

"It'd come easier, kinder, with the dress, Mr. V. V. And I wisht I had a writin'-desk, too. And a founting pen."

"Lawk's sakes, Kern, an' I've asked you a hundred times what would you do with a writin'-desk, now?"

"Mommer, I'd set at it."

"An' what time you got for settin', I'd like to know? Fairy-dreamin' again!"

"An' I'd keep notes in it in the pigeon-holes. Like it says in my Netiquette."

"You don't get no notes."

Kern was silenced by her mother's addiction to actuality, but presently said: "I'd get notes if I was a lady, would n't I, Mr. V. V.?"

The doctor assured her that she would, and that all these things would come some day. He sighed inwardly and wondered, not for the first time, where the link could possibly lie between the matter-of-fact mother and the strange child of fancy. There was nothing to do but attribute the phenomenon to Mister, the whimsical knight of the open road. The boarder asked what he should bring Kern from the party: he feared they would n't have writing-desks, it not being at all a literary set. The girl thought a rapturous moment and then asked could she have three of them marrowglasses, all in curly white paper.

Vivian promised, and departed on his duties. First there was a call at the Miggses' down the block, where the little boy Tub lay with scarlet fever, very sick; and then there was his seven o'clock office hour for workers, in which one, a teamster with Bright's disease and seven children, remained long. . . .

These matters occupied the doctor till eight o'clock: alone in his office he computed the fact roughly from his watch, a battered heirloom whose word was not to be taken literally. Good! — half an hour before time to dress. Leisure, being a scant commodity, was proportionally valued. The young man advanced to his secretary, before whose open face plain living and high thinking could be so freely indulged in.

The secretary was of fine mahogany, hand-made in Virginia in the year that Sir Edward Pakenham did not take New Orleans. It was the hero of so many travels that its present proprietor once called it a field-secretary, a pleasantry which would doubtless have convulsed Miss Mamie Willis, if only she had ever heard it. The great tall office, bare but for cheap doctorly paraphernalia,

was even more storied. A bleak grandeur clung to it still. Decayed mouldings, it had aplenty: great splotches on wall and
ceiling, where plaster had been tried through the year and found
wanting; unsightlier splotch between the windows whence the
tall gilt mirror had been plucked away for cash; broken chandelier, cracked panes, loose flooring, dismantled fireplace. But view
the stately high pitch of the chamber, the majestic wide windows
and private balcony without, the tall mantel of pure black
marble, the still handsome walnut paneling, waist-high, the massive splendid doors. No common suburban room, this: clearly a
room with meaning, a past, soul.

The look was not deceptive. Royalty had on a time sat in
this room: here granted audience to the great's higher circle, of
greatness; there, beyond that door, nowadays admitting ragged
sufferers from a fourth-class "waiting-room," slept in state
with doubtless royal snores. This, in fact, was the old Dabney
House's famous "state suite," Vivian's office the culminating
grand sitting-room, the building art's best in the '40s. A famous hostelry the Dabney House had been in its day, the
chosen foregathering-place of notabilities now long dusted to
the common level. Hither had trooped the gallant and the gay,
the knight in his pride and beauty in her power, great statesmen
and greater belles, their lovers and their sycophants. Here, in
the memorable ball still talked of by silvered ladies of an elder
day, the Great Personage had trod his measure with peerless
Mary Marshall.

A great history had the Dabney House, and now nothing much
else beside. Built upon a flouting of a common law, it had lived
to see the westward course of progress, deaf to sentiment as ever,
kick it far astern. Long since had the world of fashion deserted
it to its memories. Desolate and mice-ridden stood the fading
pile in a neighborhood where further decay was hardly possible,
enveloped by failure and dirt and poverty, misery and sin and
the sound of unholy revelry by night. 'The lion and the liz-
ard keep the courts where Jamshýd gloried and drank deep.' And
the vast moulded corridors, historied with great names, echoed
to the feet of Garlands, Vivians, and Goldnagels, and over the

boards once ennobled by the press of royal feet, a shabby young man sat writing into a book with a villainous pen, as follows:

Rent	$12.
Board	20.
Laundry	3.25

Dr. Vivian had, in short, induced himself to the casting-up of his monthly accounts, a task of weariness and travail. As to-morrow was the first day of the year, it was natural that he should thus occupy his half-hour of leisure, but as he was unmethodical by nature it was also natural that he should be casting up the account for November, December (which included Christmas) being as yet unlooked into. Jottings on loose bits of paper supplied the necessary data, or did n't, as the case might be.

The young man scratched his head, and continued:

Car-tickets	$1.25
Tobacco	.40
Soap	.15
Shaving ditto	.19
Gas	2.40
Pencils	.03

"Aha!" said V. Vivian, after a considerable interval; and penned triumphantly:

Matches	.05
Beads (Corinne)	.49

Followed a long pause.

On the opposite, or left-hand, page of the ledger there stood:

Income	50.
Receipts	6.40
Total	56.40

Vivian's dead father, though the absent-minded inventor of the turbine that would never quite work, had somehow contrived not to make away with every penny of his wife's Beirne inheritance. Very few unsuccessful inventors could say as much.

And this fact accounted for the complicating term "Income," whose regular presence in the budget was certainly a trifle awkward for the despiser of property, aligning him out of hand with the wealthy classes; but to the individual was undoubtedly most comforting, since it set a man economically free forever. You never have to do anything for money, with fifty dollars a month. Receipts were, of course, moneys taken in for services rendered. If Vivian's sick insisted on paying him a little something for his trouble, he thought it moral not to restrain them. However, the sick's attitude was commonly the reverse of the above. . . .

Ignoring "Receipts," as a highly uncertain quantity, the scheme of income and outgo commonly left a net monthly balance of about ten dollars for works of a philanthropic nature. From a strictly scientific point of view, the budget contained an unsoundness, in that it allowed nothing for depreciation of plant, so to say: the necessity for fresh supplies of a personal nature really was not duly faced in it. However, the doctor had so far eliminated all expenditures in that quarter, save only for a little half-soling matter week before last. He was confident that it would all work out very satisfactorily when occasion arose.

The trial balance to-night developed a shortage of $1.22. Before the budgeteer could precisely place it, his attention became diverted by something else, to return no more that evening. Having drawn a stray sheet of paper toward him to scribble on it "Milk for Miggs," he was caught and engrossed by other inscriptions on the sheet, noted down in the early forenoon. They ran:

Heth Works (Pickle) Art in *Factory Worker*
See Mr. Dayne — Settlement — Begin canvass not
    before Feb. 1. H. Cooney
Todd Inst. — Night School?
Socks? — Or darning
Playground. (Council Com. meets Fri. 5 P.M.)
Jack D.
Mrs. G. Loan 20c.

Through the next to the last item, Vivian absently drew a pencil mark, the weekly cheering letter to Weymouth, Texas, having been written just after the memorandum. However, the young man's eye remained fixed on the item erased. He lit his pipe, took his head in both hands and continued to stare. . . .

Dalhousie had called at the Dabney House on the night of his departure for the new country. His reappearance in the flesh proved at least that that fierce instability of character, which betrays men in moments of disaster to the irreparable rashness, was not in him. So much was a comfort, for the witch fear had ridden Vivian in the silent weeks following the Beach.

But the reparting was a heart-rack none the less. Dalhousie was no lifelong friend like O'Neill, or even like Chas Cooney. But Vivian, having made his acquaintance most informally one night in the summer, had responded at sight to the unconscious claim of weakness; he had come to feel a strong bond, conceived splendid reformatory plans. The boy's fall and disgrace, coming like a crash from the blue, had been a severe shock to him, which would last. His self-exile, while probably advisable for a time at least, had been a prospect full of sadness. If poor Dalhousie had, woven into him, a vitiating twist for self-dramatization, if he said, "My God, why can't I die?" less with the terrible dignity of ruin than like a lad portraying his idea of ruin on the stage, his native missing of the utter ring of truth never occurred to Vivian. To him this boy, broken for cowardice and cast off by his father and friends, was as tragic a figure as Œdipus.

And what made the farewell so peculiarly sad was that Dal, out of his painful bewilderment, was evidently still clinging to some sort of hope. He himself had said, and said again, that there was no hope for such as he. He admitted with bitterness his insane passion that sunny afternoon; remembered and acknowledged a wild impulse to overturn the boat, and let come what might. He paced the floor and cried out that nothing that they said of him could be too bad. And yet he hoped. He had come to the Dabney House with hope. He had given his Texas address with a falter of hope.

But of course there was no hope. Drink, the great fowler, had
bagged one more. . . .

Without, there rose a lonesome booming, far and ghostly in
the stillness of the great empty hotel. It was the Garlands'
crazy clock, memento of Mister in his prodigal bridal days.
Harried forever by some obscure intestinal disorder, the mad
timepiece stayed voiceless for days together, and then, without
warning, embarked upon an orgy of profligate strikings. Now it
struck fourteen, and fell abruptly silent.

Vivian stirred, and remembered the reception. His uncle, who
derided and castigated his Dabney House career, had said em-
phatically that he would consider it most disrespectful if his
solitary nephew absented himself from the annual greeting of
friends. The nephew, since his home-coming, had grown very
fond of the old gentleman. Yet he knew quite well that he was n't
giving up this evening solely to please his uncle.

He rose, relit his pipe, and walked about. Though useful
bones were missing from his left foot, he liked to walk: was
rather an accomplished pedestrian. In time he came to a halt
before a dilapidated little cabinet partly full of the shiny tools
of his trade. The cabinet seemed quite out of place in the tall
state chamber: but then so did the man. He did not look in the
least like a doctor (just as Miss Heth had said). The faint
scent of iodoform that he now gave off was a heterogeneity,
like a whiff of brandy on a parson.

The young man stood gazing into his cabinet, fathoms deep in
thought. That Miss Heth was responsible for a meaningless lie
which took away more than life itself from one who had loved
her truly in his way: this was a hypothesis so wild and weak
that it collapsed at the first opportunity for calm, just examination. The sight of her again, the other night, had merely
clinched the matter; driven by a glance the last nail in the coffin
of Dalhousie's hope; and by the same stroke, swept away the
last lingering trace of diabolical suspicion. But that Miss Heth
had treated Dal pretty badly before the Beach was only too
probable. The boy's bitter complainings had left small doubt
of that.

It is a world in which we must be just before we are generous. Unfortunately, there could be little question that this girl with the heavenly face had a certain touch — should we say? — of earthy hardness in her, a certain induration of the spirit. She had shown it quite plainly in her general attitude toward Dal in the hour of his need. She had shown it again, in a sort of way, in her attitude toward the Works.

Not, indeed, in her resentment at his letter. Anything but resentment there would have been unnatural, not to say inhuman and despisable, in a daughter. Of course no girl worth a pinch of salt would allow you to stand up and say that her father was a shameless homicide. Her anger there did her the greatest credit: showed beyond doubt that she was absolutely sound at heart. . . . Trouble was, of course, that she did n't know anything about the Works, and did n't want to know. She supposed that those scores of girls who went daily to her father's bunching-room had nothing to do with her.

The night was cold; V. Vivian stood warming his hands over a second-hand gas-stove, which leaked perceptibly. . . . Great heavens, how could it possibly be otherwise? Was not this the way of all the world? Let a little prosperity come to a poor peasant, and the first thing he did was to stop eating five from the same bowl. That was Tolstoy; and that was the way, through all peoples and all times, riches had meant segregation from the Common. . . . Round and round them pulsed the great warm tide of real life, and, stung by this mad blindness, men sweated and fought their lives away trying to scramble up out of the enriching stream upon a sterile little island. You could almost have forgiven them if they were happy upon their island. But happiness is born in the heart, and they who seek it elsewhere in the end hold Sodom apples in fingers through which the pearl of great price has somewhere slipped on the way. . . .

"Mr. V. V.! Ain't you dressing *yet!*" said a voice from without. "Mommer says remind you it 's after nine o'clock."

The tall young man came to earth with a thud. A startled frown gathered quickly on his brow.

"*What?* ... Then I'm late indeed. *Nine o'clock!* I don't see how it's possible...."

He seized Commissioner O'Neill's suitcase from the operating-table, with a panic show of hurry.

Kern's voice took on a cheering inflection.

"Don't you mind, Mr. V. V. All the swells 'll be late. D' you want me to help you, sir? Don't you want me put in your studs 'r something?"

Mr. V. V. set down the suitcase, dealt a mortal blow.

"I have no studs," he said, in a quiet, scared way.

A little exclamation without was followed by: "Can I come in, sir?"

"Yes, yes; come in. But this is rather serious. I confess I — don't see how it's going to work out...."

The door opened and Kern tripped in with a little kick, and a flash and tinkle of jewelry at neck and waist. She never merely walked when it was possible to dance.

"My regular shirts," said the young man, standing on the floor and brushing his hair with a worried hand, "have the buttons sewed on, of course.... Seems to me O'Neill might have thought of this contingency."

Kern repressed a desire to giggle at Doctor's air of helplessness, and controlled her itching feet. She was not wanting in the resourcefulness of the poor.

"I'll get you studs, Mr. V. V.," said she, eagerly. "Less see now — where'll I get 'em? ... I'll get 'em at Lazarus's — that's where! I'll have 'em here in five minutes, and right in your shirt."

Lazarus? Why, they shut up at six o'clock. Yes, but Willie Walter, he slept behind the counter, and was abed right now, on account of getting up so early. Just let her bang the door in the alley a couple of times, that was all. Moreover, Walter being obliging, it agreeably developed that the studs would come as a temporary loan, if desired. An evening's wear out of them, and then back on the card and into stock again, the same as new, and nobody the wiser. Lazarus would do the same.

"It's very nice of you, Corinne," said the young man, picking up the suitcase again. "Something in pearl or plain gold, perhaps. Come straight back now. I don't like at all for you to be running the streets at night —"

"Maybe I won't come back at all," said Kern, improvising a barn dance about the long office. "Maybe I'll run off with a count and go to Europe on a steamer like, and have mand'lins played under my winder by moonlight, and sit at a gool' writin'-desk all day and make up po'try."

"That would be rather hard on the count, would n't it?" said Mr. V. V., absently; and added at once: "What makes you do that?"

"Stitch in me side," said she, impishly. "Machineetis, *I* call it. Like 'pendicitis, y' know? It's gone now. I don't get tired when I dance."

Kern had a quantity of dark brown hair, covered now by a picture hat supporting a base red imitation of a willow plume; she put on the hat every night nowadays, whether she was going out or not. By two years' steady practice she was esteemed one of the best operatives in the Heth Cheroot Works; but her new passion in life was to learn from Mr. V. V. what it was to be a lady. Dearly as Kern loved beads, pins, buckles, and all that shone and glittered, her particular desire for Christmas had been a Netiquette and Complete Letter Writer, and this Mr. V. V. had duly obtained for her, though it had run to a dollar and a quarter. The little girl might have been any age or no age; she was unformed for her years, somewhat elfin of countenance, and thin in the cheek. On one of these cheeks, Dr. Vivian now laid the back of his hand, and told Kern to stick out her tongue. She did it as she did everything (except cheroot-making), like a game, sticking it out much farther than was necessary and repeatedly winking her left eye.

Vivian set down the suitcase again.

"You go to bed," said he. "I'll attend to the studs."

Kern stuck back her tongue and unwinked her eye, with something like consternation.

"I feel *very* well, Mr. V. V. — honest! I'll get 'em and come straight back, sir, — truly, truly!"

The young man reached for his overcoat. "I don't want you to go out to-night. It's just the same as if you did it for me, because you want to do it. That's what counts. Now go on to bed. You aren't well at all, I fear."

Kern turned, much depressed. "It was me thought of Willie Walter. I think you might lemme."

"You must do what I say, Corinne."

"Ain't I doin' it, no matter how hard it is, sir?"

"Don't call me sir, I've told you."

Kern sadly retired. However, she did not do exactly what Mr. V. V. said. When, after forty minutes of storm and stress, he emerged from his bedroom and shouted to Mrs. Garland to come and see him if she liked, Kern, too, came running down the hall, still in her hat. Her interest in the gay evening being so peculiarly strong, Vivian did not have the heart to scold her very hard, especially as she cried ahead the promise to go to bed the very minute he was gone. And it might be that he was secretly rather glad to have his little friend see him in his splendid regalia.

He stood under the chandelier in his decaying chamber, re-volving himself with complacence for the Garlands' inspection. It was O'Neill's old suit that he had borrowed, which, as the Honorable Commissioner had pointed out, really made a much better fit than the costly brand-new one just from Begg's. At the first sight of their boarder in it, the two women cried out with pleasure, likening him to dooks and dashing villains on the stage, well seen by them from upper galleries of the past. But with the dying of the first enthusiastic burst, Kern, the connoisseur, who had herself been clasped by gentlemen's fulldresssuits at union hops, developed a more searching tendency. By the elbow she incited the doctor to keep on rotating.

"There's *something* wrong, sir, Mr. V. V., but I can't make out just what it is."

"It's these shoes," said Mr. V. V., frankly. "I really ought to have patent leathers to look like the rest of the bloods, but these 'll do very nicely, when I have them well shined up. I'll stop by the stand at Ninth Street."

"This spot right in front of the coat don't look so *very* good," said Kern, scratching it with a small finger, which only whitened it up.

"Shuh, Kern! That!" said Mrs. Garland, who had seen the spot, but decided to say nothing about it. "Why, hot suds and a drop ammonia'll fade it out like sunshine, and nobody never know 't was there. Wait till I get my pan now, Doctor."

"I wisht the coat could set a little snugger round your neck, Mr. V. V. But mercy, who cares, when you look so beautiful anyway! And you'll have the most beautiful lady and set and talk to her, won't you, Mr. V. V.?"

"Stranger things have happened, my dear Corinne!"

"There 'll be roses and violets and little pink lights and chicking salad and conservatories and fountings all lit up. And what 'll you and her talk about, Mr. V. V., with the band playing kind of soft and settin' behind some rubber-plants like?"

"Probably something for her own good," said Mr. V. V., with a close-set mouth; leaving Kern to reflect that that was a funny way to talk at a party.

Mrs. Garland rushed in with a steaming pan, and plumped down on her knees at the unshone feet. The little girl prattled on. But the tall doctor, on his own word, had relapsed abruptly into a brown study. . . .

"It sags a little in front," Kern was saying. "Lemme just get my hand on the buckle a minute. Mr. V. V., what makes you look so mad, kind of?"

The young man started a little.

"I was thinking," said he, "that life is hard at times."

"It 's truth, Doctor. . . . Had n't his negtie ought to be tightened up a weeny bit, Kern, now?" said Mrs. Garland harshly, staring up from her adoring position. "Not but *I* think the shine of his gool' collar-button ain't pretty. . . ."

When Mr. V. V. and his gala raiment were gone, Kern skipped into his bedroom and hastily tackled the marked disorder there prevalent. She thought that an extra minute or so stolen for this purpose would not really be so very wrong. Care

THERE 'S *SOMETHING* WRONG, SIR, MR. V. V.

of the rooms was strictly included in the boarder's twenty dollars a month, but Kern was not thinking of it that way exactly.

"Mommer, what makes him have that kinder sorry look all the time, I wonder?" she said, when Mrs. Garland followed her in.

"Sorry, what you talkin' about? A pleasanter spoke gempman I never see. Hand me them pants."

"I'll fold 'em, mommer. — I don't mean speakin', but the look he's got, just the same when he's laughin' and jokin' and all. It's the look he's got, don't you notice, someway?"

"It's that foot o' his, I reckon. Pains him prob'ly. The mess he's left things . . . He'd ought to have a fulldressuit of his own, 'stead o' borrowin' that fat O'Neill's."

"Mommer, if he had one, somebody'd ask it off him. Like he gave Mister his Sunday cutaway coat. . . . How'd he hurt his foot, mommer, jever hear him say?"

"Berkler bone, *I* hear."

They worked in silence for a time.

"I'm right tired to-night. Put 'em here in his clo'es-bag, mommer. . . . Don't seem it could be just his foot. Torm Hartman's leg's right off to his hip, and he's got a fat look to him. Mr. V. V.'s sorry like he wanted to do something, and something in him knewed all the time he couldn't ever."

"Somep'n in him knewed — jever hear such foolishness! I'll take the broom to this floor. You go along to bed now. Didn't I hear you promise him?"

"Mommer, I'm going. Only I druther of went to the party," said Kern.

X

A Beautiful New Year's Party, and who spoiled it, and how; how Something is done, after all, for she tells the Man plainly that he must n't speak to her any more.

BY eleven o'clock the festivities approached their height: even the ultra-fashionable had arrived, even the ultra-conservative had not departed for bed. The affair was none of your wholesale routs. Old Mr. Beirne, who had long claimed the eve of the New Year for the hospitable repayment of his social dues, had lived to see the list of his friends shrink fast as Old Years ticked out. Nevertheless, the scene now was indubitably inspiriting. Lively groups decorated all the purview. White shirt-fronts gleamed: white shoulders did the same. The fragrance of flowers filled the air, filled likewise with the gay hum of voices. From behind a coppice of shrub and palm Professor Wissner's band of select artists continually seduced the feet. Toward the dining-room regions rose the sounds of refined conviviality. Servitors moved about with trays. Mrs. Clicquot's product fizzed, for the proper ceremonious induction of another year.

It was a most enlivening ensemble, full of pleasant attractions to the senses; and through it moved Carlisle Heth, the most beautiful lady, with a look like that of a queen in a book. In that gay company she was the proudest figure, the object of all most captivating to the eye, save one; and that one, an Olympian in evening dress, sauntered splendidly at her side.

Mr. Canning to-night made his début in the local gay world. Constant as had been his attentions for a number of days, he had hitherto held steadfastly to his valetudinarian stand against general society. He had gambolled, indeed, but he had gambolled strictly *à deux*. In his present willingness to break through his invalid rules, and appear as her acknowledged squire before the flower of her world, Carlisle's heart had recognized the crowning proof of his interest. Small wonder if in prospect this victorious evening had been starred in her mind in purple and gold. . . .

The shining pair had just arrived, lateness being reckoned very differently in Houses of Heth and Houses of Dabney. Their brilliant progress down the long gay room, stopped often for the giving and taking of greetings, left behind a wake of *sotto-voce* compliment. Cally Heth, though the familiar sight of every day, was a spectacle, or view, not easily tired of. In a company in which most had known each other from birth, her distinguished stranger and captive naturally drew even keener interest.

"Look, there he is!" whispered an excited débutante. "Oh, what a dream! . . ."

"I never saw Cally look better. If she were *only* a little taller, what a match they'd make." (This was Cally's second-best friend Evelyn McVey, herself a tall girl.)

"Wissner ought to hit up that well-known snatch from 'Lohengrin' . . ."

"Certainly, Mrs. Bronson. Delighted to introduce you — introduce him, that is. Just a little later, though. Wouldn't have me interrupt *that*, would you?"

Thus faithful Willie Kerr, somewhat harassed by the responsibilities of being next friend to a crown prince.

Backbiting among the well-bred murmurs there was of course. Mrs. Berkeley Page, the hostile one who had made the remark about the Heths being very improbable people, naturally spoke in her characteristic vein. She made her observations to her great crony, Mr. Richard Marye, who plucked a glass of champagne from a beckoned lackey, and answered:

"Whoever conceived a Canning to be an anchorite? . . . My dear, why are you so severe with these very excellent and worthy people?"

"Is it severe," said the lady, "to refuse to be cozened by gay lips and dramatic hair?"

"Aspiration," mused her elderly friend, sipping comfortably, "is the mainspring of progress. Don't you admire onward and upward? What harm can a little climbing possibly do to you and me?"

"Oh, Mr. Dick! All the harm that the tail does when it begins to wag the dog. Don't you observe how these people set up their own standards, and get them accepted, whatever old fogies like you and me may say? They *unsoul* us — that's what they do, and we may scream, but we can't stop them. Their argument is that money can do everything, and the intolerable part of it is that they *prove it.* Ah, me! — "

"Also, O temperament! O Moriarty! For my part, Mary, I'm a Democrat — "

"You're an old-fashioned Church of England man, and incidentally a great dear," said Mary Page. "And nothing on earth sickens you, and you know it, like this godless modern materialism . . ."

But who could smile more unaffectedly than Cally Heth at the bitter little peckings with which the dying order ever seeks to avenge itself on its brilliant supplanters? She passed on down the long room, stunning admirer in her train. High hope beckoned imminently to-night. By the subtle intuitions of her sex she had been notified that the steady approach of the symbol of her happiness consummate now quickened toward its shining end. . . .

Mr. Hugo Canning, having returned for a week at most, had already remained for a fortnight. And it was obviously for her sake that he had lingered. Day by day, emerging from his Payne barricades, he had sought her out: loud his feet had thundered behind, with no more promptings of hers. Of the genuineness of his interest she could feel no trace of doubt: a score of "passages" since the interesting moment in Willie's sitting-room rose to the eye of memory. And the prince of partis attracted her no less compellingly. On nearer view, he had revealed himself as full of a fascinating contrariety, various as a woman. Moods played up and down upon him, charming mysteriously. He could be distrait and silent, the portrait of distinguished boredom. And then, as by the turning of a sudden page, he was gay again, tender, witty, all ardors. . . .

More than the strains of the lovesick waltz beat in the girl's veins to-night. For this present there was no hope even of connected conversation. In the midst of the gay company the invasions of privacy were constant.

"All these nice people, and all so eager to be friendly with you!" laughed Carlisle, with some want of naturalness, as she for the dozenth time detached herself and him from a little surrounding group. "And yet you've complained to me of *loneliness!*"

"There are times, Miss Heth, when one is never so lonely as in the midst of the crowd."

"Oh! . . . Then to save you from loneliness to-night I must remove you from the crowd?"

"You grasp my meaning. I want a lodge in some vast wilderness."

"That is rather rude, is n't it? Where should I come in?"

"You come into the lodge," said Canning, and smiled faintly.

Though the smile was faint, her eyes fell before it. When she raised them, they ran upon another interruption.

"This is Mrs. Mason, Mr. Beirne's sister. You will like to meet her, Mr. Canning."

"Delightful," murmured Mr. Canning.

Because of his consistent recluseness, foregone to-night for her pleasure, Carlisle had meant rather to exhibit Mr. Canning to enraptured eyes than to subject him to a flood of undesired introductions. But because she did not want people to refer to her as catty behind her back, some sharing of her honors was inescapable. A few of her dearest girl-friends, a handful of the more prominent young men, a somewhat larger sprinkling of the older people: these were all who received the golden benediction. Evey McVey was of course among the favored few, but Mattie Allen, as usual so late in the evening, was not to be seen. She was undoubtedly "off" somewhere, probably high up on the stairs, with the most interesting man she had been able to attach.

Canning accepted all the introductions with a charming courtesy, but Carlisle detected beneath his agreeable manner a faint undercurrent of stoic weariness. The cold weather had lately touched the troublesome throat: Mr. Canning spoke to-night with perceptible hoarseness. Carlisle assured him that he had won a permanent place in Foxe's "Book of Martyrs" (of which she had heard the other day), and invited him to partake of refreshments, for they had now at last reached the doors of the dining-room. He declined, as she had done, but accepted a glass of champagne from a bald-headed Greek who was pulling corks at a small table near by. On the point of pledging his lady's health, he was invaded again, this time by resolute Mr. Robert Tellford, who held the opinion that Carlisle looked an angel this evening, and was long since addicted to celestial society.

"The wine is excellent," said Mr. Canning, clinking glasses with Mr. Tellford.

"The rooms are warm," said Robert, in about that sequence.

"People are beginning to leave, I observe," said Mr. Canning.

"Others are just coming in, I note," answered Robert, doggedly.

Carlisle laughed. "To-morrow will be a fine day. You talk like people in a play. Let's all wish each other a happy New Year. . . ."

"Duty is done," she added later, with a small sigh, when Robert had been persuaded to remove himself. "We can now give ourselves up to lives of the grossest selfishness. . . . Oh, oh, *oh!* . . . *How* would sitting down appeal to you, Mr. Canning?"

"Ice-water to Tantalus, Miss Heth. And seats are about as probable."

"*Look!*"

She nodded dramatically toward the hall and her sudden discovery: Mr. Beirne's private lair, presumably; a pleasant little retreat on the other side of the house, luring the eye through a half-open door. A little to the back, and off the beaten track, this nook seemed to have escaped the irruption of guests altogether.

"My lodge, as I live!" said Canning, with interest. "And, for once, I really don't believe we'll find a spoony couple sitting in the best place. Let's advance casually, yet with lightning speed. . . ."

They passed out of the drawing-room into the hall, the hum of various gaiety in their ears. No voices reached them from the rest-haven ahead. Carlisle was suddenly silent. A subtle and thrilling sense of expectancy possessed her, making talk somewhat difficult. . . .

However, on the very threshold of privacy, her agreeable feelings met with a cool *douche*. A brazen couple *was* already there, sitting in the best place. In this world of trouble there always, always was. The fact was disappointing enough, to say the least of it, but what made matters worse was that it was impossible merely to exclaim reprovingly, as one usually does, "Oh, there's somebody *here!*" and step back at once. Carlisle saw in the first glance that the girl in the best place was no other than her special friend Mattie Allen, already looking around over her shoulder, spying her. To withdraw from Mattie, under these circumstances, was simply not to be thought of.

She gave Canning a quick, backward, upward look which said, plainer than print, "How long, O Lord, how long?" Recomposing her features hastily, she stepped on in.

"Oh, *Mats!* It's you at last! We've been looking everywhere for you. Mr. Canning was *so* anxious to meet you. . . ."

She ended dead. The intruding "couple" had risen together, turning; and Carlisle saw, with the suddenest and oddest little sinking sensation, that the male half of it, Mattie's astounding capture, was the lame physician from the slums, he whose face and words had become inextricably a part of the most disturbing memories of her life.

She, in her radiance, had met the slum doctor's eye with a shock of recognition; she looked at once away. She felt like one who has walked singing into a malicious trap. Why, oh, why need the man have been ambushed here, of all places under the sun, obtruding his undesired presence and marplot countenance once again on her and Mr. Canning? . . .

However, if there was no withdrawing, neither was there the slightest break in the smooth outer continuity of things. Dear

Mattie (already with a sheep's eye for the king among men in the doorway) had seized the conversation even before Carlisle left it hanging.

"Hello, darling Cally! Do come in and share our lovely little snuggery. Isn't it cunning? — don't you think we were awfully smart to find it? Oh, do you know Dr. Vivian? — Miss Heth."

"How do you do?" said Cally, without a second glance. . . . "*This* is she, Mr. Canning — Miss Mattie Allen, whom you've heard so much about . . ."

Canning, hardly less piqued than Carlisle by the presence of strangers in his lodge, and unable to remember having heard the name Allen before in his life, of course rose gallantly.

"I hope Miss Allen won't think me impertinent," he said, most delightfully, "if I claim her as an old friend. . . . "

Miss Allen's response acquitted him of all impertinence. It was she who then recalled an omission, and in her sweet artless way bade the two gentlemen be acquainted. Dr. Vivian (who could not exactly recollect the steps by which he had come to be duetting in his uncle's den with Miss Allen) looked as if he expected to shake hands with Miss Heth's handsome squire; but Canning, having shot him with a quick curious glance, merely bowed, in silence. Through the minds of both men (and also of Miss Carlisle Heth) had swept at the same moment a darting memory of their last meeting. . . .

And then it was suddenly seen by all that Mr. Canning had been gathered in by his adroit old friend Miss Allen, and smartly withdrawn from the general society. And Cally was left to face alone the last man upon earth she wanted to see.

She, whose own plans had been so utterly different, had been on her guard against such a contingency as this; but Mattie's born gift for strategics had simply been too much for her. Mr. Canning had been surrounded and backed against a book-case, as it were, before anybody realized what was happening to him. . . .

"But oh, you're so dreadfully tall," she heard the voice of her gifted girl-friend, as from a distance. "I don't believe you can look far enough down to see poor little Me. . . ."

All had happened at speed: the lines of division were still just forming. And Carlisle, of course, had no idea of tamely accepting such an unfair distribution of things. As to this man, Dr. Vivian, her attitude toward him now, after the Cooneys', was simply one of cool polished politeness. She had told him what she thought of him about the Works, and he had humbly apologized for the wrong he had done her at the Beach: that disposed of him forever, and altogether to her advantage. Cool polished politeness; but she did not intend to talk with him any more, of course, admitting him as a social acquaintance; and she was, in fact, just moving after Mattie and Mr. Canning, really opening her mouth to join in their pleasant chat, when —

"I wonder, do you know if there are any *marrons glacés* tonight, Miss Heth," said the voice she had first heard in the summer-house — "with the little white jackets on them?"

The girl felt a number of things. From every point of view this inquiry, so queer yet so clearly social, so almost glaringly inoffensive, came as a surprise and an annoyance. He had merely asked that on purpose to detain her. Continuing to look at her two friends, so near and yet such worlds away, she said, coldly:

"I really do not know. I've not been in the dining-room."

"Then I may still hope," he answered, with the same air of friendliness, eager in its way. And, continuing his out-of-place remarks, he said: "I promised to bring some from the party to a little girl that — that I — well, I board with her mother, in fact. She seemed to have set her heart on *marrons*, though how she knew that such things existed passes imagination."

"I hope you'll find them, I'm sure."

"Oh, thank you," said the Severe Arraigner, quite gratefully, it seemed. . . .

Through the open door of the pleasant little room, there floated in the continual murmur of voices and the sighing refrain of the waltz. As from a great distance, Carlisle noted that Mr. Canning found Mattie agreeably amusing. (What on earth did the men see in her, with her baby airs and great pop-eyes?) But she was not thinking of her two special friends now. The flat brusquerie of her two remarks to the man had struck her own ear unpleasantly: they were neither polished nor courteous. Why was she so silly as to let this nobody, who had nothing whatever to do with her, so annoy and distract her at his pleasure? Above all, by what trick of his look had he made her feel, the moment his eyes fell upon her, that his apology had not settled the Beach episode, exactly, after all? . . .

The whole situation seemed to be growing intolerable; and suddenly it came over her that polished courtesy was not the note at all. Doubtless the trouble was that she could not forgive his remark in the summer-house, after all, no matter how generously she tried. What was needed now was to put the man down in such a way that he would take care not to come near her again. . . .

Dr. Vivian, who seemed to hold fast to his one topic, was adding: "I don't want to disappoint her, of course, particularly as she's sick to-night. Just a little touch of fever, to be sure, — but she has n't much constitution, I fear. . . ."

Miss Heth made no reply; the pause threatened to become a silence; and then he said hastily, as if to save the conversation from total wreck:

"By the way, this child — Corinne Garland, her name is — is an operative in your father's factory, Miss Heth. She's been there over two years."

Cally's head turned. For the first time she looked fully at the Cooneys' poorhouse idol. And now she remembered that she had an annihilative weapon against him. . . . Had he led up to this subject on purpose?

"Oh! . . . She works at my father's factory?"

The young man's look was plainly not controversial; no, it was as if he were pleased that at last they had tapped a vein of common interest. In one glance Carlisle's trained eye, going over him, took in his sartorial eccentricities: in particular the "shined" shoes, the large brass shirt-studs, and the "full-dress-suit" (exactly that) so obviously made for a much stouter person. She saw that the man looked absurdly out of place here, at his own uncle's. Against this background of gaiety and glitter, of music, powder and décolleté gowns, he really looked quite like a stray from some other world: only the more so in that he himself appeared quite unconscious of any alienship.

Well, then, let him keep to his own world. That, in fact, was precisely what she desired of him. . . .

"Yes, a buncher there, as they're called," he was quaintly explaining — "quite the best one in the shop, I'm told, though she's only eighteen years old. She has a record of 6,500 cheroots in one day —"

"But she has been taken sick at it, you say?"

"Undoubtedly she has a temperature to-night," said he, in an intent sort of way, desirous of giving his information accurately. "I did n't stop to take it, as perhaps I should have done —"

"And she caught her fever at the Works, you think?"

"Oh! . . . Well, of course I should n't say that. You know —"

"But of course the Works *are* full of terrible diseases, and everybody who works there quickly catches something and dies?"

Then the unmistakable hostility of her tone caught his engrossed ear. Carlisle saw his expression change a little; only it did not change nearly so much as she meant it to. He gave an embarrassed little laugh. . . .

"But oh, *please*," said the voice of Mats, near by, " do go back and tell me what *terminology* means. You don't know how *terribly stupid* I am. . . ."

"Of course, it is n't nearly so bad as that," said he. "Factory work is hard at best, you know. And conditions in it are never very good, rarely even so good as they might be, as it seems to me. But this little friend of mine that I — I mentioned, she's —"

"Why did you mention her to me at all?"

The tall young man in the fat-man's dress-suit gazed down. He pushed back his crisp hair. . . .

It was true that one from the outskirts could rise now and gird up his loins: the scribes actually called before the flap of his tent. True, in the most technical sense, that is. . . . And yet — was the passing social moment a proper occasion to shout and preach at the unlessoned upon the grim subject of their moral opportunities in this so complex world? Where was even the solitude be-

hind the rubber plants which Kern had (practically) guaranteed?
Was it kind, was it even well-mannered, to spoil a young girl's
pleasure at an evening party with bitter talk of fire-escapes and
overstrained floors? John the Baptist, God knows, should have
been a gentleman . . .

But if any thoughts like this played through the alien's
mind, he certainly wore no air of perplexity or hesitancy. He
answered without pause, in quite a gentle way:

"Well, it just seemed to come in naturally somehow. We just
seemed to drift into it. . . ."

But it was no time for gentleness now. Carlisle Heth was
whipping up her anger to destroy him. And all the time, a part
of her (the largest part, it seemed) knew quite well that she was
whipping it up: wondered why it did n't surge more spontaneously, as she had such a perfect right to expect. . . .

"But conditions *are* homicidal in my father's factory, are they
not?"

"Oh," said the man. . . . "Well, as to that — of course opinions would differ somewhat as to what consti —"

"You seem to — to have more courage in your opinions when
you 're writing letters," she flung at him, bright cheeked. . . .
"Are they homicidal?"

V. Vivian's eyes had fallen before her indignant gaze. It was
only too clear by now that she had n't forgiven him — what
wonder? — and probably never would. . . . Still, when he raised
his eyes again, the girl saw in them a look quite different from
what she had meant to arouse there. The man was feeling sorry
for her again. . . .

"Miss Heth, I consider them homicidal. I 'm sorrier than I can
say to — to worry you with all this now. Some day if you could
give me —"

"You must n't say these things to me," said Carlisle, feeling her anger to be real enough now. "I won't permit them.
And —"

"You don't imagine that I say them for pleasure," the tall
doctor interrupted hurriedly. "I 'm compelled to speak the
truth, however disagreeable —"

"Indeed? I've not noticed that you feel bound by any necessity that way."

To that he made no reply at all. But she saw, by the look he wore, that he was doing his best to convict her once again of having said something unfair and rather cheap and horrid. . . .

Turning from him, she delivered the coup de grâce, in a voice not quite so firm as she would have wished:

"I don't wish to talk to you any more. You must not speak to me again. . . ."

And she added at once, to a more congenial audience: "Oh!"

"Oh, oh! Cally!" whispered Mattie Allen, turning simultaneously, and for the first time, from Mr. Canning.

And Mr. Canning said: "Ah! — what's happened? . . ."

In almost the same moment all three had become aware that the rattle of talk and laughter outside the little room had entirely died away. There had fallen upon the house of gaiety a strange silence, in which a pin-fall might almost have been heard, and the slow speaking of a single voice, the length of the house away, was heard most distinctly.

To neither of the two girls was this proceeding a mystery. They were familiar with the New Year's Eve rites, and Mattie, after a number of pretty *Sh-h-h* gestures, whispered the explanation to Mr. Canning:

"They're reading out the Old Year. We must all go see it. It's so cunning and quaint. . . ."

So conversation of all sorts was summarily suspended. Even whispers sounded loud in the sudden hush. The four young people moved toward the door. For a moment they had almost the air of a company of friends. Young Dr. Vivian, who was nobody's friend, stood back for Miss Heth to pass out; but, seeing that she lingered beside her gallant, he turned again silently after Miss Allen, who beckoned to him *sh-h*-ingly, whose property he seemed mysteriously to have become. . . .

The alien passed out of sight, limping. If his only party that year had gone rather badly with him, it was not less so with another. Behind him in the firelit den, Carlisle looked up at Canning, color coming back into her cheek, her breast rising and falling. The sight of him, all to herself again, was more than balm to a wound, more than harbors to storm-swept mariners.

"Is there *any* rest for the weary!" she whispered. "Oh, me! Let's *go home*, right after this!"

Canning, who also wore a faint air of persecution for righteousness' sake, took her gloved hand, and she did not withdraw it.

"Do you know," he answered, with a little smile, "that's the cleverest thing I've heard said to-night. . . ."

"We can have a little party all to ourselves," said Carlisle, rather tremulously. "It's been so *horrid* to-night. . . ."

They opened the back door to let the Old Year out. They flung wide the front doors to let the New Year in. They lowered all lights to the dimness of obsequies. The gay company, standing, ranged the long room in a ghostly half-light, and old Mr. Beirne, from his immemorial post between the tall windows, read from a great book "The Dying Year," in a voice as slow and solemn as he could make it. The stately lines brought home with a certain force, rather emphasized by the festive contrast, the certain passing of all mundane things. Here was another milestone left behind, and you and I would pass this way no more. Over the long loose dim ring, your eye fell upon a familiar and friendly face, fallen suddenly a little sad; and memory stirred of the many times you had looked at that face, and with it wonder of what another year might bring to you two. Would you stand here like this, friends good and true, with hearts tuned to the same feeling, a twelvemonth from to-night? There was felt a quick, childlike impulse for hands all round and such a singing of "Auld Lang Syne" as would have brought the police on the run.

By long practice and the most accurate chronometric reckoning, old Mr. Beirne timed his proceedings to a decimal. The last line of the slow-read poem died in a deafening uproar without. Every bell in the city, it seemed, every whistle and chime, every firecracker and penny-trumpet and cannon (there was but one), to say nothing of many an inebriated human voice, hailed in a roaring diapason the birth of a new year. At Mr. Beirne's the outer tumult was echoed in the manner of the well-bred. The doors were shut, with the infant inside; the lights flew up; glasses clinked, merry healths were pledged, new fealties sworn by look alone. Gaiety overcame silence. All talked with one voice.

Carlisle Heth descended the stairs in a carriage-robe of blue-and-fur, giving and taking lively good-nights. Canning, already mufflered and overcoated, stood awaiting her near the door: over many heads she caught sight of his splendid figure and her heart leapt a little. If it had been horrid for her to-night so far, no one would have guessed it, looking at her. Her shining loveliness upon the stairs attracted considerable attention; even her best girl-friend Mattie Allen noticed it, spoke of it to Evey McVey. . . .

And then at the foot of the steps, she ran right into Jack Dalhousie's friend once more, the lame stranger whom she had just finally disposed of.

Encountering the man's eyes by mischance, she would of course have looked away at once, but her glance was trapped by the expression on his face. He was smiling; smiling straight at her. An odd smile it was, and complicated; not without diffidence, but certainly not without hope; quite an eager smile, confiding somehow, by the gift he had. It was as if he was saying that of course he knew she hadn't really meant what she said back there; and that he, for one, would never let a hasty word or two cut him off from the hope of being good friends yet.

Having thus by a trick captured her attention, he made a pleased sort of gesture toward the breast-pocket of his fat-man's coat, and, while she passed silent within a foot of him, said quite eagerly:

"*I — I got the marrons!*"

XI

In which Mr. Canning must go South for his Health, and Cally lies awake to think.

MIDNIGHT stillness hung over the House of Heth, five doors from Mr. Beirne's. Dim sounds from above indicated that Mrs. Heth, who had come in a few moments earlier, did not mean to sit up for anybody. She had, however, left the door "on the latch" as agreed. Carlisle and Mr. Canning passed within, out of the biting New Year.

It was like stepping into heaven to be at home again, after the rabble and rattle at Mr. Beirne's. Canning shut the door with something like a sigh.

"A lodge at last! We've had — well, a fragmentary time of it, have n't we? . . . That chap with the game foot is simply my hoodoo."

Carlisle winced a little. "Oh! Then you did remember him?"

"Could I forget my Beach supplanter, my giver of colds in the head? What's wrong with the fellow anyway?"

"Everything," said she. "Let's go into the library."

"Why should he remind me of a camp-meeting funeral, I wonder?" mused Canning, following behind — "or is it something I read in the book of Job?"

The girl answered with a vague laugh. Mr. Canning's odd but evident antagonism to the man she herself had such cause to dislike was agreeable to her, but the topic was not. She had had enough of the Vivians of this world for one night. She led the way through the dark drawing-room, and at the switch beyond the door turned the light into two soft-tinted dome-lamps. The library was massive rather than "livable"; it had books, which is more than can be said for some libraries; but they were chiefly books in stately sets, yards and yards of them just alike: a depressing matter to the true lover. However, it was at least

solitude; solitude enveloped with an air of intimacy vastly agreeable and compensatory. It did not seem so certain now that the
golden evening was ruined past hope. . . .

"You and he seemed to be having a terribly earnest discussion," said Canning. "Of course I did my best to eavesdrop,
but Miss Allen was so charming I caught only a word now and
then."

"He was lecturing me about how my father ought to run his
business. He always does. . . ."

She replenished the dying fire with a soft lump, and poked it
unskilfully, all but stabbing the life out of it. Canning, standing and staring half-absently into the soft glow, did not offer to
relieve her of the poker. They knew each other very well by
now.

"Only don't let's spoil our little party by talking about him,"
she went on — " he rubs me the wrong way so. And do please
take off that polar overcoat. It positively makes me *shiver*. . . ."

"Lecturing appears to be the fellow's specialty. . . . Well!"

He threw his overcoat, stick, and white gloves on the fire-
settle, turned and glanced down at her. After the long and
broken evening, he looked somewhat fatigued. Carlisle, already
seated, was just beginning to unbutton her left long glove.

"Fine hours, fine hours these, for even a play sick-man! Yet
I linger on. . . . "

"You must stay," said she, "till the last person has gone from
Mr. Beirne's."

The mantel clock stood at twenty minutes past twelve. With
a little laugh she reached up and turned its small commemora-
tive face to the wall.

"Or," she added, becoming grave, "are you really quite tired
out with being with me?"

"I was hardly thinking that," said Canning.

He dropped into a chair and stared into the fire. Carlisle
glanced at his face in profile; a virile and commanding face it was,
and to her, singularly attractive.

"My thoughts were running in the contrary direction," said
Canning. "Do you remember my saying long ago that once I

began to gambol, I was never satisfied till I had gambolled all over the place? I suppose I need a guardian, but unluckily I have one. Miss Heth, I've some sad news — sad for me, I mean. I must go south to-morrow."

Carlisle turned her head with a little start.

"To-morrow! Oh, *no!*"

"No — you're right! I *can't* go to-morrow ! The day after at the farthest, or I suppose Heber'll be down after me with a couple of sheriffs."

"But I don't understand," she said, hurriedly. "What's happened? I — I hoped you would stay till the end of the week at least."

Canning's gaze remained upon the fire.

"So did I, though of course I've known I'd no business hanging on the skirt of Mason and Dixon's line this way. I might almost as well be in my office at home — tackling the pile of work that's been rolling up while I go on with this invalid's mummery. . . . Well, Heber's found me out, as of course the clever beggar would. He's been thinking, you see, that I was in Pinehurst, at the least. I had a red-headed telegram from him this afternoon ordering me to move on to Palm Beach instanter, or he would bring my revered parents down on me like a thousand of brick — no small matter, I assure you. . . . Palm Beach — Havana, perhaps! — till winter breaks! . . . A happy New Year message, is n't it?"

"It's very sad for me," said Carlisle, looking away from him.

"Well, I can't say that I feel exactly hilarious about it, you know."

There fell a brief silence, in which the crackling of the large new coal became noticeable.

"Duty is a hard word, Miss Heth," said Canning. "A thousand times I've wished that I was n't an only son — my family's one hopeful. But I am, alas. . . . And hence the little restcure. . . ."

"Yes, it's hard," she answered. And instead of going on as some girls would, "Don't you think you could *possibly* stay a little longer?" — she added, in tones of comforting: "But of course you will enjoy Florida immensely. You know you'll find agreeable people, and plenty of fun —"

"Of course! It is my particular delight," said Canning, in his hoarsened voice, "to stay in an attractive place just long enough to fall in love with it, and then be whipped away like a naughty schoolboy."

Carlisle slowly drew off her glove.

"I'm glad you've liked it here," said she. . . . "Shall you stop again, on your way back home?"

The man's eyes turned from the fire full upon her face. His voice changed a little.

"What do you think?"

"I only know what I hope," said she; and her gold-and-black lashes fell.

The firelight played upon her half-averted face, twisted shadows into the sheen of her hair, incarnadined her smooth cheek. Whiter and softer than swan's down gleamed her round bare shoulder, her perfect neck. Canning's blood moved. He turned more fully and leaned toward her, his elbow on her chair-arm.

"Could you think that all these happy days with you have meant so little to me? . . . You've a poor opinion of me, indeed. Did n't I say in the beginning that you did not know how to be kind?"

At his tone, the girl's breath came faster. She sat in silence pulling her long gloves between slim little hands.

"You are hard, Miss Heth," said Canning, slowly. And he added, with that touch of unconscious pride with which he always spoke of the Cannings, their position and serious responsibilities in the world: "When I compel myself to think of my duty toward my father and my family, I make sacrifices which ought, I think, to win me your approval. I've a place to fill some day. . . . But since you ask, I shall think also of myself. I shall come again to the old Payne fort."

She gave him a look which said that she was not really unkind. And Canning immediately possessed her ungloved hand in both of his. Her heart fluttered at his touch; her hand seemed to feel that this indeed was where it belonged; but, on the whole, training and intuition appeared to indicate a contrary view. There was a moment of stillness, of acquiescence, in which she became aware that he bent nearer. And then Carlisle rose, with a natural air, taking the hand along with her, incidentally as it were. Standing by the fire, looking down into it, she said:

"The town will be empty without you."

Behind her, Canning had risen too, with a sort of sharpness. He was silent. And then it was borne in upon her that the proud young man was moving toward his trappings, to go. . . .

"Your friendly words are much appreciated," said he, smiling. "But I observe that I've overstayed horribly."

The girl regarded him. Hardly since the first moments in Kerr's apartment, had she heard that ironical note in Mr. Canning's voice; and yet she understood at once, and was not alarmed. Gently as she had removed herself, he had felt himself rebuffed; and he could be abrupt at his pleasure.

Nothing good could come out of this horrid evening, but there would be another. And in her heart, besides, she did not believe that he would go away day after to-morrow. . . .

"Perhaps you'll drive with me to-morrow afternoon?"

"Oh, I'd like to so much," she said, naturally, as if nothing had passed between them. "And I'm so sorry about to-night, really. You've been such a saint, and all for me. You deserve a beautiful reward, a big medal, at least, and instead, an icy five-mile ride —"

"Reward!" said Canning, wheeling, still smiling a little. "What under heaven does the inconsequent sex know of reward? Up they trip, and with one flip of a little high heel kick a man's settled plans topsy-turvy. And for this upsetting he must thank his stars if he gets in return one kind smile a week. Punishment, not reward, strikes me as the feminine idea. . . ."

"I think," she said, a little embarrassed, "the only person I've really punished to-night is Me."

And she felt a twinge, half regret, half compunction, which was not tactical at all. After all, this man had been extraordinarily nice to her, and she was letting him go feeling that she did not appreciate it. . . .

She offered him her left hand to say good-night, and invested the gesture with a sweet air of penitence.

"But don't speak as if you were displeased with me, just when I'm so sad about your going away. . . . *Are* you displeased with me — or do you like me very much?"

"I am displeased with you, and I like you very much."

As the small hand lingered with him, warming by contact, the man's clasp tightened. He brought up his other hand and folded it over it.

"I'll miss you dreadfully — you know that. . . . Very, *very* much? That's the largest amount of liking known, is n't it?"

"Then that's the amount . . . "

Outside sounded the blasts of horns and the wheels of departing guests from Mr. Beirne's: 'low on the sand and loud on the stone.' In the soft-lit room no sound broke the nocturnal stillness except the mechanism of the clock, pushing busily toward the three-quarter mark. Carlisle was looking up at Canning with eyes full of unpremeditated sweetness. Into Canning's face the blood leapt suddenly. Without other warning, he leaned back against the heavy table, and took her almost roughly in his arms.

"I'm mad about you, you lovely little witch. Do you hear? It grinds my heart that I must leave you. . . ."

The turbulence of the sudden demonstration swept the girl from her moorings. If she had seemed to invite it, it yet came quite unexpectedly. For the moment she stood still in Canning's embrace, yielding herself with a thrilled passivity, as one who, with a full heart, touches high destiny at last. And in that moment her cheek, hair, eyes, then at last her lips, felt the sting of his Catullian endearments. . . .

But the moment of bliss in culmination passed with fainting quickness. The willing ear heard not. Unsteadied intuitions began to work again, chilling the girl's blood with the knowledge of wrong here, of glaring omission. And the more her gallant murmured, it seemed, the wider gaped the sudden lack. . . .

"You've been so good to me — so dear, so sweet — charmed

away my hours as no one else could. Darling! . . . It's hard to be the stranger and the passer-by! I know you'll forget me, only too soon. . . . How can I tell you how grateful I am for all you've given me, in sweetness and happy days? . . ."

How, indeed, since this was the utmost of his wish of her?

The girl's blood warmed again with a leap, overflowing upon her fine skin. Understanding now came to her, with crushing force. Her knight made for her a pretty summary of an episode that was past. There was to come no coronation of words to ennoble these caresses: Mr. Canning, at parting, desired to thank her for her sweetness. And this was the high moment toward which she had been dancing on the fleece-pink of clouds through many days. . . .

And then his arms about her were suddenly a burning and a torture; she felt a blush sweep her from head to foot, enveloping her as in a garment of fire, shaking her with a wild mysterious shame. And she took herself, almost with violence, from the enfolding embrace.

All tenderness, Canning came after her, Pan and his fleeing nymph. . . .

"You darling, I've frightened you! Forgive my roughness. You can't know how your utter adorableness throws me off my guard. . . ."

She turned to the mantelpiece, and, laying a rounded arm upon it, buried her face from his view.

Canning had come near, intending a gentler caress; but something in the dead unresponsiveness of her bowed figure abruptly allayed that intention. The complete repulse, the girl's silent emotion, had surprised him, indeed, like a box on the ears. Well he knew the feministic curve of advance and recoil. Yet he found himself unexpectedly, profoundly, stirred.

"I'm a brute," said he, presently, with an odd ring of conviction. "You go to my head like drink sweeter than was ever brewed. I've had a hard fight all these days to keep my hands off you. . . ."

Carlisle raised her head and turned. Canning had expected to see her face stained with tears, or, more probably, flaming with (at least half-feigned) anger. His heart turned a little when he saw how still and white she was.

"You must go now, please," she said, in rather a strained voice, not looking towards him; and by some strange and subtle process of association she fell into words which she had used within the hour to another: "I don't wish to talk with you any more."

The man's handsome face flushed brightly. He said in a throbbing voice:

"I can't let you dismiss me this way. I can't endure it. Have I offended so — "

"I can't talk with you any more now. I must ask —"

"But you won't be so cruel! If I've offended, won't you make some allowance for my temptation? Am I a snow-man, to come so near and be unmoved? Am I to be a monk, because I live under sentence in a monastery? You . . ."

To do him justice, he did not look in the least like either of these things. However, Carlisle missed his look. Standing with lowered eyes, she said again, colorlessly:

"Please leave me now — I beg you —"

"But I can't leave you this way!" said Canning. "It's impossible! You misjudge me so — "

"Then I must leave you," said Carlisle; and started to go past him.

But Canning blocked her way, his face, troubled with deep concern, more handsome and winning than she had ever seen it. Only she still did not see it. He thought, with a whirling mind, that this was carrying the thing rather too far; but he saw with chagrin and a curious inner tumult the entire uselessness of more argument to-night.

"I am heartbroken," he said, a little stiffly, "that I've brought you somehow to think so hardly of me. Your thought does a great wrong to the — respect and deep devotion I feel and shall feel for you." He wobbled the least bit over these words, as if himself conscious of a certain inadequacy, but went on with his usual masculine decisiveness: "Now it must of course be as you wish. But to-morrow I shall make you understand me better."

He picked up hat, coat, and stick, defeated, yet not spoiled of his air. But as he turned to go, and looked at her for his formal bow, he was all at once aware that she wore a wholly new dignity in his sight, a subtly enhanced desirability. Unexpectedly her marble loveliness shot him through and through, and he said in a low throbbing voice:

"You darling — darling! How can I bear to part from you like this? Forgive me *now*, Carlisle . . ."

But Carlisle's only response was to move away toward the hall.

A moment later the front door shut, rather hard. Carlisle's second impassioned parting within an hour was over. She switched off the tall newel-post lamp, and went upstairs in the dark.

She was a long time in going to sleep. Not since she had the fever, as a little girl, was the great god of forgetfulness so elusive to her wooing. Not since the night at the Beach, and never in her life before that night, had the merry imps of thought so strung her brain upon a thumbscrew. Now came Self-Communion, rarest of her comrades, and perched upon her pillow.

All was plain now, by one instant of merciless illumination. She sufficed to beguile Mr. Canning's leisure for an invalid sojourn far from his normal haunts, but apart from that she had no existence for him. He could see her daily, monopolize her time, for these things happened to amuse him; he could make love to her, lead her in a hundred subtle ways to feel that her companionship was sweet to him; and then he could board a train and ride handsomely away, and woe is the word to the conquered. And by this freedom that he felt, and in particular by the license of his prodigal kisses, it appeared that she read the heart of his secret opinion of her.

Never again should he show her this opinion, at least: he should board his train with no more sight of her. On this her thought was crystal-clear from the beginning. That such short shrift to Mr. Hugo Canning was suicidally impolitic, she naturally had no

difficulty in realizing; the dread of reporting the affair to mamma
had already shot through her mind. But for the moment these
things seemed oddly not to matter. She was clearly in the grip
of one of those mysterious "flare-ups" which her mother disliked
and objected to so intensely: to such lengths borne by her recoil
from Mr. Canning's familiarity. She had met the common fate
of beauty. Flaming young men had kissed her before now. But
none had kissed her without the desire of her love, none as the
fair price exacted for a couple of weeks' lordly attentions. By
their lightness, as by their passion, Canning's kisses had seemed
to sear and scar. They had given her body to be burned. For
this was the fulness of his desire of her, her favor to wear in his
button-hole; and his thought stabbed at her, beneath his gallant's
air, that by now he had fairly earned it.

In the dark as it was, the memory of her moment of revelation
had turned the girl's face downward upon her pillow. How, oh
how, had he come to image her on so low a plane? How did it
come to be that men should have slighting opinions of *her*, of
all people, and so slap them across her face? . . .

It was the first time that such a thought of herself had ever
risen before her mind, though in a sense not the first time she
had had a pretext for it. Her painful meditations included brief
note of Vivian, the eccentric stray across her path who had once
considered her deserving of pity as a poor little thing. He, of
course, was only an unbalanced religious fanatic, whose opinions
were not of the slightest consequence to anybody, whom everybody seemed to take a dislike to at sight (except ignorant paupers like the Cooneys), and whose ideal type of girl would probably be some hideous dowd, a slum-worker, a Salvation Army
lassie, perhaps. Yet this man had felt sorry for her at the Beach;
he had done it again to-night. . . . And if he was quite out of her
world of men, was of course not a man at all as she counted men,
the same could not possibly be said of Mr. Canning, a man of
her own kind in the royal power. . . .

The thought of herself as vulnerable and vincible to the hostile
sex had come upon the girl, fire-new, with disruptive force. It was
pulling out the pin which held her life together. For if she was

a failure in the subjugation of men, then she was a failure everywhere: this being the supreme, indeed, you might say the only, purpose of her life. . . .

Below in the still house, the soft-toned chimes rang two; and, almost on the heels of that, it seemed, three. Step by step, Carlisle went back over all her acquaintance with Canning from their first meeting; and gave herself small glory. She had pursued him to the Beach; she had pursued him to Willie's apartment; and on both occasions, and since, she had used her arts to lure him into reversing the pursuit. A dozen times she had sought to lead him, so it seemed now, further than he ever had the slightest idea of going. Was it really a wonder that he, whose experienced eyes observed everything, had seen in her merely his ready plaything? Repulsed, he could wear an air of genuine tenderness, but never doubt that in his heart he was laughing at her, and had a right to. . . .

And she herself . . . Were these the pangs of unrequited love that tore her breast? In her desire to land the great catch, by hook or by crook, when had she paused to consult her heart about the glittering prospect? What else did it all mean but that she, calculating, had offered herself to him at the price of his hand, name, and enduring complement of happiness, and he, lightly responding, had rated her as worth, at most, only his counterfeit coin. Why else should the memory of the moment downstairs continually return to her like an affront?

She was of her world and time, not unsophisticated; but it chanced that she possessed a mind natively maiden. Through all her vigil, through all her questioning and novel self-criticism, her mind's-eye picture of Canning, as his arms went round her, ran like a torturing *motif*. The portrait became detestable to her. She hated him, she would hate him forever as the man who had cruelly revealed to her that love and his base brother can speak with the same voice and hand.

And next day, when a box of glorious and penitent blossoms was followed within an hour by Canning's card and presence at her door, the girl's resolution to see him nevermore held staunch.

It held to deny him a second time on the afternoon following. After that it was subjected to no more tests. And the social columns of another morning made it known to the general public that the Paynes' distinguished house-guest had departed for points south.

XII

How V. Vivian still felt the Same about the Huns, No Matter what Sam thought; also, how Kern Garland lost Something at the Works, and what made Mr. V. V. look at her That Way.

WHILE Vivian was still engaged with his sick, O'Neill, recently returned from a three weeks' industrial tour of the State, stuck his head informally through the office door.

"Oh! Busy, hey?"

"This is the last, I think. Step into the waiting-room and come in when I whistle."

In three minutes Vivian whistled, and O'Neill instantly opened the door. It looked as if he had meant to come in just then anyway, and he had.

"Say, V. V.! — step out here!" he said in a low, interested voice. "There's a whiskered bum dodging around your back hall here, and if I'm not very much mistaken, he's got your Sunday pants!"

"It's Mister," said V. V., looking round from his secretary. "Shut the door."

"Oh! — *Garland*, hey? But he's swiped your best pants!"

"They were a gift," said V. V., with a touch of soberness. "*Sh!* He'll hear you."

"Oh!" said the Labor Commissioner again, and looked a little disappointed.

He shut the door and came on in, a substantial figure in his glossy suit. It was the 30th of January, and he had been taking on flesh since October.

"Well, when'd *he* blow in? Say, he's a ringer for Weary Waggles, all right."

"Sometime in the night," replied the young man, tilting back in his swivel-chair. "Mrs. G. found him in the entryway

146

when she went down for the milk, asleep in the Goldnagels' hall-rug. I'm afraid he's only come to be outfitted again, and she will not be firm with him, no matter what she promises. . . . By the way, they were not my best trousers at all, except in a sort of technical sense. Never had 'em on but once, at a funeral. — Well, how was the lunch with the Governor?"

The Commissioner, having pushed a new brown derby to the back of his head, walked about.

"Pretty good," said he — "we had a very satisfactory talk. One of his cigars I'm smoking now. I told him what I'd noticed around the State, and gave him an outline of the legislation I want next year. Said my ideas were just right. Paid me some nice compliments. Speaking of legislation," added the Commissioner, flicking cigar-ash on the bare floor with a slightly ruffled air, "you'll be interested to hear I've been down to Heth's since I was in the other day. Saw Heth himself. . . ."

The doctor remarked that he had been thinking of Heth's, not five minutes before.

"I let Corinne go back to work this morning, you see — not that she's well again yet by a good deal, or that that's the place for her at any time. However . . . You saw Mr. Heth himself?"

"Yair. I saw him — last time I'll fool with him, too! Says he guesses the law's good enough for him. Told me point-blank he would n't spend a cent till he had to. How's that for public spirit?"

Having halted by the secretary, the Commissioner looked down at his friend in the open manner of a speaker confident of sympathy.

"Trouble is," said the friend, frowning and sketching circles over some yesterday's memoranda, "Mr. Heth probably does n't know anything about it himself. Got a lot of other interests, you see. He allows that blackguard MacQueen an absolute free hand at the Works — takes everything he says for gospel. He probably —"

"Don't you fool yourself, V. V.! Heth's too smart a man to turn over his principal business to anybody. And I'm sick and tired of jollying with him. Say, remember that letter you wrote in the 'Post' last fall?"

It appeared that V. V. did recall the thing, now that Sam mentioned it. He said introspectively:

"So you think he's still got a grudge about that? . . . Well, I'm sorry, but that letter was all true, Sam, absolutely true, in all particulars. . . . Why," said he, "what's the use of talking? You can't have omelettes without breaking eggs. You cannot."

"That's right. 'S what I came to talk about. Now, what do you say to another strong letter to-morrow, right in the same place. These —"

"*Another* letter! . . ."

"You betcher — hurt their feelings, anyway, if it don't do anything else. I guess you had it right, that a heavy dose of public opinion is —"

"Well, no," said V. V., frankly — "no. . . . Another letter would be a mistake, at just this stage of the game — a great tactical blunder —"

"Why d' you think that?" said Sam O'Neill, rather taken aback.

"Why do I think it, you say? Well, I — I know it."

"Well, I don't know it. It's a blame good thing to make these swell obstructionists feel ashamed of themselves. Let 'em see their names right in print. As for damages, Heth's shown that he's afraid to go into court —"

But V. V. waved aside the idea of a suit. "The whole thing," said he, "is merely a question of tactics. Things are going along very satisfactorily as they are. There's a drift on, a tendency — you might say. The clothing people have come in. Magees have come in. Why, they've agreed to do every blessed thing you asked — fireproofed stairways and fire-doors, ventilators and rest-rooms —"

"That makes the attitude of these others all the worse. I tell you they've practically told me to go to hell."

The good-natured Commissioner spoke with a rare touch of irritation. To have bagged all four of the offending local plants, without the aid of law and relying only on personal influence and tactful pressure, would undoubtedly have been a great card for the O'Neill administration. Moreover, Mr. Heth's manner of superior indifference yesterday had been decidedly galling.

"Well, give 'em a little more time," counselled V. V., lighting a pipe which looked as if it had had a hard life. "You must make some allowance for their point of view, Sam. Here's Mr. Heth, just to take an example, — not making much this year, you say, and mortgaged up pretty well, besides. Well! Just when he's probably getting worried about his book-keeping, down you drop on him and ask him as a favor to you to put up a new building, which is practically what —"

"He'll have to do it, too. If he don't do it now, I'll have a law next year that'll get him right in the neck."

"Exactly. *But* — mark my words, he won't wait for the law, now that we've got this drift going. Don't you be deceived by what he may say now in — in pique. Give him a little chance to adjust himself to the new idea, that's all. Rome wasn't built in a day, Sam — as you've said."

"Look here, old horse, what's struck you?"

"How do you mean, what's struck me?"

The two young men gazed at each other.

"You're pipin' a mighty different tune than you were when you wrote that letter. I've noticed it for some time."

The look of the fine-skinned young man at the desk changed perceptively. O'Neill was made to feel that his remark was in questionable taste, to say the least of it.

"I wish you wouldn't speak as if I were a band of travelling bagmen. I'm not piping or tuning in any way. I say now precisely what I've said all along. Rouse these people to their responsibilities, and you can tear up your factory laws! Different cases require different methods of —"

"Why, last fall —"

"Now, Sam — here! Arguing's no good — I'll tell you what. Suppose you just leave Heth's to me. Go ahead and hammer the Pickle people if you think that'll do the slightest good. But you leave Heth's to me for a while."

"Well! That's an order," said the Commissioner, somewhat

derisively, yet looking interested, too. "And what 'll you do with them?"

"All that I care to say at present," replied the tall doctor, apparently choosing his words with care, "is that I — ah — feel everything 's going to work out very satisfactorily in that quarter."

O'Neill stared at him, the gubernatorial cigar forgotten.

"Oho! . . . You 've met the Heths personally?"

"I 've met some of them personally, as you call it, — far as that goes."

O'Neill, puffing again, digested this information speculatively. Presently he looked knowing and laughed.

"Say, remember my saying to you, time you wrote that letter, that if you knew any of these yellow captains and horse-leeches' daughters personally, you 'd feel mighty different —"

"But I don't! I don't! You don't seem to get me at all, Sam. I 've just shown that my position 's exactly —"

"They 're a lot of Huns, and that 's why they 'll shell out thousands and modernize their plants just because you ask 'em?"

The two men eyed each other again, O'Neill good-natured and rather triumphant. V. V., for his part, was smiling just a little sternly.

"Sam," said he, "you thought I was a mad ass to write a letter a few months ago. Now time passes and you say I was quite right, and won't I please write you another in to-morrow's paper. This time, I tell you that a letter will only do harm — great harm —"

" 'Phone, Doctor!" bawled a husky young voice from below. "Aw, Doctor! 'Phone!"

"All right, Tommy!" shouted Doctor.

Rising to his height, he shot at O'Neill: "And once more you 'll see I 'm absolutely right! I don't change, my dear fellow, the simple reason being that I 've got a guiding principle that does n't change. I must answer that 'phone."

"Well, I 'll trot along with you. I 've got to get on up the hill. . . ."

They headed together for the door. By reason of the prohibitory expense, Dr. Vivian had no telephone of his own, but through the courtesy of Meeghan's Grocery just across the street (which establishment was in receipt of medical attendance gratis), the initiate could always "get a message" to him. Commissioner O'Neill, at once puzzled and somewhat impressed by his friend's air of confidence, resumed conciliatively:

"Now, jokin' aside, V. V., what's the proposition? D' you honestly think Heth can be made to clean up by your persuading his wife or daughter to ask him to? Is that it? — You met 'em at your uncle's reception, I s'pose?"

But V. V.'s reserve had fallen, like a mysterious wall between.

"You say you're at the end of your rope," said he, stepping with his long stride into the hall. "Well, suppose you give me a few months, that's all."

The two friends descended the long stairs in silence. Vivian's meditations were rather tense. He recalled the hard words of the Severe Arraignment; he remembered the unforgivable speech he had made in the summer-house; before his mind's eye rose the moment in his uncle's lamplit den when he had told the girl to her face that her father was a homicide. Sacrificing natural inclinations to kindliness, he had done and said these things. And Sam O'Neill, knowing practically nothing of the facts in the case, had the nerve to stand up . . .

O'Neill, descending, reflected that old V. V. was undoubtedly a queer one. Chuck full of hazy optimism, he was of late. Hazy optimism: O'Neill repeated the phrase, liking it. Still it was possible he might manage to work on the girl's feelings — O'Neill was sure it was the girl — whatever that was worth. He was a kind of appealing fellow, and did have connections with the swells, though it was really he, O'Neill, and Mrs. O., who ought . . .

"Well, be good," said he, as they emerged from the decayed grand entrance. "I'm breakin' in a new stenographer — troubles of my own. See you again in a day or two."

"All right. And by the way," said the tall doctor, speaking with polite restraint, "please don't get it into your head that I'm letting up on these people, or anything of that sort. As a matter of fact, my tendency is all the other way. Not to judge them too harshly — not to do the — the most serious injustice — that's what *I've* got to guard against. . . ."

He turned away, bareheaded in the mild January sunshine, and crossed to Meeghan's, where his telephone call proved to be from Rev. Mr. Dayne, desiring a personal conference later in the day. Cumbered with many cares though he was, the kind-faced Secretary of Charities had been captured at sight by Vivian's plan of buying the old Dabney House, and bringing it to life again as a great Settlement. The problem now engrossing both was how to raise the necessary money, twenty-five thousand dollars being a large sum, particularly with the benevolent field just swept clean by the Associated Charities canvass. However, the tireless Secretary seldom despaired, V. Vivian never. The young man promised eagerly to call on Mr. Dayne, whom, in common with most of the rest of the world, he admired immensely.

Hanging up the receiver, Vivian purchased a five-cent box of blacking, a commodity not ranking among Meeghan's best sellers, and returned to make ready for his professional rounds. In the closet of his bedroom, where he went for hat and coat, he was struck with the brooding sense of something lost, and readily recalled the episode of the trousers. He became conscious of a certain feeling of destitution. Undoubtedly the whole question of new clothes would have to be taken up seriously some day. For the present there did not lack a sense of economic precariousness: it was he and these trousers against the world. . . .

While brushing his hat in the bedroom, Vivian wondered if Mister had yet donned the gift articles, and how he looked in them. He fell to musing about Kern's erring parent, thinking what a strange life he led. It was many and many a year ago since Mister and society had parted company; and through all this time, it was certain that every hand had been against him. In many cities he had stood before sarcastic judges, and been sent on to serve his little time. Adown highways unnumbered he had sawed wood, when necessary; received handouts, worn hand-me-downs; furnished infinite material for the wags of the comic press. Long he had slept under hedges and in ricks, carried his Lares in a bandana kerchief, been forcibly bathed at free lodging-houses in icy winters. Dogs had chased him, and his fellow man: he had been bitten by the one and smitten by the other. Ill-fame and obloquy had followed him like a shadow. And yet — so strong and strange are our ruling passions — nothing could wean him from the alluring feckless ways which had heaped all these disasters upon him. . . .

Thus and otherwise philosophizing, V. Vivian slipped on his overcoat (which had so far escaped Mr. Garland's requisitions) and flung wide the office windows to rid his chambers of the medical smell. He had had a busy morning, his habit of having no billheads, while regarded as demoralizing by professional brethren of the neighborhood, being clearly gratifying to the circumambient laity. It was now getting toward noon, and the doctor was in a hurry. Besides calls on his sick, he was very anxious to get uptown before dinner and inquire after his uncle Armistead Beirne, who had lain ill, with a heavy, rather alarming illness, since a day or two after his New Year's reception. This call was purely avuncular, so to say, Mr. Beirne employing a reliable physician of his own. . . .

The young man picked up his doctor's bag and opened the door. At the far end of the long hall, where the Garlands' apartments were, he caught a glimpse of a skirt, just whisking out of sight. He thought he recognized the skirt, which was a red one, and called, in surprise:

"Corinne!"

There was no answer.

"Corinne!" he called, louder. "Is that you?"

Sure enough, Kern's face peeped out of a door, a long distance away.

"It's me, and it ain't me," she cried, mockingly. "I'm here *in-cog.*"

And her head bobbed back out of sight again.

"What're you talking about?" called Vivian into the emptiness. "Did you feel too weak to work?"

"Like in the books," said Kern, and stuck her head out again with a giggle. "Why, I thank you kindly," she went on in a mincing stage voice. "I'm feeling very, very, *very* well, my Lord Dook, Mr. V. V. On'y I decided I'd spend to-day lazyin' at my writin'-desk, readin' over my billy-doox from peers of the rellum, 'stead of working my hands and legs off in that nasty, *nasty*, NASTY —"

"Stop that cuckoo-clock nonsense!" called Mr. V. V., starting to walk towards her. "What are you doing here, I say?"

"I'm helping mommer soak colliflower, Mr. V. V. Honest!"

"But why did n't you stay at the Works? Come, stop this foolishness, Corinne, and answer me sensibly."

The girl's cheek rested against the door-facing. She stopped her foolishness.

"Mr. V. V., I'm fired."

A bullet would not have stopped Mr. V. V.'s advance more abruptly.

"You're WHAT?"

Kern nodded slowly a number of times. "I was n't goin' to tell you till I got me another job, and maybe never, on'y you caught me —"

"Come here," said Mr. V. V. in rather a queer voice. "Walk," he added, as she began to take the long hall at a skip.

Kern came at a walk. Eyeing Mr. V. V. as she drew near, she soon made out that he was taking it even harder than she had expected. She herself had accepted the loss of her position with the easy fatalism of the poor, though it was a serious enough matter, in the slack midwinter and following three weeks of idleness. However, after her sex, her present overweening instinct was to erase that sort-of-white look from Mr. V. V.'s face.

"It's on'y some of that sickenin' MacQueen's foolishness," she called out from some distance away — "and I was tired of workin' in that old nasty place anyway. Up and said he did n't have no job for me. Did n't have *a* job for me. So I just laughed at him and stayed round a little while, havin' a good time, and then he happened up to the bunchin' room and told me to git. So I gitted. . . . Lor, Mr. V. V.! I can find all the good places *I* want. Goodness me, sir! I 'll get more orfers of jobs —"

"Come into the office," said Mr. V. V., turning back.

In the office, Kern, acting under medical instruction, sat down on the horsehair lounge with one leg gone, and told her simple story in detail.

In these weeks, while she had gone down with mild pleurisy, been successfully "tapped" and haled back to something like an economically valuable condition, the work of the world had marched on. That another operative sat now on Kern's stool and manipulated Kern's machine might appear natural enough, as the superintendent, it seemed, had insisted with his sour smile. But this was not to consider Kern's exceptional skilfulness, known and recognized throughout the Heth Works. Replace a girl who could bunch sixty-five hundred cheroots in a single day? No, no, you could hardly do that. . . .

For this dismissal there was an explanation, and it was not hidden from the young physician. He spoke slowly, struggling not to betray the murder in his heart.

"The devil's doing this because he knows you're a friend of mine. He hits you to punish me. . . . By George, I'll show him!"

The intensity of his face, which in all moods looked somehow kind-of-sorrowful to her, made Kern quite unhappy. She was moved by a great desire to soothe Mr. V. V., to conjure a smile from him. . . .

"Lor, Mr. V. V.! What do you and me care for his carryin's on? We can get on heaps better without him than he can without Me! The Consolidated 'll jump down my throat —"

"You are going back to the Works," spoke Mr. V. V., in his repressed voice.

"Oh!" replied Kern, trying not to look surprised. "Well, then, all right, sir, Mr. V. V. Just whatever —"

"I'll give him one chance to take you back himself. I'll assume, for his sake, that there's a misunderstanding. . . . If he refuses, so much the worse for him. I shall know where to go next."

"Oh! — You mean John Farley?"

It was a shrewd guess. John Farley, sometime of the sick,

and ever a good friend of the Dabney House, was known to hold past-due "paper," of the hard-driving Heth superintendent.

But Mr. V. V., continuing to speak as if something pained him inside, only said, "I was not thinking of Farley. . . ."

The young man stood silent, full of an indignation which he could not trust himself to voice. Yet already he was beginning to put down that tendency to a too harsh judgment which, as he himself admitted, was his besetting sin. . . . Perhaps there was some misunderstanding: this contemptible business hardly seemed thinkable, even of MacQueen. At the worst, it was MacQueen personally and nobody else. No argument was needed to show that the owners would not for a moment tolerate such methods in their Works. Merely let them know what sort of thing their superintendent was up to, that was all. O'Neill should see. . . . Mr. Heth, to be sure, he did not happen to know personally. . . .

"Well, then. That's all settled," Kern was saying, eagerly, "and I'll go back to MacQueen or not go back, just which-ever you want me, and don't less think about him any more. Oh, Mr. V. V. —"

"He can consider himself lucky if he does n't lose *his* job for this day's work."

"Mr. V. V., *what d' you think?*" cried Kern; and having caused him to turn by this opening, she fixed him with grave eyes, and hurried on: "Well, there was a man here named Avery, and he was ridin' his automobile slow down a dark road and his lamps went out. And there was two men walkin' down the road, and he ran over one of them. So he turns back to see if the man was hurted, and the road bein' so dark he runs over him again. So he turns back again, scared he had killed him, and then the other man that had hopped into the ditch, he sings out to his friend, 'Get up, you damn fool, *he's comin' back!*'"

Having quite failed to follow Kern's cheer-up narrative, Mr. V. V.'s stare remained blank, engrossed; but presently he was caught, first by the silence, then by his little friend's wide and intensely expectant gaze, just beginning to fade into childlike disappointment. He promptly burst into a laugh. It began as a dutiful laugh, but Kern's expression soon gave it a touch of genuineness.

"Ha, ha!" said he. "That's a good one! Well, where on earth did you get that one?"

"Off Sadie Whirtle!" cried Kern; and springing up gleefully from the sofa, began to pirouette and kick about the bleak office.

The young man watched her, buttoning his overcoat, his specious merriment dying. . . . For all the high wages she earned, the Works was of course the last place on earth for her; but for the moment that did not happen to be the point.

"Was it not bein' a lady to say the word like he did?" said Kern, swaying about and waving her arms like wings. "I told Sadie Whirtle it was n't netiquette, but Sadie she said it was n't funny without you used the swear. And I did want to make you laugh. . . . She druther be funny than netiquette, Sadie said."

The young man picked up his bag again, his face intent. "I'm late with my calls," said he. "Tell your mother that I may n't be back for dinner."

"Sadie she heard a lady say damn once right out, a customer in the store, in a velvet suit —"

"Now stop that foolish dancing, Corinne."

Kern stopped dancing. She still looked a little pale from her illness, which had cost her seven pounds. That morning she had donned her working-clothes expectantly, but she had changed since coming in, and that accounted for her favorite red dress. The dress was a strict copy of the slender mode; she looked very small, indeed, in it. She wore a brave red ribbon in her hair, a necklace of red beads, and a long gilt chain which glittered splendidly as she moved.

"What makes you look at me that way, Mr. V. V.?"

The young man gave a small start and sigh.

"You must take better care of yourself, Corinne," said he, from the depths of troubled thought. "I shall certainly do something better for you later on. That I promise."

"Why, I feel very, *very* well, Mr. V. V., truly."

"You're much too clever and pretty to be wearing your life out at this sort of thing. . . . Much too dear a little girl. . . ."

Kern turned away. Mr. V. V. had never said such a thing to her before, and he now made a mental note that he must be careful not to do it again. He had honestly intended only a matter-of-fact statement of simple and, on the whole, pleasant truth; but Kern, with her sensitiveness and strange delicacy, too clearly felt that he had taken a liberty. All her gaiety died; her cheek seemed to flush a little. She walked stiffly past Mr. V. V. to the door, never looking in his direction.

"I'll go soak the colliflower, sir," she murmured, and slipped away into the hall.

XIII

How Life was Gray and Everything was Horrid; how Carlisle went to Little Africa with Hen; how the Man spoke to her again, just the same, and what happened then; further, reporting a Confidential Talk with a Best Girl-Friend.

HEARING the whir of a slowing motor behind her, and her name called besides, Henrietta Cooney checked her practised pedestrian's stride and looked back over her shoulder. The Heth car, with Carlisle alone in it, rolled abreast of her at the curb.

"What on earth are *you* doing, Hen," asked her cousin, but hardly as if the matter interested her much — "up here at this time!"

"Servant chasing!" cried Hen, gaily. "My favorite outdoor sport. Hortense's left us. I got out early on purpose. You're looking mighty well, Cally."

Cally made a weary little face, which seemed to say that such matters as looks were very far from being of interest to her. It happened to be the fact, indeed, that she had never felt more depressed and bereft in her life: witness her hailing Hen Cooney, whom she had never cared much for, and less than ever after the way Hen had shown her real nature about the Works. Time's chances had brought her to this, that she preferred Hen's society above the company of her own thoughts. Gray and empty had been Cally's days since a New Year's moment in the library. . . .

"But you'll not find any servants up here, my dear! — unless you expect to throw bags over their heads and kidnap them?"

"I'd like to," laughed Hen, friendly elbows on the car door. "And then give them the bastinado every hour on the hour. Think of Hortense's doing us so when we've all been perfect mothers to her for a year. But I've come up here just to get an

159

address, from Mrs. J. T. Carney, and now I'm off to Little Africa, pleasant but determined."

"Jackson Ward?"

"No," said Hen, producing and consulting a scrap of paper, "it's South Africa this time — 106A Dunbar Street. You know — down along the Canal."

"Hop in," said Cally, listlessly. "I'll drive you down there."

"Perish the thought!" ejaculated Hen, in some surprise. "You don't want to go exploring the slum districts, finding out how the other half lives. I'll like the walk —"

But Carlisle insisted, being out only because she was bored with being in, and Hen hopped in, not altogether reluctantly. By request she repeated the Ethiopian address to the chauffeur, himself of that tongue and nation; and off the cousins bowled.

"Bored? How's this, Cally? I hear on all sides that it's the gayest winter in ten years. You're not tired of parties, at your age?"

"Oh, I'm crazy about them," said Cally, indifferently, yet drawing comfort from the sound of her own voice. "But one can't have parties every hour of the day, you know. There are always chinks to be filled up, and that is where one's background comes in. My background has a violent attack of indigestion just now. Everything's horrid.—*Ohh!* Why *will* a dog take chances like that? . . ."

"How's Uncle Thornton?" said Hen, holding her hat on with a hand that looked hard-worked. "I don't believe I've seen him since that day we all came to dinner —"

"Oh, he's well, I suppose, but he's out of spirits a good deal of the time, which I *will* say is unusual for papa. I think he's probably worried about business or . . . Who was that old man that stared at me so? He looked as if I ought to know him."

"Where?" said Hen, glancing back. "Oh! — there under the tree? Why, that's Colonel Dalhousie. You know —"

"Oh!" said Cally, immediately regretting having spoken. To relieve the baldness of her exclamation, she added: "I thought he was a rather younger man than that."

"He's broken dreadfully in the last few months — that's

probably why you did n't recognize him," said Hen, cheeringly. "They say the poor old man's grieving himself to death."

Through Cally quivered an angry wonder why it was that only disagreeable things happened nowadays. Why, why, when everything else was just as abominable as possible, need that old man go prowling around the streets, stopping on corners to stare at her? . . .

She went on quickly with a tinge of light bitterness in her voice:

"I'm sure it must be business, for there's a hard-times atmosphere hanging over the house, all of a sudden, and mamma is constantly remarking that there's a limit to my extravagance, etc., etc. She and I happen to be on dreadfully formal terms just at present, which is another of the joys of home. And to cap the climax," she added, with a burst of confidence only half mocking, "I'm in an absolutely suitorless condition — not a blessed swain to my name! I was never so destitute and forlorn in my life!"

Hen, struck from the beginning with the unusual note in her brilliant cousin's manner, laughed. She perceived that Cally wished to talk about herself, and talk complainingly, and Hen did n't mind.

"First time I ever heard such a complaint in this quarter. Is J. Forsythe Avery dead without my knowledge?"

"J. Forsythe is in New York. Robert's in the sulks. James Bogue, 2d, is in bed — measles, if you please. . . . Do you ever have the horrible nobody-loves-you feeling? Rather odious, is n't it?"

"Ghastly," said Hen.

"I 'll be awfully glad to get away next month," continued Cally. . . .

Interested by the hiatus in Cally's list of missing swains, Hen desired that this conversation should go on. Like most people, the Cooneys had of course heard of, and gossiped about, the open breach between their cousin and Mr. Canning a month ago, promptly followed by the great young man's departure from town. Through the masculine half of the local world, it was

generally assumed that Miss Heth had actually rejected Mr.
Canning. It was a rare tribute to the girl's attractions that
not a few women also believed this, even though Cally's best
girl-friends, like Mattie Allen, were perfectly *sure* nothing of
the sort had happened. . . .

Hen, a Cooney, had had a special reason for wondering if this
interesting affair might not be "on" again. However, Cally,
skipping the conversation along, was talking now of the visit she
had in prospect to her friend, Mrs. Willing, Florence Stone that
was, in New York. Florrie, she informed Hen, wanted her particularly for the Lenten weeks, promising that they would spend
the sober penitential season in a hilarious round of theatres,
restaurants, and shops. It appeared that this promising invitation
had come only that morning, and Cally described it as a direct
answer to prayer.

"Goodness, Cally! You talk as if you lived in a special kind
of purgatory," said Hen. "I don't know anybody that has a
better time than you."

"Is an everlasting round of gaieties, all exactly alike, your
idea of a perfect time? What is the point or meaning of it all?"
demanded Cally, the philosopher. "The whole trouble with me,"
she added, explanatorily, "is that I have n't budged from home
in three months, and I'm simply bored deaf and dumb."

Hen might have replied that she had n't budged for three
years, but what was the use? She said instead: "When 're you
going to sail for Europe. May?"

"It remains to be seen whether we sail at all or not," answered
Carlisle, with a sudden mocking little laugh. "Mamma talks
several times a day of cancelling our passage and shipping me
off to Aunt Helen's farm for the summer. She 's been tremendously droll with me of late. . . ."

Droll, of course, was only the girl's derisive euphemism. The
truth was that mamma's attitude, since hearing of the extraordinary rupture, — which her daughter refused either to explain
or amend instantly, — had been nothing short of violent.
Jangling scenes recurred daily. . . . Perhaps, indeed, it was
mamma's relentless pressure that had brought about the gradual

shifting, amounting to a total revolution, in Cally's own attitude. More probably, though, it was only the inevitable resurgence of her own sane fundamental purposes, temporarily swept away by purblind passion.

It is one thing to kick out your symbol of happiness in a burst of senseless rage. It is quite another to learn to live day by day without it. . . . Why, indeed, should she not yield obedience to poor mamma — at the least greet Canning's return with some mark of forgiveness, a tiny olive-branch? . . .

Henrietta Cooney's voice spoke, singularly apropos:

"You don't seem to be the only one who's been bored lately, Cally — that ought to comfort you! Chas and I saw Mr. Canning yesterday, and he looked bluer than indigo. Mad, too!"

Surprise betrayed Carlisle into a naked display of interest. Turning with a little jump, she stared at Hen with a kind of breathless rigidity.

"You saw *Mr. Canning yesterday!* . . . Where?"

"Why, out on the old Plattsburg Turnpike," said Hen, certain now that the affair was not on again — "near the Three Winds Road. We happened to be taking a walk out there, and he dashed by on that beautiful big bay mare of Mr. Payne's, going like a runaway. He didn't look happy a bit. . . . You knew he was here, I suppose?"

By a very special effort, Carlisle had recaptured her poise: it was not her habit to confide her troubles to anybody, least of all to a Cooney.

"Oh, no!" she answered in a voice of careless frankness. "I don't know the first thing about his movements any more."

"Well, it seems he only came for over Sunday. A friend of Mr. Payne's told Chas he was here, on Saturday. He went off again on the noon train to-day."

"Oh! . . . Did he?"

"Looloo saw him at the station. She happened to be there, meeting a friend of hers."

Gone! — He had come, not seen her, and gone! . . . A wave of bitterness swept through Cally, impelling her to hit out at somebody.

"Of course. Is n't it *funny* how your family always sees and hears everything?"

But Hen answered, entirely unmoved, in fact with an air of modesty: "Any family can do it who keep their eyes and ears open. For instance, good old Looloo heard where he checked his baggage to: Palm Beach, if it 's of any interest to you."

"I don't believe it is, my dear. He 'll be checking it back this way again very soon, I 've no doubt. Are we going the right way for Dunbar Street?"

Hen shot at her a look of unconscious admiration. Her pretty cousin's indifferent air seemed to support the theory that she had actually rejected the prince of partis, which, in fact, was exactly what it was meant to do. Hen had never really thought that Cally had it in her. She threw her alert eye around to see where they were. The car had turned south at Twelfth Street, had crossed Centre, and was now rolling into a quarter of the town very different-looking, indeed, from Washington Street. Hen said they were all right for Dunbar Street and told Cally to cheer up. Much worse was coming, Hen said.

There was nothing personal in Hen's admonition, but the truth was that Cally, gazing fixedly at the passing sights, felt anything but cheerful at this moment. The Cooneys' tidings were staggering in their way.

What was the meaning of Mr. Canning's mysterious flying visit? That it had to do with her she did not question; and, tensely meditating, she presently found a hypothesis not unsatisfying after its kind. He had come with the hope that she would at last make some generous overture toward a reconciliation. More direct advances, after her three galling rebuffs of him, he naturally could not bring himself to make. Yet he had taken a long journey merely to put himself in her way — perhaps counting on a chance meeting, more probably expecting that she, hearing of his presence, would this time extend the sweet olive. The wormwood in it was that she would have been perfectly willing to extend the olive if she had only known. . . .

The car, pushing through a mean and shabby neighborhood, offensive to refined eyes, ears, and nostrils, now turned into a narrow street brisk with the din of business, but by no means lovely to look upon. Recalling the Cooney presence, Cally suddenly stirred with the deadly self-protective instinct of her sex, and directed Hen to cease instantly all thinking about her and Mr. Canning. She did it, needless to say, scientifically, by saying with just the plausible degree of interest:

"I meant to ask you — what on *earth* was the trouble with Hortense, Hen? I supposed she was a perfect *fixture* with you, an institution!"

"What's the trouble with all the servants in this town?" cried Hen. "I tell you, Cally, I don't know what's going to become of us. Why . . ."

She launched with zest upon the somewhat unoriginal thesis, and Cally relapsed into her own thoughts, which were full of rebellion at the bitter untowardness of her fate. . . .

Much water had flowed under the bridge of sighs since the parting in the library. Passed long since, it seemed, was that uprush of burning humiliation; subdued was the betraying flare-up (mamma's favorite word nowadays) — vanished to thin air like a midsummer madness, delirium's delusion, hardly possible to understand, much less recapture, now. A day had hardly passed, after the second rejection of Mr. Canning at her door, before the thought of whistling him back again flashed luringly across Carlisle's mind. She repelled the thought, but it recurred, and she came to dally with it, ably assisted in that direction by mamma. What had he done to warrant such absurd melodramatics? . . . More and more her mind had fastened upon the genuine tenderness, the emotion, the man had shown in his last moment with her. In love with her without quite realizing it himself, he had in the moment of parting been swept away by his feelings, and had taken a not strictly authorized kiss or two. What Sir Galahad among men was proof against such a tripping in the presence of lovely and irresistible temptation? . . .

"Hortense gave you no notice at all?" she demanded out of a dream.

"Did you ever? Why, honestly, Cally . . ."

He was to pause once again, to bid the Paynes farewell, on

his final progress back to what he had once called lights and home. That would be in April, said Cousin Willie Kerr, when his six months' sentence ran out. The distant promise brought the girl no comfort now. Why, really, should she not take this new opportunity he had given her, and dispatch him a little note, saying in a friendly way that she had wanted to see him again? By day after to-morrow, he could be at her side. . . .

It was a little note that mamma, though ignorant of the circumstances, had so specially recommended in the desolate weeks; had commanded, offered bribes for, cried for with real tears, blustered and threatened for with a purpling birthmark. In her own mind the girl had already worded many which met the situation with merely a front of sweet generosity, carrying no forfeiture of dignity, no real acknowledgment of surrender. What was the fibre of foolish hardness in her that resisted all mamma's importunities, all her own urgent wisdom?

"Five years ago," said Hen, "we paid eight dollars a month, and got really good ones. Now the greenest of them holds you up for twelve and fourteen. Hortense was simply bribed off. . . ."

Cally roused, glancing about. "Papa says," she observed, absently, "it will all end in something like the French Revolution. Heavens! What a perfectly sickening street!"

"Isn't it?" said Hen, cheerfully. "Yet it's interesting too, Cally, for this is where the city makes all its money."

Money-making, indeed, Canal Street looked. Long processions of trucks rolled up and down it, giving motorists more time than they desired to look about. All around them, as the car moved slowly on, were warehouses, new and old cheek by jowl together; commission merchants, their produce spilled over the sidewalk; noisy freight yards, with spur-tracks running off to shipping-rooms of all descriptions; occasional empty ground used as dumps, littered with ashes and old tin cans; over all a thousand smells, each more undelectable than the last.

But *April!* You might as well say in another life. How could she ever get through the days till then? . . . .

"I'm glad you're interested," she said aloud, sharply, thinking that this was exactly what came of giving a lift to the Cooneys. "I think it's simply disgusting. . . . Get us through this, William."

"It's familiar, at any rate. Let's see. Dunbar must be the next street over but one, is n't it?"

Cally, lifting a handkerchief to obliterate the adjacent odors of a gas-tank, said: "I have n't the smallest idea."

"Why, don't you like the rattle of business, Cally? Don't you like the bustle, the fine democratic air? — Why, *hello!* There's V. V.!"

Carlisle's head turned at once.

"He's signalling us," said Hen, waving back; and she nervily added: "Stop, William!"

Following Henrietta Cooney's look, Carlisle's eyes fell, sure enough, upon the tall figure of Dr. Vivian crossing the humming side-street straight toward them. Her glance caught him in the act of removing his derby, bowing in response to the cheeky salute of Hen. . . .

"Ah, he's using a cane," added Hen, below her breath. "That means his foot is bad. . . ."

"But he has no right to signal *me*," said Carlisle. "Drive on, William."

But she herself unconsciously spoke in an undertone, and the order appeared to be lost in the enveloping din. William, all but blockaded anyway, had come to a halt. Coincidentally sounded the voice of Hen, the pachyderm:

"Hello, V. V.! What're you doing way down here in the wilds? Not visiting the sick, without your little black bag?"

V. Vivian stood bareheaded at the side of Mr. Heth's (of the Works) shining car.

"How'do, Henrietta? — Oh, good afternoon, Miss Heth. No, I — I'm down here on other business this time. . . ."

Carlisle, her eyes about on a level with the young man's interesting piscatorial necktie, had acknowledged his greeting by the smallest and frigidest inclination of her head. That done, feeling outraged by this whole proceeding, she at once looked ostentatiously in another direction.

The lame doctor, for his part, appeared a little embarrassed by the rencontre, or perhaps excited, one or both.

"I — it's a very fortunate coincidence, meeting you in this way," he began at once. "The fact was, I — ah — was just thinking of you at that moment, Miss Heth, — wishing very much to see you —"

Miss Heth turned her pretty head once more, this time with a sort of jerk. So the man pretended to have forgotten that she had ordered him not to address her again.

Now her eyes fully met those of Dalhousie's friend, and in that meeting she was conscious of an odd little shock, almost like a physical impact. . . . Why was it that this impossible man, with his ridiculous opinions, his wicked untruths, and his face so full of a misplaced hopefulness, kept coming like a destiny across and across her path? What was her silly weakness, that he never looked at her with those quite misrepresentative eyes without making her angry and unhappy? . . .

She felt herself, as it were, turning pale inside, but into her cheeks there sprang a cold color.

"You wished to see me?"

"Well, do put on your hat, V. V.," interjected Hen, matter of fact, but glancing round at Cally's voice. "You'll catch pneumonia. . . ."

"Yes — thank you. . . . I'd like to enlist your help, if I could, Miss Heth. I've just come from the Works, you see," he hurried on with curious intensity — "where I went to try to right what seems to be a clear injustice. I wonder — do you remember the girl I happened to mention to you at my uncle's that night, — a buncher here at the Works? . . ."

His expression said that he was counting on her remembering. The girl in the car was looking him through and through. Hen Cooney disappeared from between them; the roar of traffic faded away.

"No, I don't remember," said Miss Heth, biting her lip a little.

"Oh! — the girl I wanted the *marrons* for? Well, it's no matter," the tall young man said, with a belying look of youthful disappointment. But he went on with undiminished eagerness:

"She's one of the best operatives in the Works, I assure you — a really valuable employee because she can get more work out of a machine than any two inexperienced girls. She's had over two years' practice, you see. This morning she reported again for work after nearly a month's illness in bed: she's had pleurisy. Well, MacQueen — the superintendent — declines to give her her place back."

"Why, what a shabby trick!" cried Hen. . . .

She looked as if she desired to say much more, but she saw that V. V.'s eyes were fixed on Cally, whose father owned MacQueen, and forbore.

Cally's breast rose and fell. She saw what was coming now. . . . How did he dare — he who had so maligned her personally, who had so maliciously thrown bricks at papa and the Works — how did he dare to turn and beg favors from the objects of his slanders? This was the supreme impertinence. Now she would say to him what would destroy him from her ways forever. . . .

V. Vivian was hurrying on, as if perceiving that he hadn't made the matter fully plain as yet: "It is quite a serious thing for her, because she can make more at the Works than anywhere else — she's a born buncher. And she and her mother are dependent on her earnings. It seems a — a great hardship that she should be thrown out this way, without any fault of her own. . . ."

"Put-on-your-hat!" ordered Hen, *sotto voce;* and again repressed further remarks seething within her.

The slum doctor, having neglected Hen's injunction hitherto, now obeyed it, though with inattention to the processes. He continued speaking, blind to all discouragements. . . . Would no one stop the God's fool, rushing with eager eyes to his doom? . . .

"I don't, of course, like to trouble you. But don't you think you could stop a moment, and say just a word to MacQueen — or to your father if he is in? . . ."

Now was the moment to demolish the irrepressible fanatic, who seemed incapable of understanding that his betters wanted none of him. And strange, oh, strange! — Cally Heth sat silent. . . . As the man reached the climax of his madness, the girl's hard challenging gaze, as if by some miracle of his ministering angels, had suddenly wavered and broken. Her eyes flitted from his face, rested fixedly on a hideous sprawling pile on the corner ahead, an abode of trade exceptionally repellent to all the senses. However, she was unaware of the detestable object, so confused was she by the odd frustrating weakness that suddenly possessed her, staying her hand in the act of delivering the mace-blow. It might be the very superlativeness of the man's temerity that disarmed her, paralyzing the hot will. It might be merely that ludicrous trusting look in his eyes, which somehow seemed to put him in the non-combatant class, like some confiding child. . . .

"I know, of course," he was concluding with unfaltering expectancy, "a word from you will make everything right at once."

And Carlisle, her glance returning toward him, but not to him, heard with disquiet and mortification her own voice saying, not indignantly at all:

"You will have to speak to my father about it if — if injustice has been done. I — I haven't time to go to the Works now —"

"Time!" cried Hen Cooney, at last assuming control of things. "Why, good heavens, Cally! It wouldn't take us any *time!* We're right there now! — and don't you think Uncle Thornton *ought* to be told how that brute's behaved . . ."

Hen intended only an argument; but it happened that her explosive statement sprang out like a switchman, finally shifting the train of the talk.

"Oh!" said Cally, staring bewildered at her cousin. "Why — where are the Works — from here, I mean? . . ."

Hen's strange look confirmed her own confused conviction that she was appearing at an annoying disadvantage all at once. And forebodings possessed her, as of one walking wide-eyed into unsuspected perils.

"You *are* lost, Cally, indeed. Why, my dear, we're right on the corner of Seventeenth and Canal now — they're leaning right up against your nose. There!"

Following Hen's nod, Cally's gaze rested again on the somewhat displeasing pile on the corner, this time with a seeing eye. Her fascinated stare took in with one sweep a dirty ramshackle building of weather-worn gray brick, spilling over the sidewalk and staggering away (as it looked) down the littered side-street: rather a small building, obviously old, certainly not fragrant, quite sinister-looking somehow. . . .

The girl felt as if the skies were falling. She perceived that there was some mistake. "Oh . . . You mean that is part of them? But the — the main part, I suppose, is —"

"No, this is all there is of 'em, Cally!" said Hen, suddenly with a kind note in her voice. And she waved upward toward a wire screen atop the ancient building, where large black letters spelled out:

THE HETH CHEROOT WORKS

"*Is that the Works?*" breathed the daughter of the Works, with a sort of stunned incredulity.

In her utter bewilderment, she was confused into glancing at Jack Dalhousie's friend, who stood silent upon the sidewalk, two yards away. Thus she surprised his translucent eyes fixed upon her with a look which she had seen there on two other remembered occasions. The eager confidence had, indeed, faded from his face, but not as she had designed that it should fade. The man had the grace to look away at once, seeming embarrassed: but in one glance she saw that he had read to the heart of what she felt, thus discovering the real birthplace of her Family. And his eyes had said to her, quite plainly, that of course he would not on any account ask her to stop now; and that, on the whole, God must pity her again for a poor little thing who did not even know where and how her own father made his money. . . .

She could have cried for the angry mortification of this moment, but perhaps that confrontation steadied her as nothing else could have done. She said hurriedly, but with some degree of naturalness:

"Well — it certainly is n't pretty — Hen! But I don't suppose factories usually are. You know, I — have n't happened to be down here for a good many years. . . ."

And then, catching the driver's eye, she nodded sharply to him to go on. In the cross-sweep of larger troubles, dismissed bunchers were naturally forgotten. The car started with a little jump.

"Why, are n't you going to *stop?*"

It was Hen Cooney who thus sounded the note of rather indignant surprise, not the man from the slums, who, understanding, stood tall and silent, lifting his old derby. . . .

Cally, looking straight ahead, replied: "I can't stop now."

That left the whole matter indeterminate; nobody was committed to anything, one way or another. Hen Cooney earned Cally's undying resentment (at least for the remainder of the drive) by crying over her shoulder as the car rolled away:

"Of course Uncle Thornton'll give her her place back! Don't you worry, V. V.! . . ."

That night the subject of the Works was touched upon again, in the course of an extended talk between Carlisle and her friend Mattie Allen, a talk ranging intimately over various aspects of life and living. It took place in Carlisle's pretty bedroom, toward two o'clock A.M. In the earlier evening the girls had brilliantly attended the Thursday German (which was always held on Mondays), and now Mattie was spending the night: a ceremony which she dearly loved, especially the eleven o'clock breakfast in bed. They routed all hands out at eight at the Allens, regardless.

The two girls, Carlisle and Mattie, were the dearest friends in the world, being perfect natural foils, each made to appear at her best by the presence of the other. Many other bonds they had also, as the fact that, while each was charming and most attractive to men, they very rarely attracted the same men, thus obviating hostile jealousies. Speaking roughly, tall, athletic, handsome, normal young men loved Carlisle; while Mattie, though rarely appealing to these demigods, made instant killings with "clever" men, literary fellows, teachers of Greek, and promising young entomologists. Doubtless the comparatively favorable impression Mattie had made on Mr. Canning at the Beirne reception was due to the fact that he, though a demigod, had thought, at times, of writing a book. . . .

"Mats," said Carlisle, apropos of nothing whatever, "have you ever heard people criticizing the Works — saying horrid things about conditions being unhealthy there, or anything of that sort?"

"Why, yes, dear, I have," said Mats at once, and sweetly. "Not very lately, though. I think there was an article in the paper about it, was n't there, a month or two ago? Why?"

"What have you heard people say?" replied Carlisle.

"Well, I can't remember exactly, Cally, but it seems to me I heard them say the Government was going to have a new law about it, or something. Why?"

This last was a popular word with Mattie, whose mind in relation to her own sex was distinctly interrogatory. All evening, mostly by indirect methods, she had been examining Carlisle in regard to Mr. Canning, and his strange visit. . . .

"Oh, nothing," said Carlisle, gently patting her face with a steaming cloth.

Mattie selected a hairbrush from her little spend-the-night kit.

"You know what perfect *nuts* it is to people," said she, "to think they have anything the least bit disagreeable on people they know."

"Is n't it?" replied Carlisle, with a repressed note of strong irritation. "Everybody has plenty of time to attend to everybody's business but their own."

Mattie glanced at her, wondering interestedly what had happened to Cally. However, she made no answer to the philosophic sarcasm, being now engaged in giving her hair one hundred and twenty-five brisk strokes before retiring, and not wishing to lose the count.

Half an hour the girls had been in the flowing negligee stage, but they were still intensely busy with the Eleusinian mysteries.

After an interval Carlisle said: "I wonder how many of the

people who criticize would put Turkish baths and — and dens in the Works if they had to do it out of their own pockets. . . . Why under the *sun* should they?"

"Of course," said Mattie. " (Eighteen, nineteen, twenty.) — I think you 're perfectly right, dear. . . ."

"If people don't like the Works as they are, why should they raise heaven and earth begging for jobs there? I wish somebody 'd explain that."

"Of course. (Twenty-five.) — And how could Mr. Heth spend thousands and thousands of dollars on such things without taking it *right out of your mouth*, don't you see? . . . Oh, *gosh!*"

"What?"

"Broke my best finger-nail — that 's all! Just the tiniest rap on the chair. Where 's the file, dear? Oh, Cally, remember, twenty-five. . . . How provoking! — I do think I 've got the brittlest I ever saw . . ."

Presently Carlisle, in a flowing silken robe, rose, went over to her dressing-table, seated herself and picked up a round cut-glass jar with a silver top. The jar contained cold cream, or something of that sort. Mattie, having filed down her nail, was now faithfully brushing again, in the forties. Her eyes followed Cally; rested upon her as she sat. These eyes, large, dark, and grave, with the sweetest, curlingest lashes, had been the turning-point in Mattie's life. She had early recognized their unique merits and values, and round them, with infinite pains, she had built up her "type." And now at twenty-three, she was sweet, artless, and full of adorable intellectual dependences, deliciously stupid (with the spectacled young men), and her favorite expression was "poor little Me."

Mattie, brushing, looked at Carlisle, and wondered if she possibly *had* refused Mr. Canning, and, if so, why Mr. Canning had skipped back just to stay over Sunday and not go near her, and why Cally was so mysterious and secretive all of a sudden. She always told Cally every single thing about her affairs, reporting in detail what was "the most" each man said to her, and always bringing her their letters to read, even Mr. Dudley's, who wrote such perfectly beautiful ones. Cally had always done the same with her, till lately, but now she was a *perfect clam*. Not a word would she tell about Mr. Canning, and to-night J. Forsythe Avery had proposed at last (Cally said), but she barely mentioned the fact, as if it were of no interest, and declined positively to repeat his words, which was always the interesting (and also the convincing) part of it. . . .

"What's the matter?" said Mattie, aloud and alertly.

Cally, sitting and rubbing cold cream (or whatever it was) had suddenly given a long sigh. At her friend's question, she turned half round, but did not cease the rubbing.

"Mats, don't you ever get sick and tired of all these things we do to ourselves to make us look pretty and attractive and — desirable?"

Mattie, looking rather shocked, said: "Why, what things do you mean?"

"Oh, these things! . . . Massage and manicure and primp! — hot baths and lotions and primp! — sleep and a little exercise to make pink cheeks and primp some more. Hours and hours every day just to coddling our little bodies! Isn't it all rather sickening, when you really stop to think?"

"I must say," answered Mattie, quite stiffly, "I can see nothing sickening about it. I think it's a woman's duty to look just as well as she can."

Carlisle rested her arm on her chair-back, and went on rubbing.

"Duty? — I wonder. Duty to whom, do you mean?"

"To everybody, to the world, to society."

"I was just trying to think," said Cally, "and it's quite fun. I believe I'll do it at least once a week after this. — What would we think of a man who spent four hours a day decorating himself, everlastingly working at himself to look pretty?"

Mattie opened her wide eyes yet wider. She was now plaiting her well-brushed hair, and looked very sweet and girlish.

"Why, that's a *very* different thing, Cally! The same qualities aren't expected of men and women — or they couldn't complement each other! Women are *expected* to be sweet and attractive, while —"

"Expected by whom?" quizzed Cally, and screwed the top down on her cold cream (if such, indeed, it was).

"By everybody," said Mattie, falling back upon her tried phrase, "by the world, by —"

"Why shouldn't it be expected of men to look nice, too, just as much? Why should we have to do the whole performance? Why shouldn't we give some of all this time to something useful, as men do? — cultivating our minds, for instance?"

"But don't you *see*, Cally? — that isn't expected of us! Men simply do *not* care for clever women," cried Mattie, who had built up a considerable social success on that very principle.

"Why should we let *them* decide for us what we're to be? Why? — Why? That's just what they do! We're human beings just as much as they are, aren't we? . . . Oh, I'm sick of men," cried Cally.

"*You're sick of men!*" echoed Mattie, aghast as at a blasphemy.

Cally nodded slowly, her lovely eyes on her friend's tremulous face.

"Oh, it's the men who make us put in all this time tricking up ourselves to look pretty. You know it, too, for you just gave yourself away. . . . Oh, Mats, wouldn't it be great to appeal to *some*body *some*times in some other way!"

Mattie, apparently on the verge of tears, murmured her complete inability to follow Cally's strange talk. Observing her, Carlisle gave a reassuring little laugh and rose abruptly. Not that it made any special difference, but she didn't care about setting her best friend's alert wits too busily to work.

"Dear old Mats! — Don't take me so dreadfully *seriously*. It's all what I read in a magazine article to-night before the German, waiting for Robert to come. He thought he was displeased with me, and came very late, on purpose. You don't seem to like it?"

"I *don't* like to hear you talk so, Cally, even in fun," replied dear old Mats, rather stiffly. "You've been strange all evening,

and you told me you did n't care whether you ever saw Mr. Canning again or not. It is n't a bit like you."

"It certainly is n't, as mamma frequently remarks," said
Cally, her laugh dying. "Well, I'm going to be just like myself
after this, never fear. . . . Gentlemen always welcome. We strive
to please."

She put an arm over her friend's shoulder, and in this true-
friendship attitude they strolled through the little entry and
connecting bath to the spare-room at the back where Mattie
always spent the night.

"I feel terribly sorry for poor Mr. Beirne," said Mattie, in a
just voice. "You know he had a sinking-spell, and they were
saying to-night he can't possibly get well."

"Yes, I know," said Carlisle, stifling a yawn. "By the way,
I must leave cards there to-morrow. Remind me. Climb in, dear.
I'll tuck you in."

"I have n't said my prayers," said Mattie, standing by the
bed. "Cally, suppose he dies and leaves a lot of money to that
cunning nephew of his! You know — Dr. Vivian — that I introduced to you that night at his house? They say Mr. Beirne's
terribly fond of him."

Cally nodded in reply, her gaze entirely blank. It appeared
that in this world there was escape neither from the nephew nor
from the topic of him.

"But what do you suppose he'd *do* with it," queried Mattie,
who was a dear romantic thing — "living off down there in the
Dabney House? Somebody told me he did n't care at *all* for
money, only think!"

"Perhaps he'd feel differently if he had any," said Cally.
"Papa says coming into money's a sure cure for Socialism and
everything of that sort."

"Why, don't you think he's terribly *sincere?* . . . Don't you
think lame people usually are, somehow?"

"My dear child, I don't see why I should think about him at
all. Besides, Mr. Beirne will leave his money to the Masons.
Now for some beauty slumber — I'm quite ready for it, too!
Sleep well, Mats dear."

They kissed, and parted for sweet dreams. At the door, Cally, pausing, said:

"Oh, Mats, go with me to Madame Smythe's to-morrow? I'm buying things for New York."

But Mats could not reply, being already at her devotions. . . .

In her own room, Cally prayed briefly with preoccupied thoughts, and rising, removed her thin blue robe, switched out the lights, raised shades and windows. In the quiet street below, a cat trotted silently, swallowed up as she watched in an immense flickering shadow from the tall street light. The girl stood a moment, looking down, a strange wish in her heart.

She wished for a confidante, some one to tell her troubles to. Mamma, of course, was impossible in this connection; you never told things to mamma, and besides, they were barely on speaking terms most of the time now. Mattie was hardly less out of the question: a girl with many excellent merits and her best friend, but the last person you would ever dream of giving yourself away to. But then you really could not trust anybody as far as that. In all the world there was no one to whom she could go and freely pour out her unhappiness and her heart.

A self-contained and self-sufficient girl, she now felt lonesomely that it would be a great comfort to talk everything over with somebody. Things seemed only to get worse by being kept locked up so tight in her own bosom. Everything was changing so, just in a little while; you could not go by the old landmarks any more. Only a few weeks ago life had been more serene, more secure and halcyon than ever before. Now, as from the clouds, one hard stroke fell after another; old established certainties exploded with a bang all about. Nothing seemed to be fixed or to be relied upon any more, nothing seemed to be settled. How had she fallen only this afternoon, supposing herself high-born of great institutions, to find herself in the turning of an eyelash merely the creature of an ugly little rattletrap! . . . But no, — no! That was simply ridiculous. Business was like that. No one had ever really supposed that a factory could possibly be anything different . . .

Agitating such matters as these, Cally Heth got into bed and pulled up the covers. She repelled the thought of the Works, as she had done all evening. Nevertheless the last thing she thought of as she dropped off to sleep was Dr. Vivian, as he stood and looked up at her from the dingy sidewalk. She wondered whether she would have agreed to speak to papa about that girl, if only the Works had n't looked so *awful*. . . .

XIV

In which Cally tells a Certain Person that she is n't Happy — very.

THE question recurred next day. The strange ubiquity of the nephew persisted. When Carlisle called about noon to "inquire" after her respected neighbor, who had lain four weeks in mysterious coma, her ring was answered and the door opened by young Dr. Vivian. He had seen her coming, through the window.

"Oh! — good-morning, Miss Heth!" said he, in a manner indicating the experiment of pleased surprise, tempered with a certain embarrassment. . . . "What a glorious day outdoors, is n't it ? — almost spring. . . . Won't you come in?"

Miss Heth replied, as she would have replied to the housemaid (who, indeed, could herself be spied just then, pausing, down the dimness of the hall):

"Good-morning. No, I stopped to ask how Mr. Beirne is to-day. We hope there is better news?"

The young man stepped at once out into the vestibule.

"Oh! That's kind of you," said he, his pleasure gaining strength. "I 'm happy to say that there *is*, — the best news. He's going to get well."

"I 'm so glad to hear it," replied Miss Heth. . . .

If, in despite of herself, there was a trace of stiff self-consciousness in her voice and air, how was she to be blamed for that? There is a breaking-point for even the most "finished" manner, and the sight of this man to-day was like a rough hand on a new wound. A great wave of helplessness had broken over her, as the opening door revealed his face: how could you possibly avoid the unavoidable, how destroy the indestructible? And it seemed that, since yesterday, he had robbed her of her one reliable weapon. . . .

The tall young man pushed back his light hair. He was smiling. The mild winter sun streamed down upon him, and his face looked worn, as if he wanted sleep.

"We had a consultation this morning — three doctors," he went on, in the friendliest way. "They 're sure they 've found out where the trouble is. A little operation, of no difficulty at all — I 've done it myself, once in the hospital! — and he 'll be walking the street in a fortnight."

"That is good news, indeed. We have been so — sorry about his illness."

"Thank you — it 's a tremendous relief to me, of course. He seemed so very ill last night. . . ."

Standing under his eye in the tiled vestibule, Carlisle produced, from her swinging gold case, not her card, but those of Mr. and Mrs. B. Thornton Heth, and extended them in a gloved hand.

"May I leave these?" she said, with the reëmergence of "manner." "My mother and father will be delighted to learn that Mr. Beirne is soon to be well again."

"That 's very kind. I know my uncle would be — will be — much gratified by your interest and sympathy."

Who shall know the heart of a woman? The thing was done, the inquiry over. The most punctilious inquirer could have bowed now, and walked away down the steps. Cally imperceptibly hesitated.

She had four times met this man, and he had three times (at the lowest computation) driven her from his presence. That thought, unsettling in its way, had leapt at her somewhere in the night: she had sought to drape it, but it had persisted somewhat stark. And now had not he himself taught her, by that hateful apology which seemed to have settled nothing, that there were subtler requitals than by buffets upon the front? . . .

The pause was psychological purely, well covered by the card-giving. Words rose to Cally's tongue's tip, gracious words which would show in the neatest way how unjust were this man's opinions of her and her family. However, the adversary spoke first.

"I 'm so glad to — to see you again, Miss Heth," he began, with a loss of ease, twirling the B. Thornton Heth cards between long thin fingers — "to have the opportunity to say . . .

That is — perhaps you'll let me say — you must n't think the Works are so — so disappointing as perhaps they may seem, just at first sight. You know —"

Her flushing cheeks stopped him abruptly; and she had not usually found him easy to stop.

"But I did n't think they were disappointing at *all!* Not in the *least!*"

The young man's eyes fell.

"Oh!" he said, with noticeable embarrassment. "I — only thought that possibly — as you — you had not happened to be in the factory district for — for some time, — that possibly you might be just a little surprised that things were n't — well, prettier. You know, business —"

"But I was n't surprised at all, I 've said! I knew exactly what it was like, of course. Just exactly. And I consider the Works — *very pretty* . . . for a factory."

She gazed up at him indignantly from beneath a little mushroom hat lined with pink, challenging him to contradict her by look or word. But he swallowed her dare without a quiver. . . . Good heavens, what girl worth her salt would endure apologies on behalf of her own father, from one so much, much worse than a stranger to her? It may be that V. Vivian liked the lovely Hun the better for that lie.

"Well," he said, compounding the felony with a gallant gulp, "I — I 'm glad you were n't disappointed —"

She could certainly have retired upon that with all the honors, but the fact was that the thought of doing so did not at the moment cross her mind. She found the conversation interesting to a somewhat perilous degree.

"I suppose *your* idea is," she said, and it showed her courage that she could say it, "that a factory ought to be a — a sort of *marble palace!*"

"No. Oh, no. No—"

"But it *is* your idea, is it not, that it 's my father's duty to take his money and build a perfectly gorgeous new factory, full of all sorts of comforts and luxuries for his work-girls? That *is* your idea of his duty to the poor, is it not? . . ."

There it was, the true call: what ear could fail to catch it? Out they came running from the city again, the old scribes with new faces; pouring and tumbling into the wilderness to ask a lashing from the grim voice there. . . . Only, to-day, it must have been that he did not hear their clamors. Surely there was no abhorrence in these eager young eyes. . . .

"Well — personally, I don't think of any of those things just as a — a duty to the poor — exactly."

"Oh! You mean it's his duty to himself, or something of that sort? That sounds like the catechism. . . . That *is* what you meant, is it not?"

"Well, I only meant that — I think we might all be happier — if . . ."

An uproar punctuated the strange sentence. Mr. Beirne's butler had chosen to-day to take in coal, it seemed; a great wagon discharged with violence at precisely this moment. Two shovelers fell to work, and an old negro who was washing the basement windows at the house next door, the Carmichaels', desisted from his labors and strolled out to watch. It was the most interesting thing happening on the block at the moment, and of course he wanted to see it.

Carlisle stared at Mr. Beirne's nephew, caught by his word.

"Oh! . . ." said she. "So you think my father would be much happier if he stripped himself and his family to provide Turkish baths and — and Turkish *rooms* for his work-girls? I must say I don't understand that kind of happiness. But then I'm not a *Socialist!*"

She said Socialist as she might have said imp of darkness. However, the young man seemed unaware of her bitter taunt. He leaned the hand which did not hold the cards against a pilaster in the vestibule-side, and spoke with hurried eagerness:

"I don't mean that exactly, and I — I really don't mean to apply anything to your father, of course. I only mean — to — to speak quite impersonally — that it seems to me the reason we all follow money so hard, and hold to it so when we have it, is that we believe all along it's going to bring us happiness, and that . . . After all — isn't it rather hard ever to get happiness that way? Perhaps we might find that the real way to be happy was just in the other direction. That was all I meant. . . . Don't you think, really," the queer man hurried on, as if fearing an interruption, "it stands to reason it's not possible to be happy through money? It's so *segregating*, it seems to me — it *must* be that way. And isn't that really just what we all want it for? — to make a — a sort of little class to ourselves, to wall ourselves off from the rest — from what seems to be — life. It elevates in a sense, of course — but don't you think it often elevates to a — a sort of rocky little island?"

They seemed to be personal words, in despite of his exordium, and V. Vivian boggled a little over the last of them, doubtless perceiving that he was yielding fast to his old enemy (as indicated to O'Neill) and once more being too severe with these people, who after all had never had a chance. . . .

Cally looked briefly away, up the sunny street. She raised a white-gloved hand and touched her gay hair, which showed that, though she hesitated, she was perfectly at ease. She had just been struck with that look suggestive of something like sadness upon the man's face, which she had noticed that night in the summer-house. She herself was inclined to connect this look with his religiosity, associating religion, as she did, exclusively with the sad things of life. Or did it come somehow from the contrast between his shabby exterior and that rather shining look of his, his hopefulness incurable? . . .

She replied, in her modulated and fashionable voice: "I don't agree with you at all. I'm afraid your ideas are too extraordinary" — she pronounced it extrord'n'ry, after Mr. Canning — "for me to follow. But before I go —"

"They do seem extraordinary, I know," broke from him, as if he could not bear to leave the subject — "but at least they're not original, you know. . . . I think that must be just the meaning of the parable of the rich young man. — Don't you, yourself?"

"The parable of the rich young man?"

She looked at him with dead blankness. Passers-by hopped over the coal-hole and glanced up at the pair standing engrossed upon the doorstep. Such as knew either of them concluded from their air that Mr. Beirne was worse again this morning.

V. Vivian's gaze faltered and fell.

"Just a — a little sort of story," he said, nervously — "you might call it a little sort of — allegory, illustrating — in a way — how money tends to — to cut a man off from his fellows. . . . This man, in the sort of — of story, was told to give away all he had, not so much to help the poor, so it seems to me, as to —"

"I see. And of course," she said, vexed anew — how did she seem *always* to be put at a disadvantage by this man, she, who could put down a Canning, alas, only too easily and well? — "of course that's just what *you* would do?"

"What I should do?"

"If *you* had a lot of money, of course you would give it all away at once, for fear you might be cut off — segregated — rocky island — and so forth?"

To her surprise, he laughed in quite a natural way. "Uncle Armistead, who's usually right, says I'd hang on to every cent I could get, and turn away sorrowful. . . . Probably the only reason I talk this way is I haven't got any. . . . That is — except just a — a little income I have, to live on. . . ."

No doubt he said this hypocritically, self-righteous beneath his meekness, but Cally was prompt to pounce on it as a damning confession. She flashed a brilliant smile upon him, saying, "Ah, yes! — it's so much easier to preach than to practice, isn't it?"

And quite pleased with that, she proceeded to that despoiling of him she had had in mind from the beginning:

"Before I go, I started to tell you just now, when you interrupted me, that I was in rather a hurry yesterday, and didn't have time to — to say to you what I meant to say, to answer your request —"

"Oh!" said he, rather long drawn-out; and she saw his smile fade. "Yes?"

"I meant to say to you," she went on, with the same "great lady" graciousness, "that I shall of course speak to my father about the girl you say was unjustly dismissed. It's a matter, naturally, with which you have nothing to do. But if an injustice has been done by one of his subordinates, my father would naturally wish to know of it, so that he may set it right."

The little speech came off smoothly enough, having been prepared (on the chance) last night. For the moment its effect seemed most gratifying. The young man turned away from her, plainly discomfited. There was a small callosity on the pilaster adjacent to his hand, and he scratched at it intently with a long forefinger. Standing so, he murmured, in the way he had of seeming to be talking to himself:

"I knew you would . . . I *knew!*"

She disliked the reply, which seemed cowardly somehow, and said with dignity: "It's purely a business matter, and of course I make no promises about it at all. If there *has* been any injustice, it was of course done without my father's knowledge. I have no *idea* what he will do about it, but whatever he decides will of course be right."

The man turned back to her, hardly as if he had heard.

"The trouble is," he said, in an odd voice, harder than she had supposed him to possess, "I did n't trust you. I —"

"Really that's of no consequence. I'm not concerned in it at —"

"I was sure all the time you would — be willing to do it," he went on, in the same troubled way. "I was *sure*. And yet last night I went off and spoke to somebody else about it — a man who has influence with MacQueen — John Farley — a — a sort of saloonkeeper. Corinne is back at work this morning."

The girl struggled against an absurd sense of defeat. She wished now — oh, *how* she wished! — that she had gone away immediately after giving him mamma's and papa's cards. . . .

"Oh!" she said, quite flatly. . . . "Well — in that case — there is no more to be said."

But there he seemed to differ with her. "I'd give a good deal," he said slowly, "if I'd only waited. . . . Could you let me say how sorry I am —"

"Please don't apologize to me! I've told you before that I — I *detest* apologies. . . ."

"I was not apologizing to you exactly," said V. Vivian, with a kind of little falter.

"I — have n't anything to do with it, I 've said! It 's all purely a business matter — purely!" And because, being a woman, she had been interested in the personal side of all this from the beginning, she could not forbear adding, with indignation: "I can't *imagine* why you ever thought of coming to me, in the first place."

"Why I ever thought of it?" he repeated, looking down at her as much as to ask whom on earth should he come to then.

"If you had a complaint to make, why did n't you go direct to my father?"

"Ah, but I don't know your father, you see."

"Oh! . . . And you consider that you do know me?"

The man's right hand, which rested upon the pilaster, seemed to shake a little.

"Well," he said, hesitatingly, "we 've been through some trouble together. . . ."

Then was heard the loud scraping of shovels, and the merry cackle of the old negro, happy because others toiled in the glad morning, while he did not. Cally Heth's white glove rested on Mr. Beirne's polished balustrade, and her piquant lashes fell.

She desired to go away now, but she could not go, on any such remark as that. Staying, she desired to contradict what the alien had said, but she could not do that either. The complete truth of his remark had come upon her, indeed, with a sudden shock. This man *did* know her. They *had* been through trouble together. Only, it seemed, you never really got through trouble in this world: it always bobbed up again, waiting for you, whichever way you turned. . . .

And what did this lame stranger have to do with her, that, of all people on earth, his eyes alone had twice seen into her heart? . . .

She looked suddenly up at him from under the engaging little hat, and said with a smile that was meant to be quite easy and derisive, but hardly managed to be that:

"Supposing that you do know me, as you say, and that I came

to you to prescribe for me — as a sort of happiness doctor . . .
Would you say that to give away everything I had — or papa
had — would be the one way for me to be — happy?"

"Happy? . . ."

He curled and recurled the corners of the Heth cards, which
did not improve their appearance. He gazed down at the work of
his hands, and there seemed to be no color in his face.

"To be happy . . . Oh, no, I should n't think that you — that
any one — could be happy just through an act, like that."

"I could hardly give away more than everything all of us had,
could I?"

"Well, but don't you think of happiness as a frame of mind,
a — a sort of habit of the spirit? Don't you think it comes usually
as a — a by-product of other things?"

"Oh, but I'm asking you, you see. . . . What sort of things do
you mean?"

He hesitated perceptibly, seeming to take her light derisive
remarks with a strange seriousness.

"Well, I think a — a good rule is to . . . to cultivate the sympathies all the time, and keep doing something useful."

Carlisle continued to look at his downcast face, with the translucent eyes, and as she looked, the strangest thought shimmered
through her, with a turning of the heart new in her experience.
She thought: "This man is a good friend. . . ."

And then she said aloud, suddenly: "I am not happy — very."

She could not well have regarded that as a Parthian shot, a
demolishing rebuke. Nevertheless, she turned upon it, precipitately, and went away down the steps.

These events took place, in the course of ten minutes upon a
doorstep, on the 31st of January. On the 27th of February, Carlisle departed, from the face of her mother's displeasure and all
the horridness of home, for her Lenten visit to the Willings.
Through the interval the dreariness of life continued; Canning
was reported in Cuba; she had abandoned all thought of a little
note. The nephew she saw no more; but it chanced that she
came to hear his name on many lips. For on the cold morning

of the birthday of the Father of his Country, old Armistead Beirne, whom three doctors had pronounced all but a well man, was found dead in his bed: and a few days later, by the probation of his will, it became known that of his fortune of some two hundred thousand dollars, he had left one-fifth to his eccentric nephew in the Dabney House.

XV

In which she goes to New York, and is very Happy indeed.

MRS. WILLING was twenty-four, handsome, expensive, lively, and intensely fond of what she thought was pleasure. Willing was thirty-two, and had a close-clipped mustache: there were ten thousand men in New York whom you might have mistaken for him at twenty paces. He was assistant something on a nineteenth story downtown, and his scale of living continually crowded his income to the wall. The Willings — there were, of course, but two of them — had the kind of home which farmers' daughters so envy the heroines of "society" novels. They lived in a showy apartment hotel in the West Fifties, kept a motor-car, and went out for dinner. In fact "out" was the favorite word in the establishment: the Willings did everything but sleep "out."

"I can't bear to stick at home," said Mrs. Willing to Carlisle. "I've always *loved* to go places."

And places they went from one end of Carlisle's visit to the other. The shops in the morning, downtown on a rush to lunch with Willing, back to Broadway for a matinee, back home at the double-quick to dress for dinner, to the theatre after dinner, to supper after the theatre. There was always hurry; there was never quite time to reach any of the places at the hour agreed.

"That's the fun!" said Florrie Willing. "Rush, rush, rush from morning to night. That's little old New York in a nutshell."

Carlisle had expected to be thoroughly diverted by the rattle, bang, and glitter in which the Willings lived, but in this she was only partially gratified. Pure restlessness, it seemed, had entered her blood: she was no sooner fairly settled in the Wrexham than she began to wish herself back home again. The vague thought pursued her, even at the places, that she was missing something;

that she had stepped aside from, not into, the real current of her
life. Dazzling indeed were some of the dining-places to which the
experienced Willings took their guest, but somehow none of them
seemed so really interesting, after all, as home. What was happening away off there on Washington Street? Suppose Mr.
Canning should return ahead of time for his farewell visit —
return and find her not there? . . .

"You're changed somehow, Cally," cried Florrie Willing, on
the third or fourth day — "I can't just put my little patty on it,
but I can see it all the same."

They had just rushed up from breakfast, which the Willings
took in the apartment café, and were now dressing furiously to go
shopping. Cally, surprised with her mouth full of hatpins, said
of course she had; she was getting frightfully old.

"You never used to rest a cheek on a pensive hand, and stare
five minutes at a time into eternity. Out with it!" said Florrie.
"You're disappointed in love."

"That's it, too. I loved a tall pretty soldier, and he rode
away."

"*We'll* never ride away, at this rate. Get a *move* on, Cally!
We've slews and slews of places to go to."

Cally, who considered that she already had a move on, did
her best to get on another one.

Young Mrs. Willing added: "Whatever became of the gay
young thing with the eyelashes you flirted so outrageously with,
the time we were up at Island Inn? What was his name — oh —
Mr. Dalhousie?"

Carlisle winced a little in spite of herself. . . . Banquo could
not have been more impossible to forget than this.

"Oh — why, he and I had the worst kind of smash-up — and
he went away somewhere. I never like to think of him any
more. . . . Let's fly!"

Fly they did, that morning and many others. It was all very
different from life at home. Born and bred in a town where
social life is large, constant, and gay, Carlisle could not help
being struck by the fact that the Willings, roughly speaking,
had no friends. One other young couple in the same hotel, the

Jennisons, appeared to be about the limit of their intimate circle: a phenomenon, no doubt at least partly explained by the fact that the Willings moved every year, or sometimes twice a year, "to get a change." Thus, in the huge rabbit-warren, they were constantly cutting themselves off from their past.

"I can't endure to poke about in the same little spot year after year," said Florrie Willing. "If I don't have something new, I simply froth at the mouth and die."

However, Mr. Willing of course had his connections downtown, and knowing his duty in the premises, he would frequently "bring up" men in the evening, brisk, lively, ambitious young fellows like himself. One of the men so brought up fell abruptly and deeply in love with Carlisle, which helped considerably to pass the time away.

"You'd better hold on to Pierce," said Florrie, talking seriously as a married woman: "He's one of the coming men — dead certain to make a pile of money some day."

Cally said she'd dearly love to hold on to Pierce, but to herself she smiled, thinking if Florrie only knew. By this time she had been a fortnight in New York, and had decided to leave at the end of another week. Whatever else the visit was or was not, it had more than justified itself by providing her with just the perspective she needed, to see things once again in their true proportions. Distance seemed wonderfully to soften away all the horridnesses. Nothing had really happened. On the contrary, against this stimulating background it was reassuringly plain that everything was agreeably settled at last, or very soon to be so settled. More and more, as April drew steadily nearer, Mr. Canning towered shiningly in the foreground of her thought.

The days passed quickly enough. She and Florrie spent many absorbing mornings in the shops, Carlisle for the most part "just looking," under the coldly disapproving eyes of the shop-ladies. But her intentions were serious at bottom, in view of three hundred dollars which papa had privately given her, at the last moment, companied by a defiant wink. (The wink indicated collusion against mamma, whose design it had been to cut her daughter off penniless for the trip.) After a great deal of looking, for she was a thrifty buyer, Cally expended one hundred and twenty-five dollars for a perfectly lovely two-colored dress, bewitchingly draped, and seventy-five dollars for a little silk suit. Both were dirt cheap, Florrie agreed. She looked four times at a dear of a hat going begging for seventy dollars, but with only three hundred you have to draw the line somewhere, so Cally simply purchased a plain gray motor-coat lined with gray corduroy, which she really needed, at sixty dollars. She also sought a gift for papa, in recognition of his liberality, and finally selected a silver penknife as just the thing. The knife, luckily enough, could be got for only $2.50.

The young broker who had fallen in love with Carlisle came up four times with Willing, called five times in between, and became host at two of the "out" evenings for the party of four. Carlisle forbore to give him any encouragement, though she rather liked his eyes, and the way his mouth slanted up at the right corner.

"I'm wild about you," said he, on her last evening, — his name, if it is of the smallest interest, was Pierce Watkins, Jr., — "I'll shoot myself on your doorstep to-morrow if it'll give you even a moment of pleasure."

Carlisle assured him that she desired no suicidal attentions.

"You're the loveliest thing I ever looked at," said he, huskily. "God bless you for that, anyway. And no matter what else happens to me, I'll love you till I die."

"Don't look so glum, Mr. Watkins dear," said Cally.

They did not go to any matinee on the last afternoon, the reason being that it was Monday and there were n't any, except the vaudevilles, which were voted tiresome. Florrie and Carlisle lunched quietly at "home"; had a rubber of bridge afterwards in the apartment of Edith Jennison (who produced for the necessary fourth an acquaintance she had made last week in the tearoom of the Waldorf-Astoria); and rushed from the table for hats, veils, and a drive on the Avenue.

Carlisle was to leave at ten o'clock. Her trunks were packed; her "reservations" lay in the heavy gold bag swinging from her side. Home, somehow, beckoned to her as it had never done before. Besides, New York, with its swarming population (mostly with palms up) and its ceaseless quadruple lines of motor-cars, began to oppress her.

"It's too full of people," she laughed to Mrs. Willing as they shot down in the lift. "It's too big. Some day it will swell up and burst."

"Why, that's the fun of it, rusticus! How I love the roar!"

"I like it, too," said Carlisle. "But I do think it's nice to live in a city where you can *some*times cross Main Street without asking four policemen, and then probably having your leg picked off, after all."

They dashed across the onyx lobby for the main entrance, as fast as they could go, Mrs. Willing remarking that they were almost too late to catch the crowds as it was. From the small blue-velvet parlor, across the corridor from the clerk's desk, a tall man rose at the sight of them, and came straight forward. For a moment Carlisle's heart stopped beating as she saw that it was Hugo Canning.

He advanced with his eyes upon her, brought her to a halt before him. If the imps of memory must have their little toll at this remeeting, the flicker passed through her too quickly for her to take note of it. It woke no palest ghost of rebellion, to walk now. The girl's heart, having missed a beat, ran away in a wild flutter. . . .

"Did my cards reach you?" said the remembered voice, without preface. "They just went up, I believe. But I see you mean to go out."

He looked a little pale under the lobby's brilliant lights, but never had he seemed so handsome and impressive. Carlisle looked up and looked down, and the sight of him there was an exaltation and heavenly fulfilment and a garland upon her brow.

"We must have passed them as we came down," said she. "How do you do? I had no idea you were in this part of the world."

He said that he was just off the train. She presented him to Mrs. Willing, who hardly repressed a start as she heard and identified his name.

"Will you come with us for a little drive?" said Carlisle. "We were just starting out to take the air. Or . . ."

Florrie Willing looked intensely eager. Canning hesitated. The feminine intuitions, of which we have heard so much, naturally divined the cause of his hesitation, and Florrie rushed into the breach.

"You're excused from our engagement, Cally!" said she, with archness, and some nobility, too. "I know Mr. Canning does n't care to parade the Avenue in our last year's model. You shall have the city to yourselves. Why not go up to the apartment?"

Carlisle glanced at Canning, who said: "You are very nice and kind, Mrs. Willing." Mrs. Willing looked at him as much as to say, "I can be five times as nice as that, if you only knew. . . ."

When she had rushed off, Canning said: "Do you feel like a little walk?"

"Oh, how nice!" said Carlisle.

"Let's stroll up to the Plaza and have tea."

They went out, turned east and came into the Avenue, where, the afternoon being fine, one million people were methodically stepping on each other's heels. However, these were people without existence, even when they jostled into one.

The moment they were out of earshot of the listening clerk, Canning said, looking straight in front of him:

"Have n't you missed me at all, Carlisle?"

"Oh, yes! I seem to have done hardly anything else."

"I've been learning your name, you see," said Canning, after five steps in silence. "You won't mind? . . . Miss Heth would be a sham, after thinking nothing but Carlisle all these weeks."

She said that she did n't mind. His presence here beside her seemed to fill every reach and need of her being: here was what her soul had cried for, through all the empty days. It did not seem that she could ever mind anything any more. . . .

"I'm very lucky to see you," she went on, quite naturally, "for I'm going back home to-night. Your six months' sentence is n't quite up yet, is it? Is it business that brings you?"

"What do you call business? Of course I've come," said he, "only to see you."

He went on, after a glorious pause: "And this is the second time — or is it the fourth or fifth? Did you happen to hear of me at Eva Payne's in January?"

"Oh, yes! Only not till four hours after you were gone."

"You'd hardly guess, though, how I've been torn between my — wish, and what it pleases me to call my pride. . . . I was in Florida and going on to Cuba for February, at least, by special request of Heber. I thought I should like to see you again before I got so far away. Only when I came in sight of your door once more, I couldn't bring myself to knock. . . ."

One interesting coincidence about the reasoning of beautiful ladies is that it is sometimes right. Continuing as they swung up the crowded street, Canning said:

"It seemed to me that . . . However, that's no matter now. Unfortunately I've the devil's own temper. To be packed off so, and then to surrender without a condition — I needed more weeks of silent self-communion for that. I've had them now, under pretty skies where the moon shines bright o' nights. I believe the breezes have blown my humors away. I'm happy to be here with you, Carlisle."

"I like it, too. . . . How on earth did you ever find me?"

"Kerr's been writing me notes from time to time, you know. In one of them he mentioned that you were away from home. I wired him yesterday from Tampa for your address."

"Dear Willie!" said Carlisle. "Do you know I'm mad to be at home again?"

They came to the shining hotel, and passed into the tea-room, which was now rapidly filling up. The doorman greeted Mr. Canning by name. An obsequious majordomo wafted him and his lady, with smiles, to the little table of his choice. Many eyes were drawn to the young pair. He was a man to be noticed in any company, but in presence and in air she was his not unworthy mate. He himself became aware, even then, perhaps more than ever then, that this provincial girl stood transplanting to a metropolitan setting with unimpaired distinction. . . .

"And tea-cakes, ma'am?" implored the loving waiter.

"Muffins," said Canning, and abolished him by a movement of his little finger.

Carlisle would have preferred the tea-cakes, but she loved Hugo's lordly airs.

He dropped his gloves into a chair, and there descended upon him a winning embarrassment.

"Tell me now, for my sins and my penitence," he said in a low voice, his strong fingers clasping a spoon, "that you have blotted away what is past."

She said that she had blotted it all away.

He went on, with considerable loss of ease: "I suppose the accursed dilettante habit has got into my blood. I needed these unhappy days and nights, for my soul's good —"

"Oh, please!" said Carlisle, her eyes falling from his grave face. "Let's not talk of it any more."

He stopped, as if glad to leave the subject; but after a silence he added with entire continuity:

"Your spirit's very fine. . . . It's what I've always admired most in women, and found least often."

The loving waiter set tea and muffins. Peace unfolded white wings over the little table. A divine orchestra played a dreamy waltz that had reference to a beautiful lady. Carlisle poured, and remembered from Willie's apartment that Canning liked one lump and neither cream nor lemon. He seemed absurdly pleased by the small fact. The topic of the Past having been finally disposed of, the man's ordinary manner seemed abruptly to leave him. His gaze became oddly unsettled, but he perpetually returned it to Carlisle's face. He appeared enormously interested in everything that she said and did, yet at the same time erratically distrait and engrossed. He became more and more grave, but simultaneously he gave evidences of a considerable nervous excitement within. . . .

If Carlisle noticed these eccentricities at all, she could have had no difficulty in diagnosing them, having observed them in the demeanor of young men before now. The case was otherwise with Canning, to whom his own unsteadinesses were a continuing amazement. Heart-whole he had reached his thirtieth year, and his present enterprise had furnished him with the surprise of his life. He was, indeed, a man who had lately looked upon a miracle. He had watched three humiliating rebuffs turn under his eye, as it were, to so many powerful lodestones. He himself hardly understood it, but it was a truth that no degree of cunning on the part of this girl could have so captured his imagination as her spirited independence of him (in mamma's vocabulary, her flare-up). A man who held himself naturally high, he had been irresistibly magnetized by her repulses of him. Rebuffed, he had sworn to go near her no more, and had turned again, an astonishment to himself, and tamely rung her bell. . . .

Canning looked and looked at Carlisle across the little table, and it was as if more miracles went on within him. Not inexperienced with the snarers, he had learned wariness; and now, by some white magic, wariness seemed not worth bothering for. If marriage was to come in question, his dispassionate judgment could name women clearly more suitable; but now dispassionateness was a professor's mean thumb-rule, too far below to consider. Of a sudden, as he watched her loveliness, all his instincts clamored that here and now was his worthy bride: one, too, still perilously not broken to his bit. But . . . Was it, after all, possible? Was it conceivable that this unknown small-capitalist's daughter, rated so carelessly only the other day, was the destined partner of his high estate? . . .

"I can't bear to think of your going to-night," he exclaimed suddenly, with almost boyish eagerness. "You know this town is home to me. I can't explain how perfect it seems to be here with you."

She mentioned demurely her hope of his return to the Payne Fort in a month or so: a remark which he seemed to find quite unworthy of notice.

"Stay over till to-morrow, Carlisle! Let's do that! And we'll take the day train down together."

"Goodness! With my tickets all bought? And my trunks packed since morning?

Canning glanced hurriedly at his watch. "I can arrange about the tickets in three minutes. As for the trunks, Mrs. Willing's maid will be only too glad to unpack them for you. Do — do stay."

She laughed at his eagerness, though at it her heart seemed to swell a little.

"And if they 've already gone to the station?"

"I can put my hand on ten men who will drive like the devil to bring them back."

"And if my mother confidently expects me for breakfast to-morrow?"

"I will write the telegram to her myself." He added: "Ah, you can't refuse me!"

Cally said: "I'm afraid you are one of the terrible masterful men that we read about, Mr. Canning. But — perhaps that's why I shall be glad to stay."

He thanked her with some unsteadiness, and said: "Where shall we dine? . . . And we could be excused from dressing, could n't we? I can't bear to lose sight of you, even for an hour."

Of course he had his way there, too. In adjoining booths they did their telephoning, he to somebody or other about the reservations, she to leave a message for Florrie Willing. Later they dined in a glittering refectory, just opened, but already of great renown. . . .

It was an unforgettable meal. So long as she lived, this evening remained one of the clearest pictures in Carlisle's gallery of memorabilia. Before the dinner was half over, Canning's immediate intentions became apparent to her. Doubts and hesitancies, if he had had any, appeared to recede abruptly from his horizon. With the serving of dessert, the words were spoken. Canning asked Carlisle to be his wife. He did it after an endearingly confused preamble, which involved his family and his natural pride in upholding and continuing the traditions of his house. Critically speaking, his remarks might have been considered too long and too much concerned with the Cannings; but of the genuineness of his love, Carlisle could not entertain a doubt. As she and mamma had planned it, so it had fallen out.

She accepted Hugo with her eyes while an affectionate servitor offered her some toasted biscuit. She accepted the biscuit, too.

It was later agreed that the betrothal should not be announced for the present, except to the parents of the contracting parties. Canning had argued strongly for a day in June, but Carlisle at length carried her point that the interval was quite too short. It was now the 20th of March. The final decision, reached on the train next day, was that Canning should join Mrs. and Miss Heth abroad, in June or July, and the formal announcement of the coming alliance should be made then, from London or Paris. The wedding itself would take place early in October.

XVI

*Of Happiness continuing, and what all the World loves; revealing,
however, that not Every Girl can do what the French People once
did.*

THE row of maiden's testimonials had received their
crowning complement. The beginning at the Beach
had touched its shining end. As she and mamma had
planned it, so it had magically fallen out.

When Mrs. Heth heard the tidings (which she did within three
minutes of Carlisle's arrival at home) the good lady hardly
restrained the tears of jubilee. Having all but abandoned hope,
she was swept off her feet by the overwhelming revulsion of feeling, and her attitude — for of course mamma always produced
an attitude about everything upon the spot — was not merely
ecstatic, but tender and magnanimously humble. For it was
clear now that the daughter had outpointed the mother at the
Great Game; Cally had justified her flare-up; and Mrs. Heth,
with eyes nobly moist, begged forgiveness for all the hibernal
harshnesses.

"You must make allowances for the natural anxieties of a
loving mother's heart," said she, in the first transports. . . .
"You've done me so proud, dear little daughter. *Proud!* . . .
How Society will open its eyes! . . ."

"So he is coming to dinner with us!" she added a moment later,
exulting with her eyes. "He will speak to your father then. . . .
It's not too late to add a course or two. And we must have out
the gold coffee-set. . . ."

Canning dined in state at the House that night, with coffee
from the gold set. Next evening, there were similar ceremonies.
Accompanying Carlisle homeward on the day following their remeeting, Canning had meant to return at once to New York; for
his long furlough had now run out, and he had felt a man's call

of duty upon him. Moreover, it was already arranged that he should come again for a real betrothal visit, sometime before the first of May. Yet he lingered on for four days now, a man magnetized beyond his own control. Radiant days were these.

In view of Carlisle's desire that her news should not tamely leak out, depriving the Announcement of its due *éclat*, some little discretion was of course necessary at this period: else people would talk and say afterwards that they knew it all along. She saw that she must still make engagements which did not include her betrothed; she must meet the archnesses of her little world with blank looks above the music in her heart, with many evasions, and even, perhaps, a harmless fib or two. Nevertheless, the lovers secured many hours all to themselves. Shut from public view in Mr. Heth's study, and more especially in long motor rides down unfrequented by-lanes they were deep in the absorptions of exploring each other, of revealing themselves each to each. And to Carlisle these hours, marked upon their faces with the first fresh wonder of her conquest, were dazzling beyond description.

Spring was coming early this year, slipping in on light bright feet. And in the House of Heth there was felt a vernal exuberance, indeed: permeating papa even, extending to the very servants. Mr. Heth had received the news of the great event with profound satisfaction, asserting unequivocally that Canning was the finest young man he had ever seen. And yet, unlike mamma, his joy was tempered with a certain genuine emotion at the prospect of so soon losing the apple of his eye.

"You know the old rhyme, Cally," said he, pinching her little ear — "'Your son's your son all his life, but your daughter's your daughter *till* she becomes a wife.' . . . Don't let it be that way, my dear. You're all the son your old father's got. . . ."

As to mamma, her feet remained in the clouds, but her head grew increasingly practical. She had been rather opposed to postponing the announcement, being ever one for the bird in the hand; but she had yielded with good grace, and within the hour was efficiently planning the "biggest" wedding, and the costliest wedding-reception, ever given in that town. By the second day she was giving intelligent thought to the trousseau — every stitch should be bought in Paris, except a few of the plainer things, in New York — and had finally decided that the refreshments at the reception should be "by Sherry." People should remember that reception so long as they all did live.

"All the Canning connection shall come," she cried, — "rely on me to get them here, — and all the most fashionable and exclusive people in the State. Every last one of them," said she, "except Mary Page."

After an interval, during which she sat with a glitter in her eye, she added explosively:

"*I'll* show her whether I'm probable!"

The remark, it seemed, had rankled even in the moment of supreme victory. . . .

Spring, too, it became, the quintessence of spring, in the young maiden's heart. Nature but symbolized the brilliant new life henceforward to be her own. And the more she came to discern her lover against his background of wealth, place, and power, the more she saw how brilliant that life was to be, the more she thrilled with the magnitude of her own accomplishment. Of himself in their new relation, Canning talked much in these days, and with an unaffected earnestness: of the high nature of the career they would make together; of his own honors and large responsibilities to come; in chief of his family, whose name it would be their pride to uphold through the years ahead. And the girl's heart warmed as she listened. What was all the storied dignity of the Cannings now but so much sweet myrrh and frankincense upon her own girlish altar? . . .

He was her maiden's ideal. He was her prince from a storybook, come true. If any flaw were conceivable in so complete a fulfilment, it might have been imagined only in this very fact of Hugo's all-perfectness. Marrying upward, in the nature of the case, involved a large material one-sidedness: that was the object and the glory of it all. Yet now, in her romantic situation, there woke new emotions in Cally Heth, and she dimly perceived that her lifelong ambition carried, through its very advantages, a subtle disadvantage to the heart. Unsuspected tendernesses seemed to stir within her, and she was aware of the vague wish to bestow upon her lover, to make him a full gift for a gift. However, it was clear that Canning had everything. For the priceless boons he was to confer upon her, she saw that she had nothing to give him in return, except herself.

With this return, Canning, for his part, seemed amply content. When the hour came when, for his manhood, he must report himself again to that office in New York which had not known his face since October, he took the parting hard. He was to return again before April was out, for a fortnight's stay preceding his betrothed's departure for Europe; yet he seemed hardly able to tear himself away. . . .

"I hope we shall have a long life together," said he, a bright gleam in his handsome eyes, "but it's certain, my own dear, that we'll never be engaged but once. . . ."

Moved herself by the farewells, she teasingly reminded him of his one-time impatience to fly back to lights and home. But Canning, straining her to his heart, replied that home was where the heart is, and was admitted to have the best of the argument.

Carlisle's world had been knocked far out of its ordered orbit. Hugo Canning, possessed by her, was so towering a fact that it threw the whole horizon into a new perspective. Between this shining state and the winter of discontent, there was no imaginable connection. Cause and effect must turn a new page, life's continuity start afresh.

So it seemed, in love's first bloom. And yet, circumstances being as they were, it was hardly possible that Carlisle should at one stroke completely cut herself off from the past, as Florrie Willing constantly did, as the French people once did, by means of their well-known Revolution.

In Hugo's absence (full as the days were with questions of the trousseau, rendered doubly exciting by mamma's princely attitude toward expense), Carlisle began to recognize once more the landmarks of her former environment. Doubtless a certain period of emotional reaction was inevitable, and with it the reassociation of ideas began. Canning was away a solid month. One day soon after his return, — it was on a lovely afternoon in early May, as they were motoring homeward after four hours' delightful *tête-à-tête* in Canning's own car, — Carlisle said to him:

"Oh, Hugo, what do you think I did while you were away? Subscribed a hundred dollars to a Settlement House! My own money, too, — not papa's at all!"

Hugo, whose intensity of interest in his betrothed seemed only to have increased during the days of absence, cried out at her munificence.

"So, you've money, in those terms — well!" said he. "Aren't you mortally afraid of being gobbled up by a fortune-hunter some fine day?"

"A *great* many people have warned me about that — mentioning you specially, by the way. But I've always told them that you loved me for my fair face alone."

Canning made a lover's remark, a thoroughly satisfactory one.

"But don't you see," he added, "this business of your having money changes everything. I must double my working hours, I suppose! I'm too proud a man to be dependent on my wealthy wife for support."

"I'm glad to know you may be prosperous, too, some day, Hugo," said she; and, after a little more frivolous talk: "Did I mention that I'm soliciting subscriptions from visiting men for that Settlement I spoke of?"

" Great heavens!" cried Canning, amused. "Why, don't you think a Hundred Dollars is more than sufficient — for one little family?"

"They wouldn't say so," said Carlisle, laughing and coloring a little, "for they're asking for twenty-five thousand dollars and have raised about two so far. What could be more pitiful than that?"

Canning, who was driving his car to-day, as he occasionally liked to do, then asked, why was a Settlement? And as well as she could Carlisle retailed her rather sketchy information: how " they" planned to buy the deserted Dabney House, make it the headquarters for all the organized charities of the city, and use the rest of the great pile for working-men's clubs, night classes, lodgings, gymnasiums and so forth. Thanks to the influence of Rev. Mr. Dayne, Mrs. Heth had been induced to lend her name as a member of the Settlement Association's organization committee. But it was from her cousin Henrietta Cooney that Carlisle had got most of her facts, at a recent coming-to-supper while Hugo was away.

Canning, listening, was glancing about him. Having made an adventurous run to-day by way of the old Spring Tavern, — he had plotted it out himself, with maps and blue-books, — they had reëntered the city by the back door as it were, and now spun over unaccustomed streets.

"I did n't know you went in for charity, my dear."

"Oh, a cousin of mine is drumming up funds for this, you see. . . ."

Not clearly understanding it herself, how could she explain the impulse which had led her to offer Hen, without being dunned at all, her royal subscription? Perhaps she had a vague feeling that this would prove, to the complete satisfaction of the public, that she and her family were far from being shameless homicides, dead to all benevolent works. It appeared that mamma had already subscribed fifteen dollars to the Settlement, on personal solicitation of Mr. Dayne, but of course you could not prove anything much for fifteen dollars.

Hugo, having turned to look at Carlisle, lost interest in Settlements. His gaze became fixed, and it said, plainer than ardent print, that, if he had many possessions, here was far the best and dearest of them. . . .

"Where 's that ripping little hat you wore yesterday? You know — a brown one, sort of a toque, I suppose — all old rose inside?"

"Why, Hugo! . . . Don't you like this hat *extremely?*"

"Rather! Only, if there is a choice, I do think I'd vote for the toque. . . . You 've gone and spoiled me by giving away how you can look when you try."

Carlisle laughed merrily. She was glad to have her lover so observant of what she wore, even though he did not know nearly so much about clothes as he imagined.

"It's not a toque at all," said she, "but I'll wear it for you to-morrow, provided you promise me now to run away from that tiresome secretary and come to lunch."

"Done! At one-thirty o'clock."

"That's the exact luncheon hour, as it happens, but I notice that many of the best fiancés make it a practice to report for duty at least half an hour before the gong. It *looks* so much better."

"Running and eating's no better than eating and running, you allege. There's some small merit in the contention. . . . What of those sterling fiancés who punch the time-clock a full hour before the whistle?"

"Oh, dear me, Hugo, are there any like that?"

"There's but one now in captivity, I believe. I — Hello! . . . Missed him, by Jove!"

"What was it? A cat?"

"Did n't you see? Our old hoodoo — that camp-meeting chap! . . ."

"Oh!"

"I wonder what ill wind he's blowing this time. . . . Poetic justice if I'd knocked him into the middle of next week."

Carlisle had involuntarily looked back, struck with a sense of coincidence, and also with the odd feeling of having received a douche of cold water. They were, it seemed, rolling along through old South Street, and behind her, sure enough, she saw the looming shape of the ancient hotel, which the Settlement Association could have for twenty-five thousand dollars cash. Of the "camp-meeting chap," however, she saw nothing: presumably, having evaded justice, he had already disappeared into his lair. Nevertheless she was effectually reminded that this man was still in the world.

"Is this where the fellow lives?" said Canning, also glancing back down the dingy street. "I thought somebody said he'd come into money from his lamented uncle."

She confirmed the conjecture, and Hugo then observed:

"Well, I'll give him a month to discover that it's his duty to God to remove to a more fashionable neighborhood."

"Oh! Do you think so?"

"Have you ever known one of these smooth religious fellows who was n't keen after the fleshpots when his chance came?"

Carlisle laughed and said she had n't, having indeed known few religious fellows of any kind in her young life. But she was struck with this new proof of Hugo's essential congeniality with her. His penetrating comment, born, it seemed, of that curious antipathy which she had noticed before, fell in astonishingly with trends of her own.

Many weeks had passed since Carlisle had decided to oust this religious fellow definitely from her thoughts, as belonging so clearly to that past upon which she had now turned a victorious back. And in these expulsive processes, she had found herself greatly assisted by the young man's confession of hypocrisy, as she regarded it, on this very subject of giving away money. Perhaps this had seemed a frail club once; she herself had hardly put much strength in it in the beginning; but she had been resolute, and time had strengthened her convincingly, according to her need. For if the man was a whited sepulchre, full of dead men's bones within, then clearly his opinions of people and their families were not of the slightest importance to anybody, so what was the good of anybody's thinking of them? . . .

Not to let the conversation lag, she had remarked, with no pause at all:

"It's strange our nearly running over him, just then and there. That old shack is the Dabney House, and you know it's he who got up the Settlement idea."

"No, I did n't know it," said Canning, slowing down to take a corner which led on to civilization. "Still," he added, "I shan't let that stay my generosity. I resolved three blocks back to subscribe five hundred — just to throw you in the shade — and I will not be deterred."

Having been duly applauded for his prodigality, he inquired: "How much, by the way, is the good doctor donating out of his forty thousand?"

"Not a cent!" said Carlisle, who had questioned Hen on this very point.

It was thus, indeed, that circumstances had given demolishing weight to her club. "If I had money I'd probably hang on to every cent," the man had said, that winter morning on his uncle's doorstep; and now he had money, a lot of it, and hanging on he undoubtedly was. Hen herself had confessed it, with a certain defiance, trying to create the impression that the man was merely reserving his funds for some other good purpose. . . .

The triumphant ring in Carlisle's voice might have struck Canning as odd, if he had happened to notice it. Still more obscure, however, were the inner processes which led him to say:

"Does he make any charge for the thought? . . . Well, it's a fine thought, all the same; a fine work. On reconsideration I raise my subscription to a thousand. Hang the expense! . . ."

There was another gay burst of felicitation, after which Carlisle became somewhat silent. Canning, bowling proficiently up Washington Street, spoke of his honored maternal grandmother, the great lady Mrs. Theodore Spencer, and her famous Brookline home. Beside him, Carlisle, listening with one ear only, considered the strangeness of life. Transfigured within, she had seemed to look out upon a new universe, yet was not this somehow the face of an old familiar, slyly peeping? Of what use, then, were clubs? When were things *ever* settled, if she could be conscious of a little cloud no larger than a man's hand even now, with the living guarantee of her omnipotence at her side? . . .

"Who was that?" said Canning, suspending conversation to bow, with Carlisle, to a passing female pedestrian.

"Oh," she laughed, a little vexedly, roused from her meditations — "just one of my poor relations."

"Ah?" said he, a trifle surprised.

A far cry, indeed, from the celebrated dowager, friend of diplomats and presidents, to Miss Cooney of Saltman's bookstore, in a three-year-old skirt. And how like Hen, instead of quietly looking the other way, to yell out some Cooneyesque greeting and wave that perfectly absurd umbrella. . . .

To Hen it was, a day or two later, that Carlisle mailed the two Settlement checks, hers for a hundred and Hugo's for ten times that amount. She licked the stamp with intense satisfaction. However, the rewards of her generosity seemed somewhat flat.

Hen, indeed, called her up immediately upon receipt of her communication, and contents noted, with excited thanksgiving. However, that was all: the checks were turned over to Mr. Dayne, and there the matted ended. Carlisle was oppressed with a sense of anti-climax. She even thought of sending another and larger check straight to Dr. Vivian.

Canning, it developed rather to Carlisle's surprise, took his business quite seriously. His indolences of the sick-leave period were now sloughed from him. He had returned this time, not merely with his favorite car and mechanic for the afternoon excursions, but accompanied by mysterious "papers" and a man stenographer; and, occupying rooms in the New Arlington Hotel, gave his mornings and even some of his evenings religiously to work.

"Why, Hugo, are you a *lawyer?*" cried Carlisle, when he first explained these matters to her.

"I am, and a pretty keen one," said he.

"And do you know how to reorganize *banks?*"

"I can reorganize 'em like the devil," said Hugo sincerely; for if a man does not want a woman to boast a little before now and then, he does not want her at all. . . .

His papers and his telegrams, his periods of engrossment in business and telephone-calls from his secretary, seemed to invest him with a certain new dignity. A subtle change in his manner was now perceptible. It was as if he had moulted some of the gay plumage of the wooing-season, and unconsciously begun to gather something of the authority of the coming head of a great house. Like many men who have long enjoyed but eluded the wiles of lovely woman, Canning clearly contemplated the married estate with profound gravity. In his absence he had communicated his good news to both his parents, though one was in Boston and the other, his father, in Washington: testifying, in short, before a Congressional Investigation Committee. He was not especially detailed as to what they had said, beyond their general expressions of pleasure; but it was clear that he regarded it as of the first importance that they should be pleased.

Matters now, indeed, began to assume a distinctly serious and responsible complexion. The days of purely idyllic romance seemed to slip behind; the engagement more and more took shape as the gateway to an alliance of institutional consequence, entailing far-reaching reactions in various directions. Mamma's remarks made it plain that, with Cally's establishment as Mrs. Hugo Canning, her own career of brilliant aspiration had reached its final goal. Even papa's future seemed to be affected to its roots. Already he spoke with satisfaction of taking a smaller house next year; ultimately of "retiring" to an undefined "little place in the country," toward which in recent years his talk had slanted somewhat wistfully. . . .

Mrs. Heth and Carlisle were to go to New York on the 20th of May, do a few days' preliminary shopping there, and sail on the 26th. Canning's visit lasted till near the middle of the month, running over his allotted two weeks. And deepening intimacy only brought into stronger relief his great advantages of position, antecedents, and experience; only showed Carlisle the more clearly how distinguished, cultivated, and superior a man she had won. With her pride, there came now, it seemed, a certain new humility. She was aware that never in the days of the thundering feet had she been so desirous of pleasing Hugo as now: when he was no shining symbol or distant parti, but the exceedingly personal and living man who was so soon to call her to the purple. She caught herself at times, with some amused surprise, in the deliberate processes — editing her vocabulary, manner, and wardrobe, for example, in the light of the preferences she intuitionally read in his eye. So, as the husbandly dignity descended upon him, she found herself possessed by something of the wifely duty. . . .

Whenever was this ticklish business of the dovetailing of two lives accomplished without some small mutual effort? No more could be said than that Carlisle felt, in rare and weak moments, a certain sense of strain. An immaterial subtlety this, properly out of the range of mamma's concrete observations. But papa's heart was tender: did he possibly suspect that his darling might feel herself just a little overshadowed at times?

He called Cally into the study one evening before dinner, and with a mysterious air handed over to her a bulky packet of very legal-looking papers.

"Why, papa! What is it?"

"Stock!" answered papa, with a chuckle. "Mostly Fourth National. There's a little more than fifty thousand dollars there in your hand, Cally."

"But — why, papa! . . . You don't mean it for *me!*"

"A little weddin' present from your old father. I meant to give it to you next fall, and then I thought, why wait? Had it all put in your name to-day."

"Oh — *papa!* . . ."

She threw her arms around his neck, suddenly and oddly touched; not so much by the gift, for she would have plenty of money soon, as by this evidence of her father's affectionate thought.

"Your daughter's your daughter till she becomes a wife . . ." remarked Mr. Heth. "It won't be that way, will it, Cally, eh?"

"Never in the world. . . . Oh, papa, how sweet — how *good* — you are to me! . . ."

"You've got a fine man," said papa, presently, patting her cheek. "But my judgment is it's always just as well for a girl to have a little money of her own. Feels independent. You'll have more when I'm gone, of course. That'll give you a little better'n three thousand a year. Non-taxable, too."

She reported her new wealth to Hugo, quite proudly, within two hours. For he had proved willing this evening to purloin night hours from his grave duties as attorney-at-law, and by telephone had easily cajoled Carlisle into breaking an engagement she had made for other society. In the nicest sort of way, Canning agreed that her father had made her a handsome dowry. He added, holding her hand tight, that she was to let him do something for her, too, on their wedding day. Of course she must have her own money; all she could spend.

"I can spend lots, my dear. You'll find me a frightfully expensive young person. . . . There are cigarettes in the drawer, Hugo. I bought the kind you like, this time. . . ."

She got one for him, struck the match herself. He watched her, loafing lordly; very handsome and dear he looked in his beautiful evening clothes.

And thence, in the lamplit privacy of the little study, — Mr. Heth having fared forth to a Convention "banquet," — the talk ranged wide. Late in the evening, it returned again to Carlisle, as the possessor of large independent funds, a topic of pleasurable possibilities from her standpoint.

She said idly: "Do you believe it makes you happy to give away money, Hugo? That's a rule I heard somewhere."

"Unquestionably one of the most refined ways known of tickling one's little vanity. . . . How full of good deeds you are these days. You're thinking of the poor again, I'm right?"

"I must have been. There's nobody else who'd take money from you, is there?"

"Oh, is n't there? I must introduce you to high finance some day."

"Well," said Carlisle, "I meant just to give it away — to anybody — just to show how free and superior you are, or something. . . . Silly, is n't it? What's your happiness rule, Hugo?"

He replied with the readiness of a man who has been over this path long ago:

"To have the capacity to want things very much, and the ability to get them."

And he squeezed the little hand he held, as if to say that he had both wanted much and gotten much.

Carlisle was much struck with this rule, which she now saw to have been her own and mamma's all their lives long. After duly complimenting Hugo upon it, she said:

"Here's another one, a man told me once: 'Cultivate your sympathies all the time, and do something useful.'"

"That's orthodox! It was a young curate with a lisp who told you, I'll wager."

"Very warm!" she laughed, struck again by his astuteness. "It was your hoodoo — Dr. Vivian! And, oh, now that I think of it, he gave me that other pointer, too, — about giving away money."

Hugo replied: "The man seems to be dripping with wise old saws, in a thoroughly inexpensive sort of way. . . . Well, we'll show him something about giving away money some day."

He was silent a moment, and Carlisle then remembered her thought of another large subscription to the Settlement, which she, for her part, could easily make now with fifty thousand dollars all her own. But Canning obliterated all such reflections by turning and taking her abruptly in his arms.

"*This* is what I want to make me happy. Darling — darling! . . ."

They sat on the shabby old leather lounge which papa had held fast to, by winter and by summer, for thirty years. Here they had sat down soon after eight o'clock, and now the soft-toned chimes in the hall had just sounded eleven-thirty. In the first days of their engagement, Carlisle had observed that Hugo was "very demonstrative." And now, at the end of their loverly evening together, he became suddenly and strangely moved, professing, in a voice unlike his own, his inability to live longer without her. Then, ignoring all their elaborate plannings, he abruptly begged her to marry him in June, as he had first asked her. . . .

"Why, Hugo!" she said, surprised and a little uncomfortable. "That's so much dear foolishness — and not a stitch of clothes made yet! October's just around the corner. . . . Do sit up, Hugo dear. There's papa, I think."

Hugo sat up. Reason reasserted its sway. But later, Carlisle remembered this moment with a dim sense of trouble, not entirely new. . . . She wondered with a certain disquiet whether all this was some everlasting difference between men and women, or whether she, Carlisle, was by nature a cold and undemonstrative sort of person? Indeed, there did seem to be a falling short in her somehow; for if not with herself and the expressions of her love, with what was she to return Hugo's royal gifts? . . .

There were three more days; and then young lovers must say farewell. In little more than a week they would meet again in New York; but still this seemed a real parting to both. It was the 13th of May, the day which marked the end of three weeks of cloudless skies. The rain long predicted by the weather sharps had come in the night, and the dreary downpour continued throughout the day. Each of the young pair seemed somehow conscious that the first chapter in their joint story had reached an end. Better days they might certainly have, but never again days just like these. . . .

"Keep well, dear heart," begged Canning at the last, "and take care of all your loveliness for my sake."

Proud of her beauty he ever was, and especially now when she was so soon to meet his mother in New York. And at the final parting, he said, visibly moved:

"Understand me, Carlisle, you are mine through all eternity. Whatever happens to you or me, this is a love that shall not die."

Saying which, having now lingered to the last possible moment, he dashed from her to his waiting taxicab — his own car having already gone by express — with just five minutes to catch his train.

From the drawing-room window, Carlisle waved her hand to him; kissed it, too, since nobody was looking. And then the car leapt forward and shot away out of sight down the glistening street. Hugo was gone, and Carlisle was alone.

She stood at the window, looking out blankly into the leaden wetness. It was just after five, and the rain poured. A curious depression settled quickly upon her, which was hardly fully accounted for as "missing Hugo already." . . . Why? Who upon earth had less cause for depression than she? No girl lived with more all-embracing reasons for being superlatively happy. What, then, was the lack in her? — or was this some lack in the terms of life itself? Was it the mysterious law of the world that nobody, no matter what she had or did, should ever long keep the jewel happiness unspotted by a doubt?

XVII

Cally crosses the Great Gulf; and it is n't quite Clear how she will ever cross back again.

BAFFLING questions these, even to young philosophers. Dismissing them as foolish, Cally Heth turned from the rain-swept window, designing to rest awhile in her own room, before dressing for a little dinner at Evey McVey's. Forsaken as she felt, she was yet not unconscious of a certain remote desirability in being alone; that is, in having a little time to herself now. It occurred to her that perhaps she and Hugo had been together rather too constantly in these weeks, going forward just a little too fast. . . .

In the hall she encountered her mother, descending the stairs in mackintosh, hat, and veil. Carlisle looked surprised, but mamma's look under the veil was roguishly dolorous, in reference to the recent farewell.

"Why, mamma, where are you going in all the rain?"

Mrs. Heth replied: "What, no tears! . . . I'm off to the old Dabney House, my dear — the first time in twenty years —"

"Oh! . . . The Settlement!"

"I promised Mr. Dayne I would go," said the capable little lady, eyeing her daughter expectantly — "it's the organization meeting and election of officers. The man has got together some excellent people for his committee. And, by the way, Cally —"

"But they have n't raised all the money already!"

At this Mrs. Heth looked still more knowing. "Confess, Cally — did n't Hugo do it? Did n't he make another big subscription after his thousand?"

Cally, arrested at the foot of the steps, stared at her mother. "Why — not that I know of. What do you mean?"

Now her mother looked somewhat disappointed, but said, snapping a glove button: "It would be like him to do it, and say

not a word to anybody. Why, there's a foolish story Mrs. Wayne
told me this morning that the whole thing had fallen through,
when Mrs. Berkeley Page came forward anonymously with a
gift of twenty-five thousand — simply buying the building outright, in fact. I don't, of course, believe a word of it. She's
exactly the kind to let her right hand know what her left was
doing. Still, I did think perhaps Hugo might possibly have done
something of the sort. He was so interested — he spoke of the
Settlement to me only yesterday. . . ."

The girl gazed at her mother, and a sudden light broke into her
eyes. Across her memory there flashed Canning's cryptic remark,
only the other night: "We'll show him something about giving
away money some day.". . . This, then, was what he had meant:
perhaps he had already done it that night. She knew that Hugo
had curiously disliked Dr. Vivian at sight, and that, by the
bond between her and him, he had somehow entered into her
own feminine feeling that to give handsomely to the fellow's own
charity (to which he himself gave nothing at all) was to show
him up completely in the interest of public morals. The gift of
such a sum as twenty-five thousand dollars simply exploded him
off the horizon. . . .

Her heart glowing toward her understanding lover, she clapped
her small hands and cried: "He did! — I remember something he
said about it now. Oh, I *know* he did!"

"I felt morally certain of it," said mamma, calmly, peering
through the plate glass of the door. "Don't tell me Mary Page
would do a thing like that. Ah, here is the car at last. . . ."

Carlisle said with sudden eagerness: "Do wait a minute for me,
mamma! I believe I'll go to the meeting, too."

Naturally some discussion followed this whimsical request.
The upshot was that Mrs. Heth, being late already, promised to
send the car back.

Cally, gloom banished, ran up the stairs, her mother's voice
following behind like a trade-wind.

"It's to be in the office of that Dr. Vivian — you know? . . .
one flight up. No difficulty in finding . . . Sure to put on rub-
bers. . . ."

The last words to be distinctly heard were: "Look for me right up at the front."

In her own room Carlisle flew about quite blithely, making ready for the unexpected excursion with odd anticipations beyond mamma's guessing. She felt grateful to Hugo, attached to him by a new tie; for he, however clearly he had understood it himself, had beautifully put her in just that position toward the religious fellow which she had so long desired to occupy: the position, in short, of overwhelming moral superiority. How easy now, choosing her own moment, to say what would dispel forever the man's odd little power of causing her to worry. . . .

The streets were slippery, the journey was from pole to pole of the town· and yet five minutes sufficed for it, bringing Settlementers to their destination. So easily does forty horse-power traverse the mile between Houses of Heth and Houses of Dabney. Cally Heth rolled up to the door of the abandoned hotel. Large and dismal it looked in the slanting rain. Archaic, too, so the modern of the moderns thought, glancing upward over the face of the shabby pile as the car halted, and William, who was ever attentive to his young mistress, sprang out with the umbrellas. It was an odd place for anybody to live, certainly; an even odder place to draw in storm the world of fashion foregathering to its bosom. Yet this indubitably was the spot. There was the little procession of motor-cars, lined against the broken sidewalk in the wet, to prove it. The girl's upward eye fell, too, upon a name, inscribed in white paint upon a window directly above the decayed grand entrance:

DR. VIVIAN

Carlisle became conscious of a certain excitement. She hoped very much that they had n't read out the names of subscribers yet.

She was late, so there was nobody to show her in. From the sidewalk she stepped under a queer little portico, which seemed to waft one back to a previous century. Here, at the vestibule step, she was obliged to move carefully to avoid treading on two dirty little denizens of the neighborhood, who knew no better than

to block the way of the quality. They were little Jew girls, —
little Goldnagels, in short, — and while one of them sat and
played at jackstones with a flat-looking rubber ball, the other
and smaller lay prone upon her stomach, weeping with passionate abandon.

Her agonized wails indicated the end of the world, and worse.
Carlisle said kindly:

"What's the matter, little girl?"

The lamenting one, who was about four years old, rolled around
and regarded the lady with a contorted face. Her wails died to
a whimper: but then, curiosity satisfied and no solace offering,
she burst forth as with an access of mysterious pain.

"Did she hurt herself?" said Carlisle, third-personally, to the
elder girl, who had suspended her game to stare wide-eyed.
"What on earth is the matter?"

The reply was tragically simple:

"*A Lady stepped on her Junebug.*"

Sure enough, full on the vestibule floor lay the murdered slum-
bug, who had too hardily ventured to cross a wealthy benevolent's
path. The string was yet tied to the now futile hind-leg. Carlisle,
lingering, repressed her desire to laugh.

"Oh! . . . Well, don't you think you could catch her a new
one, perhaps?"

"Bopper he mout ketch her a new one mebbe to-morrow,
mom. . . . *Hiesh*, Rebecca!"

Moved by some impulse in her own buoyant mood, Carlisle
touched the littlest girl on the shoulder with a well-gloved finger.

"Here — Rebecca, poor child! . . . You can buy yourself
something better than Junebugs."

The proprietor of the deceased bug, having raised her damp
dark face, ceased crying instantly. Over the astounding windfall
the chubby fingers closed with a gesture suggesting generations
of acquisitiveness.

"Is it hers to keep?" spoke her aged sister, in a scared voice.
"That there's a *dollar*, mom."

"Hers to keep . . ." replied the goddess, smiling.

But her speech stopped there, shorn of a donator's gracious

frills, and the smile became somewhat fixed upon the lovely lip. . . .

There had appeared a man's face at the glass of the old doors, and the lady, straightening benignantly to sweep on to her triumph upstairs, had run suddenly upon his fixed gaze. Nothing, of course, could have been more natural than this man's appearance there: who upon earth more suitable for door-keeper to the distinguished visitors than he, who had given his office to the Settlement to-day, in lieu of more expensive gifts? Yet by some flashing trick of Carlisle's imagination, or of his air of immobility, seen darkly through the glass, it was almost as if he might have been waiting there for her alone. . . .

But the meeting of eyes was over as soon as it began. With so prompt a courtesy did the Dabney House physician swing open the door that it was as if he had been opening it all along, as if she had n't caught him looking at her. . . .

"How do you do, Miss Heth? . . . Such a dreadful day! — you were brave to venture out."

"How d' you do?" said Carlisle, in the voice of "manner," a rising voice, modulated, distant and superior. And over her shoulder, she addressed the little Jew girls, with an air of more than perfect ease:

"Well, then, good-bye! Be sure to catch her the new one to-morrow. . . ."

She had seen that the strange young man was smiling. And by that she knew that he remembered their last meeting, and wanted to trade upon her queer weakness at that time, pretending that he and she were pleasant acquaintances together. Presently she should inform him better as to that. But why, oh, why, that small flinching at the sight of him, the very man she had fared into the downpour to explode, not pausing even to mourn her lover's going? . . .

"I'm a search-party of one," said Dr. Vivian, throwing wider the door, "for Mr. Pond. I wondered if he could have got lost, somewhere down here — he 's never turned up yet."

"Mr. Pond?"

"The director of the Settlement, you know, when it opens for business in the fall. He happened to be in Washington, and was good enough to run down to-day to make us a little address."

"Oh."

Carlisle found herself, beyond the door, in a quaint high-ceiled court, enfolded with peristyles in two long rows, and paved with discolored tiles loose under the foot. At the farther end of the court there ran away a broad corridor into the dusk, and here also, full fifty feet distant, rose the grand stairway with ornate sweeping balustrade ending in a tall carved newel-post. Obsolete and ruined and queer the whole placed looked, indeed. . . .

"Luckily," added Dr. Vivian, "I'm in good time to serve as a guide."

But Miss Heth was already walking past him with an expensive rustle, moving straight toward the stairway. For this, needless to say, was not the moment to speak that pointed word or two which should unmask the man; there would be an unavoidable vulgarity about it here, in this solitude. And even if she should get no further opportunity upstairs — well, after all, the situation spoke for itself; nay, thundered. Had not Hugo — come to think of it — struck the note of the subtler victory, he who had given magnificently and said nothing? *Noblesse oblige*, as the Gauls say. . . . .

"Oh, no, that's not necessary," she replied, walking on. "There are the stairs. . . ."

The young man fell in behind her.

"The old house is really quite bewildering, upstairs. It happened that my office was the only place available. Perhaps you will let me show you —"

"Oh, I don't think I need trouble you, thank you."

"It is no trouble," said V. Vivian.

Good sentences these, and well pronounced. With them, conversation seemed to languish. The processional pair moved across the shadowy court in entire silence. The benevolent lady led, never so securely entrenched in the victorious order, the beloved of prodigal Hugo Canning, to whom no harm should befall. After her proceeded the slum doctor: the hard marble betrayed the inequality of his footsteps. A minute more and they would be upstairs, swallowed and dispersed in the publicity of the meeting. Floor and ceiling above them brought down the sounds of a company near at hand, the scraping of a chair-leg, the muffled echo of voices. Carlisle's foot trod upon the bottom step of the broad stairway.

"I wonder if you would give me five minutes after the meeting, Miss Heth?" said the young man's voice behind her. "There's a — a matter I've wanted very much to speak to you about."

Cally's heart seemed to jump a little.

"What is it that you want to speak to me about?" she asked coolly, not turning. And, to her own surprise, she brought her other foot up on the stair.

"Well, it concerns the Works," said Vivian.

And he added at once, hastily: "Oh, nothing that you need object to at all, I hope. Not at all. . . ."

She had stopped short at the fighting-word, and turned, pink-cheeked. Certes, there was a point at which *noblesse oblige* becomes mere flabby spinelessness.

And upstairs Mrs. Heth, complacent right up at the front, craned round her neck, and thought that Cally was very long in coming. . . .

"Yes? What about the Works?" said Cally, her breath quickening.

"Oh, I don't mean to detain you now, of course —"

"But now that you have detained me?" she pursued, with no great polish of courtesy.

The young man raised a hand and pushed back his hair, which was short but wavy. It was observed that he wore, doubtless in memory of his uncle, a mourning tie of grosgrain silk, replacing the piquant aquarium scene.

"I could hardly explain it all in just a few sentences," said he, affecting reluctance, "and I — certainly don't want to give you a wrong impression. . . To begin quite at the end, I've been wondering if I — I might be allowed to make one or two small improvements there, at the Works, I mean, — in fact, out of a — a sort of fund I have."

Carlisle stared at him spellbound. She stood on the bottom

step of the old grand stairway, one gloved hand on the balustrade; and, as she so stood, her eyes just came on a level with those of the tall doctor. His hare-brained audacity almost took her breath away.

"Oh," said she. "Out of a fund you have."

And she thought wildly of accepting his offer at once, compelling him to name a definite sum, just for the fun of seeing how he would wriggle out of it afterwards.

"I'm tremendously interested in the Works, you know," the man rushed on, quite as if he found encouragement in her reply, "because I have so many friends who work there. It's to gratify my peace of mind, just to know that they have — everything they need. As I say, I happen to — to have a sort of fund — a little public fund, you might say — for — for purposes of the kind. And the idea of outside coöperation in such a matter is a perfectly sound one, as you doubtless know, a — a sound, advanced socialistic idea. It's simply the community acknowledging some responsibility where it already claims the right to regulate . . ."

At this point her stare seemed to penetrate him with a doubt, and he said, with the air of having skipped hastily and turned back:

"I mustn't detain you now to give the full argument, of course, but I assure you the idea is sound and — mutually beneficial, as I believe. Unfortunately," he added, with a certain embarrassment, "I don't know your father."

"Tell me," said Carlisle, feeling an excitement mounting within her, "how is it that you are always thinking up these plans for doing good to other people?"

Before Dr. Vivian could meet this poser, the front door opened with a bang, and a youngish man in a wet yellow raincoat came striding rapidly across the court toward them. He was a powerfully built man with a blue-tinged chin, and wore the air of a person of authority.

"Meeting not begun yet?" he demanded, without salutation, apparently addressing Carlisle. "Thought I was late."

"Ah, Mr. Pond — glad to see you," said Vivian, stepping for-

ward a little to meet the newcomer. "They've just begun —
you'll find an ovation waiting for you."

"In your office? Are n't you going up, to lead the applause?"

The doctor bowed gravely. "In my office. I'll join you directly."

"I see," said the man, nodding, having never checked his
stride.

But all that he had seemed to see with his keen black eyes was
the lovely girl posed on the last step of the ornamental stairway.
He almost brushed against her as he strode by.

The Pond person's footsteps diminished up the long stairs.
A moment later a volley of hand-clapping, sounding very near,
indicated his arrival in the meeting-room. But his interruption
and his irritating stare had accomplished no mollifying purpose
down in the court. But one end, indeed, could justify the proud
Miss Heth in lingering in a public hall with the slanderer of herself and her family.

"Does n't it occur to you," she said, hardly waiting for the
intruder to get out of earshot, "that so much preaching about
other people's business seems rather — odd, coming from you?"

Dr. Vivian now affected to look troubled.

"There was just that difficulty," said he, slowly, "that you
might think I was preaching. I'm not, this time, really —"

"Don't you know perfectly well you only said that in a — a
horrid way to try to make me feel uncomfortable?"

She paused for a reply; her excitement was growing. Her figure
was enveloped in a slim raincoat of fine gray; she wore a yellow
straw hat of an intriguing shape, and over it a white veil closely
drawn to keep the wet wind from her face. Now and then, as her
eyes moved, a descending black-and-gold eyelash became en-
tangled with this veil; that occurrence, in fact, took place at
this precise moment, creating an emergency situation of some
consequence. It was a matter of considerable public interest to
see how it would all work out. However, the girl merely raised
an indifferent hand, and plucked the veil out a little. The man
V. V. looked hurriedly away.

He was saying: "I assure you I meant nothing of the kind. However, doubtless it's natural that you should think so —"

"It seems *very* natural to me — especially here in the new Settlement building! . . . What about the *parable of the rich young man now?*"

He stood looking at her without a reply; one of his quaint looks, it was.

However, Carlisle knew positively that he did not want to improve the Works out of any fund he pretended to have, and was resolved to show him no mercy now. She had really meant to spare him, and he, mistaking magnanimity for weakness, had said what he had said. On his head be it: his deceptive trusting look should not save him now.

"Why don't you say something?" she demanded.

The young man gave an embarrassed laugh.

"Well, to tell the honest truth, I don't seem to think of anything to say —"

"Oh! . . . So the Settlement suggests *nothing* to you — as to picking the beam from your own eye?"

"Not at this moment, I think. In fact, I don't seem to grasp at all —"

"*Oh!*" said Cally, with a little gasp.

And then, stung on by his reckless hardihood, she struck to kill:

"How can you *look* at me, and pretend that you're so anxious to help other people's businesses, when you know you wouldn't even give to your own Settlement — *not a cent!*"

The two stood facing each other, hardly a yard apart, their eyes dead-level. V.V., as Henrietta Cooney called him, continued to look at her, and though he was far from a florid young man, it seemed now as if he must have been so, so much color did he have to lose. And Cally discovered that the man had somehow managed to keep, over all these brilliant weeks, that mysterious trick he had of making her feel unfair, and even rather horrid and common, when she knew perfectly well she wasn't. For the look on his unreliable face was that of one stabbed from behind in a company where he had trusted, and his eyes seemed to be saying to her quite distinctly: "Don't you worry about *me!* Just give me a minute or two, and *I'll* be all right. . . ."

But all that his actual voice said, in rather a remote way, was:

"What a terrific hypocrite you must think me! . . . I had n't realized . . ."

It was precisely the point that Carlisle Heth had been trying to establish, for a long, long time. Yet now, in the moment of triumph, her gaze suddenly wavered from his; and she heard herself, to her own secret confusion, saying hurriedly and weakly:

"At least, I understood — some one *told* me — you had n't. . . . Of course you — you *might* have given something, and — this person not have known. . . ."

But Jack Dalhousie's friend only answered, in the same detached way:

"It's unpardonable, my detaining you this way. I'd no idea . . . May I show you the way up —"

"No — *no!* Please wait! . . ."

He waited, silent. Carlisle, having paused long enough to take firm hold of her consciousness of vast superiorities, resumed more strongly:

"Perhaps I ought to explain why I — thought that. I was told that the whole thing had fallen through, when a — a wealthy subscriber stepped in and secretly gave a very large amount — had bought the building for you. So I — I naturally thought —"

"It was absolutely natural. In fact, it's quite true. . . . Shall we go to the meeting now?"

But no, something in her required that he must state in plain words the fact that would justify her accusation, alleged by his eyes to be so unjust: namely, that it was (practically) a member of her family who had done this splendid thing for him. Yet she went rather further than she had intended when she said, glancing away over the queer dusky court:

"I will tell you. Some one gave us to understand — not he himself, of course, — that it was a friend of ours who had done this . . . Mr. Hugo Canning."

He made no answer.

An uncontrollable desire carried the girl yet further. She said, in a weakening voice:

"*Was it?*"

In saying this, she brought her eyes back fully to her victim. And if ever guilt was written large upon a human countenance, it was upon the face of V. Vivian at that moment. Brightly flushed he was, with an embarrassment painful to witness. And yet, so strange is the way of life, the joy of victory once again seemed to slip from the clutch of Cally Heth. What house of cards was this she had pulled down upon herself?. . .

"Really, you must appreciate," the man was saying, in a light, dry voice, "I should n't feel at liberty to betray a secret of that sort, even if I knew. I'm sorry, but —"

But the girl's sickening sensations of falling through space broke out in faltering speech:

"*Oh!* . . . Do you *mean* . . ." She halted, to steady herself, and took a fresh start, no better than the first: "Do you mean — that —"

"I mean only, Miss Heth, that I have n't the slightest idea what this is all about. I thought," he said, in a voice of increasing hardness, "that we were talking of the Works. If, at another time, you can give me a few minutes —"

"Was it YOU?" said Carlisle, breaking through his defenses. . . . "Do you mean — it was YOU, all along? . . ."

"I mean nothing of any sort. Does it occur to you that these questions are quite unfair? — that they put me in a . . ."

She demanded in a small voice: "*Did you buy this house for the Settlement?*"

Shot down with the point-blank question, the tall young man, whose coat was so extremely polished at the elbows, died game, saying with sudden gentleness:

"No, it was my Uncle Armistead."

And then there was no sound but the steady beat of the rain upon sidewalk and roofs. . . .

Upstairs, just a floor and a ceiling away, Mrs. Heth, craning her neck for the last time, perceived that Cally had decided not to come to the meeting; also that it was just as well, viewing the inclement weather. Downstairs, almost directly beneath her, Cally stood front to front with the family enemy, her face quite white.

"Of course you understand," the enemy was saying, hurriedly and yet firmly too, "he gave me the money expecting it to be used for the public good. I've considered that I merely had it in trust, as a fund for — for these purposes, as I've explained. And this — well, you may easily imagine that it was the most perfect form of self-indulgence. . . . I 've gotten so fond of this old place . . . But I can't imagine how we came to be talking of it, and I beg that you'll forget the whole matter. I — my uncle would have been very much annoyed to — to have it known or talked about. . . ."

Not in that singular experience in the Cooney parlor, not even in the memorable New Year's moment in her own library, had Carlisle been swept with such a desire to dissociate herself from her own person, to sneak away from herself, to drop through the floor. Nevertheless, some dignity in her, standing fast, struck out for salvage; and out of the uprush of humiliating sensation, she heard her voice, colorless and flat:

"I'm sorry I said that. You make me . . . quite ashamed. . . ."

The flush deepened abruptly on the tall doctor's cheek.

"*Don't* say that! Don't you suppose I understand how absolutely natural it was? . . . Everybody'd have thought just the same, in your place. . . ."

Carlisle had turned away from his translucent eye, finding it unbearable; she descended from the stair, took an irresolute step or two over the ruined floor of the once stately court. And then she halted, having really nowhere to go, staring fixedly toward the distant doors. . . .

Mamma's nearness could not help her now. Hugo's fortifying love was no buffer against this extraordinary moment. All alone Cally stood with the contemned religious fellow who had unhorsed and disarmed her once again, and now there would be no more weapons. And there was a worse thing here than her mean looking for hypocrisy, and the discovery, instead, of a mad generosity, a princely folly. Bad enough all that seemed; very bad indeed: but Cally's painful moment seemed to cut deeper yet.

After all the struggling, had it come to this? Was the author of the Beach opinion of her a man whom she must greatly admire? . . .

Behind her stood the stairway, which led on up to mamma and the embracing security of the victorious order. Behind her also stood the man, the royal giver of the granary where finer-feathered birds now made merry among the spoils. With what speech should Cally Heth, mocked and jeered by her feeble " I'm sorry," turn now and pass him? . . .

She heard the sound of his unequal footstep, and then his voice behind her, stirred with a sudden feeling:

"Why, it's not a thing to be sorry about — how could you possibly have thought otherwise? . . . Don't you suppose I realize what cause I've given you to — to distrust and dislike me? You'd be more than human if you could forgive and forget — what I said to you one night. How could you, when it was so unforgivable? And since then —"

"*Don't!*" Carlisle said, in a muffled sort of voice. And then, clearly and distinctly: "Don't! . . . I can't quite stand that!"

She turned on the old floor, with the sound of her own strengthening voice, and came again face to face with the man, V. V. There had seemed to come to her a light. And back into her smooth young cheek trickled that color so loved by her betrothed, who had not bought the Settlement House after all. . . .

She was a brilliantly successful girl, the chosen wife of the most shiningly eligible of men; and he was a lame slum doctor in a worn-out suit, beneath her notice as a man altogether. And yet, as Hugo stood above her in all those material aspects which had always summed up her whole demand of life, so this man stood above her in some more subtle and mysterious way. And it had always been so: by bright swift flickers of intuition she had seemed suddenly to see that now. All the restlessness and discontent which the thought and sight of him had power to awake in her from the beginning came from just this; and she had never been able to put him down, no matter how she had chafed and denounced, because the final fact had always been that he, in his queer way, stood above her. . . .

And now, in this unsteadied moment, with all hope of bringing him down beaten finally to death, there had seemed to rise and beckon a finer way of bridging this gap between them. All that was best in the girl suddenly rose, demanding for once to be allowed to meet the shabby alien on his own reckless level.

"Look here," said Cally, with a kind of tremulous eagerness, "I want to tell you something. . . ."

Yes, surely it was all a matter between herself and him: she could meet his eyes now with no sense that did not add to her curious inner exaltation. Had not these eyes said to her from the beginning that they would give her no peace till she came to this? . . .

"You were right to say what you did that night. A puff of wind blew the boat over after he got out. Mr. Dalhousie never knew I was upset."

The words dropped unafraid into a perfect silence. The girl's manner was as simple, as undramatic, as possible. Yet, considering who these two were, considering the intentions with which she had entered his Dabney House not ten minutes before, no more startling words could have been devised by the wit of man.

"He never knew," repeated Vivian, in a voice suddenly mechanical.

No doubt it was by his good fortune alone that he had avoided any alarming change of expression, as he listened to the announcement which seemed to shake and stagger his visible world. The girl was soaring upon her unimagined moment of spiritual adventure. But V. Vivian stood like a man turned to stone, gazing blind into a void. . . .

Presently, out of the general chaos the young man's dazed mind stirred; leapt to life. Thought shook him through like waves of pain. It came upon him first, with crushing force, that this sweet-voiced girl with a face like all the angels had after all coldly lied, murderously lied, and maintained her lie through many months. Hard upon that, blotting it out, there swept the juster knowledge that, no matter what she had done, truth had triumphed at last; what was good in her had overcome her poor weakness. Lastly, he thought of Jack Dalhousie who, from the clouds, had received his release from prison. Yes, old Dal could come home now. . . .

"He never knew," said V. V., in his curious voice. "I'm so glad . . . This clears him . . . I never understood how he could have . . . I'm so glad to — have it settled. . . ."

If he was so glad, his face libelled him past forgiveness. But Cally Heth still soared, too high in the unplumbed blue to note, even now, what house was this she had destroyed.

"I really did n't realize at all at the time," she said, with the same simplicity. "It all happened so quickly, and it was so bewildering, and I did n't have time to think. The story about him just seemed to spring up of itself, and then it grew and grew all the time. I've worried a great deal about it, all along. . . ."

A kind of passion came into the man's face, and he said:

"Thank God, there's still time to make it all right."

Then his look brought her down a little. . . . "To make it all right?"

Vivian gazed down. He thought of what lay ahead for her now; and his heart seemed to turn within him. . . . However, sympathy was not desired of him: his lot was but to strengthen the hands of the brave.

"Miss Heth — indeed, I could envy you all the happiness you are going to give. Think — just think what it means . . . I know you must be eager — to begin, to —"

"To begin?" she echoed again, feeling somehow that their privacy was being invaded. "Why — what do you mean? . . . I don't understand."

"I jump ahead too fast, of course. But — you must be so anxious . . . to have it all off your mind, and not think of it any more. I know you must be impatient to get word to Dal at the first possible moment — it means so much to him. More than meat and drink. . . . And then there's his poor old father . . ."

Cally stared at him, speechless. There was no exaltation now; no more soaring. Rooted in her tracks she stood, yet seemed to herself to shrink and recoil from him, in her sudden self-horror. What, oh what, had she done?

And by chance at this very moment — doubtless through some Settlementer's opening a door for air — there came floating down to her the distinct voice of her mother, the strong voice of authority and no nonsense, the voice of Wealth and Permanence, of the victorious knowledge that God thinks twice before he condemns a person of quality. . . . "*In accepting the Chairmanship of the Finance Committee, I desire to say . . .*"

Cally raised a gloved little hand to her veiled lips. Plainer than speech her frightened eyes said: *Hast thou found me, O mine enemy?*

"You — you've misunderstood. No . . . no! I didn't mean that at all."

"Oh! . . . Do you mean — you don't wish to see Colonel Dalhousie — personally? Of course not! . . . It wouldn't be necessary in the least. Perhaps you would let me. . . . And as to a telegram to Dal —"

"*No — no!* . . . You mustn't go to see him. You mustn't send a telegram. I can't allow that — you've misunderstood entirely. *You mustn't tell anybody. . . .*"

They stared at each other with the same colorless faces, and again the rain became audible. In the man's too-confiding eyes, hope died hard.

"Not tell anybody? Why, I don't see . . . There's no other way of making it right, I'm afraid. . . . And you have told me. . . ."

"But I didn't tell you to tell anybody else. I didn't. I only meant to tell *you*, don't you see? . . ."

This subtlety was past the vision of the donator of the Dabney House. North, south, east, or west, he could see nothing but a seraph-faced girl whose misery it was to feel the penitential pangs, yet not be able quite to rise to the fulness of reparation. That she had reached for that fulness was to him the one thing certain in all the world. What want of delicacy in him had caused her to falter and look backward? . . .

Into the lucid gray of his eyes had come that look which

more than once before Carlisle Heth had found intolerable. Little she recked for it now. Was not this the heart of her present dilemma, that she had already followed his ocular incitements too fatally far? By what religious prestidigitation he had trapped her secret from her must remain a thick mystery now. Nothing mattered but that he, having deceitfully seemed to agree that it was all a matter between herself and him, should not now turn and betray her. . . . *Tell now?* The sudden vista of scandal horrified her. How would she ever face mamma again? How would Hugo, whose bride and pride she was, regard her then? . . .

"Don't you see?" she said, with gathering tensity — "I — I meant it as *a confidence to you*. You must n't dream of telling anybody else. . . ."

"But neither you nor I own the truth. This belongs to Dalhousie. . . ."

"Oh, it does n't! — it does n't! How can you! You misunderstand! — What I said to you gave you a totally wrong impression. He was entirely to blame for my upsetting. *Entirely!* He behaved abominably — and I —"

"*Tell now!*" cried the man, with his strange stern passion. "Once it 's done, you'll always be glad. Don't you know you *must*, now! Don't you see you can't be happy, till you let the truth be known? . . ."

There came from above the unmistakable movement of chairs, the sound of many feet. It appeared that the Settlement meeting was breaking up. The man's entreaties bounded back dead.

"I could n't! — Don't you understand? There 's nothing to tell. It was not my fault. The story was distorted, distorted, and distorted! I regretted that as much as any one. But I could do nothing, nothing to stop it. And don't you understand I could n't possibly tell this broadcast *now*, when it 's been done with for *months!* What would people think of me? Don't you —"

"What will you have to think of yourself if you don't tell?"

But the hard shot missed fire, the reason being that what she thought of herself did not matter in the least just now. She was mamma's daughter, Hugo Canning's betrothed, fighting for her own: and now that movement upstairs warned her that she had no moment to lose.

Carlisle seized the slum doctor's arm with a resolute little hand. Her voice, though panicky, was as inexorable as mamma's own.

"Promise me," said she, "that you will never repeat to anybody what I told you in confidence."

The face of the young man, which was usually so harmless-looking, had suddenly become quite stern. He looked as if he might ask God to pity her again, given a very little more. When he spoke, he spoke brusquely:

"What you ask is a conspiracy of silence. I cannot make such a promise. I cannot."

"Oh, how *can* you be so hard! You've never meant anything but trouble to me since the first minute I saw you! It is n't fair, don't you see it is n't? This has happened so suddenly — I *must* have time to think. Promise that you won't say anything — at least till you hear from me again. . . ."

Silence. And then V. Vivian said, in a suddenly hopeless voice:

"I will agree to say nothing without first seeing you. . . ."

Cally Heth dropped his arm instantly, turned from him. She fled, not up the grand stairway, but over the court for the doors, with the protecting arms of the House of Heth beyond. And none of her other routs from the family enemy had been quite like this one.

XVIII

Night-Thoughts on the Hardness of Religious Fellows, compelling you to be Hard, too; Happier Things again, such as Hugo, Europe, Trousseaux, etc.; concluding with a Letter from Texas and a Little Vulgarian in a Red Hat.

THE tireless William retraced the wet streets to the Dabney House in ample time for Mrs. Heth, but the Chairman of the Finance Committee, being in agreeable converse with fellow philanthropists, came home in Mrs. Byrd's car instead, after all. Accordingly she did not say to William, "Miss Carlisle decided not to come, Banks?" — which she liked to call William for the English sound of it — and Banks, or William, did not look respectfully surprised and say, "Yas'm, she came. . . ."

Arriving at home, the good little lady presently ascended to the third floor, where she entered her daughter's room without knocking, according to her wont. However, Carlisle had been ready for her for some time.

"You stayed," was mamma's arch conjecture, "to write a ream to Hugo, dear fellow, I suppose? . . ."

"No, I went!" said Cally, now in the last stages of an evening toilette. "Only when I got there, and peeped in, it all looked so dreary and hopeless that my heart failed me, and I turned right around and came back! Was it —"

"You did! How long were you there? There's a little too much powder on your nose, my dear — there! Did you come upstairs?"

"Oh, no! I just slipped in for a moment or two and glanced about that queer old court downstairs. Quaint and interesting, is n't it? How was the meeting?"

"Most interesting and gratifying," said mamma, sinking into a rose-lined chair. "We begin a noble work. You may go now,

Flora. I am made a governor, as well as chairman of the most important committee. . . ."

She monologized for some time, in a rich vein of reminiscence and autobiography, revealing among other things that she had rather broadly hinted, to Mrs. Byrd and others, who was the anonymous donor of the Settlement House; a certain wealthy New Yorker, to wit. However, it was clear that she saw nothing amiss, nor did she say anything more germane to her daughter's inner drama than, in the moment of parting:

"Rub your cheeks a little with the soft cloth. You look quite pale."

Carlisle rubbed faithfully, aware of a lump of lead where her heart should have been. Later she went downstairs, and then on for dinner at the McVeys'. Most grateful she was for this mental distraction; to-night she would have played three-hand bridge with papa and Mattie Allen with enthusiasm.

Evey's dinner, of course, was far ahead of three-hand. The McVeys were very rich, far richer than the Heths (theirs had been the marriage of McVey's Drygoods and Notions, Wholesale Only, and Herkimer's Fresh Provisions), and were considered "not quite" by some people, though Evey certainly went everywhere and was very refined. Accordingly, the evening's viands were of the best and the table talk at least good enough for all practical purposes. Carlisle, who was almost feverishly animated, lingered till the last possible moment: Evey actually asked her to spend the night, and she actually came very near doing it. Escorted home in a maritime hackney-coach by young Mr. Robert Tellford (whose heart had been lacerated by rumors that persistently reached him), Canning's betrothed permitted Robert to linger in the library, positively detained him in the library, till eleven-thirty o'clock: courtesies which would have run like wine to the young Tellford head but for the lady's erratic and increasing distraitness. . . .

The bibulous metaphor is here reversible. It possessed mutuality, so to say. Cally herself would drown trouble to-night with intoxicating draughts of human society. But there came a time when this resource was denied her; when the human bars closed, as it were; in short, when all the society in reach must sorrowfully put on his tall hat and go. And then there came the nocturnal stillness of the house, and then the solitariness of the bedchamber, and after that the dark.

Now the question that had rumbled all evening cloud-like in the background of her consciousness, swam and took shape in the midnight shadows, dangling before the eye of her mind in gigantic and minatory capitals:

WOULD HE TELL?

To this stark inquiry all the girl's problem came down. Gone like a fever-mist was the emotional flare-up (as mamma would have said) which had tricked her into blurting out a secret scarcely even formulated before in her own inmost soul. That mysterious moment remained merely as an astonishment. It was the strangest thing that had ever happened to her; she had simply been swept away by some unfathomable madness. And at present Nature's first law was working in her with obliterating force. *Would the man tell?* Here in the sane and ordered surroundings, with mamma sleeping and satisfied one floor below, and a long, long letter to be written to her knight among men the first thing to-morrow, there was nothing in the world that mattered but that. If Vivian would not tell, then, indeed, all was well with her. If he did tell . . .

He had said that he would not tell without first seeing her. But of course there was nothing under heaven to prevent his seeing her, or sending word to her, at any time, by day or by night. And then what?

Carlisle lay upon her back, rather small and frightened in the tall bed, struggling to pluck away the veil from the face of the menacing future. What would "telling" mean, exactly? . . .

There was a hopeful view. The whole thing was so confused, just as he himself had admitted, more than once. It might all be put on the ground of a mistake, a little misunderstanding, recently discovered. You could tell, and not go into all the mixed-up details. Jack Dalhousie would then gratefully return from

Texas (where he was really getting on much better than he had ever done at home — Dr. Vivian had practically said so); his father would quietly take him back; and it would be generally understood that Jack was not a coward now, and was greatly improved morally by the disciplinary exile, and everything would be all right. But of course the difficulty here was that somebody (like Colonel Dalhousie, for instance) might think to ask why the discovery of the little misunderstanding came now, instead of six months ago. You could hardly reply to such an one that you had just discovered the mistake as the result of a flareup, caused by a slum doctor's giving twenty-five thousand dollars to buy an old hotel. Who would understand that, when you did n't yourself? . . .

Carlisle, indeed, being a practical girl, did not linger long on the optimistic prospect. For to-night at least, "telling" seemed a matter too dreadful to contemplate. Colonel Dalhousie was an irascible and solitary widower with one son whom he had once been proud of; and this son, having been strangely compelled to take a lady's word as to his own conduct, had been disgraced by that word, cast out with his father's curse upon his forehead. Was it likely that these two would take the discovery of a little misunderstanding now with a charming quiet courtesy? — that, shouting the discovery abroad to save their faces, they would have due regard for careful qualifications and for striking the right note? The reply was the negative: it was not at all likely.

Cally knew the world's rough judgments, where all is black or all is white, and ifs and buts go overboard as spoiling the strong color scheme. And well she knew the way of horrid gossip; none better. That she, Carlisle Heth, had deliberately lied merely to save her name from public association with young Dalhousie's, and by this lie had ruined a boy who in his way had loved her well: such would be the story which the angry Colonel (perhaps coming to shoot papa besides) would throw to the four winds, to be rolled in the mouth of gossip forevermore. O what a tasty morsel was here, my countrymen! . . .

Staring fearfully into the dusk, Carlisle pictured herself as hearing such a story about Evey or Mattie: she perceived at once, with sickening sensations, how intensely she would be interested in it. Yes; once started, it would sweep through drawing-rooms and clubs like fire. With what glee would the world's coarse tongue make its reprisals upon brilliant success! Town-talk the lovely Miss Heth would be, spotted all over with that horrid tattle from which she (and Hugo) had ever so shuddered and shrunk. . . .

And against this threatened avalanche, entailing who knew what consequences, she had but the frail shield of the sense of honor — well, then, say, the sense of chivalry — of a man far beneath her world, whom she had frequently told herself that she disliked and despised.

A pale yellow ray of the moon, journeying upward over the coverlet, fell across her face. She rose, pattered on slim bare feet over the chequered floor, lowered the shade. Inside and out, all the world was still. Cally dropped down on her chaise-longue by the window, very wide awake. . . . And, gradually, since she was practical, she formed a plan of action: a plan so simple that she wondered she had not thought of it at once. . . .

A long time she had spent in trying to think how she might compel, cajole, or bribe the man at the Dabney House to pledge her his eternal silence. But she had not been able to think of any promising way: each time, she brought up confronting with painful fascination the conviction that religious fellows were hard. And out of this conviction there grew, in time, her own resolve. Well, then, she would be hard, too. She would avoid seeing or having any communication with Dr. Vivian, and if he dared to repeat *anything*, she would simply laugh it all aside. She would deny that she ever said any such preposterous thing in her life. She would *have* to do that; her duty to others demanded it. . . . And what could he do then? It would merely be his word against hers, Miss Heth's. He would be left in a most unpleasant position. . . .

In this position V. Vivian remained while Carlisle slept. However, the new day, as it pleasantly proved, brought no need for such severe measures. Many rings at doorbell and telephone

Cally's strained ears heard between getting up and bedtime, but the hard ring of Nemesis was never among them. All day silence brooded unbroken in the direction of the Dabney House. And when another morning wore to evening, and no heart brake, and yet another and another, there descended again upon the girl the peaceful sense of re-won security. . . .

In these days the House of Heth was in a continual bustle. On Tuesday next — a week to a day from the Settlement meeting — the ladies were to depart for New York, Hugo, and Europe, the Trousseau and the Announcement, to return no more till mid-September. On the same day the titular master of the house was to go off for a five days' fishing junket, thence flying to New York for the "seeing off," and soon thereafter starting out for a three weeks' business trip to the Far West. Along with the various domestic problems raised by this programme, there were all the routine duties of the season to be attended to. Cold-weather things must still be salted down with camphor balls and packed away; costly pictures provided with muslin wrappers; drawing-room furniture with linen slip-covers; rooms cleaned and locked up, doors and windows screened and awninged. Mrs. Heth went dashing from one bit of generalship to another, and tele-phoned ten thousand times a day. Nevertheless she kept eyes in her head, and accordingly she observed to Mr. Heth one starlit night, as they sat *à deux* on the little front balcony where flower-ing window-boxes so refinedly concealed one from the public view:

"I never saw a girl so absolutely naïve about showing her feel-ings. She began to droop the minute he left the house, and has n't been her natural self since. . . . Irritable! — till you can't say good morning without her snapping your head off."

"Maybe, it's the weather," suggested Mr. Heth, who wore a white flannel suit and fanned himself with a dried palm-leaf. "And I reckon, too, she's feeling sorry to leave her old father for such a long time. Four months — hio!"

"Cally's not the girl to get black rings under her eyes for things like that."

She added presently: "It's a pure love-match, which is naturally a gratification to me, who brought the whole thing about. 'Thank God, Cally, you've got a mother,' I said to her only the other day. But I do say there's such a thing as carrying love just a little too far."

Cally, meantime, while affecting no interest in summer clothes for chairs, kept as closely occupied with her own affairs, social activities and preparations for the brilliant absence, as mamma did with hers. Much time went, too, to her correspondence with Canning, who wrote her daily fat delightful letters, all breathing ardent anticipation of her approaching visit in his own city. And back to Canning, she wrote even fatter letters every morning in mamma's sitting-room, dear letters (he thought them) in which she told him every single thing except what she was really thinking about. . . .

And why should n't she tell Hugo that also? Once or twice she really came very near doing it. For as her mind had become released from her first acute apprehensions, it had seemed to insist on turning inward a little; and there grew within her a sense of unhappiness, of loneliness, a feeling of her poor little self against the world. She longed for some one to explain it all to, to justify herself before; and who more appropriate in this connection than her lover? That Hugo might have been shocked, and perhaps disgusted, to have the misunderstanding discovered to him by way of the Dalhousies' megaphone was, indeed, likely; but to have her quietly tell it to him, as it really happened, with the proper stress on circumstances and gossip, would be quite another matter. She felt almost certain that he would agree with her at once that it would be a great mistake to rake up all this now, when it had all blown over and Dalhousie was doing so splendidly down in Texas. . . .

However, Cally procrastinated. And then, Sunday morning in church, as she sat pensively wishing for a confidant, it came upon her somewhat startlingly that she already had one: Dr. Vivian was her confidant. Did he not know more about her than anybody else in the world? . . .

The simple thought seemed to cure her instantly of her wish. She had tried having a confidant and it had brought her to this;

henceforward let her keep her own counsel. (So she mused, walking homeward in the brilliant sunshine and light airs with J. Forsythe Avery, who had just conquered his pique over his rejection last January.) That her one confidant's honorable silence expressed his trust that she herself would "tell" was possibly true; but that, in this no-quarter conflict between them, was merely so much the worse for him. She would not think of him at all. She had run away from him every time she had seen him; now she had but to do it once more, and all would be as if it had never been. . . .

At the Sabbath dinner-table, which was to-day uninvaded by guests, the Heths' talk was animated. The imminent separation brought a certain softness into the family atmosphere; papa basked in it. He had spent his Sunday morning playing sixteen holes of golf at the Country Club, and would have easily made the full round but for slicing three new balls into the pond on the annoying seventeenth drive. This had provoked him into smashing his driver, as he had a score of only eighty-eight at that point, which was well below his personal bogey. Even mamma affected interest in her spouse's explanations of how it all happened.

"Of course the caddy simply slipped the balls in his pockets the minute your back was turned — they 're all thieves, the little ragamuffins," said she. "And, by the way, I have n't telephoned the bank about the silver."

Encouraged by his ladies' consideration, Mr. Heth proposed a little afternoon jaunt with Cally.

"It 's too pretty a day to stay in," said he. "Let 's take the car, eh, and run down and look at that new cantilever bridge at Apsworth?"

"Oh, papa!" said Cally, regretfully. "I promised Mr. Avery I 'd take a walk with him. He looked so fat and forlorn I did n't have the heart to refuse. I 'm so sorry."

Mr. Heth started to quote something about your daughter's being your daughter, but when Cally added, "You know I 'd lots rather go with you, papa," he changed his mind, and went off to his nap instead.

Mamma similarly departed. Cally, not feeling nappy, sat in

the library and wrote to her lover the last letter but one she would write before seeing him in New York. Her eager pen flew: but so did the minutes also, or did the impetuous Avery anticipate the moment of his engagement? His tender ring broke unexpectedly across her betrothal thoughts, and Cally returned to earth with a start . . . Good *heavens!* Four o'clock already!—and she with twenty minutes' getting ready to do!

She caught up the pages of the unfinished letter, and skipped for the stairs. In the hall there was unbroken quiet, with no sound of a servant coming. Cally paused, listening, and then remembered that it was Sunday afternoon, when even the best Africans are so very likely to have "just stepped out." Why wait? The girl went and opened the door herself, a smile of greeting in her eye, a lively apology for her obvious unreadiness upon her lip.

However, it was not, after all, the amorous Mr. Avery who confronted her. The vestibule held only an ill-dressed young girl, in a gaudy red hat, the sort of looking person who should at most have rung the basement bell, if that: and she herself seemed to realize this by the guilty little start and tremble she gave when the stately door swung open upon her. The young mistress of the house eyed her doubtfully.

"Good afternoon."

"G-good evenin', ma'am! . . ."

As she seemed at a loss how to proceed, Carlisle said: "Yes? What is it?"

The young person raised a bare hand and brushed it, with a strange gesture, before her eyes.

"Dr. Vivian he told me to give you this note, ma'am."

She added, as if suddenly moved to destroy a possible impression of Dr. Vivian as a slave-driver, flinging orders this way and that:

"He'd of brung it himself, on'y I was going walkin' myself, ma'am, and asked him to leave me take it."

If the fall was from the height of the securest moment Carlisle had known since her self-betrayal, the more stunning was the impact. Her heart appeared to abdicate its duties, with one kick; all her being drew together in a knot within her. It had come, after all. To run away was well, but she had not run soon enough. . . .

She received the note mechanically, saying: "Very well."

"Would you wish me to wait for a nanser, ma'am? Doctor he did n't say . . ."

In heaven or earth, what answer would she find to this?

"No, you need n't wait."

"Do you feel faint, ma'am?"

"Faint? . . . No, why should I?"

The young person, convicted of impertinence and silliness besides, turned red, but would not remove her gaze from the lady's face.

"The — the heat we been'havin', ma'am. I don't know — it's so sickenin', kind of. I — I fainted last week, twice, ma'am."

Something nameless in the little creature's wide-eyed gaze, timid and yet thrilled, arrested Carlisle in the act of shutting the door upon her. Was it possible that this singular messenger of Fate had knowledge of the message she brought?

"Why do you stare at me so?"

The girl replied with simplicity:

"I can't help it, ma'am, you look so sweet."

Carlisle leaned against the polished edge of the glass and oak door. The same chill little hand clenched the unfinished pages to Hugo, and Vivian's only too fatally finished note. She perceived who this girl must be, and even in this moment her thought was riveted by the wild suspicion that her secret had already been betrayed.

"You live at the Dabney House, I suppose? — you're a buncher at the Works? . . . How did you know me — that this note was for me?"

Here was a puzzler, indeed. By what instinct had little Kern known, the instant the door began to open, that this, and no other, was Mr. V. V.'s beautiful lady? . . .

"How could you be anybody else, ma'am? . . . You could n't."

"I believe I have heard Dr. Vivian speak of you. Possibly," she said, with stony bitterness, "you have heard of me in the same way?"

The girl seemed to shrink a little at her tone. "Oh, ma'am — no! To *me!* No, ma'am! He *would n't* . . ."

"But he is a great friend of yours?"

Kern raised a hand to her heart, understanding only too much that was not so. It was a glorious moment for her, and a terrible one.

"No, ma'am," said she, shaking her head a number of times. "I'm only his charity sick."

She added, as if to make the repudiation complete: "Mr. V. V.'s friends are ladies, ma'am."

"Mr. V. V.?"

Confronted by her damning slip, the young person turned scarlet, but she stood her ground with a little gasp.

"A nickname, ma'am, that *all* his sick call him by. . . ."

A fair enough rally, no doubt, but on the whole it accomplished nothing. Just in the middle of it, the lady had shut the door in the small vulgarian's face.

Carlisle clutched the two letters to her breast. The door having been shut, she was alone in the world. She went up two flights in the Sunday afternoon stillness, and locked herself in her room. Mamma should not enter here on her gliding heels.

So this, after all, was what he meant by "seeing." Having decoyed her with false hopes for five days, he struck from ambush, giving her no chance to speak for herself. Well, she would be hard, too. She would make no answer, and when he spoke, she would deny . . .

That the worst had now come to the worst, she had not entertained a doubt. Accordingly the emotional revulsion was strong when, breaking open the envelope with cold fingers, Carlisle found that the letter within was in a different handwriting from the superscription. It was not from Dr. Vivian at all.

However, her instant uprush of relief was somewhat mitigated when she saw — as she did in the first glance, for this hand had been not unfamiliar to her once — that the letter Vivian enclosed to her was from Jack Dalhousie.

Standing rigid by the window, she read with parted lips:

DEAR V. V.:

I'd have answered your letter earlier only I have n't had any heart for writing letters. Fate has knocked me out again. God knows I've tried, and cut out the drink, and worked hard, and suffered agonies of the damned, but it does n't do any good. The world is n't big enough for people like me to hide in, and the only thing I can't understand is why people like me are ever born. What's the use of it all, V. V., I can't see to save my life. The trouble all came from a fellow named Bellows, from home, a machinery salesman with T. B. Wicke Sons, you may know him, who dropped off the train here a week ago Saturday.

He saw me on the street one day, and then he went and told everybody that I was in Texas because I'd been drummed from home. Said I went out rowing with a girl and upset her and then swam off for my skin and she was nearly drowned. I've made some good friends here — or had made them, I'd better say — and one of them rode out to our place and said I ought to know what Bellows was saying, so I could thrash him before he skipped town. Oh, what could I say.

Then I saw Miss Taylor just now, she's the girl from the East I mentioned in the winter, and she asked me had I heard what they were saying. I wanted to lie to her, and she'd have believed me if I had, but you could n't lie to her, and so I said straight out I was crazy drunk at the time and did n't know what I was doing, but I guessed most of it was true. She cares a lot about those things, and I think she'd been crying. God help me. So now everything's changed here; it reminds me of home the way people look at me. Miss Taylor was the worst, she's been so fine to me. She said come to see her in two or three days, when she'd had time to think, and if she casts me off, I can't stand it here any longer, and I don't see how I can begin all over again, just when life was seeming as if it might be worth while again.

So now, you see, V. V., why I was n't prompter answering your letter. I've tried to keep my courage up like you advised, but it's too much for one man to carry. May you never know the awful feeling that you're an outcast, not wanted anywhere, is the wish of

Your unhappy friend,   DAL.

P. S. How's father, do you ever see him these days?
Don't let him know any of this.

The girl looked through the rose-flowered curtains down into
the sunny street. . . .

Dalhousie had long since become but a shadow and a name to
Cally; she had willed it so, and so it had been. Now, in his own
poor scrawl, the ghost of a lover too roughly discarded rose and
walked again. And beneath the cheap writing and the unre-
strained self-pity, she seemed to plumb for the first time the
depths of the boy's present misery. The old story, having struck
him down once, had hunted him out and struck him down
again. Where now would he hide? . . .

The too reminiscent letter had come with the inopportunity
of destiny. A little more pressure and she was done for.

But this was mere mad folly. To shake it off at once, Cally
began to walk about her bedchamber. Nothing had really happened that had not been true all along. She wished more than
ever that it had all been started differently, but it was too late to
consider that now. She must think of herself, and of Hugo and
mamma. Dalhousie's friend had done his worst, and she could
still withstand it. Once in New York, once in Europe, and all
would be as it had been before. . . .

Nevertheless, she was presently weak enough to open the
letter again. Now her eye fell upon two lines written in the
margin at the top of the first page, which she had missed before.
They were in the writing of the envelope, and read:

You can reach me at any time, day or night, through
Meeghan's Grocery — Jefferson 4127.

The words sprang up at her, and she stared back at them fascinated. The man at the Dabney House was certain that she
would tell now. He thought the resolution might come on her
suddenly, as in the night. Nominally, he left it to her; yet at the
same time he contrived to make her feel caught in a trap, with
no alternative, with this sense of enormous pressure upon her.

She remembered the man's strange, stern words to her: "You can't be happy now, till you let the truth be known."

All at once it seemed almost as if there were some one in the room with her. She looked around hastily: but of course there was no one. She became very much frightened. . . .

There came a knock on the door, and a voice:

"Genaman in the parlor to see you, Miss Cyahlile. Mist' Avery."

"I can't come down."

"Ma'am?"

"Say I'm not well and am lying down."

In the hall below, the parlormaid Annie encountered Mrs. Heth, waked from her nap by the two rings at the bell. Mrs. Heth ascended to Carlisle's room and rattled the knob.

"Cally? . . . Why, your door's locked!"

The door opened, and Carlisle confronted her mother with a white tremulous face.

"What's the matter?" said Mrs. Heth, gliding in with an expression of maternal solicitude. "Annie said you were n't well and were lying down."

"I'm not well . . . Mamma, let's go to New York to-morrow."

"Go *to-morrow!* . . . Why, *what's* the matter?"

"Nothing. Only I — I'm so tired of being at home."

Then her strained stiffness broke abruptly, and she flung her arms around her mother's neck with an hysterical abandon by no means characteristic.

"Oh, I can't stand it here another day. *I* can't! Please, please, mamma! It must be not having Hugo. I can't explain — it's just the way I feel. I'm so miserable here, I could die. *Please*, mamma! . . ."

Mrs. Heth, detecting with alarm the incipiences of a dangerous flare-up, said with startling gentleness:

"There, there, dear! Mamma will arrange it as you wish."

XIX

How it is One Thing to run away from yourself, and another to escape; how Cally orders the Best Cocktails, and gazes at her Mother asleep; also of Jefferson 4127, and why Mamma left the Table in a hurry at the Café des Ambassadeurs.

MAMMA arranged it, by Amazonian effort. New York, the colossal, received the runaway with an anonymous roar, asking no questions. Here, in the late afternoon of the first day, safe forever in a well-furnished room on a seventeenth floor, Cally Heth made her answer to Dalhousie's letter. She formally cremated the scrawl in a pink saucer which had previously been doing nothing more useful in the world than holding up a toothbrush mug.

The cremation was a rite in its way, yet required only the saucer and two matches. The letter, when well torn, flamed nicely, only a few scraps holding out against immediate combustion. There was one little fragment on top, observable from the beginning; it read:

or night
fferson 4127

These topmost bits refused to respond to poking with the burnt match, and finally demanded a new match all to themselves. Within two minutes all were reduced to fine ashes, which the priestess of the rite duly took to the window, and scattered down into the "court." Then she washed her hands, put the saucer back under the mug, and raised another window to let out the smell.

This business completed, Carlisle glanced at her watch. It was ten minutes past six, or nearly time to begin to dress. The moment was an interlude in a day which had been full of exciting activity, keyed with the joy of journey's end and lovers' meeting. An evening in similar titillating vein waited just ahead. At this moment, Canning, bidden *au revoir* some ten minutes ago, was doubtless dressing at his club, seven blocks away. Mrs. Heth, left to her own resources all afternoon, had fallen asleep in her chair, and still slept. Even the maid Flora was absent, having been given the afternoon off, after unpacking two trunks, to " git to see " her uncle, a personage of authority who served his country well by sorting letters in the New York Post-Office.

Alone in the hotel bedroom, Carlisle looked in the mirror of the mahoganized "dresser," occupied in taking off her veil and hat, and thought that Flora ought to be coming back now. Then she sniffed a little and was aware of a memorial smell from the rite. After that her mind appeared to float away for a time, and when she caught up with it again, it was thinking:

Nothing so much could really have happened, if I *had* told.

It was an academic thought for a mind which must have known very well that everything was settled now. Carlisle, assuming charge herself, promptly turned it out. Having put her hat on the bed, she began to busy herself with preparations for the evening. Flora lingering at her avuncular pleasures, she herself went to the closet and took down a dress. A capable girl she was, who could easily get out her own clothes when absolutely necessary.

Canning was dining the two ladies at the resplendent establishment of his choice, at seven-thirty o'clock; he was due to return in an hour now. All day he had been in attendance, and all day he had been the very prince of lovers. Having lunched with Mrs. Heth and Carlisle at their hotel, he and his betrothed had spent the whole afternoon together jogging about the Maytime park in a hansom-cab, — such was her whim, — with late tea at the Inn of renown upon the Drive: and through all, such talk as sped the hours on wings. How fascinating he was, she seemed to have forgotten, in these days of absence and worry. And how strong and all-conquering! — a man of such natural lordliness of mien that cabmen and policemen, proud men and strangers as they were, spoke to him with something akin to respect.

Yes, Hugo was, indeed, a rock and tower of strength. With him behind her, she had the world at her feet. . . . Heavens! What could gossip possibly do to Mrs. Hugo Canning?

Outside was the roar of conglomerate humanity. Up here in this strange bedroom, indifferent host to a thousand transient souls, it was quiet and even a little lonely. Once more Carlisle caught her mind at its retrospective misbehavior, and once more turned the key on it. Having laid out her dress on the bed, she stood and looked down into the cheerless light-well a minute, and then decided to wake up her mother. But she stopped on the way and turned back. Why wake up mamma half an hour too soon, just to hear the sound of one's own voice?

She took off her watch, and raised her hands to begin unfastening her waist. But she became engrossed in staring back at her reflection in the mirror, and presently her hands dropped.

Face and form, background and destiny, she was possessed of blessings many and obvious: all crowned now, sealed and stamped, with the love of Hugo Canning, which, he had pledged himself, was a love which should not die. What girl so entirely successful as she? Convincingly the excellent glass gave back the presentment of loveliness endowed with all the gifts of Fortune.

And yet she had run away: there was no evading that. An insignificant boy thousands of miles away had sent out a cry for help, and she, the proud and blessed, who had always considered herself quite as spunky as another person, had bolted in a panic. And she had bolted too fast, it seemed, to consider even that, with that cry, there had come a new element into the situation, disturbing to the old argument. The full reach and meaning of Jack Dalhousie's letter seemed to be coming upon her now for the first time, just when she had ritually cremated it. Out of the pink saucer had mysteriously blown the knowledge that the author of that poor composition could no more be pictured as doing splendidly down in Texas. . . .

For a third time her over-mind spied upon and detected the nether's treason; and this time Cally, turning abruptly from the mirror, was troubled. Having run away, could she not at least enjoy a runaway's peace? Why backward glances now? She had escaped Dalhousie. She had escaped Dalhousie's friend. She stood in this room the safest person in the world. No one on earth could betray her except herself.

The watch ticked loud, steadily drawing Hugo, and mamma and Flora. Up through the windows came the twilight and the rumble of the vast heedless city. Carlisle snapped on the lights. And then all at once, without warning, there closed down upon her an enormous depression, a sense as of standing on the brink of irretrievable disaster. Or it was as if she had run away, indeed, but had not escaped. Or as if, in cutting herself off from the past, she had cut away something important, which something here gave notice that it would not be peacefully abandoned. And mixed with this there was again that sense of large pressure upon her, so tangible that it was almost like a person in the room with her, sharing, dominating her councils. . . .

She was far from understanding these feelings, but she did understand that she felt suddenly sickish and quite faint; and she thought practically of mamma's little flask of brandy in her bag somewhere, if only she could find it. Then speculations on this point vanished with the recollection that she stood in the modern Arabian Nights, all the resources of the world at her beck.

Cally stepped to the telephone and called down in a small but authoritative voice:

"Send me up a cocktail at once, please. Room 1704."

"Yes, mum," replied the experienced voice far below. "What kind would you wish?"

"Oh . . . the best," said she, less authoritatively; and then rang off hurriedly, thinking how funny it was that she couldn't produce the name of a cocktail when needed, since papa shook one up for himself nearly every evening, and Hugo always ordered them when they dined together, and laughed at the little faces she made. . . .

The cocktail came, on rubber heels, and she sipped it, walking about the room and not thinking at all about dressing. A spoonful or so of the yellow concoction, and the sickish feeling vanished, and she felt instead rather devilish and fast, like the blondined villainess in a play. She was a daring woman of the new school, a Woman with a Past, who rang up hotel bars and ordered the best cocktails sent up at once. . . .

Possibly the cocktail had this moral reaction, that she no

longer sought to discipline her mind. She sipped the drink gingerly, and her thought fluttered backward and forward, full of contradictions and repetitions, as thought is in life, but now free. . . . Suppose, after all, that her past was not escaped? It was n't such an easy thing to do, it seemed. Dalhousie thought he had escaped his, but it had run him down at last, way off in Texas. Suppose Dr. Vivian now decided (in view of her being a fugitive) that it was his duty to lay the matter before Colonel Dalhousie, and the tempestuous Colonel took the next train. . . .

There was a knock at the door, causing her to start violently, and spill some of the cocktail. However, it was not Colonel Dalhousie, but only the maid Flora, who entered with that air of eager hurry so characteristic of an habitually tardy race. It appeared that the infernal powers had conspired against her promptitude in the shape of a blockade, not to mention losing her way through the malicious misdirection of a white man selling little men that danced on a string. . . .

Having learned further that the postal uncle was poly las' month but tollable now, Flora's young mistress said:

"We must dress in a hurry now, Flora. It's quarter to seven."

And then she went on through to the sitting-room of the suite, to wake her mother, thinking: "I can't go on this way the rest of my life, jumping out of my skin every time there's a knock. . . . What on earth have I been so afraid of? . . . "

Mrs. Heth slept on in her deep-bosomed chair, undisturbed by the click of switch or burst of light into her enveloping dusk. She had a magazine, face downward, in her lap; also a one-pound box of mixed chocolates, open. Her head had fallen upon her chair-back; a position which brought the strange dark little mustache into prominence, and also threw into relief the unexpected heaviness of the jaw and neck. The face of an indomitable creature, certainly, of one of those fittest to survive; but not exactly a spiritual face, perhaps, hardly a face finely sensitive to immaterial values. . . .

To gaze at a person who is unaware of being watched may be worse than eavesdropping. Arrested in the act of waking her mother, Carlisle stood for some moments looking down at her. What was there lacking in mamma that you could n't ever talk things over with her? Upon the unconscious face it was plainly inscribed that this lady would stand against telling to the last ditch. Somehow the knowledge brought the daughter no comfort. . . .

And now that she stopped to consider in calm security, what, really, if she did send Vivian a little note just before she sailed, authorizing him to tell? What had she, of all people, to fear from the clacking tattle of a few old cats? Suppose, to-morrow, she calmly said to Hugo and mamma, "I've felt all along that I did him an injustice, and now that I know he 's so unhappy, I want to set it straight." What, really, could they say that would be so bad? If there was a price for telling, it appeared now that there was a price also for not telling.

Minutes passed . . .

And then at the shake, Mrs. Heth stirred, turned, rolled a little, and opened her eyes with a start and a blink.

"I must have dropped asleep," said she.

"No!" said Cally; and she gave a sudden gay burst of laughter.

"I don't see anything so funny in that," said Mrs. Heth, yawning and sitting up. "What time is it?"

"I think it 's a perfect scream, and it 's nearly seven, and Hugo will be here at quarter past, punctually. *Now* will you fly?"

"You might have waked me a little earlier. Good gracious! . . . How long have you been in? Anything happen while I napped?"

"Not a single, solitary, blessed thing. . . . There you are! — Easy does it!"

"I'll be dressed long before you are now," was the maternal retort, accompanied by a long stretch.

And, though unchallenged, she was as good as her word. Highly efficient at the toilet as elsewhere, she required small assistance from Flora, whom she dispatched to tidy up the sitting-room instead. The good little lady was armed cap-a-pie by seven-fifteen, at which time a glance into Carlisle's room revealed much backwardness there, not concealed by the appearances of haste. Hugo would have to wait, that was clear; and just as it was clear, up Mr. Canning's name came skipping from the office.

In the tidied-up sitting-room Mrs. Heth entertained her distinguished son-to-be, during the little delay. She always enjoyed a good talk with Hugo. He was her pledge of a well-spent life, her Order of Merit, her V. C. and Star and Garter, rolled together in a single godlike figure. She beamed upon him, tugging at white gloves half a size too small. Canning tapped a well-shod foot with his walking-stick, and wished for his love.

The wish grew by what it fed on, and the banquet ran long. Half an hour passed before the door from Mrs. Heth's bedroom opened and Carlisle appeared. However, she looked worth waiting for. She shimmered a moment from the threshold, and the two in the sitting-room thought together that they had never seen her so radiantly lovely.

"I made her!" thought Mrs. Heth.

"Mine!" thought Canning.

And Cally thought, her eyes upon her lover: "*Me afraid! . . .*"

"My dear Cally! Really, I can say nothing for you but better late than never," said mamma.

"Salutations!" said Hugo, rising. "And by Jove! What a perfectly stunning dress!"

"Oh, do you like it?" said Carlisle, trailing forward, her eyes shining. "Then you won't scold, will you, if my watch *was* a trifle slow! And I should have been ready hours ago, even at that, but for Flora's over-staying at her uncle's. Tell Mr. Canning, Flora, was n't it all your fault?"

And Flora, having followed her young mistress in with the carriage-cloak, giggled into her hand as at a royal jest and said yas'm, it certny was. . . .

In holiday vein the trio departed from the suite, dropped sixteen stories in the lift, and presently came by taxicab to the Café des Ambassadeurs, where had taken place the memorable dinner for two, just two months ago to a night. . . .

Here all was glittering and gay. The Ambassadeurs, pending the arrival of something newer, was on the pinnacle of expensive popularity. At this hour everything was in fullest swing, and the impressive looking major-domo was shaking his head without hope to arriving applicants who had not ordered a table beforehand, as Hugo had done by messenger.

The Heth ladies turned into the cloak-room to remove their wraps. The air of vivacity pervading the place, or possibly it was her daughter's staccato liveliness, entered the blood of Mrs. Heth: she was imperious with the ladies' maid who assisted with the unwrapping. Carlisle, strolling about as she unbuttoned her gloves, came to the elaborate screen which sheltered the doorway and glanced out. Directly opposite, over the brilliant corridor, her gaze fell upon the glass and yellow-wood of a long-distance telephone booth.

Then she caught sight of Hugo, and smiled at him, and at the same moment mamma's voice said at her elbow:

"There's Hugo, waiting. . . . Are you ready?"

"And waiting, too," said Carlisle.

They emerged from the ladies' bower into the stir of the antechamber. Met halfway by their escort, they proceeded toward the dining-room. Advance was a little slow; there was some confusion here and even crowding, replete diners blocking the way of those just going in. Just at the door, a party of five or six managed to come between Carlisle and Canning, who was dutifully looking out for his future mother-in-law; the girl became momentarily separated from her protectors. Or perhaps it was partly Cally's own fault, precipitated by the sight of a page standing near, who certainly seemed to have been stationed there by the hand of Providence. . . .

Having stared fascinated at this page for half a second, Carlisle brought him to her side by a nod. The lad was fifteen and had seen lovely ladies in his time, but raising his eyes to this one, he acknowledged that she was a Queen.

"Call long distance for me, boy. . . . I'll write the number."

The boy produced pad and pencil, and she scribbled rapidly, a smile hovering over the sweet mouth whose slight irregularity charmed the eye beyond flawlessness.

Why, indeed, wait longer, running and sticking one's head in the sand, when here was the telephone, immediate and conclusive, when she felt now so brave and sure, and could tell mamma and Hugo this very night without a tremor? All was simple now, and highly adventurous besides. And then there was Jack Dalhousie to whom even a day or two, now that she stopped to think of it, would probably make a good deal of difference. . . .

Turning again with bright cheeks, Cally encountered strange faces; and then, in a second or two, the familiar ones of her mother and Canning, both looking back for her. . . .

"There you are!" she laughed, coming up with them again. "What an exciting jam!"

They proceeded into the dining-place and to their table, a somewhat ceremonial progress headed by three spiketails. Even in that display of beauty, wealth, consequence, and their lifelike imitations, these three, or perhaps we should say these two, drew much attention. Carlisle was conscious of lorgnettes; once she caught the whisper of the name so soon to be her own. Late as they were, the room was still crowded: the well-bred but wandering eye saw no vacant seat anywhere. There was music in the air, and the clash of cutlery, the vocal hum, and the faint tinkle of glasses. There were flushing faces and eyes that sparkled like the wine, and of it, many fragrances commingled, of flowers, chefs' *chefs-d'œuvre*, of Pinaud and Roget. Through all, too, was to be felt the hard inquisitive stare of New York, each man wondering who and whence his neighbor was, speculating under his smile as to which man of them made, on the whole, the best appearance, seemed most plentiful of his money. . . .

Pink-shaded candles stood on the little table; also La France roses of Canning's purchasing; also glasses, three more of them brought as they took their seats.

"Do you spurn your cocktail, Carlisle?" asked Canning, and when she convivially indicated that she did n't, he added, man to man: "How!"

"How,", said Cally.

She touched it to her lips, giving back his smile over the rim of her glass, and feeling gay, indeed. Two cocktails before one dinner — well!

"What kind of one is this, Hugo?" she demanded, quite knowingly.

Canning named it.

"Well, then," said she, "it was a Bronx I had before."

She did not say before what, and nobody asked. About them, as they sat in the lively hum, circled servitors without end. One fellow had brought their bit of caviare; another bore away the traces of it; another had no share of them but to fetch crisp rolls. Little omnibuses in white suits moved about, gathering up papers or napkins dropped by careless diners; bigger omnibuses in dinner jackets exported trays of dishes which the lordly artists of the serving force were above touching. Other varlets merely stood about and cooed. . . .

Dinner, having begun with the cocktails, swept on with a rattle of talk. There was debate about the theatre afterwards. The girl's eyes turned often toward the door.

"What do you think of it all, Carlisle?"

"Sweet, Hugo! . . . So simple and artless and homey!"

"Exactly," said Canning; and obtained permission for a cigarette. "But yet interesting as a vaudeville show, don't you think? What so amusing as to see human vanity displaying itself not merely without reserve but with a terrific blowing of horns?"

"Well put, Hugo!" said Mrs. Heth, who held that any kind of generalization constituted good talk. She added: "Who are all these people? How would one place them?"

Canning could indicate a celebrity or two. He had bowed several times, finding acquaintances, it seemed, even in this glittering farrago. But his eyes returned to his bride-to-be, from whom he removed his gaze with reluctance to-night. She wore a dress of yellow crêpe-de-chine, with a draped arrangement of blue chiffon, which followed faithfully the long lines of her figure; and a hat of blue straw with an uncurled yellow plume. It was a beautiful dress, though mamma considered it just a thought too low, even with a handkerchief put in.

And Cally looked back at her lover and thought: Who so honored and honorable as he? He'll only be sorry that I've waited so long. . . .

"Only," she said, aloud, "they do keep the room rather hot for the provinces, where some air is preferred. More good things to eat, Hugo? It's a collation. . . ."

"A poor one, I'm afraid. You've touched nothing."

He dispatched an army of men to adjust electric fans, turn patent ventilators, and even to do so crude a thing as open a window.

"It is all most delicious, Hugo," reassured Mrs. Heth. "I had n't noticed that the room was warm, either."

"My cheeks are burning. Touch my hand, Hugo. You see it's on fire."

All three looked up as a boy in buttons stood at Carlisle's elbow, and said:

"Got your party on the wire, mum."

"Party on the wire? What's this?" said mamma.

Carlisle laid her napkin on the table. Surprise confronted her, written large on the faces of her mother and her lover; but it did not arrest her.

"I'm wanted at the telephone. Do you mind, Hugo? I won't be gone a minute."

"*But* — you must n't go *now*, my dear!" said Mrs. Heth, astonished. "Let the boy take the number. Why — who on earth could it be, calling you *here?* —"

"I'd rather go now, mamma, if Hugo'll forgive me —"

"It's from Flora!" said Mrs. Heth, positively. "No one else knew. A telegram's come, saying your father is sick —"

Carlisle laughed and rose dazzlingly, burning without but colder than Alpine snow within.

"Not in the least, mamma dear! You see I put in this call myself. I'll explain all about it in a minute. . . ."

Explain! Why she would walk back to this table from the telephone, laughing, and saying: "Now, praise me, Hugo and mamma, for I've just been doing a deed of mercy! Do you remember that day at the Beach? . . ." Was it the fear of this that she had let plague her all these days? . . .

"To be answered *here* — at dinner — in this public place? Why, my dear Cally, I really . . ."

But Hugo, the understanding, though personally opposed to interruptions during dinner, knew the folly of arguing with the whims of the unreasoners. He had risen with Carlisle, and now said: "I'll show you the way."

Cally gave him a look of exquisite gratitude, but answered: "*Please* don't trouble, Hugo! The boy will —"

"No trouble. Let's be off before the tolls eat you out of house and home."

"Oh, no! Please don't! Could n't I have my way about such a little matter, Hugo dear?"

In this glaring publicity, the dialogue began to take on something of the nature of a "scene." Canning yielded with perfect grace.

"Of course you can, if you really prefer it. Well, then! . . . Hurry back."

"In two minutes," said she, with certainty; and smiled brightly into mamma's censorious concern.

On the heels of the proud page, Cally threaded her way among the glittering tables for the telephone and Jefferson 4127, unaware for once that she was the cynosure of many eyes. She was buoyed within, thrilled with a sense of strange adventure, baffling to analysis, but somehow comparable to that soaring moment last week. She was captain of her soul. That she was now standing by her flare-up, deliberately reattaching herself to a past which she had moved heaven and earth to cut away from her, did not occur to her, in just that way. But she was conscious of a curious inner sense of freedom, and somehow of fulfilment. And now she saw that she must have been secretly thinking of doing this for some time, nibbling fearfully at the idea. . . .

She was alone in a glass booth, with a telephone before her, receiver off its hook. She sat down, put the receiver to her ear, and said:

"Hello?"

There reached her only a faint great buzzing, the humming of distant wires, fleeting snatches of talk a long way off, striking out of nowhere back into nothing. . . . And now she was the Lady

PLEASE DON'T TROUBLE, HUGO

Bountiful, stepping aside a moment from her brilliant entourage to scatter boons to the poor and needy. Jack Dalhousie would know to-morrow morning, at the latest, by the telegram from his friend Mr. V. V., — as that little creature called him, — and whatever vexation he might be inclined to feel towards her at first, his joy and his father's would soon dispose of that. And of course he would hurry straight off with his news to that girl from the East he had fallen in love with — what a hand he was for affairs, poor old Jack! — and . . .

Out of the confused murmuring, a soft voice spoke clearly:

"Hello, New York. I got your party. What's the matter?"

A nasal voice gave answer, apparently at Carlisle's elbow:

"Well, be ca'm, little one. You people got the rush-bug worsen some full-size cities aintyer? Butt out and gimme a chanst. Hello! W'ere arey'r, Bassadoors!"

"Here I am," said Bassadoors.

"Miss Heth?"

"I am Miss Heth."

"Minute 'm . . ."

In the glass beside her Cally caught a reflection of her head and bare shoulders, and her eyes were shining, the long and slightly tri-corner eyes so piquantly fringed. A minute — that was all it would take. A minute more and she would thread her way back through the glitter to Hugo and mamma, and Hugo at least would say well-done. . . .

"Well, whatsermatter? There y' are!"

The soft voice said: "All right, Dr. Vivian. Ready now! . . . Hello! All right. . . ."

"Hello," said Cally.

Then all sounds faded away, and out of a sudden great desert of silence, she heard a man's voice, clear though it came all the way from Meeghan's Grocery, across the street from the old Dabney House, back home.

"Hello?"

Mr. V. V.!

And the moment she heard that voice, Carlisle was aware that her feeling toward the owner of it had mysteriously changed somewhere in the last week, that he stood in her mind now almost as a friend. Had he not been, by the strangeness of fate, her one confidant in the world, who now could never think of her again as a poor little thing? . . .

"Dr. Vivian? . . . Can you guess who it is? Or did the operator give me away?"

"Yes . . . I don't hear you very well . . . Where are you?"

"I'm in New York, if you please, to sail for Europe next week! We left home last night. . . . Is that better?"

"Yes . . . That's much better."

Mr. V. V.'s voice, over the long miles of wire, sounded strained and hard; but the girl noticed nothing, being full of novel thrills.

"Perhaps you can guess why I've called you up. . . . Though, you know, it was to be a secret unless you saw me again, and I really don't count a letter as seeing! . . ."

"I did n't see you," came back the unfamiliar voice. "I am to blame."

"Ah, but the letter was just as good," said Carlisle, and laughed excitedly into the transmitter. And then, having never admitted any particular sense of guilt, having felt almost no "conviction of sin" as religious fellows would term it, she went on without the smallest embarrassment: "You see, I flew into a panic for some reason, and did n't mean for you ever to see me again. I ran away! And then I could n't get his letter out of mind — I'd never taken it in that he was so miserable, really! — and I was quite ashamed of being such a coward. And so," she said, the upward-lifting lip pressing the instrument in her eagerness, "I've called up now to say I want —"

His voice broke in, not with the burst of praise and thanksgiving she had looked for, but only to say abruptly and anticlimacterically:

"I can't hear you. Will you say that again?"

However, but few words were needed, after all, to ring this climax. Carlisle said, slowly and distinctly:

"I say I want you to tell Mr. Dalhousie now — and his father, too. To-night, if you wish."

Then there was a desolating silence, out of which she heard something far off like a man groaning.

"Hello!" she called sharply. "Are you there?"

"Where are you, Miss Heth?" was Dr. Vivian's reply; and his voice was like the voice of the man who had groaned. . . . "Are you in your room at the hotel? Is your mother with you there?"

Singular words these, from the receiver of confidences and high favors. There fell upon Cally a nameless fear.

"N-no — I'm alone. . . . Why, what —"

"Could I speak to your mother a moment — first? I have some bad news. It would be better —"

"No — tell me! My mother's at dinner. I — what are you talking about? . . ."

Had he betrayed her already, then? Was the town now ringing with her name? Had Colonel Dalhousie . . .

Quite distinctly, though he evidently was not addressing her, she heard the man's hard voice say: "This cannot be borne."

And then in a different voice, there came these words over the miles from Meeghan's Grocery:

"Miss Heth — I did n't see you when I should have — and now we are just too late. I can't reach Dal now."

"You — don't mean? . . ."

"He is dead."

"*Dead!*"

And it was this girl's shame, the fruit of her long fear, that her first feeling was one of base relief. So works Nature's first law. Dal was dead; all was settled; there was nothing to tell now. And then, as by the turning of a corner, she came front to front with a sudden horror, and there unrolled before her a moment of blackness. . . .

"You must not blame yourself too hard," came the distant voice, dropping out of space like the sentences of destiny. "It's . . . cruel, the way it 's happened. But you 'll always know you had the courage and the will to set him free, when you might —"

Carlisle's hand clenched the edge of the little table where she sat.

"Tell me," said her voice, pitifully faint. "Did he ... I —
must know — Did he ... ?"

There was a roaring in her ears, but through it the words came
clear as flame:

"He went out of his mind. I know that. That could not be
foreseen. Not waiting ... he took his own life. It was this afternoon. A telegram came — from some friend of his ..."

All further words, if more there were, bounded off from the
sudden iron stillness within her. Mechanically she raised the
receiver to the hook, for was not her talk with Meeghan's quite
finished? Jack Dalhousie had killed himself. Sackcloth and
ashes would not get a telegram to him now. .... And then, some
flying remembrance of the bearer of the tidings struck through
her numbness, and she caught down the receiver again and said
indistinctly:

"I can't talk any more now. .... I'll be all right ..."

Then all thought stopped, and her head went forward upon
her hands. The yellow plume nodded bravely. ....

Outside the door of the booth was the brilliant corridor, and
beyond a glimpse of the dining-room, pretty with shaded lights,
gay with music and talk, and eyes that stared unabashed. Somewhere in there were Mrs. Heth and Canning, dining well.

The page stood near, the call-slip offered upon his tray. He,
who admired her, was aware of a subtle distortion in this lady's
winning loveliness.

"Take it, please," said she, "to the lady at the table where you
found me. And say I shall not come back to dinner."

Then Carlisle found herself in the cloak-room, which happened
to be empty except for the smiling maid. She had hardly entered
and repelled the woman's overtures, when she heard the hurried
step of her mother, brought quickly by the buttons' strange
words.

"Cally! Are you ill? What on earth's happened?"

Cally sat stiffly in a chair against the wall, her face colorless.
Different, this, from the telling she had contemplated, not five
minutes ago. What had happened, indeed?

She said in a small flat voice: "I heard some bad news — over

the telephone. A man — has died. He killed himself, this afternoon —"

Commanding even in that moment, Mrs. Heth turned upon
the hovering maid and said: "A glass of water."

When the woman had passed out of earshot, she turned again,
and put her two strong hands on Cally's shoulders.

"What man? Who was this you called up long-distance?"

"Mr. Dalhousie," said Cally's small voice. "I called up a
friend of his. . . ." She looked up fixedly at her mother and said:
"Mamma, he did it because of me."

The name of ill omen staggered the mother a little. Her voice
was half harsh, half frightened:

"Because of you! You are ill, my poor child. The shock has
upset you. You are out of your head. The boy's mind was un-
hinged by drink. Every one said so. He had broken his father's
heart with —"

"But he did this because of me. Because of what I let everybody think of him. . . . Mamma, I — I must go back home.
I'm sorry to upset everything so . . ."

The maid stood by with her tray and glass, but no hand reached
for the offering.

"Back to the hotel? Of course! — you are ill, my poor dear!
You need rest. . . ."

"I mean back home. You see I can't be here now . . . when
this has happened. I must go now, to-night. I remember the
train goes at nine-fifty-five."

Mrs. Heth, wheeling upon the maid with livid perturbation,
cried:

"Get my wraps."

XX

In which Jack Dalhousie wears a New Dignity, and the Lame Stranger comes to the House of Heth.

DALHOUSIE had been worthless while he lived. Now he had achieved the last supreme importance. The inconsiderable of yesterday wore a mute and mighty power. So he reached over the spaces, and broke the brilliant dinner-party at the Café des Ambassadeurs. So Mrs. Heth and Carlisle Heth disputed, by this new great dignity that was his, and talked in the hotel bedroom, and hurriedly changed evening attire for travelling suits. And so Hugo Canning, abruptly widowed at a railway station, was left to toss wakefully that night, ridden by deepening anxieties. . . .

For Cally had carried her extraordinary point; now that Jack Dalhousie was henceforward indifferent to all these matters.

She had said, with the deadly flatness of the mood which her mother so dreaded, that she wanted to go home to-night, and there had been no reasoning with her. Go home for what? Mrs. Heth had asked it twenty times, battling desperately against the menacing madness, now with argument and threat, now with tears and wheedlings. And Cally, proceeding dry-eyed with her dressing and bag-packing, had proved unable to produce a single solid reason.

Still, it became clear that lock and key would not keep her. The options ensuing were whether her mother should go with her, or Hugo should go, or Cally be allowed to go alone. Small choice here, indeed.

Of that evening the events following the hurried departure from the Ambassadeurs were always blurred in Carlisle's memory. To Mrs. Heth each detail remained crystal-clear as long as she lived. Upon her shoulders, as usual, fell the burden of managing everything so that the least harm should befall. Defeated, and consequently hatted and cloaked, she emerged from the bedroom at quarter-past nine o'clock, commissioned by her daughter to tell Canning everything. But what was everything, and what the mere gibberish of nervous insanity, to pass forever from the horizon with a good night's sleep? Mrs. Heth, seated before her living Order of Merit in the sitting-room, interpreted her commission with a mother's wise discretion.

Canning, at this point, knew only that Carlisle was unnerved by news of the death of a friend. In the drive from the restaurant he had been cautioned to ask no questions, hysterics being intimated otherwise. Now Mrs. Heth gave him certain selected particulars: of a man who had been in love with Carlisle some years ago, though she had always discouraged him; of a misunderstanding that had arisen between them, which he, the man, had never got over; and now of his sudden decease, which came as a shock to the poor girl, awakening painful memories, and giving rise to a purely momentary sense of morbid responsibility.

"But why," said Canning, more and more mystified as he listened, "should she want to go back home?"

"I regard it," answered Mrs. Heth, "as a tribute to the dead."

"Why, she does n't know what she's doing! . . . You must simply forbid her going."

"Forbid her!" groaned the little general, like one flicked upon a new wound.

And, before proceeding further, she was actually artful and strong enough to make the young man arrange—provisionally, she said,—about reservations, a matter which valuably consumed time.

If the good lady had now believed that all was lost, she would have instantly invoked Canning's authority, telling him everything. But as yet she would not risk that, clinging hard to the hope that Cally's sanity might come again with the sun of a new day. To-night she was for the greatest suppression possible, one eye perpetually on the little travelling-clock. However, the telephoning at last over, more details could not be avoided. It perforce transpired that the dead man was the villain of that unfortunate episode at the Beach, which Hugo possibly recalled, — he did, — and finally that it was worry over his disgrace, aided by unremitting potations, that had brought him to his death. . . .

The faint frown on Hugo's brow deepened, became more troubled. He paced the floor.

"And still," said he, "I fail to see why Carlisle must go home to-night. What does she expect to do when she gets there?"

What, indeed? Mrs. Heth mentioned again the tribute to the dead. The girl, in her shocked state, considered it unfeeling for her to remain here enjoying herself with Hugo, as if nothing had happened. Foolish? — who saw it better than she, Mrs. Heth? But that was Cally, sweet and good at heart always, yet liable to emotional fits in upset moments when opposition only made her ill. Let her have her morbid way to-night, and she would return in twenty-four hours, her own sweet natural self. . . .

Canning liked it less and less. Was not this clearly a moment when the strong mind of a man should assert itself over foolish feminine hysteria?

"How did she happen to get this news just now?" he asked, abruptly. "Who was it she called up, about what?"

He had lost sight of this point in the general flurry of sensation. It struck him now just too late to bring results. At the moment, the door from the bedrooms opened — exactly as it had two hours earlier, only with what a difference! — and Carlisle appeared on the threshold, very pale and subdued, but to her lover's eye never more moving.

"I'm so sorry to bring you into all this trouble, Hugo," she said, in a strained little voice. . . . "And when we were having such a happy time. . . ."

All thought of putting down his foot faded at once from Canning's mind, obliterated in a wave that went through him, half passion, half pure tenderness. Indifferent to Mrs. Heth, he advanced and took the girl in his arms, speaking in a manly way the sympathy with her distress which rushed up in him at that moment. And then he said words that went with Carlisle as a comfort all through the night.

"Your trouble is my own, Carlisle. I'm with you in everything now, happiness or unhappiness. Whatever happens, you know my heart and strength are yours through all time."

Carlisle, too deeply moved to speak, thanked her lover with a look. The moment's silence was broken by Mrs. Heth, resolutely blowing her nose. And then all opportunity for talk was lost in the rush for the train.

To herself she seemed to lie endlessly between sleeping and waking: and the rhythmic noises of the train sounded a continual cadence, Dalhousie's unquiet requiem. But she must have fallen sound asleep without knowing it; for her eyes opened suddenly with a start, and she was aware of the clanging of bells, the waxing and waning of men's voices, the hiss of steam and the flaring of yellow lights. Looking out under the blind, she saw that they had come to a city, which must be Philadelphia. Two hours nearer home. . . .

Now her wakefulness had a sharper quality; Cally lay wide-eyed, in a dazed chill wonder. Once in the night she pushed up the curtain, raised herself on an elbow in the stateroom berth; and her splendid gay hair, loosened with much tossing, streamed downward over her shoulders. Outside was a world of moonlit peace. The flying trees had tops of silver; meadows danced by in splotches of light and shade; once they sped over a lovely river. Strange to think, that if she had but said on that faraway day, "He frightened me so, I didn't want to call him back," — just those words, how few and simple, — she would not be hurrying home now, with everything ahead so dark, so terrifying. And, though she seemed to try a long time, she could not think now why she had not said these words, could not weigh those slight fanciful tremors against this vast icy void. . . .

She fell asleep; woke again to more clanging and hissing; slept and dreamed badly; and suddenly sat up in the berth, confusedly, to find it broad day, and the sun streaming through the little crevice beneath the curtain. Her mother was standing braced in the aisle of the little room, dressing systematically.

"We've passed Penton. You'd better get up," said the brisk familiar tones.

And she eyed her daughter narrowly as she asked if she had slept.

Home again. This time yesterday, who would have dreamed this possible? . . .

And then, after just enough time to dress, they began to pass landmarks, and presently to slacken speed; and then they were stepping down from the train, out into the hotch-potch gathering on the sunny station platform.

Both women were heavily veiled. Mrs. Heth's furtive glances discovered no one who was likely to hail them, demanding what in the world these things meant. A ramshackle hack invited and received them. And, jogging over streets crowded with a life-time's associations, the Heths presently came to their own house, whose face they had not thought to see again these four months. . . .

Mr. Heth was away, fishing, in a spot dear to his heart, but re-mote from railroad or telegraph. The House of Heth looked like a deserted house; its blinds were drawn from fourth story to base-ment. However, there was old Moses, bowing and running down the steps to open the carriage door and assist with the hand-luggage. He greeted the ladies with courtliness, and inquired mout anybody be sick. Answered vaguely on this point, he an-nounced that he had breakfast ready-waiting on the table; this, though Mr. Canning's telegraph never retched him till nea'bout eight o'clock. His tone indicated a pride of accomplishment not, he hoped, unjustified.

Having removed the more superficial stains of travel, the two women sat at table in the half-dismantled dining-room. It was a meal not easily to be forgotten, made the more fan-tastic by Mrs. Heth's determined attempts to act as if nothing in particular had happened. From her remarks to the ancient family retainer it appeared that she and Miss Carlisle had re-turned home to attend to a business matter of no great conse-quence, overlooked in the rush of departure. And she demanded, quite as if that were the very business referred to, whether the plumber had come to stop the drip in the white-room bath-room.

The butler's reply took a not unfamiliar direction. The plumber, and his helper, had come and 'xperimented round: but they had not yet stopped the drip. . . .

Mrs. Heth ate heartily, with a desperate matter-of-factness. It was half-past nine o'clock. Nothing had happened yet, at any rate. Beside her, Carlisle had more difficulty with her breakfast, hampered by her continuing mind's-eye picture of Jack Dalhousie, lying on his back on a floor somewhere. Might it be that, as this horror made telling so much harder, it also altered the whole necessity? There were plenty of arguments of mamma's to that effect. . . .

"Mr. Heth got off all right, Moses?" demanded that resolute lady. "Take some more tea, Cally. You must really try to eat something, my child —"

"I have eaten — a great deal," said Cally. And pushing back her chair then, she added: "I think I — I'll try to rest a little while, mamma. I feel — tired after the trip."

"Do!" said mamma, further encouraged. "Sleep a little if you can, my dear. It's just what you need. . . ."

But Cally did not sleep. It had seemed to her that she must be alone for a time, to try to think out what was to happen; but now she saw that she had no need to think. Of the complex nervous and emotional reaction which had brought her flying home, she had, indeed, seemed to understand nothing except that it was irresistible; her mind was like a dark cloud, refusing to yield up its meanings. Nevertheless, there seemed to be no doubt as to what she must do now. . . .

Mrs. Heth, having remained downstairs half an hour longer, ascended quietly, the beginnings of great gratitude in her heart. They were feelings born but to die. Just at the head of the stairs she encountered Cally, emerging like an apparition from the door of the family sitting-room. The girl spoke in a small voice:

"Mamma, I want to send for Dr. Vivian — to come and see me."

Mamma, just thinking that this madness was finally disposed of, was taken suddenly. Even the birthmark on her temple, which was partially exposed, seemed to turn pale. . . .

But once more Carlisle carried her extraordinary point. Ever since she was a little girl she had been subject to these incalculable fits, when punishment made her ill, but did not conquer the seven devils that possessed her. Mrs. Heth, frantic after nearly an hour's thundering, vanished into the telephone-booth, bent upon reaching Mr. Heth while there was yet time. But even now her strongest thought was that Cally was a sensible girl at heart, in the last pinch simply incapable of self-destructive folly.

Cally, also, had thought of the telephone. But the sight of it, after last night, unnerved her. She withdrew to the little desk in her bedroom.

So the word of the Lord came to the Dabney House, by the hand of an old negro gentleman.

He was standing in the middle of the floor, when Carlisle went down, an inconsonant figure amid the showy splendors of the Heth drawing-room. So much appeared to the most casual observation. Far deeper to the understanding eye went the inconsistency of this man's presence here, in an hour of appalling intimacy.

Carlisle, entering through the uncurtained doorway, halted involuntarily just over the threshold. Her eye, at least, saw all. And she was abruptly and profoundly affected by the sight of him in her familiar background, the author of the Beach opinion of her, who truly had never meant anything but trouble for her since the first moment she saw him. Time, indeed, had given the religious fellow his last full measure of revenge. . . .

Prepared speeches of some dignity and length slipped from her. Cally spoke from her heart and her fear, without greeting, in a nervous childish voice:

"I — I wanted to see you, to — to ask you — to talk with you — as to what must be done . . ."

Jack Dalhousie's friend bowed gravely. There was no victory on his face, neither was there any judgment.

"I understood," he said simply, "and was grateful to you."

He, certainly, seemed aware of no discordance in himself. He advanced with a beautiful consistency, looking as if he wished to say more. But Cally, her hand gripping the back of a spindly gold divan, her gaze fallen, seemed suddenly to find her own tongue unloosed.

"It's been so terrible," she hurried on in the same flat, unpremeditated way — "no one could know. . . . I was in New York, and we were to sail for Europe in a few days. Everything was arranged, all our plans were made, oh, for months and months. And then . . . And now I've come home — and everything is so upset — and so dreadfully complicated. And I haven't seemed able to think somehow — to decide —"

"Try not to think about it at all," said the man, with some firmness. "That's the great compensation, that you can begin to forget about it now. Won't you sit down?"

She sat down obediently, quite as if it were natural for him to be taking charge of her in her own drawing-room. And staring down at her locked hands, she fluttered on with no reference to him, with a kind of frightened incredulity, like a bird in a trap.

"It seems so unjust — so terribly *unfair*. . . . That all this could come from one little puff of wind! . . . He had gotten out of the boat. He was swimming away. And then there came one little gust. I had tied the sail, you see. He had frightened me. And now, after all these months . . . But of course I never thought — I never dreamed of — of —"

"I know; I understand. No one dreamed it. You must keep sure of that," said Vivian, in his natural voice. "I knew Dal very well indeed, you know; and I felt certain that he was — safe from this. You — you mustn't think of it as something that could have been foreseen. . . ."

He was looking down at her lowered face closely as he spoke; and went on without pause:

"You see — what upset him so was beyond your control or mine. I've heard nothing since the telegram last night. But — you may remember that he spoke of a girl in his letter, whose opinion he seemed to value. It must be that when he saw her again, she was very hard on him — so hard that he lost his grip for a moment. I can't account for it in any other way. There is another thing, too. . . . Do you think it's a little close in here, perhaps? May I open a window?"

She assented without speech, and he walked away with the step of his disability to the long windows. Into the dim great room stole the breath of the May morning, sweet with the fragrance of the balcony flowers.

The tall young man came walking back.

"There was one thing I wanted particularly to tell you. I sent Dal a message — a telegram — on Monday night. . . ."

Startled, Carlisle looked up.

"On — *Monday ?* . . . Why — I —"

"Not breaking your confidence, of course — just telling him, in a general way, to keep his courage up, that I — I thought good news was on the way. . . . It was without authority. I realized that. And yet I felt so sure that — when you had had a little time to think — that would be what you would wish. In fact, of course I knew it. . . ."

Their eyes met, almost for the first time, and a sudden constraint fell upon the girl.

"But I don't see," she said, with some difficulty — "if you telegraphed him that — on Monday — I don't understand —"

"The telegram went astray. I went to the office here last night and had them find out. It should have reached Weymouth the first thing yesterday morning. It did n't arrive till about three in the afternoon. But even then . . . You see, he could hardly have expected a reply to his letter till Wednesday. That's to-day. . . ."

These two sat looking at each other: and Cally's tongue was no longer free as a hurt child's. She seemed not to find it possible to speak at all now. The young man from the other world was going on, with his strange composure.

"So you see how much was pure blind chance, that could n't be guarded against. If he had only waited. . . . If he had only trusted you — two hours longer . . ."

Surely he had more to say, much more; yet he ended abruptly, speech being evidently not desired of him. The girl had suddenly dropped her face into her hands.

Cally did not want to look at this man any more; could not bear it indeed. His eyes, which had always seemed gifted to convey hidden meanings, had well outstripped the words of his mouth, triumphing strangely over all that he knew about her. Quite clearly they had said to her just then: "*I* would have trusted you, you know. . . ." And somehow that seemed sad to her, she did not know why. Why, indeed, should Jack Dalhousie have trusted her? . . .

Something moved in Cally in this moment which might have been the still small voice, and her weakness grew apace. She turned precipitately, put an arm on the back of the gold divan where she sat, and buried her face in it. Her struggle now was against tears; and it was to be a losing struggle. She did not cry easily. It always seemed rather like tearing loose something within her, something important that was meant to stay where it had been fixed. There was pain with these tears. . . .

The man from the Dabney House said nothing. His was a more than woman's intuition. There was a long silence in the drawing-room. . . .

But after a time, when there were signs that the tension was relaxing and the sudden storm passing, he spoke in his simple voice:

"You see your message would have been all that you meant, but for the terrible coincidence. You must n't take it — so much upon yourself. That would n't be right. Think of that poor girl out there, who is reproaching herself so to-day. And then, besides, you must know I realize that I should have seen you last week. . . . You had every right to expect that, as I was — in a measure — Dal's representative. . . . "

Cally hardly heard him.

Her back toward him, she had produced from some recess a small handkerchief, and was silently removing the traces of her tears. She had dimly supposed that there would be a long discussion; all at once it was clear that there was nothing to discuss. And she thought of Hugo, and a little of her mother, waiting upstairs. . . .

"It was too much for one person to carry alone," continued

the alien voice, sounding rather hard-pressed now. "I happened to be the one person in position to help, and I failed you ... I'd like you to know ..."

But the girl had risen, ending his speech, her need to talk with him past. Her self-absorption was without pretence. Wan and white and with a redness about her misty dark eyes, she stood facing the old enemy, and spoke in a worn little voice:

"You said you'd see his father for me, did n't you?"

The man, having risen with her, looked hurriedly away.

"Yes — of course. I'll go. At once."

And then, as if pledged to speak, though well he knew that she had no thought for him, he added abruptly: "But you must n't think of yourself as being alone with this. I promise you I'll keep the knowledge, to punish me, that if — if I'd been the sort of man you needed, you'd have settled it all long ago. ..."

"That's absurd ..." said Cally, somehow touched, but with no conception of the depths from which he spoke. ... "I never meant to tell at all if it had n't been for you."

She added, seeing him turn away, looking around the long room: "I think you must have left it in the hall."

And then, winking a little, she began to blow her nose, and moved away toward the door.

She encountered the butler, old Moses, entering from the hall. There was a yellow envelope upon his tray, though she had heard no ring at the bell.

"Excuse me, ma'am. This message just kem for you, an' I signed for it at the do'."

Carlisle thought instantly, Hugo! ... And when, having quite forgotten the man standing silent behind her, she broke open the envelope with nervous fingers, the hope of her heart was at once confirmed:

> Am coming to you. Arrive four-ten this afternoon. Wait
> for me.   H. C.

Did a tiny corner of her tightly closed mind open a little as she read? *Wait for me.* ...

She turned back to Jack Dalhousie's representative with something like eagerness, to find his eyes fixed upon her.

"Oh! — would it do any harm to wait a little while, do you think? — just till this afternoon?"

"No, no," he said, in rather an odd voice, "it will do no harm now."

"Then I'll send word to you this afternoon — at five or six o'clock," said Cally, with vague flutterings of relief, of hope, perhaps. And then, moved by a sudden impulse, she added: "I will tell you why I want to wait. I am engaged to be married. I think I should tell my fiancé, before anything is done. . . ."

To this V. Vivian made no reply. He was advancing to the door. And then as he paused before the stricken Hun, and saw the glitter of a tear on the piquant gold-and-black lashes, the young man's twisting heart seemed suddenly to loosen, and he said quite simply:

"Won't you let me say how fine and brave a thing you're doing, how splendid a —"

"Don't!" said Cally, recoiling instantly from she knew not what. "*Don't!* . . . I'm not brave — *at all!* Oh, no — that's just it. . . ."

And then, looking down, she added somewhat pitifully: "But I really didn't mean to do anything so bad. . . ."

The alien turned hurriedly away. He went without another word.

The front door shut upon him. And Cally gave a little jump, hearing above her the imperious tread of her mother.

XXI

That Day at the Beach, as we sit and look back at it; how Hugo journeys to shield his Love from Harm, and Small Beginnings can end with Uproars and a Proverb.

CANNING arrived at the House of Heth shortly after four. He had had an all-day journey in summer heat, and a bad night preceding. In the still watches following his ladies' departure from New York, he had had time for calm reflection, nothing else but time; and the more he calmly reflected, the less could he understand his betrothed's singular desire to pay this tribute to the dead. The thing grew increasingly mystifying; increasingly unorthodox and undependable, too. Moreover, the second thought reproached him that, Carlisle being so greatly upset, however unreasonably, he himself should have accompanied her homeward, in her most need to go by her side. And thinking these things, the disturbed young man had tumbled out of bed in the small hours, to make inquiries regarding trains.

He was received at the House by his future mother-in-law, who was once more the accredited intermediary. Canning was hot, sooty, and suffering from want of sleep. There were cinders down the back of his neck. Mrs. Heth had Moses prepare for him a long iced drink, with rime on the glass and fragrant mint atop. And then, as the prize of her lifetime sat and sipped, she seated herself beside him, her strong voice trembling. . . .

All hope of discreet reticence was now ripped to shreds. What chance remained of rescuing the name of Heth from the scandalous horrors of a suicide lay all in arousing this stalwart man to the imminence of the common peril. Mrs. Heth, somersaulting without hesitancy from last night's caution, flooded the dark places with lurid light.

Canning listened with consternation and chagrin. His moral sensibilities, indeed, received no particular shock, since Mrs.

Heth's narrative frankly disclaimed any wrong-doing on Carlisle's part, but attributed the misunderstanding to the excited gossip at the time. And by the same token, he was not unduly perturbed over the girl's hysterical ideas of her present duty. What struck Canning most sharply, indeed, since he was human, was the personal side of the matter: the stark fact that important developments touching Carlisle's name and happiness had been running along for some time, wholly without his knowledge, but under the direct personal superintendency of another man, this Mr. Somebody's unknown friend. So extraordinary a course of behavior seemed to reveal a totally new side of his betrothed, hitherto unsuspected. Canning would have been too saintly for this earth if he had not learned of these proceedings with the deepest surprise and vexation.

And yet — what of it? Of course there was some simple and natural explanation, which she would give when she felt better able. Doubtless she had been threatened; blackmailed perhaps. And meantime the light thrown directly and indirectly on Carlisle's distraught mood touched the lover deeply. He hardly needed Mrs. Heth's frightened hints about the necessity of gentleness with firmness in dealing with a flare-up. Had he himself not known the wilful nature of her spirit in excitement, that never-forgotten evening in the library?

And when the striker of the right note withdrew at last, and Carlisle herself appeared in the drawing-room, very white and subdued, the last remnant of a personal grievance vanished from Canning's manner. Nothing could have exceeded the tenderness of his greeting. . . .

"Did my telegram surprise you?" he said presently. "I got so troubled about you after you were gone . . . I could n't bear to leave you alone with this . . ."

And Cally said, with a quiver in her voice: "Oh, Hugo! . . . If you only knew how I 've wanted you to-day! . . ."

She meant it with every fibre of her being. Doubly he had convinced her now that he could never be shocked or disgusted with her, that in him a perfect sympathy enfolded her, covering all mistakes. That he might not understand quite yet how she felt about everything was possible, but that was nothing now, by the fact that he understood *her*, at any rate, as mamma never could.

Some discussion of the matter was of course necessary. And presently, after they had talked a little, quite naturally, of his journey and how she had slept last night, the lovers drifted on into Mr. Heth's little study, reopened against this need.

Here they sat down and began to talk. And here, in five minutes, Carlisle's heart began mysteriously to sink within her. . . .

She had been going through a series of violent emotional experiences in which he had had not the slightest share, and now required of him that he should catch up with the results of these experiences, upon a moment's notice and at a single bound. She could not realize the extreme difficulty of this feat. Nor, indeed, could Canning himself, confident by the ease with which his love had appeared to put down all personal irritations. To his seeming, as to hers, they had met in perfect spiritual reunion.

Accordingly, when he proposed that the matter be allowed to rest quiet for a day or two, till they were all in a little better frame of mind to view it calmly, he offered a temporary solution which he felt certain would seem to her as reasonable and as tactfully considerate as it did to him.

"In this moment of shock and distress," he said, with admirable restraint, "you are not quite in the best frame of mind, you see, to decide such a serious matter. Fortunately, to wait a little while and think it over quietly can do no harm to anybody now. And then, if you still feel the same way about it, of course I shall want to do what you wish."

He had had Carlisle's feelings only at second-hand, through a medium perhaps wanting in transparence. Her hesitancy considerably surprised him. To Carlisle, as was almost equally inevitable, it was as if in the solid rock of their mutual understanding there had suddenly appeared a tiny crack. She felt the reasonableness as well as the tenderness with which Hugo spoke; she wanted nothing in the world but to do what he wanted. And yet it seemed somehow a physical impossibility for her now to say that she would unsettle and postpone it all, — something, say, as if Hugo had asked her to step back into last year or the year before. And she tried to make him understand this, saying — what seemed a feeble reply to his logic:

"You see, I — I've already thought about it a good deal, Hugo ... And putting it off would only make me — miserable and ill. I can't explain very well. ... I think I could begin to — to forget about it if — when ..."

This she said over several times, in different ways, as the necessary discussion proceeded. ...

It was naturally hard for Hugo to grasp the grounds on which she rejected a mere deferment of painful discussion till to-morrow morning (for he reduced his proposal to that), or even to see why, though opposed herself, she would not readily be guided in so small a matter by his wishes. The soft chimes in the hall had rung five before it definitely came over him that the preliminaries had oddly, indeed incredibly, gone against him.

He faced the fact frankly, without perceptible sign of annoyance.

"Well, then, my dearest girl, I'm afraid we shall have to talk about it a little now. ..."

They sat side by side on papa's faded old lounge, where they had spent many an hour together in happier days. Canning held Carlisle's hand in a reassuring grasp. Her heart warmed to him anew: if he did not quite seem to understand — what wonder when she hardly did herself? — his was a love that drew its roots deeper than understanding. Nevertheless she flinched from a discussion which promised to be carried on chiefly by her overstrung nerves; and all at once she felt that she must know instantly what threatened, exactly what he thought about it.

"Hugo ... do you — don't you think I — I ought to tell?"

Far readier and surer was his voice in reply: "Frankly, darling, I can't as yet see any necessity."

How could he possibly see? — Ought to tell what? Had not her mother told him that he had to deal with the nightmare illusions of a disordered mind? ...

Canning added with great considerateness: "I've thought it all over from every point of view — and you know I'm better able to think dispassionately to-day than you are — and I simply can't persuade myself that we have any such obligation."

Carlisle thought, with a little hopeful leap, that Hugo *must* know. It was all irrevocably settled; and yet at the same time it may have been that, woman-wise, she had left ajar a little door somewhere, through which his man's wisdom might yet storm, and possess all. . . .

"But — but does n't it seem that if I — did him a wrong, I ought to be willing to set it straight?"

"Well, naturally!" said Canning, and smiled a little, sadly, to see how white and sorrowful-eyed she looked. "If you did him a wrong. But that's just the point. I'm afraid I can't agree with the somewhat extreme view this friend of the poor fellow's seems to have put forward. . . . By the way," he added, finding the natural question popping in so suitably here, "who is this man that has talked with you about it, Carlisle? Your mother did n't go into particulars."

Carlisle felt some surprise. "Oh — I supposed she told you. Dr. Vivian — you remember — who . . ."

The name took Canning completely aback.

"Vivian? — no! . . . *That* chap! . . ."

Both remembered in the same moment his quizzical complaint that this man was his hoodoo. Both felt that the pleasantry had a somewhat gritty flavor just now.

"I had n't thought of him," said Canning, at once putting down his surprise and explaining it, "because I did n't think you knew him at all. In fact, I did n't know you'd ever seen him but once, or perhaps twice. . . ."

Carlisle regretted that mamma had not explained all this. "I have n't more than three or four times. . . . Twice when I was with you, you remember, and then I met him again at Mr. Beirne's and the Cooneys' — some cousins of mine. You see — he was a great friend of — his. . . ."

"And I suppose he has worried you about this every time he got anywhere near you?"

"No," Carlisle answered, laboriously, "I don't think he has ever mentioned it — since the first. Of course I've had hardly any conversation with him — and it's always been about the Works. You know, I told you he usually talked to me about that. . . ."

He said that he remembered; and each was then aware that the harmony of a moment ago had somehow slipped away from them. Canning, indeed, instead of being enlightened by the explanation, was more bewildered than ever. How could it be that this man, her father's assailant in the newspapers, the religious fellow whom Carlisle had never mentioned but to belittle, should have been the recipient of intimate confidences which she had withheld from him, her future husband? Naturally he could not understand in the least. However, glancing at her still face, he forbore to put another question.

"Well, that's got nothing to do with it anyway," he said, lightly, dismissing the side-issue.. "Now, let's see. . . . Sit back comfortably, my dear, and we'll take it all quietly from the beginning. . . ."

Hugo had got his facts from Mrs. Heth, and nothing had happened yet to suggest that they were in any way inaccurate. On the contrary, they seemed to have received subtle moral corroboration, so instinctive was it for the lover to lean backward from the views foisted upon Carlisle by her singular and religious confidant. That he himself was capable of coloring the case, attorney-wise, to suit the common interest did not really cross his mind.

The whole issue in the singular muddle, he pointed out, seemed to be whether or not the poor fellow had known that the boat was upset. Well, who could say what he knew, an intoxicated man in a blind passion? Not Carlisle, certainly, plunged suddenly into the sea and intensely occupied with saving her life. How, for instance, could she know it if, in the instant when she was under water, the man had glanced back and — deadened by his drunken anger, admit that for him — had not returned for her? Of the dozens of people who had witnessed the disaster, not one had doubted that the unfortunate chap's desertion of her had been deliberate. . . . However, imagine that it hadn't been, exactly, imagine that the women in their excitement and resentment, and

through misunderstanding of each other's statements, had failed
to give him the full benefit of the doubt. It was still a great mistake to assume that what they had said or left unsaid had been
decisive. Public opinion, knowing the unstable character of the
man, had already judged him. Did his later life and behavior
indicate, really, that that judgment was far wrong? And as to
that night of excitement long ago, the world's rough-and-ready
justice would hardly have taken much account of Carlisle's generous theory that perhaps the man did n't know what he was
doing. By the same token, it would scarcely reopen the case
now to admit that kind conjecture. . . .

"I honor from the bottom of my heart, Carlisle," said Canning,
"your wish to do the strictest justice. Need I say that I'm with
you there, against the world? But what is the strictest justice?
Perhaps you might bring a ray of relief to the poor man's father,
and that's all. Is that really so great an object to move heaven
and earth for, at the cost of much pain and distress to all who
love you? . . ."

Having spoken at some length, Canning paused for a reply.
The pause ran longer than he found encouraging. However, he
was no more sensitive to it, to Carlisle's strange unresponsiveness
as he talked, than was the girl herself. Indeed, it tore Cally's
heart to seem to oppose her lover, pleading so strongly and sweetly
for her against herself. Yet she had several times been tempted
to interrupt him, so clear did it seem to her that he did not understand even now all that she had supposed was fully plain to
him last night.

She said with marked nervousness, and a kind of eagerness,
too: "You're so good and dear in the way you look at it, Hugo.
You don't know — how sweet. . . . But it all comes down to
whether he knew — does n't it — just as you said. Well, you see
I really *know* he did n't —"

"You're mistaken there, my dear! Only God Almighty knows
that. Don't you think we had better leave the judgment to him?"

That Canning spoke quite patiently was a great credit to his
self-control. His failure to move her had filled him with a depressing and mortifying surprise. To say nothing of the regard

she might be supposed to have for his wishes, he knew that he had spoken unanswerably.

"But you see — I really do know he wasn't such a coward, Hugo," said Carlisle, with the same nervous eagerness to accuse herself. "I — I knew him quite well — at one time. He was a wonderful swimmer, never afraid. . . . Perhaps it's only a feeling — but, indeed, I *know* he wouldn't have swum off and left me — if —"

"My dear girl, if you were really so certain of that, why didn't you say so at the time?"

Carlisle, looking at the floor, said wistfully: "If I only had . . ."

She was acutely aware that his question carried a new tone into the discussion, that Hugo had criticised her for the first time. The tiny crack in their perfect understanding yawned suddenly wider. And distressed, and pitifully conscious that it was all her fault, Cally flung herself instinctively across the breach. Her gaze still lowered, she took Hugo's hand and pressed it to her smooth cheek: an endearing thing, and done with a muteness more touching than any speech.

Canning was moved. She was not demonstrative by habit. He kissed the cheek, for once almost as if she were a child. And he said that of course she would have said so that night, except that she hadn't really been certain of anything of the sort then. That feeling came now, born of excessive sympathy and nervous shock. The mistake would be to accept these feelings for her final judgment on such a very complicated and serious matter.

So he was arguing the case for postponement of discussion once more, with excellent good sense and an even more moving insistence. . . .

If he had now but ceased his argument, turned, gathered her to his arms, and adjured her by his overflowing love to entrust herself to him, it is possible that within two minutes he might have had her weeping on his breast, in complete surrender. Body and soul, she was sore with much pounding: more than an hour ago, she needed sympathy and comfort now, loverly occupation of the desolating lonely places within her. But Canning argued, seeing nothing else to do, argued with a deepening note of patience in his voice. And when he stopped at length, it was natural that she should argue back: though she really meant this for her last attempt to convey the dim light that was in her.

"I hate to seem so silly and obstinate, Hugo. I — I can't seem to explain it exactly. But I really don't think that waiting would make any difference — in my feeling. And don't you think, if I feel I . . . could n't be happy till I — got this off my mind . . ."

Again he explained that this feeling was but a passing illusion, here to-day, gone to-morrow.

Carlisle hesitated. But Canning, seeing only silence for his pains, said with a little quickening of his tone:

"Tell me, my dear! Honestly, would such a thought as that — about your happiness — ever have occurred to you if it had n't been suggested to you by Dr. Vivian?"

Natural as the inquiry was to Canning, it jangled oddly upon Carlisle. She could not understand Hugo's recurrence to this man; it seemed curiously unreasonable, quite unlike him and somehow quite unjust. . . .

"Why, I don't know, Hugo. I — I seem to have had it on my mind a good deal lately. Perhaps he first made me think of it that way — I don't know."

"Don't you think perhaps we might have understood each other a little better all along, if you had talked it over with me before you talked to him about it?"

"Yes, I do now. I did n't seem to think . . . It all happened so unexpectedly — I never planned anything at all. And then I thought — I hoped — you would think I was doing right."

"My dear girl, nobody in his senses could possibly think you were doing right, and nobody who cared for you could want you to abandon yourself to the impulses of a moment of nervous hysteria."

He rose and paced the floor, four paces to the room. A handsome and impressive figure of a man he looked, his hands rammed into the pockets of his beautiful blue-flannel coat, his fine brow wrinkled with a responsible frown. He was seven years older than Carlisle, and, in the absence of Mr. Heth (whom neither telephone nor telegraph, prayer nor fasting, had yet been able to reach), he stood as her lawful protector and the man of her family. He must save her from the effects of her own hysterical moment, or nobody would. Clearer and clearer it had grown that he had to do with a distracted creature who, in a state of shock, had somehow passed under the influence of a man of the unscrupulous revivalist type, and upon whom, in her present mood, all reasoning was thrown away. Gentleness and firmness were the notes for dealing with a flare-up. Well, gentleness had been tried in vain. . . .

Carlisle looked at Canning as he paced, in the grip of a heartsick fear. The same comfortable, homely little room, with tight-closed door; the same evening sunshine filtering in across the faded carpet; the same situation, the same man and woman. But what was this new shape that peeped at her from behind the familiar objects? A delusion and a snare had been her first feeling of perfect unity. But was it conceivable that she and Hugo might *quarrel?* . . .

That was the one thing that could not be borne; anything to avoid that. She must give him his way, since he would not give her hers. She must agree to put it off till to-morrow, and then to-morrow he would still think she was unreasonable, and so they would put it off again, forever. She thought of Jack Dalhousie, lying on his back, but with open eyes which did not cease to question her; of poor Dr. Vivian, even now awaiting her word with trusting eyes which did not question anything; and she saw that to turn back now would be like a physical fracture somehow, like breaking her leg, and that the moment she had said she would, she would have to cry again, and afterwards she would be quite sick. And then she looked at Hugo, who was so manly and sure, who *must* be right, no matter how she felt now: and so began to nerve herself to speak. . . .

But Canning had a new thought, a new argument, which now became definite. Coming to a halt in front of her, he said in a businesslike sort of way:

"Let's see now. You want to send word to Dr. Vivian this

afternoon that he is to tell Colonel Dalhousie that you feel you did his son an injustice. Is that it?"

Checked in her drift toward yielding, Carlisle said that was what she had thought.

"Well, let's imagine what would happen then. I said just now that for you to do this would accomplish nothing, but it would of course raise a cloud of doubt, of which the Colonel would probably make the very most. He would not be so scrupulous about giving you the benefit of the doubt as you feel, at the moment, about giving it to his son. He could make a most unpleasant story of it."

Carlisle sat with lowered eyes, listening to the firm just tones. Very lovely and desirable she looked in a "little" white dress which Hugo had praised once. . . .

"And malice would seize on this story and make it worse and worse the further it travelled. If you stop to think a moment, you will easily see what a sensation the scandalmongers can make out of the materials you ingenuously wish to offer them."

He himself stopped to think; his keen mind flung out little exploring parties over the prospect he hinted at, and they raced back shrieking with vulgar horrors. Surely, surely his chosen bride could never have contemplated this.

"Carlisle, have you reflected that you would be pointed at, whispered about, till the longest day you live?"

She sat motionless, with averted face, and felt that she was slipping from her last mooring. Was it conceivable that Hugo was persuading her to hush it all up again — just because it was *easier?* . . . She and mamma had done that and thought nothing of it. But, for this moment, at least, it seemed horribly different to have such a thought about Hugo. . . .

She said in a little voice: "But if it's right, I ought n't to think about consequences, ought I?"

Canning groaned.

"How many times must I tell you that it's not right, that it's preposterous, that you yourself will say so to-morrow! . . ."

She made no reply, and then Canning, goaded on by his sense of strange impotence, spoke the depths of his secret resentment:

"Really, I should have thought that the views of your future husband would have more weight with you than those of a casual medical missionary, known to be irresponsible and untrustworthy."

Cally gave him a look full of young reproach, rose with nervous purposelessness, and went over to the empty hearthside. Much nearer now peeped that startling shape. She leaned upon the mantel and tried to think: of her duty to Hugo, of how natural it was that he should n't understand, of how all this had begun. But unhappily the tone of his last remark seemed to have set other chords quivering within her, and all that she seemed able to think of was that it was cruelly unjust for him to misjudge her so. He had promised to stand by her no matter what happened, and besides Dr. Vivian was n't irresponsible and untrustworthy. The wild thought knocked that Hugo, now that he knew the truth about her, had ceased to love her. . . .

"Carlisle," said Canning, with more restraint, "is n't it reasonable for me to think that?"

Her reply showed some signs of agitation: "Why, Hugo — of course . . . You must know your views have all the weight in the world with me. His have none . . ."

He came up to her on the hearthstone, raised her hand, and kissed the little pink palm.

"Never mind — I'm sure that's true. . . . Now, my dear, we seem unable to understand each other to-day, and trying to do so only throws us farther and farther apart. We both need rest, and time for quiet thought. You must let me decide this point for you. I am going to send word to Dr. Vivian now that you will let him hear from you to-morrow morning."

He released her hand, and turned decisively away. At that moment, the dim hall chimes began to strike six.

"Oh, no, Hugo! Please don't," she broke out, taking a little step after him. . . . "*Please!* I don't think I could bear it. . . ."

Canning wheeled instantly, his virile face darkening and flushing.

"You don't? . . . My views don't seem to matter so tremendously, after all!"

"Ah, Hugo dear! That hurts. How —"

"Tell me, Carlisle, did the idea of telling Colonel Dalhousie, for your happiness, originate with you or with this man?"

Touched once more in her spirit by his singular obsession, she replied, with constraint: "I don't remember, Hugo. Perhaps with him. But it was n't his saying so that made it true. It is the way I feel . . ."

"That brings us back to the beginning again. I have done my best to persuade you that this feeling is an hallucination."

Over and over this ground they went with quickening exchanges, Canning's patience wearing sharper at each circuit, Carlisle growing steadily whiter, but unluckily not more yielding. At last Canning said:

"You are going to trust your whole future life to me, Carlisle. It is hard for me to grasp that you refuse to trust me in this, the first thing I have ever asked of you. Tell me plainly that you mean to have no regard for my wishes."

Carlisle felt ready to scream. How had this miserable misunderstanding arisen? What was it all about? Her mind glanced back, but she could not remember, could not begin to retrace the bewildering steps. Worse yet, she hardly seemed to want to now, for Hugo could not possibly speak to her in this way if he loved her as he had said.

She said in a small, chilled voice: "That's unjust, Hugo. I have every regard —"

"So you say, Carlisle. But nothing else that you say supports it in the slightest."

The girl made no reply. And then Canning struck out:

"My entreaties carry no weight with you, it seems. Well, then I forbid you."

For the first time a tinge of color touched Carlisle's cheek.

"You forbid me?"

He had no sooner said the words than he regretted them. In the beginning nothing of this sort had been within his dreams; had he foreseen the possibility, it is probable that he would have given Carlisle her head at the start without argument. But, once the position taken, he could not bend back his pride to recede.

And to him, too, came prodding thoughts, of a bride who was revealing strange sides of her nature, strange unlovelinesses. . . .

"Good God!" broke from him. "With such excessive consideration for *two* other men, have n't you an atom for the man you are to marry? Has n't it occurred to you that in a matter seriously involving my life as well as yours, I have a claim, a joint authority with yourself?"

"Occurred to me? It has never been out of my mind."

"Yet you resent it, it seems. I say that I forbid your doing something so full of painful consequences to us both, and you show that you resent it . . . Don't you?"

"It's a surprise to me that you would want to use your authority in such a way. But —"

"Then you must have failed to grasp that this act of folly you contemplate, over my entreaty and command, would bring an entirely new element into the situation . . ."

Carlisle looked at him without shrinking now. "A new element into the situation? I don't understand. How do you mean?"

"Carlisle! Be frank! You know the effects of all this. Have you the right, when I have sought one girl for my wife, to offer me quite another?"

Pink deepened on the girl's cheek.

"I don't think I have. . . . Well, Hugo, you are free. . . ."

"*Don't say that!*" cried Canning, in a voice thick with a chaos of feeling. "It's unendurable . . ."

He turned abruptly away.

Of the two, in that disruptive moment, Canning was far the more visibly perturbed. If women think with their emotions, Carlisle's emotions, rebelling at long overstrain, had now run away with her. She was never a docile girl, as her mother well knew. To Canning she had dealt the ultimate unbelievable buffet. Through all her incredible obstinacy, through all his knowledge of the capabilities of her spirit, he had hardly doubted that one hint of betrothal restiveness would be sufficient to bring her to her knees. Now he seemed to wear her words like a frontlet, branded in the mantling scarlet of his brow. The young man felt himself falling through space. . . .

The same familiar little room, but now with a new face. Twilight began to steal into it. On the cheerless hearthside, the lovers stood, and each knew that words once spoken live forever. And looking at each other's faces each knew, and could not change it, that the lover was not uppermost in them now. They were two human beings spent with long arguing, two wills hopelessly at the clash.

In the sudden break-up of the trusted and reliable, Canning's polished style had been torn from him. He owned, laboriously and at some length, that this serious disagreement between them was terribly disturbing to him. How would it be later, if she refused now to show any regard for his urgent requests? Was it unreasonable for him to expect his chosen wife to consider the responsibilities entailed by his name and position, to share his ambition to hold both above the stings of malice and unmerited scandal?

At another moment, both the manner and matter of Hugo's remarks would have touched Carlisle profoundly. But she was beyond thinking of Hugo now. All that her fluttering heart could feel was that when he had promised to stand by her through all time, he had meant only to stand by her as long as she did everything as he told her. . . .

"No, Hugo, it is reasonable. That is what I say. I am unreasonable. I don't seem able to help it to-day."

And Hugo, with the last remnant of his unconquerable incredulities, for the twentieth time mentioned another day. A post-mortem flicker of reargument started: started, but went out, quickly extinguished by the perilous fascination of the personal. Unspoken thoughts pressed in upon them as they circled, lifelessly reiterating. These thoughts grew rapidly louder; and Canning, striving to keep his bitter hostility from his tone, gave voice:

"Of course the truth is — though I am sure you don't realize it yourself — this man has somehow got you under his influence . . . A sort of moral hypnosis . . . to compel you to do what is against your nature . . . and will bring you great harm."

At what conceivable point had the grounds of discussion become so completely metamorphosed?

"No, that is n't true. I'm not doing —"

"I suggest that in your interest . . . Otherwise I should be unable to account for the predominant part you have allowed him to play in this."

"And yet, Hugo, he was right in saying that I could n't be happy if I did n't tell the truth. And you don't understand that even now."

"I fear I've always been dull at these camp-meeting metaphors."

Now they had struck the greased road, and easy was the descent to Avernus. Carlisle said, all weakness gone from her:

"Well, I don't ask you to understand any more. You feel that I'm not the same girl —"

"I did n't say that! I asked . . . if you had the right — now — to make yourself a — different girl. By that —"

"I'm afraid I've already made myself a different girl from what you thought. You knew that when mamma told you what I had done. . . ."

Why could n't he say that he wanted her twenty times over, no matter what she had done? It would have been easy to say that half an hour ago. Canning's reply was: "I've said again and again that you've done nothing. All this malicious scandal cannot touch you unless you yourself wilfully start it."

"You seem to care less about what I am, than about what people might think I am. And yet," she added, her hand upon her heart and her breath coming quicker and quicker, "you wonder that I let somebody else tell me what I am."

The deliberate reference to the revivalist fellow stung Canning like the flick of a glove in his face.

"Dr. Vivian? He has not my disadvantage of laboring to save his affianced's name from everlasting disgrace."

"Perhaps he does n't find disgrace where you seem to look for it."

"It is cheap to be prodigal with other men's belongings. What is this man to you?"

"Hugo! — Hugo!" broke from her. "I can't bear this! . . . You must leave me."

"If I go," said Canning, trembling, "I do not return."

"It is what I wish," said Carlisle.

And her other hand came to her heart, to his glittering pledge upon her finger. . . .

Canning stood watching her, paling and purpling. How they had come to this he knew no more than Carlisle; and no more than she could he force his steps backward. In truth, the deeps of him had never so passionately desired her as now, yearning beyond reason or understanding to the untamed spirit. And yet . . . What did he know of her, whom he thought he knew so well? She had flirted with a young drunkard, fraternized with a low crank, inextricably involved herself in the scandals of a suicide. Taxed with these things, she was wantonly rebellious, contemptuously indifferent to his wishes. Lovely and wild she stood there. And yet . . .

He heard his hoarse voice saying: "Think, Carlisle. You are sure that this is what you wish . . ."

"You leave me no alternative."

"Oh, but I have . . . I do."

"Not one that I can accept."

"Then you force me to say good-bye."

"Good-bye."

His legs could not have heard the marching-order; he remained rooted where he stood. Ebbings and flowings of color mottled his handsome face.

"One last word . . . Is it to come to this? We stand . . . at the final parting of the ways. Think . . . This is what you wish?"

If he still hoped for impossible reconciliation, or if merely some instinct moved him to put the burden for the breaking upon her, Carlisle did not know. She was past arguing now.

"This is yours."

On the pink palm he had kissed such a little while ago she held out the glorious diamond he had given her in the first radiance of the engagement. Canning saw no way of escaping the offering; he accepted it with a stiff bow, dropped it in the pocket of his coat. But it was a business to which even he quite failed to impart any dignity.

He looked blindly about for his hat and stick, remembered that he had left them outside, turned and faced his love again. Between them passed a long look.

"Then . . . this is good-bye."

"Good-bye," said Cally again.

And then Hugo opened the door of papa's study and went away. And in a moment there was the sound of the front door shutting.

Was it over, then? Was the parting of lovers so brief, so final? . . .

Cally started, as from a trance. She ran out of the study and through the dark library to the drawing-room and the front windows. Just in time, she stood behind the curtains, and caught a last glimpse of Canning's receding back. Brave and dear it looked, departing.

Over and over she said to herself: "He's gone . . . Hugo's gone . . . He has thrown me over . . ."

Gone was the prince of lovers. Calamity fell upon calamity. It would be better to be dead. And suddenly all that was hard and resisting in the girl broke with the taut strain, broke with a poignant bodily throe, and she fell face downward into a great chair, weeping with wild abandon.

Here, within two minutes from the shutting of the door, her mother found her.

So the beginning at the Beach touched its farther end. It touched with the shocks of cataclysm, whose echoes did not soon cease to reverberate. The word of the Lord came to Jack Dalhousie's father, and he would not suffer in silence. Mr. Heth arrived at the House at ten o'clock that night; it was the best he had been able to do, but it was too late for a family reunion by an hour. The two women had fled away to New York, probably on the very same train that bore back Hugo Canning. And behind them Rumor of the triple head had already risen, roaring an astonishment and a proverb.

XXII

One summer in the Old Hotel; of the World's wagging on, Kern Garland, and Prince Serge Suits; of how Kern leaves the Works for Good and has a Dream about Mr. V. V.'s Beautiful Lady; of how Mr. V. V. came to sit in the still Watches and think again of John the Baptist.

AND still the world wagged on.

Calamity befell one House out of many, and the natural cycles did not stir a hair's breadth. The evening and the morning were another day, and another and another. May ran indifferent out, with blue skies and a maddening sequence of "Continued Heat." Then presently the long days had reached their length, loitered awhile, turned slowly backward. And June had become July, and midsummer lay fast over the half-empty town.

It was a summer that broke records for heat, and those fled from it who could. But in the industrious backwaters of towns, where steady work means steady bread, it is the custom of men to take the climate as it comes to them, freezing or sweating at the weather-man's desire. Mountain and ocean, awninged gardens and breeze-swept deck: those solaces are not for these. Ninety Fahrenheit it ran and over, day after day, half of June, half of July. But in the old Dabney House Mrs. Garland stood on by the steaming wash-tubs, and Kern fared daily to the bunching-room at Heth's and its air like the breath of a new bake-oven, and Vivian, the doctor, was never "on his vacation" when his sick called, and stout Mr. Goldnagel, week on week, mopped his bald Hebraic head and repaired while you waited, with all work strictly guaranteed.

Of these four it was the young physician who kept the busiest, for his work never ended. Falling back from his brief appearance in the upper world, he had been speedily swallowed again by his own environment. Routine flattened him out as never before; the problem of life was to find time to sleep.

For one thing, there was a mild epidemic of typhoid this summer, breaking out in those quarters of the town where moderate conveniences (as Mrs. Garland called them) were matters of hearsay only, and the efficient and undermanned Health Department, fighting hard, did not have the law to drive home orders where they would do the most good. But the doctor of the Dabney House needed no epidemic to keep him occupied, so acceptable was his no-bill custom — still maintained — to the unwell laity of the vicinage. Through the dingy waiting-room, old state bedchamber, there rolled a waxing stream, and the visiting rounds of V. Vivian, M.D., ran long and overlong.

Had these been pay patients, carriage trade, Receipts would have soared dizzily in these days, and handsome additions might have been made to that Beirne residue of fifteen thousand dollars, now lying useless, not even at three per centum, in Mr. Heth's Fourth National Bank. But here trooped only the unworthy with unworthy troubles, not always of the body; the poor and the sinful with their acute complaints; waiters and day-laborers and furtive sisters in sorry finery, plumbers' helpers with broken heads, bankrupt washerwomen, married grocer's clerks with coughs not destined to stop. To these through the sweltering days and nights, young Dr. Vivian ministered according to his gifts. They took his pills, his bottles and his "treatment"; they lauded but rarely took his moral counsel; and not a few spoke of loans. . . .

All July the old hotel rang with the blows of hammer and the rasp of saw, in preparation for its new birth in September, as the Union Settlement House. There came often, in the late afternoons, the Rev. George Dayne, the tireless and kind-faced Secretary of Charities, who wandered whistling over the lower floor, while his mind's eye saw, beyond the litter of boards and brick and demolished partitions, the emerging visage of a great institution. And Mr. Dayne rarely failed to climb the stairs for a little chat with the young man in the polished coat who, under promise of secrecy, had called these wonders into being.

More regular were the visits of Hon. Samuel O'Neill, desirous
of talking over the state of the Union, particularly as touching
the new advanced labor law he was now beginning to draft —
"stiffest factory legislation ever passed in the South." And
sometimes, when the condition of the sick permitted it, these
two would slip away from the Dabney House for a welcome
swim, with a growing swarm of boys behind; for Vivian had been
the best swimmer on the river in his day, and still did things from
the springboard which many lads with two sound feet could not
copy. So diversion from the medical grind was not wanting.
And once in June, the doctor lunched with Mr. Dayne at Berrin-
ger's, and twice he was dragged off to supper at the Cooneys' and
enjoyed himself very much, and once he took Sunday dinner with
his aunt, Mrs. Mason, and his little Mason cousins: only that
time he was called away from the table before dessert, and got
back to South Street just a minute before Mrs. Meeghan died. . . .

The Garlands rarely saw their boarder now except at meal-
times, and by no means always then. Kern, for her part, was off
to the Works at quarter to seven each morning, and had stopped
coming home for dinner since the heat got so bad. However, the
women observed him, and talked him over of nights as they
washed the dishes in the new detached kitchen. For the Garland
ménage boasted this moderate convenience now, directly attrib-
utable to the remarkable growth of Receipts (voluntary) which
had reached $21.75 by the book for the single month of June.
It was agreed that Mr. V. V. was not so jokey at the supper-
table as formerly, and looked po'ly, in fine, and no wonder, the
heat and all, and the way he let Hazens and Epsteins roust him
out of bed in the middle of his sleep.

Kern deplored the doctor's thinness, and hardly less, in her
secret heart, his strange indifference to his personal appearance.
She observed to her mommer that she never see a gempman go so
shabby. She longed to admonish Mr. V. V. on some of these matters, but on the whole hardly saw her way clear. However, it is
possible to do a thing or two by indirection in this world, as one
half the race has had good reason to learn. And one sultry night
in mid-July, the little buncher seemed able to talk of nothing

but the astonishing suit Jem Noonan had just obtained at the One-Price Outfitting Company for the somewhat laughable sum of $7.90. A three-piece Prince serge, warranted fast, with the English shoulders and high-cut vest, which only last week had been $15, for Jem had seen it in the window with his own eyes, but had waited around, knowing that the Mid-Summer Stock Rejuicing Sales were now about due. Such a Chance Would Not Soon Occur Again: so it said on the card in the window, and so Didymus himself would have believed, hearing Kern Garland's abandoned eulogies. . . .

And, sure enough, Mr. V. V., at length fired out of his purely civil interest, was visited with a brilliant association of ideas, as his eye betrayed. It was a matter, it will be remembered, which he had always meant to take up some day.

"Did you say the One-Price," he inquired, not without an inner sense of cleverness and enterprise, "or was it the Globe?"

Kern's heart thrilled. She was a woman, and hence the mother of all men. And this, of course, was the moment to introduce quite simply, the subject of the Genuine Mouldform Garments like the pixtures in the magazines, $15, rejuiced from as high as $28.50, and would look, oh, so fine and stylish long after the Prince serge had worn slick and faded. . . .

"But I thought you spoke of the Prince as something especially fine," said Mr. V. V., with rather a long face for the way expenses seemed to be mounting up.

"Fine for on'y a carpenter, oh, yes," said Kern, "but not hardly what you'd recmend to a doctor, oh, no."

The young man said ruefully that perhaps he had better investigate the One-Price bargains, before Jem Noonan gobbled them all up. Then his eyes rested on Kern across the table, and the light of enterprise died out of them. . . .

To take this child away from the Heth Works would be easy, indeed, but what to do with her then? That was a question which money could not answer. Kern's education had stopped at twelve. She was nineteen years old, born to work, and qualified to do nothing in the world but make cheroots.

After all, could anything more suitable happen to her than that she should take a fancy to Jem Noonan, the upstanding, square-jawed, taciturn youth who had appeared at the Dabney House in his Sunday blacks one night in May, and had reappeared regularly once a week since? Noonan was master of his trade at twenty-one, a lodge man, an attendant at ward meetings, and laying by money to embark as a contractor; he bade fair to be a power some day. And, though he seemed to be almost completely dumb, there must be something uncommon in him that he should be so drawn to the gay, dreaming little creature who was so clearly made of other clay than his. . . .

"I have n't seen Jem for some time," said the doctor aloud, casually. "How are you and he getting on these days?"

Kern gave an impish little exclamation: she never liked for Mr. V. V. to mention Jem.

"Him and me mostly get off! . . . Him and *I* mostly get off. . . ."

And then she giggled briefly, and sprang up with eyes too bright and went skipping and kicking for the detached kitchen to see if there was any hot lightbread.

But she flung over her shoulder as she vanished: "Jem he lacks 'magination. . . ."

Returning with rolls, the small diplomat reverted to the question of the Mouldform Garment, which, it seemed to be settled, Mr. V. V. was to purchase on the morrow. Kern's endeavor was to convey the idea that, in cases such as this, many men ever made it a practice to keep the old suit by, like for rainy days, and under no circumstances to give it away to the first person comes along and asts them for it. Clearly the reference here was to her father, the erring Mister, who had appeared at the Dabney House in June's first blush and was now (it was presumable) wearing Mr. V. V.'s derby down many a sunny lane.

"And the shirts they got at the One-Price Company!" cooed Kern. "And the shoes! . . . Lor, them people 're givin' away stock awmost! . . ."

However, Mr. V. V. did not purchase shoes and shirts next day, or even a Genuine Mouldform Garment. For that day was Tuesday, July 17th, the day when the professional mercury in the

Government "kiosk" set its new record, which was like to stand for many years. One hundred and one it announced, not without a touch of pride; and that day Ours was the hottest city in the United States (some said in the world), and many private thermometers showed one hundred and four, five, and six. And on that day Corinne Garland wilted abruptly in the sickening heat, and her tall machine at the Heth Works stood silent after three P.M. . . .

Kern came home and went to bed, and suddenly all the current of life in the Dabney House was changed. It was after five when Mr. V. V., returning from his rounds, heard the news, with a tightening feeling around his heart, and went down the long hall to see her.

The little girl lay silent, with feverish cheeks, and did not make a game of sticking out her tongue, which was certainly a bad symptom. However, Kern was sensitive with Mr. V. V.; she did n't like to answer his questions, would n't tell the truth in fact. It took a grizzled gentleman from the other end of town, Dr. Halstead, late physician to Mr. Armistead Beirne, to fix the diagnosis beyond doubt. Typhoid, said he, confirming the first impression of his learned young colleague. Kern Garland had typhoid.

Well, it was n't her lungs, at any rate, objects of suspicion since the pleurisy in January. Only — only — how had she ever been allowed to stay on at the Works so long? . . .

The little girl had also a nervous constitution, hardly fitted for weathering many gales. So observed the grizzled visitor, aside. And, glancing about the poor room with its swaybacked double bed, he advised that she be sent off to a hospital without delay, and so smiled cheerily at the small patient and went chugging back to his handsome house on Washington Street, having poohpoohed all mention of a fee.

But Kern cried bitterly at the threat of a hospital, and Mr. V. V. instantly promised that she should n't stir a foot from where she was. He did n't mean that she should suffer by it, either. But it would be a strange thing if he, a resident physician with the riches of the world behind him (practically speaking), could not do all that a hospital could do, and perhaps that little more beside that might make all the difference. . . .

There followed a day of intense activity, and at the end of that time — behold the power of money in the bank, so decried by transcendentalists.

Mrs. Garland slept alone in a new room containing the sway-backed double bed, and (to tell the truth) not one earthly thing besides. Kern slept in a brand-new single bed of white iron, new-mattressed and sheeted, and not far away stood another bed exactly like it. Beside Kern's bed stood a table holding glasses and bottled milk and thermometer and cracked ice and charts and liquid diet. In one of the windows stood three potted geraniums, growing nicely and bright red. Another window, where the noonday sun shone in too warmly, was fitted with a red-striped awning; and in a third — for the pleasant old room, at the extreme back of the house, had no less than four of them — a baby electric fan, operated from a storage battery, ran musically hour by hour. And through all these marvels moved the biggest and most incredible marvel of all: a lady in a blue-and-white dress and long apron, with spectacles and a gentle voice, who was paid *twenty-five dollars a week* to wait upon and give sponge baths to her, Kern Garland.

Yes, you could do something with one thousand dollars put into a checking account, and fourteen thousand more waiting behind that on a certificate of deposit. But was it not the irony of life, was it not life itself, that the little buncher, who only the other day would have thrilled to her marrow at the mere thought of all these things, should have won her lady's glories only when she was too strangely listless to care for them? . . .

Mrs. Garland feebly protested against the doctor's staggering expenditures, as in duty bound, but was silenced when he told her that, by a lucky chance, he had a fund given him by a benevolent relative for just such cases. The doctor took advantage of the interview to announce a stiff raise in board-charges, saying, in quite a censorious way, that he had been expecting for some time to hear a demand from her for such an increase. As it was, through her failure to protect her own interests, she and Kern had been doing the full duties of an office-boy for him, doing them, he might say, faithfully and well, without compensation of any sort whatsoever. This imposition must cease at once.

"Again," said he, "I am growing — somewhat heartier. I am quite aware that I eat more. I say that thirty-five dollars a month, and probably more, is the proper amount for me to pay."

And he said it so sternly, with such a superior gempman's way to him, that Mrs. Garland, feeling convicted of guilt, — and, to tell the truth, missing Kern's earnings sorely, — could only reply: "Just as you say, sir, well, now, and thank you kindly, I'm sure."

The first excitement gradually subsided, and the Dabney House settled to the long pull. Days slipped by, all just alike.

Kern's malady discouraged reading aloud. It discouraged conversation. Visitors were not allowed. But twice, without the nurse's knowledge, — Miss Masters took her rest-time every afternoon from three to seven, — rules were suspended to admit Miss Sadie Whirtle, of Baird & Himmel's, — an enormous, snapping, red-cheeked girl she proved to be, whose ample Semitic countenance gave a copious background for violet talcum, but who said nothing wittier in Vivian's hearing than "Very pleased to make your acquaintance, I'm sure" — and once to admit Miss Henrietta Cooney, of Saltman's bookstore. Hen came by from the store late one August afternoon, having heard something of the case which seemed to worry V. V. more than all his others put together. She was allowed to spend twenty minutes in the sick-room, provided she did not permit Kern to talk. Having faithfully obeyed these instructions, Henrietta returned to the office, where the doctor sat in his shirt-sleeves, humped over Miss Masters's chart.

"She's an odd little thing," said Hen, "very cute and dear with her staring eyes and her yes-ma'ams. I was telling her about the Thursday Germans, first explaining that a German had nothing to do with Germany — or has it? You know you told me she was wild about parties. She was so, so interested. . . . V. V., she's quite a sick girl, is n't she?"

"Quite sick," replied V. V. He glanced out of his weather-worn window, and said: "But she's going to be better to-morrow."

"Oh! That's the crisis, or whatever you call it?"

He answered by a nod, and Hen continued:

"She never belonged in the Works, and she certainly never belonged to that fat woman with the beak I met in the hall. She's a changeling — that's it. Speaking of the Works, V. V., I had quite a long letter from Cally Heth this week."

"Oh!" said V. V. "Oh, yes! — from Miss Heth. How is she?"

Hen, who had been strolling about the tall chamber and peeking into the instrument cabinet, noted the young man's guarded tone; and she wondered how many times V. V. and her cousin Cally had met, and what part he had played in all that affair, and in general what these two thought of each other.

"Well, she's certainly in much better spirits than when I had the note from her in July. One thing, her answering my letters at all shows it. They're in Switzerland now, at the National House, Lucerne, and J. Forsythe Avery has turned up, which is a pretty good sign of the times, I should say. He's a social barometer, you know, — the last man in the world to turn up where it would hurt his position, whatever it is. It would n't surprise me a bit to hear some fine day that Mr. Canning had sneaked back, too, now that the worst is over, and was n't so very bad at that. There's a man I'd like to have five minutes' talk with," said Henrietta Cooney. "I think I'd give him something to put in his memory-book."

Hen, having her own theory of events, gave a defiant tug to her new sailor-hat. She considered that she looked very nice to-day, and she did. She, too, had been patronizing the mid-summer sales, and beside the sailor, she had on a new linen skirt which she had got for $1.75, though the original price-mark was still on it and said $5.

"Cally," she continued, "wrote a good deal about her mother's being dropped from the officers of the Associated Charities. Well it's too bad, of course, but somebody's got to take the blow, V. V., and I imagine it's going about where it belongs. Serves her right, I say, for the sort of mother she's always been, doing her best to educate all the decent feeling out of Cally, and then trying to break her when she was doing the best thing she ever did in her life. In fact — I don't want to brag, but I expect the talk I've spread around town has had a good deal to do with the way things have gone. She married mother's brother and all that," said Hen, "but I detest and despise her and always have."

V. V. burst out laughing, and Hen observed: "Well, I'm glad I said that. It's the first smile I've seen from you this month."

She stood by the old secretary, looking down at him, and she thought what a hard life he had down here, and how his face looked too refined for this so practical world. . . .

"Now, V. V., really," said she, "why can't you leave your work to this man Finnegan for just a week and pack your little bag and run down to Aunt Rose Hopwood's farmette — really? Tee Wee and Loo are there, and everybody'll be delighted to have you. In the open air all day, sleep ten hours every night, eat your blessed head off. No mosquitoes. No malaria —"

"I can't go now, Hen. It's impossible. Thank you just the same."

He spoke quite irritably, for him, and Hen, having had this subject up more than once before, desisted and turned to go.

"Well, take some sort of care of yourself, V. V.," she said from the door. "Don't be a goose. And, by the way, be very gentle with your little friend Corinne. You know she thinks you put up the moon."

V. V. had meant to be gentle with Corinne, but in the light of this remark he resolved to be gentler still. He sat for ten minutes in abstraction after Henrietta had gone; and then, rising abruptly, picked up the chart, went down the long hall, pushed aside the light green curtain that swung in front of a door, and passed into the sick-room.

Kern lay alone with her geraniums, awning, whirring fan, and other ladylike appurtenances. Mr. V. V. sat down by the white iron bed and introduced a thermometer into her mouth. He possessed himself of her wrist, took out his silver watch and presently wrote something on the chart. He took out the thermometer and again jotted upon the chart. Then he gave the patient two tablespoonfuls of peptonoids. All this in silence. And then Kern said in a whimpering little voice:

"Mr. V. V., I'm so *hongry.*"

"I know it, poor child. Just a little more patience now: you're going to begin to get better right away, and before you know it you'll be sitting down to the finest dinners that ever you popped into your mouth. Ring the bell and order what you like — stuff, stuff, stuff — banquets all day long. And that reminds me," said he, hurrying away from this too toothsome subject — "your holiday, as soon as you feel strong enough to travel. It's high time we were making pretty definite plans about that. The question is, what sort of place do you think you'd like to go to?"

"Oh! . . . Do you mean — any place — go to *any* place I like?"

"Any place in the world," replied Mr. V. V., the magnificent.

Kern thought for some time, her eyes on the window, and then said:

"I'd like to go to some place where there's mountains and a sea." She added, as if to soften the baldness of her specifications, the one word: "Like."

Mr. V. V. thought of Marathon, which on the whole did n't promise to suit. He was visited with an ingenious idea, viz.: that Kern should go to no less than two places on her convalescent tour, one containing Mountains, the other containing a Sea! And so it was settled to the general satisfaction. . . .

"Only hurry up and get well," said the tall doctor, "or you'll find the crowds gone from Atlantic City before you get there."

He had risen, but paused, looking down at the flushed little face in which the sunken dark eyes looked bigger than ever. Thoughts of himself were in his mind; and they were not pleasant thoughts.

"Kern," said he — for he had by now fallen into the family habit, abandoning the too stately Corinne — "suppose you were absolutely well, and had a thousand dollars, what would you do for yourself with it?"

It was a game well calculated to interest the little girl even in the listlessness and apathy of fever. Kern spoke first of duck, of French fried potatoes and salads rich with mayonnaise; then, hurrying on with increasing eagerness, of taking a steamer to Europe and buying her and mommer Persian clo'es. . . .

Her medical adviser was obliged to check these too exciting flights.

"I mean more as a — as an occupation," he explained. "You know, of course, you've bunched your last cheroot. I was wondering what sort of nicer work you would like to fit yourself for — later on?"

Kern boggled a good deal over the answer to this, but finally got it out.

"What I'd truly like to be, Mr. V. V., if I could, is a writer, sort of."

"Oh! . . . Yes, yes — a writer! Well, that's very nice. A very nice occupation — writing."

The child was encouraged to go on. Staring at him with her grave investigatory eyes, she said, quite timidly:

"Mr. V. V., do you think I could *ever* be an eppig poet, sir? . . . Like Homer the Blind Bard, y' know?"

Mr. V. V.'s encouraging smile became a little fixed. Yet there came nothing of a smirk into it, nothing the least bit superior. . . . Was this the explanation of the little girl's odd yearning toward pens and desks? How came she to revere the Bard, where even to hear his name? Was it possible that Mrs. Garland's changeling had a spark in her, a magic urging her on? . . .

"Epic poet, is it?" said he aloud, cheerily. "Oh, I daresay something of the sort can be arranged. No harm in having a try anyhow! First thing, of course, is to get a good education. . . ."

And he spoke of the High School, when Kern got back from her trip, with a little brushing-up, first, perhaps, under his personal supervision. . . .

And next morning, when Kern's temperature stood down a whole degree at nine o'clock, these great plans seemed to come nearer at a bound. That day the Dabney House drew a long breath and smiled. Miss Masters was even more confident than Vivian that the hard corner had been turned. So the verdict went to Hen Cooney, who telephoned from Saltman's; and so it went to Jem Noonan, who was to be found waiting in front

of the Dabney House every evening in these days, silently
biting a Heth Plantation Cheroot, which he smoked because
Kern made them, though secretly preferring the White River
brand, made by the Trust. A great capacity for waiting had
Jem. And that was the afternoon also that Doctor mysteriously vanished from his office before four o'clock, having left
no word where he could be reached with his office-boy, Mrs.
Garland; and was still out when O'Neill called at quarter to six,
to talk about his factory law. . . .

Next day, these novel excitements continued. For when Corinne Garland first opened her eyes that morning, they fell at
once upon an imagined wonder out of fairyland. There it stood
close to her bed's head, shining gloriously in the early sun,
looking, oh, so real. . . . Kern lay extremely still, gazing wide-
eyed: for well she knew the way of dreams, how you forgot and
moved a little, and then it all winked out. But after a time,
when It did not stir or dance about at all, there came to her a
desperate courage, and she stretched out a trembling little hand.
And lo, the hand encountered a solid unmistakable. And then
Kern gave a great gasping Oh, and sat up in bed; and presently,
being very weak, she began to cry, she was so happy.

It really was the prettiest Writing-Desk in the world, a desk for
a duchess's boudoir, all made of polished rosewood, and standing
tall and graceful on four curving legs. It had an astounding lid,
this Writing-Desk had; that you either locked up or let down;
and when you let it down the lid had a shining slab of plate glass
all screwed on, thus becoming the loveliest place to write on
that you could well imagine. And the inside parts of the Desk
were running over with delightful things, notepaper and envel-
opes, and pads and pencils, and new white blotting-paper and —
true as true, dull black, with the cutest little silver belt — a
beautiful Founting Pen. Inside also were pigeonholes of the
best quality, like in the Netiquette. And in one of the pigeon-
holes there lay, sure enough, a note; not, indeed, from a mus-
tached count with a neyeglass, but from one who perhaps seemed
not less of the purple to the fevered little buncher.

This note was written in the best jokey vein throughout,

beginning, "Miss Corinne Garland, City — Dear Madam," and signed, "Your most obliged and obedient servant, Writing-Desk." . . .

It had been the intention of Mr. V. V. to call personally at the sick-room before breakfast, to see how Kern liked the arrival and appearance of Writing-Desk. But Miss Masters frustrated him at the door, saying that the child's heart was set upon conveying her thanks by formal note, and she had worried and fretted so over being refused that it seemed best to give her her way, particularly as she did not seem so well to-day. And in his disappointment over these tidings, the doctor presently forgot the desk entirely.

However, Kern's note arrived in the office an hour later, through the Kindness of Miss Masters, as the envelope advised. Mr. V. V. suspended a sentence to one of his sick in the middle to read it:

> My dear Dr. Vivian:
>
> Oh, Mr. V. V., how can I ever thank you for given me this lovely Writen Desk. I greatly appreciate your kind gift. Just putten my hands on it makes me so happy, I could cry, oh the soft feel this Pretty wood has got to it.
>
> Your kind thought of me at this time has indeed pleased me. One is never so appreciative of the thought of one's friends, if I can call you my Friend, Mr. V. V., as when one lies in pain upon a sickbed, th'o I have no pain. It 's the lovlyest sweetest dearest Desk ever was Mr. V. V., and how can me and Mommer ever make up for all you done for us. I don't know. I have every hope for a speedy change for the better in my condition, and I never dreamed Id' have a Ladys Writen Desk truly, or haven one would make me oh so Happy. My first note, dear Dr. Vivian, goes to you.
>
> With repeated thanks for your considerate thought of me during my illness, believe me, with kind remembrances,
>
> Yours very cordially,
> Your faithful friend Corinne.

The young man distributed mental italics as he read. He detected at sight the footprints of the Netiquette and Complete Letter Writer. But he did not smile once as he read and reread the odd little mosaic, and folded it at last and put it away in a pigeonhole of its own. No, his stabbing thought was only, Why did n't I do it all long ago? . . . Why? . . .

And similar things he thought next morning, and the next and next. For Kern did not get well, no matter what the calendar said, no matter how loyally Writing-Desk stood at her elbow to serve her, as It had said in the Note. Her morning temperature shot up a degree again, and there it stood day after day, and would not go down. Kern obviously grew thinner and weaker. And there came a day when the President of the Settlement Association, Mr. Stewart Byrd, came in person to the Dabney House before ten o'clock, and sent all the workmen away. He said there must be no noise about the place that day. . . .

That relapse passed, but no one could say what a day might bring forth. The young doctor looked back over the past; he bowed beneath the burden that he felt upon him. However, due credit must be given to his friend Samuel O'Neill for assisting him to bring his sober meditations to a focus.

In these days O'Neill, having got his stiff factory law drafted, was becoming concerned with the problem of landing it on the statute-books. The complexion of the incoming legislature, which met in January, promised to be conservative; and the Commissioner, breathing threatenings and slaughter against the waistcoated interests which had so flouted his warnings last winter, had decided that a preliminary press campaign would be needed — beginning, say, November 1st — to arouse public opinion to the needs of reform. The lively "Chronicle," the "labor paper," offered space for a series of contributed articles from the Commission office, always provided that "hot stuff" only was furnished, by which was meant vigorous, if not libelous, assaults upon the existing order.

Now it became the earnest wish of Commissioner O'Neill that these hot-stuff articles should be written for him by his friend V. V., of the reformatory passions and the pen of a ready writer. And, the whole subject having been discussed several times in an indecisive sort of way, O'Neill one night whacked out a jagged argument.

"I had 'em going eight months ago — was starting out for Heth's with an axe — and you asked me to leave 'em to you. I thought you had something — an idea. . . . Say, V. V., suppose we'd gone and out bagged 'em then, like I wanted — would your friend Corinne be lyin' at death's door now?"

There was, indeed, nothing precisely original in this inquiry; but, put by another, and in so bald a form, it undoubtedly came upon a man somewhat stark and hard. The two men stood talking on a street corner, where they had met by chance, and their conversation here came to an end. V. V.'s reply to Sam's question was indefinite, to say the least of it. He merely observed that he must be getting on back to the office; adding that he did n't like to be absent for any length of time just now. But he did n't say at all, by that annoying habit of reserve he had, whether or not he would agree to write the *articles!* *That* was what Samuel O'Neill wanted to know. . . .

It was September now, the third night. At his office the doctor found two calls for him, noted on a scrap of brown wrapping-paper in the rudimentary hand of Mrs. Garland. He went out again, disappearing over the Hill into that quarter of the town which was less cheering than honest slums. Returning, about ten, he found the Dabney House entirely silent: all quiet from the direction of the sick-room. All quiet, too, in the tall bare office. Very quiet, indeed. . . .

It was a strange-looking room to be a doctor's office; on the whole a strange-looking young man to be a doctor; no stereotyped thoughts, it may be, pounding through the head he held so fast between his hands. Strange entanglements were here, too, with the brilliant life over the Gulf: a life whose visible thread, it is easily surmised, will hardly lead us by this ancient secretary again.

He was all alone in the world; very much so. His father was dead; and his mother, who had married a penniless idealist for love, was dead these many years. Fifteen he was when she died . . . a long time ago. And he had had nobody since. He had just been beginning to feel close to his Uncle Armistead, and now

Uncle Armistead was dead, too. And he had no sisters or brothers. He had no wife or children. . . .

He was alone, and by that token he was free. No tie bound up the hope of others in him. Had he felt the sting of youth's rage to make things better? No bond of another's claim withheld him from spending himself to the uttermost.

All this had long been clear. Long clear also were the two paths trod by the noble army, men and boys. There were those who preached a more abundant living; and there were those who lived that living. . . . A glorious thing, indeed, it was for a man so to go his quiet ways that he became an example and model to his fellows, who were made better in that their lives had touched his exemplary one. But here, alas, was an aspiration for the saints, not for weak men with known bitternesses and passions in their blood, and all youth's furies hot upon them. And surely in that other summons there was, besides, the thrill of romance, such as the young love. There was the trumpeting to high adventure. Few there were to touch, few to remember, even the saintliest life lived in a noble narrowness, a noble silence. But the word of truth, spoken from no matter what obscurity, will rise and ring round the world, and remain forever in the pattern of men's thought. Here, indeed, was a 'bliss to die with, dim-descried.' . . .

So it was that one boy had found his heroic ideal, long since, in the grim voice crying in the wilderness. And in the years the secret picture had grown very clear, curiously full of meaning. There was descried, like something remembered from another life, an innumerable company upon a rocky plain, a little river rushing by, and in the distance a City. . . .

He had seen something of life in his time at the medical school, and before that, when he was still looking about, trying to decide what he should do. He had observed in these days of leisure, read, and burned. And he had come back to his old home-city, overflowing with fine passions, aflame with new-old secrets and forgotten truths. What speeches there had been to make in those days, what roaring things to write, what shouts to be flung from the house-tops!

And now he had been at home again over a year; he had been right here in the Dabney House a year this month. And what had he done for his faith?

He had done precisely what a weak man does, precisely what he had passionately resolved never to do. He had found life hard, and he had compromised with it. A minute routine pressed upon him, and he had suffered that routine to swamp his perspective, to drown out his fires. It was a good and useful work that he did: he never doubted that. To take the pain from a sick body, to put a coat on a bare back, this was worth a man's doing. But none knew better than he that that body would grow sick again, that back once more wear naked: and all the while the untouched causes of these wrongs festered and reinfected and spread, and a fig for your Settlements and your redoubled "relief." Was there not a bay-tree that flourished, and had he not been summoned in a vision to lay an axe to its roots? Behold, he gave his youth to spraying at the parasites upon a single small leaf.

And was it only the grinding round of work that had brought him to this compromise? Was it possible that personal considerations had seduced him, as Samuel O'Neill appeared to hint? That would be base, indeed. . . .

But no . . . No, his mind, though it seemed without mercy to-night, would acquit him of that. If he had been seduced, it was by a voice in him, confused, it might be, but strong nevertheless, and not dishonest.. He had thought that perhaps people could be more gently acquainted with their responsibilities, that in their hearts they wanted to correct their own mistakes. He had asked who appointed him a judge over men. . . .

And now there were articles to write, to publish in November, to begin to prepare now. Hard articles they must be, that broke heads or hearts, implied faiths, too, and did not care. And in the young man's ears there rang, and would not cease, the cry of a girl in great sorrow: "You've never meant anything but trouble to me since the first minute I saw you." . . . And again, in another voice: "I really didn't mean to do anything so bad." . . .

As if he hadn't known that. . . .

He was alone in the world, and by that token he was a lonely man. He had no mother or brother or sisters. He had no wife or children. . . . No, nor would have this side the undiscovered country. . . .

Abruptly the young man rose from his seat at the secretary; stood, pushing back his hair. Twenty-seven years old he was, a lame slum doctor in a fire-new suit of Prince serge, lately bought cheap at a sale; but he had a face that people sometimes turned to look at in the street.

And he spoke aloud, in a voice that might have sounded queer if there had been anybody to hear it:

"Don't I know they're doing the best they can, all the time? Seems to me I've had that proved . . . Give 'em a chance, and *they're all good. . . .*"

Far in the stillness there sounded the sweet mad voice of the Garlands' clock. It struck seven, and then two, and then fell silent. V. Vivian glanced at his watch. It seemed to be quarter to twelve, though he did not see how that was possible. He opened his office door, and stood listening. Presently he stepped through; went walking without noise down the long hall, which was pitch-black but for a dim haze of light just perceptible at its extreme farther end. When he came to this small patch, the young man lifted the curtain, and stood motionless.

A single gaslight burned in the sick-room, shaded with a green globe and turned down very low. The electric fan was silent, and the faint fever-smell was in the air. In the nearer white bed the nurse slept, with light snores. In the other, Kern Garland slept, lying almost at the bed's edge. One of her arms had wandered from the covers; the small hand was curled about the polished leg of Writing-Desk, which was squeezed as close to the bed as it would go.

Vivian went in on silent feet. Presently he sat down in his accustomed chair on the farther side of the bed. He stared fixedly at the small flushed face, which looked more elfin than ever now that the flesh was wasting away. . . .

What demerit had this little girl that she should be ordered to give up her health and life only that others might wear fine raiment and live in kings' houses? Surely it was not God who had laid that sentence upon her.

Corinne Garland and the Heth Works: it was long since these two had first seized his mind like a watchword. For here was no matter of one small girl who worked more hours than her strength would bear; no matter even of one large factory which harnessed the life of three hundred men and women and drove them over-hard. But was not this the perfect symbol of that preying of the fortunate upon the unfortunate, of that crushing inequality of inheritance, which reacted so deadeningly upward and down-ward, and more than anything else hobbled the feet of Man? By one flagrant instance, by Kern at Heth's, all the pitiful wrong-headedness was made plain. Pinned forever to the accident of economic birth, all their energies sucked up by the struggle for bread and meat, these poor were mocked with bitter "equality" which did not equalize, but despoiled of all chance to extricate themselves from their poverty. And their terrible revenge was to spread their own stagnation upward. Neither could the rich extricate themselves from their riches. The sorriest thing in the picture was that they did not desire to. Behold how blindly they struggled to cut the brotherly cord that bound them to what was common and unclean, and that cord their souls' one light. . . .

The still young man looked at the face of his little patient, and his mind went back to that day when he and O'Neill had visited the Heth Works, last October, and he had seen Kern at her machine. He had come back ablaze, and he had then written that Severe Arraignment which Mr. Heth had threatened to sue the "Post" for publishing, but never had. . . . And then . . . and then he had thought that perhaps nothing so loud and harsh would be needed. Hopeful months went by. Then trouble had come to a family, and he had stayed his hand again. . . . And now, Kern Garland, who was dear to him, whose right and need he had failed to voice. . . .

"Oh! . . . *Mr. V. V.!*"

Without warning, the little girl sat up in bed, her cheeks bright, her eyes wide and shining. Yet it seemed that she had called Mr. V. V.'s name a little before her eyes fell upon his silent figure.

"Oh, Mr. V. V.!" she repeated in a low eager voice, hardly above a whisper . . . "I been havin' the loveliest dreams! . . ."

The young man put out a hand and pressed it firmly against her hot forehead.

"Lie down, little Kern."

She lay down obediently, her face wearing a strange half-smile. Though her eyes were wide, her look was that of a person between sleeping and waking: she showed no surprise at Mr. V. V.'s being there by her bedside.

"Mr. V. V., I had on a white sating Persian dress, lowneg, and embroidery and loops of pearls put on all over it, and white sating pumps, and a fan all awstritch feathers. I was at a German — y' know? — "

"You must n't talk now, Kern. Put your arm under the cover and go back to sleep —"

"*Lemme*, Mr. V. V.! Please. It's on'y a minute to tell. Can't I, sir? . . . I was at a German, with ladies and gempmen, and there was pink lights — and vi'lins — and plants — and little presents they give you for dancin' — and flowers — and such lovely clo'es! . . . On'y I did n't have a partner. Like a stag, y' know? And then pretty soon I saw people looking at me, and kep' on looking, and one of 'em that looked somep'n like Miss Masters, on'y it was n't her, says, 'Wot's that girl a-doin' here?' she says. 'Why, she's a buncher down to Heth's.' So I walked on off and set down at my Writin'-Desk, and made out I did n't notice and was writin' notes or somep'n, like. And then I looks up and they was all coming over to me, like sayin' move on now, and then I looks off again and there was you and Miss Heth, settin' . . ."

Her listener was by no means surprised at the introduction of this name. Many times had Kern spoken of her meeting with Miss Heth, that Sunday she took the note, though Mr. V. V. did not know that from that day dated her preference for white dresses, as compared with red. . . .

"Settin' on a velvet settee you was," whispered Kern, her hand picking at the sheet, "by a founting, a boy with wings and a pink lamp on his head, pourin' water out of a gool' pitcher. And I went runnin' over to you to ast you must I go — or somep'n.

And then up comes all the ladies and gempmen and says, 'This girl don't belong here,' they says, 'she must go at once.' And Miss Heth she gets up and says, 'Not at all, this here girl is a friend of me and Doctor's.' And I says, 'No, ma'am, it's right what they say, I don't belong here.' But she says to them to leave me be. 'And do you, Co-rinne,' she says — just that away, like you used to say — 'do you, Corinne, come and set on this velvet settee with me and Doctor, and listen to this here founting play.' And I felt sad someways and I says, 'Oh, no, ma'am, it's all a mistake me being here, and these clo'es must n't belong to a workin'-girl like me. I might go to school some day,' I says, 'and be a writer sort of, mebbe; but I ain't a lady, ma'am, Miss Heth, no, nor never will be.' And Miss Heth she takes my face between her hands — yes, sir, she did, Mr. V. V., right there before 'em all — and she says, kind of surprised, 'Why, Co-rinne, I thought Doctor he told you long ago,' she says. 'You been a lady all the time . . .' And then . . . and then I woke up! . . . Was n't that funny?" said Kern. And her face indicated that she might have told more, if she had had a mind to. . . .

She lay staring, with parted lips and that same remote half-smile, as of one not yet fully returned from fairy wanderings in far lands. She did not seem to expect her inquiry to bring forth any response from the man sitting in the shadows, and it did n't, so far as words went. Mr. V. V.'s fingers had closed over her exposed wrist; presently he put the bony little arm back under the cover, rose, and went over silently to the other gas-jet where the little fixture was. The nurse, who had risen on an elbow at the first sound of voices, had lain down again at the young man's signal. She did not stir now, though perhaps she was not asleep.

Mr. V. V. returned to the bed with a cup in his hand. Kern was lying exactly as he had left her — " the wonder was not quite yet gone from that still look of hers."

"Drink this, Kernie. . . ."

She drank incuriously, with his supporting hand upon her back; was gently lowered upon her pillow again; and then she turned upon her side, wide-eyed still, but silent.

"Now, go to sleep. I 'll sit here by you. . . ."

He noted the fact of beef-tea at twelve-thirty upon the chart, and sat again in the shadows. Soon Kern's eyelids drooped, and in time she fell asleep.

But the doctor sat on in the dim room, long after his charity sick had slipped back again to her happy dreams. And as he sat, there waxed a flame in him, and he pledged himself that henceforward there should be no pausing, neither compassion nor compunction. What mattered the troubles of individuals? What mattered himself, or that Duty to-night seemed visaged like an Iron Maid? Here, indeed, there beckoned him the great good task. The day of the rocky plain and the prophet in a loin-cloth was gone; but was there less might in the printed word and the penny newspaper? Spare this child, Lord, and the wrongs done upon her shall not again lack a voice. . . .

And later, much later, when the tall young man limped back to his desolate office, he did not at once go to bed, though the small hours then were fast growing. Six weeks, and more, he had to write his articles in: but there was that in him now which would not be denied. He sat again at his old secretary, a cheap pad before him, and the words that ran from his stub of a pencil were words winged with fire. . . .

If this was a compact offered, it seemed that it had been sealed in high places. Next morning, which was the morning of September 4th, Miss Masters came smiling to the Garland breakfast-table; and all that day, for the first time in seven weeks, Kern's temperature did not move above 103. On the morning following, it slipped down another half-degree; on the third, the same; and on the fourth morning there existed no reasonable doubt that she was going to get well.

But V. Vivian, the doctor, was not one to forget his mistakes in thanksgiving, merely because the consequences had been lifted from his shoulders. If he had failed once to provide for his little friend, there should never be any trouble on that score again. So he made it all sure and definite now, by the legal-sounding paper he drew up; and Henry Bloom, the undertaker on the next block, who was also a notary public, came in and certified the signature. And he too declined his fee for his trouble, to the wealthy young testator's perceptible annoyance. . . .

That was on September 12th. And next day it was that the morning "Post" informed all readers that Mrs. B. Thornton Heth and Miss Heth, having just returned from a summer's travel in Europe, had arrived in the city, and were again at their town-house, No. 903 Washington Street.

XXIII

One Summer in Europe, which she never speaks of now; Home again, with what a difference; Novel Questionings, as to what is a Friend, etc.

IT was life's waggish way that the project conceived in the obscure dreams of an out-at-elbows young man, and born a foundling upon his money, should have been adopted at sight as the spoiled darling of fashion's ultra-fashionable. Undoubtedly, astute Mr. Dayne had had somewhat to do with this, he who so well understood the connection between social prestige and the obtainment of endowment funds. But whatever the underlying causes and processes, it was plain that the Dabney House Settlement rode the crest of the "exclusive" wave this autumn. And the fact was grasped by Mrs. B. Thornton Heth within twenty-four hours of her home-coming, so admirably was it fitted to her need.

Mrs. Heth had had time enough through the summer, heaven knew, to study out the problem of restoring the family name to its former effulgence, to decide upon the family attitude, or note, for the season ensuing. The note, already firmly struck in her summer's letters to friends, — with which she had taken immense pains, knowing from herself how closely they would be scanned, — was that poor Carlisle, shocked into hysteria by the tragedy, had magnanimously blamed herself where she had no blame beyond, perhaps, youthful thoughtlessness. Thus they were people, and in particular she was a person, severely persecuted for righteousness' sake, but resolved to bear it nobly.

So much for the note, but a passive thing at best. None saw more clearly than Mrs. Heth that a quietly resolute campaign of vindication was necessary, none more clearly that a campaign meant money in considerable sums. If you desired to prove anything, you must have money; stated in another way, you could

320

prove anything provided you spent money enough. How best to
spend large sums in this case?

Musing long upon the family attitude in dull European days
and nights, the good lady had gradually developed a complete
code of etiquette, as of funerals. Thus she had concluded that
to give an elaborate and superbly costly entertainment — ordinarily an unanswerable act of vindication — would under the
circumstances be "in bad taste." A series of small but exclusive
dinners would better strike the note on the entertaining side;
while, as for more public proof of martyrhood finely borne, she at
length decided that frank deeds of selfless charity would be about
the proper thing. She had no sooner come in touch again with the
home atmosphere than she determined to give ten thousand dollars, perfectly anonymously, to Mr. Dayne's Settlement House
Foundation.

Carlisle thought these developments odd enough, and indifferently pictured her mother's dismay, if suddenly informed whose
cause it was she was so enthusiastically pitching in to help. For
it seemed that she alone knew that the Settlement everybody was
talking about was not Mr. Dayne's at all, but Dr. Vivian's, who
wished his gift to be kept a secret. Carlisle said nothing to unsettle her mother, who possibly still thought that Hugo Canning,
the gone but not forgotten, was the royal contributor. The girl,
indeed, observed with relief that mamma's militant energies
were once more in full swing. She had spent six weeks with the
little lady when every particle of fight had been flattened out of
her, and that was an experience she was not anxious to repeat.

Cally herself was glad to be at home again, though this was a
home-coming like none other she had ever known. Four months'
use had not robbed memory of its poignancy, and the moment of
arrival at the House she found unexpectedly painful. However,
there came at once the remeeting with papa, and the first and
worst hour of reconnection with the old life again was lubricated
with reunion and much talk.

Mr. Heth had been lonely and somewhat depressed during
the summer, as his letters had revealed. But he was unaffectedly happy at having his wife and daughter back, and lingered

over the breakfast-table till nearly ten o'clock, so much did he have to ask, and to tell, about the summer.

Of that summer Carlisle never afterwards liked to talk. The first weeks of it always stood out in her mind as the most wretched period of her life. All spirit, all pluck, all dignity and self-respect appeared to have been crushed out by the disasters which had befallen her. There was absolutely nothing left on earth to be thankful for, except that the engagement had never been announced.

Through these days Cally had n't seemed to care that Jack Dalhousie had killed himself, had n't cared if the constrained tone of Mattie Allen's "steamer-letter" — which said that Mattie was terribly sorry, dear, but was vague as to what — indicated that the Heth glories had undergone a great and permanent eclipse. All her consciousness seemed sucked into the great ragged hole in her life left by Canning's going. Not till now, it seemed, had she realized to what measure her prince of lovers had twined himself into the reaches of her being. To pluck him, at a word, from her heart would have been a difficult task at best, and it was made the more difficult for her in that she did not, at first, put her will into it. For there had lingered in her a sort of stunned incredulity: she could not quite believe that their quarrel had been irretrievable, that Hugo was gone forever. In the four days' waiting and hiding in New York, even after she had put the ocean definitely between them, she multiplied her woes by keeping the small door of hope constantly open against her lover's possible return. And oh, how wretched she was through these days, how sorry, sorry for herself!

And mamma was enormously sorry for herself; and there they were, the worst companions for each other that could possibly have been found in the world. So they had sat down in London, in a modest family-hotel well off the track of tourists and of fashion; for none knew better than mamma when to draw the purse-strings tight, and the European tour, planned as a triumphal progress, had been abased to a refuge and rustication.

The average women in such a situation would, of course, quickly have pooled their sorrows for mutual comfort; but these two were fixedly held apart by their fundamental lack of sympathy with each other, and further by the disciplinary character of mamma's attitude. Whatever she wrote in her letters, Mrs. Heth's personal note was that Carlisle had wilfully brought shame and disgrace upon her ever indulgent parents, and she did not desire that the girl should be diverted for a moment from the contemplation of her errors. In their quiet quarters, they saw practically no one, did nothing but make themselves and each other as miserable as they could. They fairly wallowed in their respective seas of self-pity. And days passed when they hardly exchanged a word.

Of course so abject a surrender to the slings and arrows of outrageous Fortune could not last indefinitely. Human nature's safety-valve is its extraordinary resilience. Hope springs eternal, etc. Nevertheless, it took a small shock or so to arouse these two women at the mill from their spiritless prostration. One night in early July, Carlisle came suddenly upon the name of Hugo Canning in the foreign tattle column of a London newspaper. She read, with intense fixity of gaze, that Hugo was in Europe: in short, that Hugo was enjoying himself at Trouville, where he was constantly seen in the company of the Honorable Kitty Belden, second daughter of So-and-So, and so forth. . . .

All this time, Carlisle had been taking upon herself most of the blame for the quarrel and break. She had been distracted and unreasonable; she had never explained to Hugo sensibly how it had all happened; it was only natural that he should have misunderstood and misjudged, and in the end lost his temper and said hard things which he did not mean. And he was suffering by it no less than she: oh, be sure of that. . . . Now, as she sat alone in her bedroom, the newspaper crumpled on the floor beside her, there seemed to fall scales from her eyes, and she saw how bitterly she had deceived herself. Where was now the love pledged to last forever? Six weeks parted from her, and gaily gallivanting at the slipper-toes of happier girls, whom the breath of trouble had not touched.

Not even in this moment did Carlisle tax her once-betrothed with moral wrong in the matter of the "telling," for that whole episode had remained in her mind rather a flare-up of mysterious emotions than a case of religious "conviction of sin" and atonement. Probably Hugo had said and done what he thought was right then. But now it was clear to her, as by a flash, that he had done wrong in quite a different way, that he had committed the deadly sin of love. He had deserted her in the moment of her greatest need of him. At the first pinch his boasted mighty love had broken down; and, beneath all the disguises, it was such a contemptible little pinch at that, only that he was afraid of what people might say about her. Now he stepped the beaches of France, a squire of dames unconcerned. Should she wear her heart in mourning for a light-o'-love and a jilt? She would not. She would not. . . .

Easier said than done, no doubt. Yet Cally's thoughts had at least received a powerful new twist, which is the beginning of reconstruction. And it was only a day or two later that mamma in her turn received an arousing blow, in that debasing of her by the Associated Charities which her niece-in-law, Henrietta Cooney, had mentioned to the Dabney House.

As it happened there came a letter from Hen Cooney by the same mail that brought mamma's death-dealing one from Mrs. McVey. For Hen, who had never dreamed of corresponding with Cally before, had started up this summer with a long and quite affectionate steamer-letter, and had since written regularly once a week, the newsiest and really the most interesting letters that the Heths got at all. This letter had a private postscript, written on a separate sheet, which said:

> Cally, I don't know how you'll take it, but I think I ought to tell you frankly how matters stand. Of course there was plenty of talk, especially at first, and some of it was pretty strong. But whether you like it or not, most of the responsibility for what happened is being put on Aunt Isabel. Do you remember Mrs. John S. Adkins who was at the Beach the day it happened? She has told everybody it was Aunt Isabel who came downstairs and told her and others the story that they afterwards repeated. And then, besides, it seems to be generally understood that you were the one who wanted to straighten things out when you had no idea it was too late, and every-

body whose opinion is worth having knows it's easy enough
to slip into a mistake, but takes a lot of spunk to stand up
and say so long afterwards. Good-bye again.

HEN.

Carlisle removed this postscript, tore it into small pieces, and
put the pieces in the waste-basket under a newspaper. Later in
the afternoon she had to go into her mother's bedroom to recover
a novel which the older lady had abstracted for her own perusal.
She found her mother lying on the bed, an open letter in her hand
and on her face the marks of rare tears.

Carlisle, turning away with her book, hesitated. The two
women had not spoken a word all that day.

"What's the matter, mamma?" she said constrainedly.

Mrs. Heth, stirring a little on the bed, said, with difficulty:
"The Associated Charities met to elect new officers. I am —
omitted from the board." She added, in a voice from which she
could not keep the self-pity: "I should naturally — have been
president this year."

Her crushed mildness touched Carlisle abruptly. For the first
time in all this trouble, perhaps for the first time in her life, she
had a considerate and sympathetic thought for her mother. It
was mamma, it seemed, upon whom the reprisals of society were
to fall most heavily, yet it was she, Cally, who had caused it all.
Suppose she had been a good daughter, to begin with; suppose
she had even been an obedient daughter, and had kept her own
counsel, as mamma had commanded and implored. Ah, how
different would have been this ghastly summer! . . .

She walked over to the bed, quite pale, put her hand on her
mother's rumpled hair, and said with some agitation:

"I'm very sorry to have given you all this trouble, mamma."

Mrs. Heth looked up at her, her small eyes winking.

"Oh — I — I'm sure you meant to do what you thought was
right. But — oh, Cally! . . ."

And then she was weeping in her daughter's arms.

Perhaps the stout little lady was ready now for a reconciliation. Perhaps the strain of silent censoriousness had worn out
even her strong will. Perhaps, in some far cranny of her practical

325

heart, there was a spark which secretly admired Cally for her suicidal madness. At any rate, drying her eyes presently, she said:

"How Mary Page will gloat over this. . . . Well, we can't go on this way, my child. We'll die if we don't have some diversion. Lord knows we'll need all our strength for the fall."

And still later, she suddenly cried: "LET'S GO TO PARIS!"

To Paris they went; and there, occupying more fashionable quarters, began to look about for pleasure. The looking required effort at first and was scantily rewarded; but of course it was not long before the women's spirits responded to the more hopeful atmosphere. Soon they fell in with some lively people from home, the Wintons, who, being a peg or two lower than the Heths in the gay world, made it almost indelicately plain that they were completely unaware of anything's having happened. To Paris also came J. Forsythe Avery.

And now, in the passage of the weeks, the mother and daughter were at home again, with Carlisle finding that memory still had power to stab, and Mrs. Heth stoutly girding herself for the great fight of her life, and almost happy. . . .

If it had taken the violent break to reveal to Cally how deeply Hugo Canning had come into her life, it seemed to take this home-coming to impress upon her how definitely he had departed. There was hardly anything in the house that was not in some way associated with him, or with her thought of him. Outdoors it was hardly better: wherever she turned, she found mementoes of his absence. Strange and sad to think that he and she would ride these familiar streets no more. He had left her alone, to find her feet again in a changed world as best she might. Where was he on this day and on this, with whom making merry, her false knight who could not love as he could fear the world's opinion? . . .

It was September, and people were beginning to troop back in numbers from the holiday places of their desire. Cally's first days at home were full of meetings, with those now seen for the first time under strangely altered conditions.

She was not wanting in spirit, but she lacked her mother's splendid pachydermousness. More than mamma, she had shrunk from this first painful plunge, and now that it had come she was receptive to impressions which quite escaped the older lady. Outwardly, indeed, as she perceived with some surprise, the greetings of friends and acquaintances were much as they had always been. But she was at once conscious of a certain new quality in people's looks, a certain hard exploring curiosity, not untouched with a fleeting and furtive air of triumph. This look seemed to confront her, with varying degrees of emphasis, on nearly every face. To her sensitiveness it was as if, beneath cordial speech, everybody was really saying: "Aha!... So you're the young lady who hounded that chap into killing himself and got jilted for your pains. Well, well! Perhaps you won't be quite so high-and-mighty after this. . . ."

Even Carlisle's most intimate friends, try as they doubtless did, seemed unable to help showing that they considered her lot in the world sadly changed. So, indeed, it was. Mattie and Evey could not, for instance, begin naturally by asking, "Cally, did you have a lovely summer?" — when of course they knew very well that she had had a perfectly frightful summer. Mattie came in before eleven o'clock on the first morning, chirping affectionate greetings; but neither then nor later did she manage to convey any real sense of sympathy with Cally, or of understanding what she had been through, or even of wanting to understand. Cally would have liked to justify herself to Mattie, to talk her heart out to her, or to somebody; but Mattie's idea was clearly to keep Cally's mind off it, as you do with the near relatives of the deceased. And was it possible that even Mats's sweet girlishness showed a subtle trace of confirmation of the Frenchman's bitter maxim, that in the misfortunes of our friends there is something not altogether displeasing to us? . . .

If with Mats and Evey, so and much more so with others, less genuinely friendly. Nobody took the responsibility of open condemnation, as by "cutting" Mrs. B. Thornton Heth or her daughter. On the other hand, nobody forgot; nobody made allowances; nobody asked a single question. Judgment was obviously passed, and everybody seemed perfectly clear about the verdict. The Heths were people to be treated with respect as long as they kept their money, but between you and me, their social fortunes had received a stain which would not wear off. Hugo Canning had had it exactly right. Cally Heth would be pointed at to the longest day she lived. . . .

Cally, after the first shrinking, was possessed by a sense of anti-climax. Life had a brassy ring. She had come home with at least something of her mother's military keenness for the "campaign" of vindication, but within a day or two she was thinking, rather cynically and cheaply, that the game was not worth the candle. What difference did it all make, in her actual life? People might whisper and nudge behind her back, but their invitations seemed to come in much the same as ever, poor mamma pouncing on each as it came, with a carefully appraising eye. Wasn't there a hollowness in all this, something wanting? . . .

Untrained for analysis as she was, she had not thought of herself, in the months in Europe, as "changed" exactly. It took this recontact with the familiar environment to reveal to her definitely that her experiences of the spring and summer had not rolled through her as through an iron tube. Here were the old stimuli (as scientific fellows term them); but they failed to bring the old reactions. She was aware that the elevation of the family position, or its rescue, no longer filled her whole horizon. Old values shifted. In particular, she found her soul revolting at the prospect of another season — her fifth — another winter of endless parties, now with a secret campaign thrown in.

"I'm tired of the same old round, that's all," she said, moodily. "I want something new — something *different*."

"There's plenty that's new and different, Cally," said Henrietta Cooney, cheerfully, "if you really want to go in for it. And ten times as interesting as your old society. . . ."

"And while I think of it," added Hen, "I want to book you now for Saturday afternoon, four-thirty — open meeting at the Woman's Club on What Can We Do to Help the Poor. Don't say no. This new man Pond's going to speak, Director of the Settlement. He'll give us something to take home and think about."

This conversation took place on the way home from a meeting

of the Equal Suffrage League, to which Henrietta had borne off Cally, not so completely against the latter's will as you might have supposed. And oddly enough, Cally found that she could talk quite freely to her poor cousin, partly because of Hen's insignificance in the gay world, partly, perhaps, because of the way she had written during the summer.

"Are n't you going to the Settlement opening on Thursday?"

"Can't get away from the bookstore in time. Saturday's a short day," said Hen, her eyes on space. . . . "Look around you, Cally. You'll see lots more women than you who're sick of parties. I tell you this is the most interesting time to be alive in that ever was."

Cally smiled wearily at these enthusiasms. Nevertheless she could by now understand at least what Hen supposed she was talking about. It was as if the cataclysm in the May-time had chipped a peep-hole in the embracing sphere of her girlhood's round, and through this hole she began to discern novel proceedings afoot. . . .

Strange talk was in the air of the old town in those days, strange things heard and seen. Not a few women of the happy classes had grown "sick of parties." They grew sick of years lived without serious purpose, waiting for husband and children which sometimes never came; sick of their dependence, of their idleness, of their careful segregation from the currents of life about them. They wearied, in short, of their position of inferior human worth, which some perceived, and others began dimly to suspect, under that glittering cover of fictions which looked so wholly noble till you stopped to think (which women should never do), and dared to glance sidewise at the seams underneath. And now lately some high-hearted spirits had begun to voice their sickness, courageously braving those penalties which society so well knows how to visit upon those who disturb the accepted prejudices; penalties, it might be, peculiarly trying to women, over which some of these supposedly masculated pioneers doubtless had more than one good cry in secret.

What could be more interesting than the revolt of woman against "chivalry" in chivalry's old home and seat? That curious phenomenon was going on in Cally's town now, though acuter social critics than she had quite failed to discover it. . . .

Far rumors of her sex's strange activities reached Cally, and she listened, but with apathy. She marvelled at the freshness of interest with which Mattie and Evey McVey were preparing for the light routine which by now they knew like an old shoe. But her own mood was nothing more forceful than meaningless restlessness and discontent. Not even the unlooked-for arrival, one morning, of the dividend from the bank stock her father had given her in May, all her own, afforded her more than a flicker of the familiar joys. How employ fifteen hundred dollars so that it would bring her happiness now? Cally, after listless deliberation, took her wealth to her father that afternoon, offering it as a contribution toward mamma's Settlement donation. Her impulse was hardly sheer magnanimity; still, it was known that finance was a distinctly live issue in the House just now.

However, papa, after staring at her a moment, merely gathered her into his arms, check and all, remarking that she was a goose; and when she tried to argue about it a little, he ruled the situation with a strong paternal hand. She was to buy herself pretties with that money, he said; and there, there, he did n't want to hear any more foolishness about it. No more Alphonse and Gaspard, as the fellow said. . . .

"And, Cally," he added, pinching her cheek, "I want you to have a good time this winter, remember. You can have anything you want. Go everywhere you're invited — enjoy yourself with your friends — have a good time. D' you hear me?"

She said that she did: and as she spoke, a bitter question rose at her. Who were her friends? She had always thought of herself as having many; "hosts of friends" had always figured prominently in her inventories of her blessings. But what was a friend? Among all these people she had spent her life with, there was not one, it seemed, who cared to understand the infinite shadings of thought and impulse that had brought her to where she now stood; much less one heart which saw intuitively

All the world's coarse thumb
And finger failed to plumb . . .

Papa was adding, with an unconscious frown:

"The cash is in the bank, if your mother must have it. I'd laid it by for something else, though — make some repairs at the Works. Come in. . . . I reckon I've staved off . . ."

Considered from one angle, these fragmentary words might have been illuminating; but Cally did not even hear them. At that moment there happened the unexpected. The parlormaid Annie entered, announcing Mrs. Berkeley Page to see Miss Carlisle.

Surprise was expressed in the study. This was the lady who had said that the Heths were very improbable people. Papa opined, somewhat glumly, that she had come to beg funds for the confounded Settlement. Cally, having looked at herself in the mirror, trailed into the drawing-room with a somewhat cool and challenging civility.

But her coolness soon melted away, under the visitor's strange but seemingly genuine cordiality. It became clear that she had come in the vein of amity, and without sinister motives; though why, if not for Settlement funds, could not be imagined.

Mrs. Page was a tall, pleasant-faced woman, still on the right side of forty, a widow whose husband had left her too much of this world's goods for her ever to be classed as a poorhouse Tory; and despite the fact that she was a leader in the old-school, as opposed to the brass-band, set, many people considered her a very agreeable woman. She had amusing things to say, and she said them in the Heth drawing-room with no air of awkwardness. Carlisle, somewhat against her will, was soon thinking her extremely attractive. But the thawing out went further than that.

Talk turned by chance — or perhaps it was not chance exactly — on those growing currents of feminine activity which had nothing to do with dinners and dances: and here the visitor expressed ideas which did not seem old-school in the least. It appeared that she, Mary Page, in the period of her spinsterhood, — for she hadn't been married till she was twenty-six, a thoroughgoing old maid in those days, — had also wearied of the gay round; she had desired to *do something*. But alas, she had suddenly discovered that she was n't fitted to do one earthly thing, having been trained only to be a trimming. She said, smiling, that she had cried all one day about it. . . .

"Why is it assumed, really," said she, "that women are such poor little butterflies that amusing and being amused should absorb all their energies? I don't think of myself as a pet, do you, Miss Heth? Give us something solid to do, and the world would n't be so full of discontented women. Do you know, if I had a daughter," said Mrs. Page, "and she was n't married after three years 'out,' and had n't developed any special talent, I should send her straight down to Hartman's Business College, and have her learn typewriting. Yes, I should! — and make her get a place in an office, too, at five dollars a week! . . ."

The distinguished visitor remained twenty minutes in the improbable drawing-room, and contrived to make herself interesting. When she rose to go, she mentioned that she was staying at her mother's place in the country till after Thanksgiving, and was only in town for the day. And then, as she held out her hand, smiling in a simple and friendly way, her expression changed, and she brought up her other hand and laid it over Carlisle's.

"My dear," she began, with some embarrassment, "I wonder if you will let a much older woman say how truly she has sympathized with you in — all this trouble — and how much she has admired you, too? . . ."

Cally's eyes wavered and fell. And suddenly she divined that this, and nothing else, was what Mrs. Page had come to say.

"All of us make mistakes in this world," went on the kind voice — "all that I know do wrong. But not all of us, I'm afraid, have the courage to go back and set right what we did, as bravely as you have done."

The girl stood dumb. . . . Strange, indeed, that the first word of understanding sympathy she had had since her home-coming — barring only Hen Cooney — should have come from this worse than stranger, whom at a distance she had long secretly envied and disliked. One touch of generous kindness, and the hostility of years seemed to fall away. . . .

She raised her eyes, trying with indifferent success to smile.

But perhaps her look showed something of what she felt: for Mrs. Page immediately took the girl's face between her hands and kissed her lightly on the cheek.

"May I? . . . I mean by it that I hope you'll let me know you better, when I'm home again. . . . Good-bye."

Cally caught the gloved hand upon her cheek, and said, with an impulsiveness far from her habit:

"I think you're the sweetest person I ever saw. . . ."

And two days later, she said to her mother, though in a distinctly frivolous tone:

"What would you think of me as a Settlement worker, mamma?"

"Settlement worker? . . . Well, we'll see," said Mrs. Heth, absently. "It remains to be seen how far the best people are going in for it. . . ."

Cally laughed. She was beautifully dressed, and felt perfectly poised. It was five o'clock in the afternoon, and she and her mother were in the new vindication limousine, en route to the old Dabney House.

"What difference does that make?"

"All the difference. . . . Now, Cally, don't pick up any of poor Henrietta's equality notions, just because you feel a little blue at present. This is going to come out all right. You may trust me."

"I do," said Cally, sincerely.

After a silence she added with a laugh: "Who are the best people, mamma?"

"I am, for one," said mamma; and unconsciously her grasp tightened on the little ornamental bag where snuggled her Settlement check for Ten Thousand Dollars, securely bagged at last.

"Don't let any poor nobodies pull you down to their level with their talk about merit," said mamma. "What's merit in society?"

XXIV

How the Best People came to the Old Hotel again; how Cally is Ornamental, maybe, but hardly a Useful Person; how she encounters Three Surprises from Three Various Men, all disagreeable but the Last.

TO the Dabney House, it was like old times come back. Not in forty years had the ancient hostelry so resounded with the steps of the best people. Without, there stood lines of motor-cars in the shabby and unaccustomed street, ten times as many as there had been in May. Within — to prove at a stroke the tone of the gathering — J. Forsythe Avery himself stood conspicuously at the very door: not merely stood, but labored behind a deal table for the cause, distributing Settlement pamphlets, brochures or treatises, to all comers. He irresistibly reminded Carlisle of one of those lordly men in gold-lace outside a painless dentist's parlors. Many others of the conquering order there were observed also, almost in the first glance; chiefly congregating in the new assembly room, where the "opening reception" was under way, but also deploying in numbers all over the lower floor and the remodeled basement beneath.

It was the Heths' first public appearance since their home-coming, and perhaps even mamma felt a little bit self-conscious. But Carlisle had come with serious intentions, and a manner of determined vivacity. Let people find anything to gloat over in her appearance, if they could. Glancing about as they left Mr. Avery, she saw that the old court or lobby, where she had stood and talked once on a rainy May day, had been left intact, only renovated somewhat as to floor and walls. On one side of it now ran down a row of offices with new glass doors, the first of them marked "Mr. Pond." On the other side, a great arched doorway led into the large meeting-room, formed by the demolition of many partitions. Changed indeed it all was: yet Cally found it quite disturbingly familiar too. . . .

Beyond the arched doorway stood a little group of the best men and women: a reception committee clearly, and Mrs. Heth had not been asked to serve upon it, as she was instantly and indignantly conscious. However, she was one to bear martyrdom nobly, knowing that truth would prevail in the end; and accordingly she greeted Byrds, Daynes, and others with marked and lingering cordiality. Carlisle, passing down the receiving line more quickly, soon found herself introduced to Pond, the imported Director, according to her plan. The phrase is accurate, for Mr. Pond appeared to be panjandrum here, and people of all degree were presented to him, as to royalty. Frequent hearing of the man's name in the last few days had suggested nothing to Carlisle, but the moment she caught sight of his keen face with the powerful blue-tinged jaw, she recalled that she had seen Mr. Pond in the Dabney House before now.

The Director had turned with business-like indifference as Mr. Dayne spoke her name, but his expression as he looked at her took on a sudden half-surprised intentness which Carlisle had seen upon the faces of strangers before now. His reply to her commonplaces of greeting was:

"Where have I met you before?"

"Nowhere, I think."

Bored with the tenor of his speech, she looked at him steadily yet negligently for a moment; and then, releasing her gaze, continued: "This is the assembly room, is n't it? What sort of meetings are to held here?"

A faintly quizzical look came into the man's incisive stare.

"Do you really think it worth while for me to explain, when —"

He left this beginning hanging in midair, while he turned, without apology, to accept the humble duties of three new arrivals. Cally waited patiently. Mrs. Berkeley Page had left her possessed of an impulse, which she took to be almost tantamount to a resolution. She would give at least part of her time to doing something solid. . . .

Director Pond, turning back to her, concluded:

"When we are both well aware that you don't care a continental what sort of meetings are going to be held here?"

"Oh, but I do, you see," replied Cally, distinctly irritated. "I'm very much interested. One of the reasons I'm here this afternoon," she explained, not without an under-feeling of sad nobility, "is that I am thinking of offering myself as — as a worker."

"Oh! — As a worker."

"Yes."

"A worker. You mean it?"

She said, glancing indifferently away: "But probably Mr. Dayne is the person I should speak to about it. . . . Or — perhaps Dr. Vivian. . . ."

"What's Dayne or Vivian got to do with it? Walk a little away from the door with me — there! Thank the Lord when this mob clears out. . . . So you want to offer as a worker," said Director Pond, his face gravely authoritative. "Good. We need workers more than money now, which is putting it somewhat strongly. I am pleased that you will join us. When can you move in?"

"Move in?"

"You understand, of course, that resident workers are the only ones good for anything. You will want to live here, for a year or so at least. Naturally the sooner you can come the better."

"Live here? Here in the Dabney House? Well, no," said Carlisle, with open amusement, "I could hardly do that."

"Ah?" said he, without the slightest change of expression. "Well, that's a pity. . . . Allow me to raise my hand and point at this wall, so; and now people will understand that I'm explaining important points to a worker, and will not interrupt. Of course there is something for the non-residents to do, too. Let us see now. You can sew, I suppose?"

"Sew? . . . Well — not really well at all."

"Too bad," said he, keeping his broad back to the lively groups about them and pointing steadily at the wall. "However — I'm thinking of putting in a woman's infirmary. Can you recommend yourself as reasonably fitted for an assistant amateur nurse?"

"Oh, no! No, I could n't do that, I'm afraid. I can't bear sickness."

"Indeed? A great many people enjoy it. . . . Well! — district visitor it is, then, while we're getting acquainted with the neighborhood. But it means business, you know — six days a week visiting in the homes of the poorest, dirtiest and meanest, investigating, collecting facts under instructions you will get from me —"

"Oh! Well, no — not that. I — I'm afraid my mother would n't care to have me do that."

The man's pointing hand, which was large and strong-looking, fell at his side, and he gazed at her with a sarcasm which he no longer troubled to conceal.

"May I ask what under the sun you can do?"

"What I can do? . . ."

Under his hard and frankly belittling stare, Carlisle began to feel rather small, despite her firm resolves to feel nothing of the sort. She had heard something of this Mr. Pond in the past week: a person of some consequence in the world, it was said, several kinds of Doctor, and the author of a work on The Settlement which was considered "standard" and which Cally had meant (since last night) to purchase at Saltman's bookstore. Report made him also a man of some independent means and position, and certainly he had come with excellent letters and credentials. But Cally did not consider that these things justified anybody in being so thoroughly hateful, particularly when you could see that it was only an eccentric pose. . . .

"That," said she, with dignity, "is what I am now considering —"

"But you've already offered to help! I merely request you, in a polite manner, to state how you can help me, in my big, serious and important work. . . . Does n't it occur to you, in fact, that you are somewhat helpless?"

"Does it occur to you that you are being somewhat rude?"

"Does it occur to *you* that what you call rudeness may be exactly the sort of wholesome irritant needed by people of your class?"

"What do you mean by people of my class?"

Cally raised a white-gloved hand and put back a tendril of her gay hair. She looked at him level-eyed. The man's constant and cocksure "I," "me," "mine," rubbed her strongly the wrong way. This was Dr. Vivian's Settlement, and nobody else's. She was convinced that Vivian would have made a far better Director anyway. . . .

Mr. Pond, however, smiled suddenly. The smile largely transformed his dark face, making it look for the first time quite agreeable, and even kind.

"I mean," said he, "those who are highly ornamental, but cannot candidly be described as generally useful."

The reply, for some reason, silenced her. She thought of Mrs. Page. The man's smile faded.

"Not," said he, "that I don't consider ornaments of use. I do, in their place. Now I must get back to the firing-line. I can only add that if you are serious about wanting to help me, Miss — I'm afraid I did n't catch your name — you will lose no time in qualifying yourself to be of service. Obviously you are not so qualified at present."

He nodded curtly, and turned away. The admiring populace swallowed him up. . . .

Cally felt as if she had received a severe drubbing. She felt rebuffed, defeated, depressed, and at the same time vaguely stimulated. However, the moment for introspective analysis was not now. . . .

"Well, Cally," said motherly Mrs. McVey, drifting by, "you must feel sort of lonesome — such a turn-out of old folks I never saw. I wanted Evey to come, but she said she'd as soon go to a tea at the Needy Ladies' Home."

On the heels of Evey's mother came Cally's own, whose watchful eye had been felt from a distance before now. Possibly mamma had not forgotten what happened the last time Cally came to the Dabney House. . . .

"I saw you talking with Mr. Pond," said Mrs. Heth, a little aside. "How did he impress you?"

"He's the most conceited human being I ever saw," said Cally. "I believe he said one or two fairly interesting things."

"Well — that's not a bad recommendation. I like an important man to think well of himself. I'll ask him for my Settlement dinner Saturday, when those Cheritons stop nagging at him."

Mamma looked slightly flushed beneath her fixed smile; a look which her daughter had no difficulty in understanding. More than once this afternoon, Cally had encountered significant stares upon herself, instantly removed, which showed with amusing candour that she was the subject of conversation in those quarters. No more could she assume that this conversation and those stares were but the involuntary offerings of the multitude to beauty and brilliant success. And yet she did not seem to mind so very much. . . .

"I just gave my Settlement check to Mr. Byrd," added mamma. "He was very grateful, but not as grateful as he ought to have been."

She glided back to her position near the door. Mrs. McVey, chatting on, observed that the Pond man hadn't seemed impatient to make her acquaintance, though she had waited round some time to give him the pleasure; also that there were no refreshments but ice-water from the new ten-gallon cooler in the hall. Then she, in her turn, passed on, as J. Forsythe Avery was discerned steering in a fixed direction through the crowd.

"Are your labors ended so soon?"

Mr. Avery bowed pluperfectly, and Cally smiled suddenly. He was a pink, slightly bald young man, and had once been described by Mr. Berkeley Page as very gentlemanly.

"What are you laughing at?" inquired he, somewhat lugubriously.

"Only at something funny Mrs. McVey just said. You know how witty she is. . . . Have you handed them all out?"

"I appointed a deputy," confessed Mr. Avery, "but I labored hard for a time. Am I not entitled to — er — the rewards of labor now?"

Cally glanced away, with no more desire to smile. The look in his pink eyes had arrested her attention, and she wondered whether she could possibly bring herself to take him. She was not wanted as a Settlement worker; and he would be colossally wealthy some day. Perhaps he lacked an indefinable something that comes from grandfathers, but he had never committed a social fault in his life, unless you would hold up against him an incurable fondness for just one tiny little drop of cologne on a pure linen handkerchief. Mamma would be rather pleased, poor dear.

Then her mind's eye gave her a flashing memory-picture of Canning, the matchless, and Mr. Avery became unimaginable. . . .

"Such as what?" said she, listlessly, to his roguish hints of reward.

"I should offer my escortage for — er — a small tour over the premises, and so forth. Why not?"

"No reason in the world, except that I may not go over the prem . . ."

That word the speaker left forever unfinished. And her next remark was:

"What did you say?"

Obviously there was an interlude here; and in it Cally Heth had seen, and recovered from the sudden sight of, the strange young man Mr. V. V., upon whom her eyes had not fallen since a sunny May morning when she had sat and wept before him. He stood quite near, the founder of the Settlement, though in an obscure corner: backed there, it seemed, by a fat conversationalist in a purple bonnet. But there must have been telepathy in Cally's gaze for her one confidant; for she had no sooner descried his tall figure through the fuss and feathers than he turned his eyes and looked at her.

She had considered with mingled feelings the prospect of meeting this man again to-day; and now the sight of his face and lucid gaze brought something of that sense of shock which had attended these encounters in other days. Only now, twined with the painfulness of many associations which his look aroused, there was a sort of welcome, odd and unexpected; she felt a little start of gladness, as at the unlooked-for appearance of something trusted and familiar. How was it that she had thought so little of him in these months, through which it had seemed that there was nobody who understood? . . .

She bowed, in quite a bright and friendly way, putting down her inward disquiet; and then it was that, turning hastily again to the faithful Avery, Cally inquired:

"What did you say?"

"I suggested," said the pink and pluperfect one, "that you ought to see the gymnasium and swimming-pool at any rate. I'm informed that the pool is the largest in the State, and . . ."

But Cally had seen that the man from another world was stepping out from his obscurity; and now there sounded above the Avery periods the vivid voice first heard in the summer-house.

"Miss Heth! — may I say how-do-you-do? . . . I hadn't seen you till that moment. In fact, I had no idea you were here . . ."

"Oh, yes, indeed. I'm a Life Member, if you please," said Cally turning, looking again at the owner of that voice. "How do you do? Do you know Mr. Avery, Dr. Vivian?"

The two men bowed. Young Mr. V. V. had not long retained the slim hand which — such was his lot — had been offered to him for the first time in his life.

"Oh, Miss Kemper!" added Cally. "Do forgive me — I didn't recognize your back at all. May I introduce Mr. Avery? . . ."

And then, while Mr. Avery paid reluctant devoirs to the lady in the purple bonnet, Cally said quite easily to Dr. Vivian:

"I was just debating whether or not to make an exploring expedition over the whole Settlement. Is there much to see? — or is it mostly rooms?"

"Oh, mostly rooms," said Mr. V. V.

He seemed to begin a smile at this point, and then to change his mind about it. The smile, if such it was, ended short, as if clipped off.

"This door," he added turning to the fresh-painted portal at his elbow, "leads to one of them. . . . A fair sample, I imagine.

This one happens to be a — ah — a sort of sewing-class room, I believe. . . ."

"Oh, a sewing-class room! That must be where I was offered a position."

"Will you look at it?"

"I'd like to. Only I can't sew a bit, you see. . . ."

She stepped exploringly through the open door, into the sort of sewing-class room. V. Vivian walked after her; and behind him he distinctly heard the surprised and somewhat offended voice of the Kemper:

"Funny! I thought that was Mr. Pond I was talking to all the time."

"It's — it's a very nice place," said Cally, glancing about her as she advanced.

Not that it mattered, but it really was not a particularly nice place, only a rather dark and small chamber, smelling of paint and entirely empty save for one bench.

"Not a great deal to see, as you notice," said the summer-house voice behind her, sounding somehow changed since last year. . . . "Not much of a class could sit on the bench, I fear. Or perhaps it's this next room that's for sewing."

"Oh, I don't mind," said Cally.

And then she turned suddenly upon Mr. V. V., facing him, looking up with a sweet, half-wistful smile such as her face had never worn before for him.

"But tell me something about yourself . . . What sort of summer have you had?"

So he was brought to a halt, confronting in one of his donated rooms the loveliest of the Huns; confronting, but not looking at her exactly. . . .

"Well, it's been hot, as you know — in fact, the hottest summer since the Weather Bureau began. That was n't comfortable, of course. There was a good deal of suffering, where people could n't afford ice. . . . Personally, I've happened to be so busy that the weather did n't matter —"

"That's quite ominous, is n't it, in a doctor? Has there been so much sickness in this neighborhood?"

"Yes, there's been a lot of it. We had rather a bad typhoid epidemic, beginning in July — not easy to check in this old district, standing pretty much as it was before the war. I sometimes think there's no hope of ever cleaning it out, short of a London fire. . . . I — I hope you've been well?"

"Oh, yes, quite well, thank you. But is this district so bad — from a health point of view?"

"You should see it," said he, rather drily. "Or rather, of course, you should n't. It's more or less disturbing to one's peace of mind at times. . . ."

She was looking at him with an interested intentness of which she was quite unconscious. Never before had she seen this man free of the knowledge of menacing discussion ever pressing in the foreground; so now it was a little as if she met for the first time some one whom she had heard a great deal about from others. Her eye for externals had observed his new suit at once; in this deceptive light she considered that it looked quite nice, not suspecting that it was only the Prince, reduced; and she was thinking, with a sense of discovery, that Mr. V. V. was undoubtedly a good-looking man. A certain change in his manner she had also noted; a new touch of force, it seemed, a somewhat stiffened masculinity. What had become of that rather engaging hopeful look of his, which was the second thing she had ever noticed about him? . . .

"Perhaps I shall see it some day," she answered. "If I ever become one of your Mr. Pond's district visitors and investigators."

"Are you thinking of doing that?"

"Oh, I offered to try to do something, but Mr. Pond declined me, without thanks. He said I was perfectly useless to him — in his big and serious work. The worst of it was," she said, smiling rather ruefully, "he proved it."

She was glancing toward the door, with the moving and humming groups beyond, and so missed the sudden eagerness that briefly lit his face.

"What part of the work — if I might ask — were you — specially interested in?"

"I suppose I'm not really interested in any part. That must be the trouble. Probably it's just the usual dissatisfied feeling — when one is a little tired of parties. . . ."

Was that not yet another confidence, clearly calling for an understanding listener, for sympathetic reassurance? Nothing of the sort came to Cally; nothing of any sort. The brief pause, sharpened as it was by Mr. V. V.'s oddly formal bearing, was rather like a cold douche. And now it seemed that she must have been counting on this man somehow all along, though it was not clear as to what. . . .

"So you see my peace of mind is quite safe. Mr. Pond is right, of course. . . ." And then, thinking that this cool distance was rather absurd under the circumstances, she added in a friendlier way: "But why aren't you the Director here, instead of Mr. Pond? I should think you would be, since it's your Settlement."

But the result of that was only to bring new stiffness into the strange young man's manner.

"My Settlement! . . . Oh, I beg that you won't speak or think of it in that way. I assure you I've nothing at all to do with it, other than as one worker out of many."

Her unwarlike reply was: "Well, I have n't told anybody."

She glanced at him with a touch of bewilderment, and glanced away again, turning toward the door. Surely he had not always been like this. . . .

"Mr. Avery will think I'm lost," said Cally.

However, Mr. V. V. successfully checked her departure, saying:

"I'm sure you can be of the realest help to the Settlement, Miss Heth, if you care to be." And, then, veering abruptly, he said with his air of making a plunge: "But I must take this opportunity to speak to you of another matter. A matter which, I fear, will be disagreeable to you."

That sufficiently arrested her; she stood looking at him, with a conflict of sensations within. Faces of Settlementers appeared in the door, looked in at the bare room, passed from view again. The tall young man in the new suit pushed back his hair, with the quaint gesture he had.

"You once said," he continued, in a voice of light hardness, "that I brought you nothing but trouble. That seems to continue true, though perhaps you won't regard this as so — so serious. . . ."

Trouble? More trouble for Cally Heth?

"Why — what do you mean?"

"The question of the Heth Works — has come up again. That, at least, is the particular application. Of course many other factories are involved."

The girl was completely taken aback. "Why, I don't understand. What has come up?"

He then explained himself, in well-ordered sentences:

"The State Labor Commission feels strongly that the public good demands a new factory law at this time, requiring all owners to conform to a certain higher standard of comfort and safety for their employees. I must add that I fully share the Commission's feeling. It is considered that some publicity in the press is needed, preparing the public mind for a progressive law by showing what present conditions are. A series of articles has been decided upon, to begin about the first of November and continue daily till the legislature meets in January. I have agreed to write these articles. I thought it only fair," he ended short, "to tell you this."

The girl heard him with startled astonishment. She had never, of course, been interested in her father's factory other than as a family symbol; and that factitious interest which she had felt at times last year, born of this man's hostility, was gone long since, effaced by a tide of stronger feelings. So his sudden exhumation of the topic as a cause of war now came upon her with the harshest discordance. It seemed almost like a wanton wounding of her, somehow like sheer disloyalty in him. Surely if there were need of articles, this man might leave them to somebody else to write. . . .

Her young gaze was full of an unconscious reproachfulness.

"All that means that you are going to put some more letters in the paper attacking my father?"

"I'm afraid it's inevitable it will seem so to you."

"Oh,'" said she, it seemed involuntarily, "I don't see how you *can!*"

The young man Mr. V. V. made no reply. It may be that he did n't see how he could either. . . .

He looked away from the reproachful eyes, slate-blue to match the plumes in the hat: and there were phrases from his articles singing and kicking in his head, phrases which would cry in the penny newspaper as no voice could cry from the wilderness. Ten thousand words he had ready now, in the old secretary upstairs; hard words all, that broke heads or hearts, faiths implied too, it might be, and did not care; or did n't mean to show it if they did. And he thought, too, of a little friend he had, just pulled back from death's door, and hardly ready for her Trip now, after ten weeks. So of course there could be no flinching now. . . .

Through the door there came the continuous sounds of the nearness of the multitude, but these two seemed almost as alone in his old hotel as they had been on another afternoon long ago.

"Don't you think," said the pretty voice, still not angry — and surely anger would have been easier to meet than this — "that before doing anything so — so radical as that, you might wait a little while, believing that my father would — do what is right?"

The lame doctor brought his eyes back to her and said, slowly:

"You see, I've been worried by the feeling — that I've waited too long already."

"Too long for what? That's just what I mean. What do you think could possibly happen?"

"For one thing, Miss Heth," he said, with a faint dry smile, "the building might fall down some day."

Color came into Cally's cheek. Her feeling now was that she had made advances, spontaneous and friendly, and been smartly rebuffed. What cared he for the troubles of the Heths? . . .

"You really think my father would risk the lives of his employees, just to make a little more money for himself?"

He answered, almost brusquely: "I don't mean to judge your father. People take their views of life from the atmosphere in which they live. You appreciate that. I, of course, concede your

father's point of view. I fully understand it. I — wish it were
possible for you to do as much for mine."

She looked at him fixedly a moment, said, "I'm sorry you think
this necessary," and turned away to the door. But once again
his voice arrested her.

"Miss Heth! . . . You feel an interest in the Settlement.
You've felt a wish to help in the work — to lend a hand in some
way to those less fortunate than yourself. You — you haven't
as yet decided just what you want to do. . . ."

She had paused at the door, half-turning; their eyes met once
more. And now the whole look of the strange young man seemed
to change, and he said with sudden gentleness:

"Why don't you go to the Works some day?"

But it was late in the day to seek to improve matters with looks
and tones, with efforts to put responsibilities upon her. Cally
answered as she had answered him once before: only it was a
mark of some change in her — toward him, perhaps toward
life itself — that she spoke with a dignity which had never been
hers last year.

"I don't think I need do that to learn that my father is n't a
homicide."

For the second time also, Cally went away from the Dabney
House without the company of her staunch little mother: who
would remain in this place till among the last, contending among
the best people for the thing she held dearest in the world.

Cally, however, was well looked after by Mr. Avery, who welcomed her upon the threshold of the sewing-class room (if that is
what it was), removing himself firmly from the Kemper. His proposal was to continue the tour of the premises, but she replied
that she found Settlementing dreadfully boring, and was of a
mind to steal away for home. The disappointed pink one then
proposed to accompany her, and pay a little call, as he put it.
However, she professed an incurable dulness after her slumming,
and countered with an offer to set him down at his club, if he
liked.

It was so arranged, with the gallant, and also with mamma.

William Banks, detached by a nod from the procession of waiting vehicles over the dingy street, wheeled up to the entrance; halted with a whir; electrically self-started himself once more. Carlisle bowled off with J. Forsythe Avery, who was well pleased with this token of her regard, and resolved to make the most of it. But soon the time came when he was debarked from her conveyance; she was rid of his ponderous ardors; and Cally rolled through the twilight streets alone. . . .

There had settled down upon her a deep and singular depression. Her spirit ached, as if from a whipping. She thought a little of the Works; she had remembered that moment of somewhat painful revelation last year; but no reflection brought any doubt of her father. Long since she had reached the sound conclusion that that was the way business was; and if this fixed belief had been shaken a little now, she was hardly conscious of it. Papa, of course, did all that was reasonable and right for his work-people; it was perfectly outrageous that he should be subjected to abuse in the newspapers. Dr. Vivian, for his part, was conceded a religious fellow's strange sense of duty, though it required an effort to concede him that. Still Cally was not thinking of it from these points of view exactly. It all seemed to be quite personal, somehow. . . .

She gazed through the car-window at the familiar panorama, streets, houses, and people which she now did not see. It had been, indeed, an afternoon of snubs, such as she was hardly accustomed to receiving; and she seemed to have lost something of that wholesome defensive power she had possessed last year, the power of being righteously indignant. Time's whirligig had brought her to this, — that she had all but offered her friendship to Jack Dalhousie's friend, and he had more than repulsed her. She did feel indignant, a little; but, deeper than that, she felt wounded, she hardly knew why. After that moment of barrierless intimacy in the drawing-room, how could he bear to be so hard?

Her vesper thoughts veered a little, moved from Vivian to Director Pond, who had also brusquely rebuffed her. It was Mrs. Page's experience that Cally had had this afternoon, and she too found it humiliating. She had lately caught a distant glimpse of "work" in terms different from those which the dull word had worn heretofore: vaguely discerned activities in which the best women were coöperating usefully with men — coöperating equally as human beings, and no nonsense; not as women at all. There was something mysteriously inviting in this. She had felt a bracing absence of sex in Pond's hectoring catechism and blunt rejection of her. Yes, and in the cool declaration of war from Dr. Vivian, who had grown so hard since May. Busy and serious beings these, who would not be deterred by the flutterings of the doubtless ornamental but completely useless. . . .

"You're to go back for Mrs. Heth, William."

"Yas'm," said William, and clicked the little door behind her.

Yes, and where there was no sex, there she, Cally Heth, was n't wanted. Hard words these, but they seemed to have the ring of truth. She was wanted as a woman, she was wanted as an ornament, but she appeared to have no particular purpose as a human being. And the best prospect that life held out to her to-night was to settle down in a weary world as Mrs. J. Forsythe Avery.

Cally opened the front door, which was hospitably kept on the latch during the daytime, and stepped into the dim hall of home. Rarely in her life had she felt more dispirited. Nevertheless, when she heard a footfall from the direction of the drawing-room, and was reminded that papa had already come in, her combative blood plucked up at once. She wanted to tell her father immediately that he was going to be attacked in the papers; never fear but he would know what to do about it.

"Papa!" she called. "Where are you? I . . ."

Speaking, she had put her head through the drawing-room portières, rehung that very day: and so it was that her sentence was never ended in this world. For it was not papa who turned so quickly at the sound of her voice, and came walking so straight and sure towards her. Not papa, this splendid and once well-admired figure, now confronting her with such unmistakable feeling. No, the wonder of all wonders had happened; and the universe seemed to hang in momentary suspense as Cally Heth looked again into the eyes of her prince of lovers.

"Carlisle," said Hugo's remembered voice, "I've come back."

She stood unmoving in the doorway, her fingers tightening on the silken hanging. Her breast was in a tumult of emotions, in which a leaping exultation was not wanting. But stronger than anything else in this moment was the uprushing feeling that here was one whom she had well trusted once, and who had failed her in her direst need.

"So I see," said she.

And continuing to look fixedly at him as he advanced upon her, beginning to speak, she was shot through with a bitter thought: "He's found I'm not so badly damaged after all."

XXV

In which the Name of Heth is lifted beyond the Reach of Hateful Malice, and Mamma wishes that she had the Ten Thousand back again.

MRS. HETH returned from the Settlement "opening" a full hour behind Carlisle, and in a victorious glow such as she had not known since May. Doing good for cause, she was not one to blush too much to find it fame. Having notified Mr. Byrd of her ten thousand dollar gift to the Foundation Fund, she had proceeded with her tidings to others of the authorities, and presently met with appreciation in proportion to the funds involved. Director Pond, a decisive and forthright man, had stood upon a chair and cried the splendid donation to the assembled company, his obvious moral being that others similarly prospered by the Lord should go and do likewise. So had come vindicatory advertisement gorgeous beyond the little lady's dreams.

It was well that the world should mark this gift, for it had not been made by the mere scratching of a signature. And the colloquies preceding it had been of a thoroughly typical sort, compressing in a nutshell a whole history, in fact the whole history, of the domestico-commercial relationships of rising Houses. Settlementers might have applauded more heartily had they understood just what a deep-cutting business they were witnessing. However, they did not understand this, and Mrs. Heth, for her part, was the last person in the world to moralize upon the non-essential. Returning homeward through the night, rolling *éclat* beneath her tongue, she frankly reflected that it was worth the money. The envious would hardly be able to conceive that people who gave so magnificently to charity could have done anything really deserving of censure; no, no. Or, if such people imaginably had, then certainly the only thing to do was to forget all about it as quickly as possible. . . .

So agreeably musing, Mrs. Heth arrived at the door of the House, and received upon the threshold the great surprise of her life.

It was almost seven o'clock, so long had she lingered to enjoy and capitalize the reverberations of her triumph. Yet Carlisle, singularly enough, was discovered standing in the hall, still in her hat and gloves, just as she had left the reception an hour earlier.

Full as Mrs. Heth was of her own engrossing thoughts, her daughter's expression at once notified her that she, too, had news of some sort to communicate.

"Well, Carlisle? What're you ... Why, what's happened?"

"You've just missed Hugo, mamma."

"*Hugo!*" said mamma, paling and almost falling backward. "He's *been* here?"

In her daughter's blue eyes there lingered that gleaming exultation, not completely softened as yet by the sweeter and now due love-light.

"He wants me to marry him next month."

"Oh, *Cally!* . . ."

Fairly tumbling forward from the door, Mrs. Heth gathered her daughter in a convulsive bear-hug, murmuring ecstatic nothings. Little she thought of Settlements or picayunish donations now.

"Oh, Cally! . . . Mamma's so happy for you, dear child! . . . And me never dreaming he was within a thousand miles! All's well that ends well, *I* say! . . . When'd he come? I'm wild to see him. Where's he staying? Will he be back this evening?"

She drew away from her unwonted demonstration, leaving her hands on Cally's shoulders, and the two women looked at each other, both a little flushed with excitement.

"He's at the Arlington, to stay only till to-morrow," said she, "and he's coming in after dinner to see you and papa."

"Oh! . . . He insists on not seeing *you*, I suppose?" fleered mamma, with enormous archness.

"I won't be here, you see. I'm going to the theatre — Mr. Avery's getting up a party."

Mrs. Heth showed as much surprise as the jubilation of her countenance could accommodate.

"Why, my dear child! Break it, of course! I'll telephone him myself — a friend from out of town —"

"But I don't want to break it, you see!" said Carlisle, laughing brightly. "He can't expect to drop in after months and months and find us all twirling our thumbs on the doorstep, you know!"

"But you're *engaged to him !*"

"I should hope *not !* . . . Why, *mamma !* You must think I'm frightfully — die-away! . . . I'm *disciplining* him, don't you see ? I'm not going to make it too easy for him!"

"Oh! . . . I see!"

Perhaps she did not see exactly, and certainly she did not believe in manufacturing sporting chances in the most momentous matter in the world. But then neither did Cally, she well knew; and of her daughter's victorious skill in the matter of managing men, she had had many proofs, and now this crowning one. Lovers' coynesses mattered little in the face of the supreme fact of Canning's return.

"Well! You'll give him the whole day to-morrow, of course!... And don't you be too hard on the dear fellow, Cally. His coming back shows he's been disciplined. . . . How the cats will open their eyes!"

"Probably. . . . But don't worry about Hugo, mamma. He'll do just what I say after this."

Mamma laughed delightedly. She was of course in the woman's league for the general putting down of the enemy, Man. The two women stood staring at each other in the stately hall.

"*Next month !*" said mamma. "We can't do it, Cally! November would be better — much better — just before Thanksgiving, don't you think?"

Cally laughed merrily, and extricated herself.

"We'll have plenty of time to decide about *that.* . . . Now, I must fly and dress. I shan't have time for dinner, mamma. Will you send me up something — just some soup and coffee?"

"Certainly, darling," said mamma.

Already there had crept a certain absentness into the campaigner's voice. Her strong, constructive mind was slipping away from this present, measuring over the triumphs that lay ahead. After her darling vanished upstairs, she remained standing motionless by the newel-post, in her fixed eyes the gleam of a brigadier-general who has pulled out brilliant victory over overwhelming obstacles. The god in the machine had, indeed, forever put the name of Heth beyond the reach of hateful malice. . . .

Suddenly mamma said aloud, rather indignantly: "I wish I had that ten thousand back!"

In her own room, Cally bathed, dressed at some speed, and dined lightly between whiles. She was in a state of inner exaltation, contrasting oddly with her depression two hours earlier. Obliterated now was her conviction of her own human uselessness in a world of sexes, though it could n't be said that anything had happened to disprove that conviction, exactly. In this moment she was continuously elated by all that was signified in the fact that Hugo Canning was to spend the evening downstairs talking decorously with mamma and papa while she, Cally, loved of him, was to go off to the theatre with J. Forsythe Avery. . . .

If Canning had failed her in her greatest need, time, indeed, had exquisitely avenged her. The Lord of the righteous had delivered the prince of lovers into her hand. With his very first words in the dim drawing-room, Hugo had admitted, for the second time in their somewhat stormy courtship, his unconditional surrender. He made no mistake this time about the nature of a woman's heart; he was not logical or controversial or just; but advancing straight upon her over her decidedly forbidding greeting, he had spoken out with evident emotion:

"Don't look at me that way — I can't bear it. . . . Don't you know *now* that I love you? I love you so that I won't live without you."

Yes, Cally did know it now. She had clearly wronged both Hugo and herself in ever thinking of him as a male flirt, a light-loving jilt who too easily found balm for a heart not made for deep hurts. Busy and gay with her dressing, Carlisle thought of the Honorable Kitty Belden, and laughed musically to herself.

Yet how was it that, under so manly and sweet an appeal straight to her woman's heart, she had not instantly subsided on the shoulder of her contrite lover, with grateful tears? Cally herself hardly understood. She was, truth to tell, secretly surprised and thrilled by her own high-handedness. To what degree she and her former betrothed had remet under permanently changed conditions, it was beyond her thought to try to analyse now. Perhaps it was only the completeness of her triumph that had so fired her feminine independence. Had she met Hugo by chance, and found him lukewarm, doubt not that she would have striven to fan the embers. . . .

She had followed her intuitions, which never reason, and when she said that she was now disciplining her prodigal, she spoke out her actual feelings as far as she herself understood them; feelings, they were, which had a deep root far back in all the summer's unhappiness. There was a sentence of Hugo's last May: "*I asked one girl to be my wife; have you the right to offer me another?*" She would make Hugo pay a little more for that remark, now that she could just as easily as not.

Like Aaron's rod, the return of Canning had swallowed up all other facts of the girl's existence, or nearly all. She was lifted, as on wings, out of the slough of her despond. Nevertheless, the news heard at the Settlement recurred even now; and when Mrs. Heth appeared in the bedroom, just after eight, Carlisle greeted her with:

"Has papa gone out, mamma?"

Mamma said no, papa was in the study, though Mr. MacQueen was with him just at the moment. Something about installing some new machines at the Works, she believed. . . .

"That will do, Flora — Miss Carlisle has everything she needs. . . ." And then the good lady said, with a smile so knowing as to amount to a tremendous wink: "You are going to tell your father to-night . . . That's right, my dear —"

Cally gave a burst of gay laughter, declaring that there was not one earthly thing to tell.

"Of course, darling, mamma understands," said that lady, promptly, with her unconquerable beam.

And a few moments later she added:

"Cally, I was just thinking — no harm in being forehanded, as I always say! . . . Considering all the circumstances, what would you say to a small, dignified home-wedding, with two or four bridesmaids, and a large breakfast to the most intimate friends?"

Cally was even more amused. . . .

There hovered over her in this moment, however clearly she knew it, an immense pressure, born both within and without — pressure of her own lifelong mental habits and ideals, of her parents' wishes, strengthened by the family's late loss of prestige, pressure of public opinion, of orthodox standards, of manifest destiny, of the whole air she breathed — driving her, quite irrespective of the heart question, straight to brilliant success in Hugo's waiting arms. The wing of this vast body brushed Cally's cheek now, in mamma's cooing notes. She felt it, but only smiled. A new strength possessed her; she was her own girl now as never before.

"I'll give the suggestion due thought, mamma dear . . . I've an engagement now."

Annie knocked, announcing Mr. Avery. Cally was now fully accoutred, in a small, queer hat, and a short queer wrap, draping in fantastically above the knee and made of a strange filmy material which might have been stamped chiffon. She turned, laughing, at the bedroom door, and her mother, no sentimentalist, thought that she looked extraordinarily pretty. . . .

"Good - night, mamma. . . . *Be sure to remember me to Hugo.*"

She went off to a merry evening in which her high spirits became a matter of remark, and her friend Evey McVey considered that they were the least bit out of taste — "so soon, you know." So Hugo Canning spent the evening of his return formally reinstating himself in the good graces of papa, who did not forget his daughter's unhappiness of the summer quite so easily as mamma. . . .

But next day Hugo had his innings, according to Mrs. Heth's desire.

He had been in Washington, and had come to Carlisle upon an irresistible impulse. Steadily magnetized by the spirit of the "wild, sweet thing" who had withstood him at the price of his hand, yearning had once more conquered pride, and again he had returned, again an astonishment to himself. In view of such abasement of his self-love, he had, truth to tell, expected to find Carlisle fully ready for the immediate rejoining of their lives. But perhaps there had lingered in him a doubt of the quality of his reception, born of the manner of their parting; and her hesitation, while it shook his vanity, by no means bade him despair. After the first small shock, he had not failed to perceive the coyness of her; and why not? If her maiden's whim demanded a brief ritual of probationary wooing before verbally admitting him to her heart again, never fear but he would go through his paces with a gallant's air. . . .

The day was what photographers call cloudy-bright, turning toward mid-afternoon into fitful sunshine. The young pair lunched *à deux* at the Country Club, nearly deserted at this hour on a week-day. Hugo had stoutened the least bit under his sorrows; he was more masculine, handsomer than ever; his manner did not want his old lordliness, even now. He was not one to discuss business with a woman, but she learned of the affair which was hurrying him back to Washington, nothing less than ratehearings before the Interstate Commerce Commission, if you please. The able young man was now assistant counsel for his father's railway. However, he was to pass this way soon again, probably next week.

They sat for an hour on the club piazza looking out over smooth rolling hills, now green, now wooded, all fair in the late September sunshine. Away to the left there was the faint gleam of the river. All day Canning, in his subtle way, made love to Cally, but he was too wise to press hard upon her girlish hesitancy.

"I don't believe you've missed me much," he remarked, once, on the wooing note. "Have you?"

Cally smiled into space and answered: "At times."

"That's cheerful . . . When there's not been an hour for me, all summer, I swear it, that hasn't been singing with thoughts of you."

"You might have run up from Trouville, in July, and called on us in Paris."

His reply indicated that running, whether up or down, involved a considerable conquest of pride. And Cally understood that.

"I," said she, tranquilly, "have been growing weary of society. Perhaps that is your doing. . . ."

She told him of her experience at the Settlement yesterday, of her rebuff at the hands of Mr. Pond. Canning thanked heaven that she need not bother herself with such dreary faddisms of the day.

"You can safely leave all that," said he, "to the women who have failed in their own careers."

"And what career is that?"

"The career of being a woman. Need you ask?"

Carlisle, drawing on her gloves, observed: "That would bring up the question, wouldn't it, of what your ideal of a woman is."

"For five cents," said Hugo, "I will tell you her name."

She was pleased with the evidences of her mastery over him. The day of intimacy brought its reactions, automatically creating romantic airs. When the time came for him to go, she was sorry; and perhaps just a little uncertain in her own mind. For the re-engagement had still not taken place. The most that could be said was that an "understanding" existed, to the effect that it would take place on his return. And Canning, for his part, was not dissatisfied with this arrangement. In ten days he would come again, and take the wavering outposts by storm.

They said good-bye in the drawing-room at home, at quarter before five. Cally held out her slender little hand. Hugo smiled down at it: surely, between him and her, an odd farewell. But then, as his clasp tightened, the man's smile became a little twisted on his handsome lip.

"When I part from you again, my dear," said he, with sudden huskiness, "I swear it won't be like this."

The girl looked up at him. He raised the hand, palm-upward, with a sort of jerk, kissed it, dropped it abruptly, and was gone.

Cally remained standing where he had left her; this time she did not run to the window. She glanced at the hand which her lover had just saluted, and was conscious of a subtle want in their reunion. . . .

Hugo's presence in the body had brought up vividly that matter upon which they had broken in May. Of that matter he had said nothing, either yesterday or to-day. His manner and bearing took the clear position that he and she had simply had a lovers' quarrel, in which both had said and done things that they did not mean. But Jack Dalhousie had stood in the background of Carlisle's mind all day, and her feeling was that something rather definite should have been said about him. Possibly Mrs. Berkeley Page had something to do with this; that lady had left behind her an indefinable suggestion of invisible standards, of appraisements differing from mamma's, say. Measuring herself unconsciously with Hugo to-day, Cally had become aware that in carrying out her will in opposition to his last year, she had derived, not merely strategic, but in some way personal, strength. The old inequality had mysteriously disappeared. . . .

Mrs. Heth came gliding through the portières from the hall. Her face was one vast inquiry, lit by beams; it made an uproarious demand such as a child of three could have understood. Still, to avoid any possibility of misunderstanding, mamma briefly gave voice:

"Well?"

Cally laughed, and held up her betrothal finger, which was unadorned.

"I'm not," said she.

Mamma's face fell.

"Don't look so blank!" said the daughter, with a little laugh and shrug. "It's all going to happen next week, by the book. . . . Don't you know I'm perfectly safe?"

Mr. Heth heard Cally's business news with open indignation. She made her report to him that night, just after dinner; and she saw her father's business manner emerge sharply from beneath his genial domesticity.

The "new law" was an old story to the owner of the Cheroot Works. He kept apprised of the signs of the times; and he happened to know in some detail the provisions of the pernicious legislation the Labor Commissioner was cooking up in secret, — "that'd confiscate two years' profits from every near mill in town," said MacQueen. But the rest was news, and highly unwelcome news. To fight blackmail legislation against progressive business was comparatively simple; but a string of lies in the newspapers made a more insidious assault, injuring a man's credit, his standing as a conservative financier, his ability to inspire "confidence": valuable possessions to the President of the Fourth National Bank, and already indefinably impaired by the sensational family matter last spring. . . .

"Vivian! — That fellow!" he exclaimed, recalling not only the Severe Arraignment, but the cataclysm in the House. . . . "Why, Cally! I thought you considered him sort of a friend of yours!"

"Not that, exactly," said Cally, at a considerable loss. "Still, I was very much surprised. . . . Do you mind about the — the articles, particularly, papa?"

"I do."

"Isn't there something you can do — to have it all stopped? Couldn't you have a suit — or —?"

Her father exploded. She had touched a sore point.

"Sue! Sue a lot of paupers that haven't got a shirt to their backs! Put 'em in prison? — likely with a lot more paupers on the jury, thinkin' a successful business man's anybody's meat. *Sue!* — and what'll you get? I'll tell you! An impudent — offensive — malicious muckraking of your own private business. . . ."

Cally, looking at papa's indignant face, felt much drawn to him. However, the business conversation was here interrupted, Cally being called away to the telephone. She went, wondering intently if she could not somehow help in this threatened trouble. She had felt an impulse toward doing something useful. What more useful than assisting to shield her father from undeserved abuse? . . .

"It's only me, Cally," said Henrietta Cooney's voice, "or I, as they've got it in the grammars. I just called up to tell you not to forget the meeting to-morrow."

"What meeting, Hen?"

"I see I did well to call," came over the wire, on the wings of the Cooney laugh. "The Saturday meeting at the Woman's Club, cousin, that I engaged you for the other day. I've just heard that V. V.'s going to speak, too, which made me want you specially. Don't say no."

"Of course not. I want to go, very much."

The two girls lingered a moment to chat. Henrietta appeared characteristically cheerful, though reporting half the family sick, and Cousin Martha Heth quite low in mind with her flatfoot. And Cally's manner to her poor relation was quite friendly to-night, without any special effort. Her summer-time suspicion that Hen was actually trying to "cheer her up" had by now become a certainty (Hen did not know about Hugo, of course); and which of her own girlhood intimates had done as much? Further, the words of comfort that the hard-worked stenographer had said to her, the day she got home from Europe, had recently been endorsed, as it were, in a most distinguished quarter. A strange thought this, that there was a point of similarity between Hen Cooney and Mrs. Berkeley Page. . . .

But when Cally left the telephone she was not thinking of these things at all. She was thinking that to-morrow she would both hear and see Dr. Vivian, her father's enemy, the hard religious fellow who could so easily forget the troubles of others. Her duty on the occasion seemed to become quite clear to her. She must speak to him, try to induce him to give up his newspaper articles, or at least to leave her father's name out of them.

The day of lovers' reunion was somewhat blurred by ending with thoughts such as these. Hugo, as Carlisle had said, could not pop back after months, and repossess her mind and heart at a bound. He did it pretty successfully during the evening, while she entertained Robert Tellford and James Bogue, 2d, who cordially hated each other, in the drawing-room. But before she fell asleep that night, Cally's thoughts had turned more than once to V. Vivian, of the old hotel which was now a Settlement. Why had he asked her to go to the Works some day, and why had he done it with that strange look?

XXVI

*Concerning Women who won't remember their Place, and a
Speech to Two Hundred of them, by Mr. V. V., no less; also
revealing why Hen Cooney never found V. V. in the Crowd
around the Platform.*

IT was an interesting time to be alive, as Hen Cooney
remarked again next day. Absorbing matters were afoot
in the old town, provided that you had an eye in your
head to see them. One thing led to another with startling rapidity. Only the other day, it seemed, some one had risen and flung
against the ideals of generations the discordant cry of Votes for
Women. Rebukes for the unseemliness were copious and stern
enough. Many spoke acidly of the lengths to which childless
females would go for lack of occupation. Droll fellows of a pretty
wit giggled and asked who would mind the baby while the madam
went out to vote. Serious-minded persons of both sexes disposed
of the whole foolishness forever by saying (and wondering why
nobody had ever thought of it before) that woman's place was the
home. But few there were who perceived a symptom here; not
even when the League grew with unintelligible rapidity, and
croaking diagnosticians here or there professed to see other
manifestations not unrelated.

Cassandras remarked that women wearied of thinking "through
their husbands." The census revealed to the close student that
some women even had no husbands. It was a fact that year
before last women had appeared at legislative "hearings" for the
first time in the history of the State. These women, plague on
them, failed to fortify the wags by powdering their noses in front
of pocket mirrors while they talked, or making sweet-eyes at the
chairmen of committees. They appeared, to tell the honest
truth, with late reference-books under their arms, and in their
heads the faculty for asking the most annoying sort of questions.

More than one honest Solon was seen to stammer and turn red under their interrogations, so often stiffened by a date and a little figure or so.

And these troublesome "thinking women" had not retired when the legislature did. Editors nowadays were often surprised in their sanctums by committees of three from some pestiferous unwomanly club or other, and they had not come, alackaday, to have their handkerchiefs picked up with courtly speeches, graced with an apt quotation from "Maud." The Civic Improvement League, with a woman president, was taking a continuous interest in matters of playgrounds and parks, clean streets and city planning. The Society for Social Progress, almost exclusively feminine, was continuously astir about pure milk and factory laws, birth-rates and infant mortality, sociology and eugenics. And now here was the conservative Woman's Club, which had been purely literary and social for a quarter of a century, holding a largely attended symposium on How Shall We Help the Poor?

This latter meeting, attended by Carlisle Heth and her cousin Henrietta the day after Canning left, was no doubt a trivial and obscure occurrence. Not an earthly thing could be said for it, except that it was a bubble on the surface of an unrest which would one day change the face of human society. . . .

The two cousins, having come a little tardy, were content with seats in the next to the last row. The Woman's Club inhabited an old family mansion on Washington Street, — bought in the legendary age when land was not computed by the square foot, — and its assembly-rooms were the one-time parlors, with the dining-room thrown in by an architectural dexterity. Perhaps two hundred women could be seated here, and all seemed to be present to-day. Cally regarded serried rows of feminine backs, some of which she recognized. The little platform at the farther end of the rooms remained empty, and the place was abuzz with murmured talk. Not a back was silent, not even Henrietta's. Hen was saying enthusiastically that nothing like this could have been seen ten years ago. . . .

Cally caught widening glimpses of the Cooney meanings. She had been like a rider thrown from a gay fixed steed in a merry-go-round, who, having picked himself up and mended his wounds, looks about, and gets his first view of the carousel as part of a larger moving scene. Cally, for the first time in her life, had been glancing over the fair-grounds. Not even the knowledge of Hugo's love could now wholly turn her gaze backward.

Pending the beginning of the oratory, clubbers and guests talked to the contentment of their hearts. Cally said suddenly:

"Hen, why is it that men are so opposed to this sort of thing?"

"It's human," said Hen, "if you have the upper hand, not to want to give it up."

"You mean that men have the upper hand now?"

"Have n't they?"

A tiny little woman in the row ahead of them turned round and smiled faintly at Henrietta. She had a face like a small doll's, a button of a nose and the palest little china-blue eyes imaginable. Nevertheless, this woman was Mrs. Slicer, president of the Federation of Women's Clubs, and those weak eyes had once stared a Governor of a State out of countenance.

"Hen, they have," said she, in a fairy voice; and so turned back to her own affairs, dropping from these pages.

Henrietta presently said: "But why should they oppose it, really, Cally? If you were a man, would you insist on the privilege of marrying a helpless dependent, your mental and moral inferior? Seems to me I'd rather have an intelligent comrade, my superior for choice —"

But Hen discovered that her voice all at once sounded very loud. There was a sudden lull in the conversational hum, and then a burst of hand-clapping. The lady president of the Woman's Club had entered at the head of the rooms, followed by the orators. They ascended the platform; and when Cally saw but the Mayor of the city and Mr. Pond of the Settlement, she said at once to Henrietta:

"Why, where's your friend V. V.?"

"Somewhere up at the front, — I *hope!* . . . He was n't one of the regular speakers, you know. . . ."

Hen added in a faint whisper: "I doubt if he knows he's going to be called on —"

Being duly presented to the expectant women, his Honor the Mayor spoke first. He was a middle-aged, mustachioed Mayor, who had achieved a considerable success by being all things to a few men, but those the right ones. His reputation as an orator was well deserved, but his ability to make one speech serve many occasions had been commented upon by carpers here and there. See the files of the "Post," *passim*. To-day his thesis was organized charity, lauded by him, between paragraphs of the set piece, as philanthropy's great rebuke to Socialism. And thrice his Honor spoke of the glorious capital of this grand old commonwealth; twice his arm swept from the stormy Atlantic to the sun-kissed Pacific; five times did he exalt, with the tremolo stop, the fair women of the Southland. . . .

"The dinner-bell of the house!" said Hen, *sotto voce*, as the orator sat down, smiling tiredly amid familiar applause. "Don't be discouraged yet, Cally."

Director Pond, having been most flatteringly introduced, received an ovation, half for the man and his work, half from the wish of a kindly people to bid the stranger welcome. He spoke half as long as the Mayor, and said four times as much: so much space did he save by saying nothing whatever about the fair women of the Southland, and by absolutely avoiding all metaphors, tropes, synecdoches, or anacolutha. Mr. Pond assaulted the Mayor's apotheosis of charity, particularly as applied to his own institution. He described the Settlement, not as a dispensary for old clothes, but as a cultivated personality, an enlightened elder brother gone to live with the poor. It aspired to enrich life through living, said he, to bring light to the disinherited and the gift of a wider horizon. . . .

Mr. Pond followed his thought with more imagination than one might have thought him to possess, and with a glow on his dark face such as had not been observed there the other day. Cally, from the next to the last row, listened attentively enough; she recalled that she would see Mr. Pond this evening, perhaps sit next to him, at mamma's Settlement dinner. However, she reserved her chief interest for Hen's friend V. V., who was so merciless in his attitude toward those who were not poor. Mr. Pond spoke straightforwardly, not to say bluntly. But she pictured Vivian as shaking the rafters with his shameless homicides and God-pity-yous. . . .

"Once the bread and meat question's settled, money is of secondary importance," said the Director's deep voice. "Let's get that well into our heads. What the poor ask is that they shall not be born under disadvantages which the labor of their lifetimes can never remove. . . ."

Only these two speakers had been announced. When Pond sat down the formal exercises were over. But as his applause died away, the president of the club rose again, sure enough, — while Henrietta excitedly nudged Carlisle, —and announced an added speaker, a guest of the club to-day, whom she described as the young father of the Settlement. The president — a tall, placid-faced woman, with a finely cut chin and a magnificent crown of silver hair — had something to say about the spirit of pure idealism; and was sure that the members would be glad to hear remarks on the subject of the day from young Dr. Vivian, the missionary doctor of the Dabney House. . . .

The few kind words elicited somewhat perfunctory plaudits, despite Hen Cooney's single-handed attempt to stampede them into a triumph. The Clubbers, truth to tell, were by now disposed to leave oratory and the uplift for small-talk and tea.

"*There he is!*" said Hen, clapping splendidly.

V. Vivian stood on the platform, beside a tall oak-stand and a water-pitcher, gazing out over phalanxes of women. His youthfulness was a matter of general notice. By contrast with the Mayor's seamy rotundity and Pond's powerful darkness, he looked, indeed, singularly boyish and fair. He was undoubtedly pale, and his face wore an odd look, a little confused and slightly pained. This, combined with his continuing silence, gave rise to a general suspicion that the young man had fallen a victim to stage-fright. However, the odd struggle going on in him at his unexpected opportunity was not against fear. . . .

Carlisle regarded Vivian intently, over and through scores of women's hats. She was inwardly braced for epithets. Somewhere in the air she heard the word "anarchist"; but a woman sitting near her said, quite audibly, — "*Looks* more like a *poet*," . . . meaning, let us hope, like a poet as we like to think that poets look; and not as they so often actually look, by their pictures in the magazines. . . .

"I suppose the beginning of helping the poor," suddenly spoke up the young man on the stand, in a voice so natural and simple as to come as a small shock, "is to stop thinking of them as the poor. There are useful people in the world, and useless people; good people and bad people. But when we speak of poor people and rich people, we only make divisions where our Maker never saw any, and raise barriers on the common which must some day all come down."

The speaker pushed back his blond hair with a gesture which Cally Heth had seen before. However, all else about him, from the first sight, had seemed to come to her in the nature of a surprise. . . .

"The things in which we are all alike," said the tall youth, with none of the Mayor's oratorial thunder, "are so much bigger than the things in which we are different. What's rich and poor, to a common beginning and a common end, common sufferings, common dreams? We look at these big freeholds, and money in bank is a little thing. On Washington Street, and down behind the Dabney House — don't we each alike seek the same thing? We want life, and more life. We want to be happy, and we want to be free. Well — we know it's hard to win these prizes when we're poor, but is it so easy when we're rich? To live shut off on a little island, calling the rest common and unclean — is that being happy and free, is it having life abundantly? I look around, and don't find it so. And that's sad, isn't it? — double frustration, the poor disinherited by their poverty, the rich in their riches. . . . Don't you think we shall find a common meeting-place some day, where these two will cancel out? . . . when reality will touch hands with the poet's ideal —

And the stranger hath seen in the stranger his brother at last,
And his sister in eyes that were strange . . ."

The slum doctor paused. The confused appearance was gone from his face; he looked now introspective, quite without consciousness of himself; rather like a man listening with somewhat dreamy approbation to the words of another. And Cally, having felt her antagonism mysteriously slipping away from the moment her eyes rested upon his face, now knew, quite suddenly and definitely, that she wasn't going to speak to him about the articles.

The knowledge, the whole matter, was curiously disturbing to her. Where was the hostile hardness of the religious fellow, justifying distrust and dislike? Why should her father's attacker make her think now, of all times, of that night in Hen's parlor, the morning on Mr. Beirne's doorstep, that rainy May-day in his Dabney House when he had overwhelmed her with the knowledge of his superiority? . . .

"And — and — I think women should be especially interested in all that makes for a new common freedom," observed the youthful speaker, "for they have suffered somewhat in that way — haven't they? . . . [Applause, led by Miss Cooney.] You know the processes of history — how men, first of all by superior muscle, have made it a man's world. . . . Till to-day, large groups of women find themselves cribbed and cabined to a single pursuit, marriage: surely the noblest of all callings, but — perhaps you will agree with me — the meanest of all professions. I, for one, am glad to see women revolting from this condition, asking something truer, something commoner, than chivalry. For that, I say, steps the march to the great goal, a boundless commonwealth, a universal republic of the human spirit. It seems to me we need to socialize, not industry, but the heart of Man to his brother. Rich and poor, men and women — God, I am sure of it, meant us all to be citizens of the world. . . ."

A certain self-consciousness seemed here to descend upon the tall orator. He ceased abruptly, and disappeared from the platform, having neglected to make his bow to the chairman.

Then the moment's dead silence was suddenly exploded with a burst of clapping, quite as hearty as Mr. Pond had received, and really something like the "storm" we read about. And in the din, Henrietta Cooney was heard crying, with a passion of pride:

"Well, it's about *time!* . . . It's the first thing V. V.'s ever got — the first *tribute.* . . . A boy like that —"

Hen, curiously, was winking a little as the two girls rose. And she added in a moved voice, as if seeking to explain herself:

"Well, think of the hard life he has down there, Cally, — no pleasure, no fun, no companionship. . . . And this is the first notice of *any kind* . . ."

The meeting was over. The crowded parlors were in a hubbub. Colored servants entered, taking away the camp-chairs. A general drift toward the platform was in evidence. And Cally, standing with the others and ready to go, seemed to see no clear course at all among the disturbing cross-currents which she suddenly felt within her, impelling her now this way, now that. If she could not think of V. Vivian as hard now, exactly, a new "attitude" was obviously needed, consistent with her duty to papa. It must be that the strange young man was obsessed by beautiful but impossible ideas about the equality of the poor and so on. Carried away by excessive sympathies, he took wild extreme views. . . .

"Are you going to stay for tea, Hen?" she asked, amid the stir and vocal noises of two hundred women.

But Hen said no; getting tea for the Cooney invalids was her portion.

"We'll just stop a minute and speak to V. V.," she added, as if that went without saying.

But this time Cally said no, somewhat hastily. And then she explained that she must go home to dress, as mamma was having some people to dinner to-night. Hen looked disappointed.

"Well, there's no chance of getting near him now, anyway. Look at that jam around the platform. . . . Stay just a minute or two, Cally."

The two cousins, the rich and the poor, and looking it, strolled among the Clubbers, Henrietta speaking to nearly everybody, and invariably asking how they had liked Dr. Vivian's speech, Pond and the Mayor ignored. She also introduced her cousin right and left, and enjoyed herself immensely.

Cally, having matters to think about, again remarked that she must go. She saw Hen glance hungrily over the dense lively crowd, densest around the platform, and promptly added: "But of course you must n't think of coming with me."

Henrietta hesitated. "You would n't mind if I stayed on a minute? I *would* like just to say a word to V. V."

Cally assured her. "And thank you for bringing me, Hen. I — had no idea it would be so interesting."

The two girls parted. Hen plunged into the Clubbers to speak to Mr. V. V. Cally went out of the great doors, deep in thought. And having passed through these doors, the very first person she saw was Mr. V. V. . . .

It was incredible, but it was true. How he had escaped the handshakers was a mystery for a detective. But there the man indubitably stood at the head of the Club steps, alone in the gathering twilight, bowing, speaking her name. . . .

Had he been waiting for her, then? A certain air of prepared surprise in his greeting rather suggested the thought.

"Is your car waiting?" inquired the orator, courteously. "May I call it for you?"

Cally's heart had jumped a little at the sight of his tall figure, but she answered easily enough, as she moved toward the steps, that she was walking.

"Then won't you allow me to see you home? . . . It's getting rather dark. And I — the fact is, I wanted to speak to you."

And Cally said, far from what she had planned to say in thinking of this meeting:

"If you like. . . . Only you must promise not to scold me about the Works."

He gave her a look full of surprise, and touched with a curious sort of gratification; curious to her, that is, since she could not know how a well-known Labor Commissioner had taxed this man with "easiness."

"I promise," said he.

As they took the bottom step, he added, in a controlled sort of voice:

"Please tell me frankly — is it objectionable to you to — to have me walk with you?"

"Oh, no," said Cally.

Down forty feet of bricked walkway, through the swinging iron gates, out upon the public sidewalk, Carlisle walked silently beside the attacker of her father, the religious fellow whom Hugo Canning so disliked. About them in the pale dusk tall street-lights began to twinkle. Over them hung the impenetrable silence. It was but three blocks from the Woman's Club to the House of Heth. They had traversed half of one of them before Vivian gave voice:

"I merely wanted to say this."

And on that they walked ten steps without more speech.

"This," resumed Mr. V. V., and his voice was not easy. "You must have thought it strange the other day, when I told you the — the work I had taken up. . . . My articles, I mean. . . . I should know, if anybody does, that you — your family — have had much trouble to bear of late. . . . It seems that I should be the last person to do what will bring you more trouble — annoyance certainly, pain perhaps. . . . I felt that I wanted you to know, at least, that it took a — a strong necessity to make me go into the matter — at this time. . . . I wanted to tell you that — personally — I've been very sorry about it. . . ."

She hesitated a moment, and then said:

"I don't doubt that. . . . I haven't doubted it since I stopped to think."

And if this was disloyalty to papa, Cally felt that she could not help it. . . . What, after all, did she know about it? Surely it was all a men's matter, a mere question of "reform," in which some thought one way and some another, and each side said hard things without meaning them exactly. Probably papa would be the last person to wish her to interfere. . . .

"Thank you," he replied, it seemed with feeling in his voice. And walking on, looking straight before him, he added:

"There was one thing more . . . Ah — pardon me."

The young doctor carried a cane, but used it principally for swinging and lunging. In view of his infirmity, Cally had begun by walking more slowly than was her custom. It had soon developed, however, that he was a rapid walker, and of absent-minded habit as well, particularly when talking. So, throughout the brief walk, her difficulty was to keep apace with him.

"What you said just now — my scolding you about the Works. ... I realize that it must have seemed peculiar to you, and — and — weak — unmanly — my pursuing you so about a — a — purely business matter. Of course you must have felt that if I had criticisms to make, I should have taken them to your father — instead of inflicting them on you, all the time."

He paused; but the girl said nothing. She had, in fact, speculated considerably on this very point: how could she posssibly have any responsibility for the way papa ran his business? It occurred to her to ask the man plainly whether he considered that she had; but she did not do so, perhaps fearing that he might reply in the affirmative. ...

"I once tried to explain it, in a way," he went on, hurriedly. "I said that I did n't know your father. ... You naturally considered that merely a — a foolish sort of — claim — explaining nothing. I suppose you've forgotten all this, but —"

"No, I remember."

"Then let me say that — the other day, when I saw you — I had no idea of mentioning the Works to you, other than to explain my position — not an *idea*. ... And then, when we talked — well, I did," he said with a kind of naked ingenuousness, as if no one could have been more surprised about it all than he. ... "I can't explain it, so that it won't still seem peculiar to you. ... It's only that I do feel somehow that — that knowing people makes a great difference — in certain respects. ..."

"I — think I can understand that."

"It's generous of you to be willing to try."

"No," said Cally, pulling her veil down at the chin, and quickening her steps as he strode on, "I'm only trying to be — reasonable about it."

They were passing people now and then in the twilight street,

most of whom Cally spoke to; and once she thought how surprised Hugo would be, could he look over from Washington and
see her walking amiably in this company. But then Hugo might
have thought of these matters last year, when he said she wasn't
the girl he had asked to marry him.

"Besides," said she, suddenly, "you don't mean to say anything — *terribly* bad about the Works in the articles — do
you?"

"Yes, terribly," replied Mr. V. V., leaving her completely
taken aback.

He added, formally, after a step or two: "I — ah — shouldn't
feel honest if I left you in the slightest doubt — on that point."

But she could not believe now that his articles would be so terrible, no matter what he said, and her strange reply was:

"Then — suppose we don't talk about it."

He said: "I feel it's better so." And then they walked on
rapidly in silence.

And somewhere in this silence, it came over Cally that the
reason she could not distrust this man was because, in a very
special way, she had learned to trust him; could not dislike him
because the truth was that in her heart she liked him very much.
And people must act as they felt. And then her thought suddenly advanced much further, as if mounting the last step in a
watch-tower: and Cally saw that the question between herself
and V. Vivian had always been, not what she might think of
him, but what he thought of her. . . .

The fruitful pause ran rather long. She considered complimenting Mr. V. V. upon his speech, expressing her surprise at his
unlooked-for gentleness on the subject of the poor. How could
one who spoke so kindly write terrible articles in the newspapers,
attacking one's own father? Cally wondered, missing the perfectly obvious point of it all, namely: that when a man is a guest
at a woman's club, his particular task is to look sharp to his
tongue, ruling with a strong hand what besetting weakness he
may have for grim speech, and abhorring . . .

But the whole subject was difficult to the girl, and it was he
who broke the silence, speaking his pedestrian's apology again.

And this time, so swift and straight had they come, Cally replied, with quite a natural laugh:

"Never mind. . . . Here I am."

She halted before the white-stone steps of home, and glanced involuntarily toward the windows. Independent though she felt since day before yesterday, she would not have cared to have mamma glance out just then. . . .

"I *had n't* realized that we were here already!"

"Oh, it is n't far, as you see. . . . But it was good of you to bring me."

It was a parting speech; but Cally said it with no inflection of finality. So, at least, it seemed to be considered. V. Vivian stood drawing O's with his stick on the flagging belonging to Mr. Heth, of the Works. He took some pains to make them exactly round.

"I hope," said he, "that your — your annoyance over this matter won't interfere with your interest in the Settlement. I hope you still think of — of helping in the work."

"Oh! . . . I don't know," replied Cally, having thought but little about this since Hugo's reëntrance into her life. "Mr. Pond, you see, convinced me pretty well of my uselessness —"

"It's only his manner! — he's always so mortally afraid that people are n't in earnest. I'm certain he could find — ah — suitable and congenial work, if you — you cared to give him another chance. And I'm certain you'd like him, when you knew him a little better."

"You like him?"

"I put him above any man I know, except only Mr. Dayne."

The tall electric light four doors below, which so irritated the Heths when they sat on their flowered balcony on summer nights, shone now full upon the old family enemy. It was observed that he wore, with his new blue suit, a quaint sprigged waistcoat which looked as if it also might have come down from his Uncle Armistead, along with the money he had given away. The old-fashioned vestment seemed to go well with the young man's face. . . .

Cally stood upon the bottom step of the House, and drew her hand along the rail. It had occurred to her to tell him that she would probably go away to live; but now she only said, half-absently:

"I might think about it, and let you know later."

And then, as he accepted her tone as dismissal, and his hand started toward his hat, she spoke impulsively and hurriedly:

"Tell me, is it your feeling that this matter — the Works — makes it necessary for us to — to go on quarreling?"

The two stood looking at each other. And in each, in this moment, though in differing degree, the desire for harmoniousness was meeting the more intangible feeling that harmony between them seemed to involve surrender in another direction.

"How could it be?" said the man. "It's what I've been trying to say. But I naturally supposed that you —"

"I supposed so, too. It seems that I don't."

She looked down at her hand upon the rail, and said: "Don't misunderstand me. Of course I think that papa is doing what is right. Of course I am on his side. I think your sympathy with the poor makes you extreme. But . . . you asked me the other day to try to see your point of view. Well, I think I do see it now. People," said Cally, with a young dignity that became her well, "sometimes agree to disagree. I feel — now when we've quarreled so much — that I'd like to be friends."

The tall young man looked hurriedly away, down the dusky street. In his mind were his articles, shooting about: his terrible articles, where surely nobody would find any gentleness to surprise them. They were the best thing he would ever do; precisely the thing he had always wanted to do. And yet — well he knew now that he had no joy in them. . . .

"It's tremendously generous of you," he said, mechanically.

Cally's eyes wavered from his face, and she answered: "No, I'm not generous."

Her struggle was to keep life fixed and constant, and all about her she found life fluent and changing. Or perhaps life was constant, and the fluency was in her. Or perhaps the difficulty was all in this man, about whom she had never been able to take any position that he did not shortly oust her from it. Considering her resolution only last night, she too had thought, when she began, that she was carrying generosity to the point of downright disloyalty to papa. By what strangeness of his expression did he make her feel that even this was not generous enough, that more was required of the daughter of the Works than merely withdrawing from all responsibility? . . .

V. Vivian regarded the lovely Hun. As a prophet you might glory, but as a man you must face the music. . . .

"But I must tell you," he began, with visible effort, "that you — you will feel very differently, when you've seen —"

However, she interrupted him, raising her eyes with a little smile, sweet and somewhat sad.

"I'll look after my part of it," said she; and there was her pledge of amity held out, gloved in white. "Do you think you can be my friend?"

The light showed another change in the young man's face. He took the hand, and said with sudden strange feeling:

"Let my life prove it."

So Cally turned away thinking that she had found that rarest thing among men, a friend of women.

And Mr. V. V. walked off blindly up the lamplit street, his heart a singing and a pain.

Of one of the Triumphs of Cally's Life, and the Tête-à-tête fol-
lowing, which vaguely depresses her; of the Little Work-Girl
who brought the Note that Sunday, oddly remet at Gentlemen's
Furnishings.

XXVII

CANNING was absent more than two weeks. His attorney's business had brought entanglements before and behind; he was by no means a free man even now. Not all the powers of government could have detained him, we may be sure, had he considered such detention hurtful to the dearest matter in the world. But Canning, in the peculiar circumstances, had concluded that a period of meditation was well, that absence made the heart grow fonder; and, if human calculations are worth anything at all, his conclusions were amply justified. Through the days of their separation his chosen had constantly felt upon her the weight of that vast intangible pressure which pins each mortal of us, except the strong, to his own predestined groove. Chiefly mamma, but many other things, too, had been pressing Cally steadily from thoughts of useful deeds, of which she knew so little, toward thoughts of Mrs. Hugo Canning, of which she knew so much. For sixteen days, time and circumstance had played straight into her lover's hands. . . .

Hugo paused to be welcomed, on his way from the train. Olympian of mien, and beautifully dressed, he looked indeed exactly the sort of man who would shortly have use for the contents of the little velvet box, at this moment reposing snugly in his waistcoat pocket. Still, he had turned up the collar of his big travelling-coat, and a slight hoarseness indicated that the throat trouble which had sent him south last year had returned with the first frost.

"I can draw on it for another six months' furlough," said he, meeting Cally's eyes with gay meaning, "just as soon as I have need for such a thing."

He had come this time as the open gallant, Lochinvar in all men's sight. If his lady desired ceremonies all in order, in sooth she should have them. For the first week of his absence, he had strategically allowed himself to be lost in silence. And then the postman and expressman had suddenly begun to bring reminders of him, letters, bon-bons, books even, flowers every day, and every day a different sort. Cally greeted him wearing out-of-season violets from his own florist. And by telegraph to the faithful Willie Kerr, the gifted wooer had arranged a little dinner for his first evening, to give his official courtship a background which in other days it had sometimes lacked. . . .

"To my mind it's a bore," said he, as they parted. "Please expect to give me a little time of my own afterwards."

The occasion was no bore to Carlisle. She recognized it as one of the triumphs of her life. The material dinner could of course be no better than the New Arlington could make it; but then the New Arlington was a hotel which supercilious tourists always mentioned with pleased surprise in their letters home; that is, if they had any homes and ever thought of writing to them. And Cousin Willie Kerr, having got "off" at three-thirty with *carte blanche* for the arrangements, that night proved that the world of Epicurus had lost an artist when he had turned his talents to commerce. But of course Carlisle's triumph lay not in glowing candle-shades or masses of red and pink roses, not in delicate viands or vintages, however costly. She read her brilliance in the eyes and bearing of Hugo Canning's guests.

They sat down twelve at table. Beside Carlisle's own little coterie, there were present Mr. and Mrs. Allison Payne, who, before they had retired to the country to bring up their children, had been conspicuous in that little old-school set which included Mrs. Berkeley Page: simple-mannered, agreeable people these were, who were always very pleasant when you met them, but whom you never really seemed to know any better. And Mrs. Payne, who was Hugo's first cousin, had kissed Carlisle when they met in the tiring-room, and hoped very prettily that they

379

were going to be friends. Still more open was the gratulation of the somewhat less exclusive. Papa had been detained by business, and J. Forsythe Avery, having been asked at the last moment to fill his place, had broken up another dinner-table to be seen at Canning's. Unquestionably he must have recognized a doughty rival, but Carlisle, who sat next him, easily saw how high she had shot up in his pink imagination. As for dear Mats Allen, her late funeral note had quite vanished in loving rapture, with just that undercurrent of honest envy so dear to the heart of woman.

"He's simply mad about you, Cally! The way he looked and looked at you! . . . And he never even listened to poor little me, chatting away beside him, and frightened out of my wits all the time, he's so lordly."

This was when dinner was over, and the guests were strolling from the little dining-room for coffee in the winter garden. Cally smiled. She had observed that most of her best friend's time had gone, not to chatting to Hugo, but to lavishing her delicious ignorance and working her telling optic system on J. Forsythe Avery, who was so evidently now to be released for general circulation. . . .

Mats seized the moment to inquire, simply, whether she or Evey was to be maid of honor; and Cally then laughed merrily.

"Perhaps we shall have it done by a justice of the peace. . . . Mats, you're the greatest little romancer I ever saw. How you got it into your pretty noddle that Mr. Canning has the faintest interest in me I can't imagine. . . ."

Willie Kerr, too, paid his tribute, having momentarily withdrawn himself from mamma, whose loyal escort he was once more. Willie was a shade balder than last year, when he had played his great part in Cally's life and then sunk below her horizon; a shade more rotund; a shade rosier in the face. But he was as genial as ever, being well lined now with a menu to his own taste and an exceptionally good champagne.

"Knew he'd come back, Carlisle," said Willie, standing before a florid oil-painting he had lured her into a parlor to look at. "Said to Eva Payne in September — no, August, one Sunday it was — 'Canning'll be back soon as she gets home,' s'I. 'Don't know what happened, that trouble in the spring. Don't want to know — none of my business. But mark my words, Eva Payne,' s' I, 'Hugo Canning 'll be back.' Fact," said Willie, grinning cordially. "Funny how I knew. And don't forget, Carlisle, m' dear, 't was your Uncle Cosmo did it all! Hey? Remember that tea in my apartments? Always keep a spare room ready for Uncle Cosmo, and, by gad, I'll come and spend my summers with you."

And later, Eva Payne, the once far unattainable, asked Mrs. Heth and her daughter for luncheon on Friday — "with a few of our friends." Mamma received the invitation like an accolade. Truly that ten thousand dollars might well have remained in bank, subject to personal check. . . .

The little dinner, with its air of everything being all settled, was a huge success; a bit too huge to Hugo's way of thinking. It was eleven o'clock before he really had a word with Carlisle.

"It began to look like a house-party," said he. . . .

They were alone now in the drawing-room at home, a room whose dim beautiful lights made it look always at its best at night. Mamma had just gone up. Cally stood in front of a small plaque-mirror; she had taken off her wraps, and was now fluffing up her fine ash-gold hair where the scarf over her head had pressed it down. The pose, with upraised arms, was an alluring one; she was lithe, with a charming figure. And she still looked very young, as fresh as a rose, as new as spring and first love.

"Cally," said Canning, behind her — "I've fallen in love with your little name, you see, and I'm always going to call you by it after this — Cally, did I ever mention to you that you're the prettiest girl I ever saw. Only pretty is not the word. . . ."

Cally laughed at her reflection in the glass.

"You could never have fallen in love with me — or my name — unless you'd thought so. . . . Could you?"

"I've never asked myself. But I could fall in love with everything else about you, too, because I've gone and done it."

"I wonder . . . Anyhow none of the other things matter much, do they? I can't imagine your falling in love with a hideosity, no matter how worth loving she might be."

"Under the circumstances, why bother to try?"

"It's no bother, and it's intensely interesting. . . ."

Canning advanced a step. Carlisle's gaze moved a little and encountered his in the glass. In his eyes lay his whole opinion of one half the human world. . . .

"*Don't* look at me in that proprietary way. . . ."

Canning laughed softly. He was fully prepared for coquetry.

"Proprietary! It's the last way, my dear, I should venture to look at *you*."

She had allowed him to linger, certainly with no blindness as to what he desired to say to her. She had stood there with no ignorance that the moment was favorable. But now something seemed to have gone amiss, and she turned suddenly, frustrating whatever loverly intention he may have had.

Carlisle sat down in a circular brocaded chair, in which gold back and gold arms were one; a sufficiently decorative background for her shining *décolleté*. Hugo, standing and fingering his white tie, looked down at her with no loss of confidence in his handsome eyes.

"You've changed somehow," said he. "I have n't quite placed it yet. Still, I can feel it there."

"I'm older, my friend, years older than when you used to know me. And then I'm suffering from a serious bereavement, too. I've lost my good opinion of myself."

"Perhaps I can be of some help in restoring it to you."

"That is the question. . . . Besides ageing immensely, I'm also getting frightfully modern, you see. . . ."

And pursuing this latter thought a little, she presently replied to him:

"Oh, no — sociology, not politics. . . . I've been thinking for some time of inspecting the Works, to see if it needed repairs. How horrid of you to laugh! Don't you think a woman should take some interest in how the money is made that she lives on? . . ."

She said this smiling, in the lightest way imaginable. Small wonder if Hugo did n't guess that she had thought twenty times in two weeks of actually doing this thing she spoke of. Still less if it never occurred to him that he here confronted again the footprint of the condemned revivalist fellow, lately become his beloved's sworn friend. . . .

"Have you asked your father that question yet?"

"I thought I'd better get the advice of a prominent lawyer first. Tell me what you think?"

"The point would early arise as to how you would know, on visiting the Works, whether or not it needed repairs. You've inspected many factories, of course?"

"That's true! — I know nothing in the world about it. Of course not!"

She spoke with a sort of eagerness; but went on presently in another tone: "Do you know, I really don't know anything? . . . I've never thought of it specially before, but all at once I'm constantly being impressed with my ignorance. . . ."

And Hugo, with all his accomplishment and skill, could not thenceforward bring the conversation back where it belonged. Only the time and the place were his to-night, it seemed. . . .

"I," said the girl, "belong to the useless classes. I don't pay my way. I'm a social deadbeat. So Mr. Pond told me the other night. You must meet Mr. Pond, Hugo, the Director of the Settlement you gave all that money to last year. He can be as horrid as anybody on earth, but is really nice in a rude interesting way. He's packed full of quarrelsome ideas. You know, he does n't believe in giving money to the poor under any circumstances. Harmful temporizing, he calls it . . ." A rather wide sweep here gave Mr. Pond's views on poor relief in detail . . . "Are you listening, Hugo? This information is being given for your benefit. And oh, he wants me to learn millinery from Mme. Smythe (Jennie T. Smith, *née*) and help him start a class in hat-trimming, to train girls for shop assistants. Or perhaps I'll learn cooking instead. . . ."

"He seems to have aired his views to you pretty thoroughly," said Canning, dryly.

He rose to go, a little later, rather amused by the skill with which he had been held off. He admired the piquancy of spirit with which she took advantage of the altered positions. For him tameness was the great disillusionizer; his undefined ideal was a woman who must be won anew every day. Still, he had been rubbed a little the wrong way by the new-woman catch-phrases she had picked up somewhere, by the faintly argumentative note in her conversation. . . .

"Plans for to-morrow! . . . By the way," said Cally, glancing away to conceal a smile as she rose, "how long shall you be in town?"

"Just as long, Miss Heth, as my business here makes necessary."

"What can I say to that? . . . If I say I hope you won't be with us long, it sounds quite rude. And if I say I hope it will be very, very long . . ."

But he would not follow that lead now. His instinct, her expression warned him; and he was fully resolved that when he spoke again, it would be to land this "wild sweet thing" fluttering safe in his net. However, his laugh was not quite natural.

"I may," said he, "get a telegram calling me off, at almost any minute. Let every one be kind to the stranger within the gates. May I nominate myself for luncheon?"

He was unanimously elected. This time, at parting, he did not touch his former betrothed's hand. His bow was accompanied by a slightly ironic smile; it seemed to say: "Since you prefer it this way, my dear . . . But really — what's the use?"

Cally, snapping out the lights, felt vaguely depressed.

Next day, half an hour after luncheon, Hugo said to the greatest admirer he had on earth:

"Where did Carlisle get the notion that she wanted to go in for Settlement work?"

Mrs. Heth's reply, delivered with a beam, was masterly in its way.

"Why, my dear Hugo! Don't you know the sorry little makeshifts women go to, waiting for love to come to them?"

Hugo's comment intimated that he had fancied it was something of the sort. He then went out, to his future mother-in-

law's regret; she often wondered how it was that she and Hugo
had so few good talks.

Her two young people, as the good lady loved to call them
once more, had separated almost from the table, but soon to re-
meet. Carlisle, having spent "the morning" shopping, — that
is from twelve o'clock to one-fifteen, — had departed to finish her
commissions. Canning had a regretted engagement with Allison
Payne, downtown, to advise Mr. Payne touching some of his
investments. But he was to pick Carlisle up at Morland's establishment at four o'clock, with the car he had hired by the week;
and the remainder of the afternoon would belong to him alone.
He was to have the evening, too, at the House, following a
large dinner-party of the elders arranged by Mrs. Heth before
she knew the date of his return. And these two occasions, the
lover resolved, should suffice his need. . . .

Cally had her hour in the shops, enjoying herself considerably.
Her purchases this afternoon were partly utilitarian, it was true,
concerned with Mrs. Heth's annual box to her poor Thompson
kin in Prince William County. But she took more than one little
flyer on her own account. Nothing more had Cally said to her
father as to giving him back the fifteen hundred dollars, dividend
on her stock. Consequently she bristled with money nowadays,
and had been splurging largely on highly desirable little "extras."
And mamma, usually quite strict in her accounts, thought of
trousseaux, and only smiled at these extravagances.

Cally moved in her destined orbit. From shop to shop, she
pleasurably pursued the material. Nevertheless, she cogitated
problems as she bought; chiefly with reference to Hugo, and the
two or three hours' *tête-à-tête* that waited just ahead. . . . At
just what point should the needs of discipline be regarded as
satisfied? That was the question, as she had remarked last night.

At Baird & Himmel's these knotty reflections were interrupted for a space. In this spreading mart Cally chanced to fall
in with an acquaintance.

Baird & Himmel's was the great popular department store of
the town, just now rapidly flowing over its whole block, and building all around the usual drug-store which declined to sell. Here

rich and poor rubbed elbows with something like that human equality so lauded by Mr. V. V. and others. And here Cally had pushed her way to Gentlemen's Furnishings, her purpose being to buy two shirts for James Thompson, Jr., neck size 13, and not to cost over one dollar each, as mamma had duly noted on the memorandum.

It was ten minutes to four o'clock, as a glance at her watch now showed. Cally swung a little on her circular seat, and encountered the full stare of a girl of the lower orders, seated next her. Her own glance, which had been casual, suddenly became intent: the girl's face, an unusual one in its way, touched a chord somewhere. In a second Cally remembered the little factory hand who had brought her the note from Dr. Vivian, that fateful Sunday afternoon in May. . . .

The little creature bobbed her head at her, with the beginnings of an eager smile, which did not change her wide fixed stare.

"Good evenin', ma'am — Miss Heth."

"Good afternoon. . . ."

No more talk there had been about the Works at home, other than as to papa's plan to have Mr. and Mrs. O'Neill to dinner, to talk over matters in a friendly way. But if Cally had desired a sign of how much this subject had been on her mind since her talk with Vivian she could have found it in the mingling sensations that rose in her now. For this little apparition at her elbow — so she had learned incidentally through Hen Cooney, who knew everything — was the connecting link in the whole argument. Here, on the next seat, sat that "strong necessity" which had impelled Vivian to attack Mr. Heth in the papers.

"I remember you," said Carlisle, slowly. "I understood from Miss Cooney that you had been very sick. You don't look sick — especially."

"I been away, ma'am. On a Trip," explained the pale operative with a kind of eagerness. "Dr. Vivian he sent me off to Atlantic City, in New Jersey, and then to a hotel in the Adriondacts. I conv'lessed, ma'am, y' know?"

"I see. Now you are going back to the Works, I suppose?"

It was not a question easy to answer with delicacy, to answer and avoid all risk of hurting a lady's feelings. How explain that the Works were expressly prohibited by doctor's orders, though you yourself knew that you ought to go back? How tell of special lessons at a Writing Desk every night, such as prepared people to be Authors, when anybody could see by looking at you that you were only a work-girl, and you yourself felt that it was all wrong someway? . . .

Kern spoke timidly, though her wide eyes did not falter.

"Well — not just to-reckly, ma'am. The plan was, till I got my strength back, that I might lay off a little and go — go to School."

"I see."

The tone was cool, and the girl added with a little gasp:

"And then go back to bunchin' again, — yes, ma'am. It's — it's my trade. . . ."

Many feelings moved in Cally, and it might be that the best of them were not uppermost. Perhaps the glittering material possessed her blood, even more than of habit. Perhaps it was only her instinct warning her to take her stand now with her father, where was safety and her ordered course. Or at least it was hardly a pure impulse of generosity that made her open the plump little gold bag at her side, and produce a bill with a yellow back.

"I'm very sorry you've been ill," she said, in her pretty modulated voice. "As you probably feel that you got your illness in the Works, I should like you to take this. Please consider it as coming from my father — and buy yourself something —"

All the blood in the little creature's body seemed to rush headlong to her face. She shrank away as from something more painful than a blow. But all that she said was:

"*Oh ! . . . Ma'am !*"

It was Miss Heth's turn to show a red flag in her cheek.

"You don't want it?"

"I — why ma'am, — I *could n't* . . ."

"As you like, of course."

She dropped the spurned gift back into her bag, with studied leisureliness, and rose at once, though she had made no purchase.

Standing, she made a slight inclination of her prettily-set head. And then Miss Heth was walking away through the crowded aisle with a somewhat proud bearing and a very silken swish.

And Kern Garland swung round on her seat at Gentlemen's Furnishings, staring wide-eyed after her, her finger at her lip. . . .

No fairy coming-true here, indeed, of that gorgeous fever-dream in which Miss Heth with lovely courtesy informed Miss Garland that she had been a lady all the time. But consider the Dream-Maker's difficulties with such far-flown fancies as this: difficulties the more perplexing in a world where men's opinions differ, and some do say that she in the finest skirt is not always the finest lady. . . .

Yet times change, and we with them. It is a beautiful thing to believe in fairies. In the valley, men have met angels. Kern sat staring at Miss Heth's retreating back: and lo, a miracle. When the lovely lady had gone perhaps ten steps down the aisle, her pace seemed to slacken all at once, and she suddenly glanced back over her shoulder. And then — oh, wonder of wonders! — Miss Heth stopped, turned around, and came swishing straight back to the seat beside Kern Garland.

"That was silly of me," said the pretty voice. "You were quite right not to take it if you did n't want it. . . ."

Kern desired to cry. But that would be very ridiculous, in a store, and doubtless annoying to Others. So the little girl began to wink hard, while staring fixedly at a given point. You could often pass it off that way, and nobody a whit the wiser.

"I've happened to have the Works on my mind a little of late," added Carlisle, almost as if in apology. "But I — I'm really glad to see you again."

She perceived the signs of agitation in the little work-girl, and attributing it all to the twenty-dollar bill, saw that she must pave the way to a conversation. And conversation, now that the ice was broken, she eagerly desired, fascinated by the thought that this girl knew at first-hand everything about the Works.

"Let me see — your name is Corinne, is n't it?"

Kern's eyes, wider than ever, shot back to the lady's face. A

new wonder here! — Miss Heth said it just like in the Dream:
Co-rinne.

"Yes, ma'am," said Co-rinne, with a little gulp and a
sniff.

"And what are you doing at the Men's Furnishing counter,
Corinne?" said Carlisle, pleasantly but quite at random. "Buying a present for Mr. V. V., I suppose?"

"Yes, ma'am."

Having taken Carlisle completely aback, she hesitated and
then added timidly:

"Only a fulldress-shirt protector — for his birthday, y' know?
. . . All his sick give him little presents now'n then, ma'am,
find out his sizes and all. You know how he is, spending all his
money on them, and never thinking about himself, and giving
away the clo'es off his back."

"Yes, I know. . . . Find out his sizes?"

"Yes, ma'am. Like, say, 'Why, Mr. — why, Dr. Vivian, what
small feet you got, sir, for a gempman!' And he'll say, like, 'I
don't call six and a half C so small!' Yes, ma'am — just as inno-
cent."

A block and a half away, Hugo Canning's car whirled to a
standstill, and Hugo sat gazing at the select door of Morland's.
In Baird & Himmel's vast commonwealth, Kern Garland sat
beside Miss Carlisle Heth at Gentlemen's Furnishings, and could
not look at the lady's lovely clothes since her eyes could not bear
to leave the yet lovelier face. Kern had not confided the secret
of the protector without a turning of her heart, but now at least
the thrill in her rose above that. . . . She and Mr. V. V.'s beautiful lady, side by side. . . . It was nearly as good as the velvet
settee in the Dream — only for the founting, and the boy with
the pink lamp on his head, and Mr. V. V. . . .

An extremely full-busted Saleslady, with snapping black eyes,
deposited a lean bundle and a ten-cent piece before the work-girl,
oddly murmured something that sounded like 'Look who's ear,'
and then said proudly to Carlisle:

"What did you wish 'm?"

"Nothing just now, thank you."

The Saleslady gave her a glance of intense disapproval, pushed down her generous waist-line, arrogantly patted a coal-black transformation, and wheeled with open indignation.

"That's nice," said Carlisle, to the factory-girl. "Then the presents come as a surprise to him."

"Surprise — no, ma'am. He don't never know. Take the tags off 'n 'em, and slip 'em in his drawer, and he'll put 'em on and never notice nor suspicion, shirts and such. It's like he thought raiment was brought him by the crows, — like in the Bible, ma'am, y' know?"

There was a brief silence. Carlisle's sheltered life had not too often touched the simple annals of the poor. She seemed to get a picture. . . .

The little work-girl's face was not coarse, strangely enough, or even common-looking; it was pleasing in an odd, elfin way. Her white dress and black jacket were in good taste for her station, without vulgarity. Such details Carlisle's feminine eye soon gathered in. The touch she missed was that that cheap dress was an exact copy of one she herself had worn one Sunday afternoon in May, as near as Kern Garland could remember it.

"How long were you at the Works?" said the lady suddenly.

"At the Works? More 'n three years, ma'am."

There was another silence amid the bustle of the people's emporium.

"Tell me," said Carlisle, with some effort, "do you — did you — looking at it from a worker's point of view — find it such a very bad place to work?"

"Oh, *no*, ma'am!" said Kern. "Bad — oh, no! It's — it's fine!"

Carlisle's gaze became wider than the little girl's own. "But — Mr. V. V. says it's a terrible place. . . ."

"It's only the beautiful way he talks," said Kern, eagerly. "I mean, he's so, so sorry for the poor. . . . But lor, ma'am, we know how rich is rich, and poor poor, and so it must always be this side o' the pearly gates —"

She stopped short; and then added shyly, with a kind of anxiousness in her wide dark gaze: "An expression, ma'am — for Heaven. I — I just learned it."

The lady's look was absent. "Oh! . . . Where did you learn that?"

"Off Sadie Whirtle, ma'am — a friend of mine." The girl hesitated, and then said: "That's her now."

And she pointed a small finger at the enormous snapping Saleslady, who stood glowering and patting her transformation at another customer ten feet away.

But Carlisle did not follow the finger, and so missed the sight of Miss Whirtle. Her rising relief had been penetrated by a doubt, not a new one. . . . Would her friend Vivian have committed himself to the articles for only a foolish sentimentalism which the poor themselves repudiated? . . .

"But tell me frankly, Corinne, for I want to know," said she — "I know working must be hard in any case — but do the girls at the Works consider it a — a reasonably nice place?"

Kern knew nothing of the articles, of any situation: and at that *Co-rinne*, her heart ran to water within her. She would have said anything for that.

"Oh, ma'am, all say it's the nicest place to work in town. Yes, ma'am. . . . And some of 'em has rich fathers and need n't work at all anywhere, but they just go on and work at the Works, yes, ma'am, because they druther. . . ."

That, by a little, drew the long-bow too hard. Cally saw that the small three-years' buncher, through politeness or otherwise, was speaking without reference to the truth. And hard upon that she had another thought, striking down the impulse to cross-examine further. What an undignified, what a cowardly way, to try to find things out! What a baby she was, to be sure! . . . V. Vivian knew about the Works, though it was certainly no affair of his. This frail girl, who did look rather sick now that you stopped and looked at her, knew all about it. Only she, her father's daughter, knew nothing, wrapped in her layers of pretty pink wool. . . .

The lady came abruptly to her feet.

"I'm glad to hear it," said she. . . . "But I'm afraid I must go on now. Some one is waiting for me outside."

"Oh! — yes, ma'am!"

Kern had risen with her, though she had not learned that from the Netiquette. Much it would have amazed her to know that the heavenly visitor was regarding her with a flickering conviction of inferiority. . . .

"Good-bye, then. I hope you'll soon get your strength back again. . . . And I'm very glad I saw you."

And then there was her hand held out; not lady to lady, of course, but still her lady's hand. Poor Kern, with her exaltation and her pangs, felt ready to go down on one knee to take it.

"Oh, ma'am!" she stammered. "I'm the glad one . . ."

Miss Heth smiled — oh, so sweet, almost like in the Dream — and then it was all over, and she was walking away, with the loveliest rustle ever was. And Kern stood lost in the thronging aisle, staring at the point where she had disappeared and giving little pinches to her thin arm — just to make certain-sure, y' know . . .

This till the voice of Miss Whirtle spoke in her ear:

"Say, Kurrin, I like that! Why n't you ask me to shake hands with your swell dame friend?"

And Miss Heth, out in the crowded street, was heading toward Morland's with an adventurous resolution in her mind.

It had needed but a touch to make up her mind here, whether she realized it or not; and this touch the girl Corinne had given her. Now, too, impulse met convenient opportunity. For two weeks she had been thinking that if she *did* ever happen to go to the Works, she would make a point of going in some offhand, incidental sort of way, thus proving to herself and the public that she had not the slightest responsibility for whatever might be going on there. (How could she possibly have, no matter what Mr. V. V. thought, with his exaggerated sympathies for the poor?) Now here was Hugo waiting, perfectly fitted to her need. What could be more natural and incidental than this? She would simply be showing her father's factory to her friend, Mr. Canning. . . .

And perhaps Cally had an even deeper feeling of Mr. Canning's admirable suitability in this connection. Somewhere just above the line of consciousness, did there not lie the subtle thought that, if what she saw at the Works *should* have power to work dangerously on her own sympathies, Hugo, with his strong worldly sense, his material perfection, his whole splendid embodiment of the victorious-class ideal, would be just the corrective she needed to keep her safe and sane? . . .

When she was seated in the car beside him, and he was tucking the robe around her, Cally inquired with a deceptive air of indifference:

"You don't care particularly where we go, do you, Hugo?"

"The point seems of no importance whatever, now that I've got you."

"Then," said she, smiling, "I shall take you first to the Heth Cheroot Works."

Canning's face, which had been buoyant from the moment his eyes discovered her in the crowd, betrayed surprise and strong disapproval. That, surely, would give his afternoon a slant different from his plannings. . . .

"I bar the Works. I feel all ways but sociological to-day. Let's go to the country."

"Afterwards," said she, with the same lightness, clear proof of the casual nature of the proposed excursion. "We'll simply pop in for a minute or two, to see what it looks like —"

"But you can't tell what it looks like, even —"

"Well, at least I'll have seen it. Do give me my way about this. *You'll* enjoy it . . ."

And leaning forward on that, she said to his hired driver: "Take us to Seventeenth and Canal Streets."

The shadow of disapprobation did not lift from Hugo's face.

"I had no idea," he said, boredly and somewhat stiffly, "that you took your new-thought so seriously."

Cally laughed brightly. "But then you never think women are serious, Hugo."

It was on the tip of her tongue to add: "Until it's too late." But she held that back, as being too pointedly reminiscent.

XXVIII

THE car came to a standstill, and Cally was reminded of another afternoon, long ago, when she and Hen Cooney had encountered Mr. V. V. upon this humming corner. This time, she knew which way to look.

"There it is. . . . Confess, Hugo, you're surprised that it's so *small!*"

But Hugo helped no new-thoughter to belittle honest business.

"Unlike some I could mention, I've seen factories before," quoth he. "I've seen a million dollar business done in a smaller plant than that."

Actually Cally found the Works bigger than she had expected; reaction from the childish marble palace idea had swung her mind's eye too far. But gazing at the weatherworn old pile, spilling dirtily over the broken sidewalk, she was once more struck and depressed by something almost sinister about it, something vaguely foreboding. To her imagination it was a little as if the ramshackle old pile leered at her: "Wash your hands of me if you will, young lady. I mean you harm some day. . . ."

But then, of course, she wasn't washing her hands of it; her hands had never been in it at all.

"You'll get intensely interested and want to stay hours!" said she, with the loud roar of traffic in her ears. "Remember I only came for a peep — just to see what a Works is like inside."

Hugo, guiding her over the littered sidewalk to the shabby little door marked "Office," swore that she could not make her peep too brief for him.

She had considered the possibility of encountering her father here; had seen the difficulties of attributing this foray to Hugo's

394

insatiable interest in commerce, with Hugo standing right there. However, in the very unpretentious offices inside — desolate places of common wood partitions, bare floors, and strange, tall stools and desks — she was assured by an anæmic youth with a red Adam's apple that her father had left for the bank an hour earlier, which was according to his usual habit. She inquired for Chas Cooney, who kept books from one of those lofty stools, but Chas was reported sick in bed, as Cally then remembered that Hen had told her, some days since. Accordingly the visitors fell into the hands of Mr. MacQueen, whom Carlisle, in the years, had seen occasionally entering or leaving papa's study o' nights.

MacQueen was black, bullet-headed, and dour. He had held socialistic views in his fiery youth, but had changed his mind like the rest of us when he found himself rising in the world. In these days he received a percentage on the Works profits, and cursed the impudence of Labor. As to visitors, his politics were that all such had better be at their several homes, and he indicated these opinions, with no particular subtlety, to Miss Heth and Mr. Canning. He even cited them a special reason against visiting to-day: new machines being installed, and the shop upset in consequence. However, he did not feel free to refuse the request outright, and when Canning grew a little sharp, — for he did the talking, generously enough, — the sour vizier yielded, though with no affectation of a good grace.

"Well, as ye like then. . . . This way."

And he opened a door with a briskness which indicated that Carlisle's expressed wish "just to look around" should be carried out in the most literal manner.

The opening of this door brought a surprise. Things were so unceremonious in the business district, it seemed, that you stepped from the superintendent's office right into the middle of everything, so to speak. You were inspecting your father's business a minute before you knew it. . . .

Cally, of course, had had not the faintest idea what to expect at the Works. She had prepared herself to view horrors with calm and detachment, if such proved to be the iron law of business. But, gazing confusedly at the dim, novel spectacle that so suddenly confronted her, she saw nothing of the kind. Her heart, which had been beating a little faster than usual, rose at once.

Technically speaking, which was the way Mr. MacQueen spoke, this was the receiving- and stemming-room. It was as big as a barn, the full size of the building, except for the end cut off to make the offices. Negroes worked here; negro men, mostly wearing red undershirts. They sat in long rows, with quick fingers stripping the stems from the not unfragrant leaves. These were stemmers, it was learned. Piles of the brown tobacco stood beside each stemmer, bales of it were stacked, ceiling-high, at the farther end of the room, awaiting their attentions. The negroes eyed the visitors respectfully. They were heard to laugh and joke over their labors. If they knew of anything homicidal in their lot, certainly they bore it with a fine humorous courage.

Down the aisle between the black rows, Cally picked her way after Hugo and Mr. MacQueen. Considering that all this was her father's, she felt abashingly out of place, most intrusive; when she caught a dusky face turned upon her she hastily looked another way. Still, she felt within her an increasing sense of cheerfulness. Washington Street sensibilities were offended, naturally. The busy colored stemmers were scarcely inviting to the eye; the odor of the tobacco soon grew a little overpowering; there were dirt and dust and an excess of steam-heat — "Tobacco likes to be warm," said MacQueen. And yet the dainty visitor's chief impression, somehow, was of system and usefulness and order, of efficient and on the whole well-managed enterprise.

"If there's anything the matter here," thought she, "men will have to quarrel and decide about it . . . Just as I said."

The inspecting party went upward, and these heartening impressions were strengthened. On the second floor was another stemming-room, long and hot like the other; only here the stemming was done by machines — "for the fancy goods" — and the machines were operated by negro women. They were middle-aged women, many of them, industrious and quite placid-looking. Perhaps a quarter of the whole length of the room was prosaically filled with piled tobacco stored ready for the two floors of stemmers. The inspection here was brief, and to tell the truth, rather tame, like an anti-climax. Not a trace or a vestige of homicide was descried, not a blood-spot high or low. . . .

Cally had been observing Hugo, who looked so resplendent against this workaday background, and felt herself at a disadvantage with him. He had not wanted to come at all, but now that they were here, he exhibited a far more intelligent interest in what he saw than she did or could. Oddly enough, he appeared to know a good deal about the making of cigars, and his pointed comments gradually elicited a new tone from MacQueen, who was by now talking to him almost as to an equal. Several times Cally detected his eyes upon her, not bored but openly quizzical.

"Learning exactly how a cheroot factory ought to be run?" he asked, *sotto voce*, as they left the second floor.

"Oh, exactly! . . . For one thing, I'd recommend a ventilator or two, should n't you?"

She felt just a little foolish. She also felt out of her element, incidental, irresponsible, and genuinely relieved. Still, through this jumble of feelings she had not forgotten that they were yet to see that part of the Works which she had specially come to peep at. . . .

Progress upward was by means of a most primitive elevator, nothing but an open platform of bare boards, which Mr. Mac-Queen worked with one hand, and which interestingly pushed up the floor above as one ascended. As they rose by this quaint device, Carlisle said:

"Is this next the bunching-room, Mr. MacQueen?"

"It is, Miss."

"Bunching-room!" echoed Hugo, with satiric admiration. "You *are* an expert. . . ."

The lift-shaft ran in one corner of the long building. Debarking on the third floor, the visitors had to step around a tall, shining machine, not to mention two workmen who had evidently just landed it. Several other machines stood loosely grouped here, all obviously new and not yet in place.

Hugo, pointing with his stick, observed: "Clearing in new floor-space, I see."

MacQueen nodded. "Knocked out a cloak-room. Our fight here's for space. Profits get smaller all the time. . . ."

"H'm. . . . You figured the strain, I suppose. Your floor looks weak."

"Oh, it'll stand it," said the man, shortly. "This way."

Carlisle wondered if the weak floor was what her friend Vivian had meant when he said, in his extreme way, that the Works might fall down some day. She recalled that she had thought the building looked rather ricketty, that day last year. But these thoughts hardly entered her mind before the sight of her eyes knocked them out. The visitors squeezed around the new machines, and, doing so, stepped full into the bunching-room. And the girl saw in one glance that this was the strangest, the most interesting room she had ever seen in her life.

Her first confused sense was only of an astonishing mass of dirty white womanhood. The thick hot room seemed swarming with women, alive and teeming with women, women tumbling all over each other wherever the eye turned. Tall clacking machines ran closely around the walls of the room, down the middle stood a double row of tables; and at each machine, and at every possible place at the tables, sat a woman crowded upon a woman, and another and another.

Dirt, noise, heat, and smell: women, women, women. Conglomeration of human and inhuman such as the eyes of the refined seldom look upon. . . . Was this, indeed, the pleasantest place to work in town? . . .

"Bunchin' and wrappin'," said MacQueen. "Filler's fed in from that basin on top. She slips in the binder — machine rolls 'em together. . . . Ye can see here."

They halted by one of the bunching-machines, and saw the parts dexterously brought together into the crude semblance of the product, saw the embryo cigars thrust into wooden forms which would shape them yet further for their uses in a world asmoke. . . .

"Jove! Watch how her hands fly!" said Hugo, with manlike interest for processes, things done. "Look, Carlisle."

Carlisle looked dutifully. It was in the order of things that she should bring Hugo to the Works, and that, being here, he should take charge of her. But, unconsciously, she soon turned her back to the busy machine, impelled by the mounting interest she felt to see bunching, not in detail, but in the large.

Downstairs the workers had been negroes; here they were white women, a different matter. But Cally had a closer association than that, in the girl she had just been talking to, Corinne, who had worked three years in this room. It was n't so easy to preserve the valuable detached point of view, when you actually knew one of the people. . . .

"Three cents a hundred," said MacQueen's rugged voice.

There was a fine brown dust in the air of the teeming room, and the sickening smell of new tobacco. Not a window in the place was open, and the strong steam heat seemed almost overwhelming. The women had now been at it for near nine hours. Damp, streaked faces, for the most part pale and somewhat heavy, turned incessantly toward the large wall-clock at one end of the room. Eyes looked sidewise upon the elegant visitors, but then the flying fingers were off again, for time is strictly money with piecework. . . . How could they stand being so *crowded*, and could n't they have any *air?*

"Oh, five thousand a day — plenty of them."

"Five thousand! — how do they do it?"

"We had a girl do sixty-five hundred. She's quit. . . . Here's one down here ain't bad."

The trio moved down the line of machines, past soiled, busy backs. Close on their left was the double row of tables, where the hurrying "wrappers" sat like sardines. Cally now saw that these were not women at all, but young girls, like Corinne; girls mostly younger than she herself, some very much younger. Only they seemed to be girls with a difference, girls who had somehow lost their girlhood. The rather nauseating atmosphere which enveloped them, the way they were huddled together yet never ceased to drive on their tasks, the slatternly uncorseted figures, stolid faces and furtive glances; by something indefinable in their situation, these girls seemed to have been degraded and dehumanized, to have lost something more precious than virtue.

Yet some of them were quite pretty, beneath dust and fatigue; one, with a quantity of crinkly auburn hair, was very pretty, indeed. The girl Corinne, after three years here, was both pretty and possessed of a certain delicacy; a delicacy which forbade her to tell Mr. Heth's daughter what she really thought about the Works. For that must have been it . . .

"This 'un can keep three wrappers pretty busy when she's feelin' good. Can't yer, Miller? . . . Ye'll see the wrappers there, in a minute."

This 'un, or Miller, was a tall, gaunt, sallow girl, who handled her machine with the touch of a master, eliminating every superfluous move and filling a form of a dozen rough cheroots quickly enough to take a visitor's breath away. No doubt it was very instructive to see how fast cheroots could be made. However, the stirring interest of the daughter of the Works was not for mechanical skill.

Cally stood with a daintily scented handkerchief at her nostrils, painfully drinking in the origins of the Heth fortune. The safeguarding sense of irresponsibility ebbed, do what she might. Well she knew that this place could not be so bad as it seemed to her; for then her father would not have let it be so. For her to seem to disapprove of papa's business methods was mere silly impertinence, on top of the disloyalty of it. But none of the sane precepts she had had two weeks to think out seemed to make any answer to the disturbing sensations she felt rising, like a sickness, within her. . . .

Her sense was of something polluting at the spring of her life. Here was the soil that she was rooted in, and the soil was not clean. It might be business, it might be right; but no argument could make it agreeable to feel that the money she wore upon her back at this moment was made in this malodorous place, by these thickly crowded girls. . . . Was it in such thoughts that grew this sense of some personal relation of herself with her father's most unpleasant bunching-room? Was it for such reasons that V. Vivian had asked her that day at the Settlement why did n't she go to the Works some day? . . .

She heard Hugo's voice, with a note of admiration for visible efficiency: "How do they keep it up at this clip nine hours?"

"Got to do it, or others will."

"You expect each machine to produce so much, I suppose?"

And Cally, so close to her lordly lover that her arm brushed his, was seeing for the first time in her life what people meant when they threw bricks at papa on election night, or felt the strong necessity of attacking him in the papers. By processes that were less mental than emotional, even physical, she was driven further down a well-trod path and stood dimly confronting the outlines of a vast interrogation. . . . What particular human worth had she, Cally Heth, that the womanhood of these lower-class sisters should be sapped that she might wear silk next her skin, and be bred to appeal to the highly cultivated tastes of a Canning? . . .

If there are experiences which permanently extend the frontiers of thought, it was not in this girl's power to recognize one of them closing down on her now. But she did perceive, by the growing commotion within, that she had made a great mistake to come to this place. . . .

"Now, here's wrapping," said MacQueen. "Hand work, you see."

But his employer's daughter, it appeared, had seen enough of cigar-making for one day. At that moment she touched Canning's well-tailored arm.

"Let's go. . . . It's — stifling here."

Hugo, just turning from the bunching-machine, regarded her faintly horrified face with some amusement. And Carlisle saw that he was amused.

"I was wondering," said he, "how long your sociology would survive this air. . . ."

The peep was meant to end there, and should have done so. But unluckily, at just that juncture, there came a small diversion. The gaunt girl Miller, by whose machine the little party stood, took it into her head to keep at it no longer.

Though nobody had noticed it, this girl had been in trouble for the last five minutes. The presence of the visitors, or of the

superintendent, had evidently made her nervous; she kept looking half-around out of the darting corners of her eyes. Three
times, as the men watched and talked about her, she had raised a
hand in the heat and brushed it hurriedly before her eyes. And
then, just as the superintendent turned from her and all would
have been well again, her overdrawn nerve gave out. The hands
became suddenly limp on the machine they knew so well; they
slid backward, at first slowly and then with the speed of a falling body; and poor Miller slipped quietly from her stool to the
floor, her head actually brushing the lady's skirt as she fell.

Cally stifled a little cry. Hugo, obvious for once, said, "Why,
she's fainted!" — in an incredulous voice. Considerably better
in action were the experienced Works people. MacQueen sprang
for a water-bucket with a celerity which strongly suggested practice. A stout, unstayed buncher filled a long-felt want by flinging
open a window. One from a neighboring machine sat on the floor,
Miller's head on her lap. Two others stood by. . . .

Carlisle, holding to the silenced machine with a small gloved
hand, gazed down as at a bit of stage-play.

They had formed a screen about the fallen girl, under Mac-
Queen's directions, to cut her off from the general view. The
superintendent's gaze swept critically about. However, the sudden confusion had drawn the attention of all that part of the
room, and concealment proved a too optimistic hope. The moment happened to be ripe for one of those curious panics of the
imagination to which crowded womanhood is psychologically
subject. Knowledge that somebody was down ran round the
room as if it had been shouted; and on the knowledge, fear stalked
among the tired girls, and the thing itself was born of the dread
of it.

So it was that Carlisle, gripping fast to poor Miller's machine,
heard an odd noise behind her, and turned with a sickening dropping of the heart. Five yards away a girl gave a little moan and
flopped forward upon her machine. She was a fine, strapping
young creature, and it is certain that two minutes before nothing
had been further from her mind than fainting. It did not stop
there. Far up the room a "wrapper" rose in the dense air, took

her head in both hands and fell backward into the arms of the operative next her. In the extreme corner of the great room a little stir indicated that another had gone down there. Work had almost ceased. Many eyes stared with sudden nervous apprehension into other eyes, as if to say: *"Am I to be the next?..."*

MacQueen's voice rang out — a fine voice it was, the kind that makes people sit down again in a fire-scared theatre:

"Take your seats, every one of you.... Nothing's going to happen. You're all right, I say. Go on with your work. *Sit down. Get to work...."*

"Air," said Cally Heth, in a small colorless voice.

Hugo wheeled sharply.

"Great heavens! — *Carlisle!* ... Do you feel faint?"

He had her at the open window in a trice, clasping her arm tight, speaking masculine encouragement.... "Hold hard, my dear! ... I should have watched you.... Now, breathe this.... Gulp it in, Cally...."

His beloved, indeed, like the work-sisters, had felt the brush of the black wing. For an instant nothing had seemed surer than that the daughter of the Works would be the fifth girl to faint in the bunching-room that day; she had seen the floor rise under her whirling vision....

But once at the window the dark minute passed speedily. The keen October air bore the gift of life. Blood trickled back into the dead white cheeks.

"I ... was just a little dizzy," said Cally, quite apologetically ...

And, though the visitors departed then, almost immediately, all signs of the sudden little panic in the bunching-room were already rapidly disappearing. Work proceeded. The gaunt girl Miller, who had earned MacQueen's permanent dislike by starting all the trouble, was observed sitting again at her machine, hands and feet reaching out for the accustomed levers.

It made an amazing difference simply to be outdoors again. The last few minutes in the Works had been like a waxing night-

403

mare. But the sunshine was bright and sane; the raw clean winds blew the horrors away. Carlisle, realizing that she had been swept along toward something like hysterics, struggled with some success to recapture poise and common sense.

But she could not now quite strike the manner of one who has merely paused for an irresponsible peep. Hugo was aware of a change in her, before they were fairly in the car again. He had occasion to reflect anew, not without irritation, what an unfortunate turn she had given to the afternoon of romance, over his own plainly expressed wishes. . . .

Yet nothing could have exceeded his solicitousness. He seemed to feel that he had been neglectful upstairs, that she would not have felt faint if he had properly presided over her movements. Cally had to assure him half a dozen times in as many blocks that she felt quite herself again.

And, meantime, he conscientiously gave himself to relieving her mind of the effects of her own feminine foolishness. That queer and undoubtedly upsetting bit of "crowd psychology" they had seen — that, he pointed out, had come merely from the unusual heat, the control of the steam-pipes happening to be out of whack to-day. Such a thing did n't happen once in six months; so that surly fellow MacQueen had said. Of course, producing wealth was a hard business at best, let none deny it. Everybody would like to see factories run on the model theory, like health resorts, but the truth was that those ideas were mostly wind and water, and had never worked out yet. An owner must think of his profits first, unfeeling as that might seem; else he would have to shut up shop, and then where would those girls be for a living? They need n't work for her father unless they wanted to, of course. . . .

"You should look into a cannery some day, for sights — by which I mean that you should n't do anything of the sort! . . . Oh, get us to some quieter street there, Frederick! . . . But it was my fault for agreeing to go with you. I knew, as you could n't, that a going factory's no place for a girl delicately brought up. Those women don't mind. That is, as a rule . . ."

Carlisle responded to this sensible treatment with what lightsomeness she could muster; but the odd truth was that she hardly listened to Hugo. Heaven knew that she needed the strong sane arguments, heaven knew that he could state them all unanswerably. And yet, just as she was aware that her woman's feelings about the bunching-room would have no weight with Hugo, so she was curiously aware that Hugo's arguments produced no effect at all upon her. If she had relied upon him as a demolishing club against Vivian, the over-sympathetic, it appeared that his strength was not equal to the peculiar demand. And all at once she seemed to have gotten to know her lover very well; there were no more surprises in him. She suddenly perceived a strange and hitherto unsuspected likeness between Hugo and mamma, in that you could not talk over things with either of them. . . .

"Remember, Cally," he said, summing up, "this is the first factory you've ever seen in your life. You've nothing at all to judge by, in a business matter of this sort —"

Something in his tone flicked her briefly out of her resolve not to argue; but she spoke lightly enough.

"Yes, I judge by the way it made me feel. I judge everything that way."

"That's natural, of course," said he, with a slight smile, "but after all it's rather a woman's way of judging things than a sociologist's. Is n't it?"

"But I am a woman."

The car shook off the dust of the business district, mounted a long hill, bowled into streets fairer than Canal. Hugo's sense of a grievance deepened. Granted that she had nearly fainted, as a consequence of her own foolish perversity, it was surely now due to him that she should begin to be her sweet natural self again.

He had had quite enough of this irrational invasion of his afternoon; and so, having said just a word or two in reply to her last remark, he banished the matter from the conversation.

"Now," said he, "to fresh woods and pastures new, and a song of the open road! . . . Which way shall we go?"

Cally hesitated.

"I'm sorry, Hugo — but I think I should like to go home, if you don't mind."

"Home?"

"I really don't feel quite like a drive now. I'm very sorry — "
Canning gazed down at her in dismay.

"I knew you did n't feel quite yourself yet. You could n't deceive *me* . . . But don't let's go *home!* Why, this air is the very thing you need, Carlisle. It will set you up in no time."

But no, she seemed to think that was not what she needed, nor were her doubts removed by several further arguments from him.

Canning sat back in the car with an Early Christian expression. She had said, not five minutes ago, that she felt perfectly well; perfectly well she looked. Was it imaginable that she really took seriously the absurd little smatterings of new-womanism she had picked up, God knew where, while waiting for love to come? . . .

"Carlisle," he began, patiently, "I understand your feelings perfectly, of course, and natural enough they are to a girl brought up as you 've been. At the same time, I'm not willing to leave you feeling disgusted with your father's methods of — "

"Disgusted with papa!" exclaimed Cally, quite indignantly. But she added, in a much more tempered tone: "Why, Hugo — how could you think such a thing? . . . I assure you I 'm disgusted with nobody on earth but myself."

At that the annoyed young man gave a light laugh.

"I'm evidently about fifty years before the war, as you say down here. I can't understand, to save me, how — "

"I know it, Hugo. You never understand how I feel about things, and always assume that I 'll feel the way you want me to."

Carlisle spoke quietly, almost gently. Yet Canning's feeling was like that of a man who, in the dark, steps down from a piazza at a point where steps are not. The jolt drove some of the blood from his cheek. But his only reply was to poke his hired driver in the back with his stick and say, distantly: "Nine hundred and three Washington."

The hired car rolled swiftly, in sun and wind, toward the House of Heth. Cobblestones were left behind; the large wheels skimmed the fair asphaltum. Three city blocks they went with no music of human speech. . . .

"But I did n't mean to seem rude," said Cally, in a perfectly natural manner, "and I *am* really very sorry to — to change the afternoon's plans. I don't feel quite well, and I think perhaps I ought to rest — just till dinner-time. You remember you are dining with us to-night."

The apology, the pacific, non-controversial tone, unbent the young man instantly. Small business for the thinking sex to harbor a grudge against an irrational woman's moment of pique. Moreover, whatever this woman's foibles, Hugo Canning chanced to find himself deep in love with her. He met her advance with only a slight trace of stiffness. By the time they arrived at the Heth house, mamma's two young people were chatting along almost as if nothing had happened. . . .

However, back at home, Cally seemed unresponsive to Hugo's overture in the direction of his lingering awhile in the drawing-room. It became evident that the afternoon was ruined beyond repair. He paused but a moment, to see whether any telegrams or telephone calls had been sent up for him from the hotel.

It proved that there was nothing of the sort. The lover looked relieved. He wished his lady a refreshing rest, apropos of the evening. Beneath his feeling that he was an ill-used man, there had risen in Canning the practical thought that he had let this wild sweet thing get too sure of him. . . .

"I shall see you then," said he, at the door, "at seven-thirty."

"Yes, indeed. . . . I'll be quite myself again then. Au revoir!"

She stood alone, in the dim and silent hall. The house was sweet with Hugo's flowers. Cally, standing, picked a red rose slowly to pieces. She could pursue her own thoughts now, and her struggle was against thinking ill of her father. If it was the extreme of sympathy with the poor to regard the Works as a homicidal place, then her present impulse was plainly toward such extremity. But she dared not allow that impulse its head, fearful of the far-reaching consequences that would thereby be entailed. Yet, even from the cheeriest view, it was clear that the Works were a pretty bad place — Hugo himself had tacitly admitted that by the arguments he employed, — and if that was so, what was to be said for papa? Possibly she and mamma did have some connection with the business, but it would be simply foolish to say that they were *responsible* for the overcrowding in the bunching-room. How could she be — how *could* she? — she, to whom her father had never spoken seriously in his life, who had never even seen the Works inside till to-day? No, it was papa's business. He was responsible; and it was a responsibility indeed. . . .

It was quarter-past five. So, presently, the tall hall-clock said, on its honor as a reliable timepiece. . . . Only an hour since she and Hugo had met in front of Morland's. . . .

Still the girl did not hurry up to her rest-chamber. She wandered pointlessly from empty hall to silent drawing-room. There had descended upon her that sense of loneliness in the great world, to which in the spring and summer she had been no stranger. She felt listless and oddly tired. Presently, when she had thought about it a little, she was certain that she felt quite unwell; almost ill. The strong probability was that she had a bad sick headache coming on; small wonder, either, after nearly fainting with poor Miller and others at the Works. . . .

Cally considered whether she did not owe it to her health to dine from a tray this evening, giving Hugo to-morrow morning instead. Even as she revolved this thought — with especial reference to explaining it to mamma — there came her humble admirer, Flora Johnson, col'd, saying that Mr. Canning begged to speak to her a minute at the telephone.

"Mr. *Canning?*"

Flora said yas'm, and flashed her dazzling teeth. Her mistress ascended the stairs in surprise, wondering what reason Hugo would assign for wanting to come back.

However, Hugo's intentions were the contrary. His unhappy request was to be excused from dinner this evening.

The young man's voice over the wire was at once regretful, annoyed, and (somewhat) apologetic. There was, it seemed, the devil to pay over certain entanglements of the rate-case matter. He had found Mr. Deming, of his law firm, waiting for him at the hotel. Mr. Deming had come for a conference which could not be postponed; he had to get back to Washington by the nine-thirty train. Would Carlisle make his excuses to Mrs. Heth, and know for herself how disappointed he was?

He spoke in loverly vein, and Cally was able to answer soothingly. She mentioned that she would probably withdraw from the dinner, too; so that even mamma's table would not be upset at all. He would be much missed, of course. The suggestion emerged, or perhaps it was merely in the air, that Hugo was to come in, if he could, in the later evening.

Cally was at the telephone some three minutes. Turning away, she did not go at once to rest, though now halfway to her room. If she was not going to dinner, there was more time, of course. Or possibly her head had taken a slight turn for the better. The girl leaned against the banisters in the quiet upper hall, full of depression. And then she said aloud, with a resolution that was perhaps not so sudden as it seemed:

"I'll go and see Hen Cooney!"

XXIX

One Hour, in which she apologizes twice for her Self, her Life and Works; and once she is beautifully forgiven, and once she never will be, this Side of the Last Trump.

THE Cooneys' door was opened, after the delay usual with the poor, by Henrietta herself, this moment returned from the bookstore. Hen wore her hat, but not her coat, and it was to be observed that one hand held a hot-water bottle, imperfectly concealed behind her back.

"Hurrah! — Cally!" cried she. "We were talking of you at dinner to-day, wondering what had become of you. Come into the house, and don't mind a bit if this bottle leaks all over you. Such troubles!"

"How is Chas to-day? I just heard that he had n't been at work for a week."

"Chas? . . . Chas is better — Cousin Martha's worse — father's just the same — Looloo's dancing the floor with a toothache." Hen recited this in the manner of a chant, and added, as she ushered her Washington Street cousin into the little parlor: "But for that, we're all doing nicely — thank you!"

"Gracious, Hen! I'd no idea you had such a hospital. Why, what's the matter with Uncle John?"

"Oh, just his lumbago. He's complaining, but out and about — fighting over the Seven Days around Richmond with an old comrade somewhere, I doubt not. . . . Sit down, my dear," added Hen, who had been looking at Cally just a little curiously, "and excuse me while I run upstairs. I forgot to explain that this bottle is for mother, who's down with a splitting headache. Back in a jiffy. . . ."

Thus Miss Cooney, not knowing that for one moment, at least, her society had been preferred above that of a Canning. Such was

410

the odd little development. Carlisle, having been more with Henrietta in the past five weeks than she had commonly been in a year, had discovered her as undoubtedly a person you could talk things over with — the only person in the world, perhaps, that you could talk *this* over with. . . .

Possibly Hen, being a lynx-eyed Cooney, had somehow gathered that her lovely cousin had not dropped in merely to "inquire"; for when she returned to the parlor, having doubtless put her hot-water bottle where it would do the most good, she did not expend much time on reporting upon her invalids, or become involved in the minor doings of the day. Very soon she deflected, saying:

"But you don't look particularly fit yourself, Cally. What's wrong with the world?"

Cally, being still uncertain how far she cared to confide in Hen, met the direct question with a tentative lightness.

"Oh! . . . Well, I *did* just have a rather unpleasant experience, though I did n't know I showed it in my face! . . . We happened to look in at the Works for a few minutes — Mr. Canning and I — and I certainly did n't *enjoy* it much . . ." And then, the inner pressure overcoming her natural bent toward reserve, she spoke with a little burst: "Oh, Hen, it was the most horrible place I ever saw in my life!"

The little confidence spoke straight to the heart, as a touch of genuine feeling always will. Quite unconsciously, Henrietta took her cousin's hand, saying, "You poor dear . . ." And within a minute or two Cally was eagerly pouring out all that she had seen in the bunching-room, with at least a part of how it had made her feel.

Hen listened sympathetically, and spoke reassuringly. If her "arguments" followed close in the footsteps of Hugo, — for Hen was surprisingly well-informed in unexpected ways, — it must have been some quality in her, something or other in her underlying "attitude," that invested her words with a new horsepower of solace. And Saltman's best stenographer actually produced an argument that Hugo had altogether passed by. She thought it worth while to point out that these things were not a question of abstract morals at all, but only of changing points of view. . . .

"When Uncle Thornton learned business," declared Hen, "there was n't a labor law in the country — no law but supply and demand — pay your work-people as little as you could, and squeeze them all they 'd stand for. Nobody ever *thought* of anything different. In those days the Works would have been a model plant — nine-hour day, high wages, no women working at night, no children. . . ."

If Cally was not wholly heartened by words like these, she knew where the lack was. And perhaps Hen herself was conscious of something missing. For, having defended her uncle's Works at least as loyally as she honestly could, she gave the talk a more personal tone, skirting those phases of the matter so new-thoughty that they had never even occurred to Hugo Canning.

"Cally, are you going to speak to Uncle Thornton about it — about your going there, I mean?"

"No, no!" cried Cally, hastily. "How could I? Of course I — realize that that 's the way business must be — as you say. What right have I, an ignorant little fool, to set up as papa's critic?"

"Not at all — of course," said Hen, giving her hand a little squeeze. "What I —"

"You surely can't think that I ought to go and reprove papa for the way he runs his business — do you, Hen? . . . That I — I'm *responsible* in any way!"

Hen noted her cousin's unexplained nervousness, and it may be she divined a little further. She answered no, not a bit of it. She said she meant to speak to him, not as a business expert, but only as his daughter. It was always a mistake to have secrets in a family, said Hen.

Good advice, undoubtedly. Only Hen did n't happen to know the most peculiar circumstances. . . .

The two girls sat side by side on a sofa that sorely needed the ministrations of an upholsterer. Hen was sweet-faced, but habitually pale, usually a little worn. Her eyes and expression saved her from total eclipse in whatever company; otherwise she would have been annihilated now by the juxtaposition of her cousin. Cally's face was framed in an engaging little turn-down hat of gold-brown and yellow, about which was carelessly festooned a long and fine brown veil. Hen, gazing rather wistfully, thought that Cally grew lovelier every year.

"I'll tell you, Cally!" she said, suddenly. "Do you know what you ought to do? Talk to V. V. about all this!"

Cally repressed a little start; though the thought, to speak truth, was far from being a new one. But how could she possibly talk to V. V. without the ultimate disloyalty to papa? . . .

"No," she said, quietly, after a brief pause. "I could hardly do that."

"Why not? He's thought out all these things further than anybody I know. And he'll —"

"Hen, have you forgotten what he wrote in the paper about papa last year — what he's going to write next month. Don't you see my position?"

"I don't care what he writes in the papers! . . . When it comes to people, there's nobody so kind — and wise. And —"

"He's the one person," said Cally, resolutely, "I could not possibly talk to about it."

Henrietta, falling back on the thought she had set out with, laughed good-naturedly.

"Then, I suppose, you'll want to fly at once. He's due here at any minute, you know — in fact, he's half an hour late now —"

"Here! . . . Is he coming here this afternoon?"

This time her start was without concealment. Hen looked genuinely surprised.

"He's our doctor — I told you the other day. . . . But he does n't bite, my dear! You look as if I'd said that a grizzly bear and three mad ogres were loping down the steps."

"I never think of him as a doctor somehow," said Cally, recovering, with a little laugh. "So I could n't imagine —"

"Second largest practice in town — only I'll admit that his not charging any fees has something to do with it. In fact V. V.'s patients usually borrow anything that's loose, including his hats, suits, and shoes . . . Cally, it's like a play, for I believe there he is now. . . ."

True enough, a firm but unequal footstep just then sounded on the Cooneys' wooden steps outside. But Hen sat still, a far-away look in her eyes.

"Did you hear what Pond said, Cally, the first time he saw V. V.? — 'Who's that man with the face like a bishop that never grew up?' . . . Do you know, I never look at him without remembering mean things I've done and said, and wishing I hadn't. . . ."

She rose as the bell rang, started toward the door, hesitated, turned in the middle of the floor.

"I'd naturally ask him in here, Cally, while I went up to see if things are ready for him upstairs. Of course, if you'd rather not see him . . ."

Cally had risen too. The two girls stood looking at each other.

"No," said Cally, "I'd like to see him. Only I can't speak to him about the Works. I cannot."

"No, no — of course not, dea‾, if you don't feel like it."

Hen went out to open the door. Greetings floated in. . . .

Cally stood at the parlor window, staring out into the shabby street. Over the way was the flaring sign of an unpained dentist, making promises never to be redeemed, and two doors away the old stand of the artificial limb-maker. Cally looked full at a show-window full of shiny new legs; but she did not see the grisly spectacle, so it did not matter.

The unexpected encounter was deeply disturbing to her. There stirred in her the memory of another night when she had similarly met the slum doctor in this room, between engagements with Hugo Canning. That night he had asked her forgiveness for calling her a poor little thing, which she was, and she had charged him with wicked untruthfulness for calling the Works homicidal, which — she said it in her secret heart — they were. . . . How history repeats itself, how time brought changed angles! Strange, strange, that in the revolving months it had now come her turn to apologize to Mr. V. V. in the Cooney parlor. Only she could not make her apology, no matter how much she might want to. . . .

" . . . Stop a minute," Hen was heard to say, "and pass the
time of day . . ."

Unintelligible murmuring, and then: "D' you know who it
was that invented stopping and passing the time of day?" said
the nearing voice of Mr. V. V., gayer than Cally Heth had ever
heard it. "Take my word, 't was a woman."

"To make things pleasant for some man! — and we've been
doing it ever since. . . . Cally Heth's here . . ."

The two came in. Cally, turning, held out her hand to the
Cooneys' physician, with a sufficiently natural air and greeting. . . .

They had not met since the afternoon at the Woman's Club, a
day which had brought a strange change in their relations. But
then, each of their meetings seemed marked by some such realign-
ment, and always to his advantage. Again and again she had put
this man down, at first with all her strength; and each time when
she turned and looked at him again, behold he had shot up higher
than ever.

So Cally had just been thinking. But now that V. Vivian stood
in the room, and she looked at him, she was suddenly reminded
that he was her good friend nevertheless. And something like
ease came back to her.

When Hen had disappeared to make the sick-room ready (or
for whatever purpose she went), Cally said:

"I hope Chas is n't really going to be ill?"

"Oh, there's no trouble at all with him," replied the young
man, "but to make him stay in bed. It's all come down to a
touch of sore throat, a little sort of quinsy. We were rather afraid
of diphtheria, the other night."

"My cousins are having more than their share, just now. So
many, many invalids. . . . I hope you've been well, since I saw
you last?"

"Oh, thank you! — I've the health of a letter-carrier. At
least, I assume they're naturally healthy, though as a matter of
fact I've had three or four postmen on my list . . . I'm afraid I
interrupted you and Henrietta?"

"Oh, no! — Or rather, I imagine she was only too glad

to be interrupted. . . . I was telling her all my troubles, you see."

"Have you troubles? I'm sorry."

The man spoke in a light tone, such as is suitable for friendships. Yet he must have felt a throe then, remembering his articles: now so soon to go to the "Chronicle" office and the print that cried aloud. And the girl's case, had he but known it, was like his own, only more so. Beneath the cover of her casual talk, she was aware of thought coursing like a palpitating vein under a fine skin, threatening to break through at any minute. . . .

"Oh, so many," said Cally.

They had remained standing, for to ask the doctor to sit down had not occurred to her. The girl glanced toward the window.

"And what do you suppose Hen's prescription was? . . . That I should take them all to you."

There was the briefest silence.

"But, of course, you did n't want to do that?"

She hesitated, and said: "Yes, I do want to . . . But I can't."

That was the utmost that she meant to say. But then, as she glanced again at the lame alien whom time had so beautifully justified, more of her inner tide overflowed suddenly into speech.

"Do you know — I feel that I could tell you almost anything — things I would n't tell Hen, or anybody. . . . Oh, I could, I don't know why. You don't know for what a long time I've thought of you as my confidant, my friend. . . . Only, you see — these troubles are n't all my own. . . ."

She stopped rather precipitately, turned away a little; stood twisting a glove between her fingers, and doing her best to show by her look that she had not said anything in particular. . . .

The thoughts of these two were over hills and dales apart; and yet, by the nature of what was between them, they followed hard on the same trail. V. V. was far from possessing the Cooneys' detective gift. He saw only that this girl was troubled about something; and if his own thought never left the Heth Works, it was only because this was the point where his connection with her troubles cut him deep.

So in his ears chirped the voice of his now familiar: "Who appointed *you* a judge of people like this? Who knows better than you that they're doing the best they can? Tear up that stuff! . . ."

But aloud he said only: "I understand that, of course. And I'm grateful for the rest you say."

And Cally, five feet away from him, was learning that in some matters the business logic of it did n't help very much, that what counted was how you felt about them in your heart. If something terrible should happen at the Works *now*, if the building did fall down some day, collapsing with all those girls — did she think she could look again into this man's eyes and say: "Well, *I* had nothing to do with it ? . . ."

But neither were her thoughts for publication; and she bridged the brief gap in the conversation with a not particularly successful smile, designed to show that of course nobody was taking all this very seriously.

"But why expect to do what we want? No one can," said she. "You don't mind my fidgeting about the room this way, do you? I seem a little out of humor to-day — not myself at all, as I was told just now. . . ."

V. V. said that he did not mind.

"I wonder," she went on, "if you remember something you said in your speech the other day? — about being free. . . . It seemed strange to me then, that you should have happened to say just that, for I — I've come to realize that, in a kind of way, that's always been a wild dream of my own. . . . Don't you think — where there are so many things to think about, things and people — that it's pretty hard to be free?"

"Hard? . . . There's nothing else like it on earth for hardness."

V. V. stood grasping the back of an ancient walnut chair. It was seen that he belonged in this room, simple home of poverty; different from the girl, who was so obviously the rich exotic, the transient angel in the house.

He added: "But it's always seemed to me worth all the price of trying."

"Oh, it is — I'm sure. And yet ... It seems to me — I've thought," said Cally, somewhat less conversationally, "that life, for a woman, especially, is something like one of those little toy theatres — you've seen them? — where pasteboard actors slide along in little grooves when you pull their strings. They move along very nicely, and you — you might think they were going in that direction just because they wanted to. But they never get out of their grooves. . . . I know you'll think that a — a weak theory."

"No, I know it's a true theory."

Surely the girl could not have been thinking only of her father's business as she went on, more and more troubled in voice:

"So much seems to be all fixed and settled, before one's old enough to know anything about it — and then there's a great deal of pressure — and a great deal of restraint — in so many different ways. . . . Don't you think it's hard ever to get out of one's groove?"

"It's heroic."

She put back her trailing motor-veil, and said: "And for a woman especially?"

"It would take the strength of all the gods! . . . I mean, of course — as women are placed, to-day. Perhaps in some other day — perhaps to-morrow —"

He broke off suddenly; a change passed over his face.

"And yet," he added, in a voice gentle and full of feeling — "some of them are doing it to-day."

What his thought might be, she had no idea; but his personal implication was not to be mistaken. The man from the slums, who had mistakenly put his faith in her once before in the Cooneys' parlor, conceived that she was or might be one of these strong he spoke of; little suspecting her present unconquerable weakness.

Cally was startled into looking at him, a thing she had been rather avoiding; and looking, she looked instantly away. In

Mr. V. V.'s eyes, that strange trusting look, which had not been frequently observable there of late, had saluted her like a banner of stars. . . .

"Certainly I was not meant to be one of them," said she, rather faintly.

He must have meant only a general expression of confidence, she was sure of that; only to be kind and comforting. But to her, grappling with new hard problems, that strange gaze came like a torch lit in a cave at night. Much she had wondered how Vivian could possibly hold her responsible for what her father did, or left undone. And now in a flash it was all quite clear, and she saw that he had not been holding her responsible at all. No, this simple and good man, who let the crows bring his raiment, or not, as they preferred, had only reposed a trust in her — in Cally Heth. It was as if, that day at the Settlement, he had said to her, by his eyes: "I know *you*. Once *you* go to the Works, you won't rest till you've made things better. . . ."

But instead of this making things better for Cally Heth now, it seemed to make them worse at once. She became considerably agitated; knew that he must see her agitation, and did not mind at all. And suddenly she sat down on the sway-backed sofa between the windows. . . .

"I'm the last woman in the world ever to think of getting out of my groove," said Cally, her cheek upon her hand.

And then, with no premeditation at all, there came strange words from her, words clothing with unlessoned ease thoughts that certainly she had never formulated for Hugo Canning.

"And yet I feel that it might have been different. I've felt — lately — as if I have n't had much of a chance . . . I think I have a mind, or had one . . . some — some spirit and independence, too. But I was n't trained to express myself that way; that was all ironed down flat in me. I never had any education, except what was superficial — showy. I was never taught to think, or to *do* anything — or to have any part in serious things. No one ever told me that I ought to justify my existence, to pay my way. Nobody ever thought of me as fit to have any share in anything useful or important — fit for any responsibility . . . No, life for me was to be like butterflies flying, and my part was only to make myself as ornamental as I could. . . ."

V. Vivian, who wrote articles about the Huns in newspapers, stood at the Cooney mantel. He did not move at all; the man's gaze upon her half-averted face did not wink once. His own face, this girl had thought, was one for strange expressions; but she might have thought the look it wore now stranger than any she had ever seen there. . . .

"Maybe, it's that way with all women, more or less — only it seems to have been always more with me . . . Money!" said the low hurried voice — "how I've breathed it in from the first moment I can remember. Money, money, money! . . . Has it been altogether my fault if I've measured everything by it, supposed that it was the other name for happiness — taken all of it I could get? I've always taken, you see — never given. I never gave anything to anybody in my life. I never did anything for anybody in my life. I'm a grown woman — an adult human being — but I'm not of the slightest use to anybody. I've held out both hands to life, expecting them to be filled, kept full . . ."

She paused and was deflected by a fleeting memory, something heard in a church, perhaps, long ago. . . .

"Is n't there," she asked, "something in the Bible about that? — horse-leech's daughters — or something? — always crying *'Give, give'* ? . . ."

There was a perceptible pause.

"Well — something of the sort, I believe. . . ."

She had seemed to have the greatest confidence that, if anything of the sort was in the Bible, this man would know it instantly. However, his tone caught her attention, and she raised her eyes. Mr. V. V.'s face was scarlet.

"I see," said Cally, colorlessly, out of the silence, "you had already thought of me as one of those daughters. . . . Why not?"

"Of you! Not in my life," cried V. V. . . . "I . . . it's —"

"Why should n't you? I know that's what I am. You're —"

"*Don't* . . . I can't let things be put upside down like that."

His difficulties, in the unhappy moment, were serious. His skin had turned traitor to him, sold out his heart. And now, if

he had the necessity of saying something, his was also the fear
lest he might say too much. . . .

"If I . . . I appeared to look — conscious, when you asked me
that, it was only because of the — the strange coincidence. I —
you compel me to tell you — though it's like something from
another life."

He paused briefly; and when he went on, his voice had acquired
something of that light hardness which Cally had heard in it
before now.

"Once, a year ago, when I had never so much as heard your
name, Commissioner O'Neill and I happened to be talking about
the local factory situation, about the point of view of the owners
or, — to be exactly honest, — the owners' families. By chance
— I did use those words. And O'Neill said I was a wild man to
talk so, that if I knew any of these people, personally, I'd never
judge them so — so unkindly. . . . It was a long time before I
saw . . . how right he might be. . . . And that's what I tried to
say to you the other day — when I spoke of *knowing the people.*
I —"

"Yes, sometimes that makes a difference, I know." Had she
not felt it only this afternoon? "But I'm afraid this is n't one of
the times. . . ."

Cally rose, feeling that she desired to go. Nevertheless, glancing at his troubled face, she was suddenly moved by perhaps the
most selfless impulse she had ever felt in her life.

"Please," she said, gently, "don't mind about that. I liked
you better for it. I like people to say what they think. I've —"

"Do you? Then allow me to say that I'm not quite a bitter
fool. . . ."

The young man was advancing toward her, throwing out his
hands in a quaint sort of gesture which seemed to say that he had
had about as much of this as he could stand.

"For surely I don't think I am — I don't think I'm quite so
dumb and blind as you must think me. . . ." His repressed air
was breaking up rapidly, and now he flung out with unmistakable
feeling: "Do you suppose I could ever forget what you did
last May! Not if I tried a thousand years!" said Mr. V. V. . . .

"How could I possibly think anything of you, after that, but all that is brave and beautiful? . . ."

The two stood looking at each other. Color came into Cally's cheek; came but soon departed. The long gold-and-black lashes, which surely had been made for ornaments, fluttered and fell.

Out of the dead silence she said, with some difficulty:

"It 's very sweet of you to say that."

Cally moved away from him, toward the door, deeply touched. She had wanted to hear such words as these, make no doubt of that. Among all her meetings with this man last year, she had only that May morning to remember without a stinging sense of her inferiority. And she supposed that he had forgotten. . . .

"You see," she said, not without an effort, " I have been telling you my troubles, after all. . . . I — I 'm afraid I 've kept them waiting for you upstairs. I must go."

But she did not leave the parlor at once, even when Hen, hearing the door creak open, cried down that the infirmary was ready. . . .

If Cally felt that she had somehow confessed her weakness to Mr. V. V. — about the Works, about life — and been forgiven by him, it seemed that e en that did not quite settle it all. It must have been that one small corner of her mind refused to consider that all this was a closed episode.

She turned, with her hand on the knob.

"Shall you go to that meeting of Mr. Pond's next Wednesday — his meeting for workers? He has asked me to go."

The young man said that he would be at the meeting; that he hoped to see her there.

Cally hesitated again. Perhaps she thought of Hugo then; or perhaps the small unreconstructed corner of her mind grew more unrestful.

"I 'm not sure that I 'll be able to go," she said, slowly. . . . "Dr. Vivian — is your telephone number still the same — Meeghan's Grocery? I — I may want to speak to you some time."

Yes, it was just the same. Meeghan's Grocery.

V. V. stood looking at her from the middle of the floor, one hand raised to his hair in his characteristic gesture. His old-fashioned sort of face wore a far-away look, not so much hopeful now as wistful; a look which had been moving to Cally Heth, even in the days when she had tried to dislike him. But of this, the young man from the lonely outskirts was not aware; of the nature of his replies he had taken no note. In his ears whispered the subtlest of all his many voices: "She'll never speak to you, once that's printed. Tear it up. You've a right to your youth. . . ."

"Good-bye," said Cally, "and thank you."

"Miss Heth," said Vivian, starting, hurriedly — "I — if I — if it should ever happen that I could *help* you in any way — it's not likely, of course, I understand that — but if it *should* ever happen so — *promise* me that you'll send for me."

But the girl did not make that promise then, her reply being: "You *have* helped me — you *must* know that. . . . You're the one person in the world who has."

Cally walked home alone, in the dying effects of a lovely afternoon.

She had left the Cooney parlor in the vein of one emerging from strange adventures in undiscovered countries. This queer feeling would hardly last over the solid threshold of Home, whose atmosphere was almost notoriously uncongenial to eccentricities of that sort. But it did linger now, as Cally trod somewhat dreamily over streets that she had long known by heart. Four blocks there were; and the half-lights flickering between sky and sidewalk were of the color of the girl's own mood.

In this moment she was not troubled with thought, with the drawing of moral lessons concerning duty or otherwise. Now Mr. V. V.'s unexpected last speeches to her seemed wholly to possess her mind. She was aware that they had left her curiously humbled. . . . Strange it seemed, that this man could be so unconscious of the influence he had upon her, had clearly had even last year. Stranger yet that he, whom only the other day she had thought of as so narrow, so religiously hard, should prove himself absurdly over-generous in his estimate of her. . . . Or no, not that exactly. But, at least, it would have been absurd, if it had not been so sweet. . . .

The revolting corner of her mind seemed now to have laid down arms. Perhaps the girl's vague thought was that the feelings roused in her in the bunching-room had, after all, been unreasonable, even hysterical, as Hugo had plainly enough stated, as Hen herself had partly argued. Perhaps it was merely that all that trouble would keep, to be quietly pondered over at a later time. But rather, it seemed as if a mist had settled down over the regions of practical thought, hiding problems from view. The Works had somehow been swallowed up in that apologia she had made, Cally Heth's strange apology to Mr. V. V. for herself and her life.

Cally walked slowly along the familiar street, her thoughts a thousand miles in the blue. If the words of the good young man had humbled her, they had also mysteriously stirred and uplifted. She thought of his too trusting tribute, she thought of what they had said about women, their strength and their hope of freedom; and the misty pictures in her mind were not of herself — for well she had felt her weaknesses this day — but rather they were of a dim emerging ideal, of herself as she might some day hope to be. Vague aspirations were moving in her; new reachings of the spirit; dreams that spoke with strange voices. . . .

And, companied by these ethereal fancies, she came, before she was aware of it, to the substantial steps of Home, where began the snuggest of all snug grooves. . . .

She arrived with the intention, already well formed, of retiring forthwith to her room, and — probably — spending the whole evening there. But here, as it chanced, interruption fell across her thought. Just at her own door, Cally almost ran into a man who was standing still upon the sidewalk, as if waiting for some one: a tall old gentleman standing and leaning upon his cane. Cally came out of her absorption just in time to escape collision.

"I beg your pardon! . . ." she began, with manner, stepping back.

But then her feet faltered, and her voice died suddenly away, as she saw that this silent old man was her neighbor, Colonel John B. Dalhousie, whom she had never spoken to in her life.

The Colonel was regarding her with frightening fixity. The

girl's descent from the empyrean to reality had the stunning
suddenness of a fall: she showed it in her blanching face. Now,
as the two thus stood, the old man raised a hand and swept off
his military hat in a bow of elaborate courtesy.

"An apology from Miss Heth," said he, in a purring voice, "is
the last thing on earth one of my name would have ventured to
expect."

Doubtless the meeting had been obliged to come some day:
Cally had often thought of it with dread, once escaped it by a
narrow margin. That it should have come now, in the gentler
afterglow of this curiously disturbing day, seemed like the grim-
ness of destiny. . . . No fear of over-generosity here; no gleam
in these eyes of brave and beautiful things. . . .

"But you ask my pardon," the smooth-cutting voice went on.
"It is granted, of course, my dear. You took my son's heart, and
broke it, but that's a bauble. You took his honor, and I kicked
him out, but honor's a name in a printed book. You took his life,
and I buried him, but sons, we know, cannot live forever. What
is there here to make a father's heart grow hard?"

Cally raised her hand to her throat. She felt suffocating, or
else a little faint. From life she seemed to have stepped into the
house of dead men's bones; and here she could see at play old
emotions not met before in her guarded life: shrivelling contempt,
undying hatred, immortal unforgiveness. Nevertheless, the subtlest stroke in the naked confrontation was that something in
the father's expression, distorted though it was, reminded her of
the son, whose face in this world she should see no more.

She tried to move past the face of her Nemesis, appeared physically incapable of motion; tried to speak, and had little more
success.

"I — I'm — very sorry — for — " she said, indistinctly, and her
ears were mocked with her ghastly inadequacy. "I — I've — "

"Sorry? Why, of course you are. Doubtless the little unpleas-
antness has marred your happiness at times. But I am gratified
to know that you have other young men for your amusement,
now that my son has withdrawn himself from your reach."

The old Colonel stooped further, brought his stabbing gaze

nearer her. There were heavy yellow pouches under his eyes; his lower lip, not hidden by the stained white mustaches, twitched spasmodically.

"God looked and repented him that he had made man. I might wish that he'd made you a man — for just five minutes. But what do you imagine he thinks when he contemplates you and your work, my dear? Eh? . . . little she-devil, pretty little hell-cat! . . ."

Cally smothered a little noise between a cry and a sob. She started away, by sheer strength of horror; somehow got away from the terrible old face, ran up her own steps. Glancing whitely over her shoulder from this secure coign, she saw that Jack Dalhousie's father still stood unmoving on her sidewalk, staring and leaning on his cane. . . .

She closed the door quickly, shutting out the sight.

XXX

How it sounded like an Epitaph, but still she would not cry; how she thinks of the Beach again, and hugs a Hateful Word to her Bosom; and Hugo starts suddenly on a sort of Wedding-Trip.

IN her own room Carlisle was seized with a wild desire to cry. Her spirit, shocked past bearing, demanded this instant relief. But she fought down the loosening impulses within her, knowing their worse than uselessness; she had shed her heart's tears for this before now. And her need now was for strength; strength to meet her mother when need be, against whom key nor bolt brought privacy: strength, above all, to wipe out this mark set upon her forehead. . . .

She resisted the impulse to fling herself face downward upon the bed, which would have been fatal; kept stoutly upon her feet. And presently, summoning all her courage, she stood at the window and peeped, pale-faced, between the curtains. All was well down there now. The old avenger was gone. There were only people passing serenely over the familiar sidewalk, and the sunlight dying where she had stood and learned just now that a lie has a long life.

Yes, the Colonel was gone: and with him, so it seemed, all veils and draperies, all misty sublimations. One does n't idealize one's self too much, with curses ringing in one's ears.

Cally leaned weakly against the wall, both gloved palms pressed into the cold smoothness of her cheeks. Somewhere in the still house a door suddenly banged shut, and she just repressed a scream. . . .

Old Colonel Dalhousie did not deal in moral subtleties, that was clear. Regret, penitence, sufferings, tears, or dreamy aspiration: he did not stay to split such hairs as these. His eye was for the large, the stark effect. And by the intense singleness of his vision, he had freighted his opinions with an extraordinary convic-

427

tion. He had shouted down, as from a high bench, the world's judgment on the life of Cally Heth.

Twenty-four years and over she had lived in this town; and at the end to be called a she-devil and a hell-cat.

The girl's bosom heaved. She became intensely busy in the bedroom, by dint of some determination; taking off her street things and putting them painstakingly away, straightening objects here or there which did very well as they were. Flora knocked, and was sent away. On the mantel was discovered a square lavender box, bearing a blazoned name well known in another city. Fresh flowers from Canning, these were; and Carlisle, removing the purple tinsel from the bound stems, carefully disposed the blossoms in a bowl of water. Once in her goings and comings, she encountered her reflection in the mirror, and then she quickly averted her eyes. One glance of recognition between herself and that poor frightened little thing, and down would come the flood-gates, with profitless explanations to follow in a certain quarter. She avoided that catastrophe; but not so easily did she elude the echoing words of her neighbor the Colonel, which were like to take on the inflection of an epitaph. . . .

After a time, when the dread of weeping had waned, Cally threw herself down in her chaise-longue near the window, and covered her eyes with her hand. And now with all her will — and she had never lacked for will — she strove to take her mind from what no piety or wit could now amend: struggling to think and remember how she had tried once, at a price, to set right that wrong she had done. For other comfort there was none: what she had written, she had written. She might give her life to the ways of Dorcas; she might beat her breast and fill her hands with pluckings of her gay hair. But she could not bring Dalhousie back to life now, or face his poor father as a girl who had done no wrong. . . .

Life in the House moved on. There was a caller or two, who found the ladies excused; there was a telephone summons from Miss Evelyn McVey, whose desire it was to entertain Mr. Canning at dinner, but who now met only with a maid's message; and then, toward seven, there came mamma herself, who was, of course, not so lightly to be disposed of.

But Cally had fortified herself for the little visit, and passed the inspection without mishap. Mrs. Heth was acquiescent enough in her daughter's desire to dine upstairs, which saved the bother of hunting up another man in Hugo's stead, though involving regrettable waste of two covers already prepared. Mamma lingered for fifteen minutes making arch, tactful inquiries about the afternoon; but she noticed nothing more than was accountable for by the slight headache to which Carlisle frankly admitted. The little general's side remarks conceded no doubt whatever that Hugo would present himself very shortly indeed after dinner, for resumption of the agreeable matter in hand. They should have the library to themselves, she promised, company or no company. . . .

Cally dined at a reading-table, set by the fire. Later, when the tray was gone and she was alone again, she relapsed into thoughts which had gained unwonted lucidity and vigor.

She had been thinking of the night, a year ago this month, to which everything in her life since seemed to run straight back. She had not certainly calculated the ruin of Dalhousie that night: rather her lack was that she had hardly cared what she did to him. In that narrow circle of engrossments where she had moved, mistaking it for the living universe, the great want, so it seemed now, was that she had never been asked to measure herself by moral standards at all. What she got: this was all that people looked at here, and according to this she had well managed her affairs, snug in the snugness of the horse-leech's daughters. She had been all for the walled little island, — as she had heard it called, — the island of the upward bound, where self-propelment was the test of right or wrong, and a marriage well above her the touchstone of a girl's sound morality. On this island such as Jack Dalhousie had no merit. What simpler than to kick him off, and turn away with your fingers in your ears? . . .

Improbable people these, no doubt, if you were of those who judged people by what they did, and never by what they had;

hell-cats, perhaps, if you happened to be a father thus made son-less. . . .

Her abasement now fairly met the portrait of her sketched by a stranger two hours since; outran what another stranger had said to her, one night in a summer-house. She looked back over a year, and seemed to see herself as truly one empty within, a poor little thing; common in her whole outlook, vulgar in her soul. . . . Yes, *vulgar*. Let her hug the hateful word to her bosom. How else could she have been made to feel so again and again, by an obscure youth who had no power over anybody but that he had kept his own face turned toward the stars? . . .

And when Cally's thoughts turned toward this present, struggling to show beyond doubt that that girl and this were not one, they ran perpetually into that new cloud of her own weakness which had unrolled above her to-day, and now spread and blackened over the skies.

And yet she felt that it was not cowardice that tied her hands against the fainting girls in the bunching-room. Her strung nerves had carried it all deeper than that. She had spied on her father, found him out in guilt; he, it seemed, must for years have been leading a double life that would not bear looking at. How bring herself to confront papa, who had always been so affectionate and generous to her, with his discovered secret? . . .

If she but had some right, even, some standing from which to speak. . . . And here her new resolve was that when she saw Dr. Vivian at the Settlement next week, she would consult him directly: now asking him to say, not that she had no responsibilities about her father's business, but that she had them in abundance.

But deeper than this, beneath all the flutterings of her mind, there ran the increasing sense that, whatever the logic of it might be, responsibility was on her nevertheless: the supreme responsibility put upon free beings by the trust of a friend. . . .

Hugo, it was presumable, would be detained with his Mr. Deming until the latter's departure, or near it. He could hardly appear before nine o'clock, or even nine-thirty; and perhaps he might not come at all. Cally had felt unable to agree with her mother's theory that she was required to sit awaiting Hugo's convenience there. At all events, she had early resolved to settle the point by definitely "retiring" before his possible arrival; relying upon a worse aching head to justify her with mamma, who was not of the few to be favored with fuller confidences.

But a little after eight, when this resolve was almost ready to shape into the deed, the sensible reasoning on which it was based was suddenly upset. The maid Flora came, bringing a new message from the preoccupied lover, brief but decisive.

The business entanglements, it appeared, had only got worse with talking. Hugo, beyond all expectation, found himself compelled to go back to Washington with his law-partner to-night; possibly to go on to New York to-morrow. Would Carlisle accordingly arrange to see him now, for a few moments?

"*Now?*"

"Yas'm, he say as soon as you c'd make it convenient."

The girl had risen sharply in the first complete surprise of Flora's message; she walked hastily across her floor. But having done these things, she did not at once give the obviously due reply. She stood by her dressing-table, staring fixedly at the colored woman, the aimless fingers of her left hand continually pulling out and putting back the silver top of a squat cut-glass bottle. She appeared to be thinking, weighing pros and cons: processes surely unnecessary to a pasteboard actor, sliding smoothly toward a manifest destiny.

She stood this way so long and so silent that Flora prompted with a giggle and further information.

"Miss Cyahlile, he say if you was to answer no, to say could he please speak to you a minute on the 'phone."

Upon that Miss Carlisle was seen to replace the bottle stopper with consciousness of movement, and to turn her slate-blue eyes briefly toward the ceiling, with no movement of her head at all.

"Very well . . . Say that I'll see him at half-past eight, for a few minutes."

Flora, naturally, was not a woman without understanding the sign language of her sex. It might be that she had learned the

color of the Canning money — and she had — but her dusky
heart, like yours or mine, was not for sale.

"Yas'm — certny . . . Yas'm. Or, Miss Cyahlile — I *mout*
just say we're mighty sorry — but not knowin' he was expected,
and you feelin' po'ly an' all — you just this minute went to baid
— an' —"

"No! — do as I say," said the young mistress, quite sharply.
But, as her faithful friend turned away, she added in another
voice: "You're a good girl, Flora. . . . Be sure to say just for a
few minutes."

After the solitude and meditation came action at speed.

The maid vanished, the mistress slipped off her flowered neg-
ligée and drew hot water in the bathroom. She proceeded, with no
want of experience or skill, to make herself beautiful for her lover:
the lover who had seemed over a gulf from her this afternoon,
and now what worlds away. . . . And if the rites were done somewhat hurriedly perforce, there was no lack of conscientiousness
here. She, who had said that she had never paid her way through
life, could only pay in what coin she had. . . .

Events moved quickly. Flora, who was "on the doorbell"
to-night because of the dinner-party, was soon back to say that
Mr. Canning was in the library. She was sent ahead to make
sure that the coast was clear.

Cally, in a soft black house-dress with an apricot waist-ribbon,
went down the back-stairs. She passed through the busy pantry,
where Moses and Annie were just ready for an expert entrance
with the fish; went through the back hall, where Flora stood flashing her teeth beside the closed door of the dining-room; came to
the side door of the library. This door Cally opened, and shut it
again behind her. . . .

It was a massive and dark-beamed room, softened now with
the light of lamps and fire. Hugo stood in the middle of it, turning
quickly at the sound of the door. He, whose afternoon had taken
a course so different from his planning, still wore the clothes he
had had on then, a dark gray walking-suit which well became his
fine-figured masculinity. Over his brow there hovered a vexed
business frown, nor did this altogether vanish as he advanced

upon Carlisle, a lover's welcome springing imperiously into his eyes.

"Is n't this the deil's own luck? . . . Deming insists it all depends on me."

"You go at nine-thirty?"

"He says he'll manacle me if necessary. It's confoundedly important, you see — there are large interests involved. You know I would n't go otherwise. Don't you?"

"And to-morrow you go on to New York?"

"No! — There's only the remotest chance. I'll go bail to be back here to-morrow at five o'clock."

"Oh! . . . I — the message I got —"

"I put that in only to make absolutely sure of getting you. . . . Growing cunning, you see."

"Oh — I did n't understand," said Cally, colorlessly, continuing to look down at her pink fingernails.

She seemed to think of nothing further to say, but that appeared to make no great difference. Hugo moved nearer. If he had remembered his thought about her being too sure of him, it may be that the sight of her had rushed his senses, as it had often done before.

"You were so unlike your natural dear self this afternoon," he said, on the wooing note; and suddenly he had possessed himself of both her hands. "To-night — and we've only such a little time — you are going to make it all up to me . . . Are n't you?"

Finding herself captured, the girl hastily raised eyes dark with trouble, looking at her lover for the first time. And so looking, she took her hands from his grasp with a hastiness which might have been a little rasping to a morbidly sensitive man.

"Don't! — please don't! I — don't like to be touched. . . . I — I can only act as I feel, Hugo."

She turned away hurriedly, passed him and went over to the fireplace. There she stood quite silent before the dull red glow, locking and unlocking her slim fingers, and within her a spreading coldness.

Behind her she heard the thundering feet.

"I hoped, you see," said Hugo's voice, disappointed, but hardly chagrined, "that you would be feeling a little more — well, like your own natural self, after your rest . . . Particularly as all our plans for these two days have been so upset."

She replied, after a pause, in a noticeably constrained voice: "I have n't said that I don't feel my natural self. That's only your — your interpretation of what you don't like. . . . I — that seems to be just the trouble between us."

"Now, now! — my *dear* Cally!" said Hugo, soothing, if somewhat wearied to see still another conversation drifting toward the argumentative. "There's no trouble between us at all. I, for one, have put our little disagreement to-day out of my head entirely. I do feel that there's not much happiness in these so-called modernisms, but don't let's spoil our few minutes. . . . Why, Carlisle!" said Hugo, in another voice. "Why, what's the matter?"

She had astonished him by suddenly laying her arm upon the mantel, and burying her face in the curve of it. So close Canning stood now that he could have taken her in his arms without moving; but some quality in her pose discouraged the idea that she might desire comfort that way.

Carlisle's difficulties, indeed, were by no means over for the day. The conviction which had come upon her with the first full view of her lover's face — where Colonel Dalhousie seemed also to have set his afflicting mark — had suddenly grown overwhelming. She had made her draft for payment against an account where there were no more funds.

"Are you ill?"

"No," she answered, straightening at once. . . . "I . . . I'm afraid — this is my natural self."

"Something troubles you?" said Hugo, with penetration.

She nodded, and turned away.

She had always been capable of independent action; it was her chief strength, however mamma might speak of flare-ups. But never in her womanhood had she felt less in tune for heroics and a scene. Life was shaking to pieces all around her.

"Hugo," she began, with difficulty, playing at arranging a slide of books on the table with hands like two blocks of ice . . . "I —

I hesitated about coming down at all, but now — I think . . . As you are going away to-night, and would be coming back to-morrow entirely on my account . . . I think I ought —"

"Why, my dear! What's all this about? . . . Do you mean you've let your feelings be hurt by my going off? Why, you —"

"It is n't that."

The nature of his understanding seemed to stir something in her, and she went on in a rather steadier voice:

"I've been thinking of something you said to me once — that I was n't the girl you had asked to marry you . . . It's taken me a long time, but I've learned that that was the truth. I'm not —"

She was checked, to her surprise, by a soft laugh.

"So that's been it! . . . I never imagined — no wonder! . . . Why, Cally! How could you suppose I meant it? Don't you know I was angry that day? — off my head? Would I —"

"But it's true! I'm not that girl at all — I feel differently — I —"

"Well! Let's not waste good time in mare's nests of *that* sort. Why, dear little girl, would I be here now, if I was n't satisfied as no other man on earth —"

"But I'm not satisfied, Hugo."

Cally turned now, faced him fully, a faint color coming into her cheek. In the man's handsome eyes she had surprised an unmistakable complacence.

"I'm not satisfied," she said, hurriedly, "to know that we are miles apart, and drifting further every minute. Don't you see there's no sympathy — no understanding — between us? What interests me, appeals to me, what is really my natural self — that only annoys you, makes you think —"

"I've been at fault there, I own," he interrupted, soothingly, nodding his head respectfully up and down. "To tell the truth, I've been so immensely interested in *you*, — in Carlisle the woman, — that I have n't seemed able to make proper allow-ance for your — your other interests. I promise to turn over a new leaf there. And, on your side, I am sure, you do realize, Carlisle —"

"Hugo," said the girl, desperately, "you don't understand me. I am trying to say that I can't marry you. I cannot."

Then the faint hum of voices from the dining-room down the hall became quite audible in the library. By the ebbing of color from Hugo's virile face, Cally knew that she had penetrated his satisfaction at last; but by the look in his eyes she learned that she had lodged no conviction in him.

"I hesitated when you asked me in September," said she, slowly, and trying her best to make her voice sound firm. "I should have made up my mind sooner — I've been to blame. I'm sorry to —"

He said in a slightly hoarsened voice: "What has happened since I left you this afternoon?"

What, indeed? Everything seemed to have happened.

"Something did happen . . . But I — I don't think there's any use to talk about it."

"Tell me what has happened. I have a right to know."

"I will, if you wish — but it won't do any good. . . . I went out, to my cousins'. And at the door, as I came back, I — I met Colonel Dalhousie. He stopped me . . . expressed his opinion of me. He said things that I — I —"

She stopped precipitately, with a break in her voice; turned from him.

"Oh! — I understand . . . Poor little girl."

At the mention of the name of ill omen, Canning's strong heart had missed a beat. He had thought the old corpse buried past exhumation; the sudden rising of the ghost to walk had staggered for an instant even his superb incredulities. But with that sudden tremulousness of hers, he was himself again, or almost, with a new light upon her whole strange and unreliable demeanor. Small wonder, after such an encounter, if she was brought to the verge of hysteria, her feminine reason unseated, her mind wandering mistily over the forgotten past. . . .

He tried to take at least one hand in loving sympathy, but found that the matter could not be arranged.

"The shock has upset you — poor darling! I understand. No wonder! . . ."

"No — I'm not upset . . . I — Hugo, I can't marry you. I'm truly sorry — I've tried — but now I'm quite sure —"

"But this is madness," said Hugo's queer voice. "Don't you see it is as you say the words? . . . Not marry me — because an old ruffian waylaid you, called you — hard names —"

"No, but because what he said was true. No — of course that's not the reason . . . I must tell you the truth . . ."

Cally lifted misty eyes, beneath which faint circles were beginning to appear, and said with sadness:

"Hugo, I don't love you."

Then she watched, painfully, the last remnants of his assurance drop away from his face: and after that, she saw, with a certain fear, that she had still to make herself believed.

Hugo, supported not merely by his own justifiable confidences but by her mother's affirmations, could, indeed, put no credence in his ears. Many explanations were possible for this extraordinary feminine perversity; she had happened to mention the one explanation that was not possible.

"You don't know what you're saying," he began, huskily, out of the silence. "You're not yourself at all nowadays . . . Full of new little ideas. You've taken a whim, because an old rascal . . . whom I shall punish as he deserves —"

"No . . . That helped me to make up my mind, perhaps. But I've learned I've never loved you — since you left me last year."

Cally moved away from Hugo, not caring to witness the breaking-up of his self-control. She leaned against the heavy mahogany table, clenching a tiny handkerchief between chill little hands. If the months had brought her perfect vengeance on the man who had once failed her in her need, she was finding it, indeed, a joyless victory.

"I'm to blame for not telling you before — when you were here last month," she said, with some agitation . . . "Only I really didn't know my own mind . . . All summer I seemed to . . . just to take it for granted that — everything was the same — that I still cared for you. But — Hugo, I don't. I'm sorrier than I can say for what has been my fault. . . ."

The young man had been standing like one in a trancelike

illness, who can hear, indeed, with horrible distinctness, but can neither move nor speak. But now the increasing finality of her words seemed all at once to galvanize him; he shook himself slightly and took one heavy step forward.

"What you need is a protector, little girl — a man. I know about the summer — I suffered, too . . . Of course. And in the loneliness — you've let yourself be affected . . . The unrest of the day —"

"No, no! *Please*," said she, almost ready to scream — "don't think this is one of my new little ideas you speak of. I — it's true that we don't seem to think alike about things . . . But I'd never have noticed that at all if I loved you. I'd want to think and do only as you wished. But I don't —"

"I've spoiled you . . . letting you think you could have your way with me," said Hugo, in his thick and gritty voice. "You're mad to-night, little girl . . . are n't responsible for what you say . . ."

Flicked in her spirit, she broke across his argument with a changed voice and gaze.

"Why is it madness not to love you?"

"It's not a thing to argue about now, I say. You do love me . . . I know it. You'll marry me next month, that I swear. Why —"

"No! — when I love, I want to look up, and when I marry, I'll marry above me . . ."

That checked his queer truculence; and Cally, desperate with the need to drive home her meaning, swept on with no more nervousness.

"And — don't you see? — I've not been able to look up to you since that day last year . . . The day — I'm sorry to have to say it — when you came all the way down from New York to show me that you did n't care for a woman who was getting new little ideas about telling the truth. . . ."

Canning's face was the color of chalk, his look increasingly stony; in his eyes strange passions mounted. Now he seemed to intend to say something, but the girl's words flowed with gathering intensity.

"Why, think what you did that day, Hugo! — *think, think!*
If I needed a protector and a man, — and I did, — that was the
time for you to show me how protectors and men can act and
love. If I was wrong, it seems to me that was the time of all times
when you ought to have stood by me, protected me. But I was
right — don't you know I was? . . . I — it was the first time I
had ever thought about doing right — and *you threw me over for
it*. . . . Of course I know there was a quarrel, but — you know
perfectly well what you said. You said then, just as you say now,
that I was shocked out of my senses, did n't know what I was
saying. And then you said that people would point at me to the
longest day I lived, so the thing to do was to hush it all up, or
else I was n't the girl you had asked to be your wife. Anything —
anything — except that I should tell the truth . . . So you went
off and left me to bear it all alone. And then, when my heart had
been broken into little pieces, when I'd cried my eyes out a hundred times, then, when all the trouble was over, and people
were n't cutting me on the street, — then you came back. And
even then you never said once that you were ashamed, or sorry
for the way you'd treated me. You just came back, when I'd
fought it all out without you, and whistled, and thought that I'd
tumble into your arms. . . . Oh, it's natural, I suppose, for a
woman to lie and be mean, and afraid of what people will say —
for that seems to be the — the way they're brought up . . . But
— but —"

Her voice, which had begun to trail a little, dropped off into
silence. She turned away; made a visible effort to control herself.
And then there floated again into the still room the sounds of muffled revelry: strong Mrs. Heth making merry with her friends, a
few of the best people. . . .

"But I only hurt your feelings for nothing," said the girl, in
quite a gentle voice. . . . "Hugo, try to forgive me if I've done
you any wrong. But . . . you — you have your train to make.
Don't you think you'd better go now?"

Hugo's extraordinary reply was to seize her in his arms.

"Go? . . . Yes, and take you with me . . . you little witch.
Why, you're raving, little witch," said the hoarse, violent voice

in her ear. "Gone out of your head with notions. . . . D' you think I'll let your life and mine be spoiled for a few minutes' crazy madness? You need to remember you're a woman, that's all . . . Don't struggle. It's no use."

Her wild efforts to release herself, indeed, only drew his embrace tighter. His cheek rested upon her hair.

"Don't struggle, little witch. You've had your head too long. I'll make up your mind for you. You're going to marry me now. To-night. Don't tire yourself so. It's all settled. You belong to me — you see that now, don't you? . . ."

Now his hand was beneath her chin; he raised the still face she had kept so resolutely buried against his breast. And Cally felt his burning kiss upon her forehead, her cheek, upon lips that would nevermore be his.

"Little temptress . . . you were so anxious for me to love you last year. . . . Does n't this teach you that I'll never give you up? It's all settled now. We'll be married at once. I'll hold you this way — kiss you this way — till you learn to do what I say. Then you'll go up and put on travelling-clothes. Never mind lug . . ."

His wedding-trip ended in the middle of a word. His clasp had been weakened by that hand he had raised, and with the sudden strength of desperation his bride had broken from him. In an instant she had put the table between them.

Over ten feet of lamplit space, the lovers of yesteryear regarded each other. Both were white, both trembling. The girl now suffered a brief collapse; her face dropped into her upraised hands, through which, presently, her voice came brokenly:

"*Go!* . . . Go, I beg you . . ."

Canning stood panting, shaken and speechless. Upon him was the last measure of defeat. He had staked his passion and his pride in the supreme attack, and had been crushingly repulsed. Doubt not that he read the incredible portents in the heavens now. His face went from chalk to leaden gray.

He drew his tongue once across his lips, and said, just articulately:

"If I go — out of this room — alone . . . as God lives, you'll never see me again."

It must have been something in Hugo's difficult voice, surely nothing in the words, that set a chord to stirring in Cally. She took her eyes from her hands, glanced once at his subtly distorted face. And then she stood silent by the barrier table, looking down, knotting and unknotting her yellow sash-ends. . . .

That other night of humiliation in the library, which she had never been able to forget, had risen swiftly on the wings of memory. But, curiously, she felt no such uprush of shame now; her fury mysteriously ebbed from her. Even in this moment, still trembling from his familiar handling, still with the frightening sense of her life going to ruin about her, she felt a rising pity for her prince of lovers whom time and circumstance had brought to this. . . .

"Perhaps," said she, out of the silence, in almost a natural tone, "I ought to feel very — angry and — and indignant . . . But I don't. I only feel sad . . . Hugo, why need there be any bitterness between us? We've both made a mistake, that's all, and I feel it's been my fault from the beginning. If you seem to take me — rather — lightly . . . I must have taught you to think of me that way . . . And you'll soon see how — how superficial my attraction for you was, soon forget . . ."

Strangely, these mild words seemed to affect Hugo more than anything done or said before. In fact, he appeared unable to bear them. He had checked her speech suddenly by lifting his hand, in a vague way, to his head; and now, without a word, he turned away, walking blindly toward the door.

She, in silence, followed his going with dark eyes that looked half ready to weep.

By the door into the hall, through which she had come a little while before, the broken young man paused. His face was stony gray, touched with livid streaks. Standing, he looked unseeingly about the room, around and over her; then at last at her. It had seemed to be his intention to say something, to claim the woman's privilege of the last word. But now, when the moment arrived, there came no words.

For once Hugo must be indifferent to anti-climax, must fail to leave a lady's presence with an air. Standing and looking, he suddenly flung out one arm in a wild, curious gesture; and on that he opened the door, very quickly.

The door shut again, quietly enough. And that was all. The beginning at the Beach had touched an end indeed. Hugo was gone. His feet would thunder this way no more.

But the latter end of these things was not yet. One does n't, of course, kick out of one's groove for nothing.

Cally, returning after a time to her own room, did not go at once to bed, much as she would have liked to do that. She sat up, fully dressed, by a dying fire, waiting for what must come. She waited till quarter to eleven, so long did the dinner-guests linger downstairs. But it came at last, just as she had known it would: on gliding heels, not knocking, beaming just at first. . . .

The interview lasted till hard upon midnight. When it ended, both women were in tears. Cally retired to a fitful rest. At nine o'clock next morning, papa telephoned for Dr. Halstead, who came and found temperature, and prescribed a pale-green medicine, which was to be shaken well before using. The positive command was that the patient should not get out of bed that day.

And Cally did not get up that day, or the next, or the next. She lay abed, pale and uncommunicative, denying herself even to Mattie Allen, but less easily shutting herself from the operations of her mind.

And at night, when the troubled brain slips all control, she dreamed continually of horrors. Horrors in which neither Hugo nor mamma had part: of giant machines crashing through floors upon screaming girls, of great crowded buildings falling down with frightful uproars and bedlam shrieks. Through these phantasms the tall figure of Colonel Dalhousie perpetually moved, smiling softly. But when Cally met the doctor of the Dabney House in her dreams, the trust was gone from his eyes.

XXXI

*Second Cataclysm in the House; of the Dark Cloud obscuring the
New Day, and the Violets that had faded behind a Curtain,
etc.; but chiefly of a Little Talk with Mamma, which produced
Moral Results, after all.*

THE foolish nightmares receded; the sad faces of a dream
dwindled again into air; and she waked suddenly in the
sunshine to find herself quite well. This she knew with
the first opening of her eyes. The familiar objects in the room, the
face of the morning, wore the unmistakable *well* look. Wellness
there seemed within, too, refreshment in body, mind, and spirit.
Life called to the young and the strong, and the sunlight, streaming royally through the shuttered windows, was the ringing
reveille of a new day. . . .

But Cally Heth, having waked to life, lay on in bed. She heard
the summons, was strong to answer it; but was held back as by a
high surrounding wall. She was like a tied bird, unfolding wings
with the heart to soar, and continually brought down by the
shortness of her tether.

She had waked to overspreading gloom in the House of Heth;
but this she could have fronted cheerfully to-day, fortified to
charm it away, for herself and others. If events of late had been
sweeping her along too fast, one emotion crowded unsteadyingly
upon another, nature, stepping in, had put the gentle punctua-
tion where it was needed. Hers was the resilience of youth. And
the second cataclysm in the House, even at its worst (which was
what mamma had made it), was hardly comparable to the first.
There was no spiritual abasement this time, no sense of calamity
and worlds at end. Rather, indeed, the contrary: and it was here
that was found the seriousness of it all, in that now the smash-up
was her own deliberate doing. Cally had hardly needed her
mother's savage outbreak to make her feel how definite a part-

ing was here with the ideals and aspirations of a lifetime. She saw that one whole phase of her girlhood had passed away forever. Or, it might be, this that she had said good-bye to was the dim figure of her girlhood itself. . . .

In these thoughts there was sadness, naturally. Hugo's going had been with the noises of breakage, the reverberations of the day of judgment. But Cally had had four days to put her house in order; and she felt that she would have waked almost happy to-day, but for this stranger cloud that still hung so dark upon the horizon. . . .

It was such a day as October in this climate brings week on week, gloriously golden. Cally breakfasted in bed. Toward ten o'clock, as she was slowly dressing with the maid's assistance, word came that her mother desired her presence in the administrative bedroom below.

"Very well, Annie," said the girl, listlessly. "I'll be down in a few minutes."

The message came as something of a surprise, though a disciplinary intent was easily surmised behind it. In the interview the other night, mamma had formally washed her hands of Cally and all her flare-ups, more than intimating that henceforward they would live as comparative strangers. Since then there had come nothing from the staunch little general, who also had remained in her tent, not ill, but permanently aloof and unreconciled. Very different, as it chanced, was the note struck by papa, who had come twice a day, and sometimes thrice, to the sickroom, ostentatiously cheery in his manner, but obviously depressed underneath by the dreary atmosphere enveloping the house. Never, it seemed, had papa been tenderer or more affectionate than in these bedside visits: so that Cally, with her sense of a guilty secret, could hardly bear to look at his kind, worried face.

And she had opened her eyes on the day of wellness with the knowledge that she must put her hand to this cloud now, though she brought down the skies with it. Nothing, it was clear, could be worse than this. To-night, after dinner, she must follow her father into the study, say what she must say. Her mind had returned and clung to the solid arguments of Hen and others. She knew that the memory of the bunching-room had got upon her nerves; entwined and darkened itself with other painful things; assumed fantastic and horrid shapes. Perhaps the dreaded interview would not be so very bad, after all. Surely her father could not wear that kind look for nothing. . . .

Dressed, Carlisle stood at her window a moment, greeting somewhat sadly the brilliant day. Her desire was to stop the footless workings of her mind; to go out and do something. But all that she could think of to do was to return to Baird & Himmel's emporium and complete that shopping for the Thompson kinsfolk which had been so suddenly interrupted last week. And, that occupation exhausted, she would go on to Mattie Allen's, and probably stay there for luncheon. Tame achievements, but better than staying longer in this room.

Here on the broad window ledge, behind the concealing curtain, there stood a bowl of flowers. They were violets, dry and discolored now. The girl's eyes, just as she was turning away toward her mother, fell upon them, and she stopped, overtaken by memory. These were Hugo's flowers, his last gift to her. She herself had placed them here, that eventful afternoon five days ago, and not thought of them again till this moment. . . . Was that, which seemed like an echo from some previous life, only five days ago?

She stood looking down at the mass of sere bloom, touched the withered tops lingeringly with her finger-tips. It was her tribute to the dead, no more. The departed knight had dropped backward out of her heart with a speed and smoothness which showed that he had, indeed, had small foothold there since May. Less and less had Cally felt any impulse to judge or blame Hugo, impute "badness" to him; it was she who had changed, and never he. But how, why? . . . 'Was it something done, something said?' Strange to remember now the hurried journey to the Beach last year, that afternoon in Willie Kerr's apartment. . . .

"Throw out those flowers in the window, Flora. . . . They've been faded for days."

She went down the stairs in that inner state which her country had once found unendurable: she was half slave and half free. And on the stairs she forgot Hugo entirely. She was thinking, in her loneliness and depression, of Vivian, who had pledged his help to her; wondering if she could ask him to come and give her his help now, — at four o'clock this afternoon, perhaps, when the house would be quiet and her mother napping. Her wish was to talk with him, to show him all her difficulty, before she saw her father. She felt that she could tell anything to Mr. V. V. now. . . .

Cally tapped respectfully upon a closed door, and said "Mamma?" Bidden to enter by the strong voice within, she braced herself a little, and opened the door. . . .

Mrs. Heth sat toward the bay-window of a spacious bedroom, dignified by an alcove and bright but for the half-drawn shades. It was observed that she wore her second-best robe de chambre, and was otherwise not dressed for the inspection of the best people. So indifferently was her fine hair caught up atop her head that the round purplish spot on her temple was left plainly visible: always an ominous sign. . . .

"Good morning, mamma. I hope you're feeling better to-day?"

"Physically, I am quite well," said her mother, only half turning her head.

"Oh, I'm glad. . . . It's such a beautiful day. I hoped you would feel like going out for a drive."

"I hardly feel like going out — as yet. . . . Sit down."

Cally sat in the chair prescribed by a gesture. The eyes of the two women met for the first time since they had parted in tears. And Cally, seeing her mother's bereaved face, had to crush down a sudden almost overpowering impulse toward explanation, reconciliation at any cost. However, she did crush it down. There was nothing to explain, as mamma had pointed out in the midnight.

Mrs. Heth cleared her throat, though her voice seemed sufficiently strong.

"I understood from Flora that you were getting up this morning," said she, "so this seemed the appropriate time for me to see you, and learn something about your plans, regarding your future."

"My plans?"

"As you have so completely overthrown your parents' plans for you, I can only assume that you have others of your own."

Cally sat with her hands folded in her lap. A look of curious wistfulness flitted across her face.

"No, I have n't any special plans."

"I'm surprised to hear you say so. You surely do not expect to go on this way the rest of your natural life, do you?"

"I don't understand, mamma. Go on in what way?"

"In this way. In occupying the central position in my home, in allowing your parents to sacrifice their lives to you, in receiving lavish evidences of regard and affection which you evidently have not the slightest wish to return."

There was a considerable silence.

"I have a sort of plan there," said the girl, slowly. "I don't want you — and papa — to go on — giving me everything. I want," she said, with a slight tremor, "to take — to be just as little expense as I can after this."

"Oh! . . . Then what you want to do is to withdraw altogether from society — and go to work to earn your own living?"

Carlisle raised her eyes. "Is that what you want me to do, mamma?"

"It is not a question of what *I* want in this house any longer, it seems. . . . I am pointing out to you, Carlisle, that the independence of action you have lately taken upon yourself is a serious matter, to be looked at from more than one side. It is not becoming," said Mrs. Heth, watching her daughter's face closely, "to bite the hand that feeds you."

To this the girl had no reply. Beneath her mother's somewhat vivid metaphor, she perceived a truth, and that truth the tragic weakness of her position. But she did not know now that large books had been written about this weakness, and many more would be. . . .

Mrs. Heth having allowed the silence to continue a moment,

educationally, drew a handkerchief across her upper lip, with its strange little downy mustache, and resumed:

"With no plans of your own, you have lately thrown away the best opportunity you will ever have in your life. Now there are only two theories on which I can explain this conduct — so totally unlike your usual good sense. One is that you have permitted yourself, without my knowledge, to become interested in somebody else . . . Have you?"

"No — oh, no! . . . No, of course not."

"That I felt confident of," said mamma, though not without a certain note of relief. "Confident. . . . Yet — to touch the second point, — as you look toward the future, you do expect to marry some day, do you not?"

The daughter seemed restive under this cross-examination. She turned away from the maternal scrutiny, and, resting her arm upon her chair-back, looked toward the shaded window.

"Yes — I suppose so. . . . That seems to be all I'm fit for . . . But — since you ask me, mamma — I *would* like, in the meantime, not to be so . . . so plainly labelled *waiting*. . . . I'd like," she said, hesitatingly, "to have *one* man I meet — see me in some other light than as a candidate for matrimony."

"That," said Mrs. Heth, firmly, "will never be, so long as you retain your youth and beauty, and men retain their nature. . . .

"And why should you wish it otherwise?" continued the dominant little lady. "Despite all the loose, unwomanly talk in the air, you do realize, I see, that marriage will always remain the noblest possible career for a woman."

Cally remembered a converse of this proposition she had heard one day at the Woman's Club. She answered with light bitterness:

"When I said just now that I was fit for marriage, I meant marriage, mamma — a wedding. Of course, I'm not fit to be anybody's wife . . ." She paused, and added in a voice from which the bitterness had all gone out: "I'm not fit to be anybody's mother."

"There, there!" riposted mamma, briskly. "I think that's enough of poor Henrietta Cooney, and her wild, unsuccessful notions."

There was another brief silence; the silence of the death of talk.

"You're in a dangerously unsettled state of mind, my daughter — dangerously. But you will find, as other women have found, that marriage will relieve all these discontents. I myself," said mamma, with a considerable stretching of the truth, "went through the same stages in my youth — though, of course, I was married much younger than you. . . . Now, Carlisle, I have refused to believe that your quarrel with Hugo is irreparable."

Carlisle started as if slapped. Had mamma jerked her by a string, she could not have turned more sharply. The little general, leaning forward, swept on with hurried firmness.

"I see, of course, that you have taken your quarrel very seriously, very hard. You feel that in your anger you both said terrible things which can't possibly be overlooked. But, my child, remember that the course of true love never did run smooth. There have been few engagements which were n't broken off at least once, few marriages when the wife did n't make up her mind —"

"Mamma!" said Cally, rousing herself as from a cataleptic sleep. "You can't have understood what I told you that night. This was not a quarrel at all, in any sense —"

"I know! I understand! I withdraw the word cheerfully," said mamma, in just that tone and manner which made the strange similarity between her and Hugo. "But what I want to say, Cally, is this. Hugo is still in Washington. Willie Kerr, to whom I talked by telephone last night, had a telegram from him yesterday. Now, my child, men do not take women's angry speeches quite as seriously as you think. Hugo is mad about you. All he wants is *you* —"

"Oh, please — *please!* Don't say any more. You don't —"

"No, hear me out! See for yourself if my plan is not diplomatic and feasible, and involves no surrender of pride. I shall send Willie Kerr on to Washington this afternoon. He will go ostensibly on private business with one of the Departments, — though I will, of course, pay all expenses, — and putting up at Hugo's hotel, will meet him as if by accident. In their talk Willie, who is tact and loyalty itself, will perhaps mention your sickness, though without comment. Gradually the impression will come to Hugo that if he returns, with, of course, suitable apologies —"

"Mamma," said Cally, starting up, very white, "if you do any such thing as that I'll go away somewhere. I *will* go and earn my own living . . . I'll *go and live with the Cooneys!*"

The two women gazed at each other. Over the mother's face there spread a slow flush; the round, purple birthmark darkened. Cally spoke again, with deadly earnestness.

"I *did* think you understood about this. . . . If you persuade Hugo to walk down from Washington on his knees . . . I'll not see him."

Mrs. Heth, curiously, had been brought down in full flight: perhaps by the force of that wild upstarting, perhaps by the grisly threat about the Cooneys. Carlisle in a flare-up had always required a certain handling. The worst of the mad girl was that she was really capable of doing these unspeakable things she mentioned.

"So you refuse pointblank," said Mrs. Heth, in a muffled sort of voice, "to carry out your parents' wishes."

"About this — I *must*. I'll do anything else you want me to, anything. . . . And, mamma, this isn't papa's wish," said the girl, with some emotion. "He told me — the other night — that I mustn't think of marrying anybody I didn't care for. He said he had never thought the same of Hugo —"

Then mamma smote the flat arm of her morris-chair, and sprang up, exploding.

"*That's it!* Shove it off on your poor, generous father! . . . How characteristic of your whole behavior! Why, you ought to be *ashamed* to mention your father's name!" cried mamma; and, indeed, Cally was, though for reasons not known to her mother. . . .

Mrs. Heth walked the floor, in the grip of those agonies which the defeat of her will brought her in poignant measure. It may be that her faith in her diplomatic plan had never been triumphantly strong. Now, certainly, her purposes were punitive only, and her flowing sentences well turned to her desire. . . .

"You suppose your father's overjoyed to have his delightfully *independent* daughter thrown back on his hands — of course!" she was remarking. "True, you've heard him say a thousand times that he was going to sell his business as soon as you married and buy himself a place in the country and begin to have some pleasure of his own. But, of course, that was only his little joke! Yes, yes!" said mamma, brandishing her arms. "What he really wants is to go on slaving and toiling and worrying his heart out to keep you in pampered idleness and luxury, indulging your lightest whim without regard —"

"Mamma, mamma! — do, please!" the girl broke in. "If papa has been working so hard on my account — and I did n't know that — then I don't want him to do it any more. I wish he would sell —"

"Oh, I 've no patience with your deathbed repentances! Don't you know your father's involved in serious worries at this moment, entirely on your account? Do you think a few dramatic speeches from you can undo —"

"Worries on my account? No, I did n't know of any . . . What worries?"

Cally had stood listening with a kind of numbed listlessness, ready to go at the first opportunity, now that the real purpose of the interview was discharged. But suddenly she perceived a new pointedness in her mother's biting summaries; and she turned, with a slightly startled look in her eyes.

Her mother returned the gaze with savage sarcasm.

"Oh! You never heard of the Labor Commissioner and his hired character-assassin, I suppose! Never —"

"Yes, but I did n't know any of that was on my account."

"No, no, indeed! You thought it was just a little whim of your father's to keep his factory in a condition that 's been a scandal in the community. Fighting off legislation — bribing inspectors — just his little bits of eccentric self-indulgence. You thought that ten thousand dollars I gave to the Settlement grew on a tree, I suppose. You —"

"Mamma," said Cally, in a strained voice, "what on earth are you talking about? I want to understand. What did that money you gave to the Settlement have to do —"

"Don't you *know* he needed it for his business?" cried mamma, advancing menacingly. "I tell you he'd put it by to spend it on the Works this fall, and stop these attacks on him. And why did I have to take it from him, but on *your* account, miss? — to try to clear the family name from the scandal you brought upon us—"

"*What?*"

"A scandal," continued mamma, in a crescendo sweep, "that all but undid my lifework for the family's position, and that may yet cost your father his presidency at the bank."

The good lady easily saw that she had struck the right punitive note at last. Indeed, the question now, Cally's peculiarities being considered, was whether she had not struck it rather too hard. The girl's face had suddenly become the color of paper. The intense concentration of her gaze was painful in its way, slightly disconcerting to mamma.

"Do you mean," said Cally, in quite a shaky voice — "do you say that papa — meant to improve the Works *this fall* — and that you — that I —"

"I mean exactly what I say," said Mrs. Heth, resolutely. "And I say it's high time you were beginning to understand your position in this family, as a guide to your strange behavior. Do you suppose your father enjoys being under attack all the time? Haven't you heard him say a hundred times, that it was bad business to let things go at the Works? Where were you six years ago when he said we'd have to economize and put up a new building, and I prevented him for your sake, arguing that you were just coming out and were entitled to —"

"*Six years!. . .* Why . . . why, then I'm responsible for it *all ! . . .* Why — *I've been on his back all the time !*"

"I'm glad you realize it at last. . . . Oh, well!" said her mother, throwing out both hands and speaking with a kind of gruff tolerance, — "there's no use to *cry* about it."

"I'm not crying," said Cally.

She was, indeed, not crying as her mother had usually seen her cry; not with storm and racking. Nevertheless, two indubitable drops suddenly glittered upon the gay lashes, and now fell silently as Cally spoke.

"But I could cry," said she, "I'm so happy . . . I'm so glad, to know it's all been my fault . . .You don't know . . . I went to the Works the other day —"

"Oh, you did!" said her mother, bitterly, but enlightened a little. "And have been criticizing your father, I suppose, the father who has sacrificed —"

"He'll forgive me . . . He *must*. I'll find a way."

Mrs. Heth, flinging herself down in her chair again, said in a voice full of sudden depression: "I should say you owed him apologies, for that among other things. . . . Well, I give you up."

Cally stood unmoving, slim hands locked behind her head, staring toward the window. Gone was the albatross from her young neck, melted the cloud from the azure round. Wisdom had come with such startling unexpectedness that she could not take in all that had happened to her just now. But all that mattered was as plain and bright as the sunshine waiting for her out there. She, and not papa whom she had so wronged in her thoughts, had made the bunching-room what it was; she, and nobody else, should make it better after this. And through the splendid confusion of sensations that, mounting within, seemed to float her away from this solid floor, she heard one clear voice sounding ever louder and louder. It was the voice of the prodigal, chastened and penitent: "*I will arise and go to my father.*"

Cally turned toward the door.

Her mother, stirring from her heavy rebuking apathy, said: "Oh, there's no use bothering him now to say you're sorry. You've not thought of him all these years . . ."

"That's why I can't wait — now," said Cally. "And besides, there's something else I want to speak to him about . . . A — a business matter."

Mamma demanded an explanation. And Cally, pausing briefly at the door, turned upon that censorious gaze a face radiant as the morning.

"I'm going to give him my fifty thousand dollars to build a new Works with. . . . Won't you please help me make him take it?"

But what her mother may have replied to this request failed to overtake Cally, flying down the hall to the telephone. . . .

The bedroom conference, it was seen, had not been wholly fruit-less, after all. Mrs. Heth's last stand for Hugo — like Hugo's last afternoon — had taken a slant not anticipated by her, but at least wholesome and moral in its effects. Cally's dreaded accusing interview in the study gave place, beyond all imagin-ing, to an unpremeditated outpouring by telephone, in which her chief fear was only of making a perfect little silly of herself. And lastly, Mr. Heth, called summarily from a directors' meeting at the Fourth National Bank, was overflowed with such a wave of feminine incoherence and emotionalism as he found great difficulty in associating with his usually self-contained little daughter. . . .

Papa indeed, knowing nothing of any conference or of any dark cloud either, was treated to the astonishment of his life. When he finally understood that the house was not in flames, or his wife stricken with a deadly malady, when he began to get some notion of what all the strange pother was about, his replies, for the most part, took the following general directions: (1) that little Callipers was out of her mind with her sickness, did n't know what she was talking about, crazy, and the greatest little goose that ever was; (2) that she had no business ever go-ing to the Works, but that was all right now, and he did n't want to hear another word about it; (3) that he could n't stop to talk such foolishness in business hours, and she'd better go and lie down and rest and get her senses back; (4) that he gave her that money for herself, and when he got dependent on his little daughter, he'd let her know; (5) and that there, there, not to bother him now, we'd see, after lunch. . . .

Sufficiently vague replies these; yet they seemed to leave the daughter in no doubt whatever that the matter which had all in a moment become dear to her heart was as good as settled. For when papa terminated the conversation by smartly ringing off, she immediately called another number: Jefferson 4127, this one was, which, as the book shows (only she did not look at the book) is the number assigned to Meeghan's Grocery, down by the old Dabney House. . . .

However the untutored voice at Meeghan's reported that Doctor was out on his rounds and not to be reached before one o'clock. So Cally had to defer for a little while the happiness she would have in telling the lame wanderer across her path that, after all, his eyes had not put their trust in her in vain.

Later she sat again on a revolving seat at Gentlemen's Furnishings, eagerly purchasing shirts, cost not exceeding one dollar each, for James Thompson, aged thirteen, of up-country. It happened to be her work to do in the world, and she was doing it.

She was waited upon at the popular counter by Miss Whirtle herself, whom Cally remembered by figure if not by name; and she was so extremely agreeable and mollifying in her manner that the Saleslady's arrogance thawed away, and they were soon discussing questions of neck-sizes and sleeve-lengths in the friendliest intimacy. There were collars and neckties purchased, too, — these items Cally added on her own account, being in the vein of making presents to people to-day, — and here Miss Whirtle's taste was invaluable in assisting one to decide which were the nobby shapes and swell patterns and which the contrary. The robust one patted her transformation many times at Miss Heth, invited her at parting to call again; and later on — that night, it was — reported the whole conversation in detail in the Garland dining-room, imparting, we need not doubt, her own witty flavor to it all.

In Baird & Himmel's Cally met several other acquaintances, and finally Evey McVey, who was delighted to see her out again, but seemed to be examining her rather curiously, doubtless with reference to Hugo and what had happened in that quarter. Evey herself complained of being tired; so Cally drove her second-best friend to the McVey residence in the car, but pleaded duties at home against getting out for a little visit.

And then, bowling homeward in the brisk airs, she could return to her own thoughts again, which, as by the rubbing of an Aladdin's lamp, had suddenly become so happy and so absorbing.

Later, she must think about mamma, and with what time and solaces she could close that breach. But in these hours her thought was all for her father, whom she seemed just to be beginning to understand for the first time in her life. . . .

Now all the imaginative dreads and nightmare terrors were faded away, and she felt beneath her feet the solid sanity of Hugo's self. She had seen the Works on an exceptionally bad day; she had gone there, overdrawn and ignorant, looking for horrors; what she had actually seen and felt had been mysteriously intensified a hundredfold by her violent encounter with Colonel Dalhousie. For all that she knew, to this very moment, the Works might be, indeed (as the beautifully tactful girl Corinne had said), the best place to work in town.

But what Cally was thinking now was that, in sitting in judgment on her father, she had blindly judged him as if he were a free man — she, of all people, who had felt so poignantly the imprisoning powers of a groove. Now it appeared, as by a sudden light upon him, that papa had always been clamped fast in a groove of his own, exactly as she had been; a groove fixed for him by his place in society, by the way other men ran their cheroot factories, — for, of course, papa must do as his competitors did, or be crowded out, and the hardest-driving, meanest man set the pace for the kind ones, like papa, — and last and chiefly by the extravagances of a wife and daughter who always cried "give, give," and didn't care at all where the gifts came from. How could papa possibly be free with two costly women on his back all the time? . . . Strange that she hadn't grasped all this clearly, the minute she had recognized herself as a horse-leech's daughter. . . .

Now the first thing to do, obviously, was to get off papa's back at once. Her fifty thousand dollars would be a sound starter there; of course papa would take it, since she wanted him to so much. And her mind, as she drove, kept recurring to this symbol, kept bringing up pictures of the new Works that would be, built perfect with her money. She saw it considerably like the beautiful marble palace of her childhood's thought, the pride of Canal Street without, and within wonderfully clean, spacious and airy, and most marvellously fragrant. In this new palace of labor, faints and swoons were things undreamed of. Trim, smiling, pretty girls, all looking rather like French maids in a play, happily plied their light agreeable tasks; and, in especial, the cheeks of poor Miller (who had stoutened gratifyingly) were observed to blossom like the rose.

Yet the creator of all these wonders was well aware that she was not giving her dowry to Miller, exactly. . . .

Descending from the car at her own door, Cally encountered Mr. Pond, of the Settlement. The dark-faced Director was loafing, oddly enough, on Mrs. Mason's steps, which had once been Mr. Beirne's, four doors from home. He raised his hat about two inches at the sight of her, returned his watch and some typewritten papers to his pocket, and came forward.

"Don't run," said he, unsmiling. "I want to know plainly whether or not you are coming to my meeting to-morrow. Yes or no."

Cally laughed gaily. There was a radiance within her, and she liked this man increasingly. Several times they had met, since their antagonistic talk at the Settlement; and in the blunt Director's manner she had lately observed that creeping change which she had witnessed in men as stalwart, before now. . . .

"Don't look so fierce," said she, "for I'll not be bullied. Or at least not till you explain why you're hanging around in front of the neighbors' at twelve o'clock in the morning — you who always pretend to be so frightfully busy."

"Waiting for Vivian. And I am busy, confound him. . . . Not too busy, as you see, to take a kind interest in your welfare —"

"Oh! . . . Is Dr. Vivian *there* — at the Masons'? Why, what are *you* waiting for him for?"

"Seems to me you ask a good many questions for an idler."

He stood on the sidewalk, looking up at her with his hawk-eyes, a man yet in the early thirties, but of obvious power.

"We're going to buy second-hand benches, if you must know," continued he. "He says he can show me where to get 'em cheap. Anything else?"

"No-o — except . . . How much will the benches cost? Perhaps I — might be able to contribute something —"

"I don't want your old money," said Pond. "When are you going to be serious about serious things?"

"I think now," said Cally . . . "Only, you see, I don't know anything at all."

"I'll teach you," said the Director.

Cally, standing on the broad white slab before her own door, did not answer. Her glance had turned down the street: and at this moment there emerged from the Masons' door the tall figure of V. Vivian, the article-writer, who would never have to put anything in the papers about papa now. He saw her instantly, and over his somehow strange and old-fashioned face there broke a beautiful smile. He lifted his hat high, and, so holding it at height, posed as if for a picture, gave it something like a wave, as in double measure of greeting and good-will. A proper salutation from friend to friend; and the sunlight gleamed on his crisp fair hair. . . .

Cally's return greeting was somewhat less finished. She gave the lame doctor one look of brilliant sweetness; and then she said to him, "Oh, how do you do?" — in a voice that he could not possibly have heard. Next she said, "Yes, I'll be at the meeting to-morrow," with her back turned squarely toward Mr. Pond. And then she opened her door and went in quite quickly, leaving the Director staring intently at a crack in the sidewalk. . . .

Within, Cally perceived that she had acted rather unreasonably, missing the opportunity to tell Mr. V. V. that she desired to speak with him: but that, of course, was only because she had not wanted to interrupt and detain two busy men at their labors. The oversight, besides, was easily to be remedied; though she did not again send the clear call for Meeghan's. She decided to write a brief note instead, and did, asking her friend if he could come and give her his help about a matter — say at four o'clock that afternoon. The note was dispatched, not by old Moses this time, but by the hand of an urchin in a blue uniform, who was deep in "Lady Helen, the Fair Ghoul," as he bicycled, but apparently reached his destination in due course.

And V. Vivian, once again, was not disobedient to the heavenly summons.

XXXII

Time's Jests, and now the Perfect Apology, to stand a Lifetime in Brick and Stone; concluding with a Little Scene, which she will remember while she lives.

SHE had called him untruthful once for speaking the truth about the Works. Now she would make her apology due, to stand a lifetime in brick and stone. This Cally did for the man of the slums to-day; and this she meant him to understand without much speech, since speech, in the circumstances, would be somewhat difficult.

But then, of course, she could know nothing of those colloquies Mr. V. V. had had in his time with O'Neill, the hard-joking Commissioner, of inner conflicts he had had of late all by himself. Nor did she even take it in how far her advancing thought of him, and of all this subject, had outrun anything she had ever put into word or deed before. So she was far from imagining what a miracle she made for him this afternoon, like a midsummer dream come true; far from guessing how he, with his strange unconsciousnesses, would think of it all as just a beautiful but detached happening, a glorious coincidence. . . .

He wore for this meeting, not his holiday raiment of blue, with the sprigged waistcoat that his Uncle Armistead might have left him, but that selfsame suit she had seen upon him all last year; including that other memorable day in her life when she had come clicking down the stairs to find the tall outlander standing here in her familiar background. Only there was no feeling in her now that he was an alien in the Heth drawing-room. No, here V. Vivian seemed to belong to-day, the best and worthiest thing in the room.

To her, that was; but it was not so with others. The one speck in the perfect balm was that, to have this man here at all, she had had to manage it secretly, as if it were something discreditable. . . .

The greetings were over; they were seated; he was advised that it was about a building matter that she desired his help; and even when, as talk progressed, she placed her building lot for him at Seventeenth and Canal Streets, the doctor's manner, which was quite eager and interested and pleased at being summoned for help, showed no signs of understanding.

"Seventeenth and Canal Streets," he repeated, alert and businesslike. "Yes? It's to be a business building, then?"

"There's a building there now, but I'm going to pull that one down," said Cally. "I don't like it."

And at this moment it was that she saw consciousness burst into the unconscious; burst with the strong suddenness of an explosion.

"*Seventeenth and Canal Streets!* . . . That's the Heth Works corner!"

"That's the building I'm going to pull down. I — I've taken a dislike to it."

The tall young man came to his feet, slowly, as if hoisted from above by an invisible block and tackle. All in a moment, his face had become quite pale.

"What do you mean?" he asked, in a queer clipped voice.

"I mean . . . I don't think you will have to say anything about my father in your articles. . . . We're going to build a new Works — *now!*"

He stood staring a second like a man of stone; and then turned abruptly from her and walked away. But in that second she saw that his petrifaction was already scattering, and his face wore the strangest look, like a kind of glory. . . .

So Cally thought that he understood now; and that was all the reward she wanted. Sitting silent, she looked after his retreating back. She perceived, with a queer little twitching in her heart, that the polished spaces upon Mr. V. V.'s right elbow had thinned away into an unmistakable darning. And then it came over her quite suddenly that the reason he wore this suit to-day was probably that he had given his blue suit away, to one of his sick. She seemed quite sure that that was it. And oh, how like him, and like nobody else in the world, to give away his best one, and keep the patches for himself. . . .

And the first thing that he said, returning to her after his thunderbolt surprise, seemed also beautifully characteristic of his strange faiths.

"Well, it's wonderful," said he, in quite a natural voice. "Of course, the greatest thing that will ever happen to me. . . . And yet — it may seem strange to you — but I've felt all along — I've *felt* — that something like this might probably happen any time."

Moved as she was, Cally could have smiled at that. But when she saw the intense honesty of his face, which still wore that half-startled yet shining look, the look of a man with a sudden secret all his own, she did not smile, and her own thought was given quite a new course.

"Perhaps you're a nice sort of mind-reader," said she, gently, "for you were right to feel that way, at least as far as my father is concerned. I specially wanted you to know about that. Papa has been planning for six years to put up a new building — only last month he had arranged to spend quite a lot of money in repairs. I just came to understand all this to-day. The trouble has been," said Cally, looking up at the old family enemy with no sense of hesitation or reluctance — "I've always been too expensive, you see. I've never left him any money to carry out his plans. . . ."

She would not say anything about horse-leech's daughters, not, of all things, wanting to embarrass him to-day. But possibly his mind filled in a hiatus here, and there was no mistaking that what she said about her father impressed him profoundly.

"I . . . I really seem to have known. You might call it a sort of — of premonition — if you wanted to . . . Though you'll naturally not think I've acted that way."

Mr. V. V. stood by a spindly table, carefully examining a small but costly vase, the property of Mr. Heth, of the Cheroot Works; and now he went on with a kind of diffident resolution, the air of one who gives a confidence with difficulty, but must do so now, for his honor.

"You may remember my telling you once that I was — was sorry to write the factory articles you just mentioned. The truth

is I've hated to write them — especially as to — as to the Works.
. . . It's just the sort of thing I've wanted for a long time to
write, too. I had the argument thought out down to the bone.
Oh, they're good. . . . I — I was going to send the first lot to the
'Chronicle' this week. . . . And yet — well, it's been pulling
against the grain somehow, every line of the way. It seemed
strange . . . And now I see that I must have felt — known —
all along . . . But," said the strange young man, setting down
the vase and hurriedly running his fingers through his hair, "I
— I realize that this must sound most unconvincing to you.
Probably foolish. No matter. . . ."

But Cally felt by now that she understood him better than
he understood himself.

"No, I think I understand," said she. "And if you had n't felt
that way — don't you see? — it never would have happened."

He turned on her another strange look, at once intensely interested and intensely bewildered. But she glanced away from
it at once, and would give him no chance to ask her what that
might mean.

"I've got so much I want to tell you, so much I want to ask
your advice and help about," said she, rising, with a change to
what she regarded as an excellent business voice and manner.
"Perhaps we ought to go into executive session at once — and
let's go into the library, too! I know you're awfully busy, but I
do hope you've come prepared to make a good long visit."

The article-writer neglected to reply at all, moving after her
with his queer, startled look. . . .

So these two passed from the Heth drawing-room to the Heth
library, to talk about business: the new Heth Works, in fine.
They came into a room which was intimately and poignantly
associated with Hugo Canning. Memories of the departed
greeted Cally upon the threshold, and thereafter; only they were
not poignant now. Hugo's face kept rising mistily beside the
so different visage of the man he had instinctively disliked, his
ancient hoodoo. . . .

This was to be a meeting like none other Cally had ever had
with the stranger in her house, a *happy* meeting, troubled by no

shadow. They sat down across the great table from each other, in
good business style, as she considered; and then she began to talk
eagerly, recounting to him without any embarrassment, though
of course with some judicious expurgation, what had been going
on in her mind, and out of it, during the last five days; beginning with the afternoon she had seen him at the Cooneys', and
culminating with the long talk she had had with her father at,
and after, luncheon to-day.

And he, the only confidant she had ever had, sitting with his
patched elbow on her father's table, and his chin in his cupped
hand, attended every word with his singular quality of interest.
He was unique among all the people she had known, in that
the things he seemed to care most about were never things for
himself at all. . . .

"So that's how it stands now," said Cally, presently. "My
father was naturally surprised at first, as I've never shown any
interest in his work before, and of course he said he would n't do
it, — would n't take my money, I mean, though it's really his
all the time. But at last I did get him to talking about it seriously,
and then he grew more and more interested. . . . Oh, I know he's
going to do it! I *know* it! — That's all settled! And I do think
he'll let me have a hand in really planning it — that is, if I can
show him that I — I know anything about it. . . . Well, of course
I *don't*, you see — nothing, nothing! — and that's where my
problem begins. I've got to learn everything, from the very start,
and do it quickly. . . . Do you think I possibly can? —"

"*Books!*" he cried, throwing out both hands. "What're they
for but to teach us everything, *right away?* . . ."

In fact, her problem there was really no problem at all, it
seemed. Pond himself had at hand a fine little general library
on all these subjects; there was the State Library; there were
the bookstores of the world: all waiting for her, all packed with
meaty information. Perhaps, just as a starter, she would let
him make out a sort of preliminary check-list to-night, out of
catalogues, out of some bully advertisements in the backs of
Pond's works. . . .

"Oh, you *are* nice!" exclaimed Cally. "You can't guess what it means to be encouraged! . . . I do so want to go into it seriously."

He talked further, indicating the procedure: first her own idea of what she wanted; then an architect to sketch some plans; then a builder to figure after the architect. The thing began to shape up, rapidly, definitely. She found him an inspiriting soul. . . .

"I ought to say," she explained, quite excited, "that I mentioned fifty thousand dollars only because that was the sum I happened to have, in a lump. But we're going to make it *good*, no matter what it costs. I have a little more money of my own," said she, "about eight thousand dollars, and of course I'll put that in, too. And I know my father will feel the same way."

But no, V. V.'s belief was that the sum she mentioned would be far more than necessary. She could get a rough sort of estimate at once, if desired, given the dimensions of the lot and a general idea of the style of building she wanted. His friend, Jem Noonan, he who was just now starting out as a contractor, would be only too delighted to do some figuring on it.

"Of course the best way of all to gather ideas at the start," said he, staring through her, "is to go to the Works — go often. . . . There's no other such way of seeing what the actual needs are."

"Yes . . . Yes, of course that's true," said Cally.

But what she felt like saying was that she did n't want to go to the Works at all, unless he could go with her.

"I want to get *your* ideas now, please," she added — "everything you can think of. You can't have any notion how ignorant I am. . . . But — oh, there's one thing I wanted to speak to you about first. I suppose — even at the best — it would be some time before the new building could begin?"

Oh, a few months, no doubt, before all plans would be ready, and her father's arrangements made to move.

"Do you think the floors in this old building are very *strong*? The man who was with me the day I went there did n't seem to think so — and I did n't either! And some very heavy-looking

464

new machines were being put in the bunching-room, and I believe some more are going to be put in to-morrow."

"Oh! . . . You mean you think they might overload the floor?"

"Don't you?"

"Well — it's possible," admitted Mr. V. V., slowly, and one could see that he did n't altogether like the idea of anybody's criticizing Mr. Heth's conduct of his business. "But — ah — really I don't —"

"Could n't we fix it, in some simple way — brace up the floor somehow?"

"Oh, yes. You'd have no trouble in fixing it . . . Far as that goes."

"Don't you think you could manage to say *we* once?"

"Oh!" said Mr. V. V., pleased. "I could that! . . . I did n't know, you see, how far you cared to let me in."

Cally smiled at him over the library table.

"Has n't it occurred to you that you are in it, that you've been right in the middle of it all along?"

He gave her one of his original looks, and said: "Well, I can't say it had. . . . But it's where I'd rather be than anywhere else in the world."

"You can make nice speeches, at any rate. . . . Do you know you're the strangest man, I believe, that ever lived?"

"No, that's news. Am I? . . . Well, in what way am I so strange?"

"Oh, it's a long, long story. But I'm going to tell it all to you some day. . . . Do go on and help me about the floors. Papa won't. He did n't seem to like my speaking about them at all. He says they'd hold hundreds more machines if he only had the room —"

"Well, he *knows*. . . . He's — he's had the strain figured out. Of course."

So had Time, the master-humorist, reversed positions between Heths and Vivians. The old Arraigner, for his part, seemed to feel now that, to all intents and purposes, papa *had* put up the building six years ago. . . .

But Cally explained how floors and machines had got upon her nerves. This was, she said, *our* first point to settle. And thereupon the young man at once addressed himself to the question of remedies; sketching with his finger on the table-top, till she got note-paper and pencils from mamma's desk in the corner, switched light into a reading-lamp, and came and sat down beside him. On the paper V. V. obligingly produced an outline of the three floors of the present factory, accurately locating stairway and elevator shaft; even the point where the cloakroom was to be knocked out to give the space needed for the new machines. . . .

"How in the world do you know so much about the Works?"

"Oh — well, you see, the shipping clerk there is quite a friend of mine," said V. V. "A very nice fellow, sort of a Lithuanian, named Dolak. Don't be offended, but I — I've been down there once or twice at night."

However, he seemed stumped as to the best method of support, admitting that it was not so simple as it seemed. And presently, when he had tried and condemned columns from floor to floor, the girl said, hesitatingly:

"Dr. Vivian, do you think props — outside — would do any good?"

He turned his intent gaze upon her; he was frowning absorbedly and looking rather doubtful about it all.

"I mean iron braces running from the ground on each side of the building," said Cally — "and holding up girders, or whatever you call them, under the bunching-room floor?"

He gazed a moment, and then exclaimed:

"Oh — good! *Oh, that 's good!* . . . That would do it — do it perfectly! . . .

He proceeded with eagerness to sketch in her square-arch braces under his bunching-room floor, and he said again: "Perfect solution! . . . Why, you ought to have been a builder!"

"Oh, I — just happened to see a picture of something like that in the encyclopædia this afternoon."

Her tone was depreciatory, not suggesting that she had looked some time before she happened to see that picture. But within she was feeling the strangest, the most exhilarating thrills . . .

Oh, the dearness of being a *fellow-worker;* of praise that had nothing to do with a candidacy for matrimony! . . .

"But the difficulty," she said, "is to persuade papa to let me do it. Of course, I've no right to expect him to take me seriously. . . . I know *you* could persuade him."

That, spoken impulsively, she hurriedly covered up in conversation; begging him to go on at once and give her his ideas of what the new building should be like. She had gathered by now, that, whatever he considered wonderful in all this, it was not the fact that he, she, and her father should be, so to say, planning it shoulder to shoulder. But this fine unconsciousness of his she herself could not match; not at least till she had had more time to smooth things over with her father. . . .

However, talk of mere temporary repairs in condemned old buildings was quickly swallowed in plannings for the splendid new. Here the man from the outskirts indubitably shone; he bristled with illuminating ideas. He, it seemed, was for a four-story building, brick, with concrete floors. Much he had to say on the subject of fire-escapes and patent-doors, lunch-rooms and rest-rooms with lockers, enclosed stairways and elevator shafts; shower-baths, too, if one simply must have the best and never mind the expense. And then his pencil began unconsciously to work as he went along; and presently there emerged upon a fresh sheet of mamma's best note-paper the first visible presentment of the Works that would be. There it actually *was*, for you to gaze at, dream over; the perfect apology: the front and side elevation of a fine, dignified, business-like building, plain yet undeniably handsome, very substantial and roomy, very full of airy windows. Not like a marble palace, after all; but a child could see that nobody was ever crowded in there, nobody ever the least faint. Nothing homicidal here, Mr. V. V., look where you will. . . .

"You can *draw*, too!"

"Straight lines," said V. V., modestly. But he regarded his handiwork with passionate approbation, and finished it off gallantly with a flag flying from the roof and two stately motor-trucks (so he said) wheeling by the door.

"Oh, how beautiful!" cried Cally Heth.

And it was all so curiously exciting to her, so intensely interesting. No prospect in her life, it seemed, had ever stirred her like this strange one; a new cigar-factory, born of her purse and heart. . . .

Once, about at this point, the young man threw out with mysterious delight:

"I'll like to see old Sam O'Neill's face, when he hears about this."

In the midst of the animated talk came Annie, the parlormaid — and Cally started at the sound of the approaching feet, and hated herself for it — to say that Dr. Vivian was wanted at the telephone. The doctor seemed annoyed by the summons, though not surprised; he had had to take the liberty, he explained as he rose, of leaving word at his office where he could be found, in case of necessity — words of this sort being left, as we know, with his paid assistant, Mrs. Garland, the world's biggest office-boy.

So V. Vivian was led away by Annie to the downstairs telephone in the butler's pantry; whence he was back in a moment, looking relieved, and assuring Miss Heth that it was nothing in the least urgent or important. There was no hurry at all, it seemed. But Cally felt that the business talk was drawing to a close, with a good deal still left unsaid. . . .

Returning with eager interest to his drawing, Mr. V. V. fell to planting shade-trees of the best quality all down the Seventeenth Street side of the new building. So engaged, he observed suddenly:

"Don't worry any more about those floors, please — will you? That's all going to work out very nicely. . . . I'll get a figure from Jem Noonan right away on that plan of yours. And I'll see that it's a low figure, too, — it's got to be low! . . . Good heavens!" said V. V., eyeing his drawing with a queer little introspective smile. "We can't be expected to spend anything much on a building that's going to come down in a couple of months, you know."

She looked, smiling a little, too, at his unconscious face, fine to thinness, which had once made Mr. Pond think of a bishop who never grew up. And her look became suddenly full of tenderness. . . .

"I don't worry," said Cally, "now that I've got you to help me."

The man from the Dabney House spoke again:

"I was just thinking, out there at the telephone, that if there's no further business before the house, you might feel like beginning that long story you — you spoke of just now."

That took her by surprise. She seemed to be less and less at her ease. But now surely had come her moment to take her courage in her hands, and render him his due.

"I believe I ought to," said she, lightly — "a chapter or two, at least. For I don't think you'll ever work it out for yourself . . . And I'm glad you're that way."

He made no reply, going on carefully with his arbor-day practice.

"When you said just now that this was wonderful," said Cally, beginning to lose the light touch already — "you meant that it was a wonderful happening, did n't you? Your idea seems to be that all this just happened."

But no, Mr. V. V. denied that vigorously, and stated his logical theory: that her father had chanced to postpone his intentions, merely through the well-known fact that men get accustomed to conditions that they constantly see; but that she, going there with fresh eyes . . .

"I might have gone there a hundred times, but I'd never have thought of it as having anything to do with me — don't you know it? — if it had n't been for you."

He looked at her briefly; and she saw that his look was as bewildered as a battle-ground.

"Oh! . . . Do you mean that you *are* doing it because of — to — to avoid the — that is, on account of the articles?"

"Oh, *not* the articles! — *no!* That's just what I don't mean. I've never thought of the articles! I don't think of you that way at all . . ."

She stopped precipitately, somehow divining that she was mysteriously wounding him. And then suddenly she understood that that *was* the way he thought of himself, exactly; that he, who unconsciously moved mountains by his gentleness, somehow saw himself only in the light of his "terrible" (but still unpublished) articles. It was as if he reckoned himself as either an article-writer, or nothing. . . .

"Though it's true," said Cally, gently, with hardly any pause at all, "that through most of the time I've known you I've thought of you . . . as a hard man . . . terribly uncompromising."

His, it was clear, was not a tongue that spoke easily about himself. He finished putting a flower-box into the window of the new Works, before he said:

"I hope we need n't trouble now about anything at all that's past."

"That's what I hope, too . . . more than you could. And besides — I've always liked you best when you were gentle. And . . . it's because of what you've taught me — at those times — that I'm doing this to-day."

Again he turned his singularly lucid gaze full upon her; and now his look was absolutely startled. Color was coming into his face. His short, crisp hair, which had been parted so neatly an hour ago, stood rumpled all over his head, not mitigating the general queerness of his appearance. And yet his mouth wore a smile, humorous and disparaging.

"May I ask what you consider that I've taught you?"

"Everything I know," said Cally, lacing a pencil between her fingers.

"Why! . . . When we've never even had a real talk about it before! . . . I told you once that you were more generous than —"

"No, I'm never generous enough. That's my trouble, among others. . . . But if you think that it's a nice and happy thing for us to be putting up this building, I want you please always to remember . . . that you've done it all yourself."

There was a tense silence, out of which his voice spoke, no longer with any trace of humor.

"Don't be polite. . . . I could n't quite stand it. Do you mean that?"

"It's all a failure if you won't believe that I do."

"Then I do believe it."

This time the silence ran somewhat longer, and again it was V. V.'s voice, greatly stirred, that broke it.

"I don't understand, but I do believe it. . . . And it makes me pretty proud. By George, pretty proud! . . . Why — I 've talked a lot — but it's the first thing I've ever accomplished! *The first thing. . . .*"

His voice showed that his mind had swept away from her, over spaces; and Cally raised her eyes and looked at him. He sat gazing wide-eyed into the dull-green glow of her lamp, on his face a curious and moving look; a look humbled yet exalted, gloriously wondering, and to her the wistfullest thing she had ever seen in her life. He, who had given away his patrimony, who was giving away his life every day with a will, thought that this was the first thing . . .

All that was sweetest in the girl, all that was maternal and understanding, rose fiercely within her, stormed her with a desire to mother this man, to protect him from his own royal yet somehow infinitely sad self-denials. For this moment she felt far stronger than he. His hand, with the pencil in it, lay on the table close by her, and Cally closed her slim fingers over it with a firm clasp.

"Ah, don't say that, Mr. V. V. — don't look that way. It hurts me, in my heart. . . . Can't I make you believe that you've accomplished more than anybody else in the world? . . ."

He did not move at the shock of her touch, at the sound of his little name upon these unaccustomed lips. She was aware only of a subtle contraction, a sort of tightening going on somewhere within him. So Cally finished her small speech with her hand over his. But at just that point, a stir seemed to shake through the man; he was seen to be turning his head; and in the same breath, her moment of high strength broke abruptly. The veins fluttered queerly in the forward hand; she felt a quick flush rising somewhere within, spreading and tingling upward into her face. So Cally rose hurriedly, her hand withdrawn, and moved away. But she did her best, for her pride's sake, to

471

envelop her movement with a matter-of-fact air; and when she had got about four steps away from him, she remarked, quite distinctly:

"Don't get up. . . . I . . . want to get something."

And she did, in fact, go on to mamma's desk and attentively select three more sheets of note-paper, which would no doubt come in handy for something or other some day.

And out of the stillness behind her came Mr. V. V.'s voice, just a little husky now:

"No one ever did anything so sweet to me before."

But that only made things worse, turning a white light, as it were, on thoughts she had had before now of the loneliness of his life. So she, finding herself not strong enough to be a comforter after all, said in a resolute kind of way:

"I never like to hear my friends depreciated. So please don't do it any more. . . . What was the name of that book about factories — the one you said that Mr. Pond had?"

Silence behind her, and then: "'The New Factory Idea,' by T. B. Halton."

She noted this information carefully on one of her sheets of paper, thus proving that she was right to go and get them, all the time.

"I thought," said she, "I might see if Saltman had it. Then I could begin to cram to-night."

But no, he said that Saltman had n't it, but would order it, of course. And then the scraping of a chair-leg advised all listeners that Mr. V. V. was violating that injunction laid upon him as to not getting up. . . .

He advanced round the table-end, his hand raised in his nervous and characteristic gesture. So anyone who wished could see that deficiency at his elbow, about which he himself seemed so splendidly indifferent. He was as tall as Hugo; but Hugo, with his lordly good looks and beautiful clothes, was certainly a much more eye-catching figure. And yet, as she straightened now and looked, the knowledge shot suddenly through Cally that this doctor in his patches somehow looked, that he had always looked, rather the finer gentleman of the two. . . .

"Johnson's the publisher," said V. V., coming to a halt in front of her. And then, taking the sheets of note-paper unconsciously from her unresisting hands, he added, looking down:

"But — how'd you mean just now . . . that I — I've accomplished so — so much?"

By now Cally could smile, in quite a natural-seeming way; and this she did, full under the prophetic gaze, revealing shining white teeth and glimpses of a rose-lined mouth. And if she was a Hun, she had always been the loveliest of them, God wot. . . .

"I'm beginning to believe," said she, "that you're not such a very strange man, after . . ."

So she ended; her gaze shifting, the smile dying on her lip. For the door of the library had opened authoritatively, and that difficulty which had embarrassed her all through the afternoon suddenly confronted her upon the threshold.

Mr. Heth, of the Works, en route to his study, was briefly surprised by the little tableau he had stumbled upon. But seeing young men about the house at all hours was no nine days' wonder for him; and he came on in with quite his usual air.

"Ah, Cally! Did n't know anybody was in here," said papa; and he glanced from her, with amiable expectancy, toward the stranger. "What's this confabulation about?"

Cally felt herself turning white. She steadied herself with one hand on the writing-leaf of the desk.

"We were talking about the new Works," said she. . . . "Papa — I want to introduce a good friend of mine — Dr. Vivian."

"Oh, Mr. Heth! . . . I'm so glad to know you, sir."

Thus the fearless young voice at her side. But Cally was gazing, transfixed, at her father, on whose face the friendly greeting air was giving place to astonished displeasure, not untouched with indignation. He had stopped short in the middle of the floor, and the hand he had been automatically putting out fell dead at his side.

"Oh! — Ah! — Dr. Vivian!" said Mr. Heth, with the stiffest inclination. And then, his look going from one to the other of the two young people, he added, as if involuntarily: "*Vivian?* . . . Ah! I'd — have expected a different-looking man!

The pause then, the suspense of all action from the world, was infinitesimal. But it seemed long to Cally. And she thought she could never forgive her father if he turned away, leaving this slight upon her friend.

"Papa," she began, unsteadily, "I don't think . . ."

But once again her sentence hung unended. V. V., advancing, came then into her line of vision; and Cally saw that he had no thought for the cover of her skirt. Her father's forbidding deportment had not escaped the young man; there were both a diffidence and a dignity in his bearing. And yet she saw that his face wore like a flower that guileless and confiding look he had, the look of a man who cannot doubt that, in their hearts, all mean as kindly as he himself. He moved upon her silent father as if singing aloud an immortal faith in the goodness of his fellows: *Though he slay me, yet will I trust him.* . . .

But what his audible voice was saying was very simple, and a little embarrassed:

"I've felt that I've just come to know you to-day, Mr. Heth . . . to understand things better. I suppose it's too much to hope that you can forget what's past, all at once. But I'd be mortified to feel . . . Ah, sir! — I've felt honored by your House to-day. . . ."

That was all; the mists lifted. He saw no difficulties, and so there were none. Papa's face was thawing back, through several surprised looks, to its natural kindliness; he had taken the offered hand, in the middle of the little speech; and then, within a minute, he was saying, quite amiably, that well, well, we'd say no more about it . . . s'posed the thing to do was to let bygones be bygones. . . .

And papa's daughter, Cally, turned away quickly from that spectacle, winking furiously, and wondering when she had got to be such a baby. . . .

Strange things had been happening of late, it seemed; strange memories gathering for backward thought hereafter; novel pic-

PAPA—I WANT TO INTRODUCE A GOOD FRIEND
OF MINE—DR. VIVIAN

tures ranging in the immaterial storehouse that opens down the years. But in all Cally's invisible collection, then or thenceforward, there was never a scene that she saw so vividly as this: herself standing silent by the newel-post in the wide hall; her father, distinct and genial in the light through the open door, observing to Mr. V. V. that hard words buttered no parsnips, as the fellow said; and V. V., half-smiling at her over papa's broad shoulder, and saying to her with his eyes that of course this was the way it was meant to be, all along.

XXXIII

Her Last Day, in this History; how she wakes with a Wonder in her Heart, has her Banquet laid at the Board of the Cooneys, dreams back over the Long Strange Year; finally how she learns Something that not Everybody Knows: what it is like at the End of the World.

A MORNING in October, and she had waked to fare forth and capture, by hook or by crook, the most eligible parti who was ever likely to swim into her ken. Another morning in October, and all her waking horizon seemed filled by the knowledge that, at half-past four in the afternoon, she would meet and talk of cheroot factories with a man so little eligible that he trusted the crows to bring his raiment. In the wide world was there another person whose life's pendulum, in a twelvemonth, had swung so wildly far?

Eight o'clock now, by the little clock on the mantel: eight hours and a half to Mr. Pond's meeting for workers at the old Dabney House. One need n't be an astronomer to calculate that. And Cally Heth lay wide-eyed in her great bed, and thought how strange, how wonderful is life. . . .

In the watches her mind had gone back and back over the long year; and she had marvelled at the tininess of turnings upon which, it was all clear now, great issues had hung. She could put her finger on time after time, last year and even this, when the smallest shifting in the course would have brought her, to-day, far otherwise. 'Had she said that, had she done this'. . . Was it all the wild caprice of Chance, then, that had no eyes? Were people so helpless, the slight sport of Luck, thistledown blowing in the winds of the gods? Ah, but she saw clearer than that. Had she not felt all along how powerfully this sequence of happening and encounter had pressed toward far other ends? And the divinity that had shaped them at last, acting and reacting and giving circumstance a soul, had been only that mysterious divinity that makes human beings what they are. There was truth in the saying that destiny is only character under its other name.

No chance here, surely, that had waked her so still and shining-eyed, such a wonder in her heart. . . .

She had marked this day for diligent study. Last night an unknown hand had left at the door a hard-used copy of "The New Factory Idea," by T. B. Halton. And Cally, at the end of a second long business conference with her father, had read three chapters of the absorbing work, and slept upon the resolve to devote this morning to it altogether. But she had seen at the first look of the flooding sunshine upon the shutters, that she did not feel studious at all. Let books look to themselves to-day. Her desire was to be outdoors; to be alone, and to muse awhile. Surely nobody ever had so much, so much, to think about.

However, as a daughter one was n't altogether free; nor yet again as a member of organized society. All day the claims of the familiar encroached upon the real world within, and thoughts, the radiant aliens, had to range themselves in as they could.

She was breakfasting with her father. They were to forage for luncheon to-day, these two, and spoke of it; he naming the club, she electing her cousins the Cooneys. And here was the token of the more cheerful atmosphere prevailing this morning in the house. Mrs. Heth was entertaining a lunch-party of seven ladies, her contemporaries, at two o'clock this day. True, the invitations had been issued before the crash: but the hopeful point, as even the servants were aware, was that they had not been recalled.

They were glad that mamma felt like seeing people again; and said so. And Cally then asked her father if he had any engagement for the evening.

Mr. Heth glanced at her over his "Post," and his glance feared that he saw yet another conference advancing upon him. Yet, it was fair to say, he had not been by any means inconvincible about the new Works. Real estate was real estate, say what you would; and it might be that the violent shake-up in the family plans had made the immediate future of the business a somewhat concrete issue.

He said, guardedly perhaps: "To-night? — let's see. . . . Well, not that I think of just now."

But Cally merely wanted to propose a table of bridge in the library, he and she against a third and fourth. And papa's changed expression said at once that that was a horse of another color.

"Well, that'd suit me . . . Suit me first-rate."

Their evening was so arranged. She warned him gaily to be on his mettle; she would pick up two of the keenest players to be found. Papa, with gathering zest, admitted that practice was what he needed, most particularly as to the bids. Had a rubber at the club Saturday night, and Carmichael and those fellows took nine dollars from her old daddy. . . .

"Let's make it a standing engagement, papa — one evening a week, the same table! . . . Oh, I'd love to! . . ."

This, too, seemed remarkably suited to her father's whim. A decidedly amiable-looking gentleman he was, with his fresh coloring, spotless waistcoat and fine blond mustaches; a home-loving man, not much used to having parties given for him.

And Cally regarded him with eyes which held new depths of affection. The last moment of the interview yesterday had brought an undreamed development, strangely endearing: her father, in the nicest way, had invited Dr. Vivian to call on him at the Works this afternoon and see the plant for himself. Part of this perfect consummation had been due, without doubt, to Vivian himself, a little, perhaps, to the direction she had artfully given the conversation; but she well knew that most of it had sprung spontaneously from the father-love which had never failed her yet. . . .

"And, Cally, hunt up that book I saw kicking around here last year," said Mr. Heth, when he rose. "If we're going to do it at all, we might as well take the thing seriously, and get the bids straight."

"I'll find it, papa. We might read up a little before dinner. I'm awfully rusty."

And then her father stood by her chair, pinching her smooth

cheek, looking down at her with an odd expression, half quizzical, half grave and speculative. So she had found him looking at her last night, as she sought to explain to him how different Dr. Vivian was from the articles he wrote, and hated. . . .

"So I'm to be on my company manners with this young man, eh? Ask him won't he please be kind enough to teach an old man how to run his business, that it?"

"I did n't say that, papa dear. . . . I feel I have n't thanked you half enough for being so sweet to me . . . about it all."

"Rather surprised at my sweetness myself. . . . Well," said Mr. Heth, musing down at the apple of his eye. "There must be something a good deal out of the common about a boy who could get you so worked up about a factory, I'll say that. . . . And he certainly looks a whole lot better 'n he writes."

He quoted something about an old dog's new tricks, kissed her with tenderness, said, "Well, if we come to blows, I'll 'phone you for help," and went off humming an air.

For Cally was not to be of the Works party this afternoon. It had stood as an ideal opportunity for the two men's better acquaintance; her presence, she had thought, might only mar it. Now, gazing after her father's departing back, she rather wished she had decided otherwise. . . .

She searched and found So-and-So's "Auction Bridge." A time passed: and she was in the big bedroom, making her peace with mamma.

She had supposed the thing to do was simply to go on, as nearly as she could, as if nothing had happened. But when she saw her mother's face, marked as from an illness, she remembered nothing of any plan. She was on her knees by the morris-chair, her arms flung about the strong little figure whose dearest hopes she had spoiled: begging mamma to forgive her for being such a disappointment and failure as a daughter, for seeming so ungrateful and unreasonable, saying that she would do anything, anything to make up for all that had gone amiss.

And mamma, already somewhat propitiated, it had seemed, by the return of the money, said presently, with some emotion of her own, that she would try to regard it as a closed episode.

She, with her tireless energies, was not one to cry forever over milk hopelessly spilt. But neither was she one to temper justice with too much mercy, and her final word on the matter was a final one, indeed: "But of course you can never make it up to me, Carlisle, never . . ." And Carlisle, rising, knew even better than mamma how sad and true this was. There was only one thing that her mother had wanted of her, and that thing she had not done. Life, even on this day of song and mist, was seen to be inexorable. . . .

She was in her room for a little while, and it came to be eleven o'clock: five hours and a half . . . While she unwisely lingered there, dreamily irresolute between a walk and a drive, she was summoned to the drawing-room by a call from Mattie Allen, not seen of her since the dinner at the New Arlington last week. Mattie stayed a long time; and before she went — of course — other callers had drifted in. . . .

"Are you going to Sue Louise's bridge to-night?" demanded Mattie, continuing to inspect her with evident curiosity.

"Oh, Mats! I forgot all about it — horrors! . . . And I've made another engagement!"

"That means you don't want to go, Cally. You know it does. . . ."

Cally confessed to a certain want of enthusiasm; asked her friend if she, too, did n't weary of their little merry-go-round at times. Nothing of the sort, however, would be admitted by Mats, who was now known to be having a really serious try for J. Forsythe Avery.

"Dear," she went on before long, "do you know you seem to be changing *entirely* lately? And toward me specially. . . . I — I've wondered a *great* deal if I've done something to offend you."

Cally embraced her; spoke with reassuring tenderness. And there was compunction in these endearments. She and Mattie had been intimate friends as long as she could remember; and now it had come over her suddenly that it would nevermore be with them quite as it had been before. Must life be this way, that greetings over there would always mean farewells here? . . .

And then Mats, quite mollified, was speaking in her artless way of Hugo Canning, who had so obviously been on her mind all along.

"People keep asking me," she said, still just a little plaintive, "and I have to say I don't know *one thing*. It makes me so ashamed. They think I'm not your best friend any more."

Cally observed that all that was too absurd. For the rest, she seemed somewhat evasive.

"I feel, dearie," said Mats, "that I *ought* to know what concerns your life's happiness. You don't know how anxious I've been about you while you were sick. . . ." If there seemed a tiny scratch in that, the next remark was more like a purr: "People say that he did something perfectly terrible, and you threw him over."

"Well, Mats, you know people always get things exactly wrong."

"Then you did n't?" demanded her best friend, with a purely feminine gleam.

And Cally, ardently wishing to be free of this subject, said gaily that Mr. Canning had thrown *her* over — the second time, too! So she had told him that she had *some* spirit, that some day he would do that once too often. . . .

"Oh, you're joking," said Mats, quite pettishly. "Dear, I *don't* care for jokes."

And then, as she gazed, not without envy, at her friend's profile, so strangely sweet and gay, she exclaimed suddenly in a shocked tone: "I believe you really did do it!"

"Whisper it not in Gath," said Cally, with shining calm. . . .

It was a belief, so mamma had cried in the midnight, which nobody outside of institutions for the feeble-minded would ever hold. But Cally was struck only with Mattie's enormous seriousness. Self-reproach filled her for the interval that seemed to lie between them. . . .

"Mats, you know I've never kept secrets from you. I'll tell you everything you want to hear about it, from beginning to end. Only — not to-day."

The kaleidoscope shifted: Mattie faded out of the purview, and in her stead sat the Misses Winton, who had helped to pass the time in Europe last year, but whose presence had a contrary effect to-day. And she wondered how they could not see for themselves what a shell of a hostess they were talking at. All her being was so far away from company: one half of her continually flowing back over the months; the rest always going forward to the afternoon, and beyond; nothing at all left here. . . .

Certainly she would tease him a little about the neat way he and papa had dropped her out of the Works. "*And I thought I was the one who was doing it, too ! . . .*"

Callers gone; and then mamma, in the vein of dignity, was inviting her opinion about the color scheme of her luncheon-table. And with what an uprush of affection she responded, what eagerness to help, to be friends again! . . . And then it was time for her to make ready for luncheon herself. One-thirty o'clock; a long day. . . .

In the May-time, once, Hugo had asked her to name a day, and she had named the seventeenth of October. And now the seventeenth was here, to-day. Her wedding-day it might have been, but for this or that: and behold, her high banquet was laid at the board of the Cooneys, cold corned beef and baked potatoes, with sliced peaches such as turn nicely from the can for an unexpected guest.

Cally was glad to be with her cousins to-day. The simple and friendly atmosphere here was mightily comfortable. Never had they seemed so poor to her, never so fine and merry in their poverty. Her heart went out to them.

They were all well now, the Cooneys, and the table was their clearing-house. There was much talk, of the new Works and other matters; great argument. Two faces were missing: Tee Wee, who pursued his studies at the University, and Chas, who was lunching from a box at his desk, snowed under with work accumulated during his sickness. In their places, however, sat Cousin Martha Heth, who was described as "very miserable" with her various ailments, but whose strength at conversation, regarding symptoms, seemed as the strength of ten.

Round Cally the Cooney talk rattled on; family jokes kept

flickering up; strange catchwords evoked unexpected laughter. The woman of all work waited spasmodically upon the table; she proved to be Lugene, none other than the girl Hen and Cally had found on Dunbar Street, that day long ago. . . . Old times; so, too, when the Major told with accustomed verve how papa, a little shaver then, had brought the note from Aunt Molly down to camp, fifty years ago. . . .

Across the table sat Looloo, the best-looking of all the good-looking Cooneys. She had lucid gray eyes, with the prettiest black lashes; and Cally found herself continually looking at them. . . . Strange how expressive eyes could be, how revealing, looking things unspoken that influenced one's whole life. Imagine somebody with eyes something like Looloo's, say, to have had totally different ones; small, glassy black eyes like shoe-buttons, for instance, or to have worn thick blue-tinged glasses, like Evey's grandmother. . . .

A hand waved before her own eyes; a voice of raillery said: "Come back!"

"I'm right here . . . What did you say?"

"You were picking flowers ten thousand miles away. 'Cause why? 'Not any, thank you,' is n't the right reply to 'Please give me the salt.'"

"She's in love," said the Major, a gallant in his day.

Cally, handing the salt to Hen, said: "I am, indeed, —with Looloo. Don't you notice that she 's getting prettier every day?"

Looloo, fair as a lily, proved that blushes made her prettier still; the Major said finely, "Praise from Sir Hubert"; and Aunt Molly, giving the same truth a sound wholesome turn, observed that Loo need n't get set up, for she 'd never be as pretty as Cally, no matter how she improved.

Cousin Martha's remark was: "But to go back to what I was saying, Cally. That Wednesday night was the worst I ever spent. . . ."

And Cally felt apologetic to her poor relative to-day, a good deal ashamed before her. Her sudden impulse had been to ask papa's old cousin to come and stay in one of the four spare rooms at home (thus permitting Chas to come down from the

Cooney attic); but she had had to put that impulse down. The Heths had not built walls around their little island for nothing . . .

They were in the limousine, she and Hen, driving down to Saltman's. Hen said she would be delighted to come in that evening, and play bridge with Uncle Thornton. She was a player of known merits, rather famous for successes with hare-brained no-trumpers. And Cally, thinking what man she should ask for Hen, discovered suddenly that her thought was going much beyond a table of bridge to-night; that what she was really planning was to marry her cousin off this year. And she found herself searching about for somebody very nice for Hen, very desirable.

"Oh, by the bye," she said, presently — "I was just thinking — do you remember that corduroy suit I had last year — striped gray, with a Russian blouse?"

Hen, it seemed, remembered this suit perfectly. And Cally said no wonder, since she had worn it till she would be ashamed to be caught in it again.

"I was wondering," said she, "if you could make it do for anything, Hen. It would honestly be a favor if you'd take it off my hands."

Henrietta swept on her a look of incredulous delight.

"Cally! . . . Why, you good old bluffer! You know perfectly well that suit's a beauty, as good as new —"

"No, oh, no! Indeed, it isn't," said Cally, quite eagerly. "You've forgotten — it's worn, oh, quite badly worn. I'll show you to-night when you come. And then you'd have to cut it down, too. . . . Only you mustn't ever wear it around me, Hen, I'm really so sick of the sight of it. . . ."

So Hen presently said: "There's no use my pretending or being coy, Cally. Oh, I'd dearly love to have it. I've been wondering what on earth I'd do for a nice suit this year. . . . Why, it's like an answer to prayer. . . ."

And what had she ever done in a human world to entitle her to be bestowing last-year's suits upon Henrietta Cooney, the busy and useful? "She's worth three of me," thought Cally, "and I've been looking down on her all this time just because they're poor. I seem to be little and mean clear through. . . ." And suddenly she saw that memories had been gathering here; that Saltman's hard-worked stenographer had grown intimate and dear. . . .

Her hand closed over Hen's, and she was speaking hurriedly:

"Hen, do you know you're a great old dear? Don't look . . . I've never told you how good you were to me this summer, when I was so unhappy, and nobody else seemed to care. . . . And since I've been back, too, helping me more than you know, perhaps. I didn't appreciate it all at the time, quite, but I do now. And I won't forget what a good friend you've been to me, what an old trump. . . ."

Hen, taken quite by surprise, turned on her a somewhat misty gaze. She answered that Cally was a darling goose; with other things solacing and sweet. And then the two cousins were parting, the one to her typewriter, the other to her ease: but both feeling that a new tie bound them which would not loosen soon.

The car started from Saltman's door, and Cally glanced at her watch: it was just three o'clock. Probably at this moment Dr. Vivian and papa were shaking hands in the office at the Works. Why, oh, why, hadn't she said that she would go, too, as she had so much wanted to do? Surely she could not have harmed that meeting; she might even have helped a little.

About her were the bustle and clangor of busy Centre Street. People hurrying upon a thousand errands, each intent upon his own business, under the last wrapping each soul alone in the crowded world. And no one knew of his brother's high adventures. Men walked brushing elbows with angels, and unaware. . . .

She had had a little sister named Rosemary, two years older than she, and very lovely in the little picture of her that papa always carried in the locket on his watch-chain. Often Cally had wished for her sister; never so much as through this day. There was one, she liked to think, whom she could have talked her heart out to, sure that she would understand all, share all. But Rosemary had been dead these twenty years. . . .

"Drive me a little, William, please . . . For half an hour, and then home. . . ."

The car went far over familiar streets that she had first seen from a perambulator. She sat almost motionless, the tangible world faded out. It was good to be alone; this was a solitude peopled with fancies. Her mind dreamed back over the long strange year, while her steadfast face was shining toward the Future.

Strange enough it seemed now; but till the other day Hugo and Dr. Vivian had hardly once met in the thoughts of Cally Heth. They had hardly met in life, never exchanged a word since the night in the summer-house: so she, untrained to discernment, had supposed that they had nothing to do with each other. Now, in the last few days, it had come to seem that these two had, in her, been pitted against each other from the beginning.

Forces not of her making had cut and patterned her life; and she, driven on by feelings which she herself had hardly understood, had crumpled up that pattern and seized the shears of destiny in her own hand. The groove she had been set and clamped so fast into ran straight as a string into Hugo Canning's arms; but she had broken out of her groove, and Hugo was gone, to cross her path no more. And her mother thought, and Hugo had said almost with his parting breath, that she had been driven to these madnesses by mere foolish femininisms, new little ideas picked up from Cooneys or elsewhere.

It was true that she had these ideas; true, too, that she was not alone with them. She had been drilled from birth to the ranks of the beguilers of men, their sirens but their inferiors; and something in her, even before this year, had rebelled at that rating of herself, dimly perceiving — as she had heard a man say once — that marriage was better regarded as a career than as a means of livelihood. She had been drilled again to believe that her happiness depended on money in quantities, things had; but then, at the first pinch of real trouble, these things had seemed to sag beneath her, and she perceived dimly, once more, that she had built her house upon something like sand. And if her particular experiences here had been unique, she had seen that her experience was, after all, a common one. As if with eyes half-opened, she had divined all about her other people making the discoveries she had made; or, better yet, knowing these truths without having to discover them. She was but one of a gathering company, men as well as women, old with young. . . .

Hugo had stood rock-like across the way she was moving. And so Hugo had lost her.

But these things seemed hardly to matter now; it all went down so much deeper. Surely it was over something bigger than her "little views" that her story-book prince had locked arms with the lame slum doctor, curiously recognized by him as an adversary at sight.

They had entered her life in almost the same hour, two men so different that she had come at last to see them as full opposites. So entering together, they had both become involved with her in the first moral problem of her life, which also began in that hour. And upon that problem each had been called, in turn, to ring his mettle. One, the fine flower of her own world, with a high respect for that world's opinions and on the whole a low esteem of the worth of a woman, had found her completely satisfying as she was. The other, a wanderer from some other planet, with his strange indifference to the world's values and his extraordinary hope of everything human, had been so passionately dissatisfied with her that he, a kind man surely, had broken out in speech that had left a scar upon her memory. And upon the stranger's shocking appraisement of her, there had, indeed, hung a tale.

There were times when it had seemed that everything she had done afterwards had been but stages of an effort, months prolonged, to shake herself free from that compassionate *God pity you*. . . .

But no; she knew it was not that way exactly. Before that night she had felt vague reachings and had put them down; and similarly afterwards. Buttressed about with her island's social security, strong in her woman's faculty for believing what she needed to believe, she could easily persuade herself, or almost, that there had been only an unfortunate misunderstanding about Jack Dalhousie, that she personally had n't done anything at all. She remembered that she had all but put the matter where it would trouble her no more. And then there had come a night when she saw that the stranger, by a certain gentleness and trust there were in him, had not been able to believe his own hard words of her. This man believed that she was good; believed it because he himself was good. And the moment of that revelation had been terrible to her. She had felt in Hen's parlor the smart of coals of fire, the strange, new shame of being trusted, but untrustworthy. So there had entered her a guilty disquiet: and afterwards, however she had struggled, however Hugo's protecting strength had compassed her about, that novel sense had kept growing through the months, steadily gathering momentum. . . .

All this was quite clear to her now. Nothing had made her tell the truth about Jack Dalhousie except that one man had expected her to. Of all that had happened to her, here was the beating heart.

No one in her life had met her on this ground before. She had been expected to be a charming woman if she could, a woman as ornamental as possible. He only had expected her to be a good woman; and something in her had found the strange call irresistible. He, by the trusting eyes he had, had put her upon her honor; not her "woman's honor," but her honor; and she, who had never had an honor before, had grown one, all for him. As long as she could remember, men had paid tribute to her in all the ways of men with maids. But he alone had put any trust in her as a free and moral being; and she had bent the high heavens and all but broken her mother's heart that he should not have trusted her in vain.

She was far, far from being a good woman. Hugo certainly was anything but a bad man. Yet, when all was said, it was her expanding desire to be good that Hugo had stood against. And the collision had destroyed him.

Was this the great mystery then, the world's secret? Was this the wish that each human being had, planted away in the deeps, overlaid and choked, forgotten, yet charged with omnipotence: *the wish to be good?* Were they all waiting for somebody to pass by, sounding the secret call, to drop all and follow? . . .

Oh, wonder, wonder, that the simple faith of one good man should have power to overthrow princes and powers! . . .

The car rolled swiftly, its windows open to the sunny day. All about were the sights and noises of city streets. But the flying panorama brought no distraction: out there, men walked as trees. There blew a light autumn wind, gently kicking at Cally's veil, waving tendrils of fine hair about her face. Unaware, suffering had laid its touch upon her; this face was lovely with a deeper meaning: and yet the young girl's April-freshness clung to her still. She was in the first exquisite bloom of her womanhood. And she sat very still in the rolling car, full of a breathless wonder at the miracle of life.

It had been the year of her spirit's Odyssey. And now, when she came at last to fair haven, marvel fell upon marvel: and the quest of her heart stood saluting her from the shore. What need had she to ponder or to justify, she who, setting out to find happiness upon the shining earth, had so strangely found it among the yet more shining stars?

Very slowly, very delicately, had knowledge unfolded within her. On a day there had been pain, and nothing. On a day there had been thrilling peace, and luminous wings beating so strong, so sure. . . .

To love; to love unasked . . .

She knew that women thought this a shame to them; she had thought it so herself. Yet could it be? Had he not taught her this, or nothing, that to give was ever a finer thing than to take? Was it a shame to love what was lovable, and fine and beautiful and sweet? Ah, no; surely the shame for her would be, knowing these things now at their value, not to love them, to hold back thriftily for the striking of a bargain. Was not here, and no otherwhere, the true badge of the inferior, to measure the dearest beats of one's heart as a prudent trader measures?

So Cally Heth, the often loved and lovely, was strong to feel on her wonderful day. Beneath the maiden's invincible reserve, under the mad sweetness of this unrest, clear upon that Future which was so enveloped in a golden haze, she felt a pride in her own human worthiness, as one who now does the best thing of her life. She had always wanted to love above her: how time and this man had invested her ideal with a richer meaning! . . . Was not this the touchstone of that change within herself she had sought, that day when Colonel Dalhousie's rod had chastened her?

Many symbols of happiness had shone and beckoned about her, and she had turned her back on all of them to follow a man in a patched coat whose power was only that he spoke simply of God, and believed in the goodness of his fellows. Over the gulf that lay between their worlds, this man had called to her: and now she had made him her last full response, which was herself. He was the saint in her life; and she had found him beneath all disguises, and laid her heart at his feet.

Home again; dreams laid by. There was action for a space. Anticipation painted the world in rose.

It was after four, by the clock on the mantel. Cally stood at the window, dressed, waiting. She was bound for a workers' meeting in a somewhat dilapidated Settlement House in the slums, which only the other day had been an abandoned hotel, for cause. And never in her vivid life had she dressed with greater care. . . .

She gazed down, upon a street which she did not see. Ten minutes past four: but twenty minutes more, out of the long day. By now, he had already left the Works for the Dabney House. . . . And she was thinking that never but once had he made a personal remark to her: when he had thought, among the hard things, that she was lovely to the eye. But all that was a long, long time ago. . . .

From the door below there issued her mother's guests, departing. Two strolled away up the afternoon street; one drove off in an open car; two stepped into an old-fashioned family carriage. Then, after a little interval, Mrs. Heth herself came out with two more women; and these three drove away in the Byrd car, which had been observed waiting down there.

Cally was alone in the house. And it was good to be alone.

There whizzed up, from the opposite direction, yet another car, jerking to a standstill at the door. It caught the girl's notice; her vague thought was that it was William, come a little early. But she saw at once that this was a strange vehicle, a hired one by the look of it, and consciousness dreamed out of her eyes again. . . .

The tide of her being pulsed strong within her now. All day her strange feeling was as if an enveloping shell had, somewhere lately, been chipped from about her, revealing to her half-startled gaze a horizon far wider than any guessed before. By the new summonings that made music in her heart, by these undreamed aspirations and reaching affections, there was the thrilling seeming that always heretofore she had lived in some dull half-deadness. And she could not doubt that this port where she had arrived at last was no other than the gate of Life. . . .

"Why, that's Chas Cooney!" said Cally, suddenly, gazing down.

From the cab below there had stepped a tall young man, out upon her sidewalk. She recognized her cousin with instant surprise; and consciousness, returning to her again, set a little frown between her level brows. Chas made her think at once of the Works. How was it that he, so busy that he could not even stop for dinner, came driving up here in the middle of the afternoon? Above all, who was it that he was helping, so slowly and carefully, from his hired car?

The girl gazed with growing tensity; her hat-brim pressed the window. The downward view was unimpeded, all clear; only, things moved so slowly. However, a little at a time, the second person in the car came emerging into the sunshine.

And Cally's heart lifted with an appalling wrench as she saw that it was her father.

There had been an accident at the Works: that was clear in one eye-sweep. Her father had been hurt. He was bare-headed; a long splotch ran up his cheek, into his hair. He was dragging over the sidewalk, leaning heavily upon Chas's arm. One of his own arms hung unnaturally still at his side. More horrible than any of these things was his face, so ghastly green in the light.

And in the watcher at the window, life shocked instantly to death. For in the flash in which she saw her father's face, she knew. No need of speech; no more news to break. Had she not felt that something terrible would happen at the Works some day? There had happened a thing more terrible than all her nightmares had devised. . . .

She did not remember going downstairs at all. But she must have gone down very fast, for when she opened the door the two men were just stepping into the vestibule, Chas's hand reaching out toward the bell. . . .

One look went between her and papa. Did he see death in her face?

"You heard . . ." he said, standing there, his voice so curious. And she could have screamed for that look in his eyes.

"No," said Cally. Yet surely she had heard.

He was limping through the door toward her; dirt on his clothes; dark stains on his fine snowy waistcoat. And then his arm was hard round her neck; papa's head buried upon her breast, like a sorry boy's.

"My poor little girl."

So there had been a glimmer within, after all. It went out, with a mortal throe. All was black.

But surely this was quite, quite unreal; but one more horror of the night, the last and the worst. Ah, surely, surely, she had but to make one great effort to find herself sitting up in the dark; trembling, but alive.

"How badly are you hurt?"

"Nothing. . . . Arm's broke. . . . No one else."

Then they were standing in the wide dim hall. The door was shut, and she was holding by the knob. And she heard a voice, so small, so strangely calm.

"How did it happen, papa?"

Papa had his sound arm raised, his hand rubbing vaguely

at his lips. But it was not his own pain and shock that had bleached those lips so white.

"Floor crashed in — without warning . . . broke through. He'd made a suggestion — some braces. So I took him up to look. We were standing there . . . standing underneath. Standing there, talking. And the floor gave way . . . cracked . . . caved in on us. One machine came down. . . ."

The voice, too, seemed to cave in. And some one was squeezing her hand, very hard.

So nothing was wanting from the finished picture, not the last exquisite stroke. He, the believer, had believed even in her father's floors. It was she who had doubted, she who had asked the help that never failed. Had he not told her not to worry? . . .

But if only she had n't stopped going inside. If only her heart would soon begin to beat again. . . .

Chas Cooney was winking his keen eyes.

"He'd got clear — there was plenty of time. . . . One of the negro women was knocked over by a flying splinter . . . Things were falling all around. So he stopped for her. . . . She was n't hurt at all, when we pulled her out. . . . Of course Uncle Thornton was back in it all. A beam knocked him senseless . . ."

"Surgeon said it was instantaneous," came papa's shadowy voice. "Well. . . . It's on my head. I'm responsible. I know that."

And he sat down uncertainly, and somewhat pitifully, on the tall hall-chair. . . .

Then nobody said anything more. There would never be anything more to say. Time would go on a long while yet, but no one would ever add another touch here. This was the end of the world.

He had trusted the Heths too far.

And how strange and void it was at the world's end, how deadly still but for the faint roarings of waters far off.

She was walking toward her father. Through the roaring there came a voice, so little and so remote.

"Papa, you must come up to bed. . . . I'll telephone for the doctor."

But she did not go to the telephone; not even to her father. She brushed her hand upward vaguely, fending away the advancing blackness. And then it would have been with her as with poor Miller that day at the Works, but that Charles Cooney, who had been watching her closely, was quick and strong.

· XXXIV

*In which to love much is to be much loved, and Kern's Dearest
Dream (but one) comes True.*

BEYOND the Great Gulf, there was news coming, too:
coming with the click of hoofs on cobble-stones, and the
harsh clanging of a wagon; seeping and spreading through
the shabby street with mysterious velocity. Windows rattled
up; a word flew from lip to lip; people were running.

There came the Reverend George Dayne, of the Charities, and
hard behind him Labor Commissoner O'Neill, mopping his face
as he ran. These two were known to the neighborhood, with
their right of going in, and no questions asked. Out again came
the ambulance surgeon, shaking his head jauntily at all inquiries.
Out lastly, after an interval, issued Mr. Pond, and disappeared
into the establishment of Henry Bloom, who was known to
have loaned his camp-chairs free, the day Doctor got up this here
Settlement. . . .

Then stillness enveloped all. Nothing seemed to stir. And
no one could remember when he had seen those windows dark
before.

Within, upstairs, the two men, alike only in this one tie, stood
about, waiting; waiting for Pond's return; waiting only because
they were loath to go. What little had been for their hands to
do was done now.

The men of the yellow wagon, breathing hard as they came
up the steps, had sought out the bedroom. But Mr. Dayne
said that a soldier should lie in his tent. So they had made sure
that the three-legged lounge in the office was steady, and got a
fresh counterpane from red-lidded Mrs. Garland. Then, when
Pond was gone, the other two had thought to make ready
against the arrival of Bloom. However, they were soon brought
to pause here, finding nothing to make ready with. There was

an overcoat hung in the clothes closet, but otherwise it was entirely bare; hangers dangling empty. The men had found the sight somewhat sad.

But Mr. Dayne, who had been a parson before he was a Secretary, had said no matter. Let him go in his patches upon his great adventure. . . .

It had seemed natural to these two to be doing the last small services. There was no family here; friends' love was needed. But now there was only waiting. . . .

Mr. Dayne, in Canal Street in his own business, had been at the Heth Works in the first uproar. At intervals, he had told the story to the others: a story of one machine too many unloaded on a strained floor; of a dry beam breaking with a report like a cannon; of men and women stampeding in the wild fear that the building was about to collapse. On the second floor, but two had kept their heads; and the young doctor, for all his bad foot, had been the quicker. It was supposed that the base of the machine itself had struck him, glancing. Mr. Heth, found two feet away, was buried by a litter of débris; his escape from death was deemed miraculous. And when they brought him round, it was told that his first word had been: "Vivian hurt? . . ."

Much remained puzzling: in chief the strange amiability of the master of the Works toward the man he had once threatened to break for libel. They had stood there chatting like friends, laughing.

But here Commissioner O'Neill could give little light. Last night his friend had told him, indeed, with evidences of strange happinesss, that there was to be a new Heth Works at once. But he was mysteriously reserved as to how this triumph for the O'Neill administration had been brought to pass, saying repeatedly: "It's a sort of secret. I can't tell you that, old fellow." But O'Neill remembered now one thing he had said, with quite an excited air, which might be a sort of clue: "Don't you get it, Sam? . . . *It 's all good. Everybody's good* . . . Why, I 've known it all the time." . . .

Now the two men had fallen silent. They were in the old

waiting-room, with the office door fast shut between. Royalty had slept in this room once. It was decaying now, and bare as your hand but for the row of kitchen chairs along the wall. The minister kept walking about; kept humming beneath his breath. Once Sam O'Neill caught a line of that song: *The victory of life is won.* A strange sentiment at this time certainly; thoroughly clerical, though. It was a professional matter with Dayne; only he, O'Neill, had been really close to V. V. And he was continually burdened with a certain sense of personal responsibility for it all. . . .

"I'd like to have the doctor for that little girl in there," said Mr. Dayne.

The Commissioner, who was getting really stout these days, cleared his throat.

"How's she goin' to get on without him?"

"Ah, how?" said the clergyman, musing.

The stillness was like the silence before the dawn. Oppressive, too, was the sense of emptiness. Two men in this chamber; one small watcher beyond the door; otherwise emptiness, sensed through all the two hundred rooms of the deserted pile. Life died from the world. People forgot. Stillness, death, loneliness, and destitution. They had picked him to the bone, and left him. . . .

And then, as thoughts like these saddened the thoughts of the two men, there was heard as it were the whir of wings in his old hotel. And the crows came.

I say the crows came. They came in their own way; but so they had always come. Came in the guise of an elderly tramp, vacant-eyed and straggly-bearded, soiled, tentative, and reluctant. But what mattered things like this: since in his wings, which were only hairy arms that needed soap, he brought the raiment? Such a pile of them, too, such royal abundance. A fine black cutaway coat, a handsome pair of "extra" trousers, shirts, and shoes, and, peeping beneath all, glimpses of a pretty blue suit quite obviously as good as new.

There stood the wonder, silent and uncouth, in the doorway. Do you doubt that Sam O'Neill and Mr. Dayne knew, the moment their eyes saw, that here were the crows come? How they gazed and gazed, and how poor Mister Garland, ever retiring of habit, squirmed and shifted over an uneasy heart. . . .

He did not care to talk with gentlemen, did not Mister; gentlemen of that cloth particularly. Doubt not that in institutions men wearing such vests as this had had their cleanly will of him on winter nights. So he asked his question dumbly, with a movement of matted head and eyebrow; and when Mr. Dayne answered in a curious voice, "Yes . . . he's gone," the last expectancy faded from the rough vague face. He sidled in, timid and unwilling; laid his burden, speechless, upon a chair. And then he was shambling furtively out the door again, when the parson's hand took his shoulder.

"Why are you bringing them back now? He gave them all to you, did n't he?"

The visitor spoke for the first time, suddenly, low and whining.

"'S a Gawd's truth, Reverend, I never hooked nothin' off him, an' I was goin' to bring 'em back anyways. Nothin' wore at all, gents, you can see yourself, cep a time or two mebbe outen that there derby. . . ."

The man himself could see no point in it all except that gents had him in charge; a threatening predicament. But Mr. Dayne's gentle suasion prevailed. Out, gradually, came the little story which he was to tell sometimes in after years, and think about oftener. . . .

Mister was bringing back Doctor's things because he had never felt right about taking them.

The cutaway coat had been the beginning of it all, it seemed. The gift of so fine a Sunday coat had bewildered the recipient; he had been on the point of handing it back right there. However, nature had conquered, then and subsequently; there had accumulated a collection of clothing secretly laid away in a place he had. The man had kept asking, he said, out of habit — "more jest to see if he'd give 'em to yer like." But he seemed to feel, in a certain dim way, that there was a sort of contest on between him and Doctor.

"The innercent look he had to him, yer might say," he said, groping for words to answer the high-vested inquisitor. "Like a child like. Never scolded yer wunst . . . Just up and give yer all yer wanted. . . ."

The blue suit, given yesterday, seemed to have been conceived as a kind of test case. The man appeared to feel that, once refused, a sort of spell on him would be broken; he would then get out all his store and wear them freely. So he had told a tall story in the office: how he was surely going to settle down and be respectable this time, and was obliged to have him a good nice suit fer to git started in. . . . And Doctor had given him such a funny look that for a minute he thought sure he had him. But no, the young man had laughed suddenly, as at a joke, and said: "Well, you sit there, Mister, till I take these off . . ." Only not to tell Mrs. Garland. Took him right back, sure did. . . .

"So then I thinks," said Mister, the professional quaver returning to his voice, "it's no better 'n thievin' for to take off an innercent like him, and thinks I, I'll git the lot of 'em, and give him like a surprise. 'S a Gawd's truth, gents, like I'm tellin' yer. Nothin' at all wore but mebbe that there derby, like I up and tole yer . . ."

His word had never been doubted: this passed invention. And he was thanked, not chidden for his narrative, and Reverend said:

"He shall wear that suit for his burial. . . ."

So the crows flitted out of the door again, their errand done; and behind them was a deeper stillness than they had found.

The old waiting-room, a little dark at best, grew dimmer. Sunlight faded from the ruined floor. The glorious afternoon was drawing in. The men did not speak. And then in the lengthening silence, there floated up small noises: a door creaking open; quiet feet upon the stairs; a faint swishing as of a skirt.

The parson was standing by the half-open door.

"D' you think, sir," he spoke suddenly aloud, "there's any way to preach to a man, like just being better than he is?"

O'Neill roused, but made no answer. He had been thinking of the day he had seen this fellow Garland dodging down the hall with those trousers there. Then, becoming aware of the footsteps, he said:

"Pond back . . . Is it?"

But Mr. Dayne, looking out down the corridor, said no. After a pause, he added, in a yet lower voice:

"It's young Cooney, from the Works . . . And a lady."

A change had gone over the parson's kind face, making it still kinder. His sense of surrounding desolation ebbed from him. People acknowledged their heavy debt; paid as stoutly as they could. On the stairs there he saw, coming, the daughter of the man whose negligence had taken to-day a young life not easily to be spared.

"They're both friends of mine," added Mr. Dayne, gently. "Perhaps you will excuse me a moment?"

And he stepped out into the hall, shutting the door quietly behind him.

So Mr. Dayne thought. But under the heavy veil she wore, this was less a daughter than a woman: Cally, who had loved for a day and in the evening heard that her love was dead.

The thought behind the venture had been Chas's. Nothing required him at the House of Heth; he was for getting his sister and going to see what help the Dabney House might need. And at the last minute, she had put on her hat again, and gone too. Nothing that Mr. Dayne had felt about the loneliness of this end could touch what Cally had felt. Of whom, too, was help more required than of her, now or never any more? So they had driven three from Saltman's to the old hotel, where she had thought to come to a meeting to-day. And then Henrietta, who had come out from her typewriter strong and white as ice, methodically sticking in hatpins as she crossed the sidewalk; Hen, the iron-hearted, had quite suddenly broken down; laying her cold face in Cally's lap, weeping wildly that she would not bear it. . . .

So Cally must brave the stairs without her, must speak to who might be here. But she did not mind. Strength had come to her with the consciousness that had returned all too quickly: the dead strength of the inanimate. She was dark and cold within as the spaces between the worlds. . . .

And now the two cousins met Mr. Dayne in this strange endless corridor; and knew that no services were asked of them.

They greeted with little speech. Mr. Dayne told of the simple dispositions they were making. Chas explained how Mr. Heth had tried to communicate with Mrs. Mason, — whom Mr. Dayne had quite overlooked, it seemed, — but found that she was out of town; had telegraphed; how he would have come down with them now, but had had to stop for the setting of his arm. Uncle Thornton would come this evening. . . .

"Ah, that's kind of him," said Mr. Dayne. "He must be in much pain. . . ."

Then silence fell. There seemed nothing to say or do. How think that she could serve — mitigate these numb horrors of pain and self-reproach? All was over.

"Where is he?" said Cally, her voice so little and calm.

The clergyman told her. And then all three stood looking down the corridor to the door at the end of it: a shut door marked in white letters: DR. VIVIAN. . . . But nothing could hurt her now.

"We thought that was right," said Mr. Dayne. . . . "Will you go in for a moment?"

Briefly the girl's veiled eyes met his. He was aware that a little tremor went through her; perhaps he then understood a little further. And he thought he had never seen anybody so beautiful and white.

He added in his comforting way: "There's no one at all with him except the little girl here, Corinne, that he was kind to. . . ."

Surely there was never a loneliness like this loneliness.

"I will go, if I may," said Cally.

Chas was eyeing her, unbelievably grave, turning his hat between his hands. And then she remembered Hen, left alone, who would not be comforted.

She whispered: "Don't wait for me. . . . I'll come in a minute."

The young man hesitated; they spoke a moment; it was so

arranged. Chas was tipping away from her down the well of the stairs.

And she and the clergyman were walking up the corridor, his hand at her elbow, to the door with the white letters on it.

As Mr. Dayne's hand touched the knob, she spoke again, very low.

"Is he . . . Is he — much . . . ?"

"No," said Mr. Dayne, "the injuries were internal. There's hardly a mark. . . ."

So, opening the door softly, he left her.

And she was within, the door a step or two behind her, in front a long space, drawn blinds, and the indistinguishable twilight. Somewhere before her was the mortal man who had pledged her one day that he would prove his friendship with his life.

And how came she here; by what right?

She had perceived remotely that she was not alone. Out of the dim great stretches there emerged advancing a little figure, black-clad; advancing silent, with lowered head. Drawing near, she did not look up, did not speak: she was merely fading from the room.

The figure was vaguely apprehended, as one upon another planet. But Cally, stirring slightly as she slipped past, made a movement with her hand and said, just audibly:

"Don't go."

The girl must have paused. There came a tiny voice:

"Yes, ma'am. I'll . . . just step out." And then, yet fainter: "I was wishin' you'd come, ma'am."

It was the stillness of the world's last Sabbath. Gathering dusk was here, and mortal fear. Her limbs ran to marble. There came again the lifeless whisper.

"Don't be afraid, ma'am. . . . He looks so beautiful."

The understanding speech, the voice, seemed to penetrate her consciousness. Her eyes drew out of the dusk, turned upon the small figure at her side: the little girl he had been fond of, her father's three years' buncher. And then she heard herself breathing suddenly, faintly:

"Ah! . . . You poor, poor child! . . ."

And her heart, which had been quite dead, was suddenly alive and twisting within her. . . .

She had been engulfed in her own abyss. Tragedy was on every side, horrors pouring in, swamping her being. Feeling had drowned in the icy void. Not Hen's tears had touched her, not her father's stricken grief. But when her eyes came upon this small face, something written there pierced her through and through. Such a shocking little face it was, so pinched with no hope of tears. . . .

In the darkness of the shuttered office, two stood near who were worlds apart. And, for the first time since she had looked down from her window at home, Cally was lifted out of herself. . . .

"I — you must let me see you — in a day or two, won't you?" she said hurriedly, below her breath. "I should like so much . . . to help you, if I could. . . ."

A quiver went over the little mask; but the girl spoke in the same stony way:

"Oh, ma'am . . . it's so kind . . . I'll go now."

But the hollowness of Cally's speech had mocked the sudden sympathy upwelling within her. Her arm was upon the work-girl's frail shoulder; her indistinct voice suddenly tremulous.

"Don't think I imagine that any one can ever replace . . . You must know I understand . . . what your loss is."

Kern shrunk against the wall by the door. No moment this, to speak of what had so long been hid.

"He was like a father to me, ma'am, an' more. . . ."

And then, as if to prove that she claimed no right at all in this room, as if all depended on her establishing finally the humble and spiritual nature of her regard, she breathed what in happier days had been close to her heart:

"He was teaching me to be a lady. . . ."

Who shall say how marvels befall, and the dearest dream comes true? Was it the pitifulness of the little hope laid bare? Or the secret shrinking behind that, but surprised at last? Or was it the knowledge of a beautiful delicacy shown by this little girl before to-day?

Miss Heth's arm was about her neck, and her voice, which was so pretty even when you could hardly hear it, said, true as true:

"I think you've been a lady all along, Co-rinne."

And then the bands about Kern's heart snapped, and she could cry. . . .

The storm came suddenly, like the bursting of a dam. A bad time certainly; it was hard to be torn so, yet to make no cry or sound; in any case, distressing to others. And surely salt water could n't be good for this lovely cloth, where her face lay. . . .

Yet one does n't think overmuch of things like that, when the barriers on the great common go toppling down. And there was Sisterhood there all the time. . . .

And above the stillness and the racking, Kern heard his beautiful lady's voice once more, speaking to her own heart now, so low, oh, so broken:

"Ah, but he was teaching me. . . ."

And then Kern must go quickly, lest she disgrace herself forever; screaming aloud as she had heard women who were not ladies. . . .

The girl was gone, her head between her hands. And Cally Heth stood alone in the more than churchly stillness.

She was breaking up within. The drowned being stirred to life, with multiplying pains. And yet, in giving comfort, she had mysteriously taken it. There came to her a fortitude that was not of death.

No sound penetrated to the silent waiting-room.

The two men there spoke little. They had talked what they had to say. Sam O'Neill looked at his watch; it was twenty-five minutes to six. And, a moment later, Director Pond came up the steps, entered and said:

"Bloom will be here at six o'clock."

They spoke briefly of this. The friends of the neighborhood were to be admitted; it was agreed that this should be arranged for to-morrow morning. Pond then said:

"Is Miss Heth in there?"

Mr. Dayne said that she was. And Sam O'Neill, who had not

known who the visitor was, first looked startled and then lapsed off into heavy musings. . . .

The Director sat down on a chair by the door. His strong face looked tired.

"Won't you, a little later," he said to Mr. Dayne, "go down and say a few words to the people outside? They'd appreciate it."

The parson, biting his crisp mustache, said that he would.

Pond sat absently eyeing the pile of men's clothes beside him; and after a time he asked what they were there for. Mr. Dayne seemed less and less disposed for conversation. So it was Sam who told, in a somewhat halting fashion, of the coming of the crows. . . .

Pond, whom no one could have taken for a sentimentalist, made no comment whatever. Presently he felt Mr. Dayne's eye upon him.

"Well, would it work out, do you think?"

The Director shook his head slightly, disclaiming authority. But after a time he said:

"Not as long as men'll try it only once every two thousand years."

The parson's eyes dreamed off.

"He believed in miracles. And so they were always happening to him. . . . Oh, it's all so simple when you stop to think."

Then there was silence and the creeping twilight. Sam O'Neill stood picking at a splotch on the ancient plaster, with strong, yellow-gloved hands. Mr. Dayne walked about, his arms crossed behind him. Upon Pond there came a sort of restlessness.

He said abruptly: "How long has Miss Heth been here?"

"Oh — a — little while," said the parson, rousing. . . . "Long enough, no doubt."

The dark-eyed Director was standing. The two men exchanged a look; they seemed to feel each other. Here was a matter with which the Labor Commissioner had nothing to do.

"Well, then," said Pond, with a little intake of breath, "I'll go in."

The Director shut the door into the hall, took his hat from the chair. He crossed the bare waiting-room, and turned the knob of the frequented door into the office.

This door he opened, gently, just far enough to let himself in; he closed it at once behind him. Nevertheless, by the chance of their position, the other two saw, through the darkness of the room beyond, what was not meant for their eyes.

A simple scene, in all truth; none commoner in the world; it really did not matter who saw. Yet the two men in the waiting-room, beholding, turned away, and Sam O'Neill bit a groan through in the middle.

He had never understood his friend, but he had loved him in his way. Old memories twitched; his poise wavered. He lacked the parson's inner supports. He paced about for some time, making little noises in his throat. And then he tried his voice on a question.

"Did you ever hear him speak of John the Baptist?"

Mr. Dayne halted, and looked.

And Sam O'Neill, with some difficulty and in his own way, told of V. V.'s creed about the Huns. Of how he had maintained that they needed awakening, nothing else, and were always ready and waiting for it, no matter how little they themselves knew that. And, finally, how he had said one day — in a phrase that had been brought flashing back over the months — that if a man but called to such as these in the right voice, he could not hide himself where they would not come to him on their knees. . . .

Mr. Dayne had stood listening with a half-mystical look, a man groping for elusive truths. Now his fine composure seemed to cloud for a moment; but it shone out again, fair and strong. And presently, as he paced, he was heard humming again his strange paradoxical song, which he, a parson, seemed to lean upon, as a wounded man leans on his friend.

Her spirit returned to her body from the far countries, not without some pain of juncture. But there was no strangeness now in being in this room; none in finding Mr. Pond at her side, his saddened gaze upon her. Happen what might, nothing any more would ever seem strange. . . .

"Won't you come with me now?"

She stood, whispering: "Come with you?"

And Pond's strong heart turned a little when he saw her eyes, so circled, so dark with tears that were to come.

"Your cousins are waiting, are n't they? . . . And don't you think your father might need you?"

A little spasm distorted the lovely face, unveiled now.

She inclined her head. Pond walked away toward the door; stood there silently, drawing a finger over faded panels. Behind him was the absence of all sound: the wordlessness of partings that were final for this world. . . .

She had seen in his great dignity the man who had given to the House of Heth the last full measure of his confidence. And it was as his little friend had said. He was beautiful with the best of all his looks; the look he had worn yesterday in the library, as he went to meet her poor father.

They had slain him, and yet he trusted.

No design of hers had led her alone beside this resting-place: that was chance, or it was God. But now it seemed that otherwise it would henceforward not have been bearable. For with this first near touch of death, there had come, strangely hand in hand, her first vision of the Eternal. The look of this spirit was not toward time, and over the body of this death there had descended the robe of a more abundant Life.

So she turned quickly and came away. . . .

She was outside now. The door was shut behind. And she was walking with Mr. Pond down the corridor, which was so long, echoing so emptily. She became aware that her knees were trembling. And Corinne's fear now was hers.

She desired to be at once where no one could see her. But at the head of the grand stairway, in the desolating loneliness, Mr. Pond stopped walking. And then he held a hand of hers between two of his; pressed it hard, released it.

He was speaking in a voice that seemed vaguely unlike his own.

"It's hard for you — for your father — for all of us down here. His life was needed . . . wonderfully, for such a boy. And yet . . . How could a man wish it better with himself? He would n't, that I 'm sure of. . . . Gave away his life every day, and at the end flung it all out at once, to save a factory negro. Don't you know that if he 'd lived a thousand years, he could never have put one touch to that?"

Cally said unsteadily: "I know that 's true. . . ."

She wished to go on; but the Director was speaking again, hurriedly:

"And you must n't think that a blow on the head can bring it all to an end. If I know anything, his story will be often told. People that you and I will never know, will know of this, and it will help them — when their pinch comes. There 's no measuring the value of a great example. When it strikes, you can feel the whole line lift. . . ."

And then he added, in a let-down sort of way: "Freest man I ever saw."

There was no reply to make to these things. They went down the stairs together. Halfway down, the man spoke again:

"In the little while I 've been here, I 've seen and heard a great deal. Some day you must let me tell you — how much there is down here to keep his memory green."

The stairs were long. A kind of terror was growing within her. She would go to pieces before she reached the bottom. But that peril passed; and very near now was the waiting car, and merciful shelter. . . .

They crossed, amid springing memories, the old court where, one rainy afternoon, there had happened what had turned her life thenceforward. Then they were safely through the door, and came out upon the portico, into the last light of the dying afternoon. And here, above all else that she felt, she encountered a dim surprise.

When she had passed this way a little while before, it was as if all power of feeling had been frozen in her. Sights and sounds were not for her. So now the sudden spectacle that met her eyes came as a large vague confusion.

The shabby street was black with people.

Her affliction had been so supremely personal, her sense of this man's tragic solitariness in the world so overwhelming, that she could not at once take in the meaning of what she saw. She must have faltered to a pause. And she heard Pond's voice, so strangely gentle:

"You see he was much loved here."

Her eyes went once over the dingy street, the memorable scene. Thought shook through her in poignant pictures. . . . Herself, one day, prostrated by calamity on calamity; and in the little island-circle where she had spent her life, not one heart that had taken her sorrow as its own. And beside that picture, this: a great company, men and women, old and young, silent beneath a window: and somewhere among them the sounds of persistent weeping. . . .

And Cally seemed suddenly to see what had been hidden from her before. If he was much loved, it was because he had loved much.

Yet her confusion must have lingered. Was it so, indeed? Many, so many, to compensate his loneliness? It seemed to be important to understand clearly; and she turned her veiled face toward Pond, and spoke indistinctly:

"All these . . . Are they all . . . his friends?"

There sprang a light into the Director's hawk-eyes, changing his whole look wonderfully.

"They're his mother," he said, "and his brothers and his sisters. . . ."

THE END

The Riverside Press
CAMBRIDGE . MASSACHUSETTS
U . S . A

A HOOSIER CHRONICLE

By Meredith Nicholson

"It is one of the bravest, sweetest, most optimistic books in which, ever, plain truths of humanity and history have been mingled with the weavings of fiction." — *N. Y. World.*

"Mr. Nicholson knows whereof he writes, and the picture of the political and social life of the capital which he gives us in the present volume is vigorous and convincing." — *Boston Transcript.*

"It puts Mr. Nicholson in the front rank of American novelists who are trying to produce real literature."
— *Indianapolis Star.*

"In 'A Hoosier Chronicle' he has done something much bigger, and given us a work of fiction of a richly human sort, creating real characters and giving us a penetrating study of political life and domestic relations in the commonwealth of Indiana." — *The Dial.*

Illustrated in color by F. C. Yohn.
Square crown 8vo. $1.40 *net*.   Postage 16 cents

HOUGHTON
MIFFLIN
COMPANY

BOSTON
AND
NEW YORK

THE LONG ROLL

By MARY JOHNSTON

CHRISTOPHER

By Richard Pryce

"A refreshing book for the reader who knows and loves human nature, who delights in the quiet realities of life." — *Chicago Record-Herald.*

"The charm of the story and the leisureliness of its narration remind one of De Morgan's 'Joseph Vance,' or Locke's 'The Beloved Vagabond.' There is enjoyment on every page." — *Brooklyn Eagle.*

"He can draw characters — aristocratic old ladies, maiden ladies and ladies' maids — which are unforgettable, and he describes houses and rooms so incisively that the reader can share them with their occupants."
— *London Punch.*

"Full of quality, leisure, and the possibility of keen yet unhurried enjoyment." — *Life.*

"A brilliant piece of work, full of ripeness and an understanding of the richness of life." — *N. Y. Evening Sun.*

Crown 8vo.　$1.35 *net.*　Postage 12 cents

HOUGHTON
MIFFLIN
COMPANY

BOSTON
AND
NEW YORK